A Queen's Game

EVERYONE LIES AT COURT

ERI LEIGH

Published by Delphi Publishing, LLC 2022.
www.delphipublishing.co

Paperback: 979-8-9852409-1-7
Ebook: 979-8-9852409-0-0
Cover designed by Books and Moods.
Layout by Books and Moods.
Maps by Eri Leigh.
Eri Leigh asserts the right to be identified as the author of this work.

Scan the QR code below for a digital copy of the maps and pronunciation guide. w ww.authorerileigh.com/the-world-of-a-queens-game

The World of A Queen's Game

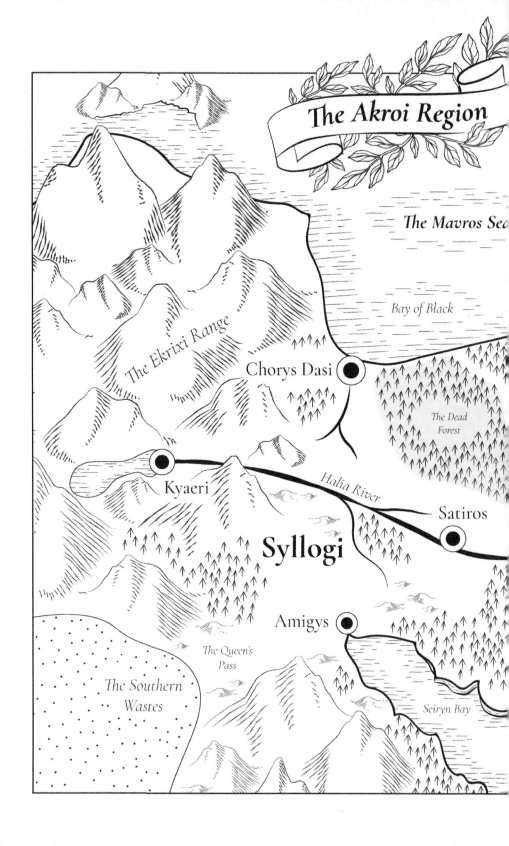

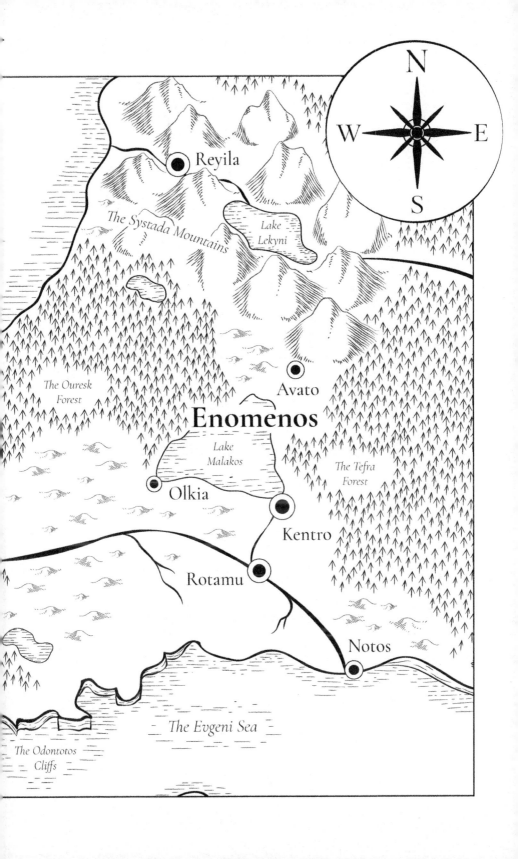

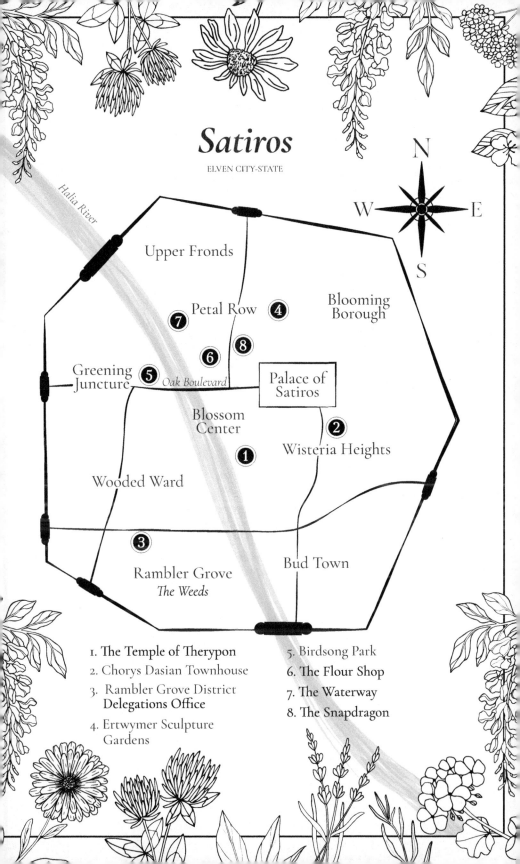

Satiros

ELVEN CITY-STATE

Halia River

N
W · E
S

Upper Fronds

Petal Row ④

⑦

Blooming Borough

⑧

Greening Juncture ⑤ *Oak Boulevard* ⑥

Palace of Satiros

Blossom Center

① Wisteria Heights ②

Wooded Ward

③ Bud Town

Rambler Grove
The Weeds

1. **The Temple of Therypon**
2. Chorys Dasian Townhouse
3. Rambler Grove District **Delegations Office**
4. Ertwymer Sculpture Gardens

5. Birdsong Park
6. **The Flour Shop**
7. The Waterway
8. The Snapdragon

Author's Note

A Queen's Game contains topics that may be upsetting to some readers. Content warnings include kidnapping, sex, domestic abuse (physical assault, emotionally abusive relationship), drug and alcohol use, depression, anxiety, suicidal thoughts, and death.

For those who fight hidden battles. You are never alone.

Part 1

"What we have been, or now are,
we shall not be tomorrow."
– *Ovid, Metamorphoses*

Chapter One

MARIETTA

BEFORE

Under the glow of a gas street lamp, Marietta Reid stood in an empty lane, looking up at her future: a bakery. She never intended to become a baker, but fate had a funny way of sorting itself out. Life seldom went according to plan. But that was what she loved about life—the unpredictable adventure of it all.

"You sure you want to do this, Mar?" Her husband, Tilan, rubbed his nape as he watched her.

She hugged him around his waist, his one arm draped over her shoulder. "Without a doubt." Marietta smiled, closing her eyes as she contemplated how this bakery would change *everything* for them.

Marietta had spent over a decade traveling between the cities of Enomenos. As a contact between businesses, her job was to bring people together. If a tailor searched for a specific type of cloth, she would find the right weaver. If a brewer looked for a particular grain, it was likely Marietta knew who grew it. If a tavern needed to organize their finances, she'd tackle them herself. It was an unconventional job that she loved. The drawback was the amount of travel and time away from Tilan.

"And here I thought you'd be jumping at the chance for me to open a bakery," Marietta said, swatting Tilan in the chest. "Aren't you sick of me being gone most of the month?"

The corner of Tilan's mouth tilted with a smile. The dark strands of his hair frayed from its knot after a long day of working in his smithy.

"Most of the month? Try the entire month because we're only together for three days. Four, if I'm lucky."

"You know what I mean." It was true enough. Often she was on the road visiting the businesses she helped. When she returned to Olkia, she spent most of her time working. That left a few days of peace with her husband—too little.

"Of course, I'd be happy if you were home more," Tilan said as he rubbed the stubble on his chin, smearing a black line into his jaw. "But you also love to help your clients."

"More than I love you?" she asked, teasing. Marietta stood on her tiptoes to brush a kiss on his marred cheek.

Tilan rolled his eyes and pressed a returning kiss to her forehead. "I want to make sure you're ready to settle down." He always considered her feelings over his own. It was another reason for Marietta to love him so much.

"Oh, it'll be about a year before I'm truly settled." Marietta twirled one of her dark curls around her finger as she inspected the bakery. "After we move in, there's still a ton of cleaning to do as well as offload my clients. I'll have to establish my suppliers, test which goods to sell, make samples, spread word about the bakery."

"Are you ready for that kind of work?"

"Do you think I can't handle it?" She shot him a smirk. "Setting up suppliers will be easy since I already have a few leads. I figured out which items I'd like to sell first." Marietta thought of the former client who taught her how to bake, and her heart ached for the old elven man. This bakery was as much for him as it was for herself.

"True," Tilan said as he nodded his head. "But what about the location? The street crowds here almost every day."

"Which makes it the perfect location." Marietta loosened herself from Tilan, walking to the edge of the building. It sat at the corner of a busy intersection in central Olkia. "Plus, there's a market only two blocks from here. That'll make the bakery a convenient place to stop while people are already out running errands. And easier for me to get supplies."

"That's also true, but are you sure you want to be in Olkia full time?"

Marietta scoffed, placing her hand mockingly on her chest as she turned to Tilan. "Silly me for wanting to be home with my husband."

Tilan shook his head. "Olkia was never your home."

She closed the space between them once more and placed her hands on his chest. Staring into the deep blue of his eyes, she couldn't stop her heart from fluttering. After five years of knowing one another—married for two of those years—Marietta still felt her idyllic love for him. "Olkia became my home because of you. Home is where you are." She stood on her tiptoes and kissed him. "Not to mention you're in this city-state because your smithy is here."

"I could always move it if you wanted to be in a different city. You grew up in Kentro. Gods, that was always your home—"

"Kentro hasn't been my home in five years, Tilan." She slid her arm around his waist once more. "Your smithy does well in Olkia. Though, your work is extraordinary enough that clients would come to you no matter which city-state we lived in."

Tilan huffed a laugh. "Always exaggerating my talent."

With a roll of her eyes, she leaned into his chest. Tilan was modest when he had no reason to be. Of all the blacksmiths and inventors Marietta had worked with, Tilan outshined them all. On the day she met him in the dim of his smithing shop, his skill had thrilled her. Weapons with ornate detail carved into the hilts and damascus steel blades etched in intricate patterns filled his store front along with more curious, whimsical creations. It was the first time Marietta had seen a music box: a metal container inlaid with precious stones that played a tinny song. Though impressive, it still paled compared to the dagger with the hilt fashioned after a dancing forest nymph: a feyrie creature rumored to roam the Akroi region long ago. The blade reminded her of her childhood—of her father's feyrie tales. Tilan had gifted it to her right after they met.

"Perhaps if you quit being modest, then I wouldn't have to be the one to brag about your work." She lifted her brow at Tilan. She paused, staring at the broad windows lining the bakery's front. "At least this wouldn't be a far walk from your smithy."

"There's that." He sighed, drawing Marietta's attention. "I want to make sure that this is what *you* want—that I didn't persuade you to leave a job that you love."

"Don't give yourself so much credit," she said. The skin around Tilan's eyes crinkled as he laughed. Though he was half a decade younger than Marietta, he had already begun aging. She knew it would happen when she fell in love with him—a human.

Marietta was half-elven. Her mother was a human from Enomenos, and her father was an elf who defected from the elven lands of Syllogi long before Marietta had been born. Humans lived the shortest lifespans while the elves lived for centuries. Half-elves, like herself, had lifespans that fell between the two. One day, she would outlive Tilan. Such a thought tightened her throat and quickened her breaths. To distract herself, she flicked him in the nose. "If I'm changing my life, it will be my decision alone. You know this."

"Gods, that's the truth."

"Then let me do this, no questions asked."

Tilan held her defiant stare. "I love you, Mar. I'd support you through anything." His gaze drifted back to the bakery. "Have you thought of a name yet?"

"A few, actually," she said with a smile. "The one I like the most is Rise Above."

"Seriously? Rise Above?" He laughed.

"Yes, Rise Above. What's wrong with it?"

"It's cheesy."

"That's the point. It's so tongue-in-cheek that it's good."

"I'm not sure how that works." He bit back another laugh.

"It's so bad that—will you stop laughing?" She swatted at his side. "It's so bad that it's unforgettable. People will remember it."

"I mean, you are the expert," he said while wrapping his arms around Marietta.

"That's right. I'm the expert." She kissed him, her heart light.

He pulled away, gazing down at Marietta. "I'm proud of you, my love."

Her heart flipped in her chest, pulled with emotion. This man would have supported her through anything. Marietta felt confident in opening her own business, but it was nice having Tilan's encouragement—to share that moment with someone who loved her unconditionally. Who didn't only think of his wants and desires.

Marietta gazed into his eyes as he pulled her into a hug in the middle of the dimly lit street. The lightness in her chest spread throughout her body. Together, they could do anything, and they would have the rest of their lives to prove it.

Chapter Two

MARIETTA

TWO YEARS LATER

Marietta groaned as she stood from the pastry case with her back tight and feet aching. Sweat coated her light brown skin, causing her stray hairs to stick. Despite the long day, she couldn't help but smile—the new pastry was a best seller again. Today made it the third day in a row that it sold out.

She threw open the door to the kitchen, finding one of her workers mopping the floor. "You're still here, Kith? I told you I could take care of the rest."

The young half-elven girl shook her head. "There's still work to do—"

"And I can get it done. Now, go. It's way past when you should have left." Marietta shooed Kith toward the back door, where she discarded her apron and hung it up with the rest. It was one thing for Marietta to exhaust herself with her own business; never would she allow her employees to do so. They were here to train under her with the goal of one day owning bakeries of their own. How would they become competent bakers if they were exhausted every day?

Crazy to think two years ago, she had opened the bakery. In that short time, it had already become a staple in Olkia. Each morning, they had a line of customers waiting for them to raise the shutters and unlock the door. Many come to place future orders, meaning Marietta was often booked a month out. Her community supported her and Rise Above, and she was eternally grateful.

Marietta took the mop and finished the last section of the bakery. Her thoughts strayed to the pastries they had prepped for tomorrow, knowing that the morning wasn't far off, though she wouldn't have traded this life for anything. The days were long and hard, but they were hers. It was always her choice on business decisions. Marietta was right where she felt comfortable—in control.

That control extended to who she trained as well. After all, she had a legacy to pass on—the methodology of baking with empathy and love. To some, a loaf of bread was simply bread. To others, it was a meager meal or a chance to share a table with loved ones. During her training, Marietta had learned that even the most mundane baked good could brighten someone's day. She took that to heart and was sure to donate what extras she had to those who needed it. Not only was that what she taught her apprentices, but they also came from walks of life that understood that a loaf of bread could mean everything to those who had little.

A booming laugh broke up her train of thoughts from the back door. Was it already that late? She wasn't expecting Tilan and Pelok for another hour.

"If you think that's bad," Tilan said, pushing open the door with his head turned back towards their friend behind him, "you should hear what Dom had to say." Tilan's voice rasped from another day at his smithy. Per usual, his hair frayed from his knot. His clothes were ashen and dirty, and his fingertips stained black.

Behind him laughed Pelok, Tilan's oldest friend. Tall and broad with dark olive skin and dark hair, he towered over Tilan.

"Though I'm sure what Dom said was nothing short of hilarious," Marietta said, wiping her hands on her apron as she approached her husband, "I would like to know why you brought this freeloader over." Her chin jutted towards Pelok, who rolled his eyes in merriment.

"Says the woman with the clogged drain." Pelok shook his head, a smile curling to his lip.

"I know I said I would do it," Tilan interrupted, pausing to kiss Marietta, "but Pelok offered to take a look. He's had similar issues at The

Dog in the past." The Dog was short for The Lonely Dog, the tavern Pelok owned and operated. The same tavern that sent her to Tilan all those blissful years ago.

Pelok had been Marietta's client when he sent her to Tilan's smithy, explaining his lack of monetary organizational skills and failing to mention Tilan's gift. What he lacked in organization, he made up with talent. Marietta accused Pelok of setting them up, but they always denied it. From the moment they met, there had been something special about Tilan, as if someone knew they'd make perfect partners for one another.

Marietta gave a half-hearted glare at Pelok, her face cracking with a smile. "At least you'll be working for free pastries."

"They aren't free if he's working for them," Tilan said, sliding his arm around her. His scent of soot, sweat, and tobacco engulfed her.

"Gods, you reek," she said, pushing him away. He laughed and pulled her closer. "You two came to be a pain while I finished up."

"And to get free pastries." Pelok already crouched down to the pipe that drained her sink.

"Better not half-ass it and call it fixed," she said without the bite of an insult.

"If I remember correctly, you broke about half my glassware by dancing on the bar—"

"I told you he still brings it up!" Marietta swatted at Tilan's chest as he laughed. "It's been five years; when will you let it go?"

"Never," Pelok said, glancing back over his shoulder with a smirk.

"You really didn't have any reason to be on the bar." Tilan loosened his grip on her and rested his hands on her hips.

"There's no better place to dance than on a bar, and I still stand by that," Marietta said, shaking her head. These two always ganged up on her, and though it grew irritating, she wouldn't have it any other way. Staring up into Tilan's face, she could only think of how lucky she was to find someone like him. Few partners would be okay with their lifestyle of long hours apart, both focused on their businesses, yet every night, they got to share a bed. They got to be together.

Life with Tilan was easy—freeing. He understood Marietta's need to be busy or why she opened another business, though Tilan made enough to support them. It made for long days spent away from one another. For two married people, they mastered the art of independence in a relationship, something she had needed as much as she needed air to breathe.

Marietta always imagined being who and what she wished. Nothing could hold her back or suppress her curiosity for life and people. She needed to do things her way, and Tilan gave her that freedom. She could decide she no longer wanted the bakery, and he would understand her change of heart. It was why they never had kids. Marietta knew they'd love any child they'd have, regardless of if they were born with more human or half-elven traits. In Enomenos, it didn't matter what you were. All were equal.

Still young for a half-elf, Marietta was in her late thirties, which meant she'd have time to change her decision. As a human, Tilan didn't have such a luxury as age worked against him. She tried not to imagine the day where she'd light her husband's funeral pyre. His human lifespan was less than half of a half-elf's. Marietta's breath hitched at the thought, and she pushed it from her mind.

Tilan held her close and brought her in for a slow, deliberate kiss. His lips were soft against hers, and her hands wove into his hair. Marietta once thought she had been in love before she met Tilan, yet every day, her husband proved how wrong she had been. Her heart still skipped a beat when he looked at her—when he murmured he loved her in the shell of her ear. She had never been so fond of someone. Artistic and laid-back, Tilan kept up with Marietta's creativity, though he possessed a much calmer demeanor. He was a rock to Marietta's emotional waves; no matter how much her excitable manner crashed against him, Tilan stayed resilient.

"Can't you two wait for me to leave?" Pelok cursed under his breath. "I came over to help you with a task, and now I have to watch you two go at it."

"Maybe it wouldn't bother you as much if you found a partner," Marietta said as she pulled back from Tilan. "I told you my friend—"

"Not interested." Pelok gave her a deadpan stare. "And you're welcome.

The drain's all fixed."

"Fixed it faster than I would have," Tilan said as he leaned against the counter.

"That's because you lack practical everyday skills. You can build machines and make elaborate weapons but can't clear a gods damned drain." Pelok stood and brushed his hands on his pants. "If it weren't for me, your whole damned building would fall to pieces."

Tilan rolled his eyes. "An exaggeration. If you have such a problem with helping, then perhaps you should quit offering."

"Then how else would I get Marietta's pastries?" Pelok turned to her with a greedy look.

"You could buy them like everyone else, you gods damned freeloader," she grumbled with a smile. Truly, it didn't bother Marietta to give him pastries every once in a while. Often she would let him be the taste tester for her experimental recipes. After filling up a small box of baked goods, she handed it to Pelok and sent him on his way.

Marietta planted her fists on her hips and stared at the kitchen. "Now that Pelok unclogged the drain, I can finish the last of the dishes."

"What's left?" Tilan picked up the bucket of dirty mop water and walked to the back door.

"Nothing for you to do."

Tilan paused in the doorway and turned to face her. "I had hoped to share a shower with my wife this evening, and if she's too busy working, then it looks like I won't get that chance."

Marietta raised an eyebrow and flashed him a smirk. "Mr. Reid, what makes you assume I'd be willing to share a shower with a man like you?"

"If I recall correctly, there's something you love doing in the shower with me," he said, calling from beyond the doorway. The bucket's dirtied water sloshed as it hit the cobblestones outside. "Perhaps I'm remembering wrong."

Her smirk broadened to a smile as heat blossomed in her stomach. "I guess there's only one way to find out." She turned to the sink, determined to get the dishes done in record time.

Tilan came up from behind her and wrapped his arms around her middle. His lips brushed against her ear as he murmured, "I love you, Mar."

She leaned into her husband and felt the tightness in her chest. "I love you too."

"Now tell me," he said, releasing her, "what can I do to help get you into that shower faster?"

Thankful for the running water of their building, Marietta settled into the pillows, still flushed from their shower. Though plumbing was available throughout Enomenos, owning a shower remained a luxury. Between her and Tilan, they could afford such comforts.

Tilan walked in, his dark hair wet and clinging to his face. He only wore his undershorts, his build slim but bulked with the necessary muscle for a blacksmith. "Busy day?" Tilan asked as he relaxed onto his side. His long hair tumbled into his face. Their late nights, which happened often, meant eating dinner apart and catching up in bed.

"Busy, yes. But also exciting!" Marietta rolled to her side, her head propped by her arm as she looked at her husband. "You remember the pastry I was experimenting with two weeks ago?"

"The one with ale in the batter?"

"Yes! That one. I had it in the case today—sold every one of them again!" she said, a smile spreading across her face.

"Mar, that's great! Glad it sold better than the cheese pastry," he said, chuckling.

She swatted his arm. "Will you stop bringing it up? I thought using blue cheese would balance out the sweetness—will you stop laughing?" She crawled to his side of the bed, swatting at him.

Tilan tried to catch his breath, speaking between gasps of laughter.

"I'm... sorry, but... who would think that stinky cheese would sell at a bakery?"

Marietta sat on top of him, looking down at her husband, whose smile lit his entire face. Her hands were gentle as she moved a rogue strand of hair that fell across his eyes, tucking it behind his round-tipped ear, and brought her face to his with a kiss, his lips soft against her own.

She sat back, still on top. "You can appreciate that I tried something new."

"That's one of the many reasons I love you, Mar." He laced his fingers with hers. "You're always trying something new."

"How about you? How was your day?"

"Same old, same old. Wit Dulath came to get his order, though he's five days late." His face dropped into a frown.

Marietta sighed. Wit was an old half-elven man and a former client of hers, whose memory worsened by the day. "I'm sorry, my love. I'm surprised the old man is still running a business. He's what, one hundred and sixty now? He should retire to Notos like the rest of the old folk." Half-elves live to about a century and eight decades, and with Wit's appetite for alcohol, it surprised her that he was still alive.

"That's because his memory is getting worse, and I brought that up to him today. Said Notos is too old for him." He laughed, the sound filling Marietta's heart. "Typical Wit."

Marietta rolled to her side of the bed and turned off the oil lamp, smiling at the nymph dagger that sat on her nightstand. Though she no longer traveled, the habit was hard to break. Ever since Tilan gifted it to her, she slept with it by her side every night.

"Sometimes, I hate these long days. I miss spending time with you," Marietta said, darkness falling upon the room.

Tilan's arm draped across her middle, pulling her close. "I know things have been busy, but we'll take a trip soon. I promise."

"A trip? And where would we go?" Marietta longed for a few days off with her husband.

"Hmm. Notos? We could visit your parents." His voice grew heavy with sleep.

"That would be nice," she said, thinking of her parents' countryside villa. "Notos is lovely this time of year, the pleasant spring weather before the summer's heat settles. And my parents would love to see you. I swear they love you more than me."

"Mm," he said, his mind drifting off to sleep.

"I love you, Tilan." Her voice was soft. A trip sounded perfect. It was the vacation they always promised they'd take together. Maybe they would go this time.

"I love you too, Mar," he murmured as sleep overtook him.

White sandy beaches, warm breezes, and the heat of the southern sun filled Marietta's dreams. Tilan held her hand as the wind whipped his hair loose from its tie. They laughed about one of their many inside jokes. She relaxed her head on his chest. Paradise, that was it; alone at last with the man who held her heart.

A loud thud stirred Marietta from her sleep, her eyes popping open. "What was that?" she asked, darkness filling their bedroom.

"Hmm?" Tilan's gravelly voice said next to her.

"I heard something." The hair of her nape rose, her heart racing from jolting awake. Out of instinct and habit, she grabbed her nymph dagger off the nightstand. As she reached for the oil lamp, someone burst through the doorway.

"Marietta!" Tilan cried, followed by sounds of struggling.

Marietta screamed as hands grabbed her ankles, ripping her from the bed. With wild flails, she swung the dagger at the attacker, and the blade plunged into flesh; the warmth of blood covered her hand. The body slumped and fell to the floor.

"Tilan!" she cried, reaching for him in the dark.

A body crashed, tearing down the curtain over their bedroom

window. Silver light outlined Tilan as he fought two bodies, his fists sure and finding their mark. "Marietta, run! Go! Get out of here!" he yelled, grunting as he wrestled his attackers.

She lunged at them, dagger in hand, as someone gripped her hair and snapped her back. Strong arms restrained her, pulling her towards the doorway.

"Tilan!" she shrieked, desperate to help him. "Tilan!"

Moonlight caught the silvered length of a knife held before her husband's throat. Marietta shrieked again, thrashing against her attacker, who pinned her arms behind her back. A cloth soaked in a sweet-smelling liquid covered her mouth as she screamed, watching the dagger slice towards Tilan. His eyes locked onto Marietta's, wide and staring.

Then her world faded to black.

Chapter Three

MARIETTA

Marietta noticed the swaying first, her body lolling from one side to another with random bumps jostling her. The clanking of metal sounded nearby with ambient chatter and the occasional laugh. When she opened her eyes, light filtering through a small carriage window blinded her, and pain shot through her head. Her skin was clammy and her chest tightened as she gasped for breath.

With a sluggish mind, Marietta leaned over, glimpsing outside to see rolling hills with brown grass sprouting green. Bodies marched in verdant fabric and metal armor in the early morning sun, traveling in the opposite direction of the carriage. What were they doing? Green, what city wore green?

Gods, she couldn't remember—not with the pain slicing through her temples and burning at her side, pulling her focus from the view. A cloying floral scent perfumed the carriage, not aiding in her pain. Marietta shifted on the padded seat, binds tying her hands behind her back. Why would her hands be bound?

Marietta stared at the floor, bobbing along with the carriage's movement as she pieced together the world around her. Their bedroom was dark besides the light from the window. There was the glint of a knife, the fear in Tilan's face, and then nothing. Panic gripped her already dry throat as tears blotted her vision.

Someone had held Marietta back, prevented her from getting to Tilan, and now she was in their custody, traveling to gods knew where. She should run, put up a fight to be free, but her limbs were made of

lead, her chest hollow. A different pain bloomed in her heart, consuming her thoughts, her body, and her soul. Tilan was gone. Dead. She didn't know how long it had been since she woke next to Tilan, and she couldn't bring herself to care. It was as if a part of her was missing. Too painful to acknowledge.

Time slipped by, the sun rising and falling, causing light to dance through the curtain of the carriage window. At some point, the clanking of armor gave way to the soft whistle of wind over the barren hills. But none of it mattered. Not while Marietta imagined the silvered streak of a dagger, Tilan's face, and the slash that ended him.

The carriage door swung open when the sun was just above the horizon, the long shafts of golden light spilling onto grassy hills beyond the bald elven man who stuck in his head. He swore as he took in Marietta. "Get the medic. She's awake."

"How long?" asked a voice from outside.

"How would I know?" The bald man stepped back.

"Well, I thought the dose would last until we stopped." A moment later, a burly elven woman stepped into the carriage. Marietta didn't spare her a glance and didn't respond when she took her chin and tilted back her head. Fight. Push back. Get to freedom. But she couldn't. Grief suffocated her very breath from the missing part of herself. Instead, she tasted the sweet liquid spill across her tongue and down her throat. The edges of her vision grew black and fuzzy until nothing took over once more with a blissful release.

Bits of awareness came, fleeting and few, shifting like sand in the wind. For a moment, there'd be brief recognition of the world. The next, life was amorphous. Bright, glaring sun. Its warmth on her skin. Her body floating over veined floors. Someone's chilled touch lifting her limbs. Her body naked. The throbbing ache of her head, the searing pain of her side. Rough, calloused hands holding her face.

The grogginess lifted before Marietta opened her eyes, her body aching and her head throbbing. Pain sliced deep into her side as she tried to roll over, eliciting a gasp. Her vision was blurry and slow to come, the room around her white and small. At her waist was a thick bandage, the material stiff as her hands ran across it. Underneath her was a narrow bed, and across the room sat a cushioned chair.

With slow, careful movements, Marietta pushed herself up, her head spinning as she hung her legs over the bed's side. The drop to the ground wasn't far, but the pressure on her legs proved too much. Marietta's legs collapsed with her weight.

The cold marble tile leaked through her thin shift dress. The pain in her side burned. Just get to the door—get to freedom.

Marietta dragged herself towards the only exit, hissing at the pain, her head spinning with it. Breaths became forced, and she paused to rest her forehead against the stone. Tilan's frightened stare flashed in her mind, robbing her of effort. Gone. He was gone.

The tap of feet on tile came from the hall, ending with the creaking of the door as it swung open. "Goodness, my lady!" a feminine voice called. A moment later, the nurse lifted Marietta back onto the bed. The large elven woman tucked the sheets around her, smoothing back her hair. "Please don't get up; your muscles are too weak, my lady."

"Where am I?" Marietta's eyes stared into the hallway beyond.

"You're safe now, my lady. Please, rest. I'll let your husband know you've awoken." She turned to leave the room.

"Wait," Marietta said, her voice only a quiet rasp, "my husband?"

Either the nurse didn't hear Marietta, or she ignored her question.

The glare of a dagger. The look of fear in Tilan's eyes. The memory flashed before her, as clear as the night it happened. She said husband. Did Tilan survive?

Were they at an infirmary in Olkia? Why wasn't Tilan in the carriage with her? She was alone from what she remembered. Or was she? His throat would need intensive healing—is that where he was?

But who would hurt them? They were known and liked in Olkia, Marietta more so throughout Enomenos. Tilan would know. He always had an answer to her questions.

The nurse returned with food and water. Marietta's stomach rumbled, unable to recall feeling such hunger as she shoveled food in her mouth. The quality surprised her for an infirmary. "Where are we?" Marietta asked between mouthfuls as the nurse fussed with her bedding.

"Satiros, my lady."

Marietta's stomach churned as she set down her fork. "Satiros?" Why would she and Tilan be in Syllogi, the elven-ruled lands west of Enomenos?

The nurse's mouth moved, but her voice became garbled. Marietta blinked as her body grew heavy. "What?" Marietta asked. She forced her eyes open, the weight of her lids too much to handle as she sunk back into her pillows.

In the doorway, a figure appeared, a man's voice speaking. Calloused hands took her own—Tilan. It was Tilan. Marietta tried to open her eyes, to fight off the sleepiness, but darkness overcame her once more.

The sleep was dreamless; the occasional voice broke through her sedation, but the words were meaningless. More than anything, Marietta felt nothing—not the time slipping by, not the pain in her body, in her heart. There was nothing. The pleasant darkness consumed her.

Marietta's eyes opened as someone left her room, glimpsing red hair tucked behind elongated elven ears. She called out, but her throat was too dry to make a sound.

Attempting to lift her head, she fell back to the pillows, the weight too much for her neck. She tried to move her arms, but they too lacked the energy to move. The bandage remained around her middle, but the pain was bearable.

Tilan was coming. Marietta needed to know he was alive despite what she saw that night.

Rousing her strength, Marietta failed to sit up. She tried again and again, wanting to get up, needing to move. Her limbs were like the boughs of a sapling—weak, unable to support any weight.

The nurse bustled through the door. "Oh good dear, you've woken again. I'm sorry you missed your husband. He's away for the day, but he'll be back tomorrow. I'll make sure not to overdo your dosage this time," she said in an assertive tone. "The traveling medic said that your drugs burned through your system on your ride to Satiros, but you would've had more on your bones then." She gestured to Marietta.

She glanced down at her unrecognizable body—frail, bonier. Her curves fell flat beneath the fabric of her shift. With wide eyes, Marietta stared at the nurse. "How long have I been here?" she whispered.

The nurse put her hands on her hips. "Oh, I don't know. About three weeks since they brought you to me."

"Three weeks?"

"The healing wracked your body. Your injuries were severe enough that we had to ask the temple for additional help. Can you believe we had a temple attendant here to help heal you? You took quite the fall down the stairs. The soldiers said that they've never seen someone fight like that with the inhalant in your system. They said you were quite the beast, expected for a half-elf." She laughed and moved to the doorway.

"Wait, what happened?" Marietta's chest tightened as she tried to recall the events that led her to that infirmary bed.

"Don't worry, my lady. Your husband will stop by tomorrow. He wants to be the one to tell you everything." She winked as she closed the door behind her.

The day dragged into evening and Marietta was alone with her thoughts. Sleep was a reprieve from the back and forth pull in her mind— Tilan. Was he alive? Injured as he was, would he be able to speak just three weeks later? But the nurse said her husband. Tilan had to be coming.

The following morning, Marietta woke to the nurse. "My lady, your husband is on his way down." She left without another word.

Relief flooded her with a heavy sigh. Marietta wanted to hold Tilan and to know what happened. Who was it that attacked him? Why were they in Satiros instead of Olkia?

Heavy footfalls sounded from the hall, pausing at her door. She watched the handle turn, her face smiling in anticipation for Tilan. The door crept open, revealing who stood beyond.

Her face fell, a sudden coldness hitting the core of her body as she realized what had happened. In the doorway was not her husband but Keyain Vallynte.

Chapter Four

MARIETTA

BEFORE

Enomenos was beautiful. Each city-state had a personality, a claim to the world, and Marietta considered herself lucky to work in each of them.

The river city-state, Rotamu, had the best ale and the most breweries, where a person could try a new drink every night for months on end. To the north, Avato had frigid winters that contrasted with its citizens, who possessed warm hearts in the mining communities. As a blossoming artisan city-state, Olkia was home to the best craftspersons in the region. Notos to the south had beautiful weather, sandy beaches, and a collection of the most curious people. As the major port city, many world-travelers came to and from the seaside city-state.

And Kentro, the place Marietta now walked, was her home. The capital sat at the center of Enomenos, bustling with industry and nightlife. Growing up here meant never having a moment of quiet, which Marietta loved.

Because her job was to connect businesses together, she had clients all over the region and often spent a week or two in each city-state. Every day was different—different clients, different places, different tasks—sharpening her mind and indulging her ever-present desire to see and know everything. No other job would give her that freedom, that independence to travel at will where no day repeats itself.

As lovely as the city-states were, they paled in comparison to the people

who lived there. Marietta loved the dynamics between the citizens—humans, elves, and half-elves—that occupied Enomenos. The physical differences between them were subtle. The elongated, sharply pointed ears of an elf were easy to spot from the round-tipped ears of humans. Half-elves, like Marietta, had a blunted arched tip that was somewhere in the middle. If someone had hair upon their face, they were human or half-elven because the elven couldn't even grow stubble.

It was a common belief that humans and elves descended from different beings. The old gods had molded the first humans, or the pili, from the earth and gave them sentience. Their children—the humans and half-elves of today—were named the pilinos. Elven had their own creation myth, believing that they were descendants of the fey. As a child, Marietta's father had shared such feyrie tales with her.

Beyond physical discrepancies, the main difference between the pilinos and elven was the length of life. Humans lived less than a century where elven could live up to six. As she journeyed down the street, Marietta smiled as she passed an elf still in their prime with a human wrinkled with age. Were they friends? Lovers? Maybe they'd been married for the last fifty years?

It wasn't often she'd see an older elf with a young human, many mindful of the age gap in romantic relationships; yet, camaraderie and friendships defied the distance in age. Even one of Marietta's dearest friends was an old elven man from Avato.

As for romance, Marietta knew if she ever loved a human, she would be unmarked with age by the time they'd pass on, outliving them by a century. To remarry after a spouse died remained common for that reason. It wasn't unusual for elves to love and marry multiple people across their six hundred-year lifespans. Not that she'd find a partner who worked with her schedule. The seamstress from Notos had ended their relationship last month for that very reason, claiming Marietta didn't make time for her. Her business came first—always.

The travel came with another drawback: being alone on the road made Marietta an easy target. Hiring a new sellsword or mercenary to escort her grew tiresome—and expensive. A friend recommended a Syllogian elven man new to town looking for permanent work. Marietta was on her way to meet him.

Marietta's cloak fell open as she approached the Drunken Drought, a tavern in the center of Kentro's entertainment district. The wintry air cut through the narrow street, the sun's last rays giving way to a clear night sky. Above her, the stars twinkled.

She pushed past the heavy wooden door and took in the familiar features of the tavern. The lighting was warm, with lanterns hanging from the ceiling and hearths illuminating the bottom floor. Idle chattering and the stale scent of ale and food made her smile.

The barkeep, an elven man well into his life with wrinkles creeping onto his face, waved her over to say hello. Marietta started for the second floor after a quick greeting and asking how his wife and daughter fared. It had been a year since she worked with the Drunken Drought. The owner had hired someone to do his finances, which meant she had done her job well enough that he could afford to hire someone.

The staircase creaked as she ascended to the second floor, reaching the balcony and leaning on it to watch her surroundings. The walkway around the second floor was wide, encircling the bottom, and gave more privacy than the packed tables on the first. Marietta preferred to meet up there, especially on nights the tavern grew busy like it would that evening. Kentro had a rich nightlife, with many flocking there for a vacation filled with entertainment. A musician would play that evening; most likely, Marietta knew who they were.

As she took a seat, an elven man she presumed to be Alyck based on his description walked in. Stocky for a full elf, a buzz of black hair, and a grin on his face. Marietta sighed as she noticed the other elf at his side. He towered over his friend with a thick wave of brown hair and cheekbones that could cut stone. Broad-shouldered with a narrow waist, Marietta noted the confident way the hulking elf carried himself.

As they approached the table, Marietta bit back her annoyance and smiled. "Hi there, you must be Alyck," she said, her hand extended to shake.

With a glance at her otherwise ignored hand, Alyck slid onto the opposite bench. "That I am. Have you ordered yet?" He raised his hand, flagging down the barmaid.

Gods, he lived up to the stereotype. Likely, he held the same views of other Syllogian elves—that pilinos were subservient to the elven. At some point in history, the elves of Syllogi deemed being descendants of fey made them more important than those who descended from the pili. Marietta found it all to be quite stupid. People were people regardless of being human, elven, or something in between; yet, across from her sat the perfect depiction of arrogance bred from a well-fed superiority complex.

Marietta dropped her hand and narrowed her eyes. "Ah, yes. The reason we're here—the ale." Sarcasm laced her tone as she shifted her focus to the other elven man. "Are you here to get drunk as well?"

The man glared at his friend. "Apologies. I didn't realize Alyck had a meeting when he invited me."

"Well, now you know. We might as well kill two birds with one stone. Get drunk, conduct some business," Alyck said, turning to the approaching barmaid. "Two mugs of ale each."

The barmaid, who Marietta was familiar with, shot her an expression— the same expression all Enomenoan women gave to each other when dealing with rude Syllogian elven men. Marietta mouthed an apology as the barmaid went back to the bar.

"Two each?" Marietta lifted a brow. Seldom was there a chance to see such an accurate depiction of a stereotype play out. "Why not make it three?"

"Now, that's a stupid question," Alyck answered, his gaze locked onto a group of women on the first floor. "The third ale would just get too warm while you finish the other two."

"The expert has spoken." Marietta shook her head and turned to the other male. "Do you also carry such ground-breaking opinions on the correct number of ales to order at a time?"

"No," he said dryly.

"A shame." Marietta took in the sharp angles of his face, noticing the dusting of freckles across his nose and cheeks. An adorable detail on such a hardened man. The features conflicted with one another. "Do you have a name?"

"I do," he said, clearing his throat as he extended his hand. "Keyain."

Marietta grasped it and shook. "Marietta Lytpier."

Keyain held on to her hand a second longer before dropping it. He turned to his friend. "Why were you meeting Marietta tonight?"

The barmaid set down the ales. Alyck grabbed one and began chugging, Marietta rolling her eyes as a bit dribbled onto his shirt. He stopped to belch and turned to his friend. "Guard job or something."

Keyain exhaled, pinching the bridge of his nose. "A guard job.... Don't you think you're being a tad unprofessional?"

"Let him be his true self." Marietta took a sip of her mug and gave Alyck a leveling stare. "After all, we'd be spending countless hours together traveling Enomenos if he gets the job."

"Oh, traveling for work? Are you a medic?" Keyain drew her gaze, settling on the bright green of his eyes.

"I'm in the business to know other people's business," she said, finding that her smile came naturally as she spoke to the more palatable man. "I help merchants and craftspeople with various problems. Some don't know how to manage their finances. Others can't find the correct product or supplier. I have clients throughout all the Enomenoan city-states, and I travel between them often, hence why I would need someone to help as a bodyguard on the road," she said, giving an unimpressed look at Alyck, who had already finished his first drink.

"This ale," she said as she gestured to their mugs, "was brewed in Rotamu—a connection I made between the tavern owner to the brewer a few years back. The owner wanted a maltier, medium-bodied ale with caramel undertones, so I found him a brewer who could supply it."

"I've never heard of anyone doing such a job for a living." Keyain looked at her a moment before he continued. "How does anyone even start something like that?"

"For one, you have to be good with people." Marietta leaned forward with a smirk. "Second, I started working at a general store when I was a teenager. I excelled at both. When the owner opened a second location, I was the one to manage it. Only took two months for me to make it more profitable than the original store."

Keyain raised his brows. "Impressive," he said, his body holding the casual confidence of someone who knew how to talk to people and was sure of every word that came from his mouth. "But why didn't you open a shop? That would've been easier than traveling and growing other people's businesses." His undivided attention drew a smile from Marietta as she tucked a loose strand of hair behind her ear.

"And live a boring life tied to one place? No, thank you." Her hand batted away the thought. "Plus, I get to meet different people. It's wonderful what you can learn about someone when you introduce yourself. With every new person I meet, I feel more complete. Even with...." She gestured to Alyck as he finished chugging his second mug, rolling her eyes as he waved at the barmaid again. At the rate of his drinking, a third ale most definitely would have still been cold.

Keyain sighed, giving his friend a look. "He's an interesting person. How long have you been working like that?"

"Six years this past fall," she said without missing a beat. "Expanding from just Kentro to the other city-states in just a couple of years, but enough about me. What are two Syllogian elves doing in Kentro?"

Keyain shifted in his seat, shooting a glance at Alyck, who watched a new group of women walk into the bar. "Oh, just traveling. Checking in on friends living here with Alyck. So I often visit around Enomenos."

Marietta rested her chin on her hand as she regarded the elven man. Her mouth curved into a smile while her brows furrowed. "Don't take this the wrong way, but even coming from a guy who looks like—"she gestured at Keyain with her other hand "—that sounds disreputable. Is it drugs or contraband?"

A quick laugh left his mouth as he glanced at his drink. "Nothing like that. I'm just a private male; my business stays close to my chest. Even if the person asking is an accomplished female who looks like," he took his hand and gestured at Marietta in the same way.

She smirked as a blush crept across his cheeks. Such bashfulness surprised her for the hardened man he appeared to be. She could have fun with that.

"Okay, but I have to ask," Alyck said, his fist pounding against his chest for a burp. "You're curvy and got a cute face. What's your situation? Got someone waiting for you at home?"

Marietta angled her head, narrowing her eyes. "Excuse me?"

"Really?" Keyain shot him a warning look.

"I mean, come on, Keyain. Is she not attractive?" Alyck gestured to her with his new mug of ale, the contents sloshing onto the table.

Marietta finished her mug and sat back in her seat. Demeaning comments from men weren't an unknown occurrence, yet Alyck's words vexed her, containing the subtlety of a rock smashing through a window.

Keyain ran his hand through his hair. "I mean, yes, obviously."

"I'd fuck her even if she is a clip." Alyck laughed while sloshing his drink down his front.

Marietta turned toward Keyain, her eyes wide from the slur. She knew Alyck was an ass, but to call her a *clip* outright was beyond inappropriate. Derived from a Syllogian elf's fear of being mistaken for a pilinos, having *clipped* ears like a human or half-elf was the worst thing they could imagine. She bit down the anger brewing in her gut. "Fitting right into the Syllogian stereotype." Marietta stood, glaring over her shoulder. "Someone will be up in a moment to kick you out."

It took little to rattle Marietta, but it took a lot to make her heated, and Alyck had the right mix of words that would piss her off. Marietta didn't glance back as she strode towards the stairs.

"Well, I'll be damned—her ass is perfect!" Alyck yelled. Keyain's heated response was inaudible as she reached the top with clenched fists. It took one prick like Alyck to give elves a poor reputation in Enomenos. There was no physical difference between the Enomenoan elves and the scum elves from Syllogi, which often meant the elves from Enomenos faced unprecedented hate, more so in the human-dominated countryside.

Marietta told the barkeep about the men upstairs, adding the comments Alyck made. The barkeep's expression darkened as he sent up the bodyguard that worked for the Drunken Drought.

Someone called after Marietta as she left the tavern. The evening turned her mood foul, and she didn't want anyone to see her so agitated. She wished to crawl into her bed with a book and forget about the evening.

The night's chill greeted her as she exited the tavern, avoiding the slush puddles that formed in the city streets. The thick wool cloak swathing her body compensated for the thin silk blouse she wore for the meeting. Her outfit may have looked the part of a successful and experienced woman but failed to keep her warm in the wintry night.

A white cloud blew from her mouth with a heavy sigh. Marietta shouldn't have met with a Syllogian elf. She knew what they were like, how they mistreated pilinos in their city-states. Did she expect Alyck not to bring his views to Enomenos?

Marietta wound her way through the city streets and, out of habit, she walked through the business district, now empty for the night. The gas lamps that lined it remained dark at that hour. Of course, Alyck wanted to meet in the evening—just so he and Keyain could prey on drunken women. Typical Syllogian elves. The Drunken Draught would ban the bastards. No business needed that malevolence in their establishment.

The smack of footfalls surprised her as cold metal bit at her throat, putrid breath filling her nose. Marietta gasped as she clawed her way out, nails tearing into flesh. The metal dug into her skin as a deep voice whispered, "Quiet, pretty."

He jerked her back, dragging her towards a dark alley. Marietta's eyes scoured the dark street to find it void of people. In her panic, her foot swung out under the attacker's leg, causing him to lose grip on her. She pushed him back and turned to run away, but she slipped on the wet cobblestone. His hand caught her hair and pulled her backward as she screamed with her heart pounding in her ears.

Another set of footfalls thundered, followed by a loud smack behind her, and she broke free from his grasp. Marietta crawled through the dirtied slush of the street, panting and her mouth dry. She turned, finding Keyain punching her assailant with his lips pulled back in a snarl.

Keyain's fist ceased when the assailant stopped moving, his hand coated in blood and his face splattered with it. Marietta's eyes widened. Was the man dead or just unconscious? The alley's darkness obscured his features, and she could only see his stilled form. She focused on Keyain's face, the blood splatter adding to his freckles.

"Are you okay?" He offered his unbloodied hand to help her up.

Her body trembled on the ground, her mouth unable to speak, but she nodded her head.

"Come on. Let's get off this street. Where are you staying?" He helped her stand and placed a hand on her lower back, guiding the still-shocked Marietta towards the light.

The keys shook in Marietta's hand as she unlocked the door to her apartment, Keyain standing at her side. It was foolish to invite a stranger into her home, yet she couldn't shake the sensation of the knife at her throat or the fear of being dragged into an alley. Sure, he had an ass for a friend, but he had saved her, hadn't he? That had to mean something. Plus, the elven man would be a good distraction and a comfort. He was alluring, among other things.

"This is it," she said, nodding to the studio apartment that was hardly a home. She unclasped her cloak and tossed it next to her travel bag, half-packed with its contents strewn across the couch.

The room became visible as she lit an oil lamp. Keyain raised a speculative brow at the tiny room. His gaze missed nothing as it scoured the apartment from the two-seater couch to the single chair at a small table next to her few cabinets that counted as a kitchen. He tilted his head curiously at the bed placed near the window. Next to it sat a stack of books acting as a nightstand. "It's... quaint. And lovely."

Marietta laughed, making quick work of her boots before dropping them beside the door. "It's a shit hole," she said, pointing to the water-stained plaster just above her.

"I wouldn't go that far."

"Then you need your eyes checked," she said, turning to face him with her hands planted on her hips.

He rubbed the nape of his neck, hesitating. "I mean, I would expect a successful businesswoman to live somewhere a little more…."

"Extravagant?"

"I was going to say clean, but sure. Extravagant."

Marietta walked to the stove and started the flame. Though a shit hole, she picked it because not only was it cheap, but it had plumbing and a gas stove. Marietta preferred to have interior gas lamps, but she couldn't beat the price. She filled the kettle, looking over her shoulder at Keyain. "Can I get you anything? Cup of tea?"

He glanced up from the stack of books he inspected. "I'm alright, but thank you."

She placed the kettle on the stove, leaning back against the counter as she watched Keyain. The elven man was a stranger, but he made himself at home as he walked around the room, attempting and failing to hide the judgment from his expression. She laughed to herself as she turned to the whistling kettle, pouring it over the leaves in her teapot. Even with Keyain's close inspection of her apartment, calm washed over Marietta. Perhaps his presence alleviated her anxiety. Or, more realistically, it was the calming chamomile scent that drifted from her brewing tea.

Marietta turned back to the room as she waited for her tea to brew, watching Keyain grimace as he examined the items strewn across the couch. "I'm only in Kentro a week at a time," Marietta said, drawing his gaze.

"And?"

"That's why my apartment is small—and cheap."

"Oh, I wasn't judging," he said, the blush climbing his cheeks again, as he stood to face her, arms clasped behind his back.

Marietta laughed to herself at his ridiculous blushing; such an adorable action didn't match the man. "You most definitely are."

"It's just surprising. You dress like someone who's well off."

"That's because I am well off." Marietta hid her smirk as she turned back to the teapot, pouring the drink into a ceramic mug. Typical Syllogian elf focused on flaunting wealth and status.

Marietta met his gaze as she crossed the room, then dropped it to his body half-hidden by his coat. Anticipation built as Keyain followed her, leaning against the opposite wall as she sat on the bed. The couch would have been more appropriate, but the bed was a dare. How would Keyain react? Thoughts darted in his eyes; she could see him trying to piece together Marietta, which thrilled her. Heat sparked at the bottom of her stomach.

"Even if you're only here part-time, I thought you'd want to live somewhere that marks your status," Keyain said.

Marietta snorted. "I have nothing to prove, no status to claim. I only own this place as a means to hold the few items I own."

Keyain shook his head, one side of his lips curving up. "You're an interesting person."

Marietta shrugged, raising an eyebrow. "Is that the best compliment you can give?

"I could insult you instead. You were foolish to go down that dark, abandoned street."

"My anger distracted me." Marietta's fingers tapped the side of her mug as her eyes narrowed on Keyain. "On a normal evening, I wouldn't have gone that way."

"No kidding; alone at night, nonetheless." He frowned, shaking his head. "I called your name at the bar."

"I heard."

"I could have walked you back."

"I wasn't in the mood to deal with you," she murmured, blowing on her tea. Even under layers, she could see the strength of Keyain's arms crossing over his broad chest.

"Look, I'm sorry about Alyck. He's a good guy, I swear."

Marietta rolled her eyes. Kicking him out sounded tempting, but the handsome elf delighted her, even as he defended his friend. "I suppose you would think good guys say clip, being from which elven city-state?"

His jaw tightened at her pointedness. "Satiros. He shouldn't have said it, but Alyck likes to… rile people up to see what they do. It was inappropriate of him, and I apologize on his behalf."

"Hmm," she said as she sipped her hot drink, her expression the same. Stupid, she should throw Keyain out and forget about him. Why would she want to keep him around when he defended his terrible friend? The slur still pissed her off, yet at least he hadn't been the one to say it. Keyain grew desperate as he shifted his weight from foot to foot, and gods did Marietta enjoy it. His need for her to accept his apology was intoxicating.

Keyain mussed his hair. "I'd like to take your job offer."

She lowered her mug, frowning. "You want it? Why?"

"I'm traveling around Enomenos already. We can travel together." He kept his head lowered but raised his eyes to watch Marietta's reaction.

"And you're willing to travel about to whichever city-state I need?" she asked with a smirk, her eyes narrowing. "What work do you do in Satiros that could be so flexible?"

"A security job of sorts. I have a few months off at a time." He smiled at Marietta's smirk, lowering his eyes again.

"Interesting," she mused. Keyain continued to shift under Marietta's dominant gaze. It was almost too easy. "What credentials do you have?"

"For one, I don't order my ales two at a time."

"A great start," she said, "but Alyck set the bar low."

"I also protected you tonight."

"Another great point." Marietta sipped her tea again, watching him stress.

"I'm exceptional with a sword."

"I'm sure you are," Marietta teased, raising a brow.

That damned blush reappeared across his cheeks, causing her stomach to tighten. "You're making this quite difficult."

"Is that a problem?"

He paused, his stare locked onto Marietta with furrowed brows and a smile. "No. Not at all."

"Good, because you have the job," she said, smirking over the rim of her mug. "But I'm paying you less because of Alyck."

"Fine by me," he said, chuckling, "your company will make up the difference."

"Is that so?" Marietta paused, deciding how that evening would go. She set her mug on the stack of books beside the bed, her heart skipping a beat as recklessness flared through her after the night's events. The attack had made her feel helpless. Getting to know Keyain more intimately would put her in control. Her eyes snapped back at him, daring. "How about we test your company tonight?" She leaned back on the bed, inviting him.

A surprised smile grew on Keyain's face as he pushed off the wall, stalking towards Marietta. One of the more stupid things she had done, she admitted, but Keyain was alluring—strong, deadly, and most likely exceptional with his *sword*. What's the worst that could happen?

Marietta's breath hitched as his finger lifted her chin, his gaze burning through her. His lips found hers, kissing with that confidence that carried him as he pushed her onto her back.

Keyain shucked off his jacket and tossed it to the floor. Marietta drew him back to her mouth, working her fingers into the muscle of his back. Though she knew how large he was, she didn't understand the extent of it until he was on top, thrusting his pelvis against her. Not uncomfortable, but also not the control she wanted.

"Sit up," she demanded.

"What?"

"Sit up and take off your shirt."

Keyain took a few calming breaths and pulled himself back. He grabbed the hem of his shirt and dropped it next to his coat.

The broad width of his shoulders extenuated the narrowness of his waist. Everything in between was hardened with muscle. Marietta's gaze traveled lower to the bulge in his pants. "I see your sword is ready to be unsheathed," she teased with her lips curling into a smirk.

"Really?" he said, his voice breathy. "That's why you wanted me to sit up? To tease me about my *sword*?"

"Not at all." Marietta pushed herself up and grabbed Keyain's chin. "I want to be on top."

Keyain returned her smirk and turned to lie back on the bed. "By all means."

Marietta straddled him, splaying her hands across his broad chest. "But I am ever so curious."

"About what?" he murmured, lifting his hips into her.

"What type of sword are we working with here? Is it a long sword? Maybe a broadsword?"

Keyain paused and gave her a look. "Seriously?"

She ran her hand down his stomach. "Maybe it's only a dagger."

"It's bigger than that," he said defensively.

"Hmm." She ran her hand over his bulge. Keyain moaned as she rubbed, feeling the length of him. "Indeed you are. Perhaps it's a bastard sword."

"You are so difficult," he said, shaking his head with a smile. "Why do you know so much about swords?"

Marietta sat back, undoing the first button of her blouse. With a hard swallow, Keyain's gaze trailed her hands. "I told you: I'm in the business to know other people's business. I'm a jack of all trades, and I know a master in at least one."

"Isn't the phrase 'jack of all trades but a master of none?'"

"Traditionally, yes." Her hands reached her navel, the silk parting to show her skin. Keyain drank in the view, his cheeks flushing. "Yet my worth is tied directly to who I know, so knowing one master in each trade is an asset." She undid the last button and slid her blouse from her shoulders.

Keyain's expression was pained as he stared at her chest. "This is hardly the time to talk about business."

"Then don't ask silly questions like why I would know about swords." Her black curls tumbled onto her breasts. She played with the end of one,

47

looking down at Keyain. "Now tell me, what is it that you want?"

"You."

"You want me to fuck you, Keyain?"

He shuddered as she said his name, ending with a nod.

She leaned forward, her breasts rubbing against his chest. Marietta moved in to kiss him, stopping just so her lips brushed against his. "I need you to use your words."

"Yes," he said, breathless as his hands gripped her hips.

She laughed, dragging her teeth across his bottom lip before sitting back. "I'll be happy to," she said, toying with the ties of her pants. "But you'll have to do some extra work."

"Gladly." He reached to undo them himself, but she pushed away his hands.

"Not what I meant. You can help with that another time." She shifted to slide her pants down her legs. "Tonight, I'm in control."

Keyain nodded his head, gaze raking over the curve of her hips and stomach. How much he enjoyed staring at her thrilled Marietta. She leaned over him once more and guided his hand between her legs. "Touch me."

The rough tips of his fingers rubbed against her center, and Keyain swallowed her moan with a kiss. His touch was feather-light as he circled her, adding to the heat that burned in her stomach. As he reached the top of her center, his fingers pressed harder on the nerves clustered there, and a moan escaped her. She shifted her hips at his hands, asking for more. His fingers stroked along her, teasing as Marietta's head fell to his chest, biting as her breath hitched.

"You're already getting so wet," he murmured as he slid his finger along the outside of her. Marietta's stomach tightened with growing heat. "Fuck, Marietta."

A smile curved onto her lips. The tension in her stomach expanded, tingling spreading from her center to the tips of her toes. Against Keyain's chest, Marietta savored the warmth and his woody scent mixed with something clean. His heart raced, adding to his groan as she shifted her hips again. Her head grew light, and her breath strained with the swipe of his finger.

"Go inside," she said, her voice far away.

Keyain slipped in a finger. "Fuck," he groaned. As he slid in a second, she shivered from the feeling of him filling her.

"And place your thumb—"

He already knew where to touch as his thumb found those nerves once more, his fingers curling inside her. She gasped as her thighs quivered around his hand. Gods, he was good—better than good. Her breath caught as his touch became more fervent, sensing how close to the edge she was. The tension grew unbearable while numbing spread to each tip of her fingers and toes. It snapped, shooting through Marietta as she rode his fingers with a cry from the pleasure. Keyain murmured her name and slipped his fingers out from her. Wetness dripped down her thighs.

"Fuck me," he moaned. "You are making a mess."

"That means you did a good job." Her voice was breathy as she kissed him. Her fingers laced into the silky strands of his hair. "Now, let's unsheathe that sword."

He shook his head with a laugh as she sat back. Marietta watched as he tugged his pants lower, revealing his cock. Definitely not a dagger. With a smile, she grasped it, Keyain groaning as she pumped her hand. "Keep going," she said. Keyain took a shaky breath and hastily threw his pants to the side. When he settled back into the bed, Marietta positioned herself on top.

"You are so beautiful," he said as he gazed up at her.

"I know." Marietta smiled. "And have you seen this ass?"

Keyain shook his head again and laughed. He abruptly stopped as she lowered herself against him. Between her legs grew slick as she glided him along. "How bad do you want me, Keyain?"

"Very bad," he said with a strained voice as he shifted his hips.

"Hmm."

"What?" he asked, his stare snapping to her.

"Very bad isn't that bad."

His expression grew pained as he asked, "Why are you teasing me?"

She slid his cock to the entrance, then slowly lowered herself down the length of him, moaning as his size filled her. "Because I can."

Marietta rocked her hips, slipping his cock in and out. She tossed her head back while she rode, enjoying the tension that built once more. Keyain's breaths became heavier as he gripped her hips. She removed his hands, lacing her fingers with his as she pinned them above his head.

"Fuck," he moaned, the muscles in his neck tightening. Through narrowed eyes, Keyain watched her with panting breaths. She smirked down at him, watching his reaction as she tightened the muscles in her center. As he tossed his head back and thrust his hips up, forcing his cock deeper.

"Like that," she said, her voice high and breathy as her body shook. Marietta moved her hips faster, moaning as she neared the tipping point once more. Keyain's hands fought against her, straining against her pin. Her grip tightened as pleasure took her, tension snapping as her vision went white behind the lid of her eyes. She came in waves, crashing from her center to the tips of her toes.

Lightheaded, Marietta slumped to his chest from the headiness of pleasure. Keyain grabbed her hips and guided her as he groaned her name. With his release, Keyain's body tensed as he cried out.

For a minute, they remained settled into one another, the sound of their pants filling the silence. "I was wrong," she said, speaking into his chest.

"About what?"

"Your sword." She pushed herself back to stare down at him. "It's definitely a great sword."

Keyain's face split into a smile as he pulled her back to him. His lips found hers, kissing her in between laughs. "You are something else," he said, brushing back the lock of her dark hair.

Marietta curled up against him, savoring the closeness of Keyain. Though a stranger, she felt comfortable lying naked in the crook of his arm. "By something else, you best mean hilarious."

"The most entertaining person I've met today."

She smiled up at him as her hand rubbed his chest. "Well, I could be more entertaining. How much longer until your sword can have another bout?"

"Seriously?" he asked. "You want more?"

Marietta pushed herself up, her curls cascading around her. "I could go all night."

A smile hooked Keyain's lips as he cupped her cheek. "I won't keep you waiting for lo—"

Marietta silenced him with a kiss.

Chapter Five

MARIETTA

The door latched behind Keyain as he stepped into the room. Marietta's heart jumped to her throat as she scurried backward on the bed. "What is this?" Marietta asked. Of all the people to attack her, why hadn't she considered him?

"Marietta," he whispered, eyes wide as he approached, "it's been so long." His hand reached out to her, but she pressed her back against the wall.

"For a good reason," she hissed. "Why am I here? Where's Tilan? The nurse said my husband was coming."

His hand fell, as did the look of hope on his face. Keyain swallowed hard as he said, "I am your husband."

"No, no, no...." If she was in Satiros because of Keyain, then her situation was worse than she realized. With bile rising in her throat, heart thundering in her chest, Marietta jumped from the bed, past Keyain. After two steps, her vision turned white, her limbs weak beneath her. Keyain caught her as she collapsed.

"Please, you must rest."

With the slight effort she could afford, Marietta pushed him away. "I asked where my husband, Tilan, is."

"Mar, I—"

"You don't use that name. Not anymore." Hot tears blurred her vision. A hasty hand wiped them away as she glared at Keyain.

"Okay," he said, holding out his hands. "You've been through a lot. It'd be best if—"

Keyain reached for her, and Marietta smacked away his hand. What right did he have to bring her to Satiros? "Why am I here, Keyain? And where in the hells is Tilan?"

"Do you remember what happened to Tilan?" he asked, taking a step towards her. "He's gone, Marietta."

Gone. Tilan was truly gone. Marietta's breath hitched as tears spilled from her eyes, mouth quivering as she yelled, "What did you do?"

"Hush, please." He reached for her again, Marietta's weak punches powerless against his embrace. Keyain's lips grazed her forehead, the touch scathing. "The soldiers said your injuries were severe, that you hit your head hard." He paused with a deep breath. "I've missed you so much."

She thrashed against him, screaming into his chest. His touch was familiar yet foreign from memories she'd long blocked out. Marietta needed to break free—to escape.

In a blur of motion, her knee found his groin, jerking up into his crotch as she darted away from him. Even in his pain, Keyain's size and strength held her to his body. As his arm shifted to her face, Marietta bit down and broke his skin. Dropped from his hold, she fled for the door. The handle was in her grip. She pulled with all her strength as Keyain's hand landed next to her head on the door, slamming it shut.

The bastard. She wouldn't stay there. Not with him. Marietta swung her hip into him to shove him out of the way, but his mass held. Her limbs were leaden as she tried again, failing in their weakened state.

Keyain wrapped her in his arms, whispering into her hair. "I know it's a lot to take in," he murmured to her. "I'm so sorry the humans have tricked you so."

"What are you talking about?" Breath snagged in her throat as she looked up at him. Was he always that tall?

"The Enomenoans took you from me. And now you're home, my wife." He whispered as he guided her back to the bed.

"I'm not your wife," she hissed.

With his strong arms, Keyain placed her on the bed as he knelt beside it with his face, keeping his face level with Marietta. "You are my wife."

He moved a stray curl of hair from her face, the gesture too personal, too sensuous.

"You're a liar," she whispered, her voice fraying with emotion. "Why am I here? What did you do?"

"I saved you, Marietta. It took longer than I would've liked, but it was now or never." His thumb rubbed over the top of her hand.

"Now or never?"

"Olkia is now under King Wyltam's rule. We besieged the city after my team extracted you."

Marietta smacked his hand away. "That isn't true."

"It is. It's a wonderful success for us in Satiros. That includes you, Lady Vallynte." A soft smile formed on his lips despite the sadness in his eyes.

"Don't call me that." The walls of the room pressed in, threatening to smother her. "If Olkia fell to Satiros, that means your King has damned my home."

"Hush, Marietta. It's alright. Please, don't cry." He pulled her tight to his body.

Numbed, she barely registered her tears that fell. Marietta struck his face with a weak effort, the hit darkening Keyain's expression. Her entire body shook. "I told you no, I would not marry you, and I made that very clear. The last time we spoke, I said I never wanted to see you again." Didn't he get over their relationship? Her voice cracked. "I married Tilan, not you."

A vial appeared in his hand from his pocket, filled with a light blue and milky substance. "I didn't want to do this, but it'll help with your emotional pain."

Marietta scrambled away from him as he brought the vial to her mouth, her voice thick. "I want nothing from you. Not now, not ever."

"Marietta, please. It won't knock you out again; it'll just take the edge of pain off. The doctor wants you to take it."

As he leaned into the bed towards Marietta, she pressed her body against the wall. With the uncorked vial in one hand, his other grabbed her jaw, forcing it open as the contents emptied into her throat.

The thick substance was like syrup, slowly dripping down and causing her to gag. Keyain held her mouth shut as she attempted to spit it out. Only when he was sure it had gone down did his grip loosen, her body falling into him as energy fled from her. Keyain placed her down on the bed, his hand rubbing circles on her back.

Some things never changed. Unattainable goals were challenges to Keyain. Anything was possible with a plan. He had tried to control Marietta's life—which she never wanted—but it seemed his efforts had paid off. Marietta was in his custody, so he would get everything he wanted.

His touch, once welcomed, felt like a thousand needles pricking across her skin. His smile and his laugh once made her chest tighten with happiness. Being in his home city-state, getting a glimpse of his other life, once would have thrilled Marietta. At one point in time, he was her most trusted friend, but now, with Tilan dead and her city seized, Marietta learned how far Keyain would go to get what he wanted.

Marietta wanted to believe the Keyain that she once knew disappeared, replaced with an evil, ruthless version of himself. But that wasn't true. His smile, his touch, and his tenderness were still the same. His affection was so much like the day she left that it was unnerving, sending chills down her spine. Keyain's cruelty had always been there; he had always been this version. She just never saw it until now. The anger subsided, replaced with a depth of sadness and mourning that left her breathless. Her reality hit her again; Keyain had taken everything from her. She had learned that hurting others wasn't above him the night they met, and yet, she would never have thought he'd be okay with attacking an entire city, killing innocents as they slept in their beds.

Sorrow washed over her, first a slow wave, then heavy crashes, threatening to drown her as breath lost its grip. Grief took her heart—for her lost city, for her friends, and for her husband.

As the drugs took hold of her consciousness, her world faded to black.

Chapter Six

VALERIYA

Valeriya brought her hand to her chin as she glared at her husband. "How sure are you? Her injuries were quite dire."

With his head bent down over his notes and dismissive of Valeriya's presence, Wyltam responded with a deep voice that didn't match his slim frame. "Keyain assured me she'd be at the victory ball, so she'll be there."

Lingering near the door, she bristled at her husband's response. King or not, he should treat his wife with more respect. The way he could easily dismiss her was one of many reasons Valeriya despised her husband. Thick red curls flipped over her shoulder as she turned. "I don't see how. They've kept her under heavy sedatives."

A sigh escaped Wyltam's mouth. Above his desk hovered a light globe that cast his office in the Royal's Suite in a golden glow. Like most days, Valeriya found Wyltam tucked away to read whatever subject he deemed worth his time. What he studied didn't matter—if only he put as much energy towards being the King.

He pinched the bridge of his nose as loose tendrils of black hair drifted in front of his face, hanging just below his eyes. "Keyain said she would be there." His voice grew sharper as the conversation continued.

"He's your friend. Wouldn't he tell you more?" Valeriya crossed her arms and stepped towards her husband. She might as well press him while he felt talkative. Somehow, the only heir to the Satiroan throne missed the charisma needed to be a leader. Silly of her to think she could help Wyltam change. An impossible task when he was never willing to meet her halfway.

"You do well enough by finding information on your own. Why don't you go learn for yourself?" The inky black of his eyes stared back at her. Since the day they met, he had been cold and guarded toward Valeriya. After years of trying, she realized how fruitless any relationship would be.

"Why do you think I went to the infirmary?" She took another step towards him. "The nurses said the injuries were serious when she arrived. The poor girl—"

Wyltam raised a hand to cut her off. "You've already explained her injuries to me." His hand lowered to the book, finger extended to a line as he looked between it and his papers.

"And I will continue to explain her injuries until you question Keyain about how she got them. Why would a minister's wife be in such a dire state?" Valeriya snapped, patience wearing thin. How dare he act like she was being unreasonable? Something wasn't right about the situation. The least he could do as *the King* was question his friend about what had happened.

Wyltam knew how to crawl under her skin and rub against each one of her nerves, which was why she never sought him out. Working with Wyltam was like trying to break chains with her hands—a fruitless effort that would never work and only left her bruised. He hindered the city-state's success, which meant he was a threat to her legacy. After all, Valeriya only agreed to the marriage to become a queen.

Her home, the Queendom of Reyila, sat in the Systada Mountains to the north. All her life, Valeriya knew her sister would ascend to become its Queen, and Valeriya had done everything in her power to stay at her side. That remained true until one thing had become clear: she would never have a legacy with the shadow her sister cast. Instead, she agreed to Wyltam's hand after learning about his aloof work within his court. Valeriya had thought there to be an opportunity to influence Satiros, but her husband had other ideas.

"That will be a private discussion between Keyain and me." The deep, dull tone of his voice was devoid of emotion.

Valeriya scoffed at his unsurprising nature. "When? Whenever it suits you?" she asked, pausing in the doorway to scowl at her husband.

"When I have the time," he replied, not bothering to look up.

"You don't think it's urgent that your Minister of Protection married a half-elf in secret?" Valeriya shook her head. As if Keyain's position of controlling the city-state guards and soldiers wasn't enough of importance, Valeriya thought Wyltam would at least care if his oldest friend hid such a secret from him. Useless as always.

His body tensed. "Why do you care if it's urgent?"

She narrowed her eyes. "You claim Keyain is your friend—likely your only true friend—yet you have little interest in his long, lost wife?"

He blinked, his expression unreadable. "Keyain made his choice."

"So you don't care that he's married to a half-elf?"

"At this point," he said, sighing, "he could marry a human for all I care."

Valeriya shook her head. Wyltam and Keyain remained friends out of formality after two centuries together. What had happened between them was somewhere between tragic and petty. Valeriya had only learned of it through gossip. "What is it with Keyain, my husband? Tell me, how was it that your childhood friend got to the highest position beside you, at such a young age, too? How do you feel about him marrying the half-elf behind your back after you helped him rise so high?" The sharper her voice grew with each word, the closer she leaned into her husband.

Despite her digging, his expression remained the same. "Keyain is many things to me, but at the moment, I find him to be a fool." He lowered his head once more, placing his finger back on his book. "You're dismissed."

Valeriya sneered, not bothering to hide her expression. How would he have seen it, anyway? His book swallowed his attention before she even turned. The door slammed behind her. Wyltam made her a queen, but it was an empty title. At most, she could affect court life. No one wrote books about queens like that. Change inspired historians to write and bards to sing; it made for a story worth telling. Valeriya would do everything in her power to ensure her life meant something—that her legacy lived long after her ashes scattered to the winds. To do that, she needed help.

The most useful thing about her sister Nystanya being the Queen of Reyila was that she still had powerful allies—her husband, King Auryon, included. Little did Wyltam know she had contacted them a few months ago, and their plan was already in motion.

Valeriya lifted her chin as she strode down the hall, each step carrying her farther from the male she despised. If she wanted to make history, then the change needed to be worthy. What better way to be remembered than to blend the pilinos and elven population of Satiros? As it stood, anyone not fully elven was considered a lesser citizen—a traditional Syllogian societal structure—yet, in Reyila, the pilinos were equal to the elves.

With her sister's help, Valeriya would reform Satiros by removing her husband from his throne and taking his place as its ruler. Then, when the dust settled, they would change Chorys Dasi—King Auryon's home city-state. It would be a mountainous moment in history, one surely to land her name in the books for years to come.

Valeriya would be remembered, even if it cost her everything.

Chapter Seven

ELYSE

Elyse paced outside her father's study, stomach clenched with apprehension. Her father didn't disclose why he summoned her, but she knew. The half-elf arrived.

What if she upset him? Her father was quick to blame misfortune on Elyse. It had always been that way. Her heart flipped in her chest, palms clammy as they gripped the doorknob, pausing as her head grew light.

"Will you just get in here?" called her father's voice, laced with irritation.

The nerves clenched her stomach again, the pain making her want to turn and run from her father. This wasn't a talk she looked forward to having, one that she often pushed from her mind to keep her anxiety at bay.

Elyse opened the door, stepping in to see her father behind his desk. His young face turned to a document he read. Papers were in ordered piles, correspondents with the other Syllgian courts. His position, Minister of Foreign Affairs, meant dealing with the city-states outside of Satiros. It also made him a prominent figure at court.

With numb limbs and a leaden stomach, she took a seat in the leather chair before her father's desk. Avoiding his gaze, she stared at her hands clasped in her lap, turning white with her grip as she tried not to shake.

"Elyse, we've talked about this. Hold your head up when talking to people." His tone was harsh. "Would you act this way with the Queen? Or around other court ladies?"

The copper tang of blood filled her mouth as she bit into her cheek.

She looked at her father, the elf who was a near mirror image of herself. With her chin now lifted, her eyes found his matching set, honey finding honey.

"It's official," he said.

"I assumed as much."

"You can't just hide in your rooms or the library."

She bit the inside of her cheek harder. That's exactly where she had planned to hide.

A sigh left his mouth, his fingers coming to his temples. "Running away isn't an option. It's a setback; he was quite the pairing for you. You got more notoriety out of it than he. But you still have your youth—Lady Grytaine is young for her marriage, and she has seven decades on you."

She nodded at her father's words, all true. What he left out was the blame he placed on her.

"Keyain is a fool," he hissed after a moment.

Elyse wanted to defend him, but she knew her father would mistake it for immature love. That wasn't the case.

When her father first shared that Keyain had already married a half-elf from Enomenos, she had been both relieved and distraught—relieved because she didn't have to wed Keyain, and distraught for how the nobles and courtiers would gossip over the failed betrothment. Elyse was the young elven lady who was about to rise so high, throttled by her betrothed's secret marriage to a pilinos. Lady Grytaine's laugh already filled her head.

"Lord Dyeiter confirmed that the law recognizes their union. Even if you had charmed him better, it would have meant nothing." The straight golden-brown strands of his hair, the same as Elyse's, shined in the light as he shook his head. "To think the fool started a war over a clip."

Keyain knew better than that. Everything he did had strong reasoning, meaning he wouldn't have started a war for that alone. No, Keyain had another reason; her father was spreading rumors again.

"Well, what do you have to say?" He leaned back in his chair, one arm gesturing out from the armrest.

"What do you want me to say?"

"Anything is better than nothing."

Her breath snagged at his disapproving expression. "I don't know what to say."

Fingers drummed on his desktop as his eyes bore through her. "I suggest you figure it out. You won't miss any time with the Queen. This situation is a setback, not a downfall."

"No," she moaned, jumping out of her seat. "Give me time, please! I can't handle that so soon after."

"The ladies are harmless; the problem is in your head. I won't let your delusional thoughts pollute your chance at staying close with the Queen."

That was another thing her father had done for her. The day Queen Valeriya's summons arrived was when her position had elevated from just a minister's daughter to Lady of the Queen's Court. The news was unsurprising to the other young nobles and courtesans. They pitied the Queen for having to deal with Elyse. Elyse pitied anyone that had to deal with her.

"I just... please. I need more time."

"Elyse, no. Keyain has slighted us, but we won't show that he has. Hold your chin high and act like it doesn't bother you, even though it does." The last bit was him implying that her attitude towards their called-off marriage was inappropriate. "You can no longer see Keyain in private," he added.

"What? He's my friend, regardless of everything." Keyain was her only friend at court, the only person she didn't drive away.

"Keyain is your formally betrothed who betrayed us by leading you on for years."

An exasperated laugh escaped her mouth. "I didn't even want to marry him!"

"Elyse, enough!" His fist pounded on the top of his desk, causing her to jump. "Keyain is my colleague, and you wanted to marry him. Now go, get your thoughts in order."

She stared at her father, the male she was a near duplicate of, yet possessed nothing of him beyond his physical features. Often her father said she was soft like her late mother. The words were an insult, but she liked them. Soft, yes, but soft didn't draw attention. Soft meant fading into the background. There was safety in softness; that was where she preferred to be.

Her eyes tore away from her father as she stood, leaving the room. Work occupied his attention before she made it to the door. Though happy she was leaving her father's presence, it irked her that work was more enjoyable. Like most people, he found most things more enjoyable than Elyse.

Her willowy body was heavy as she walked back to her room. The conversation had flared her adrenaline, leaving her drained. The library would have to wait until later; plus, going to the library meant running into other people, something else she didn't want to do.

As her mind drifted, a problem dissolved. She would at least find peace from no longer belonging to Keyain. Yes, that was desirable. No longer would she have to deal with forced conversation and unwanted attention. That torment would end with the betrothal.

The King would finally leave her alone.

Chapter Eight

MARIETTA

The soft glow of morning light bounced off the sterile white walls as the fog lifted from Marietta's mind. The drug's effects left her with no memory of what happened after Keyain forced the vial down her throat.

Focused on the ceiling, Marietta wished for the energy to escape the tiny room and the man who entrapped her. She longed for her home in Olkia, to wake up with Tilan and walk downstairs to open her bakery. Keyain ripped her away from that life. Tears returned as she closed her eyes, wishing they would stop. A heavy heart led to a clouded mind, and both made devising an escape plan difficult.

Startled from her thoughts, the nurse flitted through the door, humming to herself. She cracked open her eyes at the intrusion. "Oh, good morning, Lady Vallynte!" the elven woman said, setting down a tray of food. "Your husband will be by this afternoon to get you up and moving."

Marietta nodded, hope brimming in her chest. If Keyain took her from the room, her chances of escaping would be much higher—fewer barriers to freedom.

"After being bedridden for such a time, your body will be weak," she added, setting out a new gown of pale blue chiffon on the bed. "I told Minister Keyain to come as often as he could. Walks will help you regain your strength. Now, up, so I can get you changed!"

Marietta slid from the covers, legs wobbly as she gripped the nightstand for stability. Such weakness was unknown to her. Marietta

protested at the sight of the periwinkle fabric in the nurse's hand. "Is there something else to wear?" Such a tight garment made escaping difficult, not to mention the chafing between her thighs.

"This is what your husband chose for you, my lady," the nurse said, unzipping the fabric.

Instead, she attempted to cross her arms. "I choose my clothing, not Keyain. Is there an extra set of leggings and a tunic?"

The nurse laughed, shaking the dress before Marietta. "Minister Keyain failed to mention you have a sense of humor."

"Bold of you to assume I'm joking."

The nurse furrowed her brows. "You're a lady. You wear dresses."

"Only I decide what to wear." The little patience she had slipped away. "Not you or any *husband*." She spat the word, the betrayal to Tilan thick on her tongue. Keyain was not, nor would ever be, her husband.

"He mentioned you could be difficult," the nurse murmured under her breath. "This is all I have. There's only so much time for you to eat and to fix your hair."

"Fine," Marietta said, the submission making her want to scream. The sooner she left this gods forsaken room, the closer she'd be to escaping. Reluctantly, Marietta changed into the dress. The nurse then led Marietta to a chair and grabbed her brush.

As she reached for her hair, Marietta yanked away. "What are you doing?"

With a huff, she answered, "Brushing your hair, my lady."

"Could you wet it and use a comb? Otherwise, my curls will turn frizzy."

"A brush will have to suffice, my lady," she said, pulling Marietta back. "I don't have time to search for a comb."

Marietta held her sharp retorts, cringing as the nurse brushed. Never would she use a bristled brush on her hair, let alone when it was dry. The nurse only followed Keyain's orders, and he alone was to blame.

Finishing with a tight knot at the base of Marietta's head, the nurse placed the food tray on her lap. Though the porridge looked like paste, hunger drove Marietta to eat. Her hand shook as she took a bite.

"Good, eat your fill, my lady," she said, picking up Marietta's discarded clothing. "It'll help you regain the weight you lost while bedridden."

Marietta swallowed the tasteless porridge. "What were my injuries?"

"I won't bore you with the details, but thank goodness for the drugs that sedated you. Being awake with your injuries would have been cruel."

Yes, to be awake while in pain was the cruel part. The abduction, false marriage to Keyain, and seizure of Olkia were minor inconveniences. If hunger hadn't gnawed at her stomach, Marietta would have lost her appetite altogether.

Her mind grew foggy as she attempted to remember what happened and what had caused her injuries. There was Tilan, a knife glinting above him, the sharp sweep of its edge at his throat. Panic gripped her as her spoon clattered to the tray. Tilan was dead. A deep longing and heavy grief crept into her heart.

The nurse turned to her, Marietta watching through tear-filled eyes. "Oh, Lady Vallynte, don't be sad. Your experience must have been horrible." She approached Marietta, the nurse clasping her hands around hers. "But you're safe now, returned to your husband."

Marietta's lips quivered, her breathing coming with sharp gasps. Did she know the truth? That Keyain brought her to Satiros against her will? Or did she believe she was Keyain's wife?

"Hush, my lady," she said in a soothing voice, placing the spoon back in Marietta's grip. "Keep eating, and all will be better."

Marietta took another bite, though her throat tightened with the memory of Tilan. She wished to hug him, to feel the rise and fall of his chest against her while she played with his hair. She could imagine the stick of rolled tobacco behind his ear and the smoky scent clinging to him. Could imagine his loving smile as he looked up at her. But Tilan was gone, and never again would she get those moments. He would never craft another creation, would never tease her about her recipes; she would never be with him again. Tears rolled down her cheeks as her mind grew hazy again.

Her body was light, weightless. She fluttered through doors and hallways, passing the most curious things. To stop and inspect each statue and painting would be a dream, but someone pulled her forward by the arm. A tall person who was broad across the chest, led her through the palace. Her companion's face was unrecognizable with their features hidden beneath a gauzy white cloud.

Had she seen them before? She must have, for their guidance seemed familiar; yet, nothing came to mind. Nothing. Even the crushing grief from Tilan's death no longer weighed on her heart; the pain was nothing. She was nothing, and she welcomed it.

Time skipped with a blink and Marietta found herself in a room of gold filigree and marble statues. On a couch, she sat across from two other bodies with heads shrouded in clouds, like her companion who was beside her. A deep rumbling came from their chest, the words lost on Marietta, but a hand squeezed her arm. Golden light leaked through tall windows, lighting their clouded heads in a glow. A smile crept to Marietta's face at the shifting gauzy cloud in the sunlight, appearing like sunsets. Beautiful.

Between them was a coffee table, but Marietta's eyes locked on what held the glass top: a reptilian statue, its head supported the top on one side, and the tail flipped up, holding the other. The texture was that of scaled tree bark, from its pointed face to the legs that ended in sharpened claws. Draped across its back was a sheet of carved moss with matching bits of moss hanging from its jaw. The creature enchanted Marietta as she stared into its eyes, to the anger that radiated from them. She gasped when she felt the rage rolling off the statue, constant and threatening. It didn't want to be there. Her companion squeezed her hand, the clouded head darkening to a shade of gray. They didn't understand. It was trapped. The creature didn't belong in the castle; it craved to be free, like she once wanted.

Marietta wished to touch the reptilian creature, to run her fingers over the barked scales of its hide and soothe its anger. Shifting to stand, her companion's hand squeezed her thigh, halting her. But she needed to inspect the creature. Marietta tried moving again, this time the squeeze accompanied by a warning tone. The cloud on her companion's head turned black.

She furrowed her brows, looking between the creature and her companion. They didn't understand—the creature needed help. As a final attempt, she struggled to get up once more. Instead, her companion hooked an arm around, gripping her on the seat. Fury radiated from their body. She tried to wriggle her way out, but the grasp was too strong. Marietta surrendered and sat there as they wanted.

The pattering of rain on the window and the rumble of thunder greeted Marietta as she woke in her room. Wasn't she supposed to be doing something? Helping someone? Gods, what day was it? She raised a hand to her temple, rubbing in small circles, wishing the fog would clear.

Lights danced in her view as she sat up. No memories came to mind as she tried to recall what had happened since the last morning she woke. There was a statue, wasn't there? Or was it a person? Why wouldn't the details come?

Her mind instead wandered to Tilan, the memories searing into her heart. His laugh, the way his eyes crinkled at the edges when he smiled, were wounds in her chest. Marietta wished they had taken more time together, that they had taken a trip to Notos sooner. The regret was all-consuming, to never allow themselves a break. Never would they sit in the blistering sun with their feet in the salty water of the Evangi Sea. Their chance had passed.

What did her parents think? How had they reacted to Marietta's abduction? To Tilan's murder? Her elven father urged her never to date a Syllogi elf, and all this time she thought it was an overreaction. Did they worry about her or mourn Tilan? Gods, did they know? If they did, they would have given Tilan a proper funeral, standing beside his pyre and grieving him as family. After all, they adored Tilan.

On their first trip to Notos to visit her parents, Tilan won them over. Her father loved him from the start, fostering friendship between them. Her mother outright fell for him.

The morning after they had arrived, Tilan fixed her mother's wheelbarrow and the fence's gate. Both were things he noticed the day prior, waking before everyone else to repair them. Marietta's mother commented on how sweet he must be, but that was Tilan—always trying to help, always tinkering or designing something. Marietta didn't tell him until months later but that trip was when she fell in love with him.

Marietta hugged her legs, resting her forehead on her knees. The world lost such a remarkable person. Tilan, a man with a generous heart and thoughtful mind, ever having more to give. He was the most important person to her. He was the man who loved her truly, who gave all of himself to her. Tears fell as she wished she could hold him one last time.

Chapter Nine

VALERIYA

Valeriya sat with the ladies of the Queen's Court, concerned about the words they exchanged. They were drinking tea on the terrace above the Queen's Garden that held dense flower beds and twisting paths. It was their usual spot, but they had a new topic of conversation: the half-elf.

Lady Grytaine Lasyda gossiped with a smile plastered to her lips. "A shame that Keyain's mystery wife is so…." She paused dramatically, feigning to search for the word. "Dull, if you will." A few of the ladies hid smiles behind their hands as they failed to keep their composure. As per usual, Grytaine basked in the attention. Though she was nearly through her first century of life, she had the tact of a child. Valeriya held her sigh as she wished the lady would stop trying so hard.

Coming from a wealthy family—not a noble one—made Grytaine unique in the Satiroan court. Her marriage to Royir, the Minister of Coin, was far more bizarre, being that he was her senior by four centuries. Though there was much gossip about the courting and marriage, Grytaine learned to thrive on it. Such thick skin made her a fine fit in the Satiroan court, where gossip ran rampant. The one downfall she had, Valeriya noted, was that she didn't know when to keep her lips together.

Grytaine turned her focus to the youngest lady in the Queen's court. "Have you met the half-elf yet, Elyse?" Valeriya's expression remained pleasant as Grytaine baited Elyse once again. Withholding a sigh, she prepared to intervene.

"I haven't had the pleasure." Elyse's eyes grew wide with the attention

as her bronze skin flushed red. Such a nervous girl. Even after being in the Queen's court for five years, she remained as apprehensive as her first day.

"Pity," Grytaine said. "You should see what his wife is like."

Elyse's eyes darted to her lap as her jaw worked, and Valeriya waited just another moment before stopping them. One way or another, the girl would learn to speak for herself. Elyse cleared her throat, not bothering to lift her head. "I'm sure she's lovely."

Grytaine hid a sharp smile behind her teacup. "That's one way to describe her." A round of stifled laughs filled the terrace. "Though after meeting Lady Marietta, I can understand why you were so appealing to him."

Elyse's gaze shot to Grytaine and her lips moved, though no words came out. In her lap, her hands tore at the fabric of her dress. When it became clear she wouldn't answer, Valeriya cleared her throat. "Grytaine, your and Royir's anniversary is coming up, is it not?" The room turned their eyes from Elyse to her. "Exciting times. I'm sure you're both eager for a child."

Grytaine's smile faltered. "Quite eager, but of course there's still time." Valeriya stilled her smile at the response. It was an obvious target to aim upon, but her husband wanted another heir and grew impatient. As if there wasn't enough stress on reproduction for nobles. Valeriya had her own horrible experience as far as that went. She pushed such thoughts aside.

Lady Tryda, the wife of Satiros' Minister of Law, spoke up. "I'm sure you'll conceive any day now, my dear." Gray marked the temples of the heavyset elven female, her dark skin lined with years. After centuries at court, she always offered drops of wisdom to share. Much to Valeriya's annoyance, most of it was directed at her. As the previous Hand of the Queen to Wyltam's mother, Valeriya thought it would help bolster her position among the nobles. Instead, Tryda often shared how she could be a better queen.

"As for Keyain's wife," Tryda added, "we should look at her situation with empathy. Lady Marietta has endured more than we can imagine; it will take her time to recover. Until she is ready, perhaps we should give her the confidence that she is not her normal self."

Valeriya noted the ladies who exchanged smirks behind their teacups—Grytaine included. Someone whispered the word *clip*. After all the time spent in Satiros' court, Valeriya had hoped to change their views of pilinos for the better. With Marietta's arrival, the amount of work she had left to do became glaring. After all, if the court that presided over the city-state still slipped slurs and demeaning comments, then how would pilinos ever become equals? Irritated, Valeriya tapped her teacup. Marietta would bode well as a test for the court, to see how they accepted a half-elf into their ranks.

Of all the nobles to be accepting of pilinos, Valeriya hadn't expected Keyain. Some of the court whisperings said that Keyain developed a close relationship with Wyltam's mother—the horrid Queen Olytia, who set the strictest laws against pilinos in Satiros. Despite that, he had married Marietta. Something like hope sparked from within, that even those with the strongest hate for pilinos could change.

There was a chance, maybe, that Valeriya could use Marietta towards her goal. If she grew close with the half-elf and showed she carried her favor, then perhaps Marietta could draw relationships from the other nobles at court. Yes, that could work, but it left one glaring question: what happened to Marietta, and why was she left in Enomenos for so long? The truth of her history needed to be uncovered before Valeriya could plan on using her. That meant she had some work to do.

Chapter Ten

ELYSE

Elyse's heart threatened to burst as it pounded in her chest. Gods, she knew Grytaine would talk about Keyain's wife; yet, her mind still had blanked, unable to come up with a retort. Once again, Queen Valeriya had to step in to stop the situation from escalating—the Queen must find her irritating. After all, what lady in the Queen's Court couldn't hold their own?

Her throat remained tight as she raced to the library. Her father would learn about her reaction at tea, which meant his scolding was inevitable. Elyse tensed her shoulders at the thought of her father's raised voice, of sitting in his office as he told her how stupid she was. That's what it all led to—any other lady could handle the blow of a called-off engagement. Elyse, who struggled to look people in the eye as it was, didn't possess such skill. She was, as always, a disgrace to her father.

Voices carried from the adjacent hall, causing her to pause. She sighed, wanting to be alone. She darted across before they could say a word to her.

The worst was still to come. Keyain had kept his wife hidden away besides a few personal gatherings. What would people say once Keyain introduced her to court? She could already hear the whisperings of how once again Elyse ruined something else. It didn't matter if the broken-off betrothal wasn't her fault; Keyain held a powerful position. Elyse had more to gain from the arrangement, which meant she also had more to lose. Her breath quickened at the realization that Keyain was gone and no one stood between her and her father.

She darted around a corner, only to backpedal as she heard another

voice from down the hall. More people? Her luck had run out.

With a peek around the corner, she squinted to see Keyain escorting Lady Marietta by the arm. She seemed off. Her face was too happy, her body too loose. The only reason she moved through the hall was because Keyain half dragged her. Though her heart pounded in her chest, she followed the two. Even from behind, Elyse could tell that the half-elf was beautiful. Her light brown skin glowed in the golden light, with thick black curls tumbling down her back. Curves graced her hips and waist.

Odd. Neither anger nor jealousy lingered in her emotions like Elyse thought they would. She noticed Keyain's expression, the smile and the soft voice he used with Marietta. He was with the person he loved—someone Elyse would have never been.

Someone she never wanted to be.

Marietta stopped at a statue with a grin, but Keyain pulled her along. Grytaine had been wrong—Lady Marietta wasn't brainless, just drugged. Elyse was familiar with the drug's effects, one that made you complacent and your body light. The same drug her father forced her to take and she despised. Often she ignored her recurring head pains to avoid taking it, hiding the symptoms from her father.

Keyain and his wife rounded a corner. Elyse took one last look before turning back towards the library.

Large doors of oak and paned glass lead to the library. Beyond them lay the cavernous room, calling to Elyse. It was her safe spot, away from her father and away from all people. It was the only place in the gods' damned palace where she could breathe.

Flanking the entrance, two guards paused their conversation as Elyse approached. The one guard was a tall, dark male who always had a slight smile. If she were bolder, she'd ask him for his name; but every time she went to speak, her hands grew sweaty and her mind emptied. Instead, she kept her head down and offered a tight-lipped smile to the floor as he held the door open for her.

Like a cloud relinquishing its rain on a muggy day, Elyse took her first full breath since tea time that afternoon. Refreshing, relieving. The smell of old parchment and leather, the quiet atmosphere, and the dim golden light soothed her mood. Thank gods no one was coming to look for her here. Not yet, anyway.

She walked through the library lobby, the floors above open to the first with balconies guarded by a railing. Light globes hung above the entry, flanked by two grand staircases to both sides, rising to the two floors.

As expected, it was empty as she passed rows of bookshelves, heading to the back of the first floor. There sat her sanctuary: an alcove half-forgotten by the palace dwellers. Most took the books out of the library, never lingering long. The alcove was small but cozy, with a table settled between two cushioned benches. The top swung open to the hidden storage underneath. Elyse rifled through her stash of books, pulling out the pillows she hoarded. From her pocket, she took out a light globe and set it adrift, the alcove filling with a warm glow. With the curtains drawn shut, she sank into her spot.

What would her father make her do this time? Her betrothal to Keyain ended, so he was likely to reprimand her when gossip from tea time reached his ears. A hard pit formed in the center of her stomach, thinking of her father's punishments. Elyse was useful for sweetening his deals, loaning his daughter out as a date for his friends. Those dinners were long and unnerved her, and her father always ignored their wandering hands. At least with her betrothal to Keyain, that hadn't happened in the past five years.

She shuddered. No, she wouldn't think of it in her safe spot. With the pillows propped up behind her and her legs stretched out across the bench, she began reading. Her book offered adventure beyond the walls of the dreaded palace.

"Elyse?" a male asked through the curtain, causing her to jump. So engrossed in her book, she hadn't heard the approaching footsteps.

Her head jerked up towards the source of the voice. "Yes?"

The curtain pulled back, revealing a square-jawed male with mousy hair. She sighed at the sight of Kurtys, at his smirk and his stupid face.

"Apologies for bothering you. I saw you walk by, and you always come here. Mind if I sit?"

Annoyed, Elyse turned back to her book. "I mind." She sighed into her book as he slid into the booth across from her, closing the curtain behind him. Elyse dug her face deeper into the pages.

"I understand that you're busy," he said, "but we haven't spent time together lately."

"That's by choice."

"But you haven't given me an answer."

Looking up from her book, she flared her nose with a sigh. "I have, and it's no. I will not accept your proposal. How many times do I have to tell you this before you leave me alone?"

The young elf, still her senior by half a century, asked to marry her the day after Keyain broke off the betrothal. Unaware of Kurtys's proposal, Elyse hadn't seen the point of telling her father. For the minor noble to think her father would allow it was laughable. It didn't matter that Kurtys worked for her father.

"As many times as it'll take until you say yes." Kurtys leaned onto the table towards her.

With a scathing glare, she met his gaze. "First, you know that isn't up to me. Second, if it were up to me, I still wouldn't marry you." She lifted her book to cover her face, ending the conversation.

Fingers appeared over the top of the binding as he leaned across the table, pulling it down from her face. "No need to be so hostile." She glowered as his voice turned sultry. "I promise to make you happy, to give you every bit of what you want. You won't be thinking of Keyain's cock—"

"Out!" she yelled, slamming her book on the table.

"Elyse, don't do this to me." Kurtys spread his hands wide, his eyebrows knit together.

"Out," she yelled, pointing to the library beyond the curtain. "I've had enough with you. Leave me alone."

He snatched her hand as she pulled it away. "Please, give me a chance—"

She jerked her hand from his grip, yelling, "I said leave me alone!"

"You're an—"

The curtain snapped back, stunning Kurtys mid-sentence. Elyse held her breath, her hands and feet growing numb. "Lady Elyse, you sound distressed," said King Wyltam in his deep, rumbling voice. She hadn't been that close to him since she was still betrothed to Keyain—when he still had a reason to speak with her. Dread pooled in her gut.

"Apologies, my King," Kurtys said with a quick bend of his head. "Elyse never answered my betrothal."

The King kept his gaze on her. "I addressed Elyse, not you."

Her body shivered under his stare. Unable to take a breath, she muttered, "I wish to be alone, King Wyltam."

The King snapped his fingers. "Leave. If I find you cornering Elyse or pressuring her to marry you again, I will remove you from my court."

To watch Kurtys pale with fear was almost enough for Elyse to forget her dread. The noble scurried away, leaving her alone with the King.

King Wyltam slipped his hands into his pockets, his gaze finding Elyse. "Are you alright?"

Her throat tightened, and finding herself unable to speak, she nodded her head.

The King stared at her book. "*The History of Lyken Fulbryk*? I'm surprised you're reading about magic."

She clutched the book to her chest. "I, uh, like to read about people who travel and have seen the world, my King."

"Fulbryk lived quite the life. Are you able to follow his magic principles?"

She nodded again, her eyes wide as she gawked at him.

"Interesting, since you don't have formal training. I wonder if you'll be like your mother." He paused, tilting his head as he regarded her. "Well, carry on."

When the King walked away, Elyse released a breath as her shoulders slouched. Anxiety coiled its way from her gut to her chest, squeezing her heart. Grytaine at tea, Kurtys pressuring her, and the King's sudden appearance were all too much. Wearily, she tucked her knees into her chest, resting her head.

As much as Elyse wished to leave this life behind, she knew she could never do such a thing. This palace—this court—was her prison, bound by her father, a cruel warder wielding absolute power; but at least in that alcove, she found reprieve with reading the adventures of the well-traveled. Only there did she dare dream that one day, she too could be free.

Chapter Eleven

VALERIYA

Evening had already settled over the city as Valeriya ventured through the streets of Satiros. Light globes hung above the rooflines, casting the white-washed buildings in a glow in the fading daylight. A dense webbing of wisteria covered the side of this district's structures, their purple blooms vibrant against the pale exteriors.

Petal Row, the city district dedicated to entertainment, crawled with life. Denizens packed the sidewalks, and the trolley rolled by with its clanging bell. A mage sat at its front, using magic to push it along Oak Boulevard. Carriages passed with mages at their helm, using magic instead of animals to maneuver through the twisted streets.

Roasted meat, garlic, and other herbs permeated the air from various restaurants. The music carried through the air from music halls, a cacophony of lyres, drums, and singing voices. Some parks held outdoor theaters. If Valeriya neared them, she'd hear the actors crying out their poetic lines. She wished she had a chance to see such plays, yet her life didn't have that luxury—not when she had her legacy to build.

Instead, the greenery of the city blurred around her as she wove her way through. Gated parks sat at every block, dense with old oak and olive trees. Plants of every bloom sprouted in beds around them. As with every Syllogi city-state, statues of fey creatures rose among the foliage, stark and life-like.

When she turned down a side street, she also found it packed with meandering people. Stagnated, they took their time, enjoying the comfortable summer weather. When did she last enjoy an evening this

nice? Likely it had been during her last summer in Reyila with Katya. A smile tugged at her lips that she forced back. Thinking of her would be of no help with the task she set out to do that evening.

Shrouded in magic, Valeriya blended in with the crowd disguised as one of the palace's servants. Though being a royal was always her future, she had pursued a life as a mage to remain at Queen Nystanya's side. Her sister had other plans once she married Auryon and made him king. Convinced Valeriya was more useful in a position in a foreign court, they placed her in Satiros, where she could better use her mage abilities, unknown but powerful.

Wyltam's mother had been strict with magic practitioners. Most never had the chance to learn in Satiros, unlike the elves in the other Syllogian cities; yet, there was one thing they had in common: pilinos were restricted from learning to use magic altogether.

With an eye on the surrounding crowd, Valeriya slipped into a narrow backstreet. The scent of food grew thicker with the backs of restaurants flanking. About halfway through the alley sat an elven male on a crate. Greasy hair laid in thin strands and tied about his waist was a stained apron. At his mouth, he puffed on something pungent. An idle hand reached out front to scratch the gut hanging over his pants. Another great disguise from her contact.

The elven male grunted at Valeriya as she approached. "Oi, pretty thing like you should head on home." A gurgling noise came from the back of his throat, followed by his spit landing next to his foot.

Perhaps her contact was too good at his disguises.

Valeriya forced her voice higher and gave it a nervous shake. "Only when I've had a bite to eat."

With another grunt, the elven male stood, tossing what he smoked to the ground. He gestured for Valeriya to follow him. Before passing through the door, her eyes scanned the alley, her ears listening. No odd sounds, no odd sights. All seemed typical for that meeting.

A narrow staircase dropped Valeriya below the street. Above them, the restaurant bustled with patrons. Through the floor, the stomping of feet mixed with ambivalent chatter as her contact illuminated the dingy, cluttered cellar with a light globe. From what her eyes could see, they were alone.

"Were you able to collect information on the new half-elf in the palace?" she asked in her high-pitched voice, starting the meeting.

"I gathered a few things. Took Marietta right before the seizure of Olkia." A thick file appeared in his hand, which he gave to Valeriya.

"Did you know her?"

He nodded his head. "I know of her. Many people do. Well-known in Enomenos and used to travel for work. She worked with businesses throughout the cities, but she quit that a few years ago to open a bakery. Successful from what I hear."

"A bakery? That's quite the jump." Opening a new business while a prisoner of war was beyond unlikely. No, Valeriya could confirm that Keyain lied to the court. Marietta was never a captive. Only then, held in Satiros, had she become one. Curious, why would he lie? Why drag her to Satiros? The Minister of Law verified their marriage, yet why were they separated all this time?

Her contact continued. "When the Exisotis regrouped after the attack, no one could find Marietta. Her whereabouts were unknown until she popped up in Satiros a few weeks ago. A man was with her at the time of her abduction. Do you know anything about that? Or why they'd take Marietta?" It was his turn to get information from Valeriya.

She fought the urge to bring her hand up to her chin. "Minister Keyain brought Marietta to Satiros because she is his wife. Minister Dyieter verified the marriage license and signed it himself eight years ago. Keyain and Marietta are husband and wife under Satiroan Law."

He grimaced. "The first we heard of that. Anything about a man during the abduction?"

"Keyain's team killed a male that was with Marietta when they extracted her from her home."

The elf let out a long sigh, his disguise failing to hide the grief. "Is that so?" His fingers drummed on his arm, his stare distant at the news. With a shake of his head, he continued. "What is the King's army doing next?"

"Regrouping, letting the dust settle in Olkia before moving on to Kentro. They'll take out the heart of Enomenos, leaving the remaining three cities helpless. Have the cities negotiated with the Exisotis?" The anti-Syllogi group worked separately from the Enomenos Unionization Council. Through discreet efforts, the Exisotis operated in the background with their name unknown to most, aiding them in their necessary work.

"The governments of Olkia, Rotamu, and Notos agreed to work with the Exisotis. Kentro and Avato are still holding out, but we're confident they'll agree. The meeting next week will confirm all Enomenos is at war with Satiros."

Valeriya nodded her head. "What of the causalities in Olkia? Was the information I gave helpful?" During their last meeting, her contact asked for information to lessen the blow from their attack. Though Valeriya could benefit from Satiros' seizure of Enomenos, the idea of slaughtering innocents left her stomach queasy.

"As you said, they attacked from the west, marched right across the hills. We tried to evacuate the western district, and though plenty fled, many remained." A heavy sigh cut the grief in his face.

If Satiros attacked the city with its full force from the west, they would have slaughtered civilians. Killing families. Children. An attack on that district would have been devastating. Valeriya's heart clenched at the thought. The worst part was her husband's reason for attacking Olkia—or rather lack thereof. No one knew beyond some of the Ministers of his court.

"Do you have the papers?" her contact asked, standing up from the barrel and glancing up at the ceiling as the voices grew quieter.

Distracted, she pulled out the rolled sheets and handed them to him. He glanced at the contents before stashing them in his pocket. "Thanks for the patronage."

Valeriya followed him back up the stairs and checked the alley before stepping into it. The cool evening air was pleasant against her skin as she journeyed back to the palace, though her thoughts were dark with news of the war. Many were upset by it, viewing the seizure as a waste of resources. Why attack Enomenos now? Land wasn't a shortage for the population. As the farming hub of Syllogi, food was also plenty. Valeriya would accuse Wyltam of extending the land under his rule, but that was a ridiculous notion. No, Wyltam and Keyain were doing something and Valeriya would make it her business to find out what.

Her husband kept her blocked from much of the serious politicking in Satiros. Even the ministers she used for information were murky on the attack's details. There was only one lead Valeriya could follow—Keyain's wife. Her mysterious arrival left many questions to ask. Fortunately for Valeriya, she was in a position to get answers.

Something did not sit right about Marietta. Her injuries, her background, her secret marriage to Keyain. Did he take her as a reason to start the war? There were truths to uproot, and Valeriya would weed each one of them out. If lucky, they'd aid in her cause to thwart Wyltam. At worst, she'd have information to hold over Keyain. Either way, Marietta would play a part in what was to come.

Chapter Twelve

MARIETTA

Bright sunlight lit Marietta's room, stirring her from sleep. The brain fog that greeted her each morning still suppressed her thoughts. She was getting sick of it. Each day she woke in her room and remembered nothing of the day prior.

She swung her legs over the bed, noticing two bruises across her shins. When did she get those? Yellow welts the size of her fists as if she ran into something. The color showed they had already begun healing, but she couldn't remember how they got there. Confused, she inspected the rest of her body, trying to find any other spots that might give clues to what she did all those days. A gasp escaped her as she examined her arms. Her burn scars had disappeared. When she lifted her shift, she found the stretch marks on her hips and stomach erased from her body as well.

How did they do this? Doctors in the Enomenos never removed all the scars. To her knowledge, only the healing magic from a temple offered that. Had they brought someone here to heal more than her injuries? It was as if Keyain meant to erase her past, erase the memories that made Marietta who she was.

Who would she become if she remembered nothing of her years with Tilan? Or of baking? Or the marks of her own body? Those memories, frozen in her mind, caused her chest to ache with longing, but she would rather endure the pain of missing them than never have had the memories at all.

The smooth, unmarked skin of her arms was foreign to her. The scars were proof of her work as a baker—a damn good one. Keyain took that away from her, too.

The first severe burn she had gotten at her bakery came to mind. Alone in the kitchen, trying to prepare for the following morning, she pulled a sheet pan out of the oven, but her hand slipped. The pan landed on her forearm, pinning it between the oven door. At first, she felt nothing and yanked her arm free. Then the excruciating pain hit, causing her to scream and drop to her knees, cradling her forearm, which already blistered on both sides. Tilan burst through the back door, his breathing heavy. She remembered the panic in his face as he called out her name. When he found her on the floor, he ran to her, helping her stand. Tilan insisted on getting a doctor, though it was late. He refused to leave her in pain.

It took two months for those burns to fully heal. Every time Marietta looked at them, she remembered Tilan's reaction that night, both his fear and his wanting to help her.

Her eyes watered at the memory, her arm catching the tears as they dropped. Breath hitched in her tightening throat. It was too much. She needed to get out.

She stood, her head swimming. Still only dressed in her white shift, Marietta crossed the room and flung open the door, half surprised to find it unlocked. Small light globes lit the hallway as she stumbled into it.

Voices chattered from down the hall as her feet carried her in the opposite direction. It didn't matter where she went. The sun on her face. The wind in her hair. Those sensations compelled her to keep going. Marietta needed to feel alive.

Her movements were sluggish, her head spinning more the further she walked. The wall gave support as her body moved across it. The checkerboard pattern of the floor shifted in her vision, threatening to topple her.

Only a little farther to go. The end of the hall became closer, the sunlight from the window within reach. A glimpse of the world beyond would be enough. Gods, please, anything.

Marietta's vision faded to black on the edges, lights flashing in her eyes. Her body collapsed against the wall, tears streaking down her face. From behind her, the nurse shouted as footsteps pounded through the hall. She wanted to escape; she wanted to be free. But she couldn't do it. She was trapped.

Chapter Thirteen

MARIETTA

S oft, swishing fabric swathed Marietta as she walked arm in arm with her companion, head still shrouded in cloud. They spoke to her, but she didn't even bother to hear their words. Why listen when she could swish her skirt?

Marietta lost count of the days. Not that time mattered to her while she passed it in a dreamy haze. A giggle escaped her mouth as she moved, the open back of her dress letting her hair brush against the skin. The tip of her fingers rubbed on the dress's fabric as her companion brought her around to other clouded bodies. Some tried to talk to her, their words lost to Marietta. Instead, she smiled.

This little world was blissful. No harm could come to Marietta. Even as her companion guided her along, she felt free. The thought of Tilan's face didn't bring her pain as she imagined being in Olkia with him. Strands of his dark hair falling loose from his knot, brows furrowed as he bent over some design plans. Marietta reached out to tuck a lock behind his ear, but her hand grasped at air. Even in this world of happiness, she couldn't experience his comforting touch. A fist clenched her arm, causing Marietta to drop her hand.

After walking through the palace, the hallway opened up into a grand foyer. Statues and plants climbed the high ceiling, all encased in white marble. She wanted to examine the magnificent room, but her companion led her up a stately staircase. At the top was a ballroom set beyond a row of glass doors, clouded faces filling the room. Most were light gray, though Marietta caught glimpses of some black and white clouds.

Some clouded figures approached them, voices sounding as if she were underwater. Determined to ignore them, she looked up at the lights above. Golden orbs lit the room in a soft glow, floating above their heads.

The ceiling towered high above. Why would anyone need something so high? Impractical, yes, but also magical. Marietta tilted her head back, gasping when she saw the painted panels above them. The sections had various scenes divided by gold borders. Satyrs and other beastly creatures basked in a forest. Some danced, others hunted.

A deer-like creature with spindly antlers and a single horn on its forehead centered in one scene. Splayed on its back were wings made of leaves. The panels next to it had naked female creatures embedded into trees. They were beautiful, with long cascading hair that looked like vines. Next to them was a panel of a humanoid body. Ribbed with muscle, the creature was thick in the center but topped with a great antlered stag's head. It held its hand out to golden flecks painted in the scene.

She leaned back to view the other panels, but her companion squeezed her arm. As she snapped her head to the front of them, she saw another set of clouds stood talking. Marietta wanted to explore. There were so many fascinating creatures that filled this world.

Her companion led her to a long table where clouded faces only sat on one side. Her companion's voice rumbled in her ear as they bent her forward. Marietta flared her dress towards the two clouded figures who sat at the center of the table, dipping lower as directed.

Marietta then followed her companion to their seat near the center, their hand gripping her thigh as they sat. Before them stretched a sea of clouded faces. Her companion stood, the rumble of their voice resonating through her chest. Hands clapped all around her, the noise of heavy rainfall, a sound that always calmed Marietta. Her eyes rose to her companion, whose clouded face was white tinged with golden light. She smiled at them.

The wall behind the table caught her eyes. Thick columns of verdant stone climbed the length of the wall, entwined with golden vines. Carved white and black flowers and golden leaves studded throughout. Similar flowers grew in the forests near Avato, ones she had once picked to bring to an old, sick friend. Japsir, a former client who ran a bakery.

She smiled, thinking of the old man who inspired her to bake. The modest life he had lived, helping the sick or those whose loved ones passed away. He always sent food to them in their time of need. His kindness had touched Marietta, and she worked for him in exchange for baking lessons. During her visits to Avato, he would spend hours teaching to bake with empathy. That baking was creating joy for others, the lesson embedding into her heart.

Marietta snapped back to the room as her companion's hand fell onto her shoulder. They still addressed the room of clouded heads, their touch soothing. Marietta leaned into their hand, earning a small grasp. Her companion sat back down as the clapping subsided, food and drink following.

A servant placed a plate before her, removing a dome of gold. She jerked back in surprise; the plate crawled with wriggling bugs. She stared at it with curiosity, reaching out to grab one, but her companion's hand gripped her thigh. Instead, she turned to her glass, its contents sweet and tart as she drank it, avoiding the food.

After clearing the plates, her companion pulled out her chair, offering a hand. Marietta took it, following them to the dance floor. The fuzziness of her head grew more disorienting as the drink hit.

Her companion had one hand placed around Marietta's waist, with the other holding her hand. The gentle music, which she noticed played in the background this whole time, grew loud. Unlike any melody she had heard, she sensed the emotion placed into every note the performers played. She tried to find the musicians, needing to know who they were. A squeeze of her hand pulled her attention back.

Her companion guided her across the floor. Marietta twirled and spun, causing her to giggle, the swish of cloth tickling against her skin. Her body was light as if she were also a cloud.

That night should never end. The euphoric happiness gave her a moment of not feeling the pain of loss. She enjoyed thinking of Tilan and her friends without her grief threatening to swallow her whole. She could spin in this idyll forever.

Chapter Fourteen

VALERIYA

"**L**ook at her," Valeriya murmured to Wyltam. They sat on the dais watching Keyain and his wife dance on the ballroom floor. "She isn't a halfwit, just drugged. Keyain put her on Choke."

"Mm." Wyltam watched his best friend as he spun Marietta, his expression unreadable.

A wide grin and glossy eyes were plastered on her face, unaware of the surrounding room—both telltale signs of the drug Choke. For the first time in months, Keyain's shoulders and jaw relaxed. The love he carried for Marietta became obvious. Did he take the half-elf for more than just a war? Selfish needs, maybe? Jealous of the human who occupied her life? But why would Keyain bring Marietta to Satiros and let the court believe she was simple-minded? Why give her Choke?

Wyltam leaned over. "He's hiding something. Between her injuries and Choke, there's something he's failing to tell me. See if you can find out what it is." The deep baritone of his voice cut through the music.

"Giving me a task, are you?" Valeriya bristled. "I agree. Keyain wants everyone to think Marietta is witless. I'll see what I can find." At least if Wyltam believed she was poking into Marietta's past for his benefit, he would have fewer questions.

The information Valeriya gained from her meeting proved that Marietta wasn't held hostage. A prisoner wouldn't own a business. No, Marietta lived in Olkia on her own accord, but Keyain's marriage documentation was legitimate. Which led her to believe that Keyain

drugged Marietta because if she were sober, she would share the truth. He needed her incapacitated and the court to think she was witless so she couldn't reveal his lies. How convenient. No one in Satiros would question the half-elf's compromised mental state.

"You should invite her to tea tomorrow," Wyltam said, leaning back. An arm propped up his head as he crossed one leg over the other. His casual posture caused Valeriya to sit up straighter, holding back a sneer from her face. His kingly appearance never lasted long.

"Keyain will know it's a demand, not an ask," she responded, smiling and nodding at one of the ladies who danced past them.

"Mm," he answered.

A male of many words, her husband.

Valeriya rose, smoothing her dress. "I know you hate it, but we must dance at least once."

With a sigh, he stood and offered a hand. Wyltam led her to the dance floor as the nobles and courtesans stepped out of their way. Though he despised dancing, he wasn't poor at it. His movements were exact and lacked emotion, just like the rest of his personality. The tips of his fingers grazed her, hovering above her body. Good, she didn't like when he touched her, anyway. They both found the other repulsive. After having their son Mycaub, their already-strained relationship became near unbearable. Most of their conversations involved some level of bickering—and that was when they could stand to be around one another.

The song ended, and Wyltam stepped away before heading to the edge of the ballroom floor. Minister Gyrsh approached with his dark honey hair tumbling forward as he bowed. "May I have the next dance with my beautiful queen?"

Valeriya smiled. "Of course, Gyrsh." When her sister, Queen Nystanya, searched for allies in Satiros, Gyrsh was one of the few she could find, and that was through her husband, Auryon. As Minister of Foreign Affairs, he fostered a close relationship with Chorys Dasi, King Auryon's home city-state. Fortunately for Valeriya, the minister was enamored with the idea of having an affair with her. Which worked to her advantage, for the false encouragement on her part made him compliant with whatever she needed.

Gyrsh palmed her hips, his honeyed eyes amused. She flashed him a practiced smile as she tracked Wyltam's movements. Warmth radiated through her body as he approached Marietta and asked her to dance. Valeriya let Gyrsh take the lead as she kept her eyes on the entertaining situation. Wyltam held the half-elf close to him, his lips moving—a pointless endeavor to talk to her while she was on Choke, but it left an impact. Across the room, Keyain stood with a clenched jaw and narrowed glare.

So the game continued between them with light jabs, underhand comments, and now giving Marietta his attention. Keyain was a fool if he thought he could bring her to Satiros, and Wyltam would ignore her. Didn't Keyain remember how he treated Gyrsh's own daughter?

"You're always a pleasure to dance with, Queen Valeriya," Gyrsh whispered into her ear.

"We should do it more often," she teased, knowing it would never happen. However, Gyrsh need not know that. The minister was more likely to help her if he thought he carried Valeriya's favor.

"I'm sure we will find the time soon." He smirked, glancing over his shoulder at a group of males. "The emissaries seem to be enjoying themselves."

Valeriya noted the group but paid them little mind. The less attention she gave them, the better. "That's good to hear. I hope you show them all that Satiros has to offer."

The song ended, Gyrsh bowing his goodbye. Valeriya smiled, then parted for the other end of the ballroom floor, watching as Wyltam continued to hold Marietta. Curious, he inspected her with a slight furrow to his brows, the only sign of an expression.

Keyain's eyes remained on the two as she approached. "Come dance with me," Valeriya demanded, extending her hand to him.

He was close to saying no, likely wanting to supervise Marietta. But also because he didn't trust Valeriya—for good reasons.

"Of course, my Queen," he answered with a bow and took her hand. Keyain held her like Wyltam, his fingers grazing while his jaw remained ground shut. A smirk tugged at her lips; he was so prickly.

"Your wife sure likes to smile, Keyain," Valeriya teased, trying to keep her smirk in check. This fresh wound of his would be an entertaining means to inflict pain. "Especially when dancing with Wyltam. Just look at her," she added, glancing over her shoulder at them.

The muscle in his jaw flexed. Marietta was a convenient way to stoke the anger that burned in him. Oh, how fun for her.

"I'm glad she's well enough to come to celebrate Satiros' victory," Valeriya added. "She must join my ladies and me for tea tomorrow."

"I'm afraid she won't—"

"It's not an ask, Minister Keyain," she used his formal title for emphasis. "It's a demand."

He swallowed hard. "Yes, my Queen," he said between clenched teeth.

"Unless you'd prefer her to be a social outcast. You've kept her from us all these weeks. Why would you keep her from us for more?" Her voice was like honey, and Keyain heard through it. "Are you planning on moving her from Satiros?"

Hate radiated from his body, his limbs locked and rigid. It was almost too easy for Valeriya to get under his skin. Marietta would be a more significant piece to play than she expected by his quick reaction.

His lack of response was enough of an answer. That was valuable information Valeriya could hand to Wyltam.

The song ended, and Keyain dropped his hands, turning to find his wife. From that position, she watched as Wyltam whispered something to Marietta. Keyain interrupted, bowed to Wyltam, and grabbed Marietta from the ballroom floor.

Valeriya held much disdain for her husband, but at that moment, watching Keyain's anger roll off him in the middle of a ball, she couldn't help but appreciate his schemes. That's how they matched one another, in schemes and schemes alone.

One last task remained for the evening—the half-elf needed to be sober for tea tomorrow. The court should see who she truly was without Keyain's suppression. Plus, Marietta could share her truth with Valeriya. Why did Keyain risk his career to capture Marietta, who hadn't wanted to leave Olkia?

Outside the main room, she sent a servant for charcoal and paper. She wrote a short note, folding it into a small square. Searching the room, she found Keyain talking to one of his commanders. At his side, Marietta appeared dazed.

She approached. "Lady Marietta, a pleasure to meet you, my dear." Valeriya leaned in to place a kiss on her cheek, her hand brushing by the pocket of her dress.

Keyain stopped talking mid-sentence, watching with wide eyes as Valeriya neared. Marietta didn't react. Her hands rubbed over the fabric of her dress.

"Is she feeling alright, Keyain?" With knitted brows and pursed lips, she feigned ignorance to Marietta's drugged state.

"Perhaps she isn't," he ground out. "I'll take her back soon. I'm sure the evening was quite overwhelming for her."

"It's funny. The way you speak for her, instead of letting her speak for herself." Valeriya's voice dropped momentarily so only he could hear. "But I'll let you finish making rounds. I look forward to tea with you tomorrow, Marietta."

It amused her how easily she could rile Keyain, how clever he thought he was. As a trained warrior knowledgeable in war strategy and planning, she expected him to be better at political games. Usually stoic, his moods were often hard to read; yet with Marietta, he became a book that she eagerly consumed.

Yes, the half-elf would be the exact piece she needed, and her plan to use her was already in motion. Tomorrow, the court would meet the real Marietta.

Chapter Fifteen

ELYSE

Alcohol swirled in Elyse's cup, the red liquid her crutch for the evening. At her arm was Lord Brynden Vazlyte, an emissary from Chorys Dasi, who was in Satiros to work with her father.

Convenient he came the week of the victory ball. More convenient her father could parade Elyse on such a prominent person's arm. It was unnerving how easily he could pass her from one male to the next. Though, why should she complain? Brynden was alluring. Even without looking at him, she was aware of his confident disposition.

On an average day, anxious thoughts would pollute Elyse's mind. Brynden would be too attractive, too important, too... uninterested in her. Yet as alcohol coursed through her blood, those thoughts quieted. Left was just Elyse, the insignificant daughter of a minister.

The black silky fabric of her dress hugged her willowy frame with a square neckline that pushed up her chest. Little was left to imagination—just the way her father preferred her to dress on such occasions. *Tease and tempt, but never give* her father had reminded her before they departed from the suite earlier that evening.

That was her usual—or was before Keyain. The words were easy to follow, her father's friends being five times her age, if not more. They were always drunk with the possibility of such a young *creature*. Brynden was different. For one, he was age-appropriate.

"How fortunate that you don't want to dance," he murmured in her ear. "I was afraid we'd waste the whole evening on the ballroom floor."

The low tone of his pleasant voice caused Elyse to turn toward his

slim and structured face. His nose had a slight hook from his days as a commander in the Chorys Dasian army. Golden hues from the light globes floating above warmed his pale olive skin. "Fortunate, indeed," she said, eyes lingering on him. "Though I would dance with you if you requested it."

He chuckled, his mouth tilting up on one side. "Your father bragged that you were obedient. I didn't realize he was being so literal."

Elyse glanced at her father across the Grand Ballroom, surrounded by the other visiting Chorys Dasians. Though chatting, he glared at her and nodded to the other couples dancing. The usual dread that would pool in her stomach silenced as she offered the slightest shake in her head. *No, he doesn't want that.* He scowled and turned back to his conversation.

"Obedience is all I know," she replied, eyes turning to the emissary with a warm smile. His straight black hair was long through the middle and shorn close to his head on the sides, tied back in a knot. Peculiar. He wasn't anything like her father's other friends.

He laughed again. "Like a dog."

"Excuse me?"

"Dogs are obedient, but the last time I checked—" he leaned away from Elyse, his stare roaming her body "—you are nothing like a dog."

"Such a wonderful compliment, coming from a male who couldn't get his own date." She regretted the words as they came to her mouth, her gaze darting to her father.

"I judged too quickly," he teased, bringing his face in front of her, his eyes on her pouting lips. "You bark like a dog, but now I wonder if you bite like one." He flashed her a wicked smile.

She let out a long breath, locking eyes with the emissary. No, he was nothing like her father's other friends, who only told her how beautiful she was.

Without breaking eye contact, she threw back the rest of her drink. Brynden's brows lifted with amusement. As a servant passed, Elyse replaced her empty glass with a full one.

"That's your fourth since dinner," he commented, grabbing his own.

"Kind of you to notice," she said in a honeyed voice, offering a sweet smile.

"And you hardly ate anything."

"I don't eat meat."

Brynden's mouth tilted up on one side again. "And you didn't ask for something different?"

Her eyes darted to her father once more. "I wouldn't want to cause any trouble."

"But you're causing trouble right now," Brynden said, drawing Elyse's face back to him, confused. "Here I am, trying to have a nice evening with my lovely date, but she's more preoccupied with checking in with her father every two seconds." He tsked with a mocking pout.

"My apologies. I didn't realize my company was causing you so much misfortune," Elyse said with mocking wide eyes.

"My misfortune indeed," he teased, flashing a smile. "Tell me something interesting. What do you do when you're not entertaining your father's friends?"

"Nothing worth sharing." She took a sip of wine before adding, "Tell me about your work in Chorys Dasi."

"My friends say I talk way too much about myself, and I'm trying to change that." Brynden leaned into her. "You wouldn't want me to regress to my selfish ways, would you?"

"I would do whatever you asked of me."

Brynden rolled his eyes, turning away as he dropped her arm. "Obedient indeed."

Elyse didn't even need to look to know her father watched. Shit—she needed to pull him back in. "I like to read. And I sometimes sing," she said, her voice hushed so only he could hear in the room crowded with nobles.

Brynden looked down at his drink, then back at her. "That's hardly nothing worth sharing. I bet your sultry voice is beautiful when you sing."

She ignored the compliment as heat crept over her cheeks. "They're things I'm forbidden to share," she said, her eyes wandering over the room.

"My father believes I should be silent and ill-read. I can't go around telling his friends that I'm neither."

Brynden's hand reached for her own, his thumb rubbing against her skin. "There's a risk in sharing it, yet you exposed it to me. Was it my irresistible charm?"

A laugh escaped her as she smiled, glancing down at her glass. "You do talk highly of yourself."

"Now you sound like my friends," he said with a chuckle. "Let's find something fun to do. This ball is too boring and predictable."

"You say that like it's a bad thing—predictable."

"What if it is? Why have the same boring experience when there's the possibility for fun all around us?" Brynden hooked his arm on her, steering her in the opposite direction of her father. "Fresh air would do us some good, don't you think?"

"I think not," she said, a hint of a smile to her lips.

Brynden's head whirled to her, confusion melting back into amusement. "Oh, she can joke! Blessed by the gods, I must be!"

"Funny, you ask me not to act obedient yet mock me when I'm not." Her hand wrapped around the bulk of his bicep as they walked.

"Well, my apologies," he murmured, "you are under no such obligation to be *obedient* with me."

As they crossed the ballroom, Elyse noticed Keyain with Marietta on his arm. Queen Valeriya talked to the pair, but her eyes darted to Brynden, offering a quick nod. So subtle that she almost missed his returning one.

"You know the Queen?" she asked.

"Queen Valeriya?" he asked, looking down at Elyse.

"Yes, you both nodded to each other," she said, her brows furrowed.

Brynden laughed. "Four cups of wine have altered your perception. If I didn't know better, I'd say you were looking in that direction for your previously betrothed."

Elyse tore her gaze away, staring straight ahead. Her father had warned he might ask about this. "No, I won't give Keyain any more of my time." She finished her drink before setting it on a servant's tray.

They stepped out into the evening air, chillier than Elyse had expected. Brynden pulled her closer to his heat, the scent of juniper and citrus washing over her. He walked her across the paved patio and down a set of stairs, entering the Central Garden. Other nobles and courtesans meandered in groups in different pockets with sitting areas with thick greenery and trees, offering privacy between the groups.

Golden light globes lit the path as they wove into the garden. "Truth be told, I'm surprised Minister Keyain traded a stunning female like you in for a clip. Though I'm not complaining," he murmured. "I wouldn't have you on my arm if he didn't."

"You shouldn't say traded."

"What do you mean?"

"You are the first of my father's friends I've had to *entertain*—" she hissed the word "—since before Keyain asked to marry me. He would never admit it, but I think his intentions were good."

Brynden's arm pulled her closer. "Regardless of intention, he slighted you—deemed you less than the half-elf. Keyain is a fool; you're an exquisite female."

She slowed her steps, turning to Brynden, whose hands came to rest on her hips. "Love can make even the smartest a fool."

He smirked with a laugh. "Perhaps reading has polluted your brain. To think you'd defend the male after what he did."

"He's still my friend." Elyse searched his face, his grin playful.

The smile dropped from his eyes, though his mouth still held it. "That information should not be public," he whispered while leaning in. His arms wrapped around Elyse as his mouth grazed her ear. "Being friends with someone like Keyain will be your demise."

The warmth of his breath tickling her ear caused heat to creep once again over her cheeks, her stomach tightening. "And why is that?" she whispered.

"Because I don't want you to get hurt." He pulled back, his gaze drifting back to her lips.

Elyse grew painfully aware of his hands on her hips, the way he stared at her mouth. Gods—she'd never done *that* before. Not with someone she was interested in kissing, at least. But the way he looked at her, eyes intent on their target, left her breathless. His lips met hers, warm and soft. He inhaled and released a deep breath, his hands tightening on her hips.

Every rational thought she had disappeared with the kiss, her tongue meeting his as her stomach blossomed with heat. Gods—he was kissing *her.*

Brynden pulled back, his hand caressing her face. "Was that okay to do?"

"It's a little late to ask," she whispered, her body humming from his touch.

The one-sided smile came back as he tucked a strand of hair behind her ear. "I've wanted to do that all night, but Gyrsh kept hovering."

Gods—her father. *Tease and tempt, but never give.* "We shouldn't have done that," she whispered, crossing her arms across her middle as she stepped back.

"I think what you meant is that we shouldn't have done that so publicly," he teased, gesturing to the nobles that were within earshot. Brynden wrapped his arm around her once more. "Let's find somewhere a bit more private."

"Private doesn't make it better."

He turned to her with a frown and stopped on the path again. "I expect nothing from you."

"But my father doesn't believe that." Elyse writhed out from his arm.

"Fuck your father," he hissed. "You're an adult. If you want to go somewhere private with me, you should. Live in the moment, Elyse." His jaw was hard-set, serious, as he searched her face. Then his expression softened, his hand cupping her cheek once more. "More than anything, I wish to pull you into my lap and kiss you until my jaw aches."

He looked at her with such intensity that her breath hitched. Of all her years in Satiros, he was the first to say such of her. That she was an adult and that she could make her own choices—that she could be *free.*

Elyse grabbed the front of his shirt, drawing him to her. The heat in her stomach flared as he kissed her back, matching her hunger. "Okay," she said between kisses.

"Okay?" His eyes searched her face.

"Yes, okay. I want to live," Elyse said, alcohol emboldening her as her head felt dizzy. "I want this with you. And I want it now."

He kissed her once more before wrapping his arm around her, searching for a private spot. Brynden gave her a concerning look as her head spun. Or maybe it was the ground.

"Oh, Elyse," shrilled a voice from behind, earning a glare from Brynden. Grytaine approached up the path, alone, in a dress that revealed as much as Elyse's. "I was just wondering why you haven't introduced me to your handsome date." She winked, earning a heavy sigh from Brynden.

"Grytaine, funny to see you here in the garden. Alone," Elyse slurred.

"Lord Brynden Vazlyte, Emissary to Chorys Dasi," he answered, offering a slight bow as he held on to Elyse.

"Oh, Chorys Dasi? I hear it's beautiful this time of year. A shame that you're in Satiros." Grytaine stepped closer and showed no intention of leaving. "I'm Lady Grytaine Lasyda."

Of course, Grytaine would appear out of nowhere to be a pain, just as Elyse had a chance to experience *him*.

"Minister Royir's wife, a pleasure to meet you," he said, looking over his shoulder down the path. "I was hoping to have a private conversation with Elyse. If you will excuse us."

He pulled Elyse away, her steps clumsy as she leaned against him. Heat rolled off his comforting body, and he was so strong. And handsome.

"Please, come join my husband and me," Grytaine pleaded. "It's not every day we can talk to someone from Chorys Dasi. I insist." She flashed a false smile, placing her hand on his forearm.

He glared down at the touch before looking at Elyse with a sigh. "Of course. Please, lead the way."

Brynden's arm steadied Elyse as they followed Grytaine. "I'm afraid all the wine and no food might have clouded your judgment," he murmured. "We'll continue that another day. I promise to call on you soon." He quickly pressed a kiss onto her cheek. Grytaine raised her brows, his blatant affection odd for them not courting. Unless he meant…?

Elyse stared at Brynden as they walked. Someone wanted her to live, not just to be alive. Brynden wanted to touch her, be with her, and she wanted it, too. For once, she looked forward to the future. Not only because he promised to call on her, or because of her touch-starved state, but because for the first time since her mother's death, Elyse had hope of escaping Satiros.

Chapter Sixteen

MARIETTA

The dizzying effects from the night made Marietta's head spin as she held it, sitting on the edge of her bed. Awareness edged its way back, starting in the hallways, her body threatening to topple. Keyain had carried her back to her room.

Keyain knelt before her, whispering, "I'm so sorry I'm doing this to you." She lacked the energy to recoil from his touch as he leaned in with a kiss. Heavy footfalls crossed the floor, and then the door clicked shut.

Scenes of twirling dresses, mystical creatures, mesmerizing dark eyes, and a voice of rolling thunder swirled in her head. Where had they come from? Regardless of placing all her strength towards focusing, Marietta could recall nothing more.

The tight gown she wore grew uncomfortable the longer she sat. The green fabric with gold lace lined her body, the color causing bile to rise in her throat. Satiros's colors. Keyain was dressing her like a doll, one he could show off to the court, his faithful wife.

Fogginess threatened her vision, and even shaking her head didn't help her focus. She wanted the gods' forsaken dress off her. The zipper on the side slid down, her hands pulling the fabric off her when one hand slipped into the pocket, finding a folded piece of paper. She pulled it out, turning it over in her hands as she examined it.

Was it real, or did she imagine it?

Shaky fingers unfolded the paper to find the looping handwriting of smeared charcoal.

"Don't eat or drink what they bring you. Don't let them know you know."

Confused, she reread it once more, trying to make sense of the words. They... they were drugging her food. The words were a warning, but who in Satiros knew Marietta enough to warn her about Keyain? No one in Satiros knew her, save Keyain, but he was the one doing the drugging.

The handle jiggled as a different nurse opened the door. Marietta dove onto her bed, hiding the note underneath her pillow. As the nurse stepped in, Marietta sat on the edge of the bed, forcing her eyes to gloss over.

He said nothing to Marietta as he helped her change, as if he expected Marietta to be incoherent. How long had she been like that? The nurse left the room after changing Marietta into a plain white shift.

She glared at the door, holding her head. How and when had Keyain turned into a monster? One that killed her husband, trapped her, and drugged her into oblivion? How had he attacked the city he knew Marietta loved, then expected her to be okay with it? Expecting her to live with him in oblivion, absolving him of everything?

Burning hate swelled in her chest as she lay on the bed. Her hand shifted under the pillow, clutching the note. Whoever gave it to her knew what Keyain was doing and wanted to intervene. But why? What did they gain from helping her?

Regardless of their answer, Marietta sent a prayer to whatever god watched over her, thankful that someone had intervened. Tomorrow she would get her chance. She would escape this gods damned place.

The morning sun lit the room as Marietta woke, her hand still clutching the note underneath her pillow. The ache and fogginess lifted from her head, and her thoughts were clear. She hadn't felt this good in weeks, since before....

Pressure grew in her chest, threatening to choke her. Tilan. He remained dead. The pain of loss threatened her vision. She gripped her sides, taking a shattering breath. A piece of her was missing, one she reached out to but felt nothing. He was dead, and she was in Satiros.

As she sat up in bed, she reread the note. *"Don't eat or drink what they bring you. Don't let them know you know."* Though her emotions threatened to drown her, she needed to pull herself together. To focus.

When the nurse stepped into the room, Marietta remained sitting in bed, eyes staring at the wall. "Good morning, Lady Marietta. I expect you slept well," she said, setting a tray of food on the bed. She grabbed the discarded dress from the night before, leaving Marietta alone.

When the door shut, she jumped up, shoveling part of her porridge and fruit underneath her bed. A quick splash of her water followed, hoping that it was enough to make it appear as if she ate. Someone would find it, but she planned to be gone by the time they did.

The nurse returned as Marietta sat back down on the bed. In her hands was a light blue gown, the fabric tight and thin. Keyain was dressing her again, it seemed. What else should she expect when he thought she was still too drugged to make her own decisions?

"Must be thirsty this morning. That's the fastest I've seen you drink yet," the nurse said, humming to herself.

Shit, she overdid it.

"For a male, he has good taste," she said with a smile, glancing at Marietta. She gestured for Marietta to stand. "Pastel colors are lovely with your skin tone, and this blue will make your gray eyes pop."

The dress slipped over her head, the nurse zipping the fabric tight to her. Hugging her curves, Marietta wanted to protest. Instead, she nodded her head, doing her best to appear groggy.

The nurse sat Marietta in a chair and brushed her curls. Gods, she hadn't listened to Marietta's request to use a comb. Of course not. Marietta had no control.

The nurse ran her hands along Marietta's hairline, pulling back her strands to secure them in a tight knot. Hair covered the blunt tapered tip of her ears. Right, Keyain wouldn't want her half-elven features to show too much.

Frustrated, Marietta did her best not to smack the nurse's hands away as she layered jewelry on her. To lose the freedom of dressing herself, of styling her hair, was a defeating feeling. Keyain's control had reached new limits. Before, he would've never made such decisions for her.

A hand fell to her shoulder. The nurse said, "There, all done. You look lovely, my lady. Your husband will enjoy it." With a wink, she left the room.

Marietta wished for a mirror as she raised a hand to her hair. Her thick curls pulled taut against her head, and she longed to pull it all loose and let it fall to her shoulders. Yet another freedom that Keyain had taken away from her. She wouldn't forget this.

But she needed to focus. Today was the day—she was escaping.

Keyain's footfalls echoed down the hall before the door opened. The large elven man stepped in wearing a simple green shirt covered by a black jacket. "Good morning, my love," he murmured, approaching Marietta and kissing her cheek. His touch was as repulsing as the previous night. "You look beautiful, as always. I thought we'd go for a walk before you see the Queen today," he said. "Remember what I told you about the Queen?"

Gently, he lifted her chin and stared into her face. Never having been on drugs, Marietta thought back to the old drunks in Olkia's taverns, mimicking their half-smile and glossy eyes.

Keyain sighed. "We don't trust the Queen, do we, Marietta?"

She nodded at him.

"Very good." He looped his arm around her, leaving the room behind. She held her breath as Keyain led her out of the infirmary, passing the window she once wished to see. How long ago had that been?

Sunlight filtered through the glass panes, and below she glimpsed the greenery of a garden. A flutter came to her heart, anxiety mixed with anticipation. She was getting out.

Keyain's idle chatter faded into the background as she absorbed her surroundings. Marbled floor stretched the length of the hall. Green-veined marble columns flanked the passageway, twined with golden vines.

At the end of the hallway, a staircase built of dark wood circled to the floor below. Carved into it was an intricate forest scene with tiny beasts. The creatures enthralled Marietta. Though she wished to inspect the wood, she resisted, letting Keyain guide her down the stairs.

"I'm surprised. You usually try to stop and look at the carvings," Keyain said in a pleasant tone.

So the drugs gave her little control over her urges. Gods, what else had she done while under its effects?

The staircase opened to the bottom floor. The space was vast and cavernous, with elven men meandering about in groups, some walking to and from the open doorways. Dressed in finery, they looked the part of nobles.

A bit of green caught her eye from the far side of the room. Glass doors showed a garden beyond them, hope filling her chest. She was so close.

A few nobles nodded at Keyain as they passed, pausing their conversation. Odd. Foolish of her to think she ever knew him. All those years together, yet she never even knew his rank or position in Satiros.

Breath hitched in her throat as the reality of her situation hit her. Marietta was in Satiros at the hand of the stranger who killed her husband. Those surrounding her were all elven. She was the only half-elf. It was dangerous for her to be there; they considered her a lesser person under the law. What rights did she even have? Bile rose in her throat, the crowd of people feeling too close. Controlling her breath, she kept her tears at bay.

A spindly elf with a crop of white hair approached, his face lined and sagging with age. With his chin pointed up, he looked down at Marietta with narrowed eyes. "Good morning, Keyain and Marietta," he said with a nasal tone to his voice.

She resisted the urge to lift her chin, to stare him down the same. Instead, she forced a grin.

"Well, aren't you looking chipper today, you sweet little thing! Keyain, you got lucky to have such a tame little clip at your side," he added with a wink. The slur made her want to scream.

"I'm lucky to have her back, Royir." Keyain's arm that looped around Marietta's slipped out and folded around her waist. Her body tightened at the touch, and she tried to loosen it. She needed to keep it together. Her chance would come.

"Why, yes, we all know your occupation of Olkia was a rousing success. Though the rumors say you had ulterior motives for the invasion," he gestured toward Marietta with a smirk.

Her eyes glanced at Keyain to read his face. What did he mean by Keyain's occupation of Olkia?

"Olkia had its advantages to being first, as you're aware," Keyain said. "By seizing it, we control a part of Lake Malakos and the plains south of Olkia. But, of course, rescuing my wife from the enemy was a considering factor for mine and King Wyltam's decision."

"Of course, my dear friend. No one would blame you if she were your only reason!" He let out a bellowing laugh. "But I must be off. We must do tea again in mine and Grytaine's suite!"

Nauseous, she tumbled over their words. Keyain did attack Olkia, but why save her? There had to be a better reason than to be with her again. There had to be. Marietta had been clear that she wanted nothing to do with him. Was it revenge for leaving him? That was possible, but Keyain wasn't vengeful. Angry, yes. Often, he lost his temper, but he never sought retribution from people who wronged him. At least that was true from what she had seen. If he sought revenge, he at least wouldn't cause her physical harm. Well, beyond drugging her. That clearly wasn't beyond him.

Keyain nodded to Royir before stepping towards the doors. Outside was so close. Her heart threatened to betray her, unable to stay calm at the thought of running free. He held open the glass-paned door and let Marietta step onto a veranda. Above, purple wisteria and green vines filtered the sunlight upon a trellis.

The morning air was warm and humid but still comfortable. A gentle wind brushed against Marietta's skin. She closed her eyes while tilting back her head. It was her first breath of fresh air in... weeks? She wasn't sure how long.

With no walls closing her in, the tension in her body eased, her mind clearing. She glanced around the veranda as Keyain led her. To one side of the porch stood two elves in deep conversation. The other was towards a set of stairs that they approached. Neither way was ideal for escaping. If she waited, her moment would come.

Marietta held her breath as the garden unfolded before her. Garden beds stretched beyond her line of sight, the land dotted with trees, lush flower beds, and thick bushes. She did her best not to gawk as Keyain pulled her along. Flowers of all colors, planted in intricate patterns, expanded before her. Bees buzzed from bloom to bloom as birds chirped in the distance. Their heady scent hung thick in the air, intoxicating Marietta. Willow trees with long branches brushed the ground as a gentle breeze blew. A meandering creek gurgled as it idly cut through the garden.

Scattered throughout the flower beds were statues of mythical creatures. Satyrs playing lutes. Small antlered deer with wings sprouting from their backs. A cat-like critter with scales covering its body, frozen mid-leap through the flowers. They were creatures from childhood stories, erased from Syllogi long ago. Or so her father's feyrie tales said.

He had shared stories of how the fey's appearances differed. Some bore the characteristics of animals, having horns, tails, scales, and wings. Others contained details from the elements, like stony skin or flames for their hair. Marietta's favorite had been the ones who took after plants, with flowers and vines flowing from their body. Staring at the statue gardens, she couldn't help but think of her father and his stories—of the creatures she learned about as a child.

Marietta hesitated as they approached a satyr statue carved to be sitting on the low brick wall that lined the path. The detail carved into the stone surprised her. Its smirking expression and the glint in its eyes revealed the artist's talent.

If only Tilan could see such mastery. If only he were alive to see the intricate details. The nymph dagger was similar in intricacy, the first item of his that she had loved. Her hand extended to touch the face of the satyr, wanting to rub her thumb over the carved stone.

Keyain side-eyed her. "I know. You like the garden. We can see more if we keep walking." His voice was soft, but Marietta sensed a tinge of impatience in it, causing her to drop her hand. Of course, gawking was something she did when on drugs.

Ahead on the path was a footbridge that crossed the creek. Beyond it was a whitewashed building coated in green vines far off in the distance. Was this a courtyard garden? From what she observed, it was more vast than the largest market in Olkia. No, this must be outside the palace.

The lift of the bridge gave her better vantage to see, her eyes darting as she slowed her pace to gain her bearings. If she could find an exit point, escaping Keyain would be easier.

To her left, there was a second, much closer building. One cluttered with balconies and vines that grew up the side. In a similar design, she couldn't tell if it connected to the structure ahead of them.

As she looked to her right, past Keyain's hulking body, her heart stopped. She blinked once, twice. The garden was more extensive than she anticipated. Out in the distance, she could see walls of glass framed by whitewashed brick. No, it couldn't be the same building, could it?

But how? Keyain had said they were in Satiros. The lavish interior, the elven males in formal clothes, and the grandeur of the garden were all indicative of being within the palace. How could they fit a garden so extensive and lush with plant life within the structure? At this scale, Marietta wouldn't be able to escape. She could get lost in the garden, but Keyain would find her.

Another chance would have to come.

Keyain tilted his head, his eyes narrowing at Marietta as she closed her mouth and glossed her eyes over once more. He tipped her face towards his as his stare raked across her face. Shaking his head, he said, "Come on, Mar. We should get through the garden before the rain comes."

The deeper he led her into the garden, the harder it was to keep her sense of direction. Traveling gifted her with the skill, and she always knew her position compared to the world around her. The depth of the garden unnerved her as she grew confused with the twisting paths. She lost sight of the buildings with the plant life that grew thick around them.

Nestled among the foliage next to a small pond sat a gazebo that Keyain approached. Thick, white columns wrapped in climbing vines held a wisteria-covered wrought iron roof.

He brought her to the structure, holding her hands and looking into her eyes with a smile. The attention caused her breath to pick up again; she couldn't drop her drugged facade.

"I'm lucky, you know. To have you here," Keyain murmured, his thumb brushing her hand. "I wish I didn't need to drug you. I miss the real you, the person I have loved all this time. Only a few more weeks, Mar. Then you'll be safe at my home in the countryside." Golden rays broke through the canopy of flowers above, wrapping Keyain in shifting light, causing his green eyes to glow.

He leaned towards Marietta, her eyes open and able to see the freckles that dotted his cheeks and nose. Keyain kissed her as gently as the breeze, soft and caressing. Tilan's face pictured in her mind, his smile, his tender kisses. Her body stiffened at the touch. A sharp inhale of air came through her nose.

What did he mean by the countryside? He was trying to take her away from here, but why?

Don't eat or drink what they bring you. Don't let them know you know.

Someone in Satiros wanted Marietta to know this information— wanted to see her sober. Numbness spread throughout her body as her breathing came as sharp inhales, her heart racing.

Keyain planned to isolate her in a place where no one could intervene. She would be at his will, alone and weak. She took a shuddering breath as her mask cracked. He pulled back, his brows furrowed as he looked into her face, his two fingers finding her chin again.

Marietta tried to calm herself, but emotion overwhelmed her. Keyain had killed Tilan, taken her away to this strange place, and now would cut her off from the world. Was he going to hurt her? Was he going to make her have his children to get everything he ever wanted?

Keyain's eyes widened, his hand dropping as Marietta failed to hide her overwhelming emotions. "Marietta, what did you do?"

Chapter Seventeen

MARIETTA

Marietta needed to run, needed to escape Keyain. His fingers tightened on her chin, pulling her closer as she struggled to leave. "Damn it, Mar. You're not drugged," his voice cracked, thick with emotion.

Keyain gripped her arm as she attempted to flee, holding her in place. Panicked, she couldn't breathe, though she heaved her breaths. She fought him, pulling against his hold,

"Why... how..." he stammered, eyes searching her face for an answer.

"Oh, Keyain, Marietta! What are the chances?" a high, honeyed voice called from the path.

A mask fell over his emotions as his eyes shifted towards the voice. "Queen Valeriya, what are the chances indeed," he ground out as he dropped Marietta's chin and offered a stiff bow.

A thin elven woman in a slinky black dress appeared on the path. Her features were sharp and beautiful, almost as sharp as her eyes that glanced between the two. "Just in time for tea, as well. I would love to escort her the rest of the way, Keyain. You're very busy these days," she said, her thick red hair flipping over her shoulder. A thin crown of gold was nestled in its mass.

Keyain held his hand out in front of Marietta as if he meant to put distance between her and the Queen. His jaw tensed as he said, "I'm afraid Marietta isn't feeling well, so she must decline for afternoon tea. I should—"

The Queen raised her hand. A long sigh escaped from his nose. "Need

I remind you that this wasn't an ask? It was a demand." A smirk spread across her lips. "Come, Marietta. I've been dying to meet you."

As Marietta looked at Keyain, panic seized its last grip on her. With wide eyes, he dropped his hand and let Marietta pass. Keyain's fingers lingered on her skin as if he wanted to pull her back.

The Queen extended an arm to Marietta that she took, her limbs still numbed. "I'm pleased to see you're feeling better than last night," Valeriya said, eyes cutting to Keyain. "You seem more alert today."

Last night? Did she meet Queen Valeriya? Her tone suggested she knew Keyain had drugged Marietta. The Queen was toying with them. Marietta wanted to turn back to watch Keyain. He was a monster, but at least she could predict him. She understood him.

Why would she be dying to meet Marietta, a simple baker from Olkia? None of it made sense.

As they walked down the garden path, Marietta's breath still shook, with tears lining her eyes. Quick blinks attempted to hold them back, failing as they trailed down her cheeks.

The Queen held Marietta's arm, patting it. "Breathe. It's alright," she whispered.

Marietta gasped, but her throat was tight. She couldn't breathe. Choking, Marietta bent over and grasped at her neck. The Queen swore and led her off the path to a bench hidden by greenery, gesturing for Marietta to sit. With each shuddering breath, her vision spotted. The world spun as she beheld the Queen. It was too much.

She imagined the draw of the knife on Tilan's throat, the spill of blood as it cut through his flesh. They destroyed Olkia, her friends killed by Satiroan soldiers, by Keyain's hand. Marietta saw her friend Tristina lying dead next to her children, a pool of blood around them. Keyain's touch on her skin, his lips a violation of her body. The moments kept playing in her head, one after another.

"Hush, place your head between your knees," Valeriya said as she bent down to Marietta's face. Icy blue eyes peered up at Marietta, her brows knitted with concern. A gentle hand found Marietta's knee. "It's alright. I promise I won't hurt you. Take your time and breathe deeply."

Marietta focused on the Queen's face, grounding herself in the moment. She shook the plaguing thoughts from her mind while counting each breath. On a count of four, she inhaled, holding her breath, then slowly released it. With it, Marietta's heartbeat slowed, and her vision returned to normal. When she sat up, she looked at the Queen. "How did you know I needed help?"

"It was clear Keyain has been drugging you. I assumed he spiked your food and beverages," she said as a smirk spread across her lips. "I'm glad you got my note."

"You… why would the Queen want to help me?" Marietta's eyes grew wide as Keyain's warning rang through her head: don't trust the Queen.

But could she really trust Keyain after everything he did?

The Queen stood, bringing her hand to her chin. "I wanted to see how you'd react while sober and to learn why Keyain drugged you. Now, come. We should meet the other ladies." She turned, waiting for Marietta to follow.

Trailing Queen Valeriya through the garden, Marietta's mind raced. Why help her? To what end was helping Marietta deemed necessary to her? If she cared for her well-being, wouldn't the crown intervene in another manner? There had to be a more official procedure for someone drugging their spouse—some sort of law that prevented it. Assuming the laws here applied to someone like Marietta. She swallowed hard at the thought.

The Queen flipped her hair over her shoulder, glancing back towards Marietta. Dignity and grace, that's how she held herself with her straight back and purposeful gait. "A queen typically waits for no one, yet your husband has kept you from me. I wonder, Marietta, why that is? Was he not excited to bring his long, lost wife to court? He keeps you locked away, drugged. Why would that be?"

Marietta had thought the same question. Why would Keyain keep her drugged for this long? He was too smart to think she'd remain in that state. Did he think she'd fight him, not wanting to be in Satiros? Of course, Marietta would fight him until her dying breath, but drugs weren't the only way to suppress her.

He had mentioned she'd be safe in the countryside. Marietta assumed it was to isolate her and to restrict her freedom. Staring at the Queen of Satiros, she realized it might have been to protect Marietta from the Queen's pressing questions. What was he attempting to hide?

His marriage to Marietta. That had to be it.

He was lying to the court, had them all believing she was his wife. Keyain had to keep her drugged so the Queen wouldn't know the truth, but she saw through his lie. "I'm not sure, Queen Valeriya," Marietta said, keeping her expression neutral.

The Queen frowned, then looked ahead before speaking. "The ladies are eager to meet you. I'm sure they'll have a ton of questions, so try not to let it overwhelm you."

Heaviness pooled in Marietta's stomach. Strangers excited her under normal circumstances, learning their stories and personalities, but she didn't know their court. She'd have to walk into the room completely unprepared.

Heavy raindrops fell, causing the Queen to look up with a frown. "We'll take the long way to the Royal's Wing. This palace might sprawl, but at least they made the separate buildings connect."

Two elves guarded the door as they approached. Without their helmets on, Marietta noticed one had more masculine features and the other more feminine. Leaf-shaped pieces of leather armor dyed green spread across their shoulders and abdomens with swords hanging at their sides. The Queen ignored the guards, leading Marietta into the building.

The parts of the palace she'd seen were already dripping in luxury. Yet as she stepped into the hall, the lavishness struck her. Velvet green curtains trailed from the windows. Gold-gilded frames of artwork hung from the walls clad in expensive dark wood. Marietta felt out of place, her surroundings too formal for a mere baker.

"I know you have seen little of the palace," the Queen said, "but this is the Noble's Section. I expect you'll move in with Keyain soon enough.

Any person with a political title or land-holding noble keeps a suite in this building. Under Satiroan Law, nobles must spend at least half the year in the palace. They could be here for six months straight or interspersed throughout the year."

Marietta's eyes flicked to the Queen, recalling the days she'd travel with Keyain. He would leave for six months, never telling her the truth. "For what reason?" she asked.

"Remember titles and honorifics, Marietta," the Queen chided. "And the late Queen Olytia—King Wyltam's mother who ruled before him—had a wise philosophy of keeping her court close. It's easier to snuff the flame of rebellion when the wick is under your thumb."

Marietta raised her brows, the philosophy sounding more controlling than wise. Keeping a thumb on people would suffocate them if held on long enough. Keyain's nature was just a product of being from Satiros.

"Nobles must return when their duty calls," the Queen continued, "even if they have completed their six months. Many of Keyain's subordinates have traveled back to the palace for the war effort."

Marietta knitted her brows. How high was Keyain's position? They traveled together, ate together, slept together—he was her gods damned bodyguard; and, yet he held a high enough office to start a war and have subordinates? Unbelievable.

The hallways turned at a set of doors and led to a new section. Embossed into the floor were two intertwined wisteria flowers of purple amethyst—the Satiroan crest. Floor-to-ceiling windows lined the passage, facing the rainy garden to one side. To the other were columns of green marble laced with golden vines. A broad staircase sat at the center of the hall, made of rich wood cushioned with plush green carpet.

Marietta trailed the Queen up the stairs. "As the Minister of Protection and leader of the Satiroan army, your husband holds a very prestigious position in our court. As such, you do as well. You will be the subject of many conversations," she paused, glancing back at Marietta. "Be cautious; rumors catch like fire around here."

Marietta blinked. Minister of Protection?

Without a chance to process, servants opened a set of double doors at the top landing. The Queen's voice cut through the chatter, gesturing to Marietta. "Ladies, ladies! I brought a special visitor with me today."

A half dozen ladies all sat together, their eyes turning to Marietta as her body froze, resistant to following the Queen. This was a trap. The note may have been in Marietta's best interest, but the Queen had her own motives.

For a moment, Marietta thought that perhaps being off drugs in front of the ladies could work to her benefit—they could help her get away from Keyain; but, when she looked at their sly expressions, she knew they would be of no help. They became starved dogs just tossed fresh meat. Their intention wasn't to help but entertain themselves.

Marietta slowed her breath as she crossed the threshold, holding her chin high. She just had to get through this tea time, then she could find another way to escape. Telling the ladies the truth—that Keyain had abducted her—might make them question her sanity. After all, Keyain was their *Minister of Protection*. Marietta was a meek half-elf in their presence.

"Come, Lady Marietta. Sit with me," Valeriya said, taking a seat at a small table with two chairs. Marietta crossed the space, noting the women of the room. They wore tight gowns like her own, adorned in layered chains and necklaces. Dark powder lined their eyes.

The veranda was airy, with a tall ceiling. A humid breeze rolled in from the rain, wafting scents of wisteria, jasmine, and lavender. Below was a small garden of tumbling greenery. Beads of mist trailed off an invisible barrier protecting them from rain. At first, it confused Marietta, then she remembered—they had magic in Satiros.

The room held uncomfortable silence as Marietta took her seat. She forced a smile, trying to regain her composure. After all, how many times had she walked into a room full of strangers and won them over? Those times were of her own free will and not after Keyain abducted her, dragged her to Satiros, and drugged her into a stupor. Such nervousness was as foreign to her as the city-state she found herself in.

The Queen broke the silence with a clap of her hands, going around the room and introducing the ladies. Marietta said a silent prayer to whichever god blessed her with the gift of remembering names.

The ladies were part of the Queen's Court, all wives or daughters of various important nobles in Satiros. None of them held office positions themselves, which was irksome. In Emonemos, all genders held positions in the city-state governments. The leader of the Enomenos Unionization Council, the coalescing group between the city-states, was a human woman. Yet here in Satiros, it became clear that the ladies sipped tea while the lords waged war. Such a backward custom—not unlike their views.

The room held their breath as the Queen introduced one young elven woman, Lady Elyse Norymial. Her hair was the color of dark honey and her skin a warm bronze. With taught shoulders and fidgeting hands, Marietta recognized her nervousness. Odd—she seemed put off by Marietta's presence. A lady with pale blonde hair, Lady Grytaine, wife of Minister Royir, leaned in to whisper something to Elyse. Whatever the whisper contained made Elyse blanch.

"So, Marietta, how are you faring today?" asked one of the ladies, pulling Marietta's attention away. The lady had tight black curls that were artfully tousled and dark skin that contrasted beautifully with the silver of her jewelry.

"Much better, Lady Ymorea. Kind of you to ask," Marietta answered, keeping control of her voice.

"You were out for some time. Such injuries must have been horrid," Ymorea said, her face pouting with concern. "You've been in Satiros for over a month now and we've only had a handful of chances to talk to you."

A calm disposition remained on Marietta's face as shock registered internally. How had it already been that long? "The nurses kept me sedated for most of my time here, saying my injuries were quite dire, though I'm not sure the extent of them. My husband said the wounds were too painful for me to be awake." Disgust spread from her stomach at the thought of calling Keyain her husband, but she was only playing the part of his wife.

"That sounds like Keyain, does it not?" Grytaine turned her to Elyse, who snapped her eyes shut with dread clear on her features.

Ymorea cleared her throat with a small laugh. "Grytaine, did your father ever find his servant? I've heard six other pilinos abandoned their families this week. Can you believe it?"

Grytaine scoffed, turning to Ymorea, hands splaying across the tabletop. "It's absurd! My father still hasn't heard from the wretched half-elf after three days. Now that one of them has become a lady, they forget their place." She hesitated as the room's attention shifted to Marietta.

From across the table, the Queen's lips pursed; but she remained silent. After a long breath through her nose, checking her anger, Marietta said, "If there are so many missing, something is wrong. Have you tried contacting them or sending word to their home?"

The ladies stifled their laughter, a few exchanging looks as Grytaine regained her composure. "We don't chase down the help. If they want their wages, then they show up for work, and if they don't show up, then they're no longer employed."

"So you'd rather have *the help*," Marietta said, sarcasm lacing her tone, "come sick into your houses than to stay home? Is it that unbelievable to have sympathy for the ones who serve you? Consider taking a step out of your privileged shoes and put yourself in their position. There's a reason they didn't come to work and I doubt my presence prevents them from wanting an income. So if—"

Queen Valeriya placed a hand on Marietta's arm. "This topic has grown inappropriate for such a time."

Marietta bit back her annoyance from leaving her point half-finished. Marietta wished to push back at the Queen but hesitated at her amused expression. With a deep breath, she let it go. A rant was what the ladies hoped for, and Marietta had handed it to them.

"Instead, Marietta, you could tell us how you and Keyain met?" Lady Tryda, an older woman with dark skin and gray marking her temples, asked.

Deities damn Keyain. Such questions were why he needed to help her prepare. What had he told the court? What lies had he shared? Half-truths were better than an obvious lie, or so she thought. Would they believe their 'Minister of Protection' was her bodyguard in Enomenos?

With a sigh, she turned to Tryda. "I traveled between the Enomenoan city-states for work, which was dangerous to do alone. Keyain and I met during a meeting with a male for a guard position." It wasn't a lie; Keyain was there when she met Alyck.

"Common life is just so fascinating," said Grytaine, who looked near the same age as Elyse. How large was the age gap between her and the old man she had met earlier? "What type of work did you do?"

"I connected businesses with one another, helping to find suppliers and buyers. Sometimes I would help with managing their finances," Marietta answered, holding her chin higher after Grytaine said common.

"You're quite young to have your own business." Ymorea leaned on one arm, looking at Marietta wistfully. "And to think, our Minister of Protection sweeps you off your feet, and you never have to work again. It's a story out of a feyrie tale. You must have been excited to leave your working life behind."

"The opposite, actually," Marietta said as servants made their way between the tables to serve tea.

Laughter filled the room once more, Ymorea clapping her hands with delight. "Your husband failed to mention your humor."

Marietta furrowed her brows, and for once, she was at a loss for words. The ladies didn't take her seriously, dismissing her completely. She took a deep breath through a forced smile and turned to take a sip of her tea, thankful for a distraction.

"If only Elyse knew Keyain had married." Grytaine hid a sly smile behind her teacup.

"None of us knew," snapped Elyse, her face turning scarlet.

"Of course not," Grytaine answered, "but you and Marietta could become friends, being so close in age. Unless your relationship with Keyain is too problematic for Marietta."

Marietta narrowed her eyes. "What part of it was problematic?" Gods, was Keyain sleeping with this poor girl, leading her along when he planned to drag Marietta to Satiros?

Tryda cleared her throat. "Keyain should be the one to explain that situation, Marietta." She paused, looking out to the rest of the room, her age giving her an air of authority. "Again, ladies, remember that Marietta was gone for quite a while." She turned back to Marietta. "Keyain was unsure if you would be alright after the humans held you in captivity for so long."

Marietta paused mid-sip, lowering the cup as she stared at Tryda. "Perhaps I misunderstood. You think I was in captivity?" What in the gods did Keyain tell the court?

Worry flecked across Tryda's features. "The humans captured you, my dear," she said, each word slow as if Marietta didn't understand. "You do remember why you weren't with Keyain all this time?"

Marietta wasn't sure which angered her more, Tryda's condescending tone or Keyain's blatant lie. "I am of sound mind," snapped Marietta, "and I don't appreciate the condescension."

The ladies whispered to one another as Tryda placed a hand over her chest, brows raised in surprise.

"It's alright if you aren't," said Grytaine. "It's in your nature. Right, Elyse?"

Elyse choked on her tea, coughing, her eyes wide from the attention. "I, uh—my father said…." She cleared her throat, eyes dropping to her lap. "I don't know."

Marietta gripped her teacup at the exchange. The afternoon was out of a nightmare, surrounded by ladies who didn't take her seriously—and the Queen knew it would happen.

Queen Valeriya sat with a rigid back, frowning at Grytaine and Elyse before her gaze found Marietta. With a slight flick of her brow, she said, "Let's give Marietta some space, ladies." She faced the room, her hand coming to her chin. "Did you hear about Potyme's new play at the Ryndalf Theatre opening at the end of summer?"

The afternoon wore on; the conversation was less of a Queen holding court and more of ladies gossiping. It reminded Marietta of her bakery workers who'd spend the day chatting about news around Olkia.

"If Kennyth philandered less, he'd know how his wife really feels about him," Ymorea exclaimed. The room erupted in laughter, Marietta missing the joke.

As she sat there, the group dynamics became clear to Marietta. The ladies were fuel and Queen Valeriya sat back, observing, holding the match that could set the room ablaze. Marietta saw the power she wielded; she was more than just a queen. She was wildfire. Relentless and dangerous. The Queen took the ladies' gossip, turned it over in her head, and deciphered truth from lies. Her advice rang loud and clear to Marietta.

Her stomach rumbled. Queen Valeriya's eyes shot to Marietta, a smirk on her lips. Her skipped breakfast had caught up to her.

Without missing a beat from her story, the Queen finished her quip. "I believe we could use some treats. What do you say, ladies?" She gave Marietta a knowing look.

How had she heard? She seemed locked onto Marietta. Even though Queen Valeriya appeared not to pay her much mind, she had kept her senses open to her. Attuned to see how Marietta reacted to her court.

Servants placed a tray of pastries on the tables, breaking Marietta's heart. Sweet buns and mini pies, just like the ones she sold in her bakery. It had been so long since she last baked.

"What a sight to behold, huh, Elyse?" Grytaine asked, gesturing to Marietta.

"An elf serving a pilinos?" she answered, more a question than a statement. Her response provoked laughter from a few ladies.

Marietta steeled her emotions after her earlier outburst, ignoring the comment, and took a bite. Even in her famished state, the pie was bland, the filling was lackluster, and the crust lacked a flaky consistency.

To distract herself from Elyse, she asked, "Queen Valeriya, these are quite... interesting pies. Where did your baker come from?"

"Oh, I wouldn't know. From the same servants who make all the food, I suppose," she said, feigning disinterest in her question. Marietta caught the hint of suspicion in her eyes.

She quieted at the look, determined to draw less attention to herself. The pie lost her interest, unable to finish it even though her stomach grumbled. Who was their baker? Not someone she'd met, for they weren't that skilled.

Tea time wore on into the afternoon before it wound down. The servants cleared empty teacups and plates from the ladies.

Marietta's mind drifted to Keyain. The bastard left her unprepared for such an encounter. Foolish of him for believing he could keep her drugged. What would happen now that the court had seen her of sound mind? Gods, did he know Queen Valeriya was the one to warn her not to eat the drugged food? His earlier tone suggested suspicion.

Regardless, it was a conversation she wished not to have; it meant dealing with her situation and future. Forgotten in the countryside was not how she hoped to live, but Keyain would get his way. He always did, it seemed.

Finally, tea time ended. The ladies filed out, bidding the Queen goodbye. Marietta, unsure what to do, turned to the Queen. She dropped into a curtsy like the other ladies. "Thank you," she said, "for your time and courtesy, Queen Valeriya."

"My pleasure, Marietta, but please, wait a moment for the ladies to filter out." She had a look in her eye that sent a sense of dread through Marietta.

Confused, she nodded and waited off to the side. Tryda chatted with the Queen, clasped hand in hand.

"I'm happy to see you're not drugged—er, feeling better, Marietta." Elyse appeared behind her, fumbling with her words. "And that you're not witless, just average for a half-elf." She took off before Marietta could respond.

Gods, what was her problem? The elf was nervous. That much was obvious, but why the hostility towards Marietta? And what happened between her and Keyain? At least she gained one thing from the interaction, confirmation that the court thought she was simple-minded.

When the last lady left the veranda, Marietta approached the Queen, who stood with her hands clasped before her, smirking. "That went as I suspected, though you reacted more than I thought you would. Surprising, really. Most would remain quiet in your position." She paused, a smirk quirking at her lips. "You will be an interesting addition to the Queen's Court."

Marietta kept her face still, refraining from snapping once more. She wasn't there to be their entertainment.

The Queen continued. "Regardless, I apologize for the way the ladies acted today. It may have been too soon to include you in court life. I'll invite you to our next tea time, but there would be no offense if you don't attend." Marietta's stomach betrayed her again, the Queen looking down at her. "You must be famished, having not eaten today."

"I am, my Queen, though it is no trouble for you." She bowed her head, hoping to leave her presence, to get a moment to process the day.

"Nonsense, you were my guest, and you found the pastries unappetizing," she said with a knowing look. "A servant will show you to the kitchens if you'd like. We're between the main meal times, but the kitchens are on the way back to the Infirmary. It would be the fastest way for you to eat."

"That would be appreciated, Your Grace."

"Of course," Queen Valeriya said as Marietta turned to leave. "Welcome to the Court of Satiros."

Chapter Eighteen

MARIETTA

A servant took Marietta through the palace halls, heading towards the section she stayed in as she ground her teeth. Communication was something she excelled at—she talked to people for a living. Under normal circumstances, she lived for it; yet, in that room of elven nobility, she felt unsure of herself. Frustrated, self-doubt snaked its way into her head. Keyain had erased so much of her. Did he also take her ability to speak to people?

As for Queen Valeriya, Marietta didn't know what to think. If in a different scenario, Marietta would enjoy her company. Gods, they would even be friends. The Queen was the kind of person who saw things others didn't, whose mind missed nothing. Marietta would need to tread carefully with her. It could be used against her as well, after all.

The kitchen bustled as Marietta arrived, servants darting from task to task as voices called and laughed. The cacophony of chopping knives, the stirring of pots, and the attendants who worked them filled her ears. Her heart swelled at the familiarity of her home.

Large ovens stood against the outdoor walls and ample counter space occupied the kitchen. Workers set up at stations went about their jobs. They were of better quality than the ones Marietta had at her bakery. She and Tilan had planned to upgrade their ovens the following year.

A mix of longing and jealousy filled her. All her dreams with Tilan were dead. She would never get those ovens. It was likely she would never bake again. This kitchen taunted her, reminding her of the life she had lost. The room spun around her, her vision dizzy.

An older male elf was the first to notice her and the servant. "My lady, welcome. What can I do for you today?" He was slender with long silver hair braided back and held an air of authority.

"I've missed both meals if you have something quick for me to eat," she said, her voice far away. As she watched the busy kitchen, her mind remained stuck, remembering the life she once had.

The elf furrowed his brows. "Of course, my lady. Please, have a seat." He bowed his head and stepped into the fray of the kitchen.

Baked bread's mouthwatering scent hung thick around her as she sat at a small table across from the ovens. Marietta thought of the flatbread she made with blue cheese and how Tilan had teased her about it relentlessly. It brought a smile to her face, her eyes lining with tears.

"My lady, is everything alright?" The elven man returned with a plate of cheese, bread, and olives, setting them down on the table.

With a quick hand, she wiped away the tears. "I'm alright." Marietta should have just said thank you and let him go about his business, but she couldn't help herself. "The pies... use spirits instead of water for the crust. And when the berries aren't a good batch, add a bit of lemon and cinnamon. The lemon will brighten and cinnamon will warm the flavor." Marietta picked at the plate of food, avoiding eye contact.

"Please don't take offense, my lady, but I find myself skeptical that you would know more than my bakers," he said, his mouth frowning.

"The pie I had with the Queen this afternoon was fine, but the crust could've been flakier. And the filling tasted one-noted," she said between bites.

A heavy sigh left his mouth, his hands tightening and loosening at his sides. "I'll look at the recipe, my lady. Everyone's a critic until they do it themselves," he said with a weak smile.

Marietta stood, swallowing her bite. "Then I'll do it myself. Do you have an apron?"

The elf took a step back. "You... you can't be serious, my lady. It would be improper for you to do such a basic task." He held up his hand as he apologized.

Marietta remembered Keyain was a prominent figure in Satiros. Her lips curved into a sweet smile. "I mean no trouble, but as Lady Marietta Vallynte," she said, her throat tightening at the false name, "I'm going to ask if I can use your kitchen."

The name registered as his eyes grew wide. "Oh, Lady Marietta. My apologies, here," he said, ushering her to a spot while asking someone to grab her an apron.

Marietta gave him a list of items to get and began working on her version of the pie. Stepping into a kitchen felt so routine. All she was missing was the gossiping of her own workers around her.

The rhythm of baking came with ease, her muscles remembering the flow of her process. On a day where everything felt wrong, this was the first to feel right. She put all of herself into the pie as if it would help prove Keyain hadn't erased that part of her.

A kitchen worker brought spirits to her station, and she began working it into the flour for the pie crust. Though it was still spring, the berries appeared in season. She popped one into her mouth, the fruit tart and juicy, surprising her. Removing that much flavor from the fruit took an extraordinary amount of skill—and not in a positive way.

Marietta added the berries to a pot with water on the stove, letting them come to a boil before adding sugar, lemon juice, and a dash of cinnamon.

She took the dough and rolled it into thin sheets, draping it over the pie tin. After trimming the edge, she struck small holes in the bottom before pouring her cooled pie filling. An idea came to her as she went to add the top crust.

Marietta took a knife, cutting the dough into narrow strips to create the stalks of the vine pattern she had seen around the palace. Woven throughout the vine pattern, she added small leaves and placed them over the pie. To ensure the crust was golden brown when it came out of the oven, she brushed on egg mixed with water.

She slid the pie into the oven and wiped her hands off on her apron. Satisfied, she thought it was a pie she would have been proud to sell in her shop. Marietta paused, realizing the room had gone quiet as the kitchen workers all stood around her station slack-jawed.

The elven man's mouth hung open as he asked, "Dare I ask where a noble lady learned to bake like that?"

She bit her tongue. The truth would bring more questions. Did anyone know she was a baker? Half-truths would have to work. "One of life's greatest pleasures is making things for others to enjoy. Some ladies stitch, others paint. I prefer to bake."

"Even so, in all my years running this kitchen, I have never once seen a noble use it." His brows furrowed.

"By the sounds of it, I'm a first of many things for this court." Marietta took off her apron and folded it, leaving it at the workstation.

At her table once more, Marietta ignored the gawking workers. The pie had distracted her from her hunger, which gnawed at her once more.

The kitchen blurred as the excitement passed. No one bothered Marietta as she ate, waiting for her pie to bake. Lost in her thoughts, Marietta devoured the food, thinking of her workers in Olkia. Did one of them discover Tilan's body? That she was missing? Or did Keyain's army march on her home before they got the chance? She sent a prayer to whatever god was listening, hoping they were okay. Each of them came to her to train, dreaming of opening their own bakeries one day.

After an hour had passed, she returned to the oven. As she pulled it out, the crust was golden brown, and the sweet scent of berries and buttery crust intoxicating. The pie was one of her best. If only she could stay to confirm it, but she needed to return. Keyain would be waiting, and he didn't need to know about her performance in the kitchen. The elf found her as she set the pie on the counter to cool.

"It looks perfect, Lady Marietta," he said in an incredulous voice, his brows raised.

She smiled. "I'm sorry for taking up a spot in your kitchen. Satiros has differed greatly from Olkia. But you have offered me the greatest comfort." Her hands crossed over her chest.

"I'm happy to have brought you some relief, and I apologize. I forgot you came from Olkia. A shame what happened to it," he said, his eyes far off as he thought. "Some friends just traveled there last year. They raved about a bakery in the downtown area. It had an absurd name, like Rising Bread, or Raisin Above something…." He rubbed his chin in thought. "I can't remember. Does it sound familiar to you?"

"Unfortunately, no," she replied with a sad smile, her heart cracking with the lie.

Chapter Nineteen

MARIETTA

Marietta left the pie for the kitchen workers to eat, confident they would love it once cooled. The servant led her back to the infirmary.

She thought baking would have helped her shake the hollow feeling in her chest, but she only missed the life she couldn't have back. The thoughts caused her throat to tighten, so she pushed them away.

Keyain would be furious she had thwarted whatever plans he had made. Marietta didn't care. Let him feel as much pain as he brought upon her. If possible, she would make him suffer.

The nurse who cared for her passed in the hall, wide-eyed at the sight of Marietta. She didn't seem too surprised that she was no longer on drugs, meaning Keyain had already yelled at her.

The door of her room was ajar as she approached, the area beyond it torn apart. The mattress was bare; the sheets ripped from it, and the pillows' feathers littered the floor. Keyain sat in the chair, his forearms on his knees. As he looked up at Marietta, he clenched his jaw, eyes burning.

No one should see this side of him, herself included. Marietta pushed the door closed behind her to hide his shame. That was the temper she remembered, the one she hated.

"Well, did you have fun?" he snapped.

"The most fun I've had in over a month." She crossed her arms and leaned against the door.

The reddened skin along his neck flushed a shade deeper. "Found the Queen's little note." How Keyain had known it was from Queen Valeriya

was beyond her. Perhaps it was her handwriting or the words she shared in the garden.

Marietta stared at Keyain, forcing him to speak. "Anything to say for yourself?" he asked.

"Do you think I want to live my life drugged beyond comprehension in Satiros? Being the brainless wife of some warlord?" Marietta tilted her head as she spoke to him.

"Minister of Protection," he ground out, "and I did it to protect you."

"Protect me? You had me attacked in my home. I watched your soldiers slit my husband's—my actual husband's—throat. And you dare tell me you're protecting me?"

A sigh escaped his mouth as he rose to his feet. "If you knew the truth, you'd choose to be drugged. Unless you want your knowledge of Enomenos used in the next attack."

"What are you talking about?"

His smile didn't reach his eyes as he stepped close to Marietta. "King Wyltam wants to use you. He thinks you can be a reliable source of information." Keyain exhaled, running a hand through his hair. "I needed to get you out of Olkia. Anyone who fought back is dead, Marietta. King Wyltam ordered it. He ordered the attack. I... I couldn't live with myself if you died." Quick blinks controlled the tears that welled in his eyes.

"So you had your army slaughter people if they resisted you?" Marietta laughed darkly. "You think you saved me, but you have damned me. You stole me from my life, made sure I could never return, and drugged me so I couldn't fight back." Hot tears slid down her cheeks.

Keyain stepped closer, grabbing her hands and holding them. "I drugged you because somehow you resisted my team so much that you flung yourself down a set of stairs and nearly killed yourself. Gods, Mar, I—"

"Don't call me that!" She pushed him away from her, but he didn't budge. Keyain pulled her close, his body warm against Marietta's, his arms locking her in place.

He looked her in the eyes. "I kept you drugged because the King wants to use you. That's why you can't trust Queen Valeriya. Look at what she did today after she figured out you were no longer drugged—she told the entire court! She has her motivations, her own game she's playing."

"What would the King possibly use me for?" she hissed at him.

"You have extensive knowledge of Enomenos. He wants me to use that information as leverage over the remaining cities." A frown tugged at his lips as he rubbed his nose. "If they deemed you mentally incapable of helping, they wouldn't use you. I just needed to convince them. I could've taken you to my property in the countryside, far away from this court. You just needed to stay drugged."

"Don't you dare blame this on me. You," Marietta hissed, pushing her finger into his chest, "attacked Olkia. You brought me here. You drugged me to hide your lie. You lied to everyone and said I was your wife. All of this is all your fault."

Tears lined his eyes again as he grabbed her finger, removing it from his chest. "Legally, we are married in Satiros. Under Satiroan Law, you are Lady Marietta Vallynte, my wife."

Her eyes narrowed. Slowly she stepped out of his arms, her voice a whisper. "What did you do, Keyain?"

"I thought you would say yes," he paused, taking a deep breath. "Under Satiroan law, an elf partner can claim a pilinos partner without their consent. I was going to ask you to marry me, but…" his voice trailed off.

"But you did it without me, without my consent," she laughed. "Of course you did. You never respected me, and now I'm stuck in this cursed place with you."

"Yes, you are stuck here, with me. And if you want to survive, then you better listen to me." He stepped closer to her. "I know you're angry, and I know you're in pain." His face crumpled as he spoke, his voice cracked. "But all I want is for you to live, Marietta. It was the only way. To bring you here."

"You will always be the same, Keyain. You think you're doing what's best for me, but your actions always benefit you the most," she seethed, turning away from him.

She was legally his wife.

How dare he, after all that time. Years of begging Marietta to move to Satiros with him—to have a family. Marietta told him no, time and time again, yet he did it anyway.

Now the King of Satiros wanted to use her against Enomenos. It made little sense. Regardless, she would share nothing. What's the worst they could do, throw her in a dungeon? That didn't scare her, not when it would be temporary pain and fear under Keyain's control. She would escape, one way or another.

The silence stretched between them, Keyain mulling over her words as she weighed her options.

"What happens now?" she whispered, breaking the silence.

Keyain took a deep breath. "You'll be moving into my suite immediately."

"As your dear wife?" Her voice was dull as she spoke.

"Yes. As my dear wife."

Silence settled over them, dragging as they walked towards the Noble's Section, their arms linked. People approached the two, but Keyain apologized and kept them moving.

Marietta immediately knew which door was his: the only one with guards stationed outside it. Like the two guarding the entrance earlier that day, they wore the green, leaf-like leather armor and swords hung at their sides. Behind the guards rose an ornate double door, the wood decorated with carved wooden vines like the ones she incorporated into the pie crust.

"Here we are," Keyain said while pushing open the double doors. An antechamber greeted them, decorated with mirrors in wooden frames. Beyond the doorway was a long room, a table large enough to seat six was at the far end.

Though her apartment above the bakery was technically larger, the suite was grander with its ornate carved wood moldings, gold-gilded sconces holding light globes, the elaborately designed fireplace complete with tiny creature statues emerging from stone.

Marietta left the antechamber, stepping into the dining room with her hand dragging on the molding of the wood-paneled wall. A dark wood table sat before a hearth with chairs covered in green velvet. In the room next sat matching couches and chairs. So that was the life of an elven lord, living in excess.

Wrong—Minister of Protection.

"You live like this?" she asked, lifting one of the brocade drapes from the floor-to-ceiling windows that flanked the fireplace.

"Like what?"

Marietta turned to him, raising a brow, gesturing to the rooms. "In luxury, with no expense spared. Velvet dining chairs, really?"

Keyain gave a subtle eye roll, checking his irritation. "Is it not nice? Would you prefer the threadbare inns of Enomenos?"

"Absolutely," she said without hesitation. "At least I'd be there by choice."

She turned her back to Keyain, facing the double wooden doors inlaid with etched glass that partitioned the living room and dining room. The etching was a forest scene of deer with gnarled antlers and wings sprouting from their backs and tall, twisting trees with naked women growing from the bark. Marietta reached her hand out, gently touching the details. Such craftsmanship reminded her of Tilan.

"Must you smudge the glass with your fingers?" Keyain said behind her.

Glaring, Marietta rubbed her palm down the glass as she pushed open the door, stepping into the living room.

Gods, another fireplace? The green couches flanked its hearth with a low, dark wood table set before them. Marietta ran her hand over the fabric, as soft as velvet but as thin as cotton. Expensive.

Her gaze trailed to the bookcases lining the walls, the series of volumes and knickknacks that sat on the shelves. *History of this. War tactics that.* She clucked her tongue—unsurprising. A warlord has war books.

"What?" Keyain asked, trailing her like a dog through the suite.

"Such exciting reads." She could imagine the look on his face without having to turn around, his irritation rolling off him. Good. Suffer like she had to suffer.

Marietta walked to the far side of the room, to where a set of high-back chairs and a small table sat before ceiling-high windows, overlooking the expansive garden beyond. In the distance, she thought she saw another building, but it was hard to tell. She should've tried her luck at escaping in the gardens—at least chasing her down would have irritated Keyain.

On the far wall was a singular door, missing the fineries of etchings and carved wood. She pushed it open, finding a practical office lined with more bookcases and filing cabinets. From the wood-paneled wall hung a hand-drawn map of the entire Akroi region. Marietta walked to it, her fingers resting on Olkia, tracing the road to Kentro, to the other cities of Enomenos. The same roads on which she and Keyain fell in love.

Marietta's heart turned to ice as she turned around, glaring at the man who took everything from her. "So, this is where you do your dirty work? Start wars? Kill families?"

Keyain didn't bother hiding his irritation as he bit down on the inside of his cheek, his fingers tapping against the door frame. "This is where I read those reports, actually. The dirty work happens with the King and my team."

A nugget of information—his reports were in that room. Likely they were locked away, but what did they contain?

She walked over to his desk, her fingers tracing along the wood top to a stack of papers. "Oops," she said, knocking them to the floor.

A satisfying warmth spread out from her chest as Keyain lost his temper, swearing. "Are you a child, Marietta? Is this necessary?"

"Would you admit to having a child as a wife?" she said sarcastically, strolling past the scattered papers, past him, and out the door. Petty, so incredibly petty.

Her lips tugged into a smile. She could be so much worse.

Marietta crossed the living and dining room to inspect the other side of the living space. She stopped dead in the doorway. At its center was a four-poster bed with green brocade curtains, the mattress piled high with plush pillows and blankets. She looked around for another bedroom, her gaze settling on Keyain. "There's only one bed."

"Yes?"

"I'm not sharing a bed."

"Are we not husband and wife?" A smirk curled on his lips, the amusement not reaching his eyes as he leaned against the wall next to the doorway.

"You can sleep on the couch," she said, striding past him into the suite. "Wouldn't be the first time I made you do that."

Keyain grumbled at the memory, and she would've smiled if her stomach wasn't in knots. It was one thing to be forced to live with Keyain—it was another to *sleep* next to him.

She shuddered and turned to the bathroom, where wood paneling gave way to white marble tiles lining the room. A golden glow lit the space as she entered. "Magic must be nice," she murmured, earning a sigh from Keyain. Of course, the Syllogi nobles have magic-imbued objects for everyday use. They controlled the magic, keeping the techniques and use for their own city-states. When they did sell magic-imbued objects to people in Enomenos, it was at a ridiculous cost.

Across the wall adjacent to the bedroom was a long wood vanity with storage, marble sinks with running taps sprouting from its top, and all set before a seamless glass mirror. A stone washtub sat at the center of the room upon a dais. To its side was a small table with vials and a gold tap with a removable wash head. It was set before.... "Gods, another fireplace?" she said, gaping. It matched the carved stone of the dining-room hearth. To its left was the water closet, tucked away from the finery of the ornate bathroom.

Marietta shook her head. The lords of Satiros shit in better rooms than most in Enomenos would ever live.

She returned to the bedroom, coming to another set of doors, and found two mother-of-pearl in-laid wardrobes and a velvet-padded bench. "Yours is on the left," Keyain said just over her shoulder, causing her to jump.

A smirk lined his face as she turned to him, offering a glare. "Not too close now, lord," she said, pushing him away.

"Lord husband, if you must."

Her hands curled at her sides. Even if the suite *physically had* felt like home—which it didn't—then Keyain's presence would be enough to make it not so. Hate furled inside her as she stared at his face, the look of amusement lining his features.

"And your handmaid Amryth will bring your clothes later today."

Marietta scoffed, pushing past him in the doorway into the bedroom. "I don't want nor need a handmaid."

"Why are you fighting me on everything, Mar?" he snapped, following her.

"Don't call me that," she snarled.

Keyain sighed, running his hand through his hair. "Look, you're angry, and I know you're going to be angry, but you've seen what this court is like. You are very bright, but you don't know what you're doing—I'm going to be your only line of defense. They aren't aware of what happened to you in Olkia."

"Oh, so you're stepping in to play hero? You can't be both my abductor and my savior, Keyain," she said, squaring up to him, though she stood almost a foot below his head. "And thanks to you, I went into that tea time blind. The ladies may have mentioned that the humans of Enomenos imprisoned me, keeping me from my poor, devastated husband." She spat the words, anger and emotion building at her throat.

"If they knew the truth, that you willingly left me, I wouldn't have been able to get you." He placed a hand on her shoulder, holding her gaze. "You would have been hurt in the attack, Mar. You don't realize the whole truth of your situation."

"If you know the whole truth of my situation, then why aren't you telling me?" Marietta felt bile rise in her throat. More secrets. More lies.

When would it stop?

It wouldn't. Gods, it wouldn't end, not if she remained in Satiros. Despair clawed at her throat, the walls suddenly too close, Keyain's touch scathing.

"You're getting worked up," he said, dropping his hand. "Today has been a lot for you."

Heavy tears fell from Marietta's eyes. Her feet and hands went numb as she stood there. It wasn't just that day—all of it was too much for her. Tilan's death, being ripped from her life, being forced to live with Keyain. Gods, she'd have to sleep next to him.

A choking sob came from her throat as she crumpled, self-hate pitting her against herself. She shouldn't have cried—she should have fought. She should have screamed at him, hit him, torn the brocade curtains from the bed. Keyain deserved a headache. He deserved pain. Yet Marietta couldn't overcome her own pain.

"I know," Keyain whispered, pulling her into him, wrapping his arms around her. "I'm sorry I did this."

As he led Marietta to the bed, her breath quickened into sharp inhales. She placed her head between her legs to slow the breathing, Keyain coming to focus as he knelt before her. "Just lay in bed until this passes. Amryth will bring clothes, but I'll let her know to leave you be. Just stay in here."

Marietta nodded, not looking at him as she focused on her breathing, trying to calm herself.

"I have some meetings this afternoon, but I'll be back for dinner," he turned away but then turned back to Marietta, kissing her forehead.

The affection caused her body to stiffen. Keyain looked at her with a smile. The touch—his touch—felt familiar but wrong. So very wrong.

The front door latched as Keyain exited the suite. Marietta hugged a pillow to her chest, it catching the tears that fell.

Looking into the bedroom that surrounded her, she felt out of place, dragged into a world she didn't know or understand. This world—Keyain's world—was one of luxury, of lies. Gods, of fireplaces. There was *another one* across from the bed.

She would have laughed, but more than anything, rage grew inside her. For the grotesque wealth, for the absurd amount of fireplaces, for what it all meant—Keyain hid *all of it* for years, and Marietta bought his half-hearted lies.

All her strength diminished, wishing she could control the situation, to control her life. Marietta thought of Tilan, and her heart shattered again. Her home and her husband were gone. Only Keyain and his duplicities remained.

As Amryth filtered in and out of the room, Marietta paid her no mind. Her thoughts carried her far away from Satiros, to her home—to Olkia. To her husband.

Amryth popped her head into Marietta's view. Black skin graced her body, and dark hair twisted into tiny braids that swung as she leaned over the bed. "Is there anything else I can get you, Lady Marietta?"

Marietta shook her head.

"I'll be in the other room if you need anything." Marietta heard the bedroom door shut. She laid there for hours, lost in her pain.

That evening, Marietta ate dinner with Keyain, something she thought she'd never do again. Between them sat half-empty platters of pork in a red wine sauce, fried zucchini fritters, flatbread, and grape leaves stuffed with rice, pine nuts, and fresh herbs. Under normal circumstances, such a spread would be satisfying; yet, this wasn't a normal circumstance. The food sat like a rock in her stomach.

"Are you feeling better than earlier?" he asked, removing his napkin from his lap and placing it on the table.

"As best as I can be, considering the situation," Marietta muttered.

Keyain glanced at her with a frown. "Things will get better, I promise. I'm reworking my plan. It'd be best if you left the palace altogether," he said, sipping his drink. "The King wants the information, and I can only stall so much."

"Is the King aware that I was married to Tilan before you abducted me?" Marietta said, her eyebrows raised in mock speculation.

Keyain looked down and rubbed his nose. "No, no one is. At least not that you willingly married him, anyway. Though that's still up for debate."

"Or it's not up for debate." She set down her fork, her appetite lost.

"I don't want to get into this. Whether you like it or not, this is the situation you're in, Marietta. I'm doing my best to make this as safe as possible for you."

"By safe, you mean not letting me leave this suite before you can enact whatever new plan you concoct," Marietta said, looking out the window, resting her head in her hand.

"Unless I'm with you, of course." He reached across the table for Marietta's free hand, but she pulled away.

"And when will that be? When you have the time?"

An impatient sigh left his mouth. "I realize I'm busy, but I'll make time for you. You will stay in the suite, though. I have books in the other room and cards you can play."

Marietta stood up from the table. "War books—how fun," she said, walking into the bedroom, hearing Keyain get up and follow.

"Marietta, please don't make me out to be the enemy. What I did wasn't great, but my heart was in the right place," he said, emotion thick in his voice.

Marietta approached her wardrobe to inspect the clothes brought for her, peering over her shoulder at Keyain. "You're a lot of things, Keyain. In your heart, you're not an evil person; you just make terrible decisions." She looked back at the clothes and sifted through them.

"What's that supposed to mean?" The benched groaned as he sat.

Marietta hesitated, remembering their years together. "You always chose the wrong hills to die on. I asked you to defend me against slurs about being a half-elf, especially with your acquaintances, and you said I was overreacting. Yet if someone flirted with me, you'd make it a fight. You viewed me as a possession, not a person like you do all pilinos." A dress of pale pink, the fabric thin and gauzy, caught her eye.

The bench groaned again as Keyain stood up. "Is that really how you felt? All of this time?"

The dress dropped from Marietta's hands as she glared at the floor. "It's still how I feel. You assumed you could kill my husband, steal me from my life, and conquer my home without repercussions. Now you expect me to trust you." Dark curls fell on her back as she looked over her shoulder. "How can I trust you? You don't even see me as a whole person."

Keyain's hulking frame approached her. Marietta turned away again as he rested his hands on her shoulders.

"I have always viewed you as a person, Mar." She cringed at the nickname but let him continue. "Those acquaintances knew me because of my position here. If I had realized this is how you felt, I would've spoken up."

The nerve—how many times had they fought over this very topic when they were together? "I asked you to, so many times." She turned, surprised to see his face crumpled with emotion. The unexpected pain in his expression made her recoil.

"And I pushed you away by dismissing you, calling you dramatic." His voice was a whisper. He reached for Marietta's hands. "I am so sorry. I am so sorry I uprooted your life, and I promise to do what I can to fix it."

Marietta looked into his eyes, the green ones she loved for so long, and she didn't believe it. He had countless opportunities to rectify his actions in the past. Now, it was too late. Her hands slipped out of his as she turned back to the wardrobe. "You can't fix it because I can't go back to my life. But you could at least help me survive in your court. Trapping me in the suite won't keep the Queen away for long." Her voice had more emotion than she had hoped.

Keyain backed up a few paces. "I know. I'll find a better plan, but until I can, you'll need to stay in the suite."

Marietta rolled her eyes. He trapped her in this suite alone with him, the guards stationed outside, and the handmade he assigned. What little hope she had threatened to burn out. With that revelation, she turned back to the clothes. "There are only dresses, by the way."

"If you dig, I'm sure there are sleeping clothes, too."

"No, Keyain—there aren't any shirts or pants."

"You're a lady now and ladies only wear dresses."

She shot him a look. "I'd appreciate it if you could find me some."

Keyain sighed as her focus shifted to the wardrobe and found the strips of silk that somehow formed a nightgown. "Is this seriously what I have to wear to sleep? I'm not wearing this." She held it up to Keyain.

Red flushed his cheeks as he laughed. "The Queen sure likes to play her games. It looks like she wanted a pleasurable reunion for us."

"Do you find this is funny?" Marietta crossed her arms, brows furrowed together.

Keyain stifled his laugh. "No. No, of course not. I want you to be comfortable, but I promise to not stare at you if you wear them," he paused before adding, "even if I did, it's nothing I haven't seen before."

"That doesn't mean I want you to see it now!" She twisted away, her tone sharp. "Can you please have someone bring something more suitable to wear?"

"I would," he said, his voice getting farther as he stepped from the closet, "but if Queen Valeriya planned this, then she'll know you requested new clothes. I don't want to give her any reason to doubt our marriage."

Marietta placed her fingers between her brows. The nightgowns weren't an option, no matter if Keyain had seen her naked. As if he hadn't taken enough away, he had this power over her as well.

She balled up the silk and threw it into the wardrobe, frustrated as she looked around the closet. There had to be something else—something for her to leverage power over Keyain, to even the dynamic between them. She glanced at his wardrobe. If she couldn't ask Keyain for what she wanted, perhaps she could take it from him. A smile curled onto her lips.

Marietta stepped from the closet wearing one of his tunics that hit her mid-thigh. "Aren't you going to ask if you can take my clothing?" he asked with a lazy look on his face as he lounged on the bed.

She placed a hand on her chest, her expression mocking. "We're husband and wife now. What's mine is yours," she said, walking towards the bathroom. Marietta paused in the doorway, glancing back at him. "And what's yours will be mine."

A threat, if anything. Keyain could try to trap her in this suite, could try to control everything she said or did, but she wouldn't make it easy. No, Marietta would bleed him dry—for the life she had lost and for the life she had yet to live.

Chapter Twenty

MARIETTA

Marietta sat for breakfast the following morning. In the corner stood her elven handmaid, Amryth, unnervingly quiet. Despite the heat, she wore a long-sleeved dress, and her black box braids pulled back into a bun. Though she looked young for an elf, she held the austere expression of an old fisherman, the ones in Olkia at the fish market who Marietta could never get to smile. She cocked a brow at the handmaid and her odd manner.

Uncomfortable silence hovered between them like a heavy fog as she stood watching Marietta eat. Such a feeling was rare for Marietta. Usually she could get people to laugh, to ease them when they first met—but not with Amryth. Keyain just had to insist she had a handmaid. "You can sit if you'd like," Marietta broke the silence, gesturing to the chair across from her.

Amryth gave her a sobering look. "That would be improper, my lady." Her voice was unimpressed, as if she wished not to be there. Marietta held her laugh. At least they had that much in common.

"Oh, we wouldn't want that now, would we?" Marietta said, her tone laced with sarcasm. "It's completely normal for someone to stand while someone else eats. Not saying a word, not doing anything." Marietta popped a strawberry into her mouth. Enough food arrived to feed her and Keyain, but he had left before she woke up. She hadn't heard him leave.

Amryth narrowed her eyes. "I must insist that I stand, my lady," her tone more impatient that time. So she did have emotions.

Annoyance laced Marietta's tongue. "Right, for the good of my noble

bearing, you must stand and serve me. You should not speak unless spoken to. Stand rigid and never relax. Wipe my ass—"

"Would sitting placate you that much?" Amryth snapped.

"Yes," Marietta said, gesturing to the chair. "Is it too much to ask that my only companion for the foreseeable future acts like a normal person?"

Amryth hesitated, then crossed the room, taking the spot across from her. A headache—that's what she would be. Keyain found a handmaid as stubborn as him and likely did it on purpose. Amryth had a soldier's rigidity as she stiffly sat in her seat, her shoulders back, and sat up straight.

Marietta took another bite, looking at her companion. "There's too much food here for just me to eat. Help yourself to any of it."

"I ate before coming," Amryth said as she tilted her head to the side, "but thank you, my lady."

"Well, if you change your mind, then don't hesitate." Marietta returned to her plate.

"Handmaids don't sit down with their ladies, and they most definitely do not dine with them."

"Well, I don't like the formality, and I'm not used to servants. What I need right now is a friend."

"Unfortunately for you, my lady, I am your handmaid, not your friend. I have me a job to do, and I will see to it," she replied, her tone absolute.

Great. Of course, Keyain would trap her in the suite with someone who'd follow his every word. Gods give her strength to get through it.

After a silent breakfast, Marietta readied herself for the day. Was there a point to appear presentable if she must stay in the suite? No, but perhaps it would make her less antsy. The restricted freedom was already getting on her nerves.

Amryth followed her into the bathroom, turning the bath's faucet. "Is filling the tub necessary? I can help myself, you know." Marietta attempted to ease the irritation in her voice.

"I have a job to do, my lady."

"I get that, but please," Marietta said, waving her out, "I need to keep doing some stuff by myself to stay sane while being trapped in here."

Amryth crossed her arms, giving Marietta a stony stare. "As you wish, my lady," she sighed, walking out of the bathroom and closing the door behind her.

Marietta sunk into the deep tub, her gaze fixed upon the ridiculous fireplace. A bathroom fireplace—she wished she could hear Tilan's opinion on its absurdity.

The heat of the water soaked into her bones as she leaned her head against the side. Living in Satiros felt like wearing a dead man's clothes: nothing fit right and everything felt strange. The lifestyle, the clothing, the fireplaces. Gods, even having people wait on her hand-and-foot was uncomfortable. If servants were responsible for starting baths, then the nobles really must have had their asses wiped for them as well. Where was their need to be self-reliant? Marietta couldn't grasp it; she had always been self-sufficient. To have someone else wait on her felt absurd. Tilan had teased that Marietta was so independent that it wouldn't have surprised him if she took over her clients' businesses. There was always another way to help if she looked hard enough.

Tears formed in her eyes as she smiled to herself. He would never tease her again. Never share their inside jokes, crying from laughing so hard. Regret formed a knot in her stomach, knowing she should have spent more time with him, should have taken fewer clients, should have spent more days at home. But it was too late, and she would never see him again. The water rose above her head as she sank into the deep tub, drowning her tears.

Marietta's hair still dripped as she sat before her vanity in the bedroom, her face staring in the mirror. Except her body was different. The once rounded curves fell flatter, her cheeks sallow; even under her eyes looked bruised. It was an unknown version of herself—one she didn't like.

She worked a comb through her hair as Amryth walked in. "I can help you with that, my lady," she offered, approaching Marietta.

"No, it's alright. I can—" The comb found a knot, and Marietta yanked at it with frustration. She just wanted to look like herself.

"You're going to rip out your hair if you keep doing that." She took the comb from Marietta's hands.

The demanding tone surprised Marietta; the handmaid had some bite. Good, she wanted a genuine person with emotions as her company, not a silent overseer. She didn't fight as Amryth took over.

"Gods, your hair is tangled. How did you manage this? Was anyone combing your hair?" Amryth's face furrowed at the back of her head, concentrating on working the comb through her curls.

"My nurse insisted on using a brush on my hair—only when it was dry, too," Marietta said with a frown tugging at her lips. "I don't remember the nurses ever bathing me."

"Of course, they only brushed it when it was dry. The nurses don't know what they're doing down there," Amryth murmured under her breath. She sighed before continuing, "They have a mage assigned to the infirmary. Instead of trying to bathe the ill or wounded, they use magic to clean their patients."

"Magic must be nice," Marietta grumbled. Unlike in Enomenos, Syllogi elves are well versed in magic, keeping their secrets to their region—always the elves, never the pilinos.

"Must be," Amryth answered. "No one on the—er, none of the servants are proficient in magic."

"But you're elven," Marietta said, turning to face Amryth. "I thought all Syllogian elves knew how to do it."

She grabbed Marietta's head and turned it back to the mirror. "Only those who have a promising mental capacity can wield it."

"What does that even mean?"

"From what I know, it's based on one's ability to concentrate," Amryth said. "The more you can focus, the better a mage you are, yet the practice is restricted even for elves. Not everyone gets to learn."

Funny, Marietta always assumed most Syllogian elves knew magic, that Keyain was an anomaly of his kind. Turned out that he was more like his people than she ever realized.

Amryth made her way around Marietta's head. As she finished, she placed her hands on Marietta's shoulders and looked at her through the mirror. "How would you like your hair?"

Marietta smiled. Amryth had already dropped her title and gave her the choice of how to do her hair. "Leave it down. That's how I like to wear it."

Amryth looked like she wanted to protest but shrugged and left her hair as it was.

Marietta sat on the couch in the living room with her legs tucked up underneath her. After skimming the shelves of Keyain's dry titles twice, she only found one of slight interest—*The History of Satiros*.

Beginning with a forest that held the land before the city-state was founded, the subject quickly changed to the life of the first Queen. The text caused her mind to wander from the pages. How funny that it focused on the elven Queen, but didn't discuss how elves came to rule over the pilinos.

Since her arrival in Satiros, she had only seen elves, even in the kitchens. Curious. "I thought pilinos served the elves of Satiros, yet I haven't seen either since I've been in the palace," she asked Amryth.

At Marietta's request, the handmaid read on the other end of the couch. When she looked up, her features grew dark. "Pilinos are too low to serve nobility."

Marietta went still, feeling the roar of blood in her ears. "What do you mean?"

"There's a hierarchy. Humans are the lowest servants and are cheap help. Half-elves are a bit more... exotic. Wealthier families prefer them over humans to distinguish their wealth," she said with a tight expression. "The richest, like the nobility, can afford—in their words, not mine—actual people. So they employ full elves."

Marietta furrowed her brows and pulled her lips back in disgust. The profound hatred for pilinos ran deep in Satiros. Keyain knew this—knew that his entire city-state viewed people like herself as beneath them, and yet, she sat in his suite pretending to be a lady. The deafening roar of anger left her speechless for a moment. How could Keyain marry her at all as an elven lord was beyond her understanding. With a calming breath, she asked, "So me being a part of the court, my... marriage to Keyain. Both are an anomaly?" The word marriage struggled on her tongue.

Amryth sighed and looked like she didn't want to answer the question. "In the palace, within the court, yes. But in the city-state, not necessarily. Elves can claim pilinos as lawful partners since they don't have full personhood. The law doesn't need the pilinos's consent."

"What if," Marietta asked and then paused. "What if the pilinos is from outside of Satiros? Outside of Syllogi?"

Amryth looked across the room in thought. "I'm sure elves have tried, but it's not common. At least I have never heard of it. In theory, the pilinos would need to be a citizen of Syllogi, from at least one of the city-states, I would imagine."

Marietta nodded her head, not bothering to hide the hostility from her face. Keyain had done as such, and somehow Marietta not being a citizen didn't make a difference. "How does being a pilinos affect my position here? As a lady in court?"

"I don't know, Lady Marietta," she replied, adding the title as if she just remembered it.

Marietta remained quiet, stewing on the words. Her father came from Syllogi, and not once did he teach her about the intricacies of the social classes. Often he told Marietta to never trust Syllogian elves (the warning carrying merit since he grew up as one), but her father never went into detail. He never told her that she wouldn't be considered an *actual* person by the elves.

For him to marry her mother, a human born and raised in Enomenos, carried more weight than Marietta realized. It also showed how off-base Keyain had been when they were together. Her father had the same background, yet Marietta knew with certainty that if anyone had said a slur to her mother, they'd limp away from that conversation. The contrast between them couldn't be starker.

~Chapter Twenty–One

ELYSE

Deep throbbing pain exuded from the left side of Elyse's head, her vision dizzy, and her stomach roiling. It had been so long since her last head pain that she almost forgot how the symptoms felt.

By some good fortune, it wasn't the worst head pain she had felt. Elyse could sit in bed with the curtains drawn over the windows, blocking most of the light. A book lay unread in her lap, acting as a cover for when her father walked in. He would check on Elyse at some point, probably suspecting that her head hurt, but she didn't want to take any drugs. The effects differed from alcohol—memory loss, hallucinations, and loss of self-awareness and self-control. The last two scared her the most. With alcohol, she could control how much she drank.

Unless she was in a social setting, then it became a necessity. The ball was a testament to that. Without the drinks, she wouldn't have been able to talk to Brynden. To kiss him.

Even days later, Elyse thought about the kiss and her foolish decision to go somewhere more private. It was reckless, and if her father found out, he'd be furious. *Tease and tempt, but never give.*

Brynden's words rung in her mind—fuck her father.

The Chorys Dasian was something else. Chaotic, restless energy lurked under his skin, always looking for a quip to say something to tease or a moment of fun; that thrilled her more than it should. What were the chances Brynden would call on her again, let alone be willing to court her? At the end of the evening, he had kissed Elyse in front of Grytaine

and Royir, which he shouldn't have done unless he was interested. Maybe courting customs in Chorys Dasi were different. Maybe kissing was normal and not just shared between courting couples. Oh, gods, she hadn't considered that.

That would make more sense. After one evening, Brynden wouldn't be interested in binding his life to her. And she almost went somewhere private with him, in front of Grytaine, of all people.

Elyse raised a pillow, mock yelling into it. So stupid—gods, Grytaine would say something to her father. Dread pooled in her stomach, even as her head pain continued to throb.

There was a sharp knock at the door, not waiting for an answer before entering. Her father stood in the doorway, lips frowning and eyes displeased. "Elyse, my office. Now."

She gathered her strength, steadying herself as lights flashed in front of her eyes and pain pulsed on the left side of her head. Did he know? He must know. His face said as much.

The light of the common area blinded her as she crossed it. With a deep breath, she entered her father's office, trying her best to keep the pain from showing on her face.

He waited behind his desk, head resting on his knitted fingers, as Elyse took a seat. "Well, I found out some fascinating information," he said, eyes narrowed on Elyse.

"And what would that be, father?" she asked, ignoring the sudden dizziness that hit her.

"You tell me." He leaned back in his chair.

That was his trick: to get Elyse to admit something she did was wrong. Years ago, she learned that saying nothing was the best answer.

He gave a heavy sigh. "Honestly, Elyse. Grytaine told me about the garden."

But which part? The first kiss on the path? The kiss good night? Or worse? Silence filled the room as Elyse refused to answer.

"Elyse," her father warned, "fine, I'll be the one to say it. You were heading to a secluded spot alone with Brynden, weren't you?"

She closed her eyes, wishing herself invisible. Of course, Grytaine would tell him about it after she stopped it from happening.

"Well? Anything to say for yourself, or are you going to sit there and act like an idiot?" His temper flared, his voice rising.

Elyse raised her eyes, the light from the windows blinding. "I was being obedient," she lied, telling her father what he wanted to hear. Or so she thought.

"Oh, being obedient? You're obedient to me, Elyse, not to someone you're entertaining," he spat. "How many other of my friends have you been alone with? Was this the first time? Because we have talked about this, how far to go."

She shrunk back into the chair at her father's tone, her breathing ragged as she cast her eyes to the floor. "No one, I swear," she lied.

"Look at me when you speak, damn it," he growled. "To think, I did all of this for Brynden to think you're a whore."

The insult landed, Elyse flinching at his words. Was that what she was? The kiss on the path wouldn't leave her head. Neither would what she imagined would have happened if Brynden had her alone, kissing her until his jaw ached. Gods—she would have gone further if they had the chance.

"I'm sorry," she said, her eyes finding his face.

The anger rolled through him, his lips thinned and his nostrils flared. "How dare you try to sabotage my work? I had to find out from Royir's gossiping wife, so I'm sure the entire court knows what you are."

Tears welled in her eyes, but she blinked them back, refusing to let them fall. "I'm sorry, father," she whispered.

"Is that all you have to say? Sorry?"

Stress caused her vision to turn white, the room spinning under her feet. "I... I don't know," she stammered.

He sighed again, his tone softening. "The head pains are back, and you didn't tell me. Elyse, we've been through this. You need to take the drugs."

She tried shaking her head, unsure if she did or not. "I'm okay, really."

The drawer slid open, and she heard the clinking of glass. From it, her father pulled out the milky blue liquid she despised. Her father walked around his desk, forcing it into Elyse's hand. "Take it. Now."

With a trembling grip, she took the vial, letting the tears fall. The thick substance dripped down, churning her stomach.

"You need to listen to me, especially when an unprecedented opportunity has knocked at your door," he said, leaning against his desk.

"What opportunity?"

"It appears that Lord Brynden likes whores," he drawled. "He asked to court you, and I said yes."

Chapter Twenty-Two

MARIETTA

After a few days alone in the suite with just Amryth, restlessness wore on Marietta. "Is he always like this?" Marietta mumbled, hastily stabbing at her lunch.

"Is who like what, my lady?" Amryth asked.

"Keyain. He didn't come back for dinner. I'm not sure he even came back at all last night," she answered, chomping down on her bite, the food losing its flavor. Irritation continued to spread through her body, all directed at Keyain. How would she ever leave the suite if he wasn't around?

"He's the Minister of Protection, actively overseeing a war." Amryth sat back in her chair, crossing her arms with her face unamused. Did she actually defend Keyain?

"What reason does he have to start a war?" Marietta replied, stabbing at a grape, sending it flying off her plate. A collection of colorful swear words left her mouth as she grabbed it off the table with her hand to eat it.

Amryth lifted one eyebrow at the action. "Unfortunately, I can think of one concrete reason he would do such a thing." Marietta felt her burning gaze.

"It's not—he wouldn't…." Marietta trailed off. Amryth was unaware of the truth. Of Marietta's freedom in Olkia. "Is one pilinos girl worth starting a war?"

"Do you want an honest answer or the one I'm supposed to give?"

Marietta smirked, her irritation taking over. "How about both? How does it feel that he would've gone to war over someone like me?"

Amryth exhaled slowly through her nose with unanticipated fury glaring in her dark eyes. Marietta took another bite, making a point to avoid eye contact.

Keyain might be Minister of Protection, but his actions must have angered people. Others also had to assume Marietta was his prime reason, like Minister Royir from the other day. How did Keyain get to his high position if he wasn't respected?

The awkward silence was too much for Marietta to handle. "I hit a pain point, and for that, I'm sorry. Will you at least tell me the public opinion on Keyain's rise to power?" It was an innocent enough question, but she wanted to learn how her former bodyguard became the Minister of Protection for Satiros.

Amryth looked away, frowning. "People respect him, mostly. Just no one knows the reason for the invasion of Olkia besides the King's Council, which includes the King and his Ministers," she answered. "The one piece of information we do know is that a terrorist group backed by the Enomenos stole Keyain's wife."

A terrorist group backed by Enomenos? Marietta bit back her questions, understanding that Keyain's lies ran deep.

"If I'm being honest with you, most thought you were a rumor—a bad one at that. One of the most influential elves in Satiros married to a half-elf?" Amryth said, shaking her head.

Marietta tapped her fingers against the table. None of it made sense. Before the night she was taken, she hadn't seen Keyain in a couple of years. Why would he use her as an excuse?

Unless they had no other reason to attack.

Anger flooded her body as she imagined her friends slaughtered in the streets of Olkia. Keyain was despicable. "Do people believe Keyain deserves his position?" she asked, pretending to be half interested in the question.

Amryth narrowed her eyes at her. "Yes and no. You've heard the stories, right?"

Marietta avoided eye contact and took another bite. "Oh yes, the stories. I've heard them."

Amryth sighed. "Get better at lying if you're going to survive as a lady."

When Marietta said nothing in reply, she continued talking. "Being close friends with King Wyltam since childhood helped get him a position, but the biggest qualifier is his legacy. Keyain Vallynte is one of Satiros' greatest warriors of all time."

Marietta inhaled as she sipped water, causing herself to choke and spill water down her front. Amryth handed her a napkin. "You're lying. What war even occurred that gave him that notoriety?"

"The Orc Skirmishes," Amryth implied as if Marietta understood.

"That wasn't in the history books in Enomenos."

Amryth laughed. "Of course not. Syllogi only protects the entire Akroi Region from southern invaders, but they leave that out of your histories."

Marietta furrowed her brows. "Orcs were exterminated centuries ago."

Amryth laughed again. "That's a lie. For hundreds of years, the southern orc clans would barge through The Queen's Pass and lay ruin to the Syllogian countryside," she explained. "A century and a half ago, the Syllogi Council united to put an end to their raids. Thus, The Orc Skirmishes."

Marietta imagined the map that hung from Keyain's wall, thinking out loud, "The Syllogi Council is just the different elven courts?"

"The ruling families. King Wyltam and Queen Valeriya represent Satiros. The rulers of Amigys, Kyaeri, and Chorys Dasi are also on the Council. Did you never learn this?" Amryth asked.

"History was never my strong subject," Marietta said with a shrug. Not that she ever paid much attention to the lesson on Syllogi. Never had she thought they'd be useful to her.

"Of course, it wasn't," Amryth said, unimpressed. "During The Orc Skirmishes, the former Queen Olytia roused the army to bring greatness to Satiros over the other elven cities," Amryth paused. "Keyain was a captain in the army. It's said he took her request to heart, killing more orcs than any other soldier in all of Syllogi."

The night she met Keyain, he had left her attacker unconscious in the street. "I knew he could fight, but was he that great of a soldier?"

"Keyain was the best," Amryth answered wistfully. "And very young, for an elf at least. His parents' position helped him rise in the army, but it was his skill that made him stand out."

"How did he get to Minister of Protection then?"

"If you stop asking questions, then I'll get to it," she scolded. "When the orc clans set a trap for the elven armies, General Mykilo of Satiros fell, leaving Satiroan soldiers without guidance. That's when Keyain took the mantle, devising a plan to trick the orcs and lead the assault himself. It was the last battle of The Orc Skirmishes, the one that made the orc clans flee Syllogi."

That sounded like Keyain, taking control of the situation and making a plan. Back when they traveled together, his judgment had gotten them out of troubling situations on the road.

"What helped Keyain get to his position," Amryth continued, "was after the battle, when he placed his sword at Queen Olytia's feet in front of the Syllogian Council. He dedicated everything to her, claiming it was through her greatness that he found strength."

"Sure," Marietta mumbled. "Keyain isn't that flowery of a person. I would love to hear him admit his greatness was because of someone else."

Amryth laughed. "He can be quite arrogant. Yet Queen Olytia rewarded him for his actions. The Queen promoted him to General of the Satiroan Army, the youngest elf ever. He had been close to his fifth decade."

"Of course he was," she mumbled again, shaking her head. *A security job of sorts.* That's what he would tell her all those years ago—never *great war hero of Satiros.* The bastard's lies ran deep. "How did he go from General to Minister of Protection?"

Amryth watched Marietta's reaction through narrowed eyes. "You would think his wife would know more about his past."

Marietta avoided her gaze. No, she learned very little of his life before she met him. "He kept his past close to his chest. It's not like a half-elf like me would know the history of Satiros."

"A half-elf from the Syllogi would know their history, even if they didn't pay attention during lessons." Amryth raised a brow, well aware that Marietta was not from Syllogi but Enomenos.

"Perhaps I should go study now then," Marietta said, her tone dripping with sarcasm as she stood from the table. For a servant, Amryth knew a lot of information and knew Keyain almost too well.

The remainder of the afternoon proved once again uneventful. After spending a quiet day pretending to read, Marietta felt disappointed when Amryth left for the day. Alone with her thoughts, she paced in the suite.

Not only was she ripped from her life and her husband murdered, but Satiros's most notable warrior was the one to abduct her. Or maybe the most notable killer, depending on how you viewed it. If Keyain ever bothered to return, she'd have to question him about his past.

Marietta jumped as a hand clasped her shoulder. "Mar? You alright?" Keyain stood behind her with his jacket over his arm, his face ragged with dark circles under his eyes.

"Perhaps I should be the one asking that. Did you sleep at all?"

With a dry laugh, he bent down to kiss Marietta, to which she leaned away. Keyain tried to shrug it off, but she could read the hurt on his face. Gods, the audacity.

"I slept for a few hours in the meeting room with my team, but it wasn't very restful. Is it that bad?" Keyain asked.

"Gods, yes. And you smell. Perhaps you should wash before they bring dinner," she teased.

He rolled his eyes and sighed as he walked into the other room, the joke lost on him. Water filling the tub sounded from the other room, sparking an idea. After a few moments of waiting, knowing for sure he was in the tub, she knocked on the door, cracking it open. "Mind if I come in?" she asked, her voice soft and high-pitched.

"Not at all," he said.

Marietta walked in and realized her mistake. The brawny elven man had his lower half in the water but little else. His broad shoulders and muscled torso remained visible as he scrubbed, water dripping down his body. *Gods.* Even though she knew he was a monster, her stare lingered on him, dumbfounded.

A smirk came to his face, growing deeper the longer she stared. "There are easier ways for you to see me naked, you know."

She shook herself out of it and rolled her eyes, ignoring the heat that crept up her cheeks. "Don't mistake me for yourself, Lord '*I won't look at you, but if I did, it's nothing I haven't seen before,*'" she snapped. She was hoping to catch him off guard, yet she was the one flustered.

"Well, I have seen it before, just like you've seen this." He gestured to his body. "I still think you're the most stunning person I have ever met."

The door frame supported her as she leaned against it, staring at the ceiling. "And what? You thought I'd forgive you because we used to... mess around?"

"It was more than that," he whispered, pain in his voice. "Don't you dare make it less."

"Well, I don't know what to think anymore. Because that part of you was a lie." She glanced at him. "When were you going to tell me you're Satiros's greatest warrior of all time?"

He swore under his breath. "Amryth told you?"

Marietta nodded her head.

"It was a long time ago. But yes, I have that title."

"And you never thought to share that with me? You were happy pretending to be a basic bodyguard?" She crossed her arms, her lips pulling into a grimace.

"I never saw it as a basic job, not when it meant protecting you."

"Don't give me that as an answer."

Keyain dunked his head underwater and came back up, rising from the tub. Against the doorframe, she turned to stare into the bedroom. Keyain's heavy footfalls approach her from behind, very aware of his nakedness. "I would do anything to protect you, and I have always loved you," he whispered, standing so close that she could feel the heat rolling off his body. "Don't act like what happened between us was just casual. You loved me back, and I felt it every day I spent with you."

Tears pooled in her eyes as she left Keyain in the doorway.

"Mar, where are you going?"

"Dinner's here," she murmured.

She hated Keyain's words. And she hated that part of her knew they were true.

Chapter Twenty-Three
VALERIYA

Valeriya rocked her sleeping son in her arms, thankful for the minutes of peace. Still a toddler, his innocence was so pure, his happiness so raw. He was the bright spot among the darkness of living in Satiros, of being married to Wyltam. It had taken years to conceive him—years of pursuing Wyltam's bed—and her reward was her sweet little Mycaub.

Though she understood her fate would lead to a marriage with a male, it hadn't made that experience any less taxing. No, males held none of her interest, romantic or otherwise; yet, as Queen of Satiros, she knew the responsibility of birthing an heir. Knowing hadn't made the process any easier—for both her and Wyltam. The rift between them widened during those excruciating years.

Valeriya smoothed back the black hair from his eyes—hair like his father's. Sometimes Valeriya couldn't believe she tolerated Wyltam long enough to make Mycaub. It was worse than any layer of the hells but also her duty. Her reward was her sweet boy, who was so small, so precious, and nothing like his father beyond looks. She pressed a kiss onto his forehead.

Those moments were few and fleeting ever since Wyltam urged her to leave Mycaub with a nursemaid, a fight Valeriya had lost. Wyltam once again got what he wanted.

Valeriya wracked her brain, trying to remember the last time Wyltam had sought their son. Though Mycaub was his heir, Wyltam spent little time with him. That should bother her, but she was thankful for his absence. She didn't want Mycaub to turn out like him.

She stood and brought Mycaub over to his crib, laying the sleeping toddler inside. He stirred but continued to sleep. Gazing at her son, she found the courage she needed to do her task that evening. Everything Valeriya did was to be a better leader, to make Satiros better for all. One day, the people would know her sacrifice, and she'd be immortal by the memory of her work.

The sky darkened with the setting sun as she left the Royal's Wing, winding her way through the sprawling palace grounds. Reaching the Southwestern Gate would take half an hour unless she ran into any issues. Valeriya had to be alert as she crossed the campus, for she was the Queen, a job she enjoyed having, but it was harder for her to sneak away.

In Reyila's court, Valeriya found discreet movements yielded the best information. As the future Queen, Valeriya's sister relied on her and a half-elf named Katya to help strengthen her political position.

Katya was Valeriya's friend, training partner, and lover. The tough half-elf matched Valeriya in ferocity; years of practice turned the females into accomplished mages. Both Katya and Valeriya's mage abilities were unknown to those in Satiros.

Her heart ached for the half-elf who stood shorter than Valeriya, yet still stared down at everyone. Her cropped black hair, her turquoise eyes, her piercings, the notch missing in her ear. The details came back to Valeriya, emotion overwhelming her. No, she needed to focus, to make sure no one followed her.

At that hour, the palace and its grounds remained empty, people letting down their guard. The elven court thought no one was around at this hour, but Valeriya watched, seeing people's true colors. The dirty secrets of Satiros's court revealed themselves. She knew which marriages were doing well and which ones were not—that is how she learned of Royir's appetite for young blondes, often watching various females leave his suite when Grytaine was away.

Through Valeriya's ability to be stealthy, their secrets manifested. But remaining unseen was hard when everyone knew her face. Decades of practicing magic gave her an advantage: she could change her appearance.

True transformation magic was difficult, hard to control. To fully transform a living form took a considerable amount of *aithyr*—or magical energy. Few possessed that ability. Only the most talented, most legendary, could do so. Though Valeriya was a proud female, she wasn't too proud to admit she didn't have such ability. Instead, she knew how to work around it. Sometimes, just seeming to be a different person was sufficient.

Aware of her surroundings as she slinked through the Central Garden, ensuring no one trailed her and that the vicinity was empty, at least from what she could see. Valeriya stepped into the tangle of plant overgrowth, slipping into the shadows of a tree whose boughs curved towards the ground, creating a dome that shielded her from prying eyes. With a deep breath, she silenced her thoughts and rid herself of all emotions. Her focus remained on the thrum of aithyr energy around her, ever-present and often missed by those not trained to look.

The inexperienced didn't understand the feel of aithyr. For Valeriya, her conscious reached out like hands, dipping into the unseen power that flowed around her like a river. When her mind focused, she could pull that energy towards herself, allowing it to enter her body.

But aithyr was hard to control. It was like holding the fluidity of a river in her arms without the bucket, needing to keep the ever-moving substance restrained. Doing such took incredible mental strength, which she'd gained through her training.

While her thoughts and emotions were at bay, Valeriya pulled on the aithyr, imagining the energy within her mind. As it entered her body, she surged with power—a thick, shifting substance that moved underneath her skin. The aithyr was unruly, fighting against her and threatening to break free. The amount Valeriya needed to perform the magic made the fight worse, yet she held on, her mind forming what she needed the aithyr to become. She manipulated it, her body performing the process of magic, converting the energy into its new form. A thin blanket of energy coated her as she focused, covering her from head to toe.

When she looked down, she saw the servant's uniform covering a foreign body, knowing her face and hair had changed as well. Underneath the appearance, her body remained in its natural build. If someone were to touch her, they wouldn't feel the curves of the servant or the simple dress. They would feel Valeriya's body and the dress she wore beneath. To outside eyes, it was only her appearance that changed.

The hard part was maintaining the appearance, her mind needing to control the magic surrounding her. That's how her training gave her an advantage. She and Katya used to focus on magic while sparring with one another. Katya specialized in illusion magic, giving her the upper hand at concentrating while fighting. Valeriya was the better fighter, able to attack with weapons and magic while concentrating. The rivalry between them was intense, one that Valeriya upheld until it was no longer a competition.

She shook such thoughts from her mind as she stepped back onto the path, pretending to be the meek servant going about her duties. Valeriya wound through the elaborate gardens, making her way to the Southwestern Gate. As she neared it, she kept her head down, hearing voices chatter from down the palace hall. She darted around the corner, avoiding eye contact with the two guards that walked towards her.

"Aye, you," one of them called, a bemused grin on his face.

"Can I help you?" she asked, her voice high pitched and sweet. That was the downside to using an illusion: the magic didn't alter her voice.

"Where are you off to in such a hurry?" They stepped closer to her. The male talking had a thick neck and short, blond hair. His quiet companion was skinnier, with black curls pulled back into a tail.

"I'm busy, so leave me be. It's been a long day." The dismissive tone in her voice didn't prevent the guard from stepping into her path, holding out an arm to lean against the wall.

"Oh, you servants love to act like you're so busy. Try being a soldier like me, and then you'll have long days." He flexed his muscles for Valeriya's servant visage.

She withheld an eye roll. "You are so right, but I must be off," she said, sidestepping him. With a graceful twirl, she avoided his hand that reached out to grab her and continued down the hall. If his touch had landed, he would have felt her actual body and ruined her disguise.

"Don't be shy. You servant girls are so skittish. What's your name?" He began walking with her, his awkward friend trailing behind. She needed to lose them or else she would be late.

Earlier that day, she sent a message through magic, setting up the drop time and location to a contact. Simple messages were easy to pass with magic by harnessing aithyr and transforming it into words that echo in the target's mind. Most found that magic intrusive, and she only used it when necessary.

Valeriya turned away from the corridor that led to the Southwestern Gate. Instead, she walked towards the Guard's Garrison. Noise trailed from the dining hall as guards filed in and out from the late dinner shift, the males still trailing behind her.

"It's alright. I don't mind the quiet type. I'm sure I can get you to say a lot if you give me a chance." The guard tried to grab her shoulder, but as she sensed it coming, her body twisted away, dodging his hand.

"Leave that servant girl alone," called a demanding voice. Valeriya smirked as an officer came into view. The higher-ranked soldiers kept their subordinates in line, preventing them from bothering servant girls trying to go about their jobs.

"Yes, captain," he said, bowing his head. Under his breath, he whispered to Valeriya, "Until later, sweetie."

Valeriya let her eye roll show that time, earning a grin from him. The male elves of Syllogi were much less subtle than those in Reyila. They acted as if they had never touched a female and were desperate to do so. That was the one part of her husband for which she was thankful—he didn't possess that trait.

As she approached the gate, the guards didn't question Valeriya, since servants often came and went from the palace. Time was working against her, though, as she stepped into the street, anxious to be out after dark.

Her servant visage may be that of an elf, yet the disappearance of pilinos in Satiros alarmed her still. Since that day at tea, the original six were reported missing, and another two disappeared that week: five half-elves, three humans, and no sign of their whereabouts.

The shadows hid Valeriya as she walked on the sidewalks, staying close to the buildings. Magic thrummed around her body as she maintained her appearance, having to keep it up outside the palace, too. The risk of someone seeing her wasn't worth it, especially with what she was about to do.

She turned, making her way further into the city, weaving between streets in case anyone followed her. To her pleasure, none did.

Ahead of her was the opulent Wisteria Heights, home to the wealthiest elves of Satiros. The townhomes matched the buildings elsewhere in the city—whitewashed with vines climbing up the side. The most notable difference was the height of the structures in the neighborhood. In some wealthier spots, the houses had six floors, balconies, and ornate columns. The more work they had done to their homes, the more money they had.

Parks with open grassy areas, old trees, and elaborate gardens broke up the blocks. They were the size of markets in the wealthier sections and grew smaller as the neighborhood moved away from the palace. The cobblestone streets narrowed into sidewalks through the park, mimicking the intricacy of the palace gardens but on a much smaller scale. The golden glow emitted from light globes hung over the park, casting their light on the denizens taking a night stroll.

Valeriya thought of her task at hand. The truth was, her husband made a poor king who cared little about ruling or his people. He didn't care for diplomacy either, often ignoring the other cities of Syllogi, leaving Gyrsh to tend to affairs as Minister of Foreign Relations.

There was no time for her to dwell on her choices. If she wanted to make a lasting legacy as the Queen of Satiros, this was her chance. Change would come to Satiros, and it would be by her hand.

Valeriya wound her way deeper into the residential section, where the houses gave way to apartment buildings and markets were easier to find than parks. The drop site was down a dark-lit alley, shadows pooling in the middle. With a glance, checking for watchful eyes, Valeriya stepped into the darkness, crouching next to the wall of the building. A brick popped out of the wall with the work of her dagger, revealing a hidden compartment behind.

Not letting doubt crowd her mind, she slid the thick envelope in and replaced the brick. Valeriya left the alley, not thinking twice about the lives she just altered.

Chapter Twenty-Four

ELYSE

Late in the afternoon, Elyse sat in her usual spot in the library, curled up with *The History of Lyken Fulbryk*. History books weren't her first choice, but she recognized his name when she selected it some time ago. Who told her about him—was it her father? Or maybe her mother when Elyse was young? She couldn't recall exactly, but she remembered one thing—Fulbryk was an adventurer.

The text was heavy on Fulbryk's Ten Principles of Magic, but in between his teachings were anecdotes from his life—stories of his exploits that highlight the principles. Elyse couldn't put it down.

In the beginning, the book covered the principles and basics of magic. *Aithyr* was a new concept to her—the omnipresent energy that mages manipulated. Really, all magic was new to her. She didn't know that magic was a conversion, let alone that it needed aithyr as an energy source. Elyse tried to feel aithyr herself, to no avail. Regardless, she enjoyed Fulbryk's travels as a way to explain the principles.

The giants surrounded us, snow falling thickly and obscuring our vision. A club swung to my right, sending Abernyk flying with a sickening crunch. The snow wasn't affecting the giants, not like it affected us. I suddenly realized they were ice giants, mystical beings long lost to the lands of Syllogi.

Vicious and magic-resistant, I feared for not only my life but also of those who remained in my party. Another club swung, another sickening crunch, as they bludgeoned Ythir into the ground to my left.

I raised my hands, focusing my breath and my mind, imagining the wind I needed the aithyr to be. I grasped at the energy, letting it quicken in my conscious,

whipping it into a gust. The snow parted as air rushed from my hands. Directly in front of me, standing as tall as three full-grown elven males, was an ice giant, its club raised above my head.

As it swung, I—

A knock on the outside of the alcove pulled her from the book.

"Elyse?" called a deep voice from outside.

"Yes?" Annoyance tinged her tone. Of course, someone would bother her as she got to the good part.

"Do you have a moment?"

Her heart sunk to her stomach. "Of course, Your Grace," she replied, knocking over her long-emptied teacup as she sat up straight. Gods, oh gods—she should have known it was King Wyltam. And she had the *nerve* to use that tone.

The curtain pulled back, revealing the King. "It'll only be a moment," he said, hands clasped behind him and his expression unreadable. "Sticking with Lyken Fulbryk still, I see. Are you enjoying it?"

Enjoyment wasn't a strong enough emotion.

The King waited as Elyse shifted off the bench, smoothing her dress as she stood. "I haven't been able to put it down," she answered excitedly, pulling the curtain across. "The second principle is the most puzzling, yet also the most enthralling. By stating that it's the will of the mage that manipulates aithyr for magic, and not through the will of aithyr, implies…" her voice dropped, dread filling her stomach as her hand snapped her to mouth, turning towards the King.

Gods, for a moment, she forgot who she was talking to. How could she be so stupid?

The King had… he had a smile on his face? "And your father was adamant that you had no magical capabilities of becoming a mage. You have the right idea. Fulbryk's second principle implies that aithyr can control the mage."

Elyse's tongue numbed in her mouth, unsure what to say. That was her conclusion—that the energy could control a person, but why? The question hung on the tip of her tongue as King Wyltam gestured toward the back of the library.

"Fulbryk has other books that dive deeper into each principle, though they're drier than his histories," he explained.

The King's closeness and voice used to make her recoil, yet she found herself wanting to speak to him. "Are, uh… the books? Are they here? In the library?"

A slight smile curled onto his lips. "I have a surprise for you." They stopped before a door near the back of the library, the King turning towards Elyse. "I'm not one for words. Or gestures. Your recent interest in magic brought on an idea."

Elyse watched in silent fear as he pulled out a key and unlocked the door. As he stepped in, light globes cast the room in light. He glanced over his shoulder, motioning her to follow. But she couldn't; her feet locked in place. A sheen of sweat covered her at the thought of being alone with King Wyltam. Sure, they'd have fleeting conversations in the past, but only when Keyain was present. How would she handle a conversation alone if—

"I know you're flustered," he said, frowning. "This is only for your benefit. Please, come in."

Unsteady legs carried Elyse across the threshold. Beyond the King sat low bookcases running along the back wall. The room was a study, complete with a wooden desk and cushioned high-back chair behind it. Bookcases of varying height lined the room, some enclosed with glass. Against the back wall, the low bookcases held devices Elyse had never seen before on display.

"What is this?" Her voice was soft, her eyes growing wide.

"When I was younger, I often escaped to the library myself, to this room." King Wyltam walked with his hands clasped behind his back still. "This is my private study, containing my personal collection of books on magic. You have free rein to use it."

Her hand reached up to the leather-bound volumes to her left, seeing *Magic and Mental Strength, Fulbryk's First Principle*. "Why me?"

"I'm curious to see if you're like your mother," King Wyltam said, his eyes following her hand. "Though I must ask that no one else enter this room. Many of the materials are sensitive information and even contain my notes on magic." A smile hinted at his lips. "Though I get the inkling that you will enjoy the seclusion of this room."

Elyse walked before the bookcase, reading the titles. "What does my mother have to do with this?"

"She was the most gifted mage of her time."

Elyse's heart stilled, her fingers brushing against one of the glass objects as her heart sunk. "No, she wasn't. My father said—"

"Don't believe your father." The anger in his voice caused her to turn. "Your mother fostered my interest in magic," King Wyltam said, his gaze locked on to Elyse. "The least I can do for Anthylia is offer the same encouragement that she gave me. Do you remember Fulbryk's sixth principle?"

"*A weak mind cannot yield aithyr therefore, mental strengthening must be routine for mages*," she recited, remembering back to the chapter of Fulbryk having his friends beat him while he maintained concentration.

"Very good, Elyse. A weak mind cannot yield aithyr, and you, unfortunately, have the nerves of a skittish goat. That is the reason your father said you do not possess your mother's gift." King Wyltam's expression softened. "However, I think it's possible."

Elyse furrowed her brows. "You do?" Soft. Weak. Her father's words spun in her mind as memories of her mother's last days pulled the breath from her chest.

"Your mother was an exceptional mage. However, aithyr won against her mind. Your father believes the same will happen to you if you practice magic. I offer you this, Elyse," he said, motioning to the room. "Study here in my office and learn to strengthen your mind. If you do those things, I will train you to become a mage."

Her chest caved. "My father would never allow it, and I'm to be married."

"Are you not an adult? Can you not make your own decisions?" he asked, tilting his head. "And anyone should be lucky to have a mage as their wife."

The King considered her an adult? She blinked, her body numbing with surprise. "But what if I can't do it? What if I can't control my emotions, my mind?" Her throat threatened to close as she spoke. "What if I'm too much like my mother?"

He studied Elyse for a moment. "Life is a series of choices, Elyse. You can choose to accept things as they currently are, or you can change your life. That choice is up to you. If you cannot succeed, then at least you tried. What's the worst that could happen if you try and fail?"

The logic made sense, but the King didn't know her father. Obedience wasn't natural to Elyse; her father had forged it over a lifetime. If she were to become a mage, it would push him too far. He'd drag her back into submission, regardless if she was an adult.

Gods, but the way King Wyltam looked at her, his expression soft, understanding. Becoming a mage would give her what she wanted—a way out. Freedom.

She took a steadying breath to calm her racing heart and met the King's gaze. "I will try my best."

A pounding at her door woke Elyse from sleep the following morning as her father barged into her room. "Why are you not awake yet? Brynden will be here soon!" her father yelled, throwing back the curtains of her bed.

Shit, Brynden. He was coming to see her, and Elyse looked like— well, she looked like she was up all night, which she was.

Elyse groaned, her head heavy with exhaustion. After finishing The History of Lyken Fulbryk, she jumped into his book on the first principle of magic. Though the reading was dry, his words enthralled Elyse.

Controlling aithyr depends on a mage's ability to focus; their mental strength is what gains control, forming the aithyr into what they wish it to be.

Magic could shape aithyr into endless things if only she could calm her mind.

Her father snapped his fingers. "Elyse, are you listening to me? Brynden will be here any moment to see you. Get up. You look like a disgrace," he spat, throwing back her covers. "You're lucky someone like him even has an interest in you."

She bolted upright, staring at her father's incredulous face. How did she not wake up on time?

Elyse shook off her exhaustion, darting to the bathroom to bathe and try to make herself presentable. The brush pulled through her tangled hair as she brought it into a knot on top of her head. She cursed herself for insisting she didn't need a handmaid. The small talk with them always put Elyse on edge.

Brynden's voice sounded through the door. Gods—he already arrived? Elyse ran to her closet, tripping on her feet as she hurried. As she fell forward, her face landed on the corner of the wardrobe with a resounding thunk, her forehead throbbing.

"You alright in there?" Brynden called.

Humiliation knotted her stomach. "Yes, I'm fine!" she called back, swearing under her breath. Never was she clumsy unless it was inconvenient.

Her forehead ached, a bump already rising from the impact. Great, one more thing for her to worry about. She just needed to find something to wear. What was the weather even like?

She pulled out three dresses, holding each up against her. No, none of them would work. Gods, why was she like this? Her heart thundered in her chest, knowing Brynden was waiting for her.

She needed to just pick one—the choice didn't even matter. Elyse selected a blood-red dress of flowy fabric that hugged through the hips and a neckline that plunged low into the chest, reaching her mid stomach. The skirt had a high slit; the gap filled with lace that ran to her hip. Sleeveless was likely a proper choice since the days grew hotter, and the lace—well, hopefully, Brynden liked it. Perhaps it would make up for her barely-made face and wispy strands of hair already pulling free from her knot. Gods, she looked like a mess, but she needed to go.

Elyse stepped out of her room to find Brynden standing near her father's office. Unlike the night of the ball, his black hair was down and pushed forward towards his face with straight black locks pushed up out of the way, the shaved sides exposed. A silk collared shirt fit tight over his body, the neckline revealing the bulk of his chest. For a moment, she was silent, still surprised a male like Brynden was interested in her.

"Apologies," she said, bowing her head.

"Never a problem, Elyse," Bryden replied, her eyes rising to meet his. A smile lined his face as he added, "You look beautiful, so it was worth the wait."

The face her father gave over Brynden's shoulder suggested otherwise. She would hear about it later.

"Here," Brynden said, stepping towards her with a box in hand. "I brought you something."

"You didn't have to do that," she said with a smile, taking the gift. Her fingers lifted the lid, revealing a necklace with clear stones speckled with black. "Oh, Brynden, this is stunning."

"Diamonds native to Chorys Dasi. Mined from the mountains near my city-state," he said.

Her fingers touched the necklace, a thin chain of gold connecting a dozen stones. Glancing down at her chest, she realized she had forgotten jewelry. "Do you mind putting it on me?" Elyse turned her back to him while pulling her hair forward, holding out the necklace to Brynden.

"Honestly, Elyse," her father snapped. She thought it would be a kind gesture to want to wear it right then, but her father thought differently. Gods, he was going to lose it when she returned.

"Nothing would make me happier," Brynden said, taking the necklace.

Breath held in her chest as Brynden's arms reached around her, placing the necklace around her neck, enveloping her in his scent. Hot breath fell over her ear as he whispered, "Happy to see you're not drunk today."

The realization seized her heart. If she had woken up on time, she would have had something in her system to cope. How was she going to speak with Brynden? What would she even say? Brynden expected her to act as she did at the ball, but alcohol emboldened much of that.

Elyse turned to him, eyes wide as he stepped back. A smirk hooked across his lips as he took her in. He was amused? For what reason? She knew she looked terrible, and perhaps she wore the wrong dress.

Whore. The word crept into her mind with the sound of her father's voice, dread spilling from her. Brynden offered his arm, leading her out of the suite.

Elyse could feel the burn of Brynden's stare like a hot iron pressing on her. Her tongue turned to lead in her mouth, unable to move even if she knew what to say. Instead, she just kept a hand wrapped around his bicep, taking glances at how the white shirt was tight against his body, able to see shifting muscles beneath.

"Everything okay?" Brynden asked, turning to her as they descended the stairs to the first floor of the Noble's Section. "You're awfully quiet today."

Of course, she was quiet—what could she say to him? Elyse forced a smile, nodding while fixing her gaze on the wooden stairs. The cavernous foyer echoed with ambient voices. The bottom floor of the Noble's Section housed plush community rooms with seating, tables, game boards, and other items in which nobles and courtesans could entertain. Those rooms were the source of voices, with elves wandering between them.

"Are you sure? Because it sure seems like you're not okay." Brynden stepped onto the stair below, stopping to face Elyse. A playful smile tugged at his lips, ones that she wished she could kiss again. The light from the window cast him in the late morning light, his olive skin glowing almost as much as his russet eyes. With lips parted, Elyse stared at him, her voice dying in her throat.

"Oh, Elyse!" called an elven lady standing in one of the doorways. Elyse shut her eyes with a sigh, knowing the source of the voice. Golden hair twisted into braids on top of the lady's head, her curved body swathed in a rose-colored gown as she gestured to the two on the stairs. Lydia Rynts, a former friend of Elyse, stood in a doorway calling to her. As always, she looked breathtakingly beautiful.

Elyse wished to walk past with just a nod of the head, her usual greetings for anyone outside the Queen's inner circle, but Brynden took her arm once more and steered her towards the elven lady. She should have said something, should have stopped him, but she didn't.

"It has been far too long since you've spent time with us," Lydia said with an amused smile as they approached. Behind Lydia, nobles and courtesans lounged on couches, watching the commotion at the door. They were all stationed below Elyse, either the child of nobles or holding a small position themselves. Elyse knew their names but offered no recognition. That wasn't new, however. She spent much of the past decade dodging them.

Lydia was almost as bad as Grytaine—almost. They grew up together in the palace, their families often being at court for the same months. Elyse made the conscious choice to avoid Lydia long before her betrothal to Keyain, their friendship coming to a sudden stop after... certain events transpired.

"Lydia, it has been," Elyse responded, her body stiff and her lips pulled into a tight smile.

Lydia looked her over, and Elyse painfully remembered how unkempt she appeared. The elven lady's gaze lingered on the bump on her forehead before turning to Brynden. "And who might your handsome friend be?" She offered a hand to Brynden, looking up at him through her lashes.

Of course, Lydia would find him attractive. Who wouldn't? Brynden looked regal with his air of confidence but approachable with an amiable smile. It was as if he were meeting an old friend instead of a stranger. With a shift of his arm, his hand found her lower back. Elyse couldn't help but admire how easy it was for him to socialize as her hand trembled from the interaction. Perhaps Brynden would be happier with someone like Lydia.

He took her hand, his other never leaving Elyse. The slight gesture sent Elyse's stomach swirling, unsure if it was from excitement or guilt. "Lord Bynden Vazlyte, Emissary to Chorys Dasi. It's lovely to meet you."

From the looks of it, Lydia fell for his low, pleasant voice just as she did. "Lord Brynden, how lovely to meet you. I'm Lady Lydia Rynts. Perchance you've worked with my father, Lord Byron Rynts? He works with Minister Gyrsh." He did, though she failed to mention that he worked very much below Elyse's father.

"Unfortunately, no, I haven't. For the past few years, I have only worked with Gyrsh. To think it took this long to meet his remarkable daughter." Elyse tried not to stiffen more as Brynden leaned down and placed a gentle kiss on her temple. Whispers carried from the room beyond the doorway, sending heat across her cheeks.

"Oh, you two are courting! How exciting," Lydia said with a forced smile. "Funny, it hasn't been that long since you were still with Keyain." A glance at Brynden revealed Lydia didn't think he knew. Of course, he knew—Lydia just wanted to humiliate Elyse.

"It's unfortunate Minister Keyain wasted so much of her time," Brynden spoke up when he realized Elyse would remain silent. "I could've been courting her sooner, and then we would be already married."

Elyse's heart stopped as she gazed up at Brynden wide-eyed. Did he say married?

Lydia offered an awkward laugh. "Ah yes, if only." She turned to Elyse. "Oh, I have always loved that color on you, by the way. And I love that you're bold not only to wear dark reds in spring but also that deep neckline. Who knew courting these days meant showing so much of your body?" The smile on her face was anything but pleasant.

Anger shot to the tip of Elyse's tongue. "I love that you're bold enough to make those comments in front of Brynden. Jealousy is a poor look on anyone."

Lydia raised her brows at the comment, her mouth hanging open, though she said nothing.

Why must she be like this in front of Brynden? Why can't she hold her tongue? She was so hopelessly stupid. With dread pooling in her gut, Elyse didn't offer a goodbye as she stepped out of Brynden's arm and sped to the courtyard doors. She couldn't do this, not today. Maybe not ever.

Brynden's voice carried through the foyer. "Funny that you comment about Elyse wearing red as if it isn't the color of Chorys Dasi. If you—" The door swung shut, muffling his response.

The late morning heat was warmer than expected, offering little help as she tried to suck in air to her chest. Elyse kept her head down as she crossed the courtyard and stepped onto the cobblestone path of the Central Garden. Nobles and courtesans gawked at her from the benches surrounding a nearby fountain. "Elyse?" Brynden's voice carried from the doors.

It was so stupid. Elyse knew she should stop and let Brynden catch up, but the thought of him looking at her after Lydia's comment made her stomach churn. Because she woke up late, she didn't realize how revealing the dress was. A sheen of sweat covered her, unsure if it was from the running or her nerves. It was too much—he was too much. Too good.

Elyse rushed down the path of the Central Garden and crossed a bridge that a creek meandered underneath. What a fool she was to think she had a chance with him, regardless of his marriage comment—an attempt to be kind for her sake in front of Lydia. Brynden was confident, well-spoken, and held an important position. Gods, he had used Elyse the same way her father did, to sweeten whatever deal was between them.

"Elyse, please wait," Bryden called again, still back in the courtyard as she wove her way deeper into the garden.

Panicked, Elyse stepped off the path and into a flower bed, crossing a gap between a row of lilac bushes, and hid behind the row of foliage. A small meadow of white daisies appeared with a feline statue in the middle with a feathered tail fanned out behind it. A creek drifted at the edge of the clearing, passing under the bridge she crossed.

Elyse sat down behind the lilac bushes with her head bent to rest on her knees as she tried to catch her breath. Her father was right. Brynden was too good for her. His interest in Elyse was only sexual. It had to be— why else would he pursue her?

All she offered was a lifetime of pain, just like what her mother gave her father. No one wanted a life like that, and no one would want a life with her. The similarity between Elyse and her mother had never been more apparent. The realization made her inhales sharp, unable to breathe.

Tears fell as Elyse acknowledged that she would never be a mage either, for she would never control her emotions. This gods damned palace was her prison, and she would always be alone here with her father.

"There you are."

She jumped, not having heard Brynden approach through the bushes. She looked up at him with tear-filled eyes. Shame blossomed from her center. "How did you find me?"

Brynden shrugged. "I just knew." He crossed the space between them, crouching next to Elyse. Instead of the anger she expected, Brynden only looked concerned. "You're having quite the bad day, aren't you?" he asked with a crooked smile that crinkled his eyes, causing her heart to skip a beat.

"I'm so sorry," she whispered. "I can't do this."

The deep, rolling laugh made her chest tighten. "Do what?"

"This." Elyse gestured in the space between them.

"What is it we're doing? Walking? Talking? Learning more about each other?" His smile remained as he spoke. "I know you're an anxious person. Your father warned me, for a lack of a better word."

"Gods, of course, he did." She shut her eyes, unable to look at him.

"Elyse, it's alright. Just take a deep breath and talk to me," he murmured. "I know you were having a bad day before Lydia, so let's start before that fool opened her mouth."

Elyse's eyes popped open. "Fool? Nothing she said was wrong."

"I don't care what she said. I really don't. What I care about is why it bothered you so much." His hand stroked her shoulder as he spoke.

She looked at him, exasperated. "What do you mean, why? Have you seen me? I look like a mess and like a whore. I—"

Brynden held up his hand to stop her. "First of all, I was honest when I said you looked beautiful. You took my breath away when you stepped out of your room. Second, why would you even say that last part?" Confusion tinged with anger laced his voice.

"Because that's what you think I am, right?"

"Elyse, what are you talking about?"

She ran her hand over her hair, looking anywhere but at Brynden. "At the ball, the kiss and wanting to go somewhere private."

"Hey, look at me," he whispered, drawing her attention back to his face. His hand reached up to brush away a loose strand. "I'm so sorry I kissed you, and I'm sorry that I tried to take you somewhere private. I should've realized how much the alcohol affected you. If I had realized it would cause you this much distress, I would have never done it."

Her breath caught in her chest. "But I wanted you to kiss me—I can't stop thinking about it! And that's part of why I probably am *that*." She couldn't bring herself to say the word once more.

"I've done a whole lot more with people I knew a whole lot less, and I wouldn't ever think to call them *that*. As I said that night, I expect nothing of you." That damn crooked smile returned as he added, "Was that your first kiss?"

"I—no. Well, that I didn't regret, yes. But technically no." Gods, how did they get to that topic?

"You're saying Keyain was to marry you for five years—" he held out his hand for dramatic effect "—and he never once kissed you like that?"

She shook her head no.

"And I'm guessing you never shared a bed with him?"

"Gods, Brynden, no." She shielded her face in her hands.

"Well, I'm trying to figure out how he was your betrothed for that long and didn't even kiss you as you deserve," he said, his brows furrowed. "I couldn't be around you for one evening without kissing you." A moment passed before he added, "Five years. Really?"

"Please, can we change the subject," she pleaded, trying to stand.

Brynden's arm stopped her. "You still haven't told me all of why you were having a bad day."

As much as she didn't want to talk about it, she supposed she owed him an explanation. "I got little sleep last night, and then I woke up late. I'm so sorry for making you wait like that."

"You will always be worth the wait," he murmured. For a moment,

Elyse thought he meant it. "Why were you up late? Thinking about how I kissed you?" Brynden smirked as he leaned in.

She would regret telling him about that. "I was being dramatic when I said I can't stop thinking about it. I can, in fact, stop," she lied, knowing that it was constantly buzzing in the back of her mind.

"Are you sure? You weren't thinking about it when you were alone in your bed? Late at night? Wishing you weren't so alone?" he teased.

"Oh, my gods." Heat crept over Elyse's cheeks.

"So if it wasn't the thought of my mouth, and what I'm assuming is the rest of me," he said with the flick of his brow, "then what robbed you of your sleep?"

"I was reading and couldn't put my book down."

"Hmm."

"Hmm, what?" she asked.

"Sounds like a lie."

"Oh, my gods… No! I was reading Fulbryk's book on the first principle of magic!" she snapped, embarrassment seizing control of her. She recoiled from him, not meaning to have told him the title. Gods, if her father knew.

Brynden blinked, the teasing smirk falling from his face. "Your father said you weren't capable of magic," he whispered, his tone serious.

"I'm not," she said through her hands. "Please don't tell him what I'm reading."

"I wouldn't dream of saying a word to him. I'm just," he cocked his head, a genuine smile coming to his face, "pleasantly surprised."

"You are?" Elyse's eyes were wide as she gawked at him, her hands falling away.

"Of course. Your father spouts how he has this obedient daughter. As if you're some sort of trained mutt. But here you are, studying magic behind his back," he leaned in, his lips brushing her own. "You are anything but obedient, and I've never wanted to kiss you more."

Their lips met, Brynden cupping behind her head as he stumbled to his knees. Her lips parted, kissing him back in the way she imagined every night since the ball. Brynden was breathless as he pulled away. The way he gazed at her made her believe that maybe he did want more—made her feel that he would enjoy being married to her.

Her hand found the front of his shirt, pulling him to her face as she fell backward into the daisies. He laughed into the kiss as he braced himself on top of her, obliging her hunger. His tongue met hers, and the brief bite of her lip caused heat to pool at her center. The soft strands of his hair fell between her fingers as she reached up behind his head, pulling him closer, her mouth desperate to get more of him.

Brynden pulled back, leaving Elyse breathless underneath him. The scent of citrus and juniper surrounded her as his russet eyes glowed. "Beautiful," he whispered. "Absolutely stunning. Surrounded by these flowers, I could easily mistake you for a goddess."

He kissed her gently, first on her lips, then following the length of her jaw. She gasped as he kissed her neck, her back arching underneath him. "Goddess," he murmured into her skin. "I think that'll stick." His mouth moved along her neck, his teeth scraping against as a shudder ran through his body, Elyse responding with a moan.

"What's this—Elyse?"

She looked over Brynden's shoulder to see Keyain standing between the lilac bushes, confusion lacing his features. Dread pooled in her stomach. The gods must truly hate her.

"Nothing to see here," Brynden said with a laugh, rolling off of Elyse, leaning back on one arm.

"Who are you, and why are you on top of her?" Keyain asked, stepping closer.

"Keyain, I'm fine," Elyse said.

"If you step any closer like that, Minister Keyain, we're going to have a problem." Brynden's tone shifted. Any amusement he had left as he slowly stood up, standing in front of Elyse.

She stood, sighing. "Keyain, please—"

"So you're aware of who I am, yet you offer no name," he said, anger sharpening his words. "I will ask you one more time. Who are you, and why were you on top of Elyse?" Keyain took another step towards them.

"Why are you so worried about Elyse when you tossed her aside for a clip?" Brynden leered, trying to place her behind him with one arm.

"Brynden," she hissed, "stop this, both of you. This is ridiculous." She stepped out from behind him, trying to dissolve the situation.

Keyain took his chance as soon as Elyse wasn't in the way, charging at Brynden. Brynden waited on his toes, his movements quick as he easily sidestepped Keyain's charge. He brought up his foot, kicking Keyain in the back, sending him flying. Keyain was all brute strength and mass, a disadvantage against the quick, lithe form of Brynden.

"Stop," Elyse tried to call, her voice lost on the males.

Keyain circled Brynden as the two males moved closer to the edge of the clearing. "I thought Satiros's greatest warrior would be better at this," Brynden teased, a wicked smile on his lips that didn't reach his eyes.

With a growl, Keyain charged once more, grappling Brynden and bringing him to the ground. Keyain swung at his head, missing and hitting the dirt as Brynden tossed Keyain to the side.

Keyain held onto the front of Brynden's shirt as the two males went rolling down the hill towards the creek, ending with them crashing into it. Elyse chased after them, fear choking her voice.

Water splashed as they continued to fight. Brynden pinned Keyain's arm behind his back, his mouth finding his ear. "And to think you almost married a goddess, and now you have a clipped bitch warming your bed. Oh, how far you've fallen."

Keyain's snarls grew more animalistic, throwing Brynden off him. Brynden lost his footing as he tried to stand, slipping backward. Keyain jumped on top of him, pinning him under the water. He raised his fist, bringing it down onto Brynden's head as it crested above the water with a gurgling gasp.

"Keyain, stop!" Elyse screamed, the sounds of Brynden gasping constricting her heart.

For a moment, there was nothing but the sound of Bryden's choking, the smack of Keyain's fist, and the splashing of the creek. Elyse felt frozen, watching her only true friend beat the male she wanted to marry.

"What is going on here?" On the bridge above Brynden and Keyain stood Queen Valeriya with Lady Tryda.

"They're fighting, and they won't stop," Elyse cried, unsure what to do.

"No shit, Elyse," the Queen said with uncharacteristic crass. "I was asking them." Queen Valeriya's tone caused her to shrink back. "Keyain, get your hands off of Lord Brynden! Is this how our Minister of Protection treats foreign dignitaries?"

Keyain's hand froze in the air, his face turning to the Queen with surprise. Brynden took the chance and popped his fist into Keyain's face, the sickening crunch churning Elyse's stomach.

He swore, glaring at Brynden. "Queen Valeriya, I didn't know. I found him pinning Elyse down in the flowers, and she has that bruise on her head. I just thought..." his voice trailed off as he looked at Elyse.

Elyse's lips wobbled as she tried to steel herself. That stupid bruise. Why did he still care? He had a wife to worry about.

"You're an absolute fool, Keyain," she drawled. "Brynden is courting her, so I can only *imagine* what he was doing on top of her."

Keyain blinked and looked at the Queen, then down at Brynden, whose bloodied face held a snarl. He stood, offering a hand to Brynden, who hit it away.

"No wonder you attacked Olkia without consorting with the Syllogian Council," Brynden growled. "You're nearly as feral as your clipped wife."

"Enough! Brynden, that is enough," Queen Valeriya snapped. "I suggest you both go clean up before you return to your meetings this afternoon. Perhaps when you change clothes, you can change your attitudes and remember you are dignified nobles. Now, Elyse, come. I'll take you back to your room."

Elyse walked to the Queen, trembling. Brynden looked like he wanted to stop them, his gaze following Elyse. She couldn't meet his stare, not after this. It all happened so fast. It was her fault Keyain attacked him.

"Tryda, though I always respect your company and your opinion, I think this is a conversation Elyse and I need to have alone," the Queen said.

Tryda narrowed her eyes. "If you insist, Your Grace," she turned to Elyse. "If you need anything, you know where my suite is."

Elyse nodded, the heavyset woman taking off in the opposite direction. The Queen looped her arm around Elyse and guided her towards the Noble's Section, her floral scent blending with the flowers. The two males climbed out of the creek, the tension still taut between them.

"What do I even say, Elyse," Queen Valeriya said, sighing. "You need to grow a backbone and control of your nerves. Brynden is a wonderful male, and I think you could be a great wife for him."

Elyse cocked her head. "You know him, my Queen?" Perhaps the alcohol hadn't made her imagine their nodding across the ballroom floor.

"He's related to King Auryon, husband to my sister, Queen Nystanya, in Reyila. I've met Brynden a handful of times. He's a touch rambunctious." The Queen stared at Elyse. "If you wish to be married to someone like him, then you need to learn to speak up. You cannot sit idly by while something like what just happened unfolds."

"I'm sorry, I tried to," she whispered, shrinking into herself.

"No, stop. That is what I'm talking about." The Queen stopped walking, turning to Elyse. "Find your voice. Otherwise, you will always be a slave to your emotions. What Keyain did, assaulting a foreign noble, is grounds for them to attack Satiros. And you just stood there."

Elyse flinched at the Queen's truth. She was less than effective in their fight.

Queen Valeriya sighed. "You have a voice. Learn to wield it."

"But what if I say the wrong thing? Do the wrong thing?" Elyse whispered. "My father won't accept it."

"Your father is many things, Elyse." She paused, considering her words. "Don't take his words to heart. He designed them to hurt you and belittle you into submission. You are more capable than you know." The Queen placed both her hands on Elyse's shoulder, her gaze boring into her. "You understand, don't you?"

"Yes, I understand," she whispered.

But understanding didn't make the experience with her father more tolerable. It didn't mean using her voice would change anything. No, understanding it all created more guilt. Guilt because she was soft. She was weak.

What she needed was strength.

Chapter Twenty-Five

MARIETTA

Marietta sat in the living room, pretending to be interested in the book she read as she heard the door to the suite open. Her head whipped to Amryth with a smile—Keyain came back to let her out of the suite. Gods, when did she start sounding like a pet?

Without waiting for another second, she threw down the book, running to the other room. "Finally," she said, "you're taking precious time out of your busy day to get me out of this gods damned—" The words died in her throat when she saw Keyain.

Blood dripped from his nose, his face ragged, clothing soaked from head to toe. The broken look on his face woke something in her chest. Was it sympathy? No, it couldn't be.

"Unfortunately, no," Keyain said, walking to the bedroom as water continued to drip onto the floor.

Marietta glanced at Amryth, who shrugged and went back to reading. "Are you alright?" she asked, stepping into the bedroom.

Keyain's voice carried from the bathroom. "Yeah, I'm alright." There was a slop of wet clothes hitting the tile, followed by his footsteps.

When he came back to the bedroom, the only clothing left was his underclothes, the thin white fabric hiding nothing while wet. In an attempt to avoid looking below his waist, Marietta stared at his abdomen, finding it peppered with red welts. With cautious hands, she reached out, touching next to them. "Keyain, what happened?"

He took her hand, brushing his thumb across her fingers. "Nothing."

"So you're going to come back soaking wet in the middle of the

afternoon, covered in bruises and blood, but not share what happened?" She slipped her hand out of his grasp.

Keyain frowned, turning away and heading to the closet. "It's not something you need to worry about."

Marietta followed. "Well, I'm very curious, and you know how I get when I have to search for an answer."

Keyain grunted in response.

"Okay, then I'll have to guess. You sang for a group of your soldiers and they pelted you with rocks and buckets of water because of your lousy voice?" When he didn't answer, Marietta continued. "Or perhaps you decided to fight a fountain and you're too embarrassed to tell me because you lost." She turned the corner to the closet. "Oh! A satyr statue came alive and—" Her words cut off as she saw Keyain had ditched his underclothes.

Fully turning to her, he offered a tired smile. "Keep trying to steal peeks?" he teased, the humor not reaching his eyes.

Marietta scowled, not letting embarrassment get the best of her. "Enlighten me. I'm sure your story is more interesting than any of your books."

Keyain sighed as he pulled on new clothes. "I was cutting through the Central Garden—the big one from the other day—and I saw Elyse. A male I didn't recognize had her pinned down behind some bushes, and she had this bruise on her forehead."

Marietta brought her hand to her throat, surprised that something like that could happen in the palace. "Gods, was she alright?"

"I may have misread the situation, and he was... courting her, if you will," he said as he pulled on a new tunic.

Marietta dropped her hand. "Ah," she said, taking in the welts on his abdomen. "You lost control of your anger and attacked him?" That was just like Keyain. Back when they were together, he often picked fights with strangers for little to no reasons, acting first before questioning if it was a good idea. It seemed that he hadn't changed much.

Biting his tongue, he turned away. "No," he ground out, "the male called you a clip and your words from the other day stuck with me. If I don't stand up for you, if I let others treat you in such a way, then it's no different from saying that word myself."

Stunned silence held Marietta as she watched him continue to change. "Oh." Perhaps he could change, though a decade too late.

"Yes, 'oh,'" he repeated in a sour tone. Keyain approached, placing his hands on her shoulders. Marietta raised her head to stare at his face. "For what it's worth, I'm trying to be better. It will never make up for everything—not even close to it, but I'm trying."

Her eyes searched his face, finding the genuine pain laced in his expression. Never did she think he could reflect on his actions—or inaction—and attempt to be better. Where would they be if he tried all those years ago? "Well, thank you," she whispered, "for standing up for me."

He offered a half-smile before dropping his hands. "As I've said before, Marietta, I would do anything for you."

Keyain walked around her, leaving Marietta alone in the closet. How was he still that hung up on her? How, after all these years, has his heart stayed gripped onto her so tightly? It made little sense.

But love didn't need to. Keyain's love was always twisted—a contorted mess of wanting to be a caring partner to Marietta and wanting to do what served him best. At her core, she knew that he must have loved her. She felt it all those years on the road, living in inn after inn. Memories from those days had been some of her favorites. When Marietta left Keyain, she blocked them all out—ignored any lingering emotions she had. She assumed Keyain had done the same. Yet after being apart for years to only reunite after he abducted her, something became very clear: Keyain was still in love with her.

Such emotion should have touched her heart, yet all Marietta saw was an opportunity.

Chapter Twenty-Six

MARIETTA

Time crept on, moments blending together until Marietta forgot which day it was. After exploring every possible edge of the suite, frustration and boredom left her pacing the living room.

To escape Satiros, she needed to make a plan, but that seemed an impossible task when she couldn't leave the suite. The palace's layout was unknown to her, as was Satiros itself, meaning she had to rely on someone's help. There had to be at least one person in the entire gods damned city that would aid her return to Olkia. Marietta needed to believe that she could break free.

Deep longing filled her as she thought of returning home. Olkia would never feel the same without Tilan, but it was her home and she missed its familiarity. Maybe if she escaped Satiros, she could give the information she learned to the Olkian Guard to hurt Keyain.

His words from the other day echoed in her mind. *For what it's worth, I'm trying to be better.* She would believe it if she saw it, which was unlikely. If Keyain couldn't change before, there was little hope for him now.

"Are you going to keep pacing in the living room like a trapped animal?" Amryth asked, glaring over the edge of her book. She sat in her usual spot on the couch, never slouching, never truly relaxing.

The handmaid pulled Marietta out of her thoughts. "If I spend one more day in this gods damned suite, I will lose my mind. Keyain can't expect me to stay here like this."

"Well, try harder, I guess. Keyain's orders were for you to remain here," Amryth replied, turning back to her book. At times, Marietta

wondered if the handmaid was trustworthy. Planning an escape would be a lot easier with someone who knew the palace. However, she seemed too familiar with Keyain, leaving Marietta to wonder *how* close they were. Perhaps the reason Amryth was so high-strung with her was that she was Keyain's lover.

"Will you at least talk to me then so I don't keep annoying myself with my thoughts?" Marietta grumbled.

Amryth looked up from her book again, sighing. "What would you like to talk about?"

"Anything. Tell me anything," Marietta pleaded, still pacing the room. "What is it like living in Satiros?"

"It's fine."

Marietta gaped at her. "Just fine? That's it?"

Amryth blinked, her stare as cold as an Avato winter. "Yeah, it's fine."

"Oh, my gods." Marietta pinched the bridge of her nose, clamping her eyes shut. "Am I being punished? Is this Keyain's punishment for leaving him?"

With a tilt of her head, Amryth snapped her book shut. "What do you mean by leaving him?"

Marietta swore. "When the humans captured me," she lied. "I left his side, and that's when they abducted me."

Amryth stared, her dark eyes seeing through Marietta as silence encased them. "You're a terrible liar."

"I'm also terrible at being stuck in a tiny room all day with nothing to do but read boring books or play cards games," she yelled, exasperated. "Do you understand I lived a full life, every minute of my day accounted for? I cleaned, I baked, I ran my business—I did everything myself. Never did I sit around, reading and playing games all day. I need to be doing something, always. My life was chaotic, messy. And so incredibly busy. And guess what, Amryth?" Marietta squared her shoulders to the handmaid. "I loved every gods damned second of it."

Amryth rolled her eyes. "Calm down, will you?" The book she held thumped onto the coffee table as she stood up from the couch. Shaking her head, the handmaid left the living room, Marietta trailing behind.

"What are you doing?" she asked, peeking into the dining room.

Amryth stepped into the entryway, cracking the door. Marietta heard the low voices of the guards outside, saw Amryth laugh as she talked. Then she gestured for Marietta to come to her. "Good news. I now owe the guards a favor. We're going on a walk."

Marietta's heart skipped a beat. "Seriously?"

"Unless you'd rather stay here."

"Say no more." Marietta pranced to the door, her body jittering with energy. Half tempted to hug the handmaid, she resisted, not wanting to sully the opportunity.

The pair departed from the suite, winding through the Noble's Section with its marbled everything, velvet this and that. Marietta paid little regard to those details. Freedom occupied every bit of attention she had.

The sun's warmth on her skin was glorious. After being trapped for what felt like an eternity, she was grateful to experience any weather, including the day's heat. It consumed her, too, like her freedom, soaking in every drop of sunshine that touched her. She didn't even care about the staggering silence of the elven nobles inside, all watching her wide-eyed as she left the building with Amryth.

Outside the Noble's Section was a courtyard shrouded by trees. At its center was a three-tiered fountain, each layer an unfolded flower chiseled out of stone. Upon the petals were dancing sprites with leaves for dresses and thinly carved wings. Marietta paused to examine the details, still so impressed with the craftsmanship. If only Tilan could see.

"Come on," Amryth murmured. "I forgot the nobles would gawk at you without Keyain around."

Sure enough, when Marietta looked at the building, pressed against the glass were their faces, watching. She turned her back and followed the cobblestone path into the Central Garden.

The mid-afternoon heat only grew warmer, Marietta appreciating every drop of sweat she worked up as they walked. Never again would Keyain keep her trapped. She'd have to convince him it was alright for her to leave, especially under the watch of Amryth.

Marietta bent down to sniff a blue hyacinth, its perfume helping calm her. Mixed shapes and colors from the elaborate flower beds complemented one another, giving depth and dimension at each step. The sweet scent of freshly bloomed flowers filled the air as her mind eased itself.

The handmaid remained stiff as ever as she meandered the garden's paths with Marietta. With eyes that were always alert, she scanned their vicinity and ensured no one was following them.

Marietta stopped to examine a statue covered in climbing ivy just off the path. With the vines pulled back, she found a feline face with the body roughly the size of a child. She smiled to herself, recognizing the creature—a malk. Her father used to tell stories of this feyrie creature hunting in packs. Out of curiosity, she stepped off the path, searching through the greenery. Sure enough, she found a second malk carved to be yawning. Sharp teeth lined its mouth, remembering that they used to tear into their prey with brutal bites. "Where did these statues even come from?" she asked, returning to the path with Amryth.

Beads of sweat dripped down Amryth's forehead. "Not sure. They were always a part of the palace." The handmaid rolled up the sleeves of her jacket that covered the dress she wore underneath.

"Take off your jacket if you're warm. It feels nice to have the breeze on your skin." Marietta held out her arms, tipping her head back to let the wind tousle her hair.

"No, it's alright. I'm used to the heat." Amryth quickly wiped the sweat from her forehead.

"Oh, come on. Just take it off. Who would see if we're avoiding people in the first place?" Marietta said.

Amryth stared, then rolled her eyes as she removed the jacket, revealing the well-sculpted bulk of her arms.

"Wow, you could make Keyain jealous," Marietta teased.

Amryth laughed. "Oh, he wishes he had arms like mine." A subtle flex showed that she was competition for Keyain.

"How do a handmaid's arms make a great warrior jealous?" Marietta asked, teasing as they continued down the path.

"By training in my free time. I like to stay fit."

A handmaid that exercised seemed odd. Perhaps that's why Keyain had chosen her. Not only was she loyal to him, but Amryth could also protect Marietta—or subdue her. She frowned at the thought.

The honeyed voice of the Queen blew from down the path. "You've already ambushed me in the gardens. Why must you now pester me with questions?"

"Because she's part of your court," answered a deep voice. "You haven't met with her after insisting I interrogate Keyain."

Not having seen them yet, Marietta pulled Amryth off the path and under the limbs of the trees. The boughs, thick with leaves, hid them from sight.

"What are we doing?" Amryth hissed.

"I would rather not talk to them," she said, gesturing in the direction of the Queen's voice.

Amryth's eyes followed her hand, nodding, and stood in the shadows with Marietta.

"She did nothing to suggest she knew." Queen Valeriya appeared from around the corner, walking with an elven man.

As they approached, Marietta studied him. Slim bodied, but a wiry build, and his expression neutral with a wave of blue-black locks falling into his eyes. A flick of his head shifted his hair, revealing his face— haunted, with dark eyes marred by purple underneath; handsome, with a narrow chin and arched lips; mysterious, lacking any trace of emotion. The crown on his head revealed who he was. King Wyltam. Her husband's best friend.

Marietta's usual clients in Enomenos had been business owners. They had various levels of charm, personality, and charisma; but Marietta could read them all the same. Rarely would she encounter someone difficult to read, but it delighted her when she did. They were fun to pick apart, figuring out their personality and learning to read the subtle signs of their emotions. The King of Satiros would be such a puzzle—one Marietta knew she'd find thrilling to solve.

"Follow up on her today. I'm curious. Surely Keyain isn't hiding any more information from his best friend," the King drawled, his voice surprisingly deep and smoky.

"I'll see if she's available for tea this afternoon as soon as we get back."

"Just demand her presence," the King said, his demeanor remaining an air of disinterest as if nothing was with his full attention. That included his wife.

The Queen bristled at the response, not disguising her annoyance at his disrespect. "Of course, my loving husband," she mocked, her lips pulled in a false smile.

As the King and Queen walked the path before them, Queen Valeriya's eyes darted into the trees. Surprise lined her face when their eyes connected. "Let's go sit near the pergola," she added, ushering the King deeper into the garden.

Marietta didn't dare breathe. She held up a hand to Amryth, having her refrain from moving until she was sure they moved farther down the path. After a moment, when they were out of sight, she left the hiding place.

"What was that about?" Amryth asked.

Marietta furrowed her brows. "I'm unsure, but I assume I'll find out at tea this afternoon."

They hurried back to the suite, finding a note from the Queen. Apparently, tea that afternoon meant as soon as possible.

Amryth sighed. "I'll have a note sent to Keyain, informing him that Queen Valeriya demanded your presence, but we need to get you changed."

Marietta looked down at her plain dress, marred with dirt from the garden. After digging through her wardrobe, she pulled a cerulean gown of silky fabric with pink embroidered flowers covering the straps. The neckline dipped low in the front, with the back matching. True to elven styles, the fit hugged her hips and chest.

As she stood in front of the mirror, she grimaced at the expensive gown. A pang of guilt rattled through her chest. Marietta dressed in finery while Tilan's body rotted somewhere. With the chaos of being attacked, did anyone bother to give him a funeral pyre? Bile rose in her throat from the gnawing pit in her stomach, but she pushed the thoughts aside.

"Wear some jewelry," Amryth said from the door wall, pulling her attention back.

"But it's daytime." In Enomenos, people only wore jewelry at formal occasions and evening events.

"Trust me. You stick out from the noble ladies without it. Here," she said, walking over to Marietta's vanity, digging through a jewelry box. A dainty gold chain that dipped low in the middle appeared in her hand.

"Turn around."

Marietta obeyed, not needing to crouch down for Amryth to clasp it, being that Marietta was a touch shorter. The gold chain nestled between her breasts. She grabbed another shorter gold chain, layering them. Amryth then swept Marietta's hair half up into a knot, complete with chains woven through.

"Thank you," Marietta said quietly. "I don't know any of this."

"I know you don't," Amryth replied, her face frowning. Marietta swore she could see a touch of concern in the expression.

When she was ready, Amryth led Marietta to the Noble's Section, remaining quiet as they walked by some nobles, hands covering their mouths as she passed.

Outside on the same balcony as before sat the Queen, alone, waiting for Marietta.

"Lady Marietta, welcome. Glad you could come on such short notice," she announced, her expression saying more.

"Thank you for having me, Queen Valeriya," Marietta responded with a curtsy before sitting down. A servant set two cups of tea on the table. With a hand, the Queen dismissed them, including Amryth. The handmaid gave her an uneasy look as she left.

"For such an expansive palace, it feels small sometimes, does it not?"

she said while sipping her tea and looking out over the balcony.

"That it does, Your Grace," Marietta answered, holding her shoulders back and her head high, ready for the Queen's game to begin.

"I heard a little rumor about you."

"What rumor would that be?" Marietta offered a soft smile, amused by the idea. As the only pilinos at court, there was sure to be a handful of rumors floating around about Marietta.

The Queen gave a knowing look. "That you are quite the baker. Is that true?"

Marietta kept her face calm, unsurprised the Queen learned that. Gods, she even sent Marietta to the kitchens herself. "It is, Your Grace. I learned to bake in Enomenos."

"Curious," she paused, taking a sip of tea, her eyes unwavering from Marietta. "You said you helped businesses around Enomenos for a living."

"I did that as well, and I also learned a hobby or two," Marietta said, her words true. Marietta had just turned one hobby into a new career.

"Is that so?" She paused, sipping her tea. "I heard your baking skills were quite extraordinary. Some may even say you're as good as a trained baker."

"Well, now you're just trying to flatter me," she said with a gentle laugh.

"Oh, you'll know when I'm trying to flatter you." Her mouth slashed a smile, her icy blue eyes holding suspicion. "I did some digging into your background and learned that you owned a bakery."

Marietta held her tea before her lips as she looked at the Queen. "Perhaps your sources are wrong."

"My sources are never wrong. I promise you that," she said with a smirk.

Marietta broke eye contact and looked out over the garden. Queen Valeriya had realized Marietta could bake, and she had known that when she sent Marietta to the kitchens. She played right into the Queen's hand.

"Owning a bakery? Quite the freedom for a captive," the Queen said, her eyes narrowing. "Correct me if I'm wrong, but prisoners don't get to have successful careers as a baker or otherwise."

"Maybe there wasn't much choice in my career change."

"The rumor also said that not only were you a spectacular baker, but that it was your passion. That doesn't seem like a forced career change."

Marietta tilted her head, asking, "Are you not passionate about the things you have a talent for, my Queen?" She picked up her tea and took a sip.

Queen Valeriya contemplated her answer, her face pensive as she stared into the garden as dark clouds rolled in. "I suppose I do. I also did some other digging into your background in Enomenos. Who is Tilan Reid to you?"

Marietta choked on her tea, sending her into a coughing fit. The Queen said she dug into her background but hearing Tilan's name on her lips.... Gods, Queen Valeriya realized Tilan was her husband. She bit down on her lip as her coughing subsided.

Queen Valeriya continued, "Yes, I know. He is someone to you. I may have discovered that the human was your husband."

Marietta's thoughts raced. "It was a forced marriage by my captors," she lied, the action knotting her stomach.

"Is that so? You're telling me this man forced you to marry him and to open a bakery?"

"That's the truth, Your Grace."

"And this Tilan Reid... he was a blacksmith, was he not? You met him through your previous business?"

Marietta kept her face straight at the memory. "That's correct."

The Queen paused, glancing at Marietta. "So you also were aware of his position in the Exisotis?"

For a moment, there was silence. "Of course. I lived with Tilan, didn't I?" she answered with quickened breath. What in the gods was the Exisotis?

"Then please, enlighten me. Tell me about your captors. What were the Exisotis doing?" she asked with a wicked smile, knowing she backed Marietta into a corner.

Marietta sat stewing. The Queen had more information than she realized.

Queen Valeriya cocked her head, red curls falling over her shoulder. "The Exisotis is a resistance group, opposing Syllogi for the oppression of pilinos with the goal to usurp the leaders of the Syllogian Council, like my husband and I. You didn't know that Marietta, did you? Or that Tilan, a man you willingly married after your marriage to Keyain, was a member of this group?"

Marietta's chest ached as she let out a heavy breath. The Queen had won and now rubbed salt in the wound. "Tilan was just a blacksmith, not a part of a resistance group." Whispers of the group had reached her ears, but never the name. Tilan was in the Exisotis? No, it wasn't true. It couldn't be.

"I wouldn't be so sure. Tilan held meetings in his smithy, and we have proof." The Queen sipped her tea, then continued. "Regardless of your feelings, it would appear that you were under the influence of the Exisotis."

Marietta's mask cracked as tears swelled in her eyes.

"Just admit it," Queen Valeriya whispered, bringing a hand to her chest. "You loved this Tilan. You loved a man who ranked so high in the Exisotis. I promise to keep it just between us."

"It's a lie," Marietta said in a cracked voice.

"It isn't, and I know it isn't, Marietta."

"Why would I trust you?"

Queen Valeriya leaned forward, setting her teacup down, whispering to Marietta. "I mean you no harm. I believe you know nothing about the Exisotis, which is all I need to share with my husband. The other parts are for me to understand you better." As she spoke, her hand found Marietta's. "You are in my court, and I can't help you with the other ladies if you aren't honest with me."

All logic told her not to trust the Queen. Gods, even Keyain told her not to trust her; yet, at that moment, Marietta could feel the Queen's sincerity. There was honesty in her tenderness.

She swallowed hard. "I loved Tilan, and I chose to marry him."

"You know what, Lady Marietta?"

"What, Your Grace?"

"You don't love Keyain and you never wished to marry him. But why would he risk his career to save you? That's what I can't figure out," she said, her voice trailing as she thought.

Marietta felt hollow, unable to bring herself to lie. "Keyain never stopped loving me. Even after I left him."

The Queen pulled back. "Even after you left him..." she repeated, her eyes darting with thought. "That explains why he never married Elyse. Betrothed to the girl for five years, but the wedding never occurred. Keyain's union to you remained unknown until you showed up, drugged into unconsciousness a few months ago." The Queen paused before adding, "Bruises covered your body, and you had a gash across your side. Who gave you those injuries?"

Marietta brought a hand to her abdomen, feeling for a nonexistent scar. The moment of Tilan's death flashed—someone had grabbed her by the hair. "Keyain's soldiers. The team sent to get me."

Queen Valeriya tapped her fingers on her chin as she said, "It's funny. Keyain was adamant that your human husband was hurting you, citing that's why he needed to extract you as soon as possible."

"No. Tilan would never have harmed me." She took a shattering breath and whispered, "it was Keyain's soldiers that slit his neck."

Heavy tears fell as the memory played over and over in her mind. Tilan was dead, and she was having tea with the Queen of Satiros. Her stomach churned and bile climbed her throat.

The Queen pulled out a handkerchief and handed it to Marietta, the two sitting in silence. Consumed by her thoughts, Queen Valeriya stared out into the garden.

Marietta might regret her honesty, but she had the information, the sources—she already knew her answer. Was Keyain aware of how informed Queen Valeriya was? And what does her having that information mean? She took a deep breath, attempting to push her emotions down.

"Marietta, you don't want to be here," the Queen whispered.

The response held at the end of her tongue; she had already said too much.

"Did anyone tell you Keyain and King Wyltam are close friends?"

Marietta looked at Queen Valeriya. "I learned they were childhood friends, not that they're still friends. Keyain left that out," she replied. Specifically, when he blamed King Wyltam for the attack on Olkia.

"Not surprised. It seems we both have found ourselves in marriages to males we can't trust." She looked over at Marietta with a sad smile. "And like you, I wish I wasn't here. I wish they hadn't ordered their attack on Olkia."

No words came to Marietta, her brows knitting together in confusion. The Queen's face seemed to age with the heaviness of her thoughts. They were similar, trapped in Satiros, playing this game to stay alive.

The door busted open, a piercing scream breaking the silence. "Mama, mama!" a dark-haired child cried, a servant following him. Marietta jerked her head towards the child, not realizing that the Queen was a mother, the child the prince.

"Oh, Mycaub. What's wrong, my dear?" Queen Valeriya stood and walked to the child, hushing him in a tender tone. The Prince quieted as the Queen rocked him, his screaming reduced to sniffles. "Princes don't cry, my love," she murmured to the child.

Marietta held back her shock. Queen Valeriya, the fiery queen with a sharp wit, folded into a doting mother. She reminded her of her friend Tristina calming her two sons in Olkia.

"I hate to cut our time short, but my son needs me. I look forward to picking up our conversation another day," the Queen said, quickly exiting the balcony and leaving Marietta alone.

Marietta stood there, unsure what to do after their tea time abruptly ended. The Queen had given her heavy information. Tilan was a part of a resistance group? No, he was a leader. It couldn't be true, but she had someone she would ask.

"Marietta, are you alright?" Amryth quietly said as the other servants came in to clear their tea.

She dabbed under her eyes again, replying, "I'm fine. The Queen was asking about my past. It wasn't easy to talk about."

"Well, you nearly cried off all your makeup. Let's get you back to your suite," Amryth said, her face worried.

Amryth led her from the room, Marietta's mind sifting through what she had just learned.

Chapter Twenty-Seven

MARIETTA

Confusion and disbelief continued to fill Marietta's mind as they returned to the suite. Silence stretched between her and Amryth, whose eyebrows knitted with concern. As the door closed, she asked, "Do you want to talk about what happened?"

The question surprised Marietta, not expecting a handmaid to ask about her time with the Queen. With a shake of her head, she walked into the living room and sat in front of the window. Silently, she stared at the rain falling on the Central Garden. At some point, Amryth brought over a blanket and draped it on her lap. Marietta gave her a pitiful smile at the kind gesture.

"I'm going to give you some time alone," Amryth said, breaking the silence. "If you need anything, have the guards send for me." With a gentle squeeze on Marietta's shoulder, she left the suite without another word.

The sky grew dark, Marietta not bothering to light the suite. Queen Valeriya's information was hard to accept. Tilan was no ordinary blacksmith—he had the creative ingenious to be an inventor as well. Organizations of any kind held little of his interest, let alone secret ones.

Of all their years as a couple, he never struck Marietta as a liar. Sure, Tilan was a private person and as independent as Marietta, but that was part of how their marriage worked. Separate lives during the day, but each evening they spent together. There was ample opportunity to lie, yet Marietta knew Tilan. Would he have kept that big of a secret from her?

Guilt and shame pitted her stomach and brought heat to her face. Who was she to question her dead husband's past?

What Marietta needed was the truth, and fortunately for her, Keyain was the person to ask. As the Minister of Protection, he would have information about the group and he made it clear he met Tilan before.

"Marietta? What are you doing?" Keyain asked, startling Marietta from her thoughts. Outside grew dark, globes of gold drifted above the hazy, mist-covered garden, offering the only light. She turned to face Keyain as he lit the room.

"Oh, just sitting." Marietta stood, leaving the blanket on the chair.

"Wow," he said, taking in her entire body.

"Wow, what?"

"You look beautiful. The jewelry was a nice touch." A smile grew on his lips but faltered as she stepped into the light. "Were you crying?"

"I had a rough afternoon." Marietta crossed her arms, not meeting his eyes.

"What happened? What did Queen Valeriya do?"

"We had tea." Marietta took a steady breath, thankful that tears didn't come. Perhaps at that point, she had none left to give. "Queen Valeriya had some enlightening information to share."

"What kind of information?" Keyain asked, stepping forward with a hand reaching out, brows furrowed.

Unable to stare at him, Marietta turned away, wrapping her arms around herself. "Tell me about the Exisotis."

Keyain swore under his breath. "Marietta, we're not having this conversation."

"So it's true."

"I said we're not—" A knock on the door stopped the reply as servants entered with dinner. "We're not talking about this," he finished, whispering. "You'll feel better after eating."

Dinner made her feel worse. Marietta sipped on wine and picked at the braised goat and vegetables, but her appetite was nonexistent. Keyain chatted about nothing important and every few minutes, Marietta would nod to something he said. That satisfied him enough.

What she needed was information on the Exisotis and what Tilan's role was. The uncertainty led Marietta's mind to question every detail of their life together—the late nights at the smithy, knowing random people around town, what he did when she was traveling. Gods, even how they met seemed suspicious. And if Tilan could hide the Exisotis from her, what else did he hide?

The servants cleared the remnants of dinner and left. Keyain sat across from Marietta, frowning, as she offered simple replies. With a heavy sigh, he stood up and walked to a cabinet. From it, he pulled out two glasses and a decanter of a dark liquid.

"Here," he said, pouring a glass and handing it to her. "Go change; get comfortable."

Marietta took it and stared at the amber whiskey inside, an idea coming to mind. She drained the glass of the burning alcohol and set it back on the table, gesturing for more. The idea would not be enjoyable.

"Oh, it's that kind of night." Keyain finished his drink and refilled both while Marietta left to change in the bedroom.

In the living room, Keyain sat on the couch with his legs propped up on the table. He slung an arm across the back. Keyain sat up straighter when she came into view, his jaw slacking.

Marietta stood in a scrap of indigo silk and lace that covered little of her body. Aware of how much skin showed, she bent over, grabbed a drink, and took a sizable sip. As she sat down on the other end of the couch, she stretched her legs out towards Keyain. "I felt bad for borrowing your clothes."

"You don't need an excuse. You look... comfortable." His gaze remained locked on Marietta as if the sight would vanish if he looked away.

"Comfortable?" She raised a brow.

"Well, yeah. And beautiful, but I already said that once tonight. I didn't think you'd want me to repeat it."

"What lady doesn't love to hear they're beautiful?"

"Fair. You, Marietta, are the most beautiful." In one hand, he held his drink, sipping the whiskey, and his other fell onto her bare leg. Instinct urged Marietta to move away from his touch, but she fought it, her plan working.

"I am also the most comfortable. Perhaps the Queen had my comfort in mind when she sent me silk nightgowns?" She tried slipping into their familiar banter.

"Oh, most definitely, it was purely a practical decision. I'm not even enjoying it one bit," Keyain said, looking down at his glass with a blush before glancing back at Marietta.

Marietta laughed, watching Keyain continue to drink as she drained the last of the whiskey. She stood, leaning to place the empty glass on the table, letting Keyain see exactly how little the nightgown covered. When she sat, Marietta draped her legs over his lap, tucking her head into the crook of his arm. Keyain tensed for a moment, then relaxed, his hand finding her leg once more, fingers grazing the skin.

"This is nice," she said quietly, gazing into his face.

His lips parted as he leaned in, kissing her. Marietta cupped his cheek, kissing him back, ignoring the resentment in her chest. Keyain had killed her husband and forced her to Satiros, and there she was, kissing him as if she could ever forgive him. The plan—it was just for the plan.

There was a thud as Keyain reached to set his glass down, not breaking his face from her own. One arm slid behind her bent knees, the other finding her lower back, shifting Marietta to seat her in his lap.

Marietta's lips and tongue slid over Keyain's, the oaky flavor of the liquor fresh. He pulled back with a molten gaze, his chest rising and falling with heavy breaths. Keyain shifted Marietta so that her legs straddled his lap.

The buzz of alcohol silenced the rancor in her head, allowing her to block out who she kissed. Instead, she focused on kissing along his jaw. Under the nightgown, Keyain explored her body, his rough and calloused hands pawing at her curves. When she reached the shell of his ear, she moaned softly as he caressed her ass. "Mar," he said, his voice rough.

Little fabric remained between them as she straddled him, his excitement clearly pressing through his pants against her. She pulled back, grabbing his chin and turning his head to the side as she kissed along his neck. Keyain's head tilted back as his breathing quickened, near moaning with her effort.

"Are you enjoying this?" Marietta asked.

Keyain's eyes were half-closed as he nodded.

"You want me to keep going?" she murmured into his skin. Keyain's body writhed, his grip tighter as he nodded again.

"Then tell me about the Exisotis."

"What?" Keyain asked, breathy and scowling.

A rock of her hips caused his head to drop back again. "Just share what you know, then we can keep going." She grabbed his hands, placing his grip on her hips as she continued to move.

"Mar." Keyain's voice was gravelly and filled with a warning, caught between what he wanted to do and what he should do—exactly where Marietta wanted him. Pride be damned. She needed to know the truth.

The nightgown rose as she led his hands up her body. Keyain cupped her breasts, thumbing the tips. "You just have to give me some information, and I'll be yours. I promise." She smiled at him playfully, her voice like honey.

"Marietta, I can't. Not no-" He stopped mid-sentence to let out another moan, her hips grinding as Keyain tried to lift off her nightgown.

"Not so fast. You can have all of it. Just talk to me." One hand held his chin, and the other one explored the hardness in his lap, earning a writhing shake.

"Marietta, please," Keyain said, his head dropping back.

Her mouth found his neck again, working her way to his ear as she moaned Keyain's name. He panted, straining against his self-control as he thrust his hips.

"Tell me, Keyain."

"No." Anger laced his voice as he held her away from his body.

"This is what you want, right?" Marietta reached to cup his face, but he snatched her hand.

"Not like this." The muscle in his jaw tightened as he ground his teeth. With gentle and exact movements, he lifted her off and left the couch. He kept his back to her as he leaned against the fireplace, attempting to regain his composure.

"Keyain, please tell me."

He shook his head. "You don't understand what you're asking."

"When Queen Valeriya asked about Tilan, saying he was in the Exisotis, I didn't have an answer. So tell me, because that information is the only way I can defend myself here." Marietta stood, her voice rising.

"Queen Valeriya didn't know about Tilan until you said something. And you think I want to give you information about *him* while you grind on top of me? Are you kidding?" Keyain faced her with his upper lip curled. With a deep breath, he grabbed his glass off the table and started for the other room.

"Maybe if you thought of me as a person instead of an object to have, then I wouldn't need to put on a show for you," she said, her words like venom dripping from her teeth.

Keyain paused in the doorway and turned around, his eyes shadowed with a sneer on his lips. "So that was a little show. Congrats, Mar, you gave an excellent performance—the most convincing one you've had since arriving in Satiros. If this marriage doesn't work out, then maybe I'll drop you off at a brothel. You'd be a great whore with an act like that."

"I didn't ask to be here, Keyain. You took *everything* from me for your own selfish, little needs. I was only an object for you to possess back then, and you haven't changed at all," she yelled, her face snarling. "Like I would ever marry you. Tilan loved me for who I was, something that you could never do. You will never compare to him."

Keyain ground his jaw harder, gripping the glass before chucking it at the wood-clad wall, smashing it to pieces, his breathing ragged. "You want to know about the Exisotis? You want to know the truth?"

The quiet of his voice sent chills down Marietta's spine as he stepped towards her, hands clenched at his side. "Tilan was a leader in this lovely group. Their goal was to take out not just the Satiroan nobility but the whole Syllogian Council. And guess what else—he wasn't as great as you thought! Do you know how he was going to overthrow the Syllogian

Council, Marietta?" The space between them narrowed as Keyain stalked closer, ending until he was within inches of her face. Marietta held his glare with her own, refusing to back down.

When she didn't answer, he continued. "The Exisotis, including Tilan, built an army to attack and kill not just the people of Satiros, but all of Syllogi." A dark laugh escaped his mouth. "He is no different from me."

"Even if it's true, at least he loved me more than just for vanity."

"Think for a moment, Marietta. I was already Minister of Protection when we were together. You might not have realized it then, but certain people recognized me and my position. You were unaware that you dated a high-ranking nobleman and decorated hero of Satiros." He paused with a vicious glare. "But guess who did, Marietta?"

"No," she whispered. Her hand shook as she brought it to her lips. "You're lying." It wasn't possible. There wasn't any way Tilan knew Keyain, that he was a part of some secret organization. Tilan had promised he didn't know Keyain. Her stomach lurched as tears filled her eyes. He didn't lie.

"Please, say it with your pretty little mouth that was just all over me, that I could have so easily enjoyed all over my body. I want to hear you say it." He gave her a wicked grin.

Marietta turned away from Keyain, but he grabbed her chin, forcing her to meet his glare. "Your sweet, beloved Tilan knew exactly who I was. Tilan knew what you meant to me, knew I had those marriage papers signed." Keyain sneered, his eyes wet, though no tears fell. "Tilan and the Exisotis used you to hurt me, Marietta. And look, they still are."

"You're a liar," she yelled, pushing him away. Even with all her strength, Keyain didn't budge.

"Oh, I'm not. Use that pretty little head. When you were traveling, it was easy for him to hide. I tried to tell you, tried to warn you. But you wanted nothing to do with me. And when the tensions between Syllogi and the Exisotis became too tense, Tilan started suggesting that you find a job that traveled less, right? Saying sweet things like 'I miss you, stay with me longer.'"

"It's not true. Tilan loved me," Marietta said, uncertainty lingering in her voice. Keyain's words only furthered her own questioning.

Keyain chuckled and walked to his study. Keys clinked together, and then a drawer slid open. He returned with a stack of papers in hand and pushed them at Marietta.

Marietta flipped through the documents, dates marking the pages and describing Tilan's movements—everywhere he went. She paled at a date listed before she had met Tilan. The document transcribed a conversation between him and their friend Pelok. It mentioned both Keyain and Marietta by name. If she and Tilan hadn't met at that point, then....

The papers fell from her shaking hands as she looked wide-eyed up at Keyain. Tilan had only pursued her for the benefit of the Exisotis. His love was a lie. Every kiss, every utterance of how much he cared was a lie. Marietta's breath quickened as her vision darkened on its edges. A sharp pain struck her chest as she tried to suck down air.

As if her world hadn't already been toppled, this information was a final blow to who she used to be. If Tilan lied about the circumstances of them meeting, then did he lie through the entire relationship? Did he ever really want to be with Marietta? She shook her head as the tears streamed down her cheeks.

"Tilan used you, Marietta. He used my love for you as a weapon against Satiros." His voice cracked as he continued, "And I've thought of you every day since you left."

Pain from her heart shattering caused her voice to shake as she whispered, "Don't you dare act like you're a victim—you were an awful partner. Your temper is still a short fuse, and I've seen you break a dozen glasses like that back in the day. You even believe elves are a superior race! Did you think I would marry someone who thinks they're above me because of the body they were born in?" Marietta laughed darkly. "At least when I was with Tilan, I felt loved for every minute of every day. Even if it was a lie, he still made me feel more loved than you ever did."

The insult landed, Keyain curling his shoulders inward with his face faltering. "Just go to sleep. I'm done with you."

Marietta stormed to the bedroom, slamming the door with all the strength she had remaining. Collapsed against the door, she curled into a ball, resting her head on her knees. Despite all the tears she already shed, shaking sobs struck her as the pain of Tilan's truth took hold.

Chapter Twenty-Eight

MARIETTA

Keyain never came to bed. Alone, Marietta tossed between the sheets as her mind sifted through the information.

The name of the group, The Exisotis, was previously unknown to her. Bits of information came up in conversation, leading her to understand they were a group of radicals against Syollgi and based out of Enomenos. Marietta never realized it was an actual organization or that her husband was one of them.

Tilan had never expressed strong opinions about Syllogi more than the average Enomenoan citizen. Perhaps that was on purpose, to hide his involvement with the Exisotis. After all, he was a *leader*—which alone sounded like a farce. Tilan was never one for commitment or leadership, which brought up a good point. Tilan hated all kinds of commitment and obligations, yet he still married. Gods, was she really this blind?

On top of it, Tilan swore he didn't recognize Keyain, but that was a lie. After they started seeing each other, Keyain began harassing Marietta, and Tilan acted as if he didn't know who he was. But Tilan knew. He knew the entire time who Keyain was and never said a word to Marietta. A hollow chasm opened in her chest.

When she closed her eyes, she saw Tilan's smile, the one that caused his eyes to crinkle and brighten. The phantom touch of his arms wrapped around her, his soft kisses and playful jokes added to the pain. Were they all a lie? All those moments. Were they faked, so she would love him? Her memory of Tilan had tarnished as his face was no longer a comfort. Instead, the memory of him churned the bile in her stomach.

The entire night, Marietta slept restlessly, trying to grapple with her reality. Tilan was a liar, Keyain was a murdering thief. Both had done so much wrong, altering Marietta's life in incomprehensible ways. What was true? Every facet of her life had holes if she looked hard enough.

Before the sun had risen, Keyain entered the bedroom, moving between the closet and bathroom. She kept her back to him as he got ready for the day. He didn't approach her.

Thoughts drifted to her years with Tilan. How many signs did she miss? The late nights, the time he had when she traveled—it all made sense, but why would Marietta search for evidence when she didn't suspect him of secrets?

A knock on the door shook Marietta from her thoughts, morning light filling the room. A servant brought food, but Marietta sent her away, unable to stomach anything. Even water left her gut feeling uneasy.

No one came to find her until the late afternoon.

"Marietta?" Amryth called tentatively. When there was no reply, she added, "Are you okay? The serving girls said you hadn't eaten, and the guards last night heard Keyain yelling. I sent for someone to clean the broken glass in the living room."

"I'm fine," she said, her voice hoarse from crying.

"Marietta?" The curtain of the bed pulled back. When Marietta didn't answer, the bed shifted as Amryth sat at the edge. Her voice was soft. "Talk to me. What did Keyain do?"

"Nothing," Marietta said without lifting her head.

"It helps to talk about the things that are bringing you pain. Just talk to me."

Marietta sat up, aggravated. "You want the truth? My husband is a fraud."

"Keyain?"

"No, not *that* husband. Tilan, my husband, before Keyain abducted me from my home." Marietta hugged her knees to her chest.

"Is that so?" Amryth asked, her expression unreadable. "Tell me about your abduction."

"Soldiers came in the middle of the night while Tilan and I slept, pulling us from our bed. I tried to fight, to get to Tilan." Marietta's voice cracked at the memory. "He had fought two people and then I saw the knife come slashing down at him before I went unconscious."

"You never wanted to be here?" Anger laced the handmaid's words.

Confused by her tone, Marietta answered, "No, and I still don't. Keyain and I were together before I met Tilan, but I broke off that relationship. Keyain stalked me when he found out about Tilan." There was a danger in telling Amryth, but Marietta didn't care to be cautious. Queen Valeriya already knew, so what was one more?

Amryth stood and paced the room, her lips pursed and brows furrowed. Her hands fidgeted with the ends of her braids. "Can you recall how many attacked you?" Her voice was harsh as she turned her face away from Marietta.

"I don't remember. Four? Maybe five? What does that have to do with anything?" she asked.

"And you or Tilan killed at least one attacker, right?"

Marietta paused, remembering her dagger plunging into someone, the warmth of their blood on her hand. "Yes," she whispered. Knots formed in her uneasy stomach—she had forgotten about that.

Amryth was silent, avoiding Marietta's confused look. "Have you noticed I'm not like other servants?" she asked, her voice low.

"I've noticed." The curtness of her manor, the muscles, and her relationship with Keyain were unusual.

"I'm one of Keyain's soldiers in the Elite Guard, not a handmaid. Assigned to not only protect you but to ensure you stay under a watchful eye at all times."

Marietta felt as if Amryth slapped her.

It made too much sense. "You're one of Keyain's soldiers." Marietta's voice trailed off.

"In his Elite Guard and my spouse recently passed too." Tears trailed down Amryth's face, her gaze finding Marietta. "She died on the mission to extract you from Olkia. I just discovered it was for some pilinos girl who doesn't want to be here. You weren't being tortured or held captive. Keyain lied." Anger rattled her voice.

Marietta stared, quiet and unsure what to say. Amryth was prickly, but overall, she enjoyed her company. The handmaiden—no, soldier—was becoming her friend, she realized as her heart broke again. Everything was a lie.

"My wife died because of you. She died because Keyain hid the truth. Now you're here saying you didn't need saving. Deyra died for nothing." She laughed darkly, her breathing ragged. "I can't deal with this right now."

Amryth turned and walked out of the room. The hallway door closed with a resounding thump, leaving Marietta to her thoughts.

Marietta drifted like a ghost through the suite, her mind unaware of the time that passed. Guilt was like lead in her bones, weighing her down.

Keyain should have never brought Marietta to Satiros. There were obvious reasons, like the unimaginable horror of abducting her and murdering Tilan. But also, his actions had negatively affected others. Elyse was to marry him, which explains the elven lady's odd behavior at tea. And there was Amryth's wife, who died at Marietta's blade.

A shiver snaked its way down her spine as she remembered the thick, hot blood coating her hand moments before Tilan's death and her unconsciousness. Until then, Marietta assumed the person lived. She wasn't a trained fighter, so taking a life seemed so unrealistic. But she had killed someone. Because of Keyain.

The tears came slower, her swollen eyes somehow having more to offer. Her life wasn't supposed to turn out like this. Marietta should have been closing her bakery at that time, cleaning up before Tilan came home. Unless it was a late night for him. Unless he was with the Exisotis.

The life she lived prior was becoming a nightmare and a source of pain. Lies piled on lies from both Tilan and Keyain. A fool she was for trusting either, for wanting to believe them and never looking too deeply for the truth. If she ever could escape Satiros, she wouldn't be such a fool again.

Marietta stood with her arms crossed before the bedroom windows when the suite's door opened, followed by Keyain's heavy footfalls. Golden light filled the bedroom as he entered, then a pause in his steps and a heavy sigh. Marietta didn't bother turning around. The fight from the night before lingered between them.

Everything she had said was true. Between the two liars, Tilan made her feel more loved. Perhaps that was why it hurt so much. Her time with Keyain was fun and fast, but Tilan was her partner, ingrained in her social and work life. Tilan grounded her, gave her a foundation, a home to come back to after traveling. Keyain left for large chunks of time—apparently to be the Minister of Protection.

A knock at the door signaled the servants arriving with dinner. Keyain walked to the other room as the clattering of plates and silverware sounded. Marietta cautiously approached the doorway. Platters of baked fish, fresh flatbread, and an array of roasted vegetables permeated the air, tossing Marietta's uneasy stomach. Still in her clothes from the night before, she watched as Keyain ate from the doorway.

With a glance, he acknowledged her, rolling his eyes. "Showing that little outfit again for me, huh?"

She crossed her arms, leaning against the door frame. All this time, Keyain knew Amryth's wife died saving Marietta, and he still kept Amryth assigned to her. Gods, he lied when he said she was a handmaid. As she stared at Keyain, all she could do was frown.

"Either sit and eat or go lay down. I don't care which," he said, his eyes not leaving his plate.

"I know." Her voice felt hollow and far away.

"Know what?" He tapped his fingers against the table.

"Amryth. She's your soldier on your Elite Guard."

"Yeah, not that hard to figure out." He gave her a pointed, unimpressed look with raised brows.

"I know about her wife, too."

"What about Deyra?" Keyain resumed eating, the conversation unimportant to him.

"I killed her. The night your soldiers took me, she was there. I killed her with a dagger." The stillness of her voice surprised Marietta. Such a confession should have eased the weight, but Keyain's obvious dismissal made it too much to bear.

"It's not like you did it on purpose, Mar." He spoke with food in his mouth, still looking at his plate.

He said it as if Deyra wasn't his soldier, as if Amryth's pain meant nothing. "No. And I guess you wouldn't care." Leaving Keyain to eat alone, she turned around and crawled into bed, falling into a restless sleep.

Days blurred together in a timeless void of Marietta's thoughts. She spent most days in bed, waking up and wishing she hadn't. Servants encouraged her to eat so she would eat a little. Every couple of days they would get her into that tub to bathe, get her to change into a new nightgown. But she wouldn't speak, never smiled.

Why live when such a life condemned her? A chance to escape wouldn't come, not when Keyain assigned Amryth to prevent such a thing. Even if Marietta escaped, how could she go back to Olkia and face the pain of Tilan's lies? How many of her friends were in the Exisotis? How many of them knew Tilan married her for the Exisotis?

Everything had holes; everything caused suspicion. The times Tilan would step outside to smoke with a stranger at a tavern. The late nights at his smithy. When his acquaintances found out she was his wife, their attitudes had changed. Were they Exisotis too? Marietta had likely met many of the members but never knew.

It tainted her memories of Tilan, rotten with holes from the deceptions that she would never learn. The truth he could never share.

Was his happiness fake, too? Did he dread coming home to her every night to a woman the Exisotis forced him to marry? Perhaps he loved another woman. Was it her he wished to be with, and he had just pretended with Marietta?

Keyain was untrustworthy, but Marietta saw the documents. She saw how detailed the reports were. Queen Valeriya only solidified the truth by knowing Tilan's name.

Tilan knew him—knew Keyain was a minister of Satiros. And the day Keyain nearly broke down Tilan's apartment door to take Marietta, Tilan knew.

Tilan knew.

Tilan lied.

And lied.

And lied.

Marietta's memories flipped before her until there was nothing else.

Chapter Twenty-Nine

MARIETTA

BEFORE

"Keyain, stop!" Marietta cried as he kissed down her neck, pushing her onto the double-wide bed. Just arriving in Rotamu, they were getting settled in the room for a week-long stay in the double river city. Dust and dirt from traveling from Kentro coated their clothes, Keyain not caring as they rolled onto the covers.

For a moment, Keyain pulled back, leaning on one arm as he gazed down at Marietta. The golden afternoon light shined through the windows, casting Keyain in its glow. With a hand, he cupped her face, a thumb brushing over her cheek. "I love you, Mar."

That was new. Marietta couldn't help but smile, thinking of her grumpy bodyguard who gave way to protective partner in just a few months. Keyain cared deeply for her though he could be a bit possessive at times. Her heart fluttered as she said, "I love you, Keyain."

His kisses came slowly, passionately, his hands reaching for the hem of her tunic, pulling it up over her head. "Life is so much more enjoyable with you in it," he said while kissing down her neck once more.

Marietta's stomach flipped as her smile widened. Keyain was never one for sentimental words, yet he continued. "Freedom like this, to love and to travel, is made so much sweeter by your company. I can't believe there was ever a time in my life where I didn't have you," Keyain said into her skin, pausing to kiss her collarbone. "Your vibrant energy for life is

refreshing. Your enthusiasm for your business and people is commendable. How you balance it all—the traveling, the work, the people—and still make time for me is unbelievable. I love you, Marietta, and I am utterly and completely yours."

Keyain kissed her again while his hand cradled her head. Marietta pulled back, holding his face. "Such flowery words from someone who hates sharing how he feels," she teased, causing his smile to deepen. "It's funny to think of how much of a killjoy you were at first, not wanting me to drink or dance, not wanting any mischief," she said, lifting her mouth to his. "But you learned to trust me, and I can see that your concern came from a place of caring. Despite your rough, aggressive exterior, inside you is a large heart that somehow I'm lucky enough to have a spot in." Marietta sighed, looking up at Keyain. "You are a pain in my ass," she said, earning a laugh from him, "but I am yours. I love you, Keyain."

Keyain slowly kissed down her body, removing her leggings as he went and discarding his clothes. With the confession of their love fresh on their lips, they didn't stop until the sun hung low in the sky.

The past five months had been a blur for Marietta. She'd gained a handful of new clients, some needed more attention than others, and then there was Keyain—an unexpected piece she hadn't planned on. He wasn't *just* her guard for long. After their first night together, Marietta had tried to keep things professional, clearly stating that the position wasn't *that* type of job; yet somehow, through the tension that was ever present when they were together, she had fallen for Keyain. Despite his blunt way of handling situations and dealing with people, Keyain was a refreshing foil, helping Marietta think logically about her business. Plus, on the road, Keyain had proven himself more capable than any guard, especially after the first attack in the countryside.

Marietta laid on her side, staring at Keyain while their bodies were still slick with sweat. "The freckles kind of take away from the aggressive manly look you're going for," she said, reaching out her fingers to trace them.

Keyain pretended to bite her fingers, laughing. "You mean aggressive *male* look." He flicked the elongated tip of his ears and said, "These don't count as *manly*. Quite clearly, I'm an elf."

Marietta rolled her eyes. "You know what I meant. Male and female sound too much like breeding animals. It's brutish."

"Maybe here, but you wouldn't catch anyone from Syllogi saying *man* or *woman* when referring to elves." He hesitated, biting his lip. "Speaking of Syllogi, we need to talk about something."

"That sounds serious." Marietta tried to joke, but her stomach dropped.

"It's not bad, I swear," he said, leaning on his side to face Marietta. Keyain brought Marietta's hand up to her mouth, kissing it. "I have to leave at the end of the week."

"What? Why?" Marietta furrowed her brows. "You wait to tell me this now?"

"I'm sorry I waited to tell you." Hesitating, he ran his fingers through his hair, deciding his words. "I need to go home for a while."

"Satiros? For how long?"

"Six months."

Marietta jolted up, looking down at him. "Six months? And you waited until a week before to tell me?"

"I know, I know. Marietta, I am so sorry. But I hired guards, already reached out to a few people I trust. And I paid for everything, you just—"

Marietta cut him off. "Why do you have to go back? Why for so long?"

Keyain tried to cup her face, but she moved away from his touch. "I have a job, Marietta. I can only do so much on the road."

"And this job is what, exactly? I'm assuming it's still drugs of some sort since you *still* won't tell me," Marietta said, tightening her lips. "I'm willing to overlook whatever it is because I don't believe you're harming people or doing anything too despicable. But you need to tell me something, Keyain."

"I love you, but I can't. One day I will, I promise. Right now, you're better off not knowing."

She fell onto her back, gazing at the wooden ceiling above. "Is this the part where you ask me to come with you?"

Keyain leaned over, his finger lightly circling her skin. "I could never ask, not with your business, but you are more than welcome to come with me. I'd love to show you Satiros, to tell you everything."

Marietta closed her eyes and sighed. "You know that isn't possible. I can't take six months off, as much as I would love to learn something about your life," she said, glancing at Keyain with a tight smile.

Silence overtook them as they laid together, Marietta stewing about his blatant lack of notice. Finally, she said, "Alyck won't be one of the guards, right?"

Keyain laughed uncomfortably. "No, he wouldn't make it an hour before you killed him, and I prefer to keep my friends alive."

Marietta smirked. "I would rather risk it by myself than rely on him. So no worries, he'd be alive and well in whatever city-state I ditched him in."

He rolled over, laughing a kiss onto Marietta's lips. "Well, let's head to dinner. I think you and I could both use our first-night-in-town drinks." He shifted up, looking over his shoulder at Marietta. "Plus, there are some people I'd like you to meet."

A tavern sat on the bottom floor of their inn, making their trip to dinner quick. Marietta's stomach fluttered, never having met anyone from Keyain's personal life. As they changed for dinner, he had explained that they're some friends from Syllogi, who would also return at the week's end.

Which meant he planned to meet them here, yet he didn't tell her until that evening. Annoyed, she tried to let it roll off her shoulders, but it irked her. How could he say that he loved her, then take off for six months? It's been less than six months since they've met.

The tavern was hot and stuffy, crowded with travelers and natives to Rotamu. Stale alcohol, roasted meat, and yeasty bread permeated the air, making Marietta's stomach growl. The first night in every city was always her favorite. A recoup from traveling before she met with her clients, always celebrated with good ale and better food. Marietta laced her fingers with Keyain as they walked through the dining room of chattering denizens.

Marietta waved to a handful of people she recognized, but didn't have time to greet them as Keyain wove his way through the long wooden tables. He came to a stop at a booth where two elvish folks were sitting. An elven man with dark skin and a bald head flagged them down from across the room. Next to him sat a pale elven woman with chestnut hair and a tight smile on her angular face.

"Peryn, Rynka, it's been too long," Keyain said, sliding into the booth across from them, Marietta following. "I'd like you to meet my partner, Marietta."

Surprise lined their faces as they looked between Marietta and Keyain. "We weren't aware you'd found a partner, Keyain," the man said. "I'm Peryn. This is Rynka." The elven woman kept a tight-lipped smile, nodding her head. Marietta didn't miss the fervent glances she gave Keyain.

"It's lovely to meet you both. Have you visited Rotamu before?" Marietta asked, slipping into the conversation.

"Yes," Peryn answered, "but briefly. This will be our longest stint in the city. Keyain, I'm assuming you've told Marietta when we're leaving?" The question irked Marietta, for she had only just found out.

"I have. She knows it's about six months." Keyain turned to Marietta. "They're traveling with me back to Satiros."

"Does that mean Marietta won't be joining us?" Rynka asked, her gaze turning to Marietta.

"Unfortunately no, she has her empire to run here." Keyain smiled as he wrapped his arm around her. "Marietta helps businesses in all the cities of Enomenos. Six months would be—"

Marietta cut him off, hating that he spoke for her. "Six months is too long. Every week I'm in a new city meeting with my clients."

At the edge of her vision, Keyain ground his jaw. He knew better than to speak for her.

"Oh, a business owner, Keyain?" Peryn said, grating Marietta's nerves as he drove the conversation back to him. "I was a little surprised to learn you're partnered with a clip, but it seems she comes with quite the pedigree."

Marietta's head jerked to Keyain. As if the slur wasn't enough of an insult, he added *pedigree* on top of it as if she were an animal. Was this the company Keyain kept? Could he seriously love her if this is how they'd talk about her? Marietta glared at Keyain, waiting for him to correct his friend.

The correction never came. Instead, the three kept talking. A few hours ago he confessed his love for her, but now didn't speak up against his friends? Sure, the slur stung, but it was nothing compared to the hurt of Keyain's inaction.

Perhaps he didn't want to stir the pot so soon after meeting his friends. That had to be the reason. He had stood up for Marietta when they were in the countryside a few weeks back. Humans in a small town between Avato and Kentro had called her ill-blooded for being half-elven. He was feral in his response, threatening to hurt them all. Keyain cared for her, so there had to be a reason to say nothing this time. With a sigh, she decided to swallow through the insult, and she would discuss it when they went back to their room.

They ordered drinks and dinner, the elves talking about Satiroan politics, which proved boring. Marietta's mind wandered to her clients that week. There was an alchemist in Rotamu that she was to meet for the first time. A mutual acquaintance gave Marietta the recommendation but knew little of their practice. The elven woman's business was struggling, and a friend of hers grew concerned that the alchemist's operations would go under.

Marietta had done her research and learned she had a drinking problem, which she knew was likely the cause of the business' failing; and that wouldn't be the first time Marietta helped in such a scenario. The problem with gaining notoriety over the last six years was that people talked. The elven woman wouldn't be the last person she would have to help with such a problem, even though being a counselor or a doctor wasn't part of her job. She couldn't say no to helping someone.

"Marietta," Keyain said, touching her arm, "don't be rude. Peryn asked you a question."

Marietta shook her head, forcing a smile. "Apologies. I was thinking about my clients. What was the question?" Keyain's hand fell to her thigh, giving her a warning grip. He wasn't happy, which did nothing for her mood. The audacity he had at times was enough to set her off. Keyain was, as always, a pain in her ass.

"That's alright. Clips often have trouble focusing. That's just in their nature. I was asking—"

Marietta cut him off. "We don't say *clip* in Enomenos. It's a slur and one I am asking you not to address me, or any other pilinos, as such." With practiced patience, she kept her voice calm as anger burned under her skin.

"Marietta," Keyain snapped.

"I didn't mean any offense," Peryn said, his smile tight. "In Syllogi, we say clip as it isn't a slur."

"It is one, whether or not you're from here. Just because Syllogi is ignorant and believes pilinos' lives fall below full elven one's doesn't mean the rest of Akroi is as ignorant," she said, not hiding her anger. Keyain's hand gripped harder as she pried it from her leg.

Rynka and Peryn shot looks at Keyain. "I didn't realize your partner had such strong feelings against Syllogi," Rynka ground out, her eyes burning.

"Apparently, she has had too much to drink." Keyain gave her a warning look. "I have never heard her say anything bad about Satiros or Syllogi myself."

Marietta gaped at him, knowing full well she had made fun of him to his face about being a Syllogian elf. Keyain was lying, but why?

"I'm just going to make this clear for you three," Marietta said, splaying her hand on the gnarled wood tabletop. "Clip is a slur. It is insulting. You don't get to decide whether it is or is not. Elves are not superior—they never were and never will be. One day, your bodies will burn just like the rest of ours. I suggest during your week in Rotamu you learn how to empathize with those who look nothing like you because clearly you never have."

Marietta left the booth, turning around adding, "I would say it was great meeting you, but unlike some people here, I'm not a liar." She glared at Keyain before stalking off to the stairs, heading up to their room.

Keyain returned to their room not long after Marietta, slamming the door behind him. "Are you kidding me?" he yelled, his face red.

"I should be the one asking that," Marietta said, crossing her arms. "You honestly believe clip is an okay way to refer to me?"

"We've been through this—that's how people refer to pilinos in Syllogi, Mar!" Keyain dragged a hand through his hair, turning away from Marietta with his jaw tight.

"I don't give a fuck where it's said. It's an insult, and you were in the wrong. If you can admit I'm your partner—which, by the way, seemed unbelievable that you'd ever date a half-elf—then why can't you stand up for me? Why can't you treat me like I'm a whole person?"

Keyain whipped to Marietta, his nostrils flared. "I know you're a whole person, Marietta. And yes, it probably was jarring for them to see me with someone like you but—"

"Someone like me? You mean a clip?" Marietta rolled her eyes and went to her pack, pulling out her nightclothes. "Half-elf is just as easy to say, only it admits that part of me is elven. Wouldn't want to taint the word elven with my filthy, part-human blood," she said sarcastically.

Keyain walked over to her. "Marietta," he said, grabbing her arm.

She jerked back from his grasp. "If you ever—*ever*—try to grab me like that again, then you can travel Enomenos by yourself." Marietta stepped closer to him, placing her finger on his chest with a furious glare. "Do you understand?"

"I don't want to fight." Keyain bit his tongue, biting back tears. "This is our last week together for a while. I don't want to end our amazing journey to be like this."

Keyain's arms wrapped around Marietta, folding her into a hug. Pettiness wasn't above her, and she thought of shoving him away and insulting him some more, but she couldn't bring herself to do it. Gods knew Keyain deserved a huge blown out fight. After everything, she should just leave him and tell him to not return to Enomenos; yet when she looked into his face and saw the emotion in his expression, that anger cooled. She hated herself for it, wishing she could stay heated, could hate him for not standing up for her.

The funny thing about love was that once it took root in one's heart, it was hard to weed out. Keyain made her furious, not just at him but with herself. Despite that feeling, she knew that she loved him. The good of him outweighed the bad. And now, whether she was ready for it, Keyain was leaving in less than a week.

Perhaps six months away would do them some good. After all, living out of inns together for the past few months had been an awful lot like being married. Marietta would gain some independence back.

She didn't want to part on a sour note, no matter how in the wrong he was. "Okay," she whispered into his chest. Keyain pressed a kiss on the top of her head.

"I love you, Marietta. I promise to always support you, even when it doesn't seem like I am."

Marietta bit back her retort, deciding not to fight. "I love you, too. And I'm really going to miss you."

Chapter Thirty

ELYSE

"**R**emember to not make a fool of yourself today," Elyse's father said, picking fuzz off a navy jacket as he ignored the heat from the early afternoon sun. "Last time was enough of an embarrassment for a lifetime. I need not remind you what the consequences would be."

The implication lingered between them, and Elyse swallowed hard. No, she wouldn't think of the consequences. "I'll be on my best behavior, father." She hated the words, and she hated her father for expecting them.

After Keyain and Brynden's fight, referred to as *the incident*, it surprised Elyse that Brynden wished to call on her again. More surprising was her father agreeing to let Elyse leave the palace.

The Chorys Dasians stayed at a townhouse nearby, though Elyse questioned why they wouldn't stay in the designated section of the palace for foreign dignitaries. But who was she to question? She'd get to visit with Brynden and enjoy a day of freedom. No palace. No father. No watchful eyes. Excitement bubbled at her center, a mixture of nerves and giddiness.

Her father ordered a handmaid back full time for Elyse since Brynden wished to continue pursuing her hand in marriage. Though she dreaded sitting through the awkward silence, Elyse was thankful for their expert touch.

Much to her surprise, she felt beautiful. People claimed she was a beauty, and Elyse knew they didn't lie, but she was uncomfortable in her skin. She could not see what others saw. It was as if her clothes or hair never fit her, like they belonged to a different person.

Except for that afternoon, in her gown of pale blush, striking against her bronze skin. The tight-fitted lace corset bodice flowed into a tulle skirt with slits well up her thighs. A sweetheart neckline complemented what few curves she possessed. The sleeves started mid-arm, billowing out in the sheer fabric and gathering again at her wrists. The handmaid twisted her hair up with loose strands of honey brown hair falling free; her shoulders laid bare.

For once, her father had nothing to nitpick on her appearance. That alone set her nerves at ease. Well, that and the liquor. Three cups, to be exact, kept them eased as well.

An ostentatious carriage pulled up to the curb outside the palace, painted black with red and gold filigree adorning the trim and doors. At the helm sat a mage who propelled the vehicle with magic.

The door flung open, revealing Brynden, his straight black hair pulled into a knot, extenuating the planes of his face. Draped on his body was a silk shirt with a deep neckline dropping to his navel with ruffles. Similar to her dress, the sleeves billowed out and were tight at his wrists. A gold chain hung deep into his neckline, with a small gold medallion hanging from the end. Handsome, but like the carriage, ostentatious.

Elyse suppressed a laugh as he bowed dramatically, a full smile lining his face. "Oh, my dear Elyse, how I have missed you so."

Before she responded, Brynden slipped one hand behind her head, the other at her waist, pulling Elyse into a kiss. His grasp was firm, his kisses soft as he started with her lips and moved to her cheek, causing heat to flood her face.

Her father cleared his throat as he stood right next to them.

Brynden pulled back with a mischievous grin. "Hello, my goddess," he murmured, lacing their hands together.

"Brynden, it's good to catch you outside our meetings." Her father stepped up, offering his hand. In his plain clothes, her father looked subdued next to Brynden.

"Gyrsh, always a pleasure." Brynden took her father's hand. "I've looked forward to spoiling your daughter all week."

"Don't spoil her too much. I wouldn't want Elyse to forget her place."

Elyse didn't miss the warning in her father's words. She was lucky she even had this opportunity with him.

Brynden pulled her close, the juniper and citrus scent becoming stronger. "Well, it's a good thing her place is at my side," he said with a wink. "But we should be off."

Before her father could answer, Brynden led her to the carriage. A slight limp in her gait caught Brynden's eye, though he didn't comment. Instead, he offered a hand as she entered the carriage. With a last glance back, her father gave her a look that said she should be grateful. Grateful didn't cover it.

Inside the carriage, Brynden lounged across from Elyse on an upholstered seat as the carriage rolled forward. The neckline of his shirt hung loose, revealing his olive skin and the sculpted shape of his body beneath. She had seen glimpses of his chest before but now she could confirm how toned they were. Though he was no longer in the army, he remained fit.

"See something you like?"

"Just admiring the interesting choice in shirt." A smirk came to her lips.

"I believe you're admiring more than just the shirt, my goddess. After our last encounter, I figured you'd appreciate a deep neckline. As you see," he gestured to his chest with a hand, "I won't be outshined by your remarkable fashion choices."

A laugh escaped from Elyse as she rolled her eyes. "Minutes into spending time with me and you're already teasing." The banter was easy, lighthearted—just like the night they met.

"Sassy today, are we? My friends will enjoy that."

Elyse tilted her head. "Friends? It won't be just us?"

"I wish it were just us, but I've assured your father chaperons would be around so no one will find me on top of you in a field again." His russet eyes gleamed with amusement. "You met them at the ball."

Gods, her father introduced her to the Chorys Dasians, but alcohol made her forget. "Perhaps you can remind me of their names. That was some time ago."

"It would be my absolute pleasure to tell them my beautiful date forgot their names because my alluring nature distracted her," Brynden said, pulling open his shirt more.

"Oh, my gods…."

A genuine smile came to his lips. "It's cute that you say that."

"Say what?"

"Oh, my gods this, gods that. If I didn't know any better, I would say you're one of their followers." A dark eyebrow lifted as he spoke.

"Just because I don't follow them doesn't make them not real."

"You're absolutely right," he said, sitting up and placing his forearms on his knees. "But being real doesn't make the gods as all-powerful as they would like us to believe."

Brynden dropped to his knees before Elyse, placing himself between her legs. Heat crept across her cheeks again as his face became inches from her own. "I digress—we won't spend the entire time with my friends."

"What's that supposed to mean?"

"Just because your father thinks there will be constant chaperoning doesn't mean there will be." He smirked and added, "I'll be on my best behavior, I promise. If kissing you at the ball sent you over the edge, then I can't imagine what straddling you in a field of flowers did for you."

Elyse's heart heaved in her chest, but the liquor emboldened her words. "If I told you I already forgot about it, how would you feel?"

"Hurt, because you would be lying. There is no way you forgot." Both of his hands crossed over his heart with dramatic flare. "It brings me much joy knowing you feel better today." Brynden leaned in. "Perhaps you're well enough for another kiss?"

Elyse leaned forward, her lips locking with his and Brynden caressed her cheek, his lips soft.

"Hmm," Brynden said, pulling back. "That's what I thought."

"What?"

"Alcohol. Couldn't get through one afternoon without drinking?" He raised an eyebrow in speculation with a crooked smile.

"After last time, my father didn't want to risk it, so he had me drink a glass or two," she said as she avoided his gaze. She hated that he knew, hated that she even needed it to talk to him.

Brynden's thumb brushed across her mouth as he cupped her cheek. "There's nothing to worry about. Unless I'm so unbearable that you need to drink to get through the afternoon."

"Gods, no. You are more than bearable. I just... get nervous. And you're so perfect. And handsome." What was she saying? "I enjoy your company and don't want to mess this up."

"There is nothing you can do to mess this up, goddess."

Her breath snatched, not realizing how much she needed that reassurance. Elyse glanced at her lap then back at him as her smile grew.

The carriage came to a stop as Brynden kissed her again. "Remember to repeat the part about me being perfect and handsome to my friends. They'll be thrilled that someone is feeding my ego."

With one last kiss, he stood, exiting the carriage with an extended hand to Elyse.

Brynden escorted her to the staircase that led to the townhouse before them. Six stories high in white-washed stone clad in green vines, it looked like any of the homes along the street, except for the columns and ornamentations added to the outside, painted in crimson and gold like the carriage.

"May I welcome you to my home away from home, my goddess?" Brynden led her over the threshold, beholding the cavernous foyer.

Black tiles patterned the floor, meeting the dark wood wainscoting of the walls. A rug of crimson, black, and gold sprawled below them depicting scenes of elves on ships, of a minotaur howling.

A grand staircase curved from the second floor with a crimson runner lining the steps. Banisters of rich, dark wood lined the staircase, the ends capped with a carved bull head.

"Though I'd love to give you the grand tour now, it'll have to wait until I show you your surprise upstairs." Brynden winked as he strolled over to a living room, only partially separated from the entry.

Elyse followed him, though her gait slowed by the frustrating pain in her hip. Staying a step behind Brynden, she hoped he wouldn't notice it again. "Surprise? What surprise?"

Black clawfoot couches and chairs centered the room, surrounding a low table of similar style. Brocade curtains of crimson hung from the floor-to-ceiling windows overlooking the courtyard. Bookcases lined the wall, complete with leather-bound volumes and trinkets. Elyse examined some closer titles.

"How would it be a surprise if I told you?" he teased with a bemused smirk, walking past the living room, aiming for a glass-paned door.

"Give me a hint then," she said, tearing her eyes away from the books to follow.

"It's more of an *experience* than an object."

Elyse's eyes grew wide. He didn't mean…."Experience, as in physical? Physical, uh, touching?"

The smirk on his face grew into a full smile as he laughed. "Someone has quite the dirty mind. Perhaps wishful thinking led you to such a conclusion?" He took her hand as she approached. "As much as I would love to *physically touch* you, my surprise is not that."

Brynden leaned in, kissing her on her cheek. "But let's join my friends for a bit, so we're not lying to your father."

The afternoon sun greeted them as they stepped into the courtyard, the stone tiles continuing underfoot. Rose and juniper bushes lined the outdoor space and landscape beds broke up the tiles. Beyond a simple fountain, voices and laughter carried from deeper in the courtyard.

Brynden slipped his arm around Elyse as they approached three familiar males sitting on low couches around a table beneath a shaded pergola.

Lounged on one of two couches was a male with dark skin with black curly hair, the sides faded. His angular face had a full smile sitting over a square jaw, amusement dancing in his eyes. "There you two are. We were just taking bets on whether you two join us or head upstairs."

In one chair nestled between the two couches sat a fair-complexioned male with blond hair. As they approached, his wide-set eyes locked onto Elyse. She tried her best to avoid his invasive staring, feeling uncomfortable.

The last male sat in the other chair. Handsome, he had brown skin with a wide nose and eyes angled up to the outside. His dark hair curled loosely to his shoulders. He scowled at Brynden.

Brynden offered his hand as she sat on the cream-colored couch. "Yeah? And who's losing coin today?" He sat beside Elyse, an arm draping on the back of her spot.

The same male answered. "Daryn and I lost. Sylas bet you'd find us first," he said, gesturing to a male with brown skin. The scowl remained on his face. The dark-skinned male and Daryn flicked a gold coin each at Sylas.

"I can always count on Sylas for believing the best in me," Brynden said with a mock smile, placing his hand over his heart.

"It was less what I believed you'd do and more what I'd hope you'd do." Sylas gave a pointed look. "Gyrsh was clear that I need to keep an eye on you two."

Brynden chuckled, his arm wrapping around her. "All Gyrsh needs to know is that I'll treat Elyse like the goddess she is." Sylas's scowl deepened, causing Brynden to laugh harder.

"Unfortunately, the night of the victory ball, my alluring nature dazzled Elyse enough that she forgot your names," Brynden said, leaning in to kiss her cheek.

The dark-skinned male laughed. "I'm sure that's a lie. You couldn't have been lucky enough to find a female that willingly strokes your ego."

"I am the luckiest male there is that she even considers me, let alone strokes my ego," Brynden said, looking down at Elyse with a smile. "So, go on. Introduce yourselves."

The dark-skinned male was the first to speak up. "Lord Oryck Ramstyn of Chorys Dasi. New Emissary for my city-state and a first timer in Satiros."

"Lord Sylas Tygenbrook. Both Emissary to Chorys Dasi and

nursemaid to Brynden." With added flavor, Sylas rolled his eyes, causing Brynden to laugh.

"And I'm Lord Daryn Comstych, Emissary to Chorys Dasi," said the male with pale skin, his eyes locked onto Elyse. "I have worked with your father since he started his position as Minister of Foreign Relations. He had quite wonderful things to say about you."

Brynden waved his hand at Daryn. "All a lie. She's anything but the obedient daughter he has made us all believe. Elyse has been reading Lyken Fulbryk."

Elyse snapped her head to Brynden, a warning sitting on her lips. If her father found out, the consequences would be worse than after *the incident*.

Oryck sat up at that. "Is that so? After he made such a big deal about her being incapable of magic?"

Brynden looked down at Elyse. "Go on; tell them."

Elyse paused, her heart racing despite the alcohol. "I just finished his book on the second principle and started the third last night."

"So you understand the second principle—of not letting aithyr control the mage?" Sylas asked, Elyse unsure if it was mocking or curiosity.

"Sylas," Brynden warned.

"It's alright. I know a little about my mother, how aithyr affected her. That's why I haven't tried reaching out to it," she said, staring at the table nestled in the center of the seating area.

"Which is why I wanted her to try Mage's Eye today. To see if she could," Brynden said.

"No, absolutely not," Sylas glowered. "Gyrsh would have our heads if we smoked with her."

"How about we let her decide? Elyse?"

Her wide eyes stared back at Brynden. "What's Mage's Eye?"

Oryck laughed, adding, "Gyrsh really does keep her sheltered."

Heat crept across her cheeks, hating not knowing and hating being laughed at for it. As if it were her fault.

"Enough," Brynden said with a glare at Oryck, causing the laughter to die in his throat. He turned back to Elyse. "Mage's Eye helps calm and focus the mind, allowing mages to better access aithyr. Since your thoughts often overwhelm you, I thought not only could it help you with magic but also help with your nerves." He smiled at Elyse, a hand reaching up to her cheek.

"You left out the part where it can be addictive." Sylas crossed his arms, his full lips a thin line.

Brynden looked over his shoulder at Sylas. "I also left out that in Chorys Dasi, people use it to help with anxious thoughts, regardless if they are a mage or not." He turned back to Elyse, clasping her hand. "It is up to you if you'd like to try. We'll have to flush the alcohol out of your system first, though."

From the corner of her eyes, she noticed the three males share glances. Determined to ignore them, Elyse asked, "And it won't make me see anything weird? Or make me complicit?" The blue, milky drug her father gave her came to mind, sending a chill down her spine. That was the last thing she wanted.

Oryck scoffed with surprise. "How do you know what Choke is but not Mage's Eye?"

"Is that what it's called? My father makes me take it for head pains and I hate it." She glanced at Oryck, then back to Brynden, who frowned. "So if your drug is anything like it, I don't want it."

Sylas swore under his breath, drawing Elyse's gaze. He tucked strands of his hair behind an ear, the metal piercing his flesh catching the light as displeasure spread across his face. Did he ever smile?

Brynden squeezed her hand. "Mage's Eye is nothing like it. Choke is a serious drug meant to incapacitate and make you under someone's influence. Gyrsh told me about how severe your head pains get, but Choke?" He shook his head. "Mage's Eye will calm you. You will remain aware of yourself and your surroundings."

Her entire life was within the walls of the palace, sheltered from such experiences. She felt stunted, cheated out of her life. Everything was predetermined, and she didn't have freedom of choice. But Brynden gazed down at her, giving her one. "If you can promise that, then yes, I'd like to try it," Elyse said with a hammering heart. It would be the first of many new experiences if she and Brynden married.

"I promise, with my whole heart and my whole being." Brynden kissed her before adding, "And now to flush the alcohol from your body." He stood, offering his hand to Elyse.

"I still think this is a terrible idea," Sylas said, picking something off his black shirt.

"You think all my ideas are terrible ideas," Bryden responded, leading Elyse back inside. The three males chuckled as the door closed behind Elyse.

"How are you going to flush the alcohol?" Elyse asked, following Brynden down a hallway off the sitting room.

"Magic-infused medicine. It flushes toxins out in an instant. I keep some of this stuff on hand for nights I've drunk too much," he said, turning to Elyse. "Makes you sober in a snap. Also, it's good to have on hand when doing drugs."

"And you do drugs often?" she asked with a speculative brow.

"Occasionally. When the moment is appropriate, like today," he said, winking.

"You live quite the life." Elyse bit her lip, a tinge of jealousy in her words.

"And you will too, if I get any say in it." Brynden gave a broad smile as he stopped in front of a door, leaning against it. "But first, I'd like you to tell me why you're limping."

Despite the alcohol, her breathing picked up and her limbs went numb. "It's nothing. I'm just clumsy and hurt my knee."

"There's no need to lie. I can tell it's not your knee, nor your ankle. What did you do to your hip? Are you alright?" His brows furrowed with concern.

A practiced sweet smile curled on her lips as she placed her hand on his arm. "I'm alright. No need to worry about it. We should be quick, though. I don't want them taking any more bets on whether we'll come back or be upstairs."

Brynden laughed, pausing as if he had more to say, but pushed open the door. "One of the side effects of flushing your system requires a toilet." He gestured past the door as the room lit, revealing a restroom. "So I'm going to give you the vial and let you take care of it. All you need to do is drink and give it a minute. I have to run upstairs, but I'll be back to grab you, alright? Just wait for me here."

Before she could answer, he gave her a quick kiss and headed down the hallway. Elyse stepped into the bathroom, locking the door behind her. The liquid in the vial looked like water, nothing similar to *Choke*. Without another thought, she downed the vial and waited until her bladder suddenly felt as if it would burst.

Once she finished, she waited in the hallway for Brynden, her head clear from the alcohol's effects.

"My lady." She turned to find Daryn staring at her with his weird, wide eyes again. "It's good to see you again."

Did Daryn follow them? "Have we met before?" Unease settled into her chest.

"Once, about a decade ago. Your father hosted a handful of us from Chorys Dasi. You were acting so obedient that night, Gyrsh having us believe it was his raising. Now I know it was Choke."

Of course he did. She glared at Daryn for bringing up the memories of those nights, ones that often happened before Keyain. If the ball wasn't so public, Elyse assumed her father would have drugged her then to be Brynden's date.

"I have a favor to ask, and it's going to sound odd. Can you keep it between just you and I?" Daryn took a step closer, causing Elyse to step back.

"That depends."

"Can I smell you?" he asked, taking another step.

"Excuse me?" Of all the favors she expected, *smelling her* was not one of them.

"I… uh. Brynden said you have a specific scent, and I was curious."

"No, you cannot smell me," she snapped, brows furrowed, her glare deepening. "What kind of favor is that?"

"I know it's odd," Daryn said, taking two steps, cornering Elyse. "But please, it could even be your arm."

"This is highly inappropriate," she said, pressing herself against the wall. "What would my father say if he knew you were asking me this alone in the hallway?"

Where was Brynden?

Daryn laughed, nervousness laced throughout it. "Gyrsh would blame you, would he not? For turning down a simple, harmless favor of his contact from a foreign entity?"

Gods, he was right—he would blame her and punish her. Daryn took another step towards her, a hand brushing back his blonde hair.

Where in the hells was Brynden?

"Please," Daryn asked again. "I'm just curious to see if Brynden was correct."

"Correct about what?" Elyse asked.

"If you smelled like us."

"Why would I smell like you? Please step back." Her heart pounded faster as he leaned in close, and she shoved her arm into him. "Stop this."

Daryn grabbed her arm and brought it to his face, inhaling. Elyse watched with horrified eyes, unsure of what to do.

"Daryn, what are you doing?" Sylas stormed down the hall, his wide nostrils flaring as he gave a menacing stare to Daryn. After meeting the male sitting down, Elyse didn't realize how large he was. Broad-shouldered, about a head and a half taller than Daryn, and absolutely terrifying with the snarl on his face.

"Az was right. She smells like us," Daryn said, turning to Sylas.

Elyse took her chance and pulled her arm out from his grasp, pressing further back into the wall. What in the gods is wrong with him?

Sylas grabbed Daryn and slammed him into the opposite wall, pinning his shoulders. "You idiot," he hissed, "that was uncalled for."

"But she smells like peaches and honey and cream. Like *us*," Daryn said, exasperated. "After Gyrsh said—"

Elyse tilted her head. Why would she smell like any of those things?

"What is this?" Brynden walked towards them with a small box under his arm. "Do I even want to know what Daryn did to terrify my lady so?"

"I'll give you the full details later," Sylas growled.

Elyse turned to Brynden, arms wrapped around herself. "He was trying to *smell* me, stating you thought my scent was of food."

A smile came to Brynden that didn't reach his eyes. "And what else?"

"He grabbed my arm so he could smell me after I told him no."

Brynden walked towards the group, handing the wooden box to Elyse. "Please hold this for a moment, my goddess."

He stalked towards Daryn as Sylas backed off, crossing his arms with a disapproving grimace. Brynden grabbed Daryn by his shirt, jerking him back into the wall. "If you ever so much as lay a finger on Elyse again without her permission, then I will break both your hands. Do I make myself clear?" Despite his anger, Brynden kept his voice calm and low, his eyes boring through his friend.

"Yes, my—," Daryn said, cut off by Brynden slamming into the wall.

"Get your shit together or you will need to leave. Understood?" he threatened.

Daryn only nodded his head, biting back his reply. Elyse shook where she stood, something glass rattling in the box Brynden handed her.

Her mind raced as she followed the three males back to the courtyard. Why would Brynden tell them how she *smelled*? And of things she most definitely didn't smell like, let alone like *them*.

Between Sylas and Brynden's anger, the silence was almost unbearable, their rage similar to that of her father's. Brynden had lost his temper twice over minor things—was he always like this? Was she jumping from one controlling male to another?

No, because he didn't want her to be some complicit wife. At least that much was obvious. But what else did she know of him?

She knew little of Brynden. That was her third time spending time with him, and he was already so protective of her. None of it made sense.

Brynden courting her after meeting her once, continuing to court her even after *the incident*. What was his angle? Elyse wasn't worth the hassle.

Silence still encased their group as they returned to the courtyard, Oryck looking between them all. "I missed something. Tell me what I missed."

"Nothing." Brynden flashed a smile and opened the wooden box. Inside was a leafy mixture smelling like burnt resin. He filled a few pipes before handing one to Sylas and Oryck.

Oryck raised his eyebrows to Daryn, gleaning something had angered Brynden.

"So Elyse, my goddess, all you have to do is inhale," Brynden said, holding a pipe in his hands towards her. "Have you ever smoked before?"

She shook her head. It was all new to her, and she couldn't believe she was doing it.

"Well, you'll experience a little burning in the chest, but it should adjust after a few times. Here, try it." Brynden handed her the pipe. From his fingertips, a small flame appeared that he dipped into the pipe. "Inhale."

Magic. Of course, Brynden could do magic.

Suppressing the shock of his ability, Elyse brought the pipe to her mouth, inhaling. Smoky resin and peppered smoke filled her lungs. A cough racketed through her chest, causing her to fumble with the pipe, but Brynden steadied her hand.

The effects came slowly at first, her thoughts still racing, but the impending doom that always lingered over her head lessened and... she was okay.

There was no doom, no stress. She looked at Brynden, who puffed out a cloud of white and turned to her, and her breath caught. The crooked smile returned, his eyes ablaze with an emotion Elyse couldn't place.

"How do you feel, goddess?" he said, keeping his voice low as the other males chatted and smoked.

"Like a great weight lifted from my shoulders. I didn't even know I was holding it until it was gone." She rolled her neck, closing her eyes as her head tilted back in the sun. She smiled at the lightness in her heart, in her chest.

"If I could see that smile every day for the rest of my life, it still wouldn't be enough." Brynden leaned over to kiss her cheek.

"If you could show me everything the world has to offer, then I would smile like this every day." She peeked one eye open towards Brynden, his smile still caught on his face.

"Once more should be enough for you." Brynden handed her back the pipe.

She smoked again, the effects stronger the second time around after her coughing subsided. All her worries vanished—even the ones that always ebbed at the edge of her mind. The sense of being watched, the unease in it, vanished as well.

Was this how normal people felt?

As she looked at the Chorys Dasian males laughing as they smoked, the friendship and relationship they had, Elyse knew she was missing something. A lot of things. Life's simple pleasures of sitting around with friends, joking, and enjoying the moment, were foreign to her. Elyse's heart ached for it. Her hand grasped Brynden's, and she squeezed. "If you can give me a life like this," she whispered to him, "then I will love you until the end of time."

"Of what? Smoking?" he teased, pulling her close to him.

"Moments of peace, of laughter, of friendship. The freedom to be happy and to enjoy life." Elyse turned her gaze to his russet eyes. "I want to live and to love, Brynden. I want to experience everything that's been kept from me."

Brynden swallowed hard, his gaze roaming her face. The world subsided as they stared at one another, an unspoken understanding passing between them. His lips ticked up in a smile and he glanced down, then back at her. Brynden opened his mouth to speak, but his response was cut off.

"You two are awfully quiet over there," Oryck said. "Are you walking her through aithyr?"

Brynden hesitated, pulling his gaze from Elyse. "I don't think I need to walk her through anything. If Fulbryk can keep her up through the night reading, then I think she's ready."

Elyse nodded, remembering her reading. Aithyr was all around them, ever-flowing and ever-present. All she needed to do was have her mind reach out and....

She gasped, not registering what someone said, followed by some chuckles. Instead, she focused on the flow of aithyr all around her. The paths were faint and hazy white. A strong, thick current of energy flowed in front of her before snaking up and over the house. Smaller streams of energy wove through the courtyard, swirling around the males.

Elyse's mind pulled at a smaller stream first, the aithyr drawn to her. Energy entered her body, causing her to gasp again, but the energy stayed thrumming inside.

But what should she do with it?

Thinking back to Fulbryk's, she imagined transferring the energy to her hand, creating fire as Bryden did.

Her hand burst into flames as her surroundings came back into focus. Brynden jumped back while someone else yelled. The flames covered her hand and the cuff of her sleeve. Heat danced over her skin as she watched in amazement. She'd done magic.

Despite being soft and weak like her father suggested, this moment proved otherwise. She could do it. The magic felt incredible, all-empowering. With that kind of power, she could have the freedom to do whatever she wished. She laughed as the flames flickered up from her hand.

Water appeared from Brynden, dousing her hand and sleeve. "Are you okay? How bad is the burn?"

"What are you talking about?" she asked, observing her unmarred skin and dress. "I didn't let it hurt me."

Sylas swore and sat forward in his chair. "And you never touched aithyr before just now?"

"No, but I felt it all around us. I could see what it looked like. Through here—" Elyse sat forward, tracing the strong current of aithyr with her arm "—there was a big stream. I just tried a smaller stream that was closer, though."

Brynden stared at her with his mouth agape. The other males held similar expressions.

"What?"

"Gyrsh is a bloody liar. Your talent could outshine your mother's," Sylas stated. "Even with drugs, most mages can't get that clear of a reading on aithyr, let alone on their first time. Can you create the flames again? And hold it as you did?"

Elyse nodded, focusing on the aithyr once more. That time, she dipped into the strong current, expecting its strength and pulling out a small amount of energy. Like before, she imagined her hand lit in flame and transferred the energy.

Flames licked up her sleeve, heat encompassing her skin but it did not burn.

Bryden reached out his hand to the flame. "It's not an illusion, Sylas," he said, laughing.

"Elyse, can you toss it up and catch it back in your hand?" Sylas asked, his brows furrowed with his attention locked on her.

She bit her tongue as she tossed her hand, focusing on the energy. The flames formed a ball as she tossed it in the air, catching it as it fell.

"Well, I'll be damned." Sylas sat back in his chair, confusion mixed with his scowl as he regarded Elyse.

She let the flames sputter out as the aithyr she held burnt away. "What does this mean?"

"It means I'll have the most beautiful and most talented wife," Brynden said. "That was incredible."

Elyse turned to Brynden with wide eyes, his words registering. He winked before pulling her close to him, his scent and touch mixing with excitement in her chest.

Brynden intended to marry her.

The afternoon wore on with Brynden, Sylas, and Oryck calling out different ways to manipulate aithyr, Daryn consciously remaining quiet. She summoned water, like Brynden, and a wind that blew back his hair. Sylas challenged her to try an illusion—changing the clothing she wore. Her ability to keep using aithyr faltered after an afternoon of effort, and she could change only the color to black.

The effects of Mage's Eye wore off, but Elyse's mood remained light and cheery, slipping into easy conversation.

Brynden called for food and drink, and servants arrived with a platter of olives, cheeses, bread, and meats. They also brought carafes of dark red wine, filling their glasses to the brim.

Elyse picked around the meat, catching Oryck's attention. "Not a fan of goat?"

"Oh, I don't eat meat," she answered, taking a sip of the tart and full-bodied wine.

"Why's that?" Sylas asked between bites.

She hesitated, turning to Brynden.

"Is there a reason?" he asked.

"The scent and flavor make my stomach churn," she offered a tight-lipped smile to Brynden, who gave her a curious look but didn't press further.

Not long after, the sun dipped below the roofline, casting the courtyard in the shade. Brynden clapped his hands. "Well, my friends, I think Elyse and I have done our due diligence on being chaperoned. Now, if you will excuse us, I have a surprise for her upstairs."

Sylas tried to scowl, but a smile cracked through. "Have fun, don't be too long. We have a meeting tonight."

Brynden swatted a hand at him as he led Elyse inside the townhouse.

Chapter Thirty-One

ELYSE

After a quick tour of the townhouse, a question burned at the end of Elyse's tongue, but her stomach churned each time she went to speak. Daryn's behavior made her uncomfortable, and no one bothered to explain it. They all acted as if nothing happened but it did happen.

Who asks to smell someone they didn't know?

Who asks to smell someone they *did* know?

Gods, to think Daryn was also at her father's dinner parties when she was still a child. Unaware of herself and her surroundings, Elyse didn't remember those evenings. Her father would dress her up and place her on the arm of a friend or colleague, softening whatever deal he wanted. The memory of it then made her breath quicken.

"Fascinating," Brynden said, shaking Elyse from her introspection.

"What's fascinating?"

"I can see a thousand thoughts that cross your mind in an instant and yet you share none. You think more and say less than most people." The crooked smile returned to his face as he stopped in the wide hallway of the sixth floor. "Since the night of the ball, I've been dying to know those thoughts."

Elyse broke from his stare with a laugh, rolling her eyes. "Trust me, you do not."

"And why would that be?"

Because they were erratic and dark, but she couldn't tell him that. Elyse hesitated, finding her words. "I'm like shattered glass."

Brynden lifted a brow. "Explain?"

"I'm in tiny, broken pieces and if you try to help put them back together, you're likely to get hurt."

Brynden stepped close, lifting her chin to meet his gaze. "Not true. You are more like a raw diamond fresh from the ground. Resilient, even when mistreated. Led to believe you are nothing before being shaped. But that means you're full of potential, your true form not yet known. When you figure out the way you want to be cut, your true nature will shine."

Tears welled in her eyes as her breath caught. "I wish that were accurate; I'm soft." Weak.

"Would you be standing here today if you were?" Brynden's arms wrapped around her waist, pulling her close. "Would you do things like magic and reading Fulbryk's if you were soft? No, Elyse. I don't know all your pain, but I can see it in you. I've noticed its weight on your shoulders, like that weight lifted earlier today."

Elyse looked up into his face as a tear fell, his fingers brushing it away. "Why are you so kind to me? I don't understand."

Truly, she did not. Brynden owed her nothing—not time, not energy, not kindness. Regardless of the mess Elyse was, he still wanted to be with her.

"Well, my curiosity began at the ball. My young date, daughter of a foreign minister, arrived with a few drinks already in her system—yes, I noticed immediately," he said, smirking.

Elyse bit the inside of her cheek, thinking she had hidden it well.

"That was the first odd thing. The second was your gaze drifting to your father to see if he was checking on you—and he was. I saw the disapproving looks as if you were doing something wrong, which you weren't." Brynden lifted his brows, his mouth pursing. "And then you revealed you read and sing, that your father *forbade* you to share. His adult daughter."

Brynden shook his head, staring down the hall. "If I'm being honest, I asked to court you because it seemed like you have never had any fun."

"So, all of this is because you pity me?" Gods, she was so stupid.

Of course, it was. From the beginning, she realized that Brynden being interested in her after one night was—

"There you go again." Brynden's voice shook her from her head. "The thoughts flying through your mind, I can practically hear them standing this close."

"If this is all for pity, then you've done more than enough." Elyse made to step away, but Brynden held on.

"Maybe it was at first, or so I thought. My mind hasn't known peace since the day I met you. Your pouty lips and honey-colored eyes plague my every thought. I often wonder what you're reading or who you are with. Whether being on top of you, kissing you left you up late at night," he said, smirking.

"Oh, my gods…" Elyse said, her eyes snapping shut. She still regretted telling him she couldn't stop thinking about their first kiss. If she was honest with herself, she also thought that day in the field. But instead of the fiery happiness it should have brought her, she only felt dread. Her father marred that entire day.

"And before the fight with Keyain, when I found you huddled in those flowers, my heart broke, and I realized I cared for you more than pity." Brynden tucked a stray hair behind her ear.

Elyse's breath caught. She could count on one finger the people who have said they cared about her. Brynden might be a stranger but the more she learned of him, the more she found herself hoping. Hoping to leave Satiros and to live happily. Hoping that someone would love her.

"When you admitted to studying magic, betraying your father's wishes, I saw you were forming your own future, and I wanted to be a part of it. So yes, pity was the catalyst, but I'm here right now for you, Elyse." Brynden kissed her forehead and pulled her tight into a hug. His juniper and citrus scent filled her.

Elyse pulled back, staring up at him, her heart rattling in her chest. No one has ever given her much thought, much consideration beyond her face value. A lovely ball of nervous energy, doomed to be insane like her mother.

But Brynden saw. He paid attention. The feelings she felt fell dead on her lips. What could she say to match his intensity?

Elyse hesitated. "Why did Daryn want to smell me?" The need to know caused her to blurt out the question.

"That was not what I expected you to say," he said, taking her hand once more. "Try to forget it for now."

Elyse pulled her hand from his grasp. "Daryn said you thought I smell like honey, peaches, and cream. That I smell like *you* Chorys Dasians." Brynden turned with a frown. "Tell me why he would say that when I smell like none of those things."

Brynden sighed, running a hand over his hair as he thought. "I truly do not know how to explain this, Elyse, but you smell like that to me."

"But I don't smell like those things."

Brynden shrugged. "I can't explain it. You just do. Perhaps our Chorys Dasian noses are different; they can smell things that aren't there. But please, I'm very excited about your surprise."

Unhappy with his answer, Elyse took his hand and strode down the hallway. Honey, peaches, and cream? Was it possible for someone to smell something that was not there?

Within minutes they approached a door, Brynden opening it to a room with a wall of windows. Light from the setting sun turned the gauzy white drapes into gold, the room glowing with radiance.

To one side were plush, ornate couches and chairs of cream and crimson. What sat on the other side caused Elyse to pause with curiosity. "A piano? That's quite the expense for a townhome you don't live in full time." Pianos were for important occasions. Elyse had heard a rumor of one residing within the Royal's Wing.

"I am a male of expensive taste, my goddess. And I am also a male of many talents."

Brynden led her to the black wooden piano, inlaid with gold and mother-of-pearl in swirling details. Before it was a matching bench that he sat on, patting the open spot. "Come, my goddess. I have a request."

Elyse took a seat, giving Brynden some space to move as his fingers slid across the ivory and black keys, filling the room with the bright, clear sounds of the instrument. Awestruck by his playing, Brynden's talent was unexpected, though it was nothing more than warming up his hands.

"You like to sing." He gazed at her with a crooked smile. "I like to play the piano. Would the goddess be so gracious to gift me her voice this evening?"

Elyse's heart hammered in her chest because of his expression shrouded in golden light and that she has never sung for anyone but her mother. "I don't know that many songs—or popular ones. Nothing you could play along to."

"Ah, I had a feeling you would say that. Even if it's just a child's nursery rhyme, I wish to play along with your voice. I've wished to do so since the moment you told me you like to sing."

Elyse's heart swelled, thinking of the songs her mother used to sing. "There is one I loved as a child that always brought my mother to tears. However, I don't remember the name."

"If you sing the first couple lines, I may know it." His fingers glided over the keys with ease.

"What if you don't, and I sound foolish singing alone?" Elyse asked, fidgeting with her cuffs.

"Though I doubt you would sound foolish, you won't know until you try. Experience this with me." Brynden's eyes blazed as he took in Elyse.

She nodded, trying to shake her nervousness. With a deep breath, her sonorous singing voice called out, reciting the song from her childhood.

"*In a land lush with magic and life, our old family keeps. With open ears and open hearts—*" she paused, hearing the piano notes step in time with her singing.

Brynden stared at her with wide eyes, lips parted. "The number of times you have surprised me today is astounding. That is a very old song. How did you learn it?"

Elyse returned his incredulous stare. "My mother. We sang it all the time, and I would sing it to her when she could no longer do so herself."

Brynden shook his head, smiling. "If you start again, I'll jump in with the piano."

Elyse took a shaky breath and started the lines again. *"In a land lush with magic and life, our old family keeps. With open ears and open hearts, we can hear their weeps."*

The piano played along with the slow, melodic pace of her voice, her heart filling with the memories of her mother. *"Lives of thrall and hailing calls, urging to fight that which binds, us to a land that will never be home unless we search our like kind.*

"Through moonlit trees and beachy seas, by twinkling star at night, we wander a-through strangers' worlds, by vigorous will and might. Call thee who lost, on thee who fight, on thee who set worlds alight, and draw on the spirits of the fallen to set our worlds a-right.

"Of feigned descent shed elven blood, one guided by self and a heart of gold. We sing these mourning songs so our stories ought not untold. Rise shall be the favored, a champion for a world lost. One whose choices preferred the bold, free us for that of life cost."

Elyse opened her eyes as the piano ceased, Brynden's gaze fixed on her. "You have the voice of a goddess, a blessing to my ears. Your existence is a gift that I am completely unworthy of." He caressed her cheek. "If you would have me as your husband, then I promise you freedom, a life of happiness, a life of laughter and adventure. I promise you will no longer just be alive, but live. If you will have me, Elyse, I will give you the world. Let me be a part of your future."

"But you don't even know me. You don't—"

"I know everything I need to know," he said as his powerful arms pulled her into his lap, his juniper and citrus scent engulfed her.

"But what if I'm too much to deal with and you—"

"I can handle anything you throw at me." Brynden leaned towards her face.

Gods, this wasn't up to her. "Brynden, you're making a mistake."

"Then let me make it because you would be the greatest mistake of my life." Brynden kissed her, confident as he pulled Elyse tight to his body.

Elyse's head spun, unsure what to make of the proposal. Her father would decide, but gods… she wanted it. If that day was a taste of what her life could be, then she would greedily drink every drop Brynden promised. "You still need to ask my father," she said, pulling back from his face. "That isn't a decision I can make."

"I'm asking if *you* want to be my wife. I have ways to ensure Gyrsh agrees if that's what you wish. But it is up to you—it's your decision," he said while kissing along her jaw.

Her decision without her father. A life free of his lectures and punishment. A life of Brynden sweeping her off her feet, showing her everything she has missed. A life married to *him*, in Chorys Dasi, *living*.

The answer was clear. "Yes," Elyse whispered, her hand cupping his face.

His russet eyes glittered, smiling as she kissed him. Soft at first, as if she needed to hold herself back from him, but then she let go. Brynden would save her from Satiros, and she let go of any reservation she had, kissing him frantically as if stopping would make the proposal untrue.

He met her eagerness, kissing down Elyse's jaw, then her neck with teeth grazing her skin. Arched against him, she let out a breath, shifting her back to his front. His mouth continued to her bare shoulders, her core heating as tension built.

"Is this okay?" he murmured into her skin, a hand at the tie of her corset. Through the slit of her skirt, she felt the other hand grasp her thigh.

"Yes," she gasped, her blood like fire in her veins.

Brynden loosened the ties and the fabric fell, the afternoon light coloring her exposed skin golden. His hands reached around her, the rough tips of his fingers tracing lines on her breasts as he continued to kiss her neck and shoulder. "I want to give you every experience. I want to make you feel everything good in this world." Elyse gasped as his fingers brushed over the tips.

"Please," she moaned, arching into him again as pleasure shuddered through her body.

Brynden cradled her in his arms, holding her as he stood and crossed the room. With careful movements, he lowered her to the couch, laying himself on top.

Elyse's hands hooked behind his head, pulling Brynden close. The taste of wine was heavy on his lips, his hair like silk between her fingers. Brynden drove his hips against her as the soft kisses traveled down her neck and onto her... oh, gods. Elyse arched when he kissed her breast, his tongue flicking the tip. A hand traveled up her skirt, fingers tracing up the inside of her thighs.

Chaos filled her. Thoughts disappeared and her hesitation gone, leaving heat flaring in her center and crackling under her skin. Each of Brynden's movements set her alight, causing her to gasp and shudder.

His grazing hands ventured higher, toying with the edge of her undergarments as his free hand lifted her dress to her waist, leaving little to hide behind. Pleasure ripped through her core as he pressed against her, his fingers rubbing and teasing.

"Is this okay? You look terrified," Brynden said, looking up with his liquid stare. He swallowed hard, breathing as heavy as her.

"Don't stop," she gasped.

A wicked smile came to his face as he gazed at her, his fingers slipping under the scrap of fabric remaining between them. She sighed a breathy moan as his fingers filled her, causing her back to arch again.

Soft lips brushed the inside of her thighs as his fingers moved, his thumb brushing the cluster of nerves outside. Tension coiled tighter, almost too much for her. When his fingers curled against her inner wall, her pleasure snapped with a cry, squeezing Brynden between her thighs. Her hips bucked as it coursed from her center to her limbs in euphoric waves.

"You're dripping for me, my goddess," Brynden murmured against her skin as he peeled back the bit of fabric remaining. "I wonder if you taste as sweet as you look."

Elyse whimpered as his lips moved up her thighs, Brynden's kisses growing harder, less restrained. Hunger took over as his mouth claimed her, his tongue hot against her center. A strangled cry left her mouth once more, and Brynden pulled back, kissing around the sensitive area, teasing.

"Please," she heard herself say, her voice far away.

A deep laugh emanated from him. "I love it when you beg." The flick of his tongue sent a jolt through her, her legs quivering.

A knock at the door pulled Elyse out of it, her heart racing from the heat of the moment.

"We're busy," Brynden growled without lifting his mouth from her. Elyse glanced down to find Brynden's gaze fixed on her.

The knocking came again.

"I said we're—"

Sylas stood in the doorway, irritation lacing his features.

Elyse snapped her arms to her chest, thankful that Brynden blocked Sylas from seeing the rest of her.

The male looked at Brynden, then at Elyse. "Sauntyr arrived. So did Gyrsh. He's asking where you two are at."

Gyrsh. Her father.

"Oh, fuck. Oh, gods." Elyse jerked away from Brynden. Memories of her father's anger after *the incident* played in her mind. Her breathing turned ragged. At least the fight wasn't her acting against his wishes.

But to be alone with Brynden in a room, unsupervised?

Elyse swore under her breath as she stood, turning away from Sylas so she could hide her chest. The dress dipped lower on her back as she shifted to pull it up with one hand.

Brynden's hand stopped her, his grip firm. "That's why your hip hurts." His voice was a deadly calm, the malice in his tone clear without Elyse needing to turn around.

"Please, let go."

Brynden pulled the dress lower, gasping as he took in her hip, side, and below. His breathing hitched as Sylas closed the door.

"Stop, you're embarrassing me," she cried, tears welling in her eyes. Brynden didn't need to see that shame. Her father's anger bruised into her skin.

"Why?"

"Because I don't want you to see!" Her anger lashed out as she jerked away from his grasp, pulling the dress up.

When Elyse turned to him, fully covered, his stare was icy, his jaw set. "No. Why is there a bruise from the top of your hip to down below your ass?" He stood from the couch, Sylas calling his name in warning. "Gyrsh? From him, right?"

Elyse froze, not letting her tears fall. She felt humiliated, holding her loosened dress around herself, answering questions she never wanted Brynden to ask.

"I know it was him." Brynden's voice cracked with emotion. "Why? And how?"

Elyse's lips quivered, and she closed her eyes. "It was my fault you and Keyain fought. I embarrassed him. Not being ready, running from you. He learned every detail because people from court told him. It was my fault, he was—"

"No," Brynden snapped. "Stop. There is no reason for it. None." He paced before the couch, his breathing heavy.

"Brynden," Sylas warned, trying to get his attention.

"It wasn't your fault—you even tried to stop it."

"Brynden," Sylas warned again, walking towards them.

He ignored his friend. Brynden ceased pacing, tapping the tip of his boot against the floor, revealing a blade that popped out of the heal. "I'm going to kill him." Elyse's breath caught from both the surprising weapon and the imminent threat.

"Az!" Sylas yelled that time, tearing Brynden from his thoughts. "Get your shit together. You're terrifying her."

Brynden turned his gaze to Elyse, fear and anger lining his face with wide eyes. "But he can't... he's been doing this all along, hasn't he?"

Elyse clutched her dress tighter to herself as Sylas approached, her breathing ragged. "Az?" she asked. "That's twice today your friends have called you that."

Sylas stepped closer, causing her to recoil. With his hands splayed in front of him, he said, "It's a childhood nickname abbreviated. And please, let me help. Someone needs to tie your dress." Gone was the irritation in his face from when he entered, replaced with softness, concern.

"Is that true, or are you lying like the smell thing?" Elyse asked, letting him approach.

Sylas stiffened at the comment, looking at Brynden, who was wide-eyed.

"I didn't lie. I just don't know how to explain it." Brynden took a shaky breath. "And Az is a nickname for those closest to me, and I won't use it when conducting business."

Unconvinced, Elyse nodded. Why would he lie? Maybe he wasn't about the scent thing. She might have smelled like that to him, though it made little sense. And Az was a simple enough name to be a nickname for anything.

"What we need to focus on," Sylas said as he tied up her corset with gentle hands, "is getting you two downstairs. Now. Your uncle doesn't enjoy starting late."

"Uncle?" Elyse turned to Sylas, the scent of amber and pine trailing from him.

"Sauntyr is his uncle and he just arrived from Chorys Dasi, here to meet with us and your father," he said, frowning and taking a step backward.

"Elyse can't go back to him." Brynden strode past to look out the window. "Not tonight, not after this."

"Then we'll retrieve her from the palace after the meeting, for which she cannot be here. We'll work out the *details* with Gyrsh after the meeting while your uncle is here." A handkerchief appeared in Sylas's hand, offering it to Elyse. "Here, wipe your face."

She nodded, thankful for the gesture. "Do you think I can actually come back here? My father won't allow it."

A slight smile came to Brynden's lips. "I have a way around it. A way that will force him to agree. When we head downstairs, don't acknowledge your father."

"But that would be odd if I didn't."

"Not if I'm the one introducing you to Sauntyr," Brynden said confidently, offering her a small bit of hope.

Elyse kept her chin high as they walked into the sitting room, a small smile on her face. She clutched onto Brynden's arm, careful to avoid her father's burning gaze.

A slight touch on her shoulder came from Sylas. "Relax, you're doing fine. Brynden and I are here to help. You're not alone," he whispered.

Thankful for his encouragement, she offered him a smile and mouthed a thank you. From over his shoulder, Oryck had a bemused look on his face, as if he knew he had missed something yet again and was hoping to see the drama unfold.

"Ready?" Brynden murmured, guiding her through the small group of strangers.

"Yes," was all she managed. Every nerve in her body was aware of her father's glare, Brynden striding right past him to his uncle.

"Ah, there you are," said an older male, traces of gray trailing through rough, tied-back hair. Though he addressed Brynden, his intense stare was on Elyse. Thin scars crossed over the top of his nose, one end curling as he smiled at her.

"Uncle, glad you made it safe." Brynden clasped his hand, keeping one arm around Elyse. "May I introduce you to Elyse?"

As Brynden instructed when they journeyed downstairs, Elyse took the male's hand and tilted her head down. "Lady Elyse Norymial. A pleasure to meet you."

His eyes darted to Elyse's father, then to Brynden, before falling back on her. "Elyse, I have heard of you. I'm Lord Sauntyr Vazlyte. It's a pleasure to meet you as well." He turned his attention back to Brynden. "She isn't staying for the meeting, is she?"

"No, uncle," Brynden said. "I'm about to send her home. But I'd like you to meet my betrothed before she left."

Surprise flickered across Sauntyr's face, eyes glancing again to where her father stood. "I was unaware of such a union." The male grabbed her hand, pressing a slow kiss into the back of it. When he rose, a slight smile lined his lips and he gave a subtle nod to Brynden. "May I be the first to welcome you to our family."

"Thank you, Sauntyr," she said, trying to shake the nervousness from her voice.

Brynden squeezed Elyse's arm, kissing her cheek as they left his uncle. With long, quick strides, he led her to the entryway and down the front steps to where a carriage waited. "You were perfect, absolutely perfect."

"Well, it angered my father. I could feel him watching us," she said, fidgeting with her cuffs.

"But it's done. My uncle gave his blessing for us to marry, which is what I was hoping would happen."

"So I can come back with you tonight? Here?" Elyse's eyes widened with hope. She wouldn't survive with her father after what happened tonight.

"Yes," he said, pulling her close. "I'll come to get you when I can, and we'll give you a separate room, of course. Wouldn't want to start too many rumors. Though perhaps I'll wander my way there to finish what we started earlier."

Elyse shook her head. "I wouldn't expect anything less." She hesitated before adding, "Thank you."

"For what, my goddess?" His thumb stroked the back of her hand as they stood there clasped together.

"For not only giving me hope but following through on it. To think—" her words choked. "Thank you," she whispered into his chest as she leaned into him.

"Thank you for surviving this long, for giving me this chance to be with you," he murmured into her hair.

And she felt Brynden meant it, that he truly was thankful she was alive and there with him. The pain and torment she experienced were contrasted by the brightness her future offered. Elyse could be a mage, wife to a male who adored her, and free from Satiros.

As Brynden gave her one last kiss, closing the carriage door, she saw her father in the townhouse's doorway. Thankful didn't describe how she felt towards Brynden when she saw her father's expression, the pure malice swallowing his features. Elyse had only seen that expression once before.

The day her mother died.

Chapter Thirty-Two

ELYSE

Warmth filled Elyse's chest as she combed through King Wyltam's bookshelves and collected her notes on Fulbryk's principles of magic. Brynden only mentioned one night at their townhouse, but she had the inkling that it would be longer.

After pacing in the suite for an hour, Elyse had decided she would need her notes and books. Unsure of when the Chorys Dasians would arrive, she has hastily ventured to the library.

The reality of the situation hadn't hit her yet, that she was to marry Brynden. That he would take her away from that gods forsaken palace. The hope of a better future made everything look brighter, her steps lighter.

The choice was a touch impulsive, Elyse had to admit. She didn't know him well, knew nothing of Chorys Dasi. But it would all work out, because anything was better than her current life.

A knock sounded, bringing Elyse out of her thoughts. Curious, she cracked the door. "Brynden? How did you find me here?" With furrowed brows, she attempted to block the doorway.

Still donning the ridiculous ruffled shirt, he gave her a wide smile, picking her up with a hug. "There's my future wife. I arrived at your suite only to realize you weren't there. Where else would my goddess be if not in the library? The guards pointed me in the right direction. Now I am here." A soft kiss met her lips as he set her back down.

"Gods, you reek of alcohol. Are… are you drunk?"

Brynden shrugged with a smile. "We had a drink celebrating our betrothal. Or maybe more than a few drinks, but I'm fine." He kissed her

on her forehead.

Based on smell alone, it was many drinks. She sighed with a shake of her head. "I'll be ready to leave in a moment. Wait here while I collect a few things." She hurried back into the room.

In the desk drawer, Elyse searched for her notes on *The History of Lyken Fulbyrk*. The information in her next book dove deeper into the third principle and wanted to refer to it as she read.

Brynden staggered through the doorway. "What is this?"

"Not mine, and you're not allowed in here." Elyse walked to him, pushing him out with a gentle effort. "Please, just wait out here."

His strong arms wrapped around her, his gaze missing nothing. "But I wish to see where my dear goddess spends her days. Let me indulge in my curiosity."

"It's not my rule, Brynden," she said, trying to push him out. Somehow they ended up further in the room, his eyes scanning the books. "I will get in trouble if we don't leave."

"By who?"

"By... the person whose room this is." She attempted to push him towards the door and horribly lost.

"Interesting," he said, grabbing an unfamiliar object on the bookshelf. Geometric glass with a series of symbols on its face.

"Please put that back. You need to leave the room."

Brynden placed the object in her hand, causing a series of symbols to glow. "Fascinating," he said as he craned his neck to watch. "I wouldn't have thought that." He spoke under his breath, a smile spreading wider on his face.

"You need to leave, Brynden," Elyse said, pulling her hand back. She glanced at the door, nervous that someone would catch him in here. The King had been clear—no one else was allowed. Now Brynden ignored her as she tried to usher him out. Her stomach dropped, feeling helpless against the situation.

With a sly grin, he grabbed the object from her hand and dropped it, the glass shattering at her feet. "Let's keep that a secret."

"Brynden!" Elyse took a step back, her mind racing at his behavior. "What are you doing? Why aren't you listening—" Shards littered where she walked, causing her to lose balance. Elyse slipped backward, glass tearing into the skin of her forearms as she landed on her back.

"Oh, fuck. Elyse, are you alright?" Brynden said, kneeling to offer his hand.

"Get away from me!" She scurried back, away from his outstretched hand. "If this is how you act when you drink, then I need to reconsider my future."

"Goddess, you're bleeding. Let me help you."

At the raise of his hand, Elyse flinched. The reaction was involuntary, one her body knew to do, and it caused a flash of grief in Brynden's expression.

The stark reality hit her. Elyse didn't know him, didn't know how he acted when drunk or how often he drank. Foolish. She would jump from one bad situation to another. She shook her head as tears began to fall. "You should leave."

"Sylas is waiting for us," Brynden said, holding out his hand.

She stared at it, shaking her head. "He's waiting for you."

"No, don't act like that." He laughed, the sound weak as his expression changed from worry to fear. "I promise I didn't mean anything by it, goddess."

Elyse swallowed hard, mustering up a glare as she stared at his face. "You need to leave. Now."

"That would be a wise decision." A deep voice came from the doorway. King Wyltam walked slowly into the room, hands clasped behind his back. "Elyse, perhaps I wasn't clear."

Her limbs numbed at his appearance, the sudden fear of losing magic, the last thing that gave her hope. "He wouldn't listen to me. I tried to get him to leave."

King Wyltam's stare landed on her arms, to where blood seeped from the glass digging into her flesh.

"It's alright. We were about to leave." Brynden tossed a glance over his shoulder as he reached for Elyse. She pulled her arm out of his grasp.

In a few quick strides, King Wyltam loomed over Brynden's shoulder. He grabbed him, jerking him back with a force she hadn't anticipated. "Who the fuck are you?"

Brynden scrambled from the grip, fighting to push back but fell short as they reached the door. King Wyltam raised his hand and a blast of wind struck Brynden, sending him flying into the library beyond the doorway.

"King Wyltam!" Elyse pushed herself up, breath caught in her chest. Brynden groaned as he picked himself up. A menacing glare held his expression.

"Who is he, Elyse?" the King asked. "What is he doing here?"

"Brynden Vazlyte of Chorys Dasi, my betrothed," she said, her voice small as she approached on unsteady legs. "Or was my betrothed." Brynden's face fell at her words.

"And Brynden, a foreigner, is in my personal office because you invited him?" the King continued.

Elyse took a steadying breath as her heart raced. "Of course not. I was collecting my things when he came in."

"I came to escort Elyse," Brynden said, eyes locked on her.

"Escort her?" King Wyltam inspected Brynden from head to toe, his eyes narrowing. "Explain to me, *Brynden* from Chorys Dasi, why I find you in my personal study with my noblewoman wounded?"

"You're studying magic for King Wyltam?" Brynden shook his head. "Elyse, we should go—"

The King held out his arm in front of Elyse, as if she would walk to him. No, the male that she thought she'd marry was someone different.

"You come to my court, break into my office, and damaged not only my property, but also hurt Elyse." The King paused, glancing at her. "She claims you were betrothed, which is news to me."

"That's because Gyrsh and I just settled it."

Gods, how much did he drink? Brynden swayed where he stood.

"Good, I just sent a message to Gyrsh. He'll be here in a moment, and so will Keyain. They'll love to hear your reasons." The King placed his hands in his pocket, his expression unreadable even as he threatened Brynden.

Panicked, a chill washed over her body. Not her father, not when she was so close to being free of him. "King Wyltam, please," Elyse pleaded. "It was an accident with an object on the shelf. I dropped it, then slipped in the glass."

"Elyse?" Keyain's voice called out, his heavy footfalls sounding. "You're bleeding. What happened?" In a crumpled tunic covered by a jacket, Keyain appeared and halted as Brynden came into view, his gaze turning feral. "You. What did you do?"

"Keyain, it was my fault please—"

"Of course it was your fault, you stupid girl." Her father arrived behind Keyain, the fury on his face joined with a new red welt. "Betrothed less than a couple of hours and already ruined it?"

"You don't talk to her." Brynden took a staggering step towards her father, lips pulled back and his finger pointed. "You're lucky Sylas pulled me off you or else I would have—"

"Are you saying you attacked another minister?" Keyain said, reaching for the sword at his waist.

Elyse stepped forward, the King's hand reaching out to keep her back. "Keyain, please—"

"Gyrsh deserved it. Unless you think it's okay for him to be hitting her." Brynden steadied himself, fury clear on his face.

Keyain turned, his eyes growing wide. "He's doing it again?"

"You knew? You fucking knew and left Elyse with him?" Brynden suddenly became calm, turning to her. "Let's go. Someone at the townhouse can heal you."

"No," the King, Keyain, and her father all said at once.

"She's my betrothed," Brynden argued. "I'm not leaving this fucking palace without her."

"If you keep this up, you won't be leaving at all." Keyain's hand fell to the hilt of his sword. "And Elyse sure as fuck isn't going anywhere with you."

Elyse watched in silent horror as the males debated what they wanted of her—debated her future—while refusing to listen to her. Waves of fury rose from her gut to her head, causing a roaring in her ears. No more. She wouldn't sit by any longer.

"Stop it!" she screamed, her breathing ragged. "I've had enough of you all deciding for me what I can and can't do! Stop making my decisions and stop talking like I'm not here. I don't belong to any of you." She glared first at Keyain, to Brynden, then at her father. "I'm done."

Elyse sidestepped around King Wyltam's still out-stretched hand, offering a sympathetic glance at Brynden. "I don't want to marry you, not after this." She stormed towards the library's exit.

"Elyse, please," Brynden called, his voice cracking.

"Don't move," Keyain growled. There was scuffling and a loud thud, Elyse not bothering to turn back.

The King's voice carried through the library, loud enough for her to hear. "Gyrsh, we get to have a nice long chat, it seems." Though she had never seen the King show much of any emotion, his words dripped like venom.

The stinging in her arms subsided from her attention as she passed rows of shelves, mind spinning. Sure, Brynden was drunk, but why didn't he listen? When she pushed him back, why did he fight?

She was incredibly, helplessly stupid. An hour ago, she couldn't contain her happiness. A future with a handsome male sweeping her off her feet. A new city of freedom, a life worth living. How foolish was she to think it would happen?

Silent tears streaked her face. The life she lived that day—sitting around with friends, magic, singing, being *wanted*—it was all a lie, things she could never have. But since she tasted the freedom of that life, her future stuck within Satiros became more damning.

She would die here.

She would die.

Anxious to be far away from the library, Elyse hurried through the exit with her head down, bumping into someone.

"Oof, sorry—Elyse?" Sylas stopped, gazing into the library and then to her arms, his face paling. "What did he do now?"

"Nothing." Elyse walked past him, but his hand caught her shoulder.

"Elyse, please. You're bleeding. What in the hells happened?"

She swallowed hard. "Brynden is a drunken ass. Clearly I made a mistake by accepting his offer to marry me."

His jaw tightened as he sighed. "Where is he now?"

"In there with my father, Keyain, and King Wyltam."

Sylas swore, his hand pushing back the curls that hung in his eyes. "You need to see someone for your wounds."

"You need to go grab your friend before Keyain draws his sword."

"Are you okay to walk by yourself? Oryck can grab Az, and I can take you to get help." Sylas's brows were drawn together, his voice gentler than she expected from a male who spent the day scowling and rolling his eyes.

"The infirmary isn't far. I'll be fine by myself," she said, giving him a sad smile. "Just get him out of here before he does anything else."

Sylas nodded, hesitating before entering the library. The indistinguishable yelling from the males echoed down the hallway as Elyse took off.

Even with healing, Elyse's arms ached. The stinging from the cuts irritated her, but she refused to take medicine for the pain, even when the nurse dug through the wounds looking for shards.

Across from her was another pain. Keyain ran through the night's events with her. Again. For the fifth time. Elyse stifled a yawn behind her hand as Keyain recited his questions. "And at no point, you felt threatened by Brynden?"

"No."

"Even as he resisted you after you told him to leave? When you fell?"

"No, Keyain."

"Okay. And earlier in the day, when he saw your bruise, he wasn't forcing himself on you?"

"For the last time, no."

"Look, Elyse, I understand that you're upset, but we need to talk," he said, setting his notebook and charcoal into his lap. "How many times has Gyrsh done this since the end of our betrothal?"

"Once." Elyse left out the times he had threatened to inflict harm.

"Is that why you want to marry Brynden?" The question was a trap, one set in the middle of questions she was routinely answering at that point.

"No, but it helped make the decision easier." That part was true enough.

"Okay, I'm going to lay out the situation from how I see it. Your father, who is abusing you again, introduced you to Brynden, a foreign lord only he knows. You meet him three times, then decide to marry him, a stranger, and move to a city-state you don't know. Then—"

"If you're going to patronize me, then you can just leave."

Keyain furrowed his brows, frowning. "Just listen, please. Brynden has fought me, hit your father, and nearly launched himself at King Wyltam in the library. We know nothing of this male, save for what your father tells us, which at this point means nothing."

"Just say what you mean."

Keyain brushed a hand through his hair, mussing it, giving Elyse a sobering look. "King Wyltam and I talked. Brynden is banned from the palace and your betrothal is over."

"Funny," she drawled, picking at her nails. "I thought I ended the betrothal, but sure. Let's give you credit." Her heart squeezed at the thought. The decision to walk away from her only chance to be free of Satiros was painful, and she didn't even get the credit for deciding it.

Keyain nodded his head. "Something is off about him, Elyse. I don't know what you saw in him but he's completely unhinged."

Elyse laughed dryly, shaking her head. "I would do almost anything to leave here, Keyain." Her voice cracked with emotion.

"What do you mean?" Keyain asked, his tone softening.

"This palace, this court—it's a prison. If I stay here, I won't make it."

Elyse's heart ached as she spoke the truth. "Brynden was my chance to escape, to be free."

"You want to leave Satiros? And not just your father?"

She took a steadying breath as tears fell. "How is that news to you? How could you, the person who knows me better than anyone else, my only friend, not understand how much I hate it here?"

Keyain stared at her in silence, contemplating his words. "Perhaps you would hate it less if you made friends with the other—"

"Fuck you," Elyse snapped, her glare cutting to Keyain. "Did you forget why I don't talk to them? How you wanted to *investigate* what happened that night? I will never forgive her." She swallowed hard. "Now that you have Marietta, I'm truly alone again."

"Is that what this is all about? Me ending our betrothal?"

"Is that a joke? Our betrothal was never real, not when you were already married to Marietta. And I never wanted to marry you, not really."

"You and Marietta have that in common," he said, wiping his face with his hands, sitting back. Guilt flooded in her chest, not knowing of his marriage problems. "Would all of this help if you didn't have to live with Gyrsh? If you didn't have to interact with him?"

Could she keep going if he wasn't in the picture? Elyse tore at a hangnail, the skin stinging. "What would that look like?"

"Tomorrow, King Wyltam will submit the paperwork to Minister Dyieter about you emancipating from your father. You would move to your own room within the Noble's Section. Gyrsh could not talk to you or approach you, but you would also lose any financial support from him.

"In exchange for room and living expenses, you will work for King Wyltam regarding magical research in secret and stay your title of Lady." Keyain sighed before continuing. "As for your position on the Queen's Court, that is at Queen Valeriya's discretion, though I don't think she'll remove you."

"And I could keep studying magic?" Hope blossomed in her chest. If anything else, she would have magic. Being a mage would be a greater freedom than some emissary's wife, right? It had to be. Though the loss of

Brynden hurt, the possibility of her new future dampened the pain.

"Yes, though I want to ask when did this start happening?" Keyain shifted in his seat, his brows lowered and pulled closer together.

"A bit ago. He saw me reading a book on magic in the library and offered his resources." She hesitated, then added, "He mentioned my mother had been a mage."

Keyain nodded his head. "She was. From what I heard, she was extraordinary."

"So you knew as well but never told me." Elyse dropped her hands to her lap, the hot burn of anger rising to her cheeks.

"It was better for you to not know, especially with how…." His voice trailed off as he stopped himself.

"How she wasted away?" Elyse shook her head. "I'd rather know than be ignorant."

Keyain ingested her words, no emotion breaking through his mask. "Will you comply with the emancipation? We can have your stuff moved into a new room by tomorrow afternoon. Tonight, you can remain in the infirmary."

Elyse slumped back against the wall on the bed. "Sure," she said, her mood deflated. How many people knew about her mother? That Elyse could be like her? Even Sylas had known of her mother's skill. The frustration built in the back of her throat, tightening as emotion swelled. She was a puppet, and the men in her life held the strings. Elyse swore to give everything into being a mage so she could cut those strings. No husband, father, friend, or king would decide for her again.

Keyain nodded as he stood. His hand clasped her knee before walking towards the door. "I'm really sorry, Elyse. For everything. If you're looking for a friend, I think Marietta could use someone. Like you, she only has me in this court. You're the only person I would trust with her."

Gods, being friends with his wife after they were betrothed was an agonizing thought. Even if Marietta didn't resent her, there was still the humiliation. Grytaine would thrive with insults. She nodded. Keyain patted her knee and left the room, leaving Elyse with her thoughts.

There was no more Brynden, no more Chorys Dasi. There would be no more days like that afternoon, where she could sit around with friends, feeling relaxed—feeling alive. The thoughts ached; but at least she had magic, and she wouldn't have her father.

There was a chance that, maybe, she could survive a bit longer.

Chapter Thirty-Three

MARIETTA

Tilan's deceptions tore through Marietta, and her life continued in a haze around her. Servants came and went. Keyain came and went. Everything in between was lost, faded to her. Nothing mattered. Her life was a lie.

During the days she felt best, which were still plagued by the silent, unyielding pain threatening to consume her, she would wander through the suite. Keyain kept a blanket and pillow on the couch, opting to sleep separately from her.

Marietta didn't mind. It didn't matter either way. Keyain would get what he wanted in the end. That was the point of her being there, after all. What else did she have to live for, if not whatever future Keyain planned?

Because she had nothing else. No home. No friends. No business. Lies built that life. Consumed it. Returning to it wasn't an option, not when she now knew the truth.

So she drifted through the suite, present only physically as she dug deep into the hollowness of herself, hating every memory that flashed before her.

One afternoon, she sat in her vanity chair placed before the bedroom window. Thick fog hovered over the Central Garden, a slight mist coating the glass with a layer of dew. She watched as moisture would gather, form larger droplets, and then drip down the pane. Over and over. Dripping like tears. Like blood. Continuous with the unrelenting fog.

"Mar," Keyain whispered, a hand falling on her shoulder.

She barely heard him, barely noticed his touch, continuing to stare at

the window.

With a sigh, Keyain knelt next to her, a hand cupping her face. She stared past him, eyes locked to the dew that dripped.

"Mar, we can't continue like this. You can't continue like this." He brushed the hair out of her face.

His voice sounded far away, echoing in her mind as she blocked him out. To look at Keyain was to remember all the lies, all the pain.

"Come, join me for dinner. You need to eat more." He stood, his hand running through her hair. Keyain waited a moment, leaving when she never answered.

The afternoon sunshine fell onto Marietta as she stared out the window, watching a gentle wind blow through the greenery of the Central Garden. As late spring gave way to early summer, courtiers wandered through the paths, enjoying the season's kind weather.

That time of year usually excited Marietta. When the cold of winter was far behind, and the promise of the endless sun for the months ahead energized her spirit. But she felt nothing.

Last spring, her bakery was busy with wedding celebrations. In Enomenos, sunny weather was a good wedding day omen, meaning most couples waited until the start of summer to wed. Marietta would bake cakes, pies, and other treats for the revelry that followed ceremonies, often staying late to celebrate because she was never just the baker. She was always a guest, too.

Stress left Tilan on edge, and Marietta thought it was from her busier-than-usual schedule and his work. To help, she baked his favorite treat, tart lemon bars with a vanilla crust. The apology brought a smile to his face, and he said she had done nothing wrong. Tilan assured her that he loved her more than anything and considered himself the luckiest man to have such a thoughtful wife.

That was a lie. Work didn't bring him stress—at least not smithing. His work with the Exisotis would have increased with the impending war.

In hindsight, Marietta could clearly see all the signs. Stressed plagued him not because she was busy and going out every night but because he knew the threat of Keyain was looming. As tensions grew with Satiros, the possibility of him making a move grew more and more likely; yet Tilan never told Marietta. He had let her believe all was right with the world. Why did he lie to her? Why did he have to lie?

"Gods, Marietta," someone hissed behind her. Amryth appeared at her side, a hand falling to her shoulder. "Keyain said you were sick, not that you were wasting away. You haven't been eating, have you?"

When she didn't answer, Amryth knelt next to her. "When's the last time you bathed?"

Marietta continued to stare out the window, wishing Amryth would leave. Since her secret was out, Amryth wore the leather armor of the guards. She had her box braids pulled back into a tail. Marietta sighed when Amryth pulled her out of her seat, leading her to the bathroom. When she helped Marietta out of her nightgown and into the tub, she didn't protest. The sooner she let it happen, the sooner she'd leave.

"Now I know something is wrong," she murmured. "Lady independence who doesn't need help with anything is letting me do something for her."

Marietta let out a sharp breath, irritation from the comment lingering. If she came to mock her, then she could leave.

Amryth laughed as she tilted Marietta's hair back into the water. "You can continue not speaking, but I know that resentful sigh."

She cut her a glare but didn't give her the satisfaction of responding.

"This is the longest I've heard you stay silent," she said after a moment, working oils through Marietta's curls. "Perhaps if I look outside, I'll see pigs flying."

Marietta's grip on the side of the tub tightened.

"Or maybe all the flowers in the Central Garden are dead. A pilinos serves as Queen of Satiros—"

Marietta jerked away, her anger winning against the dulled senses that plagued her. "Why are you here?" she snapped, turning to Amryth.

"There she is," Amryth said, offering a smile. "The Marietta I've come to know wouldn't mope and remain silent. Whatever happened between you and Keyain must have been dreadful." She turned Marietta's head forward, then dipped her head back to rinse. "I came to apologize."

Marietta scoffed, her gaze finding Amryth. "I should be sorry. Your wife died because of me."

"She died because of Keyain," she said, running her hand through Marietta's hair. "Because he lied to us about you."

Marietta shifted out of her grasp, turning to face her. "But I held the knife; I stabbed someone with it, and I don't know if they lived."

Amryth's hands dropped, her brows furrowing. After a moment, she closed her eyes and took a deep breath. "Though I don't know if you truly had done it, I forgive you. You were defending yourself, something I'd also do in your position."

"But she was your wife! How are you not upset?"

With a sad smile, Amryth shook her head. "I'm devastated. Each day I wake up and am forced to remember that she's gone." She paused, taking a breath. "I've been seeking help at the temple of Therypon—the goddess of healing and pain. A friend took me to her after it all happened."

Marietta shook her head, tears falling. "But that doesn't absolve me—"

"Stop, please. I've made my peace through Therypon's help." She handed Marietta a bar of soap with a washcloth, her eyes cast upwards. "I'm still mourning, of course, but it doesn't feel like I'm..." Her voice trailed off, eyes searching for the right word.

"Suffocating?"

"Yes," she said, looking back at Marietta. "The grief is no longer suffocating, which I guess you've also been experiencing."

Marietta hugged her legs, setting her head on her knees. "I don't know what happens next. Whatever life Keyain planned, I don't want to live it. I'd rather be...." Her voice trailed off as emotion choked her.

Amryth hushed her, a hand rubbing across her back. "There's always a way forward. If you're feeling up to it, I can take you to Therypon's temple. She isn't a fix-all solution, but that suffocating feeling? It'll ease, I promise."

Marietta nodded her head. "I would like to go, even if it's getting out of this room."

"And wearing something other than silk nightclothes," Amryth said with a chuckle.

"Do a lot of people go to her temple?" Marietta asked, remembering her friends in Enomenos who went to the temples. Rarely did they ever share their experiences. That was partially because she never asked.

"I would say over a third of the city-state visits at least one of the temples on a regular basis."

Marietta jerked her head at that. "Of just the pilinos population?"

"Including them, but also the non-noble elves of Satiros. Those who are of middle and lower status often visit the temples or actively worship one of the deities."

The non-noble elves don't reject the temples, unlike Keyain. Her heart deflated at the thought, sinking back into the water. "He'll never let me go," she whispered.

"I can talk to Keyain about going," Amryth said, "but it'd be best to hear it from you."

With the washcloth lathered, Marietta scrubbed herself. "Keyain doesn't listen to me."

"Well, there's no harm in asking him," Amryth said, standing to grab a towel.

But Amryth didn't know Keyain, know how controlling he could be. Gods, he wouldn't let her out of the suite, so how would she leave the palace?

She shook the thoughts from her head, ignoring the doubt that clawed its way back in. Something had to change—Keyain had said as much. Marietta struggled to ignore the hope that rose in her chest.

Amryth remained for the afternoon, letting the silence remain between them. The quiet was peaceful, welcoming. At one point, Marietta asked about the goddess Therypon and how she helped. And though the goddess couldn't heal away emotional pain, what had helped Amryth was praying to her in the temple's silence and clearing her head of thought and emotion.

It sounded like it could help Marietta, but Keyain would say no, wouldn't he? When they were together in Enomenos, it was clear he found the temples and their followers untrustworthy. After all his effort to keep Marietta locked in the suite, would he really let her go?

You can't continue like this. Those were Keyain's words, but did he mean them?

When the sun began to set, Keyain returned to the suite with his button-down shirt already untucked and hair disheveled. Marietta waited for him to notice her at the dining room table, sitting with a book left unread next to her.

He furrowed his brows as he reviewed the open file in his hands before giving Marietta a double-take. "Mar, you're up." He closed the files as he approached and set them down on the table. "And dressed."

"Amryth came by."

Keyain sighed, mussing his hair more. "I told her to stay away after…."

"Of course you did," Marietta said, a frown tugging at her lips.

"I see she got you out of the nightgowns. Did you eat today too?"

"Yes, a little."

"A full meal?"

She thought back to the handful of grapes and cheese Amryth goaded her to eat. "More than usual."

He nodded his head, a smile hinting at his lips. "That's good—an improvement. Are you feeling better?"

She sighed and gestured to the seat across from her. "Can you sit so we can talk?"

With furrowed brows and a nervous glance, he sat down. "Is everything alright?"

Part of her didn't want to bother asking, wanted to resign herself to wasting away in bed as she had for days. But after an afternoon with a friend, another part of her stirred. Marietta wanted control over her life and wouldn't let anyone or anything take her agency away.

She met Keyain's gaze, holding her chin high. "As you said, I can't continue as I have been, but I'm content with wasting away."

His hand reached across the table to hold her own, concern laced into his expression. "How can I help?"

With a squeeze of his hand, she said, "I need to talk to someone, to get out of this suite, Keyain. Amryth mentioned she's been visiting the Temple of Therypon and that they've helped her—"

"For fuck's sake, Mar," Keyain said with a sigh, pulling his hand back from her. "The temples are just cults."

"But they helped Amryth with the death of her wife. If you want to help me, then let me go to the temple to find peace."

"I'll have a doctor from the infirmary sent to the suite," Keyain said, standing. "I know you didn't like the drugs, but it's better than what you've been doing."

Marietta stood with him, her chair knocking backward. "No, Keyain. I want to go to the temple, not be drugged out of my mind."

Keyain stared at her, letting the anger ease from his features before speaking. "You can not, and will not, go to the temple; you will not set foot outside the palace. Do you understand?" Without waiting for a response, he turned towards the living room.

Marietta followed at his heels, arms crossed at her chest. "No, I don't understand. You ask how you can help, and then you deny the one thing I ask for after you caused all of this!"

He stopped at the center of the living room, Marietta bumping into him. "I'm sorry my actions have affected you so negatively."

She scoffed at his audacity—affected her negatively? He stole her life.

"The city isn't safe right now. With the missing pilinos—" His words cut off, and he offered a glance back at Marietta before continuing to his office.

Marietta's heart paused in her chest. "What missing pilinos?" she asked, trailing him into the office.

Keyain licked his lips as he placed the files into his desk drawer, locking it with a key.

"What missing pilinos, Keyain?" she asked again.

He hesitated, lines bracketing his mouth as he thought of his words. "Fifteen pilinos were reported missing in the past month, most of them being half-elves. I will not risk your safety."

"But you'll risk my life here in the suite, waiting for me to rot away?"

"I'll take my chances here, where I can protect you."

"Then come with me," she said, trying to hold on to hope. "If you take me, then you'll know I'm safe."

"No," he snapped. "We're done talking about this." Keyain moved to the door, but Marietta stood at the center, blocking his way.

"This is what I want." She swallowed hard, looking into his face. "I'm asking you for help and you're refusing. You've taken everything from me, Keyain. What will it take for you to help me?"

He placed his hands on her shoulders. "Not this."

The hope that blossomed in her chest uprooted, and Marietta cursed herself for letting it grow in the first place, for the tears it now caused. She turned from Keyain and continued to the bedroom, closing the door behind her.

She had no control over herself, over her future. Keyain had the final say on it all. Frustration caused Marietta to tear the now loose-fitted dress from her body, to tear her hair from its bind, ignoring the pain of strands ripping from her scalp. She dug her nails into her skin and sunk to her knees as her breaths came sharp. She felt nothing and everything, the pain of being trapped, of being at the Keyain's whim. Before her abduction, she chose everything—her clothes, where she went, what she did. To have such control only to lose it made the hurt greater.

Marietta knew that this was her fate, brought on by the hands of Keyain and what he believed was protecting her. What she needed was help, but what she received was damnation.

Chapter Thirty-Four

VALERIYA

Valeriya suppressed a hiss as her handmaids wrestled with her thick mane of red hair, attempting to twist it into two braids before her vanity. The tugging did nothing for her mood, already soured thinking of the mess between Az and Elyse.

After talking to Gyrsh earlier that week, who seemed entirely too dismissive of Elyse's emancipation, she got the full details of what happened. Valeriya tried to warn the girl that Az could be difficult. Perhaps it was for the better. Elyse was timid and nervous, and though the two could make for a strong union between Satiros and Chorys Dasi, Valeriya had her doubts that the marriage would be a happy one. After all, this wasn't his first fast courting—far from it. His love was oil and time was a flame, quick to burn but not long lasting. She'd have to check on the girl, to see how she fared.

The attention it drew to the Chorys Dasians frustrated Valeriya. Not only had they drawn Keyain's attention twice now, but Az had made direct contact with Wyltam. Even if he hadn't been banned from the palace, Valeriya would have made it clear to keep him away. The brazen attitude that made him entertaining also made him a liability.

A hiss escaped her mouth as the one handmaid found another knot, earning an immediate apology from the female. With a wave of a hand, Valeriya dismissed it. She always hated her hair and its knots and tangles. Back in Reyila, she always wished she could chop her hair short like Katya, for ease of movement and stealth, but her hair was so thick that it would have just stuck up at odd angles.

Katya.

No, she wouldn't think of her.

Valeriya turned her focus to Marietta, who was missing from court again. She hadn't seen or heard from her since they had tea a few weeks ago. Of course, Marietta had learned a lot of information during that conversation, but nerves still clawed at Valeriya's stomach. Something was wrong. The only hint Keyain would offer was that she fell ill. The tightened muscle in his jaw had revealed Marietta caused him some tension. Whether it was a worry for her health or their marriage, Valeriya wasn't sure.

Tea time with Marietta had been fruitful, at least. The half-elf confirmed she wasn't held against her will in Olkia, that she loved Tilan freely and married him after leaving Keyain.

The most interesting bit of information she learned was that Marietta broke off her and Keyain's relationship. Though Valeriya didn't know the details, it was clear Marietta held disdain for him. Something was there at the root of their relationship, a detail shrouded in secret. It was almost as if Marietta never wanted to marry him, or perhaps made a foolish mistake out of young love. Valeriya couldn't discern Keyain's motivations in all of this. Yes, he cared for Marietta, but how likely was it that they separated long ago? Marietta had remarried even.

Regarding the attack on Olkia, the only information she had came from Gyrsh and Royir. Though on the King's Council of Ministers, both were murky about the details around the reason for the seizure. The one thing they agreed on was that Keyain and Wyltam searched for *something*. Other than that, there was only Marietta and her ties to the Exisotis. Perhaps that's why Keyain brought Marietta to Saitros after all these years, because he needed a convenient reason to start a war.

If that was truly the reason, then Keyain and her husband were more cruel than she even knew. How many had died because they searched for an unknown thing? What could be so important that it was worth the lives lost? Valeriya gripped the arms of her chair, wishing she knew *why*.

A servant marched into her room, rousing her from her thoughts as her handmaids finished her hair. "Queen Valeriya," the servant said, bowing, "King Wyltam requests your presence at your earliest convenience." He turned about and left the room.

Valeriya sighed, placing her fingertips on her brow. Why must he always send a servant when she was just three rooms over in the suite? She smoothed the silky black fabric of her slip dress as she stood and went to her husband. He probably couldn't be bothered to get up from his research.

Wyltam, per usual, was in his study doing exactly what she predicted. Black hair hung in his face as he wrote a note from the book displayed before him.

"Good morning, my husband," she said with a slight bow of her head. She glided to a padded wingback chair before the desk.

A single hand floated up, signaling for her to wait as he finished writing. Valeriya bristled, not hiding the irritation on her face. Being married to Wyltam was like being married to a corpse. He was cold, lacked emotion, and stiff when he talked to her. Even after being married for how many years, he still hadn't warmed up.

Wyltam set down his charcoal utensil and finally acknowledged her. "Valeriya, thank you for coming." He sat back in the chair, his head resting on a hand.

"Of course," she said, forcing the disdain from her voice as if any normal husband and wife requested to talk to one another. "I was hoping to ask you about the missing pilinos situation and the rumors surrounding it."

Wyltam blinked slowly, shifting in his chair with an unreadable expression on his face. "Which rumors?"

"Some of the ladies in the Queen's Court mentioned a little over a month ago that six pilinos went missing, then another two were reported missing a week later." She paused, waiting to see if her husband would chime in, and unsurprisingly, he didn't. She sighed and continued. "Have they found any of them? Were there any more?"

Wyltam sat for a long moment, quiet, his eyes lost in thought. Speaking to him was near pointless when his mood wasn't talkative. Valeriya sighed and went to stand.

"Seven more have gone missing. None of them have been found."

Valeriya collapsed back into the chair, her heart sinking. At first, she hoped it was just half-elves escaping to freedom. Valeriya didn't blame them for wishing to leave Saitros; yet so many had gone missing in a short amount of time, leaving Valeriya uneasy. "And are you doing anything about it?"

"Keyain's guards are handling it."

Valeriya huffed a dry laugh, not finding the matter humorous. Keyain handling the situation meant it wasn't being handled at all. He was the perfect second to Wyltam.

"What I would like to talk about," he said, shifting so that one leg bent and his foot rose to rest on the seat, "is our own missing half-elf from court."

Valeriya bit back her annoyance at his posture. At least no one was around to see him this time. "What would you like to know?"

"Where is Marietta?"

"Haven't you asked Keyain? After all, he is your friend."

Wyltam stared at her through his expressionless eyes, yet she knew she hit a nerve. "He tells me to not worry about his wife."

"Funny," she said, smoothing the fabric of her dress. "He had more to share with me."

"And?"

She fought the smirk that wanted to curl on her lips, enjoying getting under Wyltam's skin. "She's ill. Keyain said she's been bedridden for weeks."

"Funny," Wyltam drawled. "I checked with the infirmary, and they haven't been informed of her illness."

Valeriya cleared her throat, sitting up straighter. To not check the infirmary was an oversight on her part. "So you're giving me another task? To check in on her?" Truly, she wished to do it, but she would never admit that to Wyltam.

"I'll take care of this one, actually." With a wave of his hand, he added, "You're dismissed."

Marietta had been through enough. Likely she grieved for the life she lost and for a husband she didn't know as well as she thought. Her husband's prying into the matter would just make it worse. "Wyltam—"

He cut her off with a raised hand, pointing towards the door as his head bent back into his book. Valeriya sighed, leaving the room and closing the door harder than she ought to have.

Afternoon sun lit the hallways of the Minister's Chambers as Valeriya made her way to her meeting with Gyrsh. Not often was she privy to political meetings, but every once in a while she was called in to check on Satiros's *hospitality*. The notion that it was her sole political responsibility outside the Queen's Court vexed her, as if she cared about the tedious needs of foreign dignitaries. Gyrsh had a team of nobles working under him that handled that.

As she walked, nobles paused their conversations to bow their heads in her direction. She kept a pleasant smile on her face, trying to acknowledge each one. Better to win their favor now, for one day they will be the nobles underneath her.

Two males walked towards her down the hall, deep in conversation. With coiffed golden hair and an amiable smile, it was easy to understand how Adryan Pytts rose to his position as Minister of Commerce. Quick to laugh and able to win the hearts of many, the short male proved his personable nature with every action he took. The male he walked with was older, his dark skin wrinkling and his black hair flecked with gray. Leyland Fedyr held the Minister of Vassals position and oversaw the non-noble population as well as managed the relationship with the temples.

In all, there were ten males on the King's Council of Ministers, all overseeing various areas of their city-state. They were an integral part of how their government ran, being that Wyltam gave them little oversight. Even for important decisions, he allowed them to vote instead of acting like a king and leading his people. Though how could she complain when it allowed Gyrsh to work with her?

In her position, all sorts of rumors of courtesans and nobles reached Valeriya's ears. Ministers were not excluded from such gossip. More than a few times, her ladies had shared that Leyland had been sleeping with a pilinos. Others had said he had a pilinos bastard, which was why he advocated for them. From the gossip, Valeriya distilled he did his due diligence as the minister who oversaw them. What she would like to find out one day was his stance on giving them full citizenship. If he was in favor, then she could have another ally for the future.

With that in mind, she approached the males. "Minister Leyland, Minister Adryan, how wonderful it is to run into you."

"Your Grace," Adryan said with a bow, "how wonderful indeed. Seldom we see you around this part of the palace."

"What a shame that is," she said.

"Indeed, my Queen," answered Leyland. "Gyrsh mentioned you'd be checking the status of our hospitality for the Chorys Dasians today. An important job to be had."

Valeriya forced her smile. "That indeed. Who better than the Queen to make our guests feel welcomed?"

"And what a wonderful queen you are," Adryan added. "The epitome of grace and generosity."

"Flattering me today, are we? Do you need something brought up with Wyltam?" she asked.

"Fortunate for us," Leyland said, "King Wyltam trusts our judgment on most things. Adryan just likes to curry favor with important persons."

Yes, Wyltam, with his blind trust for his ministers. Not wanting to do the work himself, he often relies on his council to take care of things without his oversight. Ever a wonderful king.

"Alas, that is true." Adryan flashed her a bright smile. "Though I think it'll take more than simple blandishments to become Queen Valeriya's favorite."

"Yet you still try," she said, her smile coming easy. How that male could ease anyone astounded her. No wonder he oversaw the businesses within Satiros. "Blandishments never hurt," she said, taking a step away from the pair.

"And they say flattery will get you nowhere." Adryan laughed and bowed his head. "Good day, my Queen." Leyland bowed his head and continued on with him.

Something about Adryan had never sat right with her. He held the ear of many of the ministers and could sway favor among them. Persuasive people such as him proved to be dangerous adversaries and Valeriya didn't know how he felt towards pilinos. If he held an opinion opposite of hers, it could ruin their future plans. A vexing thought.

Down the hall, she found Gyrsh's meeting room with a half dozen of his subordinates hard at work. A large table anchored the room with stacks of papers organized into neat piles across its surface. That was Gyrsh, keeping a strict and orderly protocol with his team. It was always odd to see him in such a powerful position for how much he liked to fawn after her. She cleared her throat, gaining his attention.

"Ah, Queen Valeriya," he said, "how wonderful it is for you to join us. Come, please sit."

"Minister Gyrsh, a pleasure as always."

"You," Gyrsh said, pointing at one of his subordinates, "get the Queen her cup of tea." The young male jumped up with the order and served her as she sat down.

"How have things been going with our friends from Chorys Dasi?" she asked, blowing over her cup as Gyrsh took his seat. The rest of his team followed suit.

"Trade negotiations are going well," he said with a slight smirk to his smile. Of course, trade relations weren't the real reason for their visit. Though a good portion of his team was aiding with the plan, it was still a poor idea to talk so openly about it. "I think we'll come to a swift agreement."

"That's good to hear," she said, bringing her hand to her chin. "Have they had a chance to see the city?"

Gyrsh nodded to one of his stewards. "Kurtys, if you will."

The name jogged a bit of gossip she had heard from Grytaine at tea one day. A smile curled onto her lips. How cruel was Gyrsh to this boy?

"My Queen," he said, his mousy hair falling forward with his bow. "As you had suggested, I offered to take them to the Ertwymer Sculpture Gardens. They showed no interest and instead focused on visiting a few taverns. Besides that, they show little interest in seeing Satiros."

Such news didn't come as a surprise, though she'd had thought they'd take a tour of the city-state's gateways and river system. That had been in the plan, at least. "Perhaps Lord Brynden has been too preoccupied by other sights Satiros offers."

Kurtys blinked at her words, failing to hide his discontent. The poor male had asked for Elyse's hand many times only for her to deny him and court Brynden after meeting once. Now, Gyrsh had him showing Brynden around Satiros. Satisfaction spread out from her chest; playing with Satiroan nobles never grew old.

"If that's a mention of Elyse," Gyrsh said, anger underlying his tone, "I would like to put on the record that her interference with the Chorys Dasians has not distracted them from our work, though Lord Brynden has been playing a lesser role in negotiations."

Playing a lesser role? Elyse had diverted him then. Valeriya made a mental note to follow up on that.

"How unfortunate that their betrothal fell apart," she said, sipping her tea. "As her father, you must have been disappointed."

Gyrsh flared his nose at her words, trying and failing to hide his anger. "As you are aware, Elyse emancipated from my estate and is no longer considered my daughter." He took a sharp breath, his grip tightening on his quill. "Anyone who continues to pursue her hand is advised otherwise because she no longer has any financial bearing."

Though he didn't look at Kurtys, the male flinched. His words had been a warning for him. How curious that not only did he still wish to court Elyse, but that Gyrsh would sabotage anyone who tried. Perhaps he thought if no one offered their hand then she would go back to him. The fool; he was a terrible father.

Kurtys cleared his throat and continued on with his update. Valeriya plastered on her fake smile, knowing none of it mattered. One day soon, she would replace these wasted afternoons with actual work—actual change. These males did not know what they were in for. Valeriya looked forward to the day she could show them.

Chapter Thirty–Five

ELYSE

E lyse stifled a yawn as she nodded to the two guards outside the library that she didn't recognize. Since moving to her own suite, it was easier to wake early and head to the library without raising her father's suspicion. Though the sun just crested above the horizon, Elyse looked the part of a court lady with her hair tied into a half knot and black lining her eyes.

One freedom of living on her own was the choice of clothing. The dress she wore was chiffon of pale gray that cinched at her waist, the neckline dipping low. The tulip skirt appeared as if she had a normal slit until she walked, the fabric falling to the sides and revealing more of her legs. It was a style that would have been too odd for her father.

Elyse would be thankful during her afternoon walk in the gardens for less cloth on her body. Plus, she liked the way her leather slippers and legs peeked out as she walked through the palace and to the library.

When Elyse arrived, her mind was still sluggish, with only having had one cup of tea. She jumped when she opened the door, finding the King in the office looking at her notes and a new stack of books on the desk.

"Elyse, I didn't realize you came in so early." King Wyltam set down her notes and placed his hands into his pocket, his eyes heavy with sleep and marred by dark underneath.

"Good morning, King Wyltam," she said with a curtsy. "I spend my mornings reading and the afternoon practicing." Ever since the experience with Mage's Eye, Elyse practiced feeling for aithyr and other techniques

from Fulbryk's.

He nodded, looking down at her papers. "These notes are intriguing. Usually, those who study magic write line after line of text from the book. You drew diagrams and pictures instead."

Elyse bit the inside of her cheek. "Drawing helps me memorize the visual details."

"Clever. Were you good at your basic studies as a child?"

"My scores were less than average," Elyse said, the admittance not burning as much as she thought it would. "I struggled to memorize text. When I tried to draw out my notes, the tutors would scold me."

King Wyltam raised a brow, one side of his mouth lifting. "Typical. Funny how tutors know so much but also so little. Some, like yourself, cannot learn from text alone and I found in my teachings that visual aids go a long way. To figure that out on your own shows great promise."

"You speak too kindly, Your Grace."

"I don't. I speak the truth." The King's hand spread her notes across the desk to read. The uncharacteristically slight smile remained on his face as he retrieved from his pocket a metal tin. "Ink is often unforgiving and slow to dry. I can see your smudges—and your frustrations."

Gods, he saw the angry scribbles where she made mistakes, hashing them out hard enough to nearly tear the paper.

"I prefer charcoal, but being left-handed means it'll smudge on my page; so, I had these made," he said, shaking the tin, causing a rattling noise. "They work well for taking notes. Charcoal wrapped in paper, enchanted not to smudge unless intentionally done with the paper end of the utensil." King Wyltam set the tin on the desk next to her notes. "Borrow my set for the time being. See how you like them. If you prefer them over ink, I'll have some stocked in here for you."

Elyse bit back her shock at his observation and kind expression. "Now, you are too kind. Thank you, my King."

He waved his hand, turning back to her notes. "Enough of the titles. When it's just you and I, Wyltam will suffice. If you're to work with me, I prefer less pageantry."

Surprised, she couldn't hide her reaction that time. "Of course, understood."

Wyltam then placed his hand on the new stack of books on the desktop. "I know you're still focusing on Fulbryk's principles, but work these texts into your studying. Fulbryk is good for groundwork and theory, but the new material provides better physical instructions. My goal for you is to have you training with magic by the end of next month."

"As in training with you? By the end of next month?" That wasn't a lot of time.

"Me, or one of my mages. Or all of us," he paused, staring at her a moment while he considered his words. "The mages I trained do well in stealth but not so well in court life. Elyse, you have the perfect position in court as a lady born to a high-ranking noble but yet to marry. You possess the high capability to learn magic, and it is my belief that you will excel at it. You're in a unique position to help me with court intrigue. My goal is to have you be my eyes and ears in the other Syllogian city-states."

Her heart sunk. Of course, learning magic came with a price. She could visit the other city-states but only by the King's hand. Foolish of her to think she'd gain true freedom. Even so, freedom at the end of a leash was better than a cage.

Wyltam came around the desk, leaning against its edge with his arms crossed. "If we can get your nerves under control and improve your proficiency with magic, then you may become one of the greatest allies of my kingship."

"So I would travel to the other city-states at your request?" she asked, her heart swelling. She imagined the castle of Kyaeri nestled in the Ekrixi Mountains flanked by waterfalls that feed the Halia River. The travel and adventure she wished for could be in her near future.

"You would, and you would play the dazzling, young courtier as you have with the Chorys Dasians."

Elyse closed her eyes, taking a deep breath as embarrassment flooded her. "I'm so sorry again—"

"That's enough," he said, cutting her off. His expression softened.

"None of it was your fault. The incident brought much to my attention that I had been ignorant to, and for that, I'm thankful."

Elyse only nodded, unsure of what to say.

"You have much potential, Elyse," Wyltam said, pushing off the desk and heading towards the door. "But with that potential comes the opportunity for disappointment. Only you decide the outcome."

"I won't let you down, my—Wyltam."

"Be careful to not make promises you can't keep," he said. "And if you ever need me, I've enchanted the room to alert me if you call out my name or if anyone without permission enters. Just call for me, and I will come."

As he made for the exit, one lingering question made her speak up. "Not that I'm in a position to question," she said, fidgeting with her hands, "but why? Was it just because of my position at court?"

Wyltam paused in the doorway, his eyes landing on Elyse. "When I was younger than you are now, I started to study magic and its possibilities. On my own, I could only learn so much. It took a mentor for me to reach my full potential." He sighed, his expression softening to a sadness Elyse never had seen on him. "Your mother was my mentor and she made the biggest impact on my life. The least I could do was help the daughter she adored."

It was as if the air was knocked out of her. "You knew her that well?"

He nodded his head, giving a sad smile. "She was like a mother to me. Between you and me, I'm happy you're free from your father. Gyrsh used to be a good male," he paused, shaking his head, "but that was a very long time ago."

Elyse nodded, unsure what to do with the information.

"It's funny," he added, "for how much you look like Gyrsh, it was always your mother I saw." And with that, Wyltam stepped out of the room, the door clasping behind him.

Elyse walked around the desk and slumped into the chair. He thought she was like her mother—he could see her mother in her. That alone brought a smile to her face. Wyltam believed in her, believed that she could be a spy. To travel to the other city-states as a noble lady by day and his secret mage by night was something out of a book, a life she could only dream of.

Her imagination ran wild, imagining all the scenarios she would be in, the places she would see. Elyse would get what she wanted, to leave Satiros, but only if she learned to control her nerves.

The late afternoon sun filtered through the curtains, a gentle breeze carrying the fresh early summer air. Elyse's new suite was smaller than the one she shared with her father, but comfortable with a combined living and dining room, bedroom, bathroom, and office. The previous occupants left behind the threadbare furnishings.

Across from Elyse sat Queen Valeriya on the faded golden yellow couch. Steam rolled off the cup of tea she sipped from, her posture pin-straight, and her eyes watching Elyse. She did her best to keep her chin up. "I'm glad to see you're all settled into your new suite," she said, her tone warm. "Does the independent life treat you well?"

"It does, Your Grace," she said with a smile.

"I heard the details of your father's behavior, and I have to apologize for not knowing. Are you sure you're alright?"

The Queen felt the need to coddle her again. "I assure you I'm alright."

"Even about Brynden?"

Elyse's gaze dropped at the mention.

"He's like a caged bull. Even if there are barriers keeping him in place, he still thrashes against the sides." The Queen set down her tea, clasping her hands in her lap. "There will be other chances for marriage, don't you worry."

"If I choose to marry at all." She bit her lip, regretting the words. How would the Queen react to such an idea?

A smile lined her lips as she huffed a laugh. "A modern female you are. I'm sure there will always be a position at court for you, regardless of your relationship with Gyrsh. That being said, I'm more than happy to have you continue joining us in the Queen's Court."

Dread filled Elyse. She'd still have to go to tea time and face all the ladies. "That is kind of you."

"I find you very intriguing, Elyse. You are quiet and unassuming, yet you have had two betrothals to two prominent males before you've reached your third decade."

She winced at the truth.

"I don't mean that as an insult." The Queen brought her hand to her chin. "You are so young and full of potential. Even if court life is overwhelming for you know, you'll have decades to adjust. I can't wait to see what kind of female it makes you."

Elyse smiled and swallowed hard. "It'll be interesting to say the least."

"Give yourself credit. In my time as a royal, I have never seen a lady in such a position at as young of an age as you. Why do you think Grytaine attacks you the way she does?"

"I'll be better about standing up for myself," Elyse said as she closed her eyes.

"You'll get there one day, I'm sure." The Queen picked up her tea. "You threaten Grytaine."

"That makes little sense."

"She's young, like you, and she was the youngest lady in my court until you came along. She didn't grow up as a noble, so she has to fight her way to gain connections. Even without your father's estate, you still have connections. You have a history with my ladies."

Grytaine likely had a difficult time gaining favor among the nobles where Elyse never had to work for it. Such relationships were always given to her. That didn't excuse her attitude, however.

"As for Brynden," the Queen continued, "perhaps it wasn't the best match right now, but that doesn't mean it couldn't work out in the future. You are not the final version of yourself yet. Future you might be able to wrangle a bull."

Elyse smiled and nodded at her words. Perhaps future her would be better suited, but Elyse wasn't worried about that. What left her on edge was her position with Queen Valeriya and King Wyltam. The Queen would keep her on her court, and now, she worked for the King. Never had she heard of a lady in her position—or even a lord. She would become close with both royals. The thought should excite her, should mean that she had a bright future; but she was apprehensive. Having friends in powerful places drew attention, something she never wanted.

Even then, attention was not the same as status. It wasn't the same as a noble's wealth. Elyse traded both those things for freedom, and that was worth more than any boon her father gave or any male's attention.

Even Brynden's.

Chapter Thirty-Six

MARIETTA

Marietta remained in bed, though the sun had long since risen. The day of Amryth's visit and the speck of motivation it birthed had passed, leaving her alone in the suite once again. No one visited. She didn't leave, and she continued to spiral.

After that day, Marietta noticed items missing from the suite. The fire poker from the hearth, scissors from her vanity, the letter opener from the bookshelves, and other sharp things disappeared. It made her laugh—Keyain had the foresight to prevent Marietta from self-harm, yet he wouldn't help her.

On a day of sunny weather with a gentle breeze tousling the trees of the garden below, Marietta tried to open the windows, to let fresh air into the suite and feel the wind over her skin, only to find them locked. As much as she pried at them, the locks wouldn't budge.

Keyain confined her to the tiny space, alone and desperate, wishing she'd one day wake up and realize it was a nightmare, or never wake up again. To lose control of her life was to lose control of herself. At her very core, Marietta was confident and independent, and without her own control, she found herself a shell of who she was.

So she let herself go, dwelling on the memories of her past life. Tilan was at the center of thought most days, questioning if they were ever truly in love. Did it count as love if she never knew the real Tilan? Sure, he supported her dreams and her goals and stood with her through everything. But how much of that support came down as an order from the Exisotis? To keep her happy and away from Keyain?

The doubt hurt her more than anything. Losing such surety in her life was foreign, as was the second-guessing, yet how else should she feel? Tilan lied from the beginning, and that lie became the basis of their relationship, conceived to make Keyain suffer.

Marietta rolled over in the silk sheets, watching the clouds drift beyond the window. She should get up, perhaps bathe and change her clothes, but she wouldn't. She should distract herself from the negative thoughts, but what was the point? Until Keyain enacted whatever plan he had drafted, all Marietta could do was wait.

Lost in her head, she hadn't heard the door open nor the footsteps into the suite.

"Lady Marietta?"

The voice startled her, deep and baritone—one she remembered from the garden. Marietta jumped from the bed. King Wyltam stood in the doorway with his hands in his pockets and a frown on his face.

He averted his gaze from her nightgown, clearing his throat. "Apologies for not sending word prior to coming. I was hoping to speak with you a minute."

"Of course, King Wyltam," she said, bowing with a hand covering her chest as she leaned forward. Marietta grabbed a robe from her wardrobe, wrapping the silk around her body as she ignored her heart racing in her chest.

Why did the King wish to speak to her? And gods, when was the last time she washed? Her hair was in tangles as she ran her fingers through her locks, walking out to the dining room where he waited.

The King stood in the doorway to the living room, hands clasped behind his back. He turned to Marietta. "I was hoping to sit in here, but it appears Keyain has been sleeping on the couch." He walked over to the dining room table and pulled back a chair. "Please, have a seat."

The King of Satiros, the city-state that deemed pilinos lesser to elves, pulled out a chair *for her*. Confused, curiosity sparked from the King's audience and kind gesture.

Marietta sat, letting him push in her chair before he sat across from her. His gaze raked over her face, then to her body, not even attempting to hide his stare. "You look terrible," he said after a long moment.

An incredulous laugh left her mouth, a single breath, at his pointedness. The King was right, she knew, but the brusque manner of his observation was surprising.

"I do not mean that as an insult," he said, pausing. "Your face is gaunt; under your eyes are near black. Unbathed, undressed, and most likely underfed, based on the weight you've lost since the ball."

Marietta narrowed her eyes. "What ball, Your Grace?"

"Not surprising that you don't remember; Keyain gave you a drug that would prevent you from knowing what was happening around you." With a shake of his head, the black hair that fell into his face flicked back. His eyes were dark, nearly black, as she searched them, looking for any emotion.

"He drugged you and now leaves you neglected." A flash of anger came across his features, gone before Marietta could fully register. "One would think he'd treat his wife better, especially after all you've gone through; yet you have deteriorated since coming to Satiros, and for that, I deeply apologize."

Marietta bit back her surprise as the King bowed his head. "You shouldn't be the one apologizing, Your Grace."

The King cocked his head. "You're right. I shouldn't be. Has he tried to intervene at all?"

With a dry laugh, Marietta sunk into her chair, crossing her arms across her chest. "He offered to drug me again. That was his solution."

Anger flecked through the King's expression once more, his eyes searching the room as he thought of his words.

"I asked to visit the Temple of Therypon," Marietta said to break their silence, drawing his attention. "He refused to let me go."

His fingers drummed on the tabletop, an expressionless mask falling over his face. "In Satiros, it is illegal to bar someone from attending a temple. Keyain knows this and knows you don't know the laws."

Marietta gripped her forearms, not bothering to hide her grimace.

"Keyain always gets what he wants, regardless of the law."

The King considered her words, once again his eyes darting back and forth in thought. Such silence from someone would bother her if it wasn't the King. Though he had the authority to dismiss Marietta, he considered her words. He put thought into his answer.

King Wyltam was nothing like a king, at least from what Marietta thought a king should be. His presence alone was abnormal; yet he sat before her, dressed in fine but plain clothing, all black as if he were in mourning. Even the crown on his head was a simple circlet of gold.

Beyond that, he took a moment to talk to her, to listen to what she said. A king should be busier, should not have the time for such a visit. Perhaps he felt the need to because he was friends with Keyain.

"Keyain doesn't know I've come," he said after a moment. "As no one does. Leaving the palace would put you at risk, given the unrest in the city. Should you visit the Temple of Therypon, which you have a right to do, don't travel plainly through the streets."

"Are you giving me permission to leave?" Marietta asked, her heart skipping a beat. If the King allowed her to go, what could Keyain say?

"You do not need permission when the law states you are free to go," he answered. "However, I'd advise you to make plans with Keyain."

Her hope faltered. "As I said, he'd break the law to get what he wants, and what he wants is me locked in this suite without contact." She should have hidden that disdain for him in her voice, but she couldn't, not after weeks of being trapped.

"You're angry with Keyain for more than his neglect," noted the King. "I wonder, is it because he waited to save you or because he saved you at all?"

How easy it would be to tell the King her truth, that she didn't marry Keyain, that she loved another? Yet the Queen hadn't told her husband such a truth, so why should she? "How could I be angry now that I'm safe, Your Grace?" she lied.

A small smile cracked his expressionless mask. "Everyone lies at court, Lady Marietta. As an outsider, I had hoped you'd be different." He stood, regarding Marietta. "Let me know if that changes."

The King walked to her chair, pulling it back so she could stand. "Talk to Keyain, and if he doesn't listen to you once more, I'll intercede on your behalf."

Marietta was at a loss for words—the King himself was now involved with Keyain and his plans to isolate her. She could be free, at least to go to the temple.

"I hope the next time we speak is less bleak," he added before turning for the antechamber.

"Thank you, King Wyltam," she said, adding a quick curtsy.

He turned to face her in the doorway. "I am simply doing what Keyain has failed to do."

After a day of contemplating what to say to Keyain, she thought it best to sleep on it, mull it over before approaching him again. She could tell him she was aware of the law, that he can't keep her from going to the temple, but again, Keyain would break it. And how would she let the King know if he did?

Instead, she spent the afternoon crafting a plan, the words she'd say to him. Because remaining in the suite was no longer an option—any moment longer trapped in the small space would send her over the edge.

She ignored Keyain when he returned to the suite and didn't join him as he ate dinner, though he gave a half-hearted attempt to get her to eat. Instead, she roused herself to bathe, taking her time in the bath and letting the heat soak her bones.

It was a small luxury, with the lavender-scented oils in such a large tub, and it helped her clear her head as much as she could. Tilan was still at the fringe of her thoughts, lurking as he always did, but she had a small goal to focus on: the temple.

After allowing her hair to dry a bit, she sat at her vanity. A comb broke up her tangles, so she took to setting her curls, encouraging the coil of the strands, when Keyain walked in.

"You've bathed," he said, leaning against the bed frame off behind her, his face reflecting in the mirror of her vanity.

She glanced at him a moment, then focused on her hair once more, determined to ignore him. Anger was just below the surface, waiting for her to lash out with frustration.

"It's a good sign," he added after a moment. "Almost like you just needed time to process and not a temple."

Her anger won out. "I wouldn't want the King to stop by again and find me so *neglected*," she snapped, eyes focused on the curl she wrapped around her fingers.

"I found out after the fact, and I'm sorry he surprised you." From the corner of her eye, she watched Keyain rub the back of his neck, stalling his words. "Sometimes he likes to show up, to make sure things are okay. I talked to him a few days ago, and I mentioned you needed some time to adjust."

Determined to ignore him, she said nothing.

"Mar," he said, approaching her with a hand on her shoulder. "I'm so sorry I put you through all of this. I promise that this was to protect you—because I love you."

Keyain crouched next to her chair as she worked, his eyes bearing into her. "Did you know I thought of you every day we were apart? I thought of you when I struggled. When I felt nervous, it was you I saw to steady myself. I thought of you when I felt at my happiest. When I was at my saddest. Your face, your laugh—they were both with me all this time." Keyain paused, taking a deep, shuddering breath.

His hand fell on her leg. "When I learned you were seeing someone new, I accepted it. It hurt, obviously, but I took solace knowing you were doing your best to be happy." Trembling, he paused for a breath. "But when I learned who you were with, I lost control of myself. Wyl locked me in a room to keep me from riding to Olkia until I calmed down."

He swallowed hard. And yet Marietta said nothing, content to listen.

"I was distraught, Mar," he said, his voice tight. "I had to sit here and imagine what the Exisotis would do. It broke me, Marietta."

He leaned forward, resting his forehead against her thigh. "When we finalized the attack on Olkia, I had to save you from the Exisotis. I begged Wyltam, risking my career to rescue you," his voice cracked, thick with emotion. "That's when he learned you were my wife. I showed him the marriage certificate I signed when I thought you'd move to Satiros. He agreed that having the wife of one of his ministers kidnapped by our enemy was a risk and was furious when he learned how long you'd been in their custody."

Keyain waited for Marietta to respond, but she only offered silent tears that slid down her face as she secured a silk scarf around her hair.

"Tilan knew me. The Exisotis knew me, too. I tracked them for years— had tracked Tilan since he began building weapons for the Exisotis." He shook his head, still pressed against her. "You weren't supposed to see Tilan die. I didn't want that memory to haunt you, even if he's an evil man. That day at his apartment, I realized how deep his deception went." His voice cracked again. "And I was so scared. My only regret is not saving you sooner."

On the day he referred to, Keyain nearly broke down the door to Tilan's apartment and tried to take her away. An event Marietta thought about since learning the truth, remembering Tilan denying he knew Keyain. Tilan lied, and she'd believed him with her whole heart.

Even then, Tilan was with the Exisotis. The lies had been present from the beginning, forming the foundation of their relationship. The truth revealed cracks that were always there, waiting for their relationship to crumble.

Keyain was out of line with how he warned Marietta, tracking her through the cities as she visited clients. Yet he'd tried to warn her. He'd attempted to help her.

"Please say something," Keyain begged.

There was nothing she could say. Marietta's hand fell to his neck, where skin met hair, and she rubbed gently, earning a deep sigh from Keyain. He looked up at her, the green in his eyes vibrant against his red, swollen skin. "I love you so much."

In his own twisted way, she knew Keyain loved her and had always loved her. Parts of her would always feel that affection back for him, but their time was done. Too many fights. Too many hurt feelings. Too many incidents that made Marietta feel small. Staring into his eyes, she felt it all: the good, the bad, and everything in between. Perhaps for one night, though, she could entertain the idea of letting Keyain be sweet to her. It would at least soften the question she'd inevitably ask tomorrow.

For the first time in so many nights, Marietta led Keyain to the bed and fell asleep in his arms.

The bedroom glowed with morning light as Marietta opened her eyes. Wrapped around her was Keyain, his deep breathing indicative of sleep. Marietta rolled over, lying face to face with him. As he slept, he looked peaceful, no sign of the anger that seemed to be always a breath away. The splattering of freckles across his nose and cheeks were as she remembered them. For a moment, she let herself imagine they were at an inn, that they would head down to breakfast soon. The ache in her heart for those days came suddenly to her.

After Marietta left Keyain, she blocked out those memories, too painful to remember. The emotions, the love she had for him, didn't make a difference. Keyain imagined a very different future for them, one Marietta would never agree to, yet there she was, in his arms once more. She was angry, and rightfully so, but Keyain was doing what he did best—protect. Though, if he could fight someone to defend her and could repeat his protection narrative to her time and time again, then why couldn't he understand the help she actually needed? Even after she told him verbatim?

Marietta traced the line of his jaw with her fingers, sweeping against his cheeks and lips. A face so familiar, one she woke up to a thousand times with a kiss each morning. Why couldn't he understand?

Back then, he was the Minister of Protection but never told Marietta. If he had, she would have ended their relationship immediately, which meant she understood why Keyain hid it. He was always honest about keeping his job a secret, so he never did lie to her. But leaving out that he was the King of Satiros' best friend and a minister was a glaring oversight.

The fact he hid it still angered her, but at least he didn't lie. In that way, he treated her better than Tilan.

Keyain's eyes fluttered open, still heavy with sleep as his body grew taut with a stretch. Her hand cupped his face, Keyain turning to kiss her palm. "Good morning," he said, voice rough with sleep.

"Good morning." She dragged her hand through his sleep-mussed hair, smoothing the brown strands.

It was then she decided that she'd ask him one last time for the temple. After his words of love, his confession clearing some tension between them, there was a chance Keyain would understand. "I know that you love me," she admitted, and Keyain took her hand in his own. "And I know you would protect me against anything, but you aren't listening, Keyain."

His thumb brushed across her knuckles, his smile faltering. "I always listen to you."

She sighed, closing her eyes. "You listen, but you don't understand. So, please, truly try to hear what I'm saying." She opened her eyes, meeting Keyain's gaze. "You can't decide everything for me. If I say I need something, then you should help me get it, not choose if it's a need or not."

"But you don't understand Satiros or how this court works," he whispered. "You don't realize what it's like."

"How will I ever learn if I'm locked in here, isolated from everything?" she said, pulling her hand from his grasp, but he gripped tighter. "By keeping me confined, you choose what to tell me, only sharing information that is convenient for you. Like the law that allows anyone to visit the temples. The King told me."

"Yes, that law allows anyone, under any circumstances, to visit the temples, but it doesn't protect you from being attacked." Each word came faster than the last. "If I lost you, if you ended up like those other pilinos—" His voice cracked as panic set in his eyes.

"Then it's your job to help get me there safely, not lie to me and forbid me from going."

"It's not that simple."

"What isn't simple, Keyain?" She sat up, staring at Keyain with a grimace.

He ground his jaw, rolling onto his back, and his eyes searched the bed's canopy. "These attacks started the week of the ball—after your first very public appearance." He swallowed hard, averting his eyes. "There are rumors that your presence inspired the foulest of the elven population to… to take action."

Marietta felt gutted. As if everything up until then wasn't awful enough, the guilt of those missing people tore into her chest. She blinked, stammering, at a loss for words as tears fell.

Keyain sat up, wrapping her into his embrace. Marietta didn't fight it. Instead, she rested her head on his bare chest as he smoothed back her hair. "I know," he said, his voice tight. "This is why I didn't want to say anything—why I don't want you in the public eye."

"But it isn't my fault, is it?" she asked, turning her face to Keyain.

He brushed back a lock that broke loose from the silk scarf covering her hair, his lips tugging into a deeper frown. "No, don't go down that line of thinking, Mar."

"But it is—"

"No," he said, his eyes burning. "You are not responsible for their deaths; you have every right to be here as my wife, as a lady of the court."

"But only elves serve on the court."

"Not anymore," he whispered, shaking his head. "Your anger towards me for marrying you in secret is completely justified, but so is your presence at court. You are my wife, a half-elf, and you are a lady of Satiros. If the extremist used your existence as an excuse for vile deeds, then the blame is on them." He cupped her face, his mouth set to a tight line. "You have done nothing wrong. Your existence and your presence are not wrong."

Marietta's lips trembled. "I don't belong here, Keyain, and you know it. That's why you keep me locked away."

He shook his head, nostrils flaring. "No, I keep you away from the

Queen and King, from prying questions and eager eyes. You belong here, just as any wife of a lord."

Keyain took a long breath, his eyes searching the room. "Tonight," he whispered, "I'll get you out for a walk. It'll be short, but we can make them longer as the court adjusts to your presence."

"You don't have time for that, do you?" she asked, her voice bitter.

"I'll make time," he said, kissing her forehead. "I promise."

Keyain left for the day, leaving Marietta alone once more. His promise meant nothing—not until it happened. Marietta knew not to get her hopes up as she readied herself for the day, as she absently flipped through the book, occasionally gazing out to the garden beyond.

And she knew that when she sat at the dining room table, waiting for Keyain to return for dinner, that it still didn't mean the walk would happen. He was busy, a minister overseeing an active war. Yet it didn't stop her disappointment when the meal arrived without Keyain, when the sun had set, and the sky grew dark. She readied herself and got into bed, alone.

In the morning, he gave her his apology when the room was gray with the first morning light, promising to take her on a walk that evening. But Marietta didn't see him again until the following morning, offering more apologies and more promises.

After a week of neglected promises, she steeled herself. No longer would she wait. If Marietta needed help, she'd have to rely on herself to get it. A week to the day of Keyain's first promise, Marietta sent a note to Amryth.

She would leave that suite, whether Keyain knew it or not.

Chapter Thirty-Seven

MARIETTA

Within the hour, Amryth arrived. "I came as soon as I could," she said, leaning against the doorway to the dining room. "Is everything alright?"

Marietta swallowed hard, pacing back and forth. "Keyain won't let me leave."

"Do you want me to talk to him?"

"It won't matter," Marietta said, pausing. "The King visited me, told me that the law allows for me to go to the temples, but even his visit didn't convince Keyain."

Amryth stared for a moment, watching Marietta with a blank expression. "So you sent for me," Amryth said, pushing off the doorway, hands clasping before her.

"Yes," Marietta whispered.

"Though he's my superior."

Marietta faltered her stare, biting her lips as she paced once more. Gods, this was a terrible idea; she was too loyal to Keyain. Amryth was the obvious choice, but not the only one. The King might visit again. He might overrule Keyain on the matter, but what if he didn't visit? What if he couldn't be bothered by a miserable half-elf like her? Gods, when did she start thinking of herself that way?

"Marietta," Amryth snapped. "Did you even hear what I said?"

"No, but I don't want to put you in a position—"

"I'll take you."

Marietta's heart stopped once more. "What?"

"I'll take you to the temple."

"But Keyain—"

"You have a right to visit the temple."

"What if he demotes you? If you lose your position?"

"Well, I'm already breaking his rule of not visiting you," she said, offering a tight smile. "I do what's right, regardless if my superiors believe it is or not."

Marietta nodded, her chest swelling. "How do we do it then?" she asked. "How do I leave?"

"Don't worry. I came prepared." Amryth undid her green cloak, flapping it out. "How fast can you change?"

After changing into a simple dress that hung on her now thin frame, she met Amryth by the door. "Whatever happens, just follow my lead," she said, not waiting for Marietta to respond. She stepped into the hall with Marietta in tow. The guards posted outside paused, exchanging glances.

"No one said Lady Marietta would leave the suite today, Amryth," said a male with rich, dark skin and a scowl fixed on his features.

"Special instructions to get her on a walk since she hasn't left in weeks," she said, placing her hand on Marietta's back to encourage her to go.

The guard glanced at his companion, a lighter-skinned male with a similar scowl and a hooked nose. "Makes sense. We were wondering how sick she was. Glad to see you up, my lady."

Marietta nodded, trying to smooth the confusion from her face. The guards were always posted outside the door, so it made sense that they would notice something was wrong. Did they seriously believe her to be sick? Is that what Keyain told them?

Amryth ushered her away before she could respond. With luck, they exited the Noble's Section without encountering anyone. Within a few minutes, Amryth stopped in the Central Garden. She handed her cloak to Marietta. "Put this on."

Marietta took it as the rain began to fall, the cool droplets dotting her skin. She gasped at the sensation, casting her face towards the sky as she donned the cloak. Gods, when did she last feel the rain on her skin? The wind in her hair? Without another comment, Amryth pulled up Marietta's hood and took her hand, dragging her through the garden towards a part of the palace she didn't recognize.

Guards in similar cloaks walked past, some with intent, others milling about with laughter in their throats. The sight was almost overwhelming, seeing that many bodies at once, though they stayed in the halls. She tried to focus on Amryth's back, not to stray too far behind as they raced towards the exit.

Two woman guards approached them as they neared a set of doors, but Amryth shrugged them off, saying Marietta was a new recruit in training. The excuse seemed good enough for them.

Outside the garrison, the surrounding wall stretched to both sides farther than Marietta could see. Guards stationed at the gate, swords at their hips and papers in their hands, waved them through as Amryth approached. As they stepped onto the sidewalk next to the cobblestone street, she sighed and picked up her pace.

If the hallways filled with guards were overwhelming to her senses, then the city was an assault. Crowds of people packed the walkways, calling to one another over the ambient sound of the city. Marietta gripped the back of Amryth's armor as they wove their way through, growing dizzy at the bodies pressed in around them.

How funny that a few months in confinement had changed Marietta. Just three months prior, she could walk into a crowd and control it at will, make a friend or two in the process. But after the quiet loneliness of the suite, her heart rammed into her ribs, and her grip grew sweaty, holding onto Amryth.

A horseless carriage rolled by, and Marietta almost lost Amryth as she gawked. There were no horses—or any other animal—pulling it, right? Or had she lost her gods damned mind?

White buildings laced with greenery loomed over them as they ventured deeper into the city. Nestled between the structures were pockets of trees surrounded by neat fencing. Marietta craned her head to catch a glimpse of a statue, but they didn't stop. Instead, they turned down a narrow side street.

Overhead, purple wisteria draped between the tall buildings, blocking a portion of the misty weather that fell. Fewer people patrolled the side street, making it easier for Amryth to navigate. She turned for a moment, her eyes still looking forward. "Not too much farther now."

The street opened up to a wide avenue, which they quickly crossed, dodging another horseless carriage. At the head sat a man, hands held in front of him and eyes focused in the direction he traveled. Though confused, Marietta was happy she didn't mistake the earlier carriage. Perhaps she wasn't losing her mind after all.

The rain started to fall steadily as they turned down another street. Marietta gasped as she saw the temples, all columned with steps climbing from their raised landing down to the circular street. Through gaps in the crowd, she glimpsed a temple of red-veined marble with vibrant crimson banners hanging between ornate columns. The one across from it was of taupe stone and gray banners.

The color of the temples pulled at her memory, reminding her of the temple districts found in Enomenos. Though she had friends in the temples, she never remembered which god or goddess belonged to which color. Her parents never joined a temple, so Marietta grew up without knowing much about them. As she grew older, her friends had shared more details, but she never had a reason to practice. Even as some of the colors tugged at her memory, nothing surfaced.

Statues dotted the fronts of each temple, the ones from the black stoned temple being the most notable. At street level, they passed a carved man crying out in pain as he gripped his chest. The temples in Enomenos didn't have those.

Amryth led her to where the crowd was thickest. Marietta caught the gaze of a smiling woman in a yellow tunic, breath catching when she saw her ears. A blunted arch like her own. A half-elf in Satiros—someone like her.

They approached a temple of white stone, columned with cerulean banners, marked with a black serpent, hanging beneath a relief depicting a brutal fighting scene. Cypress bushes and other greenery broke up the stone steps and building, dressing the white stone in bright shades of green. Before the entrance, towering above her there was a statue of a woman nearly as tall as three men. The relaxed face had a slight smile on her full lips. A wide nose sat beneath large, rounded eyes, and a hand extended out before her, beckoning to Marietta. With her gaze locked onto the statue, Marietta nearly tripped going up the steps, but Amryth caught her.

The statue's eyes seemed to follow her, call to her. They were gentle, kind, yet realistic and showed the pain she felt.

Beyond the columns, at the top of the stairs, was a double set of opened doors. A dark-skinned man in a blue tunic and silvered armor stood to the side laughing with a man in plain clothes. Scruff lined his face, thinner than what grew on a human, but the presence of facial hair was enough of a clue—he was a half-elf, the second she'd seen in Satiros. Marietta met his gaze as they walked through, his smile dropping with a look of shock.

Amryth held up her hand. Less a hello and more a warning. "Later," was all she offered as she pulled Marietta into the building.

Ornate statues lined the antechamber to either side, the space wide and open. Scenes of people receiving healing lined one wall, scenes of people screaming in pain lined the other.

Amryth guided her down the bright hallway, passing more attendants in bright blue, some robed, others donning a tunic, and a few in armor, like the man out front. The deeper they went, the stronger the scent of eucalyptus and peppermint grew.

The hall ended in a towering room, benches lining the space with people sitting in silent prayer. They all faced the altar at the front of the room. A statue that matched the figure out front towered above them, her face the same. However, inside the temple, she knelt on one knee with waves of hair flowing away from her body and her hand extended to lie flush with the ground. A person in the same blue as the others occupied the hand, kneeling before the statue.

Amryth pulled Marietta to an unoccupied bench. They sat among the worshippers, who remained quiet with their heads tilted to the ceiling. Marietta followed their gaze, finding a window high above splattered with rain and the gray clouds beyond it.

"Have you ever prayed at a temple?" Amryth asked, keeping her voice below a whisper. Though people filled the room, it remained silent besides the soft pattering of walking and the occasional sniffle.

"No," she whispered. Many of her friends in Enomenos were followers of the gods, but she never bothered. She lived a fortunate enough life that there was never a need to seek them out.

"Relax your shoulders, place your feet firmly on the ground, and set your hands palm-side up on your thighs to accept the goddess." Amryth took up the seated stance. "When in position," she whispered, "close your eyes and tilt your head toward the ceiling. Try to empty your mind. Reach out to the goddess, and she will help you."

Marietta nodded again, settling herself onto the bench and following Amryth's instructions. With her eyes closed, every breath became noticeable, every scuffle of feet, clearing of throats. All the sounds were louder than the silence she had experienced for days.

Keyain would be furious if he found out she had left. She sighed, shaking her head as she sat on the uncomfortable bench, shifting from side to side. After all the anticipation for the temple, now that she was there, anxiety squeezed her chest. It begged her to hurry, urging her to return to the suite. Keyain's wrath wasn't something she wanted to experience. When anger took him, he lost all rational thought. He had smashed glasses, punched walls, ripped the curtains from the windows. There were a handful of inns in Enomenos she couldn't show her face at anymore because of him.

Would he take his wrath out on Amryth? Or would the King protect her since she was following the law, preventing one from being broken? She lifted a lid to stare at Amryth, her stoic face calm as she sat with closed eyes. She risked her position for Marietta—risked her livelihood so she could be here.

"Acknowledge that your mind is wandering," she muttered. "Then dismiss the thoughts and try again. Think of nothing, of no one."

Marietta closed her eye once more with a sigh. How could she think of nothing? There was always something on her mind.

Yet she tried, the effort fruitless. She'd clear her thoughts, focus on the dark of her lids, the breathing in her chest, but then thoughts crept in. Taking Amryth's advice, she acknowledged her mind wandering, then brought it back to nothing.

The cycle continued, Marietta's breath growing deep, the tension in her shoulders easing. At one point, there was nothing—no thoughts, no emotion. There were only her breaths, the black of her eyelids, and the presence of a goddess watching over her.

At some point, Marietta became aware of the nothingness, the sudden burst of thought startling her. Her eyes opened to the dimmed interior of the chapel, devoid of any person.

The lightness of her body surprised her. The tension she's held for weeks loosened as she rolled her neck. Even the stone bench didn't make her ass hurt, nor her legs stiff. Gods, she felt alive. Not the over-the-top jumping for joy alive. But functional. Each breath wasn't a fight, each thought not racing.

Only then did Marietta realize the extent of her grief, of that suffocating emotion the robbed her of her senses. She took a deep breath and turned to look for Amryth.

"Welcome back!" A chipper voice startled her. Marietta clutched her chest as she found a tiny brown-skinned half-elven woman next to her, staring with large eyes. A thick black braid of smooth strands fell over her tunic in the cerulean blue of the temple.

"Who—" Marietta stopped herself as she heard yelling from down the hall towards the entrance.

"I'm Deania, a cleric to Therypon! I was making sure you'd finish praying to the goddess on your own," she said, her voice high-pitched and sweet, almost childlike. "And look, you did it!"

Marietta furrowed her brows, a question resting at the tip of her tongue.

"LET ME IN NOW." The bellowing of a voice carried down the hallway. Gods, was that Keyain?

"That why I'm sitting here!" Deania laughed. "I'm your last line of defense in case they couldn't stop him from barging in."

Gods, oh gods. Marietta jumped up from the bench, hurrying towards his yelling. She knew this could happen, that Keyain would find out she went to the temple. He'd be furious and take it out on whoever was near him.

"DO YOU KNOW WHO I AM?"

Keyain stood in the antechamber's doorway, red-faced with bulging veins in his neck as the half-elven man she saw earlier held him back with one hand. "You know the rules, lord. This is a holy place; we stand separate from the law," the half-elf said with a modulated voice, even with Keyain snarling in his face.

The half-elven man stood as high as Keyain but didn't possess the same bulk. Curly black hair hung from the top of his head, the sides a faded shave, and his skin a dark brown.

"Then you know that's my wife in there, wrongfully taken from the palace," he said with a growl, glancing over his shoulder at Amryth. She leaned against the far wall of the antechamber with her arms crossed, her face unamused.

"As I said," the half-elf answered, "just let her finish. It shouldn't be much longer now."

"Do you understand how late it is?" Keyain yelled again, pushing him.

His effort had no effect as the half-elf stood his ground. At his hip was a sword, one he didn't reach for even as Keyain fought him. "Look, I get it. You're worried, it's late, and your wife was missing. But you have to see it from our point of view. Marietta was a mess when she came in, and she chose to come here. As an attendant to the goddess Therypon, I have a duty to ensure she gets the help—"

"Marietta had all the help she needs at the palace," Keyain hissed, cutting him off before he could finish.

"That's funny because Amryth said you allowed your wife to become a shell of a person in just a few months." The half-elf gave a speculative look. Keyain swung at him, but the man stopped Keyain's fist with his hand. "If you are getting any more violent tonight, we will remove you from the premise."

"I dare you to try," Keyain growled back.

Deania came to Marietta's side. "No need. Look, Marietta finished!" She took Marietta's hand and shook in the air like they were celebrating.

"Mar!" Keyain tried to push past the half-elf.

"Keyain, what're you doing here?" Marietta said in a taut voice.

"Come on, let's go. I told you that you didn't need a cult's help." The word cult was spat from his mouth as he glared at the half-elven male.

"Buddy, look at her. Marietta is much better now than when she came in." The half-elven man faced her, his jaw square and stubbled with scruff lining his full lips and wide nose. A tattoo curled up the side of his neck that Marietta couldn't make out from that distance.

"She wanted to come. King Wyltam even gave his permission." Amryth stepped forward, placing her hand on his shoulder.

He ground his jaw in frustration. "Mar, please." Keyain made to shove past the half-elf again. "Move. I'm taking her home."

"Marietta decides if she's ready, lord." The half-elf held him back, earning another snarl from Keyain.

"Is that another rule of your cult worshiping?" Keyain yelled in his face.

"No. That's me making sure Marietta feels safe leaving with you. We've seen domestic disputes like this before." He gave Marietta a concerned glance.

Keyain snarled again, attempting to shove past the half-elven man's hold.

Deania grabbed Marietta's arm and softly asked, "Are you comfortable going home with him tonight? It's okay to say no."

"I do... but things need to change, Keyain. I need my freedom—to not be locked in a room all day," Marietta paused, trembling. "And I want to come back. I'm not fixed by any means, but I feel like I'm finally taking my first breath after months of suffocating."

"We'll see, Mar. Please, let's just go home," Keyain said, eyes wide with worry.

"Do you promise to let her come back?" Deania spoke this time. Her voice stayed sweet but firm when addressing Keyain.

"We'll talk about it when we get home."

"Say you promise now. It's what she wants," the half-elven man spoke, still keeping his calm tone.

Keyain glared at him, his eyes alight with anger like she hadn't seen in a long time. "I promise," he said through gritted teeth.

The half-elf and Keyain stood back as Marietta passed through into the antechamber door.

"Be safe, Lady Marietta. You will always find peace and safety at the temple of Therypon. We look forward to seeing you again." The half-elf's words felt true as he spoke.

Chapter Thirty-Eight

VALERIYA

Slouched against an alley wall, Valeriya caught her breath after overhearing a passing guard say someone found Marietta at the Temple of Therypon. Relief flooded her, releasing the tension coiled in her chest.

If her memory served correctly, many flocked to Therypon for both mental and physical healing. For Marietta to go there meant she was in a worse condition than Valeriya first assumed. Guilt knotted her stomach. Perhaps learning of Tilan in such a way wasn't helpful to Marietta's already stressful life changes. No—this was on Keyain. Valeriya may have misjudged Marietta's reaction, but it was Keyain who was responsible for helping her.

To think Keyain let the situation get to where the girl had to flee the palace. Part of her believed the Exisotis came to get Marietta before Valeriya wielded her in court. It was only a matter of time before they would appear, whether Wyltam or Keyain believed they would. Marietta was one of their own.

The other part feared she was abducted, left to the fate of the other missing pilinos in Satiros. What would the crown do if a lady at court disappeared? Maybe that's what it took for Wyltam and Keyain to take action.

The evening breeze blew past, tossing the two braids woven down her back, reaching mid-waist. Though no one passing would see them, or the black leggings and top she wore. No, they would see a curvy half-elf walking along at night; the illusion magic would hold as long as Valeriya

maintained her concentration.

Deep within Greening Juncture, Valeriya paused in an alleyway to catch her breath. She had intended to reach the Weeds, the only section of the city where pilinos could live, to see if she could find her. Now that the danger had passed, Valeriya turned to make her way back to the palace.

"Interesting times for you to be out alone," slurred a deep voice as bodies appeared at the entrance of the alley.

Valeriya hid her sneer. Drunk males preying on a helpless pilinos stoked her anger. Typical. "Only trying to make it home."

Her steps were slow as she approached, her heart steady. In the dim, she made out three males who leered down at her half-elven form. A breeze caught the overbearing scent of alcohol that wafted from them. Three against one. In theory, Valeriya would be at a disadvantage, but she had the element of surprise on her side.

"Few of your kind making it home these days." A short male with choppy blond hair stepped forward, sizing her up. "Makes a dark alley a dangerous place for you."

What were the chances that these were the elves responsible for the missing pilinos? A wrathful smile curled to her lips as she pulled aithyr into her body. "Whatever do you mean?"

She stood a few feet from them now. One male ducked his head and stepped out of the alley. "All good," he called back to his friends.

"You could disappear like those other clips." He took a step to her right, the last of the trio stepping to her left.

Such words were implication enough for Valeriya. "I don't believe that for a second."

The males closed in. "You're a brave little clip, aren't you?"

Valeriya laughed as a sly smile slid to her face. "The problem with marking a target you don't know is that you run the risk of underestimating them."

The male to her left lurched forward, grabbing her wrist. In a fluid motion, she kicked the male in his knee and grabbed his arm, twisting as the male cried out in pain. Valeriya released the energy stored in her body through her grasp. Purple, crackling electricity danced around his limb as he dropped to the ground.

"The fuck?" The male behind her took a bewildered step back, stumbling.

"Nothing is ever as it seems," she said, pulling out a dagger. The light globes from the main street reflected on its glinted edge.

The male turned to run but Valeriya chucked her weapon. The metal found the soft spot behind his knee, the male collapsing. She chuckled as she approached the male sprawled on the ground, his panting the only sound. "Where are the missing pilinos?"

"Wh-what?" he stammered, cowering as she stood above him.

"Don't act stupid." Valeriya kicked, feeling the crack of his ribs. Wyltam had said that Keyain would take care of their disappearances but Valeriya knew that was as good as doing nothing. This was her chance to find them. "Tell me where they are and what you're doing with them."

"I don't know what you're talking about!" The male flinched as she kicked him again.

"I warned you. Don't—" A dull blow knocked into the back of her skull, her version going white from the pain. She joined the male on the ground, groaning as she tried to stand.

"What in the hells is this?" The male who attacked her from behind stood over her with furrowed brows. "She looks exactly like…."

The male on the ground next to her scrambled back. "She looks like Queen Valeriya."

She glanced down at her body, realizing her illusion dropped with the hit to her head. "Shit," she hissed, rolling into a crouched position.

Though it was unlikely anyone would ever believe that the Queen attacked them in an alley, it wasn't a rumor she was eager to have going around. The best way to remain discreet for her and her sister's plan was to give no hints of Valeriya's mage abilities—which included any rumors. With a sigh, she resigned herself to the task she must complete.

Aithyr coated her body in her disguise once more as she sized them up. "As I said, an unknown target can be the most dangerous one." Valeriya glared at the two males who pulled knives out. "You've chosen poorly this evening."

With a quick motion, Valeriya threw the dagger at the male to her left, trailing its trajectory. The male hit the blade away, but Valeriya was on him before he could attack. With one foot placed behind him, she used her body's momentum to shove, causing him to trip, and she pulled another dagger to her hand.

"Stupid bitch," the male said as he thudded to the gravel and stones of the alley.

Valeriya jumped on him, pinning his arms down with her knees as she aimed for his jaw before he could speak again. Her punch landed, sending pain through her hand and earning a crack from his jaw. As she went to hit again, crackling lightning danced around her fist.

The male bucked, throwing Valeriya off him. Before she responded, he stood, drawing his leg back, and kicked her in the chest. Pain bloomed with a snap. He drew back his leg and kicked again, landing in the same spot. Valeriya grabbed his leg on his next kick, pulling him back to the ground. The male had seen who she was—incapacitating him would no longer be an option. Her dagger found its mark between his ribs, fresh blood coating her hand.

A panicked cry came from the end of the alley. The other male crawled towards the main street with her dagger still penetrating the back of his knee. Valeriya jumped up, closing the space between them.

"Please," he begged. "I swear—"

Valeriya grabbed him by his hair, placing the edge of her dagger against the pulse of his neck. "One last chance. Tell me what you've done with the missing pilinos."

"Help!" he shrieked, fighting against her hold. "Help—"

The blade cut deep, silencing his cries.

Valeriya dropped her dagger by the unconscious male, the one she knocked out with magic. At least he had lived, meaning the guards would have one of them to question.

Footfalls sounded from the main street, followed by the barking of orders. Valeriya faded into the dark of the alley, taking off before someone would see her.

She had never taken a life prior to this. The blood on her hands and the stillness of their bodies haunted her as she traveled through the city streets. Though she had trained to become a mage, she never believed that she would need to kill anyone. Now, she'd killed two. There was one slight solace to the edge of guilt she felt: pilinos would stop disappearing. That terror ended at the edge of her knife. The thought steadied her as she raced toward the palace.

Chapter Thirty-Nine
MARIETTA

A warm, humid wind blew past Marietta's face, the petrichor scent thick in the breeze. A smile crept onto her face even as Keyain gripped her arm, leading her down the temple steps. City guards waited at the bottom, Amryth remaining at Marietta's side instead of falling in line with the rest. The chirp of crickets cried from small pockets of greenery that dotted the cityscape.

Her body no longer felt the relentless weight she'd been carrying for months. She got herself out; she got herself free. Though Keyain's rage was a breath away, held back by only his need to appear calm in front of others, Marietta continued to smile as he wove her through the cobblestone city streets.

Light globes drifted overhead with their warm glow. Flower boxes sat beneath windows, spilling over with blooms of every color. Mature oak trees dominated tiny parks as they passed, surrounded by greenery and statues like the ones in the palace. Marietta longed to stop and explore the fascinating city, but Keyain pulled her along.

"Amryth, give us some space," Keyain said, making the soldier step in line with the other guards. Once she was out of earshot, he hissed, "What the fuck were you thinking? You've made a spectacle of yourself, escaping the suite amid pilinos vanishing on the streets. You could've been the next victim, Marietta."

"If you had taken me to the temple yourself, then this wouldn't have happened." Marietta's eyes wandered to the Satiroans walking the streets. An elven lady leaned over to her companion, hand over her mouth, as they

stared in their direction. They weren't the only ones to take notice of their party.

"You shouldn't have gone to the temple at all," he snapped. Keyain took a heavy breath, reining in his anger as he noticed the people gawking and pulled her closer by wrapping an arm around her middle. "This is an absolute embarrassment," he said under his breath.

Marietta laughed, unable to help herself. After months of trapping her in the suite, letting her deteriorate into the shell of who she used to be, Keyain remained more worried about his public image. "Wouldn't want anyone to know that Satiros' greatest warrior married a feral clip," she said, the slur causing him to recoil.

"Enough, Mar," he said after a moment. "We'll deal with this once we're home."

Home. The idea was laughable. That tiny suite was not her home but her cell. No matter how many comforts Keyain gave her, it would remain as so.

Silence settled between them as they returned to the palace. The guards dispersed once they were inside the halls, and Keyain wasted little time hauling Marietta back to their suite. He shut the door behind him, turning to Marietta. "Sit down," he ordered, gesturing to the dining table.

His tone sparked a flame of anger in her chest. Vexed, she walked to the table, crossing her arms as she leaned against it.

Keyain sighed, pinching the bridge of his nose. "Fine, stand for all I care," he said, exasperated. "What do you have to say for yourself?"

"Excuse me?"

"An apology would be nice, at least."

Marietta gave an irritated laugh. "I owe you nothing, the least of all an apology."

He sulked, arms crossed over his chest as his hulking frame towered over her. "You owe me an explanation then—something I can tell the King and Queen after half the guard was sent into the city to search for you."

"Are you not listening?" she asked, pushing off the table. "Have I not been telling you I need help? That I wanted to go to the temple for help?"

"You're the one not listening," he said, leaning down towards her. "There are ways to help you in the palace—"

"And where is that help, Keyain?" She took a step towards him, craning her neck to stare into his glaring face. "What have you done to help me since I've been here?"

"Well, you were on drugs, but Valeriya—"

"Queen Valeriya gave me what I wanted," she snarled. "I don't want to be drugged, unaware of the world around me. I want to live—I want to be present. This," she said, gesturing between them, "needs to change. You stripped me of everything—"

"I saved you, Marietta," Keyain said, grabbing her shoulders with a slight shake. "I gave you the truth. Aren't you happier knowing?"

"Learning the truth was devastating!" She shifted from his grip, glaring at him. "I was struggling, alone, confined to just my thoughts. You couldn't even be bothered to take me out of this gods damned suite!"

Keyain recoiled from her yelling, his face grimacing. How funny that she, who stood barely to his chest, could make Satiros' greatest warrior flinch. Such power bolstered her, Marietta's words growing sharper. "I'm done. I'm done waiting for you, done being alone, done being at your whim. You've stripped me of myself, and I will put myself back together," she said, stepping towards the bedroom door. "Go ahead and think you've saved me, Keyain, but you didn't. You've damned me, and now I'll save myself."

"Marietta, we're not—"

She shut the bedroom door, cutting off his sentence. Keyain slammed his fist, the table thudding in response, followed by the clinking of glasses. Typical. He always turned to alcohol when he felt negative emotions.

Marietta leaned against the door with her eyes closed as a smile laced her lips. Tomorrow she would get out. Tomorrow she wouldn't be alone.

Tomorrow, she would be one step closer to being free.

Part 2

"Be patient and tough; one day this pain will
be useful to you."

– Ovid, Metamorphoses

Chapter Forty

MARIETTA

The sun came out the following morning; the weather matched her new optimism. A note waited for her at the table, an invitation to join the Queen for tea at noon. Of course, she likely heard of Marietta missing the day prior. She should have expected such a request.

Marietta took her time with breakfast, savoring the taste of the fresh figs with her yogurt. Though she couldn't eat much, her stomach filling up fast after a month of poor eating, each bite kept the smile on her face. Likewise, she spent the morning getting ready, soaking in the tub until her fingers pruned. She even allowed the handmaids to help, appreciating their quiet enthusiasm towards Marietta's change. Peace nestled into her core, her head remaining free of racing thoughts and negative attitudes. Things were about to change for her; she could feel it.

In the late morning, Marietta lounged on the high-back chairs in the living room, half reading, half staring out to the Central Garden. A knock at the door tore her from her thoughts as Amryth entered the suite.

"Look at you," she said with a crooked smile. In the peaceful atmosphere of the suite, her leather armor and sword at her hip were almost jarring.

"A bit of an improvement from a nightgown," Marietta said. "Figured if the Queen wants to see me for tea, then perhaps I might wear something less revealing."

Amryth snorted, taking the chair across from her. "With the court styles, I'm not sure if it is less revealing."

Marietta glanced at the low neckline of her dress and laughed with her. It was a bit excessive, but the dove gray fabric was soft against her

skin and the embroidered leaves and white flowers along the straps looked pretty. At least the Satiroans had good taste in clothing.

"What brings you here so early?" Marietta asked, setting her book on the table between them.

"To make sure nothing went wrong after Keyain brought you back last night." Her expression said more than her words, with worried brows and a grimace tugging at her lips.

"You haven't seen that side of Keyain before, have you?"

"No," Amryth said, staring out into the garden. "I've known him my entire life. Keyain is stoic, quiet; always the collected, fearless leader. Easy to smile, yet always a big deal if someone can get him to crack a laugh."

"He was like that when we first met." Marietta gave a weak smile at the memories. "A hard-ass, too good to dance and let loose."

"Did he ever let loose?"

"With the right mix of alcohol, he did," Marietta said, her smile slashing into a smirk. "Once, I got him to dance on the tables with me at a tavern in Avato. He was so embarrassed the next day."

"Quite the difference to how he is in Satiros."

"Yeah," Marietta said, nodding her head, her smile fading. Keyain was nothing like himself in those days.

"His actions and words were inexcusable last night," Amryth added, drawing back Marietta's attention. "It doesn't matter that you're his wife, or that you left without him knowing—he let you waste away and his behavior was highly inappropriate."

"Can you say that about your superior?"

Amryth laughed darkly. "Can I respect him as my superior when he threatens temple attendants? When he drags you through the city, not bothering to hide his anger after letting you deteriorate?"

"I guess not. That temper was part of why I left him."

Amryth reached out to hold Marietta's hands, her expression growing serious. "Do you feel safe with him?"

"Keyain would never lay a hand on me." Marietta avoided Amryth's gaze.

"Sure, but there are other ways he can hurt you. I already know you're not here by choice, so your position is at his whim. Does he yell at you in private like he did last night?"

"Only once since I've been in Satiros. But I yelled, too, fought back against him."

Amryth shook her head, her frown deepening. "You yelling doesn't put it on equal footing. He has all the power in this situation. I fear for you. And not just me—Deania and Coryn from the temple agree."

"Coryn?"

"The half-elf who held Keyain back last night. He and Deania were the attendants that helped me when I first visited," Amryth said, squeezing her hand. "They also expressed that if you are ever in danger, the temple of Therypon will intercede on your behalf."

"Gods, I'm not in that much danger."

"There's never been a half-elf at court, Marietta. Many aren't happy about it—about you. Keyain protects you from the brunt of it." Amryth paused, her face pensive. "If things get worse again, please come to me. I can help you—Coryn and Deania can help you. You're not alone."

The swell of emotion caught in Marietta's throat, not realizing how much she needed to hear someone say those words. "And if Keyain prevents the temple from helping again?"

"Then he'll be breaking the law. Deania and Coryn know you wish to return, so they'll know when to come knocking." She hesitated, uncertainty flashing across her features. "I hope it never comes to this, but the temple can also claim you under their protection if your position turns dangerous again. It can be a messy situation, but we're here if you need it."

Marietta choked on her words, and tears blotting her vision. "Thank you."

"Of course," Amryth said, squeezing her hands.

"Would you join me on a walk before my tea time with the Queen?"

A smile broke across Amryth's face. "I would love to."

Marietta savored the sun's warmth on her skin as she walked with Amryth through the Central Garden. Never again would she go so long without that sensation, a promise she made to herself.

As the time inched closer to noon, Amryth led Marietta back towards the Royal's Wing, leading her past the stairs that she took to the balcony where she usually met the Queen for tea. The invite said to meet in The Queen's Garden, which was at the center of the Royal's Wing. A bright hallway next to the stairs ran to a glass-paned door flanked by guards. Amryth gave her a quick hug before taking off for her shift.

Alone, Marietta pushed open the door to find a small courtyard. Lavender lined the sandstone tiles, its pattern spiraling towards the center to a towering fountain carved into the shape of an oak tree. Water trickled down from the boughs, sounding like rain, and when the sunlight caught the droplets, they shined like gems.

Wisteria hung from a trellis that overhung a path on the far side of the courtyard. Marietta followed it, hearing the screaming giggles of a child coming from beyond. It led to a large grassy area surrounded by dense trees and plants. The small black-haired child from before ran in the grass, the nursemaid chasing him.

"Marietta, I'm pleased you could come." The Queen sat in a cushioned chair resting below a gauzy white umbrella, casting her in the shade. "I hope you don't mind Prince Mycaub playing while we talk. I reserve this time for him, yet I heard you were feeling better...." Her voice trailed off as Marietta approached. A frown came to her face as she took in Marietta's thin frame.

Marietta noted the tight navy dress she wore with a high neck and long sleeves, unusual for hot weather. "Thank you for inviting me, Queen Valeriya." She curtsied before taking a seat.

"It's been quite some time since our last meeting. I grew worried when you turned down my requests for tea. Keyain waited to share you were sick until I found out from other sources." The Queen stared at Marietta, her expression insinuating she understood what made her ill. Her voice faded to a whisper as she frowned. "Look at you, so thin."

"It was a rough time," Marietta said, confused by her concern, "but I'll be alright, my Queen. How have *you* been?"

Queen Valeriya looked at her son off in the distance, his high-pitched squeals of laughter breaking their silence. Her fingers drummed on the arms of the chair. "Marietta, do you know where I am from?" Her gaze followed the toddler as he ran through the grass.

She had never thought of where she came from, even after she admitted she didn't like the King. "I assumed you were from one of the city-states of Syllogi."

Queen Valeriya shook her head. "I was raised in Reyila, the mountainous elven queendom north of Enomenos. Much is different here than there. In Reyila, we welcome all. Human, elf, half-elf. I have even met people from the orc clans of the far south." A small smile tugged at her lips, then dropped.

"Wyltam approached my sister, Queen Nystanya, with his proposal to marry me. After my sister had married her husband, Auryon from Chorys Dasi, she thought it'd be beneficial to tie our family to another ruling family of Syllogi. We thought that Wyltam would see me as an equal, that I would help command at his side." Queen Valeriya laughed, though no humor touched her expression. "I was naïve in both my belief that Wyltam would see me as his equal and that I could change Satiros, to blend its citizens like Reyila. The transition to Satiros was difficult. I was in a political marriage to a stranger in a city-state I didn't understand; the hardest part was having different views from my husband." She looked at Marietta, her eyes filled with sadness. "The people of Satiros think that because elves have the longest life span that we are the dominant race. They believe pilinos exist to be subservient to elves."

Marietta's heart thrummed in her chest, remembering learning of the elven-ruled Reyila. She hadn't realized they were mixed like Enomenos— that their elven viewed pilinos as equals. Queen Valeriya was like Marietta, away from her home, and married to a man with different beliefs. "Keyain seems to also carry that belief." Marietta bit her tongue, regretting her words. Why would she share that?

The Queen paused for a moment. "Do you understand how odd it is that you and Keyain are married?"

Marietta laughed carefully. "Now that I'm here, I understand."

"How do you feel about his views—of Satiros' views?" The Queen raised her brows, giving Marietta a pointed look.

"Oh, I just love them," she said, her tone dripping with sarcasm. "There's nothing more heartwarming than knowing the man I'm married to believes I'm less than a person to him." She should have held back, not be so frank in her frustrations, but after Keyain's refusal to help her, Marietta could only feel bitterness that sparked the sarcasm.

"Unsurprising that you feel that way considering his mistreatment."

Marietta and the Queen jumped at the sudden deep voice that sounded behind them—King Wyltam. Startled, Marietta jumped from her seat, turning to the King with a curtsy. "King Wyltam, it's good to see you again." Like the day he visited Marietta, he wore all black, and on his head rested a simple crown of gold.

"That it is. I'm happy to see you're well enough to dress."

Queen Valeriya made a slight sigh at the comment, though Marietta was unsure if the King meant it as an insult. Unlike most people, she had a hard time gauging his tone and reading his expression. It was as if nothing excited, bored, or angered him. His demeanor was like stone—no, colder. An icy, expressionless mask with piercing black eyes that missed nothing as they searched Marietta.

The King turned to Queen Valeriya. "Take Mycaub inside. I wish to have a moment alone with Marietta." Coldness crept through his deep tone as he spoke.

"Though we haven't had tea yet?" she bristled, walking to stand next to Marietta. She sighed, clasping her hands before her. "It seems your time is accounted for, Marietta. We'll have to do tea another day." Without waiting for a response, she took off toward her son, scooping the giggling child into her arms before entering the Royal's Wing.

Once alone, King Wyltam cleared his throat. "I see you're still lying, though the sarcasm is a nice change." The King's gaze continued to rake over her as he stepped forward, narrowing the space. "You still appear gaunt but the blackness under your eyes has eased. Are you feeling better after your excursion yesterday?"

Marietta searched his expression for any sign of mocking, yet found none. "A little, yes."

"Good." His stare landed on the side of her face, his hand reaching. "May I?"

Confused, Marietta nodded as the King brought his hand to her hair, tucking it behind her ear. The chill of his fingers brushed the blunted arched tip, causing Marietta's heart to race.

"A half-elf in court. If only my mother were alive to see it." The edge of his lips hinted at a smile, beautiful and threatening. Marietta exhaled as he dropped his hand, taking a step back.

"I'm sure if she were alive, then I wouldn't be standing here, Your Grace," she said, letting the bold words slip from her mouth, though she knew little of the late queen.

A small laugh escaped King Wyltam, the brief look of amusement flashing on his features. "You don't realize how right you are." He offered his arm. "Please, walk with me."

Marietta hesitated, then took his arm, letting the King lead her to a path that wove through lilac bushes and boxwoods among the trees. The King of Satiros first made a personal visit and now escorted Marietta within the royal's private garden. The thought was nauseating. Why her? Why his consideration at all?

"Your existence surprised us all, not knowing Keyain married, nor that his wife was held hostage," he said after a moment. "Curious that after the horrendous experience you must have had in Enomenos, he allowed you to suffer alone in that suite." The black of his eyes found Marietta. "Did you get the help you needed yesterday?"

Marietta thought of the temple, of its eucalyptus and peppermint scent, of the goddess's serene face carved into stone, of the two half-elves, Deania and Coryn, who risked Keyain's threats to help her. "I did," she said, a smile touching her lips as she stared down the path. "More than I knew I needed."

"That's good to hear."

From walking at his side, she felt the rumble in his chest as he spoke. "May I ask you a question, King Wyltam?"

"Please do."

"Why is that good to hear?" She turned to him, tucking her hair behind an ear. "You're the King of Satiros, and you've spent more time with me than you ought."

Paused in the middle of the path, the King was inches from her as he stared through the waves of dark hair. "A few reasons, really," he said, his gaze searching her face. "For one, you are the wife of my closest friend and that should be reason enough." He lowered his face to hers as he murmured, "And you may have information that proves useful."

Marietta scoffed, trying to pull away from the King, but his arm held. "Unfortunately, I know nothing." Of course, she was just of use to him. As if she would share anything about Enomenos with the man, leading the assault on her home.

"Forgive me, I've offended you."

Marietta furrowed her brows at his apology, a thousand questions surfacing in her thoughts. In an instant, he was both insulting and kind. She couldn't decide if the King mocked her or took her seriously. "You're a king. You don't apologize."

"All kings rule in their own way."

His arm loosened, letting Marietta put space between them as she stood before the King and his undivided attention. Never had she met someone so conflicting, unable to read him and unsure whether to dislike him or not. "I'm sure you are too busy to care what happens to me; yet, here we are."

"Yes," he drawled, "here we are. Me, a king ruling a city-state in war, and you, wife of the male leading the war. A wife who despises her husband after he risked his career to save you."

Icy dread filled Marietta as the King regarded her, his hands clasped behind his back, his stare unceasing. So that's what this visit was about.

The truth that Keyain hid that now Marietta was burdened to carry.

"I don't despise Keyain," she lied. Gods, she did—more than despised—but the King shouldn't know the truth after Keyain lied.

King Wyltam raised a brow and began circling Marietta. She held her chin high as he stood behind her. Breath danced across her ear, the deep of the King's voice barreling through her. "Liar."

"Excuse me?" Marietta went to turn to him, but the King's hand clutched her shoulder.

"As I said, everyone lies at court, Marietta, but I had higher hopes for you."

"I'm not lying—"

"Another lie. Perhaps this meeting was for nothing if you can't share a shred of truth with me."

Is that what he thought this was? A meeting? Marietta doubted there had ever been a pilinos alone with the King for *a meeting*. Having the King's attention was a danger—one she wasn't sure was worth the risk. Unnerved, Marietta stood on the path with the King at her back. The chirping of birds and rustling of leaves were the only sounds besides her heavy breathing. "What is it you would like to know, King Wyltam?"

"Many things, but let's start with what I do know." His hand fell from her shoulder, Marietta spinning to face him as he spoke. "You do not wish to be here, and you do not love Keyain. Loveless unions are common for nobility," he said, pausing as he leaned closer to her, "but Keyain loves you—and his love goes unrequited."

Marietta held her tongue.

"Though you wish to leave Satiros, I cannot send you back to Olkia." He paused, his expression unreadable. "What do I do with you?"

"A good question," she said, her tongue sharpening. "What do you do with someone you have no use for?"

A small smile cracked the King's expression. "I never said you couldn't be of use. Keyain made a fool of me by keeping your marriage secret. From what I can gather you don't think fondly of your marriage, so I come to you with a proposal."

Nerves knotted her stomach. "And what would that be, King Wyltam?"

"Seek retribution; give Keyain grievance for his actions by accepting my flirtations."

Marietta laughed, unable to help herself. "What kind of proposal is that?"

His demeanor hardened. "You know Keyain, and you understand how deep his jealousy runs."

Marietta shook her head, looking off into the garden. "You're asking to flirt with me in order to spike Keyain's jealousy."

"Do you not hate your husband?" the King asked. "Quick to anger, possessive of you? Accept my advances—kind words, small presents, my attention—and you can be the source of what pains him."

The idea was tempting, to make Keyain helpless against his friend, to anger and irritate him where it hurt most. Gods, maybe she should accept; yet, it was a game—one that used Marietta. She wouldn't allow herself to be used as such. "You think of me as a pawn," she said, breaking their silence. "One you can manipulate as you please. Yes, I am beyond livid with Keyain for more reasons than you can fathom, King Wyltam, but now that I have a bit of freedom, I won't ruin it by stoking his anger."

"Even knowing that my word carries more weight than his?" he asked. "I can intervene if he tries to lock you away again. I can stop his removal of you from the palace."

"I would hope you'd intervene regardless of this arrangement." She crossed her arms, glaring at the King. "Find someone else you can use to agitate Keyain. I want no part in it."

The King released a slow breath, his gaze darting over the garden. "You're being stubborn. Perhaps, if given time to think on it, you will warm to the idea."

"I think not," she said. "My time in Satiros is strenuous enough without your attention."

"All I ask is that you think on it."

"Fine." All Marietta wanted was to be free of the garden and his presence.

King Wyltam regarded her for a moment longer, the muscle in his jaw tightening, before turning to face the garden with his hands clasped behind his back. "You're dismissed, Lady Marietta."

Chapter Forty-One
MARIETTA

Once again, tea time with the Queen led Marietta to spiral; yet this time had no tea or queen—just the King and his ridiculous plan to agitate Keyain. Irritated, she paced in the hallway to the Queen's Garden. Why would the King offer Marietta retribution against Keyain? His Minister of Protection? His offer made little sense. Even if she were willing to be his pawn, why would agitating Keyain benefit him?

Marietta had witnessed Keyain's wrath and jealousy. Often in the last weeks of their relationship, he would act out violently against those who talked with her, unable to control his emotions. He became near-obsessive, clingy, and overprotective. Hate burned in her chest at the memory. No, the King's deal would only make her situation worse.

Not having a reason for the King's proposal nagged at her mind. This went deeper than Keyain hiding his marriage. He might have made King Wyltam look foolish, but whatever his actual reasoning went beyond that. The question burned at the tip of her tongue: why?

Not being able to gauge the King's emotions left her at a disadvantage. He was an emotionless void, cold and fathomless; yet, her mind lingered on the moments his icy demeanor melted with a small smile, amusement in his eyes. Sure, he was cold, but he was also intriguing. An enigma. A threat. A headache.

"Marietta? Is everything alright?" Amryth said, approaching from down the hall.

"Just a very odd afternoon." Odd didn't even describe it.

"You're rattled like last time." Amryth's expression said what her words didn't. *Did the Queen do something?*

"I'm alright but I can't go back to the suite like this. I need a distraction." She ran a hand through her hair. "Can I show you something? Something you can't share with Keyain or anyone else?" She itched under her skin to move, to be busy.

"You think I'd tell him anything at this point?"

Marietta smiled. "No, I suppose you wouldn't. Can you take me to the kitchens?"

"Welcome back, Lady Marietta!" called a voice as they entered the bustling kitchens. The older elven man from her last visit approached with a smile. "That pie was splendid! We made the changes you had suggested."

Amryth looked at Marietta with furrowed brows.

The tension in Marietta's shoulders eased. "You don't know how happy that makes me," she said, smiling. "Though I'm afraid I forgot to ask for your name the last time I visited."

The old elven man dropped into a bow, silver hair gleaming in the light. "Chef Emynuel, my lady."

"A pleasure to see you again, Chef Emynuel. Do you mind if I take over one of your workspaces?"

The chef gestured for her to go ahead before returning to his work. With a quick smile to Amryth, Marietta went to the pantry for the ingredients.

"Are you going to explain or will I have to guess?" Amryth said at the door, her arms crossed.

Marietta thrust a bag of almond flour at her and turned back, gathering other supplies. "This is just something I need to do."

Amryth shrugged her shoulders, looking annoyed to hold the bag, but carried it back to the station.

A plume of flour rose as Marietta added her dry ingredients to a bowl. In another, she whisked together softened butter with sugars. The kitchen workers used a magical item that mixed ingredients with no effort. Marietta heard of the device, but she was baking for the familiarity of her methods.

She folded the dry ingredients into the butter and sugar mixture before adding the eggs, mixing the batter until smooth. Once added to a round pan, she slid it into the oven and patted the flour off her dress.

"Well, that was surprising—I haven't seen you smile like that ever," Amryth said with a softness in her eyes.

"Baking brings me joy. That's why I stopped helping businesses and opened a bakery. That and the long hours of traveling were taxing for Tilan and I." Marietta cupped her chin, leaning on the counter.

"I'm glad I got to witness a genuine part of you. You've seemed empty of a person since you've been here."

"Because I have been. Losing Tilan, even with his lies," Marietta said, emotions choking her words, "hurts. It hurts so much." She bit the inside of her cheek, eyes blinking so tears wouldn't fall. "I miss him. I miss the life we had built. Being here, in this kitchen baking, reminds me that I had that life. That I could make my own decisions—that I had freedom."

Amryth considered her words. "You mentioned before that Tilan was a fraud. What did he lie about?"

With a glance around the room, ensuring no one paid attention to their conversation, Marietta dropped her voice. "I knew less about my late husband than I thought. According to Queen Valeriya and Keyain, Tilan was a leader of the Exisotis—Keyain even had documented proof."

Amryth let out a long sigh. "That part I was aware of, unfortunately. When Keyain briefed us on the mission, he shared that a leader of the Exisotis captured his wife. I thought you knew he was in the Exisotis."

"I didn't," Marietta said quietly, dragging her finger through the loose flour that remained on the counter. "And I also learned Tilan knew Keyain. That the Exisotis planned for Tilan to marry me to use against him." A shaky breath exhaled from her. "Our relationship started with a lie."

Amryth placed a hand on Marietta's arm. "Did you ever once feel like he didn't love you?"

"No. Never."

"Then perhaps, even given the circumstances, he really did love you."

The sounds of the kitchen filled their silence, Marietta remembering her days at the bakery. "When I decided to open the bakery, I was most excited to sleep next to Tilan at night. To see him every day, to not be away from him."

As another swell of emotion tightened her throat, Marietta focused on slicing almonds for the cake. When Marietta had needed help prepping, Tilan closed his smithy for two weeks to help her. And she loved it—two weeks of just them and the excitement of a new business.

The day the bakery opened, friends and old clients lined the street. Tilan was with her, helping her, supporting her. There were so many people to be thankful for, tears coming to her eyes as their faces flooded her memory.

"All the people I cared about in Olkia—I don't know if they're okay. I don't know who's alive." Tears dropped as Marietta stilled, her hand gripping the knife as she stared at the countertop.

"You lost more than your husband that night. You lost a family, a community." Amryth patted Marietta's back. "I'm so sorry this happened to you."

Marietta took a deep breath, slowing her tears. "The temple helped. It reminded me that people care, that life goes on, and I have to keep trying to survive." She peeked into the oven, seeing the browning of the cake, and pulled it out.

"That's what it did for me," Amryth said after a moment. "Helped guide me on my journey to heal."

On a stovetop, Marietta brought honey and water to a boil into a sweet, sticky syrup while the cake cooled.

"I can't thank you enough, Amryth," Marietta said, looking up. "You saved me, and I'm forever grateful."

"I only wish I never left."

Turning to the cooled cake, Marietta shrugged and drew a knife around the edge of the cake pan to loosen the edges, then flipped it over onto a plate. She added the almonds to the honey syrup and then spooned the mixture over top of the cake.

That was her favorite cake recipe, reminding her of sunny summer afternoons. The sweetness of the honey and the nuttiness of the almonds made the perfect combination. It was her go-to recipe because she could always get the ingredients in Olkia.

Marietta cut the cake into slices, sharing it with Amryth, Emynuel, and whoever stopped to see what she made.

"This is spectacular." Amryth covered her mouth, which was still filled with her first bite. Emynuel and his team murmured in agreement. Marietta smiled to herself, happy to have made something for them to all enjoy.

An afternoon filled with laughter, swapping of stories, and helping the staff gave Marietta a chance to work through her frustration, to reset her mind. Much was different in Satiros, but for one afternoon, she could pretend she still lived a normal life.

Chapter Forty-Two

MARIETTA

BEFORE

Nervous behind the counter of her bakery, Marietta fretted after spending the last few days baking and preparing for her first day in business. Pastries, cookies, and sweet buns filled the case below the counter. The small fortune she paid for the enchanted cabinets would preserve the quality of her baked goods.

"Ready, my love?" Tilan walked up from the kitchen, the apron around his waist wet from washing dishes. A few loose strands of dark hair broke free from his knot that he pushed away with a hand.

He had been a tremendous help, stocking the shop and readying it to open, even closing his smithy to help her prepare for her opening. If her projections were correct, she'd make enough income to hire a few workers in the coming weeks.

"For the first time in my life, I don't know if I did enough." Marietta frowned, staring out at the seats and tables placed at the front of the shop. The building sat at the corner of two main streets in Olkia's central district. Through the broad windows that overlooked the streets, she could see the uptick in morning foot traffic.

"Who is this version of Marietta?" Tilan said, teasing. "Never thought I'd see the day you questioned your own work. You sent your former clients flyers, told all your friends about your opening. Gods, you even handed out samples in the market—that was just to get the word out. Per usual, you've done more than most people in your position."

Marietta shrugged off the compliment. Gods, she really wasn't acting like herself. It was hard to, knowing that the work she had been putting in would culminate in how her bakery did this week. If it was a flop, how could she just go back to helping others' businesses? Who'd want a failed business owner to help them?

Anxious to distract herself, she looked around for something to fix. The last batch of bread was nearly done in the oven as its scent filled the front of the shop. Marietta passed Tilan to the kitchen in the back, which was double the size of the storefront. Plenty of storage lined the walls and underneath workspaces, and one wall had four different ovens stacked two by two.

The bread looked perfectly browned as she pulled the loaves from the oven to cool. A specialty box built next to the window drifted the hot bread's scent to people walking on the street—one of Tilan's creations. The location would receive a lot of foot traffic that she planned to utilize.

"Being nervous is natural, especially when doing something new. Just don't spoil it for yourself," Tilan said, carrying the racks of hot bread.

"I'm not used to feeling nervous," she muttered. "I'm still excited but I'll feel better after we get past the first few days."

With shaky legs, Marietta walked to the front of the shop and unlocked her doors. A peek into the street sent her jaw dropping. People lined up outside, waiting for her to open. She snapped the door shut and looked at Tilan, her eyes wide.

"What is it?" he asked.

"There's a line of people."

Tilan stared at her. "That's a good thing."

"But it's a line of people."

"Mar, you have to let them in."

She peered out the window. "What if I over-sold the quality of my baking?"

"Then everyone who has had your lemon bars must have shit for taste buds." Tilan slung a rag over his shoulder. "No one in their right mind would be disappointed in those."

"You have to say that; you're my husband."

Tilan rolled his eyes. "I have no such obligation to lie to you."

"So, if they're bad…."

"Marietta, they're great."

"Okay, but what about the bread?"

"It's bread. People like bread."

"What about—"

"Mar." Tilan's voice was soft but assuring. "You're a damn good baker. Let those poor people in."

Her heart stuttered as she stared at her husband. Nothing had ever made her this nervous. Not when she started her last business, not when she married Tilan. To put herself so boldly out there meant she had farther to fall. Even with her uncharacteristic anxiousness, Tilan stood by to get her through it.

Alright. She could do it. With a deep breath, she opened the doors and greeted her guests to her bakery, Rise Above. The customers filtered in, the faces of her friends mixed into the crowds. They would take a moment in the craziness to talk as she hustled behind the counter.

"Well, I'll be damned," said Pelok's booming voice as he got to the front of the line. "Looks like the business savant is officially a baker."

Marietta rolled her eyes as she smiled. "Don't sound so surprised."

He held up his hands. "I'm not, I swear. It's good to have you around all the time."

Marietta reached over the counter to hug him. "It's good to be around. What can I get you?"

"Do you have any glasses?" he asked with a grin.

"Seriously?" Marietta gave him a leveling stare.

"It's only fair if I break about half of yours."

"Pelok, my friend." Tilan slung his arm around Marietta as he approached. "You come to my wife's bakery on the day she's opening, and you're heckling her about the glasses again?"

"Gods, it wasn't even that many." Marietta shook her head, knowing it had been at least four dozen glasses that shattered at his tavern because she decided to dance on the bar. Well, it was because she *fell* while dancing on the bar.

Pelok scoffed. "It was that many—"

"I won't hesitate to kick your ass if you don't drop it." Even from behind, Marietta could tell Tilan smiled with the words. The two men had been friends since they were children.

"There will be no ass kicking in my bakery." Marietta slid out from under Tilan's arm. "Now, the alley behind the bakery is another story." Marietta grabbed a box and began filling it with Pelok's favorites.

"Fine. I'll accept baked goods as payment for the glasses." He grabbed the box from Marietta.

"Gods damned leech," Tilan muttered under his breath as he walked away.

Pelok laughed and tossed a few coins into Marietta's outstretched hand. The man could act like he only wants to heckle her, but she knew the truth. Pelok came because he was proud and excited for Marietta, even if he showed it in his own way.

A half an hour passed when a body collided with hers. "Look at this place! Gods, Marietta!" Tristina, her closest friend, wrapped her in a tight hug. Her bob of ash blonde hair bounced as she turned her head to check out the space. "Two weeks ago it didn't look like this."

"Well, we've been at it non-stop." Marietta hugged her back, taking a moment to catch her breath with her friend.

"I offered to come and help—Kole did too."

Marietta shewed away the words. "Who would've watched the boys?" She shook her head, knowing either Tristina or her husband had to take care of their sons. "I put these to the side for you."

"Are those the pastries you brought over for tea a few months ago?" Tristina grabbed her arm. "I've had dreams about those custard tarts. Will they be here tomorrow?" she asked, taking the box. "Because I'll need more by then."

Marietta laughed and took her money before Tristina went on her way. The half-elven woman matched Marietta for her energy, which often meant dancing at taverns until they needed to close for the night. Her heart warmed at the memories.

Patrons came and left the shop all morning. A long line snaked out the door when Marietta heard a small voice on the other side of the counter. "Mrs. Reid, do you have the chocolate cookies?" A small half-elven child named Brady asked, clutching his human mother's hand and standing between her and his elven father.

The Pystier family were the city's healers. The husband, Hyf, worked with his siblings to help heal the sick in and around the city-state, often at little cost to their patients. They were a cornerstone of their community.

"Of course, I have those chocolate cookies—I know they're your favorite!" Marietta threw in a few extra baked goods for them.

The faces of her community blurred in front of her, all coming to support her. Marietta could've wept from joy if she wasn't busy running back and forth, helping customers. Tilan continuously refilled the cabinets from their stock in the back. She sold everything by the late afternoon.

Marietta placed a closed sign on the door, locking it behind her. She leaned against the door. Her body was sticky with sweat.

Tilan laughed as he walked over to Marietta and picked her up in a swinging hug. Though his body was slim, smithing kept him strong. "All that worrying just to sell out of everything early." His kiss was gentle and loving as he held her in the bakery's front. "I'm proud of you."

Marietta leaned into his touch, half from exhaustion, half from being in love with this man. Through everything, he had been more than supportive. "I'm surprised so many people came." Marietta was still in awe, even as her body ached from a day of being on her feet with no break.

"I'm not surprised. The people of this community love you, Mar. You've made a bigger impact on them than you realize." Tilan offered her another quick kiss before disappearing into the back.

Marietta stood in the center of the storefront with her hands on her hips, surveying the damage. She needed to sweep and mop the floors, wipe down the cabinets, and count the money in the register. That didn't include all the baking she'd need to do for tomorrow.

Tilan returned with a bottle of wine and plates of food. "Take a seat, my love. First, we celebrate. Enjoy this moment."

They sat in the chairs at the front of the bakery, sipping on wine and eating a meal a friend had dropped off for them. Marietta looked around her bakery, and her heart swelled with love. She had made the right decision.

Chapter Forty-Three

ELYSE

Fluffy white clouds drifted through the sky, offering a reprieve from the sun's heat as Elyse crossed the courtyard. Courtiers milled about in the shade, most ladies with a parasol to help with the hot weather, but she paid them no mind as she strolled past, even as someone called her name. Gods, must there always be someone trying to talk to her in that damned palace? Not acknowledging the call, Elyse picked up her pace, stepping into the winding garden paths.

Nothing positive ever rose from those conversations, just more fuel for whatever mocking they deemed entertaining for the day. It was a shame Grytaine wasn't born as a lady at court—she would have fit in well with the younger nobles. Elyse could only imagine what they'd all have to say after her second failed betrothal, only lasting a couple of hours. Brynden had—no, she wouldn't let herself think of him.

Oh, but she could imagine Grytaine saying, *"First Keyain, now the Chorys Dasian? A shame, you'll have to find suitors in Kyeari or Amgiys who might not have heard of your reputation."*

The worst part was she would be right—everything she said had a bit of truth that Elyse could see. The other courtiers' words were the same, and she couldn't handle hearing them out loud when she already thought about them every damn day. So instead, she fled.

Hydrangeas, rock roses, and other flowering shrubberies, thick with blooms, lined the paths as she ventured deeper to the heart of the Central Garden. After living in the palace for most of her life, she knew the labyrinthine layout and the best hiding spots.

Off the path, Elyse took a dirt walkway that wound through knee-height lavender, yarrow, and boxwoods that led to a gap in the towering willow tree and its low-hanging boughs. Underneath the shade of the tree, Elyse leaned against the gnarled trunk, looking at the pond that stretched out to the other side.

The nearby frogs croaked as the willow's leaves rustled in the breeze, and the pond's water lapped onto the bank. Elyse took a deep breath, trying to clear her mind, her body growing more relaxed. The racing thoughts would help with nothing, and she needed to control them if she wished to become a mage.

"Fuck, Elyse."

She jumped, whipping around to where she entered the willow to find a scowling Sylas standing there, breathing heavy.

"What do *you* want?" she snapped, giving him a matching scowl. The last thing she needed was another rumor about her and the Chorys Dasians.

"Brynden said you were fast, but—" Sylas leaned his hands on his knees, then stood up straight, smoothing his black shirt. "I called your name. Did you hear me?"

"I did, and I chose to ignore it."

He shook his head, exasperated. "What is wrong with you? What's with the attitude?"

"Attitude? What's with stalking me?" She did have an attitude, but she didn't want to talk about Brynden.

"I'm doing *you* a favor here," he said, his scowl deepened.

"How is this a favor?"

From his pocket, he pulled out a piece of paper. "I'm no longer just Brynden's nursemaid, but also his errand boy."

"What is that?"

"A letter."

"Why do you have a letter for me?"

Sylas closed his eyes, swearing under his breath. "Because he wanted to apologize."

"For what? Being drunk and disorderly? For causing a scene that ended with another very public end to a betrothal?" Elyse should check her attitude, but frustration gave way as she spoke.

"You're angry."

"Yes, I'm angry."

"At him? Or Keyain and King Wyltam?"

"Oh, my gods. Yes, all of them," she snapped, crossing her arms. "I'm tired of being treated like an object, pushed from one hand to another. Brynden proved he would claim me just as they have."

"Because he wants you as his wife."

Wants. As in, *still wants.*

"Though I'm free of my father, Brynden will now have to ask King Wyltam for my hand, which he will not get."

Sylas sighed, pinching the bridge of his nose. "That's his next step in this asinine plan to win you back—to ask the King for your hand."

King Wyltam would turn him down, undoubtedly, for she was an asset to his crown. Elyse bit her lip to keep from saying something she would regret and held out her hand.

Sylas crossed the space and gave her the letter with a softened expression. Was it compassion? Sympathy? Whatever it was, Elyse preferred the scowl that matched her own emotions. She cut him a look, pausing before unfolding the paper.

Like a sailor drifting lost at sea, shipwrecked and alone, my body thirsted—an aching need for water, though surrounded by it. A goddess came, blessing me with her rain, quenching my thirst, and offering me salvation. Oh, how parched I was, so close to death, yet unaware until she bestowed on me her gift.

I drank greedily, happy to take my fill and rejoice in the goddess' blessing, but forgot to offer my gratitude, swept up in my own salvation. Within a blink, she disappeared, cast away by my negligence and selfishness, and again, I was alone in my suffering, with only myself to blame.

Having drunk the goddess's blessed rains, to fill myself with her gift, to then have it taken away, made the parchedness return with fervor. To have and have lost, only then did I realize the depth of my gratitude.

So each day, I call upon the goddess. I pray to her to return, if not to quench my thirst, then to offer the thanks she so deserved. To show her that I, a parched male, forgot myself and turned blind to that which was gifted. To express the impact the goddess had made, though my time in her presence was short. To let the goddess know that, each day, my aching need reminds me I have lost something divine, for I was swept up within myself.

So each day I pray to her.

And pray.

And pray.

Hoping the goddess deems me worthy of her presence again.

A lump formed in her throat, emotion choking her at the unexpected words of Brynden's letter. "He's poetic."

"He's dramatic," Sylas said, a smile curling to one side of his mouth.

Elyse reread the letter. "He couldn't have just written a normal apology?"

Sylas laughed, a full smile coming to his face. "Nothing he does is normal. Everything he does is extravagant and over the top. He wanted you to know that the only way to make peace with a goddess is through prayer, so he wrote one."

She shook her head, trying not to smile. "But does he mean it? Does he regret being a drunken ass? For claiming me like every other male in my life?"

"In his own way, yes," Sylas said with a shrug. "By the way you left the library, he understood you were upset enough to call off the marriage, though he wasn't sure exactly which part did it. He's been manic at the townhouse, replaying the entire day with me repeatedly, and I, unfortunately, know too much about you two now."

"Oh, my gods… how much did he tell you?" she said, blushing.

"You're acting bashful when I found him headfirst in your skirt? When I was the one to retie your dress?"

Elyse clenched her eyes shut, sighing. "I try to block that part out."

"Well, besides that, he shared what you said after we smoked—that you would love him forever if he could help you experience life, things that you missed," he said, frowning as he looked out over the pond.

"I did say that." And she had forgotten about it from all of that day's excitement.

"He also told me about your singing—that goddess was an accurate name for you based on your voice alone," his gaze slid to Elyse. "And he told me of the song you sang for him."

"You know it too?"

"I do, and it's surprising that you know it, that your mother remembered it enough to teach you." Sylas was quiet, his face settling into a scowl. "He's obsessed with you."

She smiled, looking down at the letter. "And he still wants to marry me?"

"For now," he said, considering his words. "Obsession isn't love. It holds no assurance for tomorrow."

Elyse nodded, her smile faltering. Obsession wasn't love. "You're his friend. Aren't you supposed to tell me things he wants me to hear?"

"If he brings you to Chorys Dasi and grows bored, I'll be the one to pick up the pieces."

The words stung, ripping right into Elyse's heart. "Ah, selfish motivations cloaked in kindness. Thanks for the lecture. You can go now." Elyse gave him a leveling stare, gesturing to the path.

"It's the truth, no matter how much it hurts to hear. I'm not your adversary."

"Sure, but you are an ass, and you can leave."

Sylas rolled his eyes, stalking back towards the path. He stopped between the boughs. "When can I get your response?"

"Response?"

"Brynden's expecting you to write him back."

"I didn't realize that," she said, biting her lip. Her love of reading didn't translate to a love of writing. Gods, what would she say? Her heart raced at the thought of talking to him again, though I would be just through letters.

"Usually when someone writes you a letter, they expect a letter back."

"Give me two days, and I'll meet you here, under the willow." That should give her enough time to figure out a response.

"Under the willow," he said with a nod. "I'll see you in two days, Elyse."

Chapter Forty-Four

MARIETTA

Marietta sat at her vanity, quietly working on her hair and face as Keyain hovered behind her, pacing. "Are you sure you want to go back to the temple today?" he asked.

"Gods, for the last time, yes." Marietta closed her eyes with a sigh. "Don't you have meetings or something else to do with your time?"

"I rescheduled them for later so I could see you off," he said, the sounds of his footsteps approaching.

"Of course you did," she grumbled, already in a sour mood from Keyain's fretting.

"And there are handmaids who can—"

"Keyain," she snapped, turning in her chair. "You need to stop."

He stood with his arms crossed, lines bracketing his mouth. "I'm allowed to worry," he said. "This is something perfectly worth worrying about."

"Well, keep it to yourself." Marietta turned back to her vanity, hooking a simple pair of gold earrings through her ears. "You already have how many guards coming with Amryth and me?"

"Four."

"That's four more than necessary."

"It's not nearly enough, considering you've insisted on walking to the temple." Keyain approached, setting his hands on her shoulders. "You should at least take a carriage."

"I want to see the city."

"You can see it from a carriage."

"Keyain!" She stood up, startling him, and seethed as she walked to the door. "You have to let me do things my way."

"Of all the ways you've changed, why couldn't your stubbornness have been one of them?" he snapped, following her out. "There are people in the city who want to hurt you."

Marietta turned to him, exasperated. "I'm sure there are people in the palace who wish to hurt me, too! You are more than welcomed to escort me yourself."

"You know I don't—"

"Have the time, yes, I know," Marietta said, brushing him off and walking to the front door. She opened it to find Amryth standing with her hands behind her back, face unimpressed, with four other guards.

Much to Marietta's displeasure, Keyain stood behind her with his hand clamped onto her shoulder. "If any of you fail to protect Marietta, consider yourselves demoted."

"Keyain, I swear to gods!" She turned to him, incredulous. "You picked these guards yourself!"

"Yes, but—"

"But nothing," she said, stepping out into the hall. "I'll see you at dinner."

"Marietta, wait."

She pinched the bridge of her nose, pausing her steps. "Can I please leave?"

Keyain turned her around, cupping his large hand to her cheek as his thumb brushed across it. "I love you. Please, be safe." He kissed her forehead before she jerked away, leaving him behind.

What right did he have to be this nervous? Yes, pilinos had disappeared from the streets, but not in the morning, and not when they were walking to a temple. Of all the ways Keyain could act, a simpering anxious husband was by far his worst. The sooner she got away from him, the better.

Marietta already felt on edge after a week of his coddling. Where was this caring when she refused to speak? When she didn't want to live? Of course, the only thing that had changed was her trip to the temple and the King's attention. Marietta didn't doubt that King Wyltam talked with him about the temple, about all the guards dispatched to find her. It probably sparked his need to overdo the protective husband act.

Over the past week, ever since the temple incident, he grew more irksome to be near. Dinners were the worst where Marietta listened to him drone about court this, guards that. It was almost as if he wanted her to take the King's offer, which sounded better each day. If King Wyltam sparked Keyain's jealousy, how much worse would his coddling get? No, accepting the King's flirtations made Keyain miserable—which would only make her more miserable.

On the streets of Satiros, Amryth nudged her, shaking Marietta out of her thoughts. She pointed to a small park across from the palace, where cypress and wisteria fought for coverage and a statue of a creature sprouted. Though they didn't stop, Marietta could make out the head and wings of an eagle, spread tall and wide.

If she were free, if she had a say in what she could do, Marietta would inspect every inch of the city-state. Each statue drew her eyes, and the businesses beckoned her to visit their storefronts and meet the owners; yet Keyain's guards remained close and ushered her towards the temple, not stopping to examine the colorful array from the other places of worship.

The guards waited at the bottom step when they arrived, opting to keep an eye outside. Marietta hooked her arm through Amryth's and ascended the temple stairs.

The inside was quiet as they entered, with fewer worshipers milling about in the early morning. As they walked into the chapel, Deania, the tiny half-elven woman from her last visit, was whispering to a few other attendants, her face taut with worry.

"Go ahead without me," Amryth said, gesturing to the benches. "I'm going to check in with Deania."

She kept her eye on the group as Amryth approached, watching as they glanced over at Marietta and walked back down the hall. Alone, Marietta sat on the bench, staring up at the goddess' statue. Her outstretched hand remained devoid of supplicants, and Marietta felt the temptation to kneel in it. Odd. Why would she? Marietta was just there to pray, to get away from the palace and Keyain. The temple was her peppermint-and-eucalyptus-scented sanctuary, where she could sit and feel free for a while. No lord or royal breathed down her neck, just her in the serenity of the empty chapel.

With her eyes closed, palms facing towards the ceiling, Marietta let her mind wander. In the quiet, she thought of Tilan, of his crinkled eyes and dark hair fraying from its tie. Of his laugh, his smile, his creations. The things she loved of her husband only existed in her mind, and though they threatened to crush her very being to think of, she'd rather risk the pain than let them die with her memory.

She swallowed the knot that formed in her throat and was thankful no one was around to hear her sniff back her tears. For him, she would persist. For Tilan, she chose to live, so the memory of him could live on.

Her watery eyes cracked open, the tears distorting the face of the goddess as she watched. A sudden warmth began to grow in her chest as if she drank hot tea on a cold winter afternoon. It was surprising, yet comforting, and she welcomed the sensation. Marietta closed her eyes and leaned into the warmth.

The world slipped away from her, no longer feeling the bench beneath her or the ambient noise from the temple. Only the scent lingered. It jogged a memory of days with her mother as a child. The markets in Kentro they had shopped at, with Marietta clasping her hand as they had perused the herbalist stalls.

She took a deep breath, imagining her mother hugging her, the warmth of her body so close. One day, she would do so again. With another breath, Marietta relaxed her shoulders more, letting the warmth in her chest flood her body.

When she opened her eyes, she stood in the backyard of her parents' newer home in Notos. The smell of basil, rosemary, sage, and thyme floated through the air from her mother's herb garden. The sky was bright blue with hazy white clouds drifting by, offering little shade from the sun, yet she didn't feel its burn on her skin. She tried to call to her parents in the house, but it was fuzzy, out of focus, as was everything beyond her immediate vicinity.

"Hello, child," a warm, earthy voice said within her.

Marietta blinked, and the goddess from the statue appeared before her. Therypon. Dark, onyx skin glowed in the sun, her sharp, high cheekbones catching the light. Her eyes were black in the center, large and round, reminding Marietta of a doe with the way they glistened.

"What is this?" Marietta said to her, her voice an echo in her head.

A warm wind whipped across the yard, causing the goddess's black waves to swirl around her, falling past her waist. A gauzy white gown surrounding her body blew taut against her, revealing her thin frame. *"Share with me the thoughts that plague your mind, that cause you to suffer so. Talk about the things that bring you pain."*

Marietta hesitated, running her hand through her hair, but it passed through nothing, as if she weren't really there. Was she supposed to air all of her grievances to an entity she didn't know? It felt odd, yet Therypon had helped Amryth therefore she could help her. "As of late, everything brings me pain. My present life is that of a nightmare, forced to live with the man who killed my husband. My past life is riddled with holes, with lies of Tilan and the life we lived together. And my future…." Marietta laughed, though no humor sounded in its tone. "There isn't one. Not if I continue in the palace."

The warmth returned to her chest as Therypon extended her hand to Marietta. *"Your truth, Marietta, has yet to show itself to you. Not knowing clouds your future, making it hard for you to continue."*

"You know my future?"

"I do not know the exact future, but I know your truth. The web of lies spun around you causes your pain, ensnaring your very soul. Only the truth will set you free." The goddess' voice was smooth, refreshing.

"I want to be free; I want to feel like myself, but how do I find the truth?"

A smile came to the goddess' face, the warmth and love reaching Marietta. *"Seek it."* Like a cat nestling in for a nap on her chest, so too did the warmth settle deep within Marietta as the goddess said, *"Seek the truth, Marietta."*

From her chest, the warmth spread through her body, and for the first time since she arrived in Satiros, Marietta felt a sense of peace.

Her parents' house and the goddess faded to black, leaving Marietta's head empty and calm. No thoughts raced through her mind, no stress tensing her shoulders, just the simplicity of her breath, the basic feeling of being alive.

At one point, she must have nodded off for when she woke, people in prayer filled the benches, some in street clothes, others wearing the blue of Therypon. Marietta craned her head, looking for Amryth. She didn't see her. Instead, at the hallway's entrance stood Coryn, the half-elven man from before, who signaled for her to follow.

Confused, she stood, her legs prickling as blood returned to her limbs. Gods, how long was she sitting there?

His face was grave as she approached, but he said nothing, just turning towards the exit. The bickering came first, the voices carrying down the hall. Then she heard the crying of someone, the soft weeping and sniffle.

Coryn picked up his pace, Marietta close on his heels. At the temple's entrance, Amryth stood an inch from a guard's face, snarling. "She's safe for now. Keyain isn't going to demote you, Jyrad."

In the corner of the antechamber, Deania held a human woman in her arms, her eyes red and swollen.

"What happened?" Marietta asked as she stepped around Coryn.

"Thank gods you've finished," Amryth said, her words quick. "We have to get you back to the palace."

"Tell me what happened." Marietta looked past Amryth, finding the four guards who escorted them that morning, as well as another half dozen who lingered on the steps below. Wide-eyed, she turned to Amryth.

"They found one of the missing half-elves," Deania spoke, her voice taut. "My friend, she—" Her breath heaved as she held onto the crying woman in her arms.

"We can confirm someone is targeting and murdering half-elves."

Coryn stood at her shoulder, his tone harsh, anger underlining it. "They found her body behind the temple this morning."

"So we need to get back," Amryth said, beckoning her forward. "Keyain already had guards on the scene and sent more to escort you back."

Unsteady legs carried her to Amryth's side, the world jarring and off-kilter. Was it a coincidence? It had to be.

Therypon's warmth flickered in her chest as she left the temple, Marietta desperate to hold on to it as she walked back to the palace.

Chapter Forty-Five
VALERIYA

The guards had said the scene was gruesome, too terrible to disclose the details; yet they did anyway. Valeriya had listened as they described the body behind the Temple of Therypon: a female half-elf, the body mutilated with 'clip' carved into her forehead. Anger and guilt wove through her stomach, blanketing her in shame. Either the males she killed hadn't been the murderers, or the one she left alive got away. Did they ever question him? Did they have any suspects at all?

Perhaps Wyltam had answers. If she were lucky, he'd feel like sharing them with her. However, he summoned her, and likely he had his own agenda that had nothing to do with the welfare of their people.

Mid-summer approached with the heat of the season upon them, and Valeriya walked into the shared living space to find Wyltam sitting before a fire. She suppressed her scoff as he lounged in the chair with one leg down, the other tucked to his chest and his chin propped up by his fist. It wasn't enough that his posture was unkingly, but his black hair hung in his face, too.

"Husband," she said, taking the seat across from Wyltam. As the heat of the fireplace rolled off, droplets of sweat formed on Valeriya underneath her long-sleeved and high-neck dress. Bruises covered her chest and ribcage from her fight in the alley. They grew too dark to be covered with makeup and maintaining the magic to cover them would grow tiring.

"Your taste in clothing has been interesting as of late," Wyltam drawled, staring into the flames in the hearth. His air of disinterest, even when probing her with his suspicions, was immaculate. Though he asked

her to join him, she was still not worth his time.

A sigh escaped her mouth as she crossed her arms, patience already wearing thin. "Was there anything specific you wanted, or are you just sharing your opinion on seasonal fashion?" Tiredness ebbed her mood, making her short when she should have bitten her tongue. By the subtle smirk that came to his face, he knew he'd gotten under her skin already.

"Do I need a reason to spend time with my wife?"

He was toying with her. After she deemed the question unworthy of an answer, Wyltam chuckled and shifted in his seat. "What do you think of Marietta?"

Valeriya rubbed her temples, rubbing the tension that built in her skull. "She's innocent and ill-prepared for court life. Perhaps Keyain should have never brought her here."

"You think that? What should he have done with her?" Wyltam inspected his tunic as he spoke, not looking in her direction.

"Locked her up in his manor on his lands or left her with the Exisotis. At least she was ignorant of who they were and who she married."

Wyltam's gaze slid to her, his eyes narrowing. "When did you talk to her about that?"

Shit, her contact gave her that information, the realization causing her stomach to drop. Wyltam would have never told her that. "Oh, I didn't. Marietta mentioned Keyain told her, and we talked about it over tea. The poor girl was so shaken. No wonder she let herself rot away in that suite."

For a moment, he stared at her, his fingers tapping on the armrest of his chair. As always, his expression remained blank, hard to read, as if she were staring at a wall. "It seems Keyain makes for a poor husband. Marietta looked worse than I expected."

Valeriya agreed with his observation, but would never admit they agreed on anything. "How are you handling Keyain having a wife?" she asked. The question seemed innocent, but Wyltam stiffened in his chair.

"What are you insinuating?"

With a shrug, she glowered at her husband. "I'm sure the entire situation has been hard. After all, you two used to be so close."

Knowing his full past, close was only one way to describe their relationship. Never had she brought it up so boldly with him. The thought of Wyltam and Keyain together was laughable. How could they work together after all the drama?

"And what of Marietta? You have a soft spot for half-elf females, do you not?" he asked.

Katya. How did he know about her? Valeriya forced her body to still, not reacting to his question.

Another chuckle came from her husband. "Perhaps we perform our marriage duties tonight to solve our wayward thoughts. Mycaub would be a wonderful older brother, would he not?" Rage flared in Valeriya as Wyltam cut her a glare. "Go ahead, take off your dress, Valeriya. Let's see what you're hiding."

She bit the inside of her cheek, checking her anger. Their relationship was never physical, only necessary to reproduce an heir to the throne. The experience had been the final rift in their already-distant relationship. Before Mycaub, they were just two strangers married to one another. After two years of trying, they became people who detested the other's body. Even the scent of Wyltam was enough to churn her stomach.

Valeriya wanted to blame their relationship strains on that alone, but the divide between them was present from the beginning. She hated him and he hated her.

With a wave of a hand, his stare deep into the flames, he said, "You're dismissed."

Chapter Forty-Six

MARIETTA

A note addressed to Marietta arrived in the afternoon, the crown's crest of two intertwined wisteria sealing the envelope with purple wax. Marietta couldn't help but laugh when she read the contents.

> *Lady Marietta,*
> *As a lady of our court, you should know about the city-state you preside over. With me as your guide, I extend to you the opportunity to see Satiros on a carriage ride in two days' time. As always, if Keyain is available at noon, he is welcomed to join us. Alas, if his job obligations command his time, then I would be honored to take you alone.*
> *I await your reply.*
> *King Wyltam*

If Keyain's job obligations command his time. Gods, when didn't they? Of course, King Wyltam was well aware of that, making the letter a dry mockery of Keyain. She'd be lying if she said she didn't enjoy it; yet that didn't mean she'd join him. No, a private carriage ride with the King felt like she would play into his hand, taking part in the deal to flirt with Marietta to torment Keyain. Though she longed to see the city-state, her want to cause less trouble was greater.

Marietta waited for Keyain to return that evening, sitting at the dining room table with a glass of wine in hand. The note from the King lay

in front of her. As Keyain bent down to kiss her, the paper caught his eye. "What is this?" he asked, picking it up. The muscle in his jaw tightened as he read, red creeping up his neck. His gaze darted towards Marietta, then back to the letter before he placed it down on the table.

She watched the emotion seep through his stilled expression. Anger, as always, flecked across his features, joined with something more somber. Was it regret?

"The King is kind to offer me such an experience," she said, eying him over the rim of her glass. The deep red of the wine matched the growing flush of Keyain's skin.

"He doesn't offer it to just anyone," he grumbled, ripping off his jacket, flinging it to the back of the chair. "First the unplanned visit, now this."

"Not quite."

"What do you mean, 'not quite?'"

"I saw the King last week during tea with the Queen," she said, holding back a smirk.

"When were you going to tell me about that?"

"Oh, it slipped my mind."

Keyain's shoulders tensed as he stared at the letter. He fought with the first few buttons of his shirt, swearing when his fingers fumbled. "What did Wyltam have to say?"

The question remained casual on the surface, but Marietta could sense his uneasiness underneath. The King knew precisely how to rile Keyain, yet how far did this anxiety of his run?

Marietta stalled, biting her lip and turning away as if she were abashed. "He wished to see me alone and sent Queen Valeriya away. He was happy to see me dressed and out of the suite." She paused, turning to him. "Is he always so... friendly?"

The flush crept up to his cheeks. "What do you mean by friendly?"

She turned her back to him to hide her lie. "I didn't know he could be so flattering. Had plenty of compliments to give."

"Don't believe a word he said."

Marietta snapped her head back towards him. "Excuse you."

"Not what I meant, Mar."

"Is it so hard to believe that the King would compliment me?"

"No, you are stunning—always." He ground his jaw, hand mussing his hair. "Wyl has done this before, with… other females. Not as bold, usually. He—" Keyain shook his head. "He would always compliment and make them uncomfortable. But never this," he said, pointing to the note. "That is new." He paused with a breath. "And after the incident at the temple—"

"There wasn't an incident."

"They found a body behind the temple," he said, taking the seat across from her. "And on the day you were to visit. It's not a coincidence."

"It was a coincidence. You can't prevent me from leaving the palace again." Marietta crossed her arms over her chest. The nerve he had.

"It wasn't a coincidence and you're not leaving—" Keyain paused as the servants knocked, entering with their dinner. "You're not leaving the palace for a carriage ride with Wyl," he continued in a hushed voice.

"You don't get to make that decision." She nodded her thanks to the elves, who set down the platters before they turned and left.

Silence settled between them, the food engrossing Keyain's attention. They had talked about this; he couldn't continue to control her. And yes, finding the body of one of the missing pilinos was tragic, but Marietta wasn't in danger, not when Keyain would surround her with guards any time she stepped foot outside of the suite. Who would dare try to abduct her when she was that well-protected?

Determined to make it clear to Keyain that she alone could decide for herself, she would accept the King's invitation. It might play into whatever scheme the King planned, yet it was the perfect opportunity to show control. She'd send her response in the morning.

Breaking the silence, Keyain rambled about court news, something about someone being pregnant out of wedlock. Marietta held back her surprise, not from the news but at the fact Keyain entertained such gossip. The conversation lulled as Marietta nodded along, feigning amusement at his stories. By the crestfallen look on his face, he gathered she didn't want to talk. What he should have realized was that Marietta didn't want to talk to him.

"Have you done anything interesting as of late? Anything exciting on your walks with Amryth, or that you've read?" he asked, taking a sip of his wine. Keyain was trying—she'd give him that.

"Not really." She pushed the remaining vegetables on her plate around.

Keyain nodded. "Well, if you're looking for another way to spend your time, Elyse may ask you to visit with you soon. Just you and her."

Surprised, Marietta knitted her brows. "Elyse? You mean your formally betrothed?"

Keyain blew out a breath. "She and I were never going to marry. I couldn't, not when I already had a marriage certificate signed to you."

"So you were misleading her."

"I wasn't misleading her," he said with such seriousness that it took Marietta back. "Her father, Gyrsh, is a complete asshole." Keyain ran a hand through his hair as he ground his jaw. "I just found out that he started hitting her again—that's why I faked the betrothal. Because Gyrsh wouldn't dare to lay a hand on her in case I found out."

Marietta's heart sank. "But she's an adult—she has to be close to my age."

"That's odd to think about. Elyse is near to her third decade, so not much younger than you." He quieted, biting his tongue. "We all treat her as a child when, at her current age, you and I were together. And you had your business well-established by then." He sighed, letting his head fall into his hands. "Fuck, that's what she meant."

"What?"

"Nothing. I just realized something," Keyain said, looking up at her through his hands. "Thank you—for talking to me tonight. I know none of this is easy for you, but I still enjoy your company, for what it's worth."

Marietta nodded; he only just then realized the woman he was betrothed to was an adult. No wonder Elyse's behavior was so erratic—the very man she was to marry thought of her as a child. Her father abused her, though she was an adult.

Did Elyse have anyone besides Keyain helping her? Marietta considered that thought. "If she initiates it, I'll go. But I'll let her be the one to reach out."

"Thank you, Mar," he said, dropping back in his chair, a range of emotions on his face. "Thank you."

Marietta woke to Keyain getting ready, the sun not yet cresting above the horizon. Light spilled through the doorway of the bathroom, illuminating the room. Keyain emerged dressed in a casual tunic and pants when he noticed her awake. "Go back to sleep, Mar."

"Why do you wake so early every morning?" Marietta's voice was thick with sleep.

"I train with the guards before my meetings," he said, crossing the room to shuffle through a pile of clothes.

"A minister trains with the common guard every morning?"

"As Minister of Protection, I oversee both the guard and the army. How can I keep their respect if I let myself slack off?"

"And here I thought being the greatest warrior of Satiros would earn you respect."

Keyain huffed a laugh, turning to Marietta. "You'd be surprised. That was also a century and a half ago. Titles fade if you can't back them up."

A century and a half. He earned that title well before Marietta had been born. "A funny thing, age between the races. I often forget how old you are."

"Well, I'm not that old," he said, walking to Marietta. "I'll see you this evening." Keyain kissed her forehead and took off from the room. A few minutes later, she heard the suite's door close.

Silence encased Marietta as she stared at the canopy above the bed. Did Keyain realize the difference in their lifespans? Half-elves lived a fraction of years of an elf's. In the end, she would only be a blip in his life, and perhaps that was the reason he could so easily rip Marietta from her own.

Not letting her thoughts dwell on that idea too long, Marietta rose and readied herself for the day, hours before she would do so normally. After sending her response to the King, Marietta selected one of Keyain's books and sat in the living room. She stifled a yawn while she read *The History of Satiros*—or attempted to, at least. After waking up early, her tiredness caused the dry material to be drier. Even her strong tea didn't help. How did Amryth stay awake reading such books?

"In the first years of Queen Olytia's rule, she proved to be a capable ruler of Satiros. Through strict laws and restructuring her court, she brought security and hope to her people, driving incoming refugees from all over the Akroi region to live in the city-state. Her name became synonymous with idealism, a future where all could praise her—"

Satiroans praised the late queen like she was a deity? Never would someone view a city-state leader or the Enomenoan Unionization Council members more than who they were—an elected official. They didn't receive special treatment because they did not differ from anyone else, held to the same standard as all. Was that the difference between having a monarch rule? Do people learn to praise instead of holding leaders accountable? Gods, that was a dangerous line of thought. Kings and queens get their ego stroked at the cost of their people. Was ego the sole reason for such praise? Or was it to maintain the power of their throne? Marietta shook her head. It was too early to tackle such thoughts.

"Her name became synonymous with idealism, a future where all could praise her for the everlasting change in Satiros. Under her rule, she strengthened the laws against pilinos, solidifying their role in society. Some ill-informed critics—"

Ill-informed critics? Marietta flipped to the cover of the book, laughing. Did Queen Olytia write this herself? The book was an ode to her greatness because of placing pilinos scum in their lowly place. Of course, Keyain had this on his shelf.

A soft tapping sounded from Keyain's study, so subtle she may have missed it if she focused on reading. She must be hearing things. The palace was old and bound to make noise. Marietta reopened the book to her spot, but the tapping came again. Curious, she set aside her book and tip-toed to the study when it stopped once more.

A panel of the wooded wall swung open, Marietta gasping and taking a step back as Queen Valeriya stood in the passageway, donned in simple pants and shirt. "Hello, Marietta."

Her mind blanked, registering what she saw. The Queen of Satiros appeared in a hidden doorway, not dressed like a queen.

Queen Valeriya read her expression and laughed. "Surprised? I have something to show you."

Marietta shook her head, bringing a hand to her temple. "What is this?"

"I need your help, Marietta. I'll explain more if you come with me."

"I don't understand." Marietta glanced around the room.

"Shocking, I know, but this," she said, gesturing to the passage behind her, "ensures we're alone."

Marietta took a hesitant step forward. "How did you even know about this hidden door?"

"A queen's secret, if you will." A smirk came to her face, yet she offered no further explanation.

"And if I don't come with you?"

"Then you'll miss a great opportunity to inflict Keyain pain. Do you love Enomenos, Marietta? Do you wish to help?"

That caught her attention, her pulse quickening. "Yes."

"Then come. I have much to tell you."

Marietta hesitated, remembering Keyain's warning about the Queen. But what did he know? Marietta had fewer reasons to trust him. Shaking off her nerves, she followed Queen Valeriya through the door, the wood-paneled wall clicking shut behind her.

A small light globe sat in the Queen's palm, illuminating the narrow staircase that spiraled down. Marietta followed the Queen in silence.

Gods, this was a terrible idea. Why would the Queen want Marietta to help Enomenos? Beyond hating Keyain and the King, what reason did she have to aid the region? Perhaps it was a trap, yet curiosity drove her forward, eager to learn what waited at the end.

Queen Valeriya strode ahead of her, looking nothing like the conniving Queen in gowns during tea. Marietta's stomach knotted as she realized that this was the real side of her.

The stairs ended deep beneath the palace. The light globe lit the dark passageway as they continued forward, taking off down the hall and turning onto a connecting walkway. After making a few more turns, they arrived at a hallway lined with wooden doors. They stopped at one of them, Queen Valeriya pulling out a key from her pocket and unlocking it. They stepped inside, locking the door behind them.

The room was small, with odds and ends along the walls. In the middle sat a table covered in papers. The Queen moved a box to block the bottom of the door frame and then lit a few more light globes around the room.

"What is this?" Marietta asked, awe mixed with nervousness.

The Queen walked around the table, stopping across from Marietta, splaying both hands flat on the surface, her weight leaning into them. Her red hair looked like fire in the golden glow. "Marietta, how much do you care about Enomenos?"

"Very much, you know this," Marietta said, confused.

"I do, which is why I know you'll keep what I'm about to say between just us." Queen Valeriya lifted her chin, her eyes shining in the light. "For the past year now, I've been talking with the Exisotis."

Marietta laughed but silenced herself at her serious expression. "No, you haven't."

"I worked with them to prevent the slaughter of Wyltam's army at the hands of Keyain." She paused, taking a deep breath. "But I was unable to prevent it with the information I had."

"Slaughter? Keyain didn't say it was a slaughter." As much of an ass as he was, he wouldn't lie about something like that, would he?

"Why would he tell you anything?" she asked. "And what he does tell you, how do you know it's the truth?"

"I know about this." Marietta held the Queen's gaze. "Keyain wouldn't lie to me about the city I love, the people I love."

"Ah, yes," the Queen drawled, rolling her eyes. "The male who took you from your home, forced you to marry, and kept you drugged would never lie to you."

Her sarcastic tone hit a nerve in Marietta as she clenched her fist. "And why should I believe you, Queen of the city-state that attacked my home?"

"Because I was the one to help you when Keyain kept you drugged."

Marietta bit back her retort. Queen Valeriya prevented her from being drugged further, told her the truth about Tilan. "Why are you calling it a slaughter?" Her voice was smaller than she had hoped.

"The Satiroan army moved through and killed everyone who didn't surrender. It was a bloodbath." The Queen swallowed, her gaze falling to the table. "My sources in the Exisotis said thousands of civilians died."

Marietta leaned onto the table for support as the room spun. Keyain said they attacked a section of the city, but if it was a slaughtering—oh, gods. Her friends. Her community. It couldn't be true. "Why are you telling me this?"

"I didn't have the right information," she said, her voice strained. "I couldn't prevent it on my own. And you, Marietta, you are with Keyain every day. Only you can steal information from him."

Her heart throbbed in her chest. "What kind of information? And how?"

"Reports, even if it's glimpses of them. If you can steal them, then all the better."

Marietta laughed mirthlessly. "He doesn't trust me to leave the suite, let alone be near his work."

"Then distract him," Valeriya said, cocking her head. "He loves you; that much is clear. Use his love against him. Earn his trust and lower his guard." She paused, a slow smirk coming to her lips. "If you can play the part of a loving wife, it would not only help with that, but could be a distraction for Keyain."

"I tolerate him as much as I can already. Why would he need to be distracted?"

"To drive a wedge between him and Wyltam." The Queen spoke quickly, her hand moving to her chin. "If we can separate them, if we can deteriorate their relationship, then the whole court will suffer. Marietta, we could do damage from the inside while making a difference with the Exisotis."

Marietta could affect the war. She would have to suffer Keyain's attention, but she already saw the cracks in his relationship with the King. All she had to do was pry it open. If she could do that, then she would be close enough to Keyain that he'd let down his guard, meaning she could steal information.

"Okay," Marietta said, meeting the Queen's gaze. "For the community I lost, I can fake being in love with him again. But I need your word that it'll work." Marietta exhaled slowly. "This will open up a wound that healed years ago. It can't be for nothing. It has to work."

The Queen stepped around the table, grasping Marietta's hands, her eyes earnest. "That is a promise I can keep. Together, you and I can sabotage this war, and at the end, I will turn Satiros into Reyila, where pilinos are equal."

Emotion clogged Marietta's throat. To change not just the lives of those she cared about, but of all those she had yet to meet, was more than she could ask. "Then I promise to do my best, Queen Valeriya."

"When it's just us, Valeriya will suffice." She dropped Marietta's hand, her lips curling up to one side. "After all, we will be working together." Valeriya took a step away, leaning against the table again. "You'll have to be a better liar. Keyain can't learn you're up to something, and you always have a tell."

Marietta winced. "Am I that bad?"

"Yes, you're pretty obvious. Your expressions always reveal your emotions except for when you lie."

"How do I fix that?"

"Just act the part. Pretend you're the sweet, devoted, demure wife of the elvish nobility, the dream wife existing to bear him kids." Her tone was sarcastic, and she rolled her eyes. "Or imagine him as someone you love, as someone you could say or do those things to. Just dive into it, don't think about anything else. Make yourself believe that you feel those emotions."

"I can try," Marietta said, looking down at the table, noticing a paper with neat rows of numbers. She grabbed it, recognizing the ledger. "What's this?"

"The crown's income and costs from the army. It's long to parse through. Here." Valeriya handed another stack to Marietta. "Those are the papers I managed to grab, though they're a few months old."

The army cost Satiros a vast sum of gold. Mentally, Marietta tallied up the costs, realizing the number written on the sheet was incorrect. How did the Queen get these documents? Marietta skimmed through the rest. "Do you have something to write with and a paper?"

Valeriya handed her charcoal and a blank sheet. Marietta started making her adjustments on the new page and compared it to the numbers listed on the original documents. After some time, she had adjustments for the month's tracked expenses.

"Who's in charge of these?" Marietta looked up at Valeriya, her hands still hovering over the paper.

"Royir. He's Minister of Coin."

Marietta thought of the old elf she met in the hallways with Keyain, the one who called her a clip. "He's made a ton of errors, claiming that the losses aren't that severe, but according to my numbers... they're losing a ton coin. The army is costing them a great deal." She pointed at the numbers she wrote off to the side.

Valeriya laughed. "Of course it is. This is the exact number that Satiros is losing?" she asked, pointing to Marietta's notes.

"It is."

Valeriya rolled up the papers. "I can work with this."

"You'll give my notes to the Exisotis?"

The Queen hesitated. "Yes, I will. I don't know what they'll do with it, but this is a weak spot that they can exploit," she said, placing the papers in her pocket. "We should head back before anyone notices that you're missing."

Back in the suite alone, Marietta paced, thinking over the plan she made with the Queen—no, Valeriya. There was danger in trusting her, in agreeing to steal information and hand it to her. After all, how did the Queen of Satiros have a contact in the Exisotis?

Valeriya hated her husband. That much was clear. But did she really wish to tear apart the court she ruled over? To help the pilinos, Marietta guessed she'd have to break apart the court and start fresh. None of the presiding males would ever agree to change.

The part Marietta hated to admit was that tricking Keyain into thinking she fell back in love with him would be beneficial, regardless of the Queen's intentions. By distracting the two people in charge of the war, the Exisotis and Enomenos could attack while Satiros was weak.

It just meant sacrifice on Marietta's part. Not that she had a difficult life in the rich palace, but to kiss Keyain, to act as if she loved him after he murdered Tilan, would rip open old wounds and likely create new ones. But like she told Valeriya, for the people she loved, she would give everything, even her life. Marietta hoped it wouldn't come to that.

Chapter Forty-Seven

ELYSE

Only two days for Elyse to respond to Brynden's poetic apology. Two days. She was hopelessly stupid if she believed she'd come up with something worthy in that short amount of time. Set before her was a blank sheet of paper, as it had for the previous two hours, on the wood surface of the desk in the King's office.

Keenly aware of how close it was to noon, Elyse pulled at her hair, slumped back in her seat, staring at the blank page. What Brynden had written was beautiful. How would she even come close to such an eloquent response? The answer was she couldn't.

Frustrated, she picked up the charcoal again and began to sketch their first kiss on the night of the ball. Perhaps dwelling in that moment would inspire words to come to her. The thrill of the moment. The heat of her stomach. The hope of freedom. The more she drew, the clearer she translated the night to the page. Brynden held her, his face against her own as they kissed in the Central Garden.

She set down the charcoal to examine her work. The likeness of their faces and their bodies were, in her opinion, perfect. Perhaps if she added the garden around them and the drift globes above….

By the time she finished, it was close to noon. The drawing wasn't a letter, but she was proud of it, something she would want to keep in memory of that evening. However, it seemed like it missed a message. What did the moment mean to her that Brynden didn't realize?

Hope.

That moment was when hope blossomed in her chest. Hope to be free,

to live a better life, of a better future, perhaps with Brynden. In her best attempt at calligraphy, she wrote the word that surmised her feelings.

Elyse kept the folded drawing tucked deep into her pocket as she darted across the palace. She was late to meet Sylas, but at least she had something to give him.

A thin layer of sweat coated her body as she reached the willow. Sylas leaned against its trunk with a deep scowl on his face. "You're late."

"I know," she said, out of breath. "I was finishing up my letter."

Sylas let out a sigh, stepping towards Elyse. "Perhaps next time, finish before you're supposed to meet me, so I'm not waiting for you."

Elyse cut him a glare as she handed over the paper to him. "Sorry that I was late, but not everyone can write poetry like Brynden. How in the gods was I supposed to follow that up?"

Sylas rolled his eyes. "You could have written one word and it would've been enough. If only you could see the manic fool he's become since being banned from the palace and barred from seeing you."

"Wait, you're not going to—" She was too late. Sylas unfolded the drawing.

With one brow raised, he looked it over with a scowl. "You did just write one word." He laughed, breaking the stony demeanor on his face.

"Well, I didn't intend for anyone but Brynden to see it," she snapped. "What is wrong with you?"

"I have to check everything exchanged between you two to make sure nothing... inappropriate is said."

"Gods, was that Keyain's stupid rule?"

"No. Sauntyr's." Sylas shook his head with a smile hooking his lips. "This is going to drive him crazy."

Elyse closed her eyes with a sigh. "I know, it's lousy compared to what he made—"

"No, you misunderstood me. You're talented at drawing, and that alone is going to send Brynden over. Is this a picture of something that happened or that you hope to do?"

"That was us the night of the ball. The kiss that gave me hope."

Sylas glanced down at the paper, then back at Elyse, pursing his lips. "I don't mean to sound like an ass, but don't get your hopes up."

"Well, you sound like an ass," Elyse said, crossing her arms.

"Just because Sauntyr gave his blessing, it doesn't mean his sister would."

Sister? Elyse didn't even realize Brynden had a sister.

Her expression must have said as much, causing Sylas to roll his eyes, swearing. "You didn't know he even had a sister, did you? What about a brother?" When Elyse didn't answer, he continued. "His sister is the matriarch of the family—even Sauntyr listens to her. Which means you must get her blessing still to marry him, and I honestly don't think you'll get it, Elyse."

She turned her back to him, staring out at the pond. Though she ended her future with Brynden, the truth of the situation stung. "Don't worry. Brynden won't get the King's blessing either, so I don't have any hope left." Brynden wouldn't receive it with the King's plans for her. The admittance crushed the small part of her heart that had still relished the thought.

"I figured as much," Sylas grumbled, staring out at the pond next to Elyse. "But I can read the hope on your face when we talk about Brynden. I'm sorry about what I said last time, about him growing bored and me picking up the pieces. Brynden is impulsive, never stays on one thing too long. Even though he's my friend, I don't think he'll make a good husband—ever. You have been through enough."

Elyse scoffed. "So you get to decide if he's a suitable match for me or not?"

Sylas cut her a glare. "No—what I'm saying is the male you see now will not be the male you get in the future. You're young. There are hundreds of years left in your life."

"So forget him?"

"No, Elyse. Just wait. There's no rush to marry him, so don't plan on leaving Satiros with him, okay?"

His scowl softened into a frown, concern showing. Why did Sylas care for her, anyway? Elyse nodded as she wrapped her arms across her middle, avoiding his gaze.

"I have to run to a meeting, but I'll find you when Brynden has his response." Before he left the willow, Sylas added, "You really are talented, you know. The drawing is perfect. He'll love it."

Elyse just waved a hand, letting him leave without another word.

Hope to be with Brynden reignited after reading his apology. That somehow, despite everything that happened, they could still be together. That Elyse could leave Satiros with Brynden and become his wife.

Hope was a deceitful feeling.

Chapter Forty-Eight

MARIETTA

Marietta cursed herself all morning after Keyain lingered in the suite, asking if she was sure she wanted to go on the carriage ride with the King. With a lot of patience and Valeriya's goal fresh on her mind, Marietta eased Keyain's worrying. And by that, it meant she kissed him on the cheek before he left, causing him to grin with a flush. The action made her stomach churn. But she could do it, and she would, if only to watch Keyain's face when he realized it wasn't real. Gods, when did she become so cruel?

The carriage ride with the King posed a slight hiccup for her winning Keyain over, being that he had found out through King Wyltam that she had accepted his offer. When she sent her reply, she didn't know Valeriya would appear in the wall to conspire against Keyain.

An entourage of guards escorted Marietta to the front of the palace, her curls loosened around her head. The fabric of her dress was soft and comfortable with slits in the legs, which she was thankful for when they stepped into the sun's heat.

The driver hopped down from his perch, his skin dark and long black hair tied into a tail. Without a word, he opened the door for Marietta, revealing the King sitting inside. Ominous, he sat quietly, his gaze peering out the window. Rocking the carriage, the guards climbed into position on the outside. Marietta took a seat as they rolled forward, startling her. There wasn't a jerk of motion like with horses.

"Magic," the King said in his deep voice, his dark eyes now observing Marietta.

"Excuse me, King Wyltam?" Marietta held back her attitude at his lack of greeting.

"Magic propels the carriage. The driver is a mage."

Marietta glanced towards the cab wall where the driver sat on the outside. "So there are no horses, Your Grace."

"None in the city, at least."

She shrugged, taking her first good look at the King. His shirt was of black silk, the neckline showing a bit of his chest. Nestled in his dark hair was the thin crown of gold. "Must be nice, not having to dodge horse sh—" Marietta bit her lip, stopping herself from finishing the sentence. She was with the gods damned King, and she was talking about horse shit. What was wrong with her? "Your Grace," she added, averting her eyes.

One side of his mouth twitched with amusement. "For those who walk the streets, I'm sure it's a pleasant feature of our city-state."

A minute passed where neither spoke. Apparently, a tour of the city was visual, not verbal. She stared out the window at the rows of plain white buildings and their black roofs. The only source of color came from the plants that blossomed on most of them.

Marietta glanced back at the King, who watched her with an expressionless gaze. Hating the silence, Marietta asked, "What is this part of the city called, Your Grace?"

"Petal Row," he answered, looking out the window. "The district is known for its entertainment. Taverns, theaters, museums, gardens, and more occupy the area. When the city was founded, our oldest tavern, The Lily Pad, was the only business in the district. Throughout the…."

Gods, it was as if he read from a history book. Not realizing the verbal tour would feel like a lecture, Marietta nodded, focusing on every other word as she viewed the people on the street. All elven, all in fine clothing. Though she shouldn't be surprised by it, she felt crestfallen by the lack of pilinos. As they neared a bridge, Marietta perked up.

"This is Bellflower Bridge. Built in…."

She sunk back into her seat. Perhaps this was a mistake.

"After we cross Bellflower Bridge, we enter Greening Juncture, known for its—" The King paused as she stifled her yawn. "Apologies, Marietta. Am I boring you?"

Marietta searched his face for annoyance but found the same icy expression. "I should be the one to apologize, Your Grace," she said with a tight smile. "This is just different from my expectations."

"How so?"

"You sound rehearsed. Like you're reading it from a history book."

"Well," he said, gesturing out the window, "it is our history."

"How about you share one fun fact with me?" she asked, giving a polite smile. "Something not so... from a book."

The King gazed off to the side, his eyes darting back and forth as he thought. Just as Marietta was about to speak again, he broke the silence. "Wisteria is not native to Satiros. Instead, it was transplanted here and cultivated during my great-grandfather's reign. His wife, native to the lands across the Dyreste Mountains, brought it as a wedding present. Since then, it became popular within the city-state and eventually became the city's crest."

Marietta blinked at him. "How is that a fun fact?"

"All facts are fun."

Marietta tried to hold back her laugh but failed. The King cracked a smile, the sight odd on such a usually cold face. It almost made him approachable.

"I'm guessing you aren't one for reading and research," he said, meeting her gaze.

"Oh, I enjoy reading, just not history books." Unless there was history in the dirty books she often swapped with her friends in Olkia.

"Then which types of books do you enjoy?" he asked. "Adventure?"

Marietta bit her lip, nodding. "Yes, adventure. But what do you think of your city-state?" she asked, eager to change the subject.

"You want to know what I think of Satiros?"

"I do. I'm curious what your favorite places are, the type of people the King busies himself with." She leaned on her hand, her arm propped up by the window of the carriage.

The King nodded, his gaze shifting to the city. Marietta waited in silent fascination as he thought of an answer. The silence would grow irksome normally, but he gave her question some thought. How was that man best friends with Keyain?

"Though I'm not one to venture in public often," he said, his eyes shifting back to Marietta, "I would say my favorite place is the Ertwyrmer Sculpture Gardens. Most statues in the Central Garden are tame compared to some in the sculpture gardens."

"I'd love to see them sometime," Marietta said. "Are they as detailed as the ones in the palace?"

"They are," he said with a quirk of his lips. "I could show you one day if you would like."

"I hope you do." She smiled at the King, at the idea of being outside the palace and finding more curious statues.

"The type of people I busy myself with are those in government positions," he added. "And even that is too much."

Her smile grew, realizing his quietness was not him uninterested in her but him being one to tire of people. "It seems you and I are opposites."

"How so?"

"I love being around people and wish I knew more of your court and its people." She leaned forward, her smile sharpening. "And you wish to be around none of them—to be alone."

"Is that such a bad thing?"

"Not at all."

Her answer must have been the right one, for he smiled, his gaze locking on hers before staring out the window once more. "Just beyond Bellflower Bridge sits Birdsong Park, the largest park in the city-state proper. I would share a fact about the park, but I fear I'd bore you."

Marietta shot him a smile, thankful he had a sense of humor about her not wanting a history lesson.

As they crossed over the Halia River, the park came into view. The stonewall of the river's shore lined one edge and the boulevard they traveled on lined another. Trees of every kind canopied much of the walkways lined with bushes and other greenery. On such a sunny day, a walk through a shady park would have been pleasant. "I'd listen to every fact you had to share if we could see it up close."

"It would be too unsafe, given the current situation with the missing pilinos," he said while shifting his left foot to the seat, his knee tucked close to his chest. "The view from the carriage must suffice."

Marietta hid her growing smile. Such a casual posture didn't suit someone in court, let alone a king. It was almost comforting, as if the formality wasn't for him, either.

"A view from the carriage isn't the same as experiencing it, you must admit. The wind in your hair, the sound of rustling leaves—especially on a day like today." She shook her head. "It'd be wonderful. Though my favorite thing to do in such a park is people watch—something I have done little of in the palace."

"Why is that?"

Marietta resisted rolling her eyes. "Keyain, mostly. But even when I walk through the Central Garden, most courtiers gawk at me. Makes it hard to watch someone when you have their full attention."

The King huffed a dry laugh. "Unsurprising, but you misunderstood me. What's enjoyable about people watching?"

"Oh," Marietta said, surprised that he wished to know. "Well, each person has their own story, their own way of viewing the world. Our unique experiences forge us into who we are." She gazed out the window, getting one last glimpse of the park as they passed. "I can't help but wonder who strangers are."

White-washed brick gave way to multi-colored stone facades as they traveled into the next district. "I've never thought of it that way," King Wyltam said, breaking the silence.

"When you view life as a puzzle and each person a piece of it, it's hard to find the truth if you only see one side of a person."

"How similar you and I are," he mused, a smile hinting at his lips. "I also view life as a puzzle, but my pieces are what make the world function.

Where do we come from? How does the world work?" He paused as if he was considering his words. "What is the source of aithyr?"

"How peculiar that a king ponders such questions," she teased. "Such interests must be difficult to pursue in your position. I wonder what type of person you would be without your crown." If she and Valeriya were successful, then perhaps Marietta would see such a thing.

Outside, elven folk mostly walked the streets, but she did see pilinos trekking among them. Expensive-looking clothing seemed left behind in Petal Row, the denizens of this district dressed in practical, less formal attire.

"I often wonder about that myself."

Marietta jerked her head back towards the King, a question sitting at the tip of her tongue. Why would he have such thoughts? Did he not want to be king? Yet she remained silent, watching as his thoughts took over, his eyes darting back and forth. King Wyltam was odd, peculiar, nothing like she would expect a king to be, let alone a friend of Keyain. Keyain was grounded by reality, of seeing the future and how he can plan his way to it. The King, well, he pondered life's big questions. How frustrating it must be that he couldn't explore such ideas.

The carriage turned, heading south according to the direction of the sun. Like the park, leafy trees populated the area, replacing the lush wisteria from the fancier parts of the city. The further they traveled, the more pilinos she saw. A few people turned towards the carriage; yet she knew they couldn't see her inside.

What would they think of a half-elf in the lone presence of the King? Gods, what did they think of a half-elven lady? Perhaps they thought she betrayed them, basking in the wealth of noble life while those who looked like Marietta were treated as lesser, but the man who sat across from her was to blame, too busy thinking of life and not of those he should serve.

Irritated, she swallowed a sigh. Marietta would change the Satiroan society, though. Together, she and Valeriya would deliver the Exisotis the information, and they would break the Satiroan court from within, starting with Keyain.

She peeked out the window in the direction they headed, and her brows furrowed. The buildings grew tall and narrow, looking as if the structures were smashed together haphazardly, like a cheap quilt stitched and patchy. Plants crowded the balconies, the vines and brambles twisting every which way, cascading down the buildings' facades.

The cobblestone road ended at the knobby buildings, and beyond she could see dirt streets crowded with people. As they approached, she could see the stunted and rounded tips of ears. She could see the facial hair on the men—a feature of only those who are pilinos. But there was no elven. Her lips pursed, her irritation building as she turned to the King. He was already watching her with his normal icy expression settled over his face.

"Rambler Grove. The only district in which pilinos can live. Most citizens refer to it as The Weeds." He glanced at his shirt, plucking something off and letting it drop to the floor. It was clever, the casual arrogance of such a gesture, as if talking about the only district for people like her wasn't worth his full attention.

She dug her nails into her palms as she glanced back. "Couldn't let them spread out of the district, so you had the buildings built higher to fit more, huh?" She should have hidden the disdain in her voice while talking to the King, yet she left caution behind.

"Historically, yes." From the corner of her eyes, she watched him shift back into a seated position. "The pilinos' population seems to grow by a third each year. Only half of The Weeds' inhabitants are native to Satiros. We have many pilinos from the other cities hiding within our city-state."

"As if it's better here," she mumbled, glaring at the chaotic buildings. Enomenos wouldn't allow such shoddy structures, deemed too dangerous, too carelessly built. Past the buildings, she noticed people pulling carts— and then it hit her. "You don't let them have horses." Marietta turned to King Wyltam with an incredulous laugh. "The elven can learn magic, afford to hire mages for such tasks, so not having beasts to pull wagons and carts isn't an issue." Her words boiled out of her from the rage that built inside. "But for them—" she jabbed her finger into the glass "—you don't allow for any aid, so they pull it themselves."

His dark eyes hardened at her tone. "As you said, not having horse shit in the city is enjoyable for many."

Her nails nearly broke through her skin for how hard she pressed. So this was the proper Satiroan experience for a pilinos, to lose out on the privilege of magic in a city ran by it. Gods, she bet if she were to walk through the streets of The Weeds, she would find gas lanterns lining the walkways in place of the fancy light globes.

"Life is better for those outside the city-state walls," the King added. "Though all pilinos outside the walls are natural-born citizens of Satiros."

"Why would that matter?" The question came out sharper than she intended, but the King didn't acknowledge it.

"Those who flee the other Syllogian city-states do so illegally. There's a universal law, agreed to by the various queens and kings of Syllogi, that if a criminal of one city-state is in another, they have the right to extradite them." He paused, cocking his head at Marietta. "But in Satiros, I don't allow the other city-states' guards inside our walls."

"And why is that?" she ground out.

"Too many resources spent on tracking them, making sure they don't take anyone they're not supposed to take," he said in such a casual manner as if it were an annoyance and not an immoral act. "So, our guards focus on protecting the pilinos living outside the walls, ensuring that those who were born here can live peacefully within their means."

"And you don't care if you have *criminals* living in your city?"

"No," he drawled. "As long as they commit no crimes here. We have an obvious space issue, but they make do."

Marietta laughed again. "Unbelievable."

"Is there something wrong, Marietta?"

She shook her head, watching the last bit of the district pass by. Pilinos were forced to cram into a single spot, and he dismissed it as an obvious space issue. As if they didn't matter. As if they were an afterthought. Did no one in the Satiroan government care about these people? Marietta knew the answer. The people running Satiros haven't set the precedent of caring, and now they grew more apathetic to pilinos. Then again, why would they care about people they deemed lesser than themselves?

They crossed over the Halia River once more, traveling in silence. The buildings shifted back to white, the signs indicative of trades folk and their businesses. Based on what she's learned thus far about Satiros, she knew that only the elven had such shops and that the pilinos were their grunts. She didn't have to ask.

In Satiros, she could have never opened her bakery unless it was in The Weeds. What kind of money do people make in such a stunted district? They had to make less than their elven counterparts. So how much gold filtered through their community?

She crossed her arms, glaring out the window, and wished they would hurry. A park passed by, the slope of green grass leading to... a building?

Marietta leaned forward, pressing her face to the glass as she looked down the street. Her jaw dropped. They were townhomes—opulent and extensive townhomes. Though they shared walls, the lawns of grass and flower beds and manicured hedges stretched before them. The sprawl of the homes and their land were insulting. To have so much space, to have such lavish homes while they forced the pilinos to live in close quarters, was despicable.

"The last district we will see today is Wisteria Heights." King Wyltam broke their silence, his deep voice just above a whisper. "Home to Satiros' wealthiest. Some lords own a second home in this district, as do some nobility from the other Syllogian city-states."

Ornate columns of marble; wrought iron fencing on the balconies; rich, dark wood doors; elaborate garden displays surrounding statues. Each detail was more insulting than the last.

"I believe some of the high-ranking guards under Keyain live here as well, if I'm not mistaken."

Keyain's guards. Those given high positions *by him* and allowed to live in such extravagance. He played a hand in this—all of this. Marietta took a deep breath through her nose, exhaling slowly to calm the flame of anger inside her, stoked by the disgusting show of wealth.

She would break apart their court for not just every life lost in Olkia, but for each one suppressed in The Weeds, too. Marietta would steal, she would lie, and she would become cruel if it meant helping them. And for the man who brought her here, she would break him. Keyain allowed all of this to happen—thrived off his city-state being this way. And the King. She turned her narrowed gaze towards him. He neglected the most vulnerable of his city-state. The wedge that Valeriya wanted to create between Keyain and Wyltam? Marietta would become it, for he gave her a unique opportunity. She could use Keyain's jealousy against him.

King Wyltam met her stare. "Something on your mind?"

"Does your offer still stand?"

His expression remained unreadable. "Of course."

She lifted her chin. "I have a few stipulations."

"And what would those be?"

"I have questions, ones Keyain will never answer. I accept your flirtations if you answer those questions."

He blinked, his gaze roaming her face. "Counteroffer: You accept my flirtations and we agree to answer each other's questions." He paused, leaning forward so his forearms rested on his knees. "We trade a truth for a truth."

Unsurprising. Marietta knew the King wanted information from her; yet she knew nothing that would harm Enomenos. They were terms she could accept. There posed but one problem. "Here's my counter, King Wyltam. Keyain would never believe it if I just accepted your flirting, your gifts."

"How do you suppose we solve that?"

She leaned forward, mirroring the King's posture. "If you want to make it believable, then I must act like you make me uncomfortable. That you're doing it against my will."

A laugh escaped his smiling lips, surprise lining his features. Marietta's heart stopped at the sight and sound. How strange of someone wearing an expressionless mask to suddenly remove it. How strangely charming.

She hated it.

"Cruel and clever; you are nothing like I expected." The brief smile faded back to his impassive expression. "But there's logic in your reasoning to which I can agree. Consider it part of the deal." He held out his hand to Marietta, waiting for her to grasp.

The deal was a tad foolish, knowing every word the King would share could be a lie; yet she could pluck the truth from his words if it came to that. Marietta wanted answers. One way or another, she would get them, all while using Keyain's weakness against him.

For the first time since stepping into Satiros, Marietta felt like herself. Confident, independent, making a deal that would put her in control.

She grasped the King's hand and shook.

King Wyltam locked eyes with her. "I look forward to working with you, Marietta."

Chapter Forty-Nine

ELYSE

Elyse approached Keyain's suite, stomach aching with apprehension. Just because Marietta said she would accompany Elyse to the library that afternoon didn't mean she *wanted* to go. Perhaps Keyain guilted his wife into it.

Two guards stood outside his door, surprising Elyse. That was new. The male on the left nodded to her in greeting. Elyse remembered meeting him once with Keyain. She returned with a tight smile as nerves knotted her stomach, and she knocked on the door.

A moment later, Marietta answered, her round face lit with excitement and black curls loose around her head. "Thank gods," she said, stepping out of the suite. "I've been dying to get out of there. Amryth—the guard who's usually with me—was on an assignment this week, so you're a blessing."

Elyse blinked, taken aback by her excited chatter and lack of greeting. "Oh, of course, Lady Marietta."

"Just Marietta. Titles grow tedious after a while." She looked up at Elyse. "Shall we, my savior?" Marietta looped her arm through hers and started down the hall.

A surprising laugh escaped Elyse's mouth. How was Marietta this okay in her presence? How was this not awkward for her?

They descended to the first floor of the Noble's Section, heading towards the Central Garden. "You would think Keyain would at least come and *walk me*—" she emphasized the words with her hands "—when Amryth's busy. Being trapped in that room is dreadful. Would not recommend."

"Recommendation noted." The nerves knotting Elyse's stomach loosened, Marietta putting her at ease. "I'm glad I called on you when I did. Keyain mentioned you're alone here in court, like me."

"Alone is one way to put it. Others might say an anomaly. Many of the courtiers aren't eager to befriend the first half-elven lady."

"Trust me. You're better off without them." Elyse bit her tongue, not sure why she felt the need to say such a thing.

"Is that so? Please elaborate because that would be the first bit of useful information I have received about this gods damned court."

"Well, they're all liars; they live for gossip."

"Unsurprising," Marietta muttered.

Elyse glanced at the scowl on her face. She couldn't help but smile. "None of them are worth your time. Once you're in the Queen's Court, you no longer fit in with them."

Marietta's head snapped to Elyse, eyes roaming her face. "That's what happened to you. You don't get along with them anymore."

Stunned silence held Elyse at how quick she could read that from her. "Uh, no. I choose not to interact with them."

Marietta nodded her head. "And you also don't get along with them. Perhaps one day you'll share why that is." She gave a pensive look, playing with a lock of her hair. "Between you and me, those who consider me less because I'm a half-elf don't deserve my time."

A smile spread across Elyse's face as they stepped into the sunshine, the summer's heat hitting her like a wall. Marietta tipped her face toward the sun, grinning.

Across the courtyard, groups of courtiers lounged near the fountain in the building's shade. All too aware of their pressing stares, Elyse led them to the garden path that cut to the library. She halted at the sight of Sylas, who stood before the path's entrance in deep conversation with two females who stole glances in their direction.

Gods, of course, they were standing right there, and of course, she and Marietta drew their attention. "Let's go this way," Elyse said, pulling Marietta away towards the farther path.

"We can just ask them to move if that's what you're avoiding."

"I'd rather not talk to them right now."

Marietta studied her face, then whipped her head back to the group. "Well, it looks like the man is heading right for us, anyway."

"Oh, my gods… I don't need any more rumors."

"What do you mean?" Marietta asked as Elyse half dragged her into the gardens, quickening her pace.

"He's from Chorys Dasi and is friends with Brynden."

"Who's Brynden?"

Elyse slowed to look at Marietta. "You really don't hear any of the court gossip, do you? Not even from Keyain?"

A dark expression crossed Marietta's face. "Keyain only tells me what's convenient for him. But please, tell me about this Brynden."

"Yes, Elyse," drawled Sylas. "What do you have to say about Brynden?"

With her heart racing and mood plummeting, Elyse spun around to dismiss Sylas with a scowl, but Marietta already threw him an icy expression. "And who might you be?" she asked.

With his own scowl, he raised a brow. "Lord Sylas Tygenbrook, Emissary to Chorys Dasi, errand boy to Lord Brynden."

Marietta observed Sylas from head to toe, pausing on his face with a smirk. "A pleasure to meet you, Lord Sylas," she said as she stuck out her hand. "I'm Lady Marietta Vallynte, a curious friend of Elyse."

Sylas hesitated, then took Marietta's hand.

"Tell me, *errand boy of Lord Brynden*," she said, crossing her arms, "why you wish to start rumors by hounding us on our walk?"

Elyse's mouth went dry. She had no intention of telling him that.

"Is that why you keep running from me, Elyse?" Sylas asked, pulling a folded piece of paper from his pocket. "Even though Brynden wrote you another letter?"

Marietta's stare cut through Elyse as she stared wide-eyed at Sylas. "I just… you were talking… and after Brynden…" Gods, why couldn't she talk? Elyse's throat tightened as she struggled with her words.

"I seem to be missing some details," Marietta said, dragging her gaze to Sylas. "Elyse believes that you chasing after her in a public manner will start rumors, and you are a friend of this Brynden who apparently wrote her a letter."

Marietta narrowed her eyes and glanced at Elyse. "Ah, perhaps a love letter. From the look on your face, something bad happened between you and this Brynden. Or his love goes unrequited? And by Sylas hunting you down, you think the courtiers will start rumors about you and Brynden?"

Elyse furrowed her brows under Marietta's intense gaze. Gods, she was so close, except...

"No," she said excitedly. "You're anxious that they'll start rumors about you and Sylas! Rumors about *another* Chorys Dasian who's interested in you."

Heat crept across Elyse's cheeks, marveling at Marietta's deduction. "Yes," she whispered, avoiding Sylas' gaze.

"That's what you're worried about?" Sylas said, attempting to step into her line of sight.

"Yes, Sylas!" Elyse snapped, turning to him. "I know how this court thinks. If you're chasing after me or they saw us together, they'll think I'm just trying to get another husband."

"Funny, because I just left that conversation saying I need to deliver a letter on behalf of Brynden to you," he said, thrusting the paper to her. "I'm not trying to embarrass you."

Shame pitted her stomach, realizing that Sylas would do his best to deflect such rumors. Elyse grabbed the paper. "Thanks, you can go now."

"Brynden asked that I watch your reaction as you read so I can share it with him later," he said with a laugh. "And to answer any questions you may have."

"Gods," Marietta murmured, the smirk coming back to her face. "This Brynden is pining after you, Elyse."

"I would hope so, considering she accepted his hand in marriage," Sylas said dryly.

"Oh?" Marietta gave her a grin.

"Not oh. I ended the betrothal." Elyse avoided their stares by glaring at the paper in her hands.

"And yet he still sends you love letters," she said, glancing at Sylas.

"I'd like to return to my conversation with those two ladies if you would please just read the letter." Sylas looked over his shoulder with a sigh.

With a glance towards Marietta's eager face, Elyse unfolded the paper.

Hope is a blessing from my goddess's lips, her hands offering me the sweetest gift. I am once again finding myself unworthy. You have heard my prayers, my calls to you desperate and pleading, wishing to be deemed worthy of your presence. Though you speak in images and single-word meanings, your voice permeates through it all. Oh, how I long to beg on my knees to you, my honey-eyed goddess.

I would give you my hands in prayer to have your divine honey coating my fingers.

I would sing your praises on my lips to taste your juiciest peach drip on my tongue.

I would give my body in sacrifice to feel your sweetest cream spill from your divine being.

I long for you, my goddess, my heart aching every day to supplicate at your temple.

Each night I pray anew with guided hands, begging for the goddess's relief. To be in your presence would be to give in to my every need. A kiss from your lips would be enough to break me. A touch of your hand would be enough to own me. A shudder from your body would be enough to claim me.

Though only the fates know what tomorrow holds, I hope for a future where I pray daily to you, my goddess.

This is my promise.

Elyse didn't breathe—no, she couldn't. Heat flooded her face as she clutched the letter to her pounding chest. He didn't mean….

Marietta snorted, bent over with laughter. "You must let me read it after that reaction! What did that man write to you?"

Elyse's wide eyes turned from Marietta to Sylas, whose scowl disappeared, a broad smile lighting his face. "Please tell me you didn't read this," she whispered.

"Unfortunately, I read every word, though it was worth it for your reaction." Sylas rubbed his chin as he laughed. "As I said, he's obsessed with you and going crazy in that townhouse."

Elyse read it once more, only making it halfway before clenching her eyes shut. "Oh, my gods."

"Brynden also wanted me to ask if you understood it all. Do you know what *your divine honey* is?"

Marietta's hand struck out, grabbing Elyse's arm with a grin on her face. "My gods, Elyse. Hand it over, *please.*"

Elyse hesitated but gave it to her. "I figured out what he meant, Sylas," she snapped, wrapping her arms around her middle.

"What about *your juiciest peach* or *your sweetest cream?*"

"Oh, my gods…. will you please stop?" she pleaded.

Marietta laughed again, her eyes scanning the page. "Elyse, you are such a lucky lady. This Brynden is beyond pining for you."

The smile died on Sylas' face. "He's obsessed, at least for today."

Marietta looked up from the paper, catching Sylas' gaze. A silent conversation passed between them, Marietta nodding her head. "I see. Well, having someone write such smutty things to you is quite fun, is it not?" she said, elbowing Elyse.

"I don't want to talk about this," she said, taking the letter back from Marietta and placing it folded in her pocket. "Come by the library in a few days, Sylas. I don't want to keep drawing attention to us."

"Noted," he said, frowning. "I'll see you in a few days. Lady Marietta, it was wonderful meeting you like this." With a slight flick of his brow, he turned on his heels and left the ladies on the path.

A giggle escaped Marietta. "Does the goddess wish to continue to the library? I would love to hear every detail about this Brynden whose heart you possess."

With a groan, Elyse looped her arm back through Marietta's. "Please don't tease me about this. Things didn't end well."

"No more teasing, I promise. But if you'd like someone to talk to about what happened, I'm all ears," Marietta said with a genuine smile.

Elyse stared at her moment, debating on what to say. Would she treat her like Grytaine and hold this over her head? Or was it, as Keyain said, Marietta needed a friend just as she did? If Keyain loved Marietta, then she must have been a good person. She was already unlike anyone else at court or anyone else she has met.

The anxiety in her stomach remained at ease as Elyse took a breath and started recounting what happened with Brynden as they continued to the library.

Chapter Fifty

MARIETTA

To fall in love again would be devastating. The uncertainty and yearning that accompanied courtship were exhausting, and Marietta saw its toll on Elyse. Even with such a brief history between her and the pining Lord Brynden, a relationship that blossomed and decayed in a matter of weeks, it weighed heavily on Elyse's mind. Marietta understood the hurt of her loss of it. Though Elyse was an adult, she had experienced little. Perhaps losing Brynden stuck in her mind for that reason.

As they combed their way through the library shelves, Marietta distracted Elyse from her anxiety. With a clear head, Elyse could share what happened with the unfortunate betrothal—a far cry from the lady she met at tea so long ago.

Sylas played a steadying role for Elyse as well. From what Marietta gleaned, Brynden was a person to love too quickly, too brightly, only to let it fade to nothing. *He's obsessed, at least for now.* His words were clear, his expression saying what his mouth did not. If she were to marry Brynden, he would grow bored and turn into a wayward husband. How curious that, as Brynden's friend, he felt the need to warn Elyse.

"If you go to Chorys Dasi with Brynden," Marietta said as she pulled a book from a shelf, looking over her shoulder to Elyse, "keep Sylas close."

Elyse shot her a nervous glance. "Why?"

"Because he cares about you, or at least cares about what happens to you. I think you'll find safety in him."

She scoffed, rolling her eyes. "Perhaps, but Sylas has the worst attitude.

I'm not sure he likes me all that much."

"You'd be surprised," Marietta said. "He wouldn't warn you about Brynden if he didn't."

"Or he's saving himself from a headache later. I believe Sylas said he'd be the one picking up the pieces if Brynden grew bored."

Marietta nodded her head, turning back to the shelf. She had surmised as much, considering he introduced himself as Brynden's errand boy, a hilarious but damning title. "Regardless, even if he feels some obligation to help you, at least someone there will have your best interests at heart."

Elyse leaned against the bookcase, staring at the titles. "Though part of me wants to be with him, I'm thankful it's over. Brynden is fun, but I know little about him."

Her words sounded hollow. Elyse could keep telling herself that, yet she didn't see her expression when she talked about him. She still wished to be with him. "Nothing wrong with enjoying his attention, though. Too bad they banned him from the palace. I'm dying to hear what he's like in bed," Marietta said, smirking.

"Oh, my gods."

"There's nothing inappropriate with being sexual. I wonder if Brynden is all talk or if his actions live up to the beautifully filthy words he wrote for you."

Elyse hesitated, a smile coming to her lips. "We almost did something. Well, technically we did something." Redness covered her cheeks as she spoke, averting her gaze from Marietta.

"Oh? Is that so? Please give me those details."

"After he asked for my hand, he—well, he *gave* me his hand, if you will."

Marietta's smile grew wider, a laugh bursting from her, watching Elyse turn to a glowing red. "So he already experienced the goddess' divine honey coating his fingers. How delightful," she said with a smirk.

"And he went to use his mouth—"

"Yes? To taste the juiciest peach—"

"But then Sylas barged in, so... that was all. And the most I've ever experienced."

Gods, by her age, Marietta already had a few partners. "The gods are cruel, to give you enough to want, and then rip it away. Maybe if you had chaperones, you could see him again, even if you don't get time alone. I'll talk to Keyain to see if us four can go out into the city together."

A bemused grin came to her face. "Do you think he'd agree?"

"I'm sure I can convince him," she said, pulling out a book, inspecting the inside cover. "Plus, I'd love to meet Brynden. Can you imagine him saying such filthy things in front of Keyain? Oh, it'd be so funny."

Elyse snorted, reaching for a book. "I don't think he could handle it. He once caught me reading this book," she said, handing it to Marietta. "Known for its... sexier scenes, if you will. Which, of course, I didn't know when I brought it to read in front of Keyain."

Marietta's smile grew as she laughed, flipping through the pages. "I can only imagine how that went."

"Oh, he was flustered when he had to explain to me to keep it hidden from other people when I walked with it," Elyse said, laughing. "That was the first and last time I brought a smutty book to read in front of him."

Marietta snapped the book shut, tucking it under her arm. "Imagine his surprise when I return to the suite with it then," she said, walking down the row of books. "Do you think he'd be more horrified if I read him lines from this book or Brynden's letter?"

"Brynden's letter, without a doubt in my mind."

The two giggled as they decided which lines would make Keyain the most uncomfortable. Laughter echoed through the shelves, carrying deeper into the library, with tears coming to Marietta's eyes. She hadn't laughed like that since... since she last saw Tristina. Her friend who was the first to turn any event into a party. As she watched Elyse, she couldn't help her heart aching for her. Perhaps with the young lady, she had found another friend in Satiros. Where Amryth was all seriousness, Elyse was easiness despite her anxious tendencies. Her friends. The thought warmed Marietta through the center, the edge of loneliness creeping away.

"How curious," King Wyltam's voice drawled from behind. "I was unaware you two had found camaraderie."

The ladies spun to face the King. "King Wyltam," Elyse said with a curtsy. "Marietta was kind enough to join me this afternoon for a break from... scribing."

Scribing? Why would a lady be scribing?

The movement was subtle, but Marietta watched the King's brows twitch, the only emotional hint he offered. "Of course, Elyse. I hate to cut your time short, but I wish to speak to Marietta alone."

Elyse stiffened, clearly uncomfortable with the dismissal. "Of course, Your Grace." She offered a quick curtsy to the King, taking off down the aisle, offering a worrisome glance over her shoulder at Marietta. Even with her usual anxious demeanor, the reaction was odd.

King Wyltam stood before her with his expressionless mask and cold eyes, his gaze lingering. In all black clothing, he fit into the warm glow and somber colors of the library. "Marietta, I hope you remembered our deal."

"How could I forget?" She threw him a sharp smile, tucking a loose strand of hair behind her ear. "It's not every day the King who attacked my home offers me a deal." Stupid, bold words; she should have kept her mouth shut. The King may have given her the opportunity to hurt Keyain, but she didn't need to be polite to him.

Warmth came to his eyes as laughter broke through his cold facade, like ice cracking over a lake—sudden and jarring yet still fascinating. "I see you're feeling hostile today. Perhaps you can hold your tongue and join me for a walk."

"Perhaps I can, King Wyltam." Marietta gave him a tight smile.

"Here," he said, holding out his arm, "let me hold your book."

"Thank you, but that won't be necessary." Marietta dismissed him, tucking it under her arm and the other wrapped around his bicep.

"Humble me," he said. "Though I'm the King, I can still be courteous."

Courteous, sure, but did he know the reputation of this title like Keyain had? It would be wise to hold the book herself, shield the title, in case the *sexier scenes* gave the book notoriety; yet, with the King unyielding with his held-out handle, she did, in fact, humble him by placing the book in his hand.

King Wyltam tucked it under one arm as Marietta took the other. If he recognized the name or its contents, he didn't comment. Thank the gods.

"You two were making quite a bit of noise with your laughter." King Wyltam inspected Marietta's face, a hint of curiosity dancing behind his eyes.

"Apologies. We didn't mean to cause a commotion." If Marietta meant to, they would have been louder.

"No apology needed. I'm just pleased that you could make a friend in court."

Marietta suppressed an eye roll. It was almost as if the court avoided interacting with Marietta, preferring to gawk from afar. "And I'm just glad you only made Elyse a touch nervous by being alone with me. Do you make everyone in your court as nervous or just the young ladies?"

The reaction was subtle, controlled. The slight pursing of his lips. A flick of his brow. Even his body seemed to still. "Whatever you are insinuating, I would advise against it." His gaze faltered, looking towards the end of the aisle instead of at Marietta.

They wound their way out of the library, Marietta watching the King's face, willing for more emotion to break through. A glimpse of anything but the icy mask. "Of course, but why would her demeanor change so drastically when you appeared?"

Marietta almost missed the guttering of his eyes as he stared ahead. Was he trying to hide his emotions, or did showing emotions make him uncomfortable?

Gods, it was both.

"I had hoped Elyse would be less nervous around me by now." He paused, considering his words before his stare slid back to her. "Being the King is a powerful position that often leaves people holding their tongue."

Marietta rolled her eyes. "Your position has never caused me to hold my tongue."

King Wyltam held the door for her as they stepped outside. The slight glint in his eye returned with a smirk. "No, it hasn't. Such petulance surprises me. Never would I have thought Keyain would marry someone like you."

"And never would I have thought I'd marry Keyain."

King Wyltam halted on the veranda before the doors, turning to Marietta. "Did you not marry him by choice?"

Did he really not know? By some miracle, did Keyain not share that detail of their marriage? Her smile grew, realizing she could leverage that question with their deal. "Truth for a truth, King Wyltam?"

"Alright, truth for a truth. How did you and Keyain marry?"

"I believe the law is that an elf can marry a pilinos without their consent, is it not?" Resentment laced her narrowed glare and sharp tongue. Resentment for Syllogi, for Keyain marrying her without her consent, and for the laws that allowed it.

The King resumed walking, stepping into the garden's path with his arm still locked on Marietta's. "That is true. However, you'd have to be from Syllogi, which you are not."

So Keyain lied on the marriage certificate, to make it seem like Marietta was from Syllogi, not Enomenos. How would that slip through? Though intrigued to know the answer, she held back her questions for the most urgent ones. "Why do you view pilinos as lesser people?"

The King raised a brow. "I do not view half-elves or humans as lesser people."

Marietta tsked. "The deal was to answer truthfully."

"I'm being truthful. I believe pilinos are as much of a person as any elf. However, those are the laws I inherited; I did not make them."

"But you could reverse them."

"Though I am king, I still answer to the people I rule." Tiredness edged the inky black of his eyes, the dark circles underneath appearing darker. "Many would revolt such a sweeping change. Gradual change is easier for people to handle, like adding a wider variety of city-states to ally with Satiros—city-states that have a different dynamic between elves and pilinos."

"And how does attacking Olkia help you achieve that?" The question snapped out before she could stop herself.

"I believe it's my turn to ask a question," the King said, a bemused expression on his face. "How did you meet Keyain?"

Marietta exhaled through her nose, staring down at the King. She despised him for attacking her home, then having the nerve to look amused. She bit back her anger, answering the question. "Through work. Traveling through Enomenos on my own was dangerous, so I hired a bodyguard."

"Do you expect me to believe that the Satiroan Minister of Protection was a bodyguard?"

A crooked smile twisted into her lips. "I believe it's my turn to ask a question. Why did you attack Olkia?"

The King hesitated, leading Marietta further into the gardens, crossing a bridge that overran a creek. For the slimmer frame of the King, it surprised Marietta that his arm underneath felt hard and lean. Why would a king have muscle and then hide it? Were his enemies that much of a threat? They would be if they were in the palace already.

"If I'm being honest with you—"

"Which you should be."

The King leveled her with a cold stare. "Satiros seized Olkia for two reasons. One, to force the conversation between the Enomenoan governments and Satiros to become one entity. I have requested meetings from both local city-state governments and the Enomenos Unionization Council. No one was interested in our proposition." The King glanced at her before continuing. "Two, to find The Shepherd, leader of the Exisotis, or, at the very least, his family. Keyain searched for years to no avail."

Marietta scoffed and pulled her arm from the King's but his grip held. "Neither are good reasons to attack innocent people."

The King stopped walking. "Where would you hear such a thing like that? Attacking innocent people?"

Under his cold, narrowed stare and the tightening grip on her arm,

Marietta refused to cower, lifting her chin. "You slaughtered the people of Olkia, did you not?"

The King brought a hand to her chin, gripping it with gentle fingers. "Not your turn for a question, Marietta. Who told you that we slaughtered people? That we attacked innocents?"

Gods—the Queen did, but Marietta couldn't share that. "Keyain," she said without hesitation.

His grip tightened on her chin. "We agreed to share truths. Now tell me, who told you this?"

Marietta curled back her lips at the King, tugging away from his grip, glowering; yet he held true, staring at her through his emotionless mask. It worried her to share the truth, that the King could discover that she and Valeriya were working with one another. As he stared her into her face, she had little hope of sharing a convincing lie. Reluctantly, she uttered, "Queen Valeriya."

With a sneer, his grip loosened. "Of course. This is a court of lies, Marietta, and sitting at its center is my wife. I urge you to take her secrets with a grain of salt."

Marietta exhaled at the King's reaction. He was used to Valeriya saying such information. What did that mean for working with her? Did she often reach out to members of the court and share her secrets? Gods, likely not if she worked with the Exisotis. King Wyltam couldn't trust his wife, but Marietta could. "Noted," she said, tearing out of his grip. To her dismay, he grabbed her hand. To more of her dismay, heat rushed to her cheeks as he stood closer to her.

"Your turn, Marietta." His deep voice was just a murmur, eyes locking onto her lips.

Marietta tilted her head, confused by the sudden change in his tone.

The King lifted his other hand. "May I?"

She swallowed hard, nodding her head. Gods, she hated him. Hated his handsome face. Hated the way he made her heart skip a beat. King Wyltam was a monster, sinking in his claws. Part of her didn't want him to let go.

"Why are you punishing Keyain?" she asked, her voice smaller than she'd hoped.

The gentle touch of his hand moved to her ear, tracing the stunted arch. King Wyltam leaned in. The breath on her ear made her want to push him away, made her want to pull him closer. The deep rumbling of his hushed voice nearly pushed her over the edge. "Because I loved him and he betrayed me."

The King loved Keyain and was using her against him. Gods, what did she agree to?

He tucked a lock of her hair behind her ear, bringing her hand up to his mouth. "You are very beautiful, Marietta."

She didn't dare breathe as he kissed her knuckles, locking eyes with Marietta.

"Wyltam, what is this?" Keyain's harsh voice sounded from down the path.

King Wyltam took a step back, Marietta catching the brief smirk that hinted on his lips. "Keyain, what a surprise."

Marietta's head jerked towards Keyain as her stomach dropped. Keyain stood on the path with two males, to whom he turned and dismissed before approaching with a burning glare.

"Marietta," he ground out, "what happened to your trip to the library with Elyse?"

"It was cut short."

"Yes," King Wyltam drawled. "Elyse needed to return to work, so I offered to escort your wife. Is that a problem?"

Blood rose to Keyain's face, and the muscles in his neck tightened. "Not at all, but I can take her from here." He held out his hand like she was a dog. Marietta forced herself not to scowl.

The King's hand landed on her shoulder. "That's quite alright. I would love nothing more than to return Marietta to your suite," he said, pausing as Keyain flared his nostrils. "Unless you want to take her back instead of focusing on your duties?"

That was the game. Not only was he flirting with Marietta to aggravate

Keyain, but making him choose between his position and her. It was a cruel plan; one Marietta couldn't help but envy the King for concocting.

"I have time before my next meeting. Come, Marietta." A demand.

Perhaps it was a game for her, too—forcing her to keep up the charade of not wanting to be near the King and trusting Keyain. She wished to curse Keyain, yet her feet reluctantly walked towards him.

The King's arm caught her, spinning her to face him again. He leaned in, whispering, "Our conversations stay between us." Though his voice was soft, Marietta felt the threat underneath. "And though this isn't an adventure book, I believe you'll find a few of these chapters quite entertaining."

Gods, he knew about the book. Marietta closed her eyes with a breath and snatched the book from the King's outstretched hand.

He stepped away, a smirk breaking through his facade. "Go along. You're dismissed."

Chapter Fifty-One

ELYSE

How should she respond to a smutty letter?

How would anyone respond?

Elyse was still at a loss, even as she read the letter for what felt like the hundredth time. Brynden made what he wanted clear—and gods, she wanted it herself; but how does she put that want into a drawing? How does she convey that message?

Elyse leaned back in the desk chair in her suite's office. Not having much gold to her name, save for what the King gave her, Elyse hadn't bothered furnishing it beyond the desk. Pushed up against the window, Elyse stared absently out at the palace walls. The suite she had shared with her father was one of the coveted spots facing out into the Central Garden. However, her new suite was a spare smaller one they had available, thus the lackluster view. She didn't mind, though. The view wasn't worth more than putting up with her father.

Staring back at her sheet of parchment, Elyse picked at her nails as she thought. Though she had stopped believing she and Brynden would marry, she still wished to *be* with him, to relive the experience in the piano room. She wished she could give herself to him.

Perhaps she could.

Elyse jumped up from her seat, darting to her bedroom, and grabbed a mirror from off her vanity. People weren't her strong suit with drawing, but she would at least try.

As she sat at her desk, staring into the mirror, she began drawing.

From inside the King's study, silence encased Elyse. She sat at the desk with her eyes closed, breathing deep, as she practiced the mental exercises from Wyltam's books.

Over the past two weeks, Elyse had worked through the stack Wyltam had left for her. The first listed breathing and mental exercises, like the one she now practiced. Each day, she had taken breaks to sit in silence, clearing her mind of any thought, any emotion.

The book had warned that it could be difficult but not to become frustrated. Each time Elyse's mind had drifted, the book instructed her to acknowledge it, then pull it back. Every day, she would inhale through her nose, releasing it slowly through her mouth. Over and over, until her mind had emptied.

Elyse's first attempt failed miserably. Not only had her thoughts wandered, but she became aggravated from letting it happen, yet she continued to try twice every day and learned to sit with a clear mind.

Of all the ways she expected magic to improve her life, she hadn't expected it to help with her anxious thoughts. Between the mental exercises and the separation from her father, her head remained clearer than it had ever been.

Thinking of nothing, Elyse sat behind the desk in silence as something brushed against her mind. Her first instinct was to jerk away, but the sensation was familiar. She had experienced it before—with Mage's Eye at the Chorys Dasian townhouse. Accepting the mental brush, she leaned into the energy, gasping as she became aware of the tendrils of aithyr. With Mage's Eye, Elyse had seen the distinct paths of the magical energy, like hazy white rapids of a river. Without it, Elyse only sensed them flowing around her, like how she couldn't see a gust of wind but could feel its movement on her skin.

Like the day at the townhouse, Elyse reached out, using her mind to pull at a tendril. The aithyr came effortlessly, filling her body with thrumming energy. When she opened her eyes, she imagined the aithyr as wind gusting from her hand.

Air blew from her palm, scattering the papers across the desktop. With a laugh, she stared at her hand, unable to believe she did it. Her toughest hurdle to becoming a mage was herself—her mental strength. That moment proved Elyse could overcome it, that she could clear her mind and control her emotions. That she could become the spy Wyltam wished her to be.

After working hard to improve herself, to feel such an accomplishment was empowering. No longer was she the weak and insignificant daughter of a minister; she was the budding mage of the King. If she continued down that path, no one and nothing could stop her.

Magic was power beyond what she could imagine, sweeter than any marriage. With it, she could control her positioning in the world, no longer needing to rely on others for strength. In that way, it was also freeing. Though she might be at the King's beck and call while working for him, outside her duties, she could be whatever she wished. She could do whatever she wished, see whatever she wished.

A knock drew her from her thoughts. "Elyse, it's Sylas."

Her smile dropped. Gods, right. The drawing. This one was a risk, one that would tell Brynden of her intentions, but she remembered what Marietta had said, that exchanging smutty letters with Brynden was fun, enjoyable.

With that in mind, Elyse grabbed the folded sheet and approached the door. Sylas stood with his arms crossed, and he looked... handsome. His curly hair was loose down to his shoulders, one side tucked behind his ear as if to show his piercings. Coupled with his tight-fitting silk shirt and black embroidered jacket, he dressed too nicely for an average day in the palace.

"What's with the elegant attire?" she asked, leaning against the door frame.

"Turns out Brynden isn't the only one attracted to Satiroan females," he said with a bemused grin. "I'm accompanying a lucky lady for lunch this afternoon."

Elyse bit back her surprise. Of course, Sylas would find someone at court. "May I ask who?"

"Lydia Ryntz. She's a friend of yours, right?"

Elyse's limbs numbed and she nearly dropped her drawing. "No."

Sylas narrowed his eyes, the usual scowl coming to his face. "No, you aren't friends with her? Or no, I can't court her?"

"Both," she hissed. "Lydia is not my friend—has not been my friend for years. You can't court her; she's horrible."

Sylas raised his brows. "Lydia mentioned you view your friendship with her differently—"

"She has a horrible habit of deciding what others should think." Elyse hesitated, unsure whether to share more, but sighed and gave in. "I spent most of my childhood questioning my own thoughts, my own memories of events because she told me I remembered them inaccurately."

"Well, you are erratic in your thinking—"

Elyse shoved the drawing into his chest. "Take this and go, Sylas." She knew he was an ass, but this was different. Perhaps he would be a perfect match for Lydia.

"I'm sorry," he said, unfolding the drawing. "I didn't mean to—"

"Don't open this one," she snapped, restraining from pulling the paper from his hands. If she were to rip it, then her hours of work were for nothing.

"You know the rules."

Heat crept up her cheeks and chest as Sylas opened it, then quickly folded it closed. "You're playing a dangerous game. Are you sure you want to give him this?"

Elyse sighed, hating herself for being embarrassed. The drawing was perfect, a self-portrait of her from the chest up, nude, with hair covering most of her breasts. Written at the bottom was the word *dream*. "How else do you respond to a filthy letter, Sylas?"

"You didn't need to match him for content," he said, placing it in his pocket. "A clothed self-portrait would have sufficed."

"Just leave, Sylas. Enjoy your date—you two are a perfect match."

Elyse turned before seeing his reaction, closing the door to stifle any reply. The drawing was a bit impulsive to send to Brynden. She knew he'd love it, but she also hoped it wasn't a mistake.

Chapter Fifty-Two
VALERIYA

Valeriya traveled the streets of Satiros, the city's alleyways and buildings growing narrower, the rooftops rising higher as she journeyed into Rambler Grove. The district was more like its nickname—The Weeds. Scraggly, with tall, spindly buildings made of whatever material was available. Life bloomed from every nook and cranny, be it a well-planned space for housing or dense urban gardens for its denizens. The resilient residences proved they could grow anywhere and through anything. What started as a mocking name for the district became a symbol.

When Valeriya arrived in Satiros—two weeks before her public arrival date—she snuck into the city disguised. Disgusted, she found The Weeds and its dense living conditions. Over the past seven years, she had visited a handful of times per month to support the pilinos businesses in the district. Not all battles were fought with magic and swords. By stealing the crown's coin, she funded the district. When her and her sister's plan came to fruition, the pilinos would need resources to help uplift themselves; otherwise, wealth could keep them trapped in a status below the elven.

In a different form from her other trips into the city, she donned the visage of an older half-elven female she knew in Reyila. Gray marred her temples, magic shifting her body to look curvy, and she wore the plain face of the steward of Reyila's castle. By rotating who she appeared as in The Weeds, she minimized the risk of people recognizing her and asking too many questions.

While the rest of Satiros was beautiful, she admired the practical

aesthetic of the district, where they left no space unused. They turned parks into community food gardens a few years back, thanks to Valeriya's anonymous donation. With the food prices marked up for pilinos and less lucrative careers, many couldn't purchase the nutrition they needed.

The ever-growing refugee numbers didn't help with the shortage of food and space. Over the past couple of years, the population grew by a third, making the already limited area tighter. With every donation Valeriya made, she hoped to give them a chance to thrive in Satiros, to set them up for the future.

A few people nodded their heads at Valeriya as she wound through the packed streets, thankful the cloud cover snuffed the sun's heat. Even with the shade, sweat layered Valeriya's skin. Not much further was her first stop—the refugee intake building.

A human boy with a crop of curly brown hair almost ran into Valeriya, but she dodged his clumsy movements. He offered a quick apology before darting down an alley. She could only smile. To give such a boy the freedom to be careless was worth every risk.

With each visit, The Weeds' denizens reminded her more of Reyila. Her heart longed to show Katya what she accomplished in her short time in Satiros, wishing to hear her husky voice encourage her to keep going. After killing those males, she wanted Katya's assurance that she was on the right path. Perhaps Valeriya should just message her, though they promised to cut off their relationship. Would she want to speak with Valeriya? Would she still care?

Occasionally through magic, she received a message from Nystanya, brief words exchanged between the two. Her sister was proud, saying that Valeriya had to continue working with Chorys Dasi and change would come; it was only a matter of time. All she could do was listen and hold her head high.

Valeriya arrived outside a brown brick building that sat at the center of The Weeds, deep within the district and away from elven eyes. When she entered, she met the tired stares of dirt-covered refugees. A young half-elven girl was sniffling next to her human mother, who tried to hush the girl. A half-elf in a white vest made their way to each refugee, taking their name and statement. Another handed out food and water to the small group that occupied the space.

"I have a donation to drop off," Valeriya said to the half-elf with the clipboard.

The round-faced female spared her a glance. "Go on back. Lily will help you."

Valeriya offered her thanks, stepping through a narrow doorway into a makeshift storage room beyond. A small human female barked orders at two males as they arranged care kits for the refugees. "No, no—that pack is for the mother and daughter. This one is for the old man," she snapped, earning a glower from one of the males.

"Are you Lily?" Valeriya removed a canvas knapsack from her back.

"Aye, I am. What do you want?"

Valeriya hid the smile tugging at her lips. Such anger and petulance wouldn't be possible for someone like her anywhere else in Syllogi. "Food donation," she said, handing over her pack filled to the brim with loaves of bread and hard cheeses. At her waist, she removed a heavy coin purse. "And a monetary donation."

Lily gave her an uneasy look, taking both bags. She glanced at the food and handed it to one of the males. "Distribute this among the current kits." Without waiting for an answer, she turned to the coin purse. The bag slipped from her hands as she looked inside. Valeriya caught the bag before it hit the floor, only a few gold coins getting loose.

"That... that's at least five hundred gold." Lily's jaw went slack, the males whipping their heads in their direction.

"Five hundred and fifty, to be exact," Valeriya said with a smile. That haul was the largest sum she had swiped from the royal coffers, and only half of what she took this time. "All to provide refugees with the room, food, and clothing they need to get off their feet."

"But how?" Lily said, taking the bag back and shaking her head. "This is more than any single half-elf can make, even in Satiros."

"The fewer questions you ask, the better." Valeriya offered a sincere smile. "Not stolen, but a blessing, if you will."

"Gods must bless us on this day," Lily said, running a hand through her ash blonde hair. "Thank you. What's your name?"

"Consider it an anonymous donation."

Lily glanced at Valeriya, then back at the gold and the food. "Well, it's appreciated. With so many refugees arriving every week, we've been running low on supplies." The coin jingled as she shook the bag. "This will make an immense difference. From all of us, thank you."

"Just trying to help," Valeriya said, turning to leave. By helping, she ensured the future for them all in Satiros—ensured her legacy as the Queen who reformed the city-state.

With a light heart, Valeriya strode through the city streets to her next destination. Clustered in groups off to the side of the main walkway, she gleaned information from conversations.

"It has to be a hoax. Is she really a half-elf?" someone said.

"Yes! From Enomenos, married to Minister Keyain," their friend answered.

"No, it's a lie. She's just an elf with odd ears, not half-elven."

"Well, I heard it from an elf who worked in the palace. They said she even knew how to bake in the kitchens!"

Valeriya felt a smile tug on her lips as she paused. "She's real. Lady Marietta was a baker in Enomenos." The two half-elves gawked at her as she strode away.

"But what does that mean for us?" the one asked excitedly.

That was why Marietta needed to be protected. Of course, her life mattered, as did her well-being. However, her proximity to Keyain's information made her a useful ally, and more importantly, she sent a message. A high-ranking member of Satiros' court married a half-elf. Whether Keyain realized it or not, he was starting a revolution. Plus, Marietta was a calming presence among the disappearing pilinos. Four more bodies were found, the latest one being a human male with clip carved across his forehead, left to bake in the sun on the shore of the Halia with his body mangled and deprived of clothing. At least no more pilinos had gone missing since.

Marietta's presence distracted them, gave them hope despite the horror that threatened them. In The Weeds, they would come to learn Marietta's name for the change she represented. Valeriya would be the Queen who accepted her, gave her a place among the nobles. Yes, Marietta's life mattered to many.

The streets thinned out as she neared the edge of the district where it bordered Wooded Ward. Valeriya approached one of the few opened buildings. The sign above the door read *"District Delegations."* The room beyond was expensive for The Weeds but drab for elsewhere in Satiros.

Rich brown wainscoting made of wood covered the lower half of the wall, the top covered in white wallpaper painted with green vines. In a frame on the wall hung the Satiroan crest, two down-turned purple wisteria blooms curving into one another with the city's motto, *"Ever Blooming."* Its presence was mocking. The crown didn't care about The Weeds or its denizens, at least, not beyond the service they provided to the elven population.

Valeriya passed a few open doorways where males and females talked in hushed voices in parlors. Coming to a door at the end of the hall, she knocked twice.

"Come in," called a voice.

Inside, Valeriya found the lead district delegate of The Weeds. A squat half-elven man with thinning, mousy brown hair and a pair of spectacles resting at the bottom of this bulbous nose. He looked up at Valeriya from his papers. "Ah, you," he said, sitting back in the chair with a smile. "It's been a while since your last visit, Blythe."

The name she used from her previous visit took her by surprise for a moment, but she recovered. "It has, Alderan. I see you spent my donation wisely; the streets are looking immaculate." Everyone knew of the district's frustrating potholes. With horses prohibited in the city and the lack of magical equipment available to pilinos, the last issue they needed was pocked dirt roads to pull their carts.

"Things have been smooth, so to say."

Valeriya chuckled, but realized the male didn't mean it as a joke. Covering the laugh with a cough, she added, "Well, I'm glad to hear it." She strode toward his faded wood desk with another coin purse in her hand. "And the education funds? How are those holding up?"

"Not well," he said, rubbing the stubble forming on his pointed chin. "For a while, we had enough to keep each child supplied with materials, but with the increase in refugees, the budget is tight."

"That's why I made my last donation. I thought it'd help for the foreseeable future." The fact the money hadn't gone as far was troubling.

"None of us foresaw a half-elven lady in court," he said with a tired smile. "The number of refugees over the past months has spiked. Many believe life in Satiros is about to change for pilinos, despite recent events." His tired smile faded.

Curious, Marietta's reputation has already made its way to the poorest populations in Syllogi. "Do you not think change is coming?"

Alderan let out a long breath. "A younger version of me would have said yes, but I know better now. Between the war and the missing pilinos...." He paused a moment, rubbing the small circular pendant hanging on his neck. "To me, the half-elven lady's presence is more of a warning to Enomenos—that they'll steal their loved ones if they fight back, that they'll turn to violence to keep us suppressed."

If Valeriya were a betting female, she knew what that pendant symbolized—and why he said *loved ones*. Alderan was Exisotis.

"Perhaps they intended her to be a warning," Valeriya said, smirking, "but we can also decide what her presence means, regardless of who died for her to be in Satiros."

Alderan blinked, realization coming to his features that she referred to Tilan Reid, which was the confirmation she needed. The Exisotis infiltrated the lower governments of Satiros. That information would be useful for her sister.

"Who are you exactly, Blythe?"

"I am who I need to be," Valeriya said, lifting the coins. "Which right now is the funder of The Weeds' educational system." She tossed the bag onto his desk.

With an uneasy glance, Alderan opened it, shaking his head. "Once again, you come when I need you most, so who am I to ask questions?" He laughed and pulled the strings tight. "I don't know who you are, but it seems we keep like company."

"Like enough," Valeriya said, smiling. "All children deserve proper education." She turned to leave, pausing in the doorway. "And they will need that education for the future. Change is coming, Alderan. Let's make sure your district is ready for it."

Chapter Fifty-Three
MARIETTA

After the King's taunting in the garden, Keyain asked Marietta to stay in the suite until Amryth came back from an assignment. When they had returned to the suite that afternoon, he was so shaken, so furious, that calming him down was a struggle.

Keyain had cursed Wyltam, saying he was out of line and beyond inappropriate. Of course, from his vantage point, it would have appeared incongruous; but Marietta knew the truth, that she intended for situations like that to occur. King Wyltam's timing of the entire day was impeccable. The kiss on her hand, the placing of her hair behind her ear, caused Keyain to release his jealousy in a way she hadn't seen in years.

Marietta could see how it worked into Valeriya's plan as well, pinning the two men against each other. The thought made her smile, that she finally crafted a way to give herself control in this court. Not only did she help the Queen, but she also found a way to further their plan by her own means. The divide in Keyain and the King's friendship had widened already.

What irked her, though, was King Wyltam's confession. The King loved Keyain, and she planted herself at the center of their drama. Of all the ways she imagined their relationship deteriorating, she hadn't considered love or lack thereof. Perhaps because Keyain never talked of his love life prior to Marietta, though it wasn't all too surprising that he'd been with a man. Most in Enomenos are attracted to more than one gender.

Yet a question had burned at the back of her mind, one she almost

asked Keyain when they returned to the suite. Did Keyain ever love the King back, or was the King bitter when Keyain never returned his feelings?

Regardless, Marietta would stick to the plan despite what trouble it could bring her. That included handling Keyain's burning fit of jealousy that day after the gardens. Even holding his hand hadn't worked. It took a kiss. Not on the lips, thank gods, but on his cheek while Marietta caressed his face. Only then did he stop and breathe. Nauseating work, but it could have been worse.

The week alone in the suite had included her pretending to find his court gossip entertaining and lying about not being bored. She read the book from the library within an afternoon. The sexier scenes Elyse referred to were, well, tame. When Keyain saw what she was reading, he acted affronted. Marietta had to remind him that they had much wilder nights than what was in the book back in the day. The idea that the content was scandalous made her laugh. If only Elyse could read the books she had left in Olkia.

Other than that, her week dragged on, each day making her antsier than the last. The morning Amryth returned, she wasted no time in getting out of the suite. They strolled an unfamiliar section of the castle, where marble statues lined the hallway. A coiled serpent sat on a pedestal with its head raised, a pair of horns curling back from its face, its tongue flickering. She stopped to inspect the details, failing to remember the creature's name from her father's feyrie tales.

"Are you still not going to share what your task was?" Marietta asked.

"Gods damned fool's errand is what," Amryth grumbled. "I offered to help with the search of the missing pilinos, and Keyain took that as I'm open for whatever tasks he needs."

"What did he have you do?" she asked again, raising her brows.

"Nothing worth sharing," she said, waving her off, her leather armor shifting smoothly with the motion. "I checked in with Deania at the temple last night. She knew half of the missing pilinos, and so far, the ones whose bodies have been recovered were all her friends."

"Deities above, that's tragic." Marietta clutched a hand to her chest.

"Is she alright?"

"She says she is, but I know she isn't." Amryth paused, crossing her arms to lean against the pillar. "What I find more concerning is that she's hiding information. The murderers almost abducted another friend of hers during the height of the disappearances. They never reported it to the guard."

"Can you blame them?" Marietta said with a tight smile. "It's not as if they're treated well."

"Though that's true, Keyain is putting all his resources towards this." She paused, toying with one of her braids. "The reason they didn't come forward was because of what they saw. Two male elves cornered them, but the details were confusing. In the dark, they could only see the most glaring features, which were described as one having a set of gray, feathery wings sprouting from his back. The other male had two horns circling the sides of his head from his temple."

Marietta furrowed her brows. "Costumes, maybe?"

"But why costumes? Why wear such distinct features that also make it difficult to move?" Amryth shook her head. "It makes little sense, and her friend knew that, hence why they didn't go to the guard."

Amryth pushed off the pillar, leading Marietta further down the hall. A massive statue pulled her attention. The bottom was that of a horse, from the torso up was human. "It sounds like something from a feyrie tale," she said, nodding to the sculpture. "Like a centaur or satyr."

Amryth scoffed. "Right, as if the statues were coming alive and attacking pilinos specifically."

Marietta laughed, taking her arm to skip down the hall, happy to distract Amryth from the dour topic. "If you could be any creature from a feyrie tale, what would you be?" She stopped, twirling out the pale pink of her dress to face Amryth, the dual slits in her skirt reaching to her hips.

"What kind of question is that?"

Marietta shrugged, twirling again. "A fun one. I think you'd be a gorgon."

"Seriously? Because of my hair?" She almost looked offended.

"No, because your gaze can turn anyone into stone." Marietta laughed, getting Amryth to crack a smile. "Your unimpressed stare turns me to stone—and you like me. I can't imagine what it looks like when you don't like someone."

Amryth smirked. "Let's hope you don't find out."

"What do you think I'd be?"

"A satyr," she answered without missing a beat. "Because you're impulsive as all hells."

"And I like to dance." She twirled again, finding herself at the end of the hall where it opened up to a new room. Marietta stood, mouth agape.

"Welcome to the Glass Garden," Amryth said, stepping past her. "I knew you'd like it."

The enclosed garden had statues of satyrs and delicate water nymphs, carved frolicking in the waters, water spouting from the tips of their fingers. A massive rock outcropping from the wall centered the fountain. At its front was a cave inhabited by a beautiful female creature with a haunted expression, its mouth gaping as if she screamed. The angles of the face were too sharp to be human, elven, or anything in between. Water spouted out the eyes and mouth, down her naked body.

The glass ceiling high above let in the afternoon light. Crystal orbs floated above the fountain in the sun's rays and created rainbows in the mist. Colors danced across every surface from the refracted light.

Around the exterior were trees and flowers planted in containers with thick vines coiled up the stone walls and columns. The perfume from the blooms blended with soil and wet permeated the air. The fountain's babbling water aided Marietta's sense of peace. "How have I not seen this?" she asked. "It's unbelievable."

"It's one of the most beautiful spots in the palace." Marietta jumped at the deep voice from just over her shoulder.

"Gods," Marietta said, clutching her chest where the fabric dipped low. "King Wyltam, you scared me." She offered a quick curtsy. At her side, Amryth dropped to a knee, her right hand fisted over her heart.

"Apologies, Lady Marietta," he said, his expression showing nothing of an apology. "I didn't intend to sneak up on you." He looked past Marietta. "Amryth, you are dismissed. I wish to speak to Marietta alone."

Amryth glanced at Marietta for a second with her nose flared. Gods, she didn't want to leave, especially after hearing what happened with her previous outing with the King; yet, she was dutiful, nodding her head once before she stood and went back down the hall.

"I've always loved this room," the King murmured, looking up at the female creature at its center.

"That's surprising, King Wyltam," Marietta said with a dip of her head. "You don't strike me as someone who appreciates art."

A laugh loosened his icy demeanor, the sound like rolling thunder. "And what makes you say that?"

Marietta despised the King and what he stood for, yet she felt compelled to stare. With his skin pallor and black eyes and hair, he was drab; most would overlook the beauty in him. But Marietta saw how he contrasted with the world around him, like the way dark storm clouds could make a rainbow brighter. In all her travels, she had met no one quite like him.

Fascination and anger fought in her gut. Anger for what he represented, regardless if he did not hate pilinos himself, or for allegedly not slaughtering the people of Olkia, because his inaction was just as incriminating. Her fascination was the inability to grasp him as a person, as if he existed behind shifting smoke, letting brief glimpses show through. Curiosity drove her to keep looking for those glimpses.

"Art seems frivolous," she whispered, taking in his features. "And you don't strike me as a frivolous person, Your Grace."

"All beauty is frivolous. The world could be ugly, and yet all would function the same," he said, glancing at her. "No, I don't appreciate art, but I enjoy the secrets these statues hold."

Marietta tilted her head, her gaze finding the inky blackness of the King's eyes. "What secrets do they hold?"

He smiled—not smirked—but smiled, cracking the cold features with something warm, something personal. The sight made Marietta breathless. "No one knows who sculpted the statues. There's no record; no book holds the name. Yet throughout Syllogi, these statues are prevalent, exposed to the elements, yet remain unmarred. I can't help but think of who—or what—carved them."

Marietta studied the statues, lingering on the nearest satyr. The carved stone was flawless, every detail exact and realistic. Pure euphoria exuded from the smiling face, Marietta sensing it in her core. The female creature at the cave held menacing anger in her expression. The pure, undiluted rage cut deep within Marietta, much of what mirrored her own emotions. "These statues might hold secrets, but they hold something deeper."

"And what would that be?"

"Pure emotion, like crashing waves," she said, turning to him. "Just look at their faces, so expertly carved that I can't help but sense what they feel."

The King's eyes narrowed. "And what emotions do you feel? Are they all the same?"

"No. The satyrs are euphoric, carefree. The female creature in the cave holds rage so deep, so heavy, that I have nothing I can compare to it."

"A naiad."

Marietta smiled. "I remember my father sharing the stories of naiads. I always loved the one about Callithyia."

The King raised a brow at her. "That is a very uncommon feyrie tale to recall. What do you remember of it?"

"I'm surprised you even know of it." Marietta turned her attention to the fountain. "Callithyia was a naiad to a water fey of the elemental domain, ordered to protect one of the fey's rivers. The feyrie tale said she was beautiful enough to draw the attention of a powerful arch fey who stole her from her river. Callithyia tried to escape, but the arch fey caught her. As punishment, he transformed her into a white cow, thinking being a beast would dissuade her from ever leaving his side again. However, Callithyia was determined to be free of his control, be it as a naiad or as a beast. When she eventually escaped, the arch fey sent his minions after her, so she was destined to roam forever in order to remain free."

"It's a dour story to be a feyrie tale you love," noted King Wyltam.

"I'd argue that it's inspiring," Marietta said, glancing at the King. "That no matter what body you are in, your freedom is worth fighting for."

"Quite a parallel to you."

Marietta took a deep breath, the likeness not lost to her. For the King to point out the comparison sent chills down her spine. "They're just stories, anyway."

"Stories hold meaning. Just because they're imagined doesn't mean they don't hold significance." The King paused, stepping to Marietta's side. "Do you believe they ever truly existed?"

"The fey?" she asked, turning to him. "I'm not sure. My father always said it was possible that they had existed, even though no one alive had ever seen them. We have all these stories, all this knowledge about them. Do you know about the domains?"

A slight smile hinted at his lips. "I do. Elemental, beastial, botanical, and ethereal. Each of the domains responsible for their own ilk and creatures."

"Exactly. Sometimes their world seems too complex, too elaborate to be stories." Marietta said, turning to the satyr statue before them. "When I first saw the statues in the Central Garden, I couldn't help but be in awe. Their renditions were always how my father described such fey creatures. I wish I could meet the artist." Their skill was similar to that of Tilan's, to the detail woven into the nymph dagger that she loved.

The King's smile deepened as he inspected the nearest nymph. "They were indeed a master of their craft, and I'm glad they caught your eye. You and I are more alike than I thought."

"You've said that twice now," she said, raising a speculative brow. "You honor such a lowly half-elf as me by making such a comparison." She gave him a mock bow. She shouldn't be so carefree with the King, but what was the harm?

King Wyltam exhaled a slight laugh, looking in the opposite direction as if he wanted to hide it. To get a laugh from such an austere man delighted her. Perhaps he wasn't a storm cloud after all.

"Come," he said, holding out his arm, "walk with me."

The fabric of his black shirt was soft against her skin as Marietta took his arm. From the corner of his eye, he stared at Marietta with a light smile lining his lips. He flipped his head to fling his hair away from his face.

Marietta noted he had no entourage, no guards at his side. Wouldn't Keyain make sure soldiers protected the King? Yet King Wyltam was alone in the Glass Garden as he was in the Central Garden the week prior. Under her grasp was the King's hidden strength, leading her to wonder how capable he was of defending himself.

"I'm lucky I get your company once again after Keyain kept you hidden for a week." The King leaned in close to her head. "Seemed our plan worked a little too well."

"I think it worked perfectly," she said, shrugging. For a moment, she thought back to King Wyltam's gaze as he kissed her hand. Her next step hit the edge of the stone path, her ankle rolling as she gasped.

The King caught her, one arm tucked around her middle, before helping her stand. "Careful now," he murmured.

She tried to shrug it off with a stride, but the pain caused her to curse. "I can't put any gods damn weight on it."

"Such a filthy mouth for a lady."

Marietta cut him a glare.

Offering a small smile, the King said, "If you'd like, I can carry you."

She looked down at the dual slits of her skirt, knowing that if the King cradled her, the fabric would fall away to the top of her hips. "How about you help me walk to a bench?"

"Of course," he said, lifting his arm.

Marietta placed her weight on the King, wincing as she stepped. He eased her onto a stone bench beside a manicured row of boxwood. Bushes of purple-flowered thyme and basil grew in planters flanked on either side. King Wyltam sat beside her, his leg touching hers. She peered down at her throbbing ankle, hissing as she tried to move it.

"It's swollen already," the King noted, leaning down to inspect. "Here, rest it on the bench. Raising it should help with the swelling." He stood as she protested.

"I will not make you stand while my leg takes up the bench," she said, scoffing.

The King sat down once more. "Then put it on my lap." He looked down at her ankle, his dark eyes glancing back at her.

"I am most certainly not putting my leg on your lap." She leaned away from him with a scowl. "It'll be fine as is."

"It'll only get worse, so either I stand so you can place your leg across the bench, or I sit so you can place it across my lap."

"Is that a demand from the King?" she said, mockingly.

"Actually," he said with a tilt of his head, "it is. Now pick one, or I'll pick for you."

She sighed. "Fine, sit."

The King raised her leg, Marietta having to turn, so she stretched across the seat. She leaned back on her hands to support herself, careful of the skirt of her dress and where it fell open. Such proximity in the dress would have made her uncomfortable. However, if the King loved Keyain—found someone like Keyain attractive—then surely such a show of skin wasn't an issue for her.

"Under different circumstances, I would say this is inappropriate," she said.

"Curious, what circumstances?"

Marietta gestured at her leg. "At least you don't find me attractive."

The King glanced down, then back at her. "Please explain to me why I would not find you attractive?"

"Because you loved Keyain, and fortunately my body is completely different from his."

"Quite presumptuous of you. I find different aspects attractive depending on the gender. For example, I like women with curves." His gaze drifted to her thighs for a moment. "And prefer men or non-binary persons with brawn." A playful smile held his lips as he stared at Marietta. "That being said, I do, in fact, find you rather attractive."

"Then this is too inappropriate." She moved her leg, but the King's hand fell, stopping her.

"I'm only trying to help." The King frowned, removing his hand. "I can stand if you wish."

She sighed, clenching her eyes. "Fine—it's fine."

"You're quite flustered."

She opened her eyes, finding one side of the King's mouth lifted to a smile. "I'm fine."

"Fine enough to continue trading truth for truth? I do believe it's my turn."

"Ah, yes," Marietta said, her eyes narrowing. "Right after you admitted you loved Keyain."

"And you too loved him at one point," the King reminded her, causing Marietta to glower. "How did Keyain become your bodyguard?"

Marietta sighed, tilting her head back to watch the mist furl above them. "I traveled all over Enomenos and hiring a new guard every week grew tiresome; so, I searched for someone permanent. I was to meet with a Syllogi elf named Alyck, and he brought along Keyain. Let's just say Keyain and I hit it off, and he offered to take the job."

The King was silent for a moment. Marietta noted the slight pursing of his lips, the twitching of his brow.

"Do you not believe me?" she asked

Amusement flickered in his eyes. "I believe you, Marietta, but you wasted your next question."

She gave him a leveling stare. "That's not very honorable."

"Fine," he said, shrugging. "You're lucky I'm such a gracious and honorable king."

With a dramatic eye roll that earned a laugh from him, Marietta thought of her next question. "You said you did not slaughter the people of Olkia, so what happened during the attack?"

The King's gaze drifted out towards the fountain. "While the majority of the army stormed the western side of the city, the attack was just a distraction. We deployed discrete teams to capture the leaders of Olkia and the Exisotis. When the city guard realized what happened, we offered mercy if they set down their weapons. Very few fought back."

She searched his face, looking for dishonesty, for Queen Valeriya had said it was a slaughter. If that was truly what happened, did the Queen lie?

"Which city-state in Enomenos is your favorite?" King Wyltam asked, pulling Marietta from her thoughts.

She laughed, surprised at his question. "That's your next question?"

"Indulge my curiosity," he said, leaning in to her. At that distance, Marietta could see his eyes weren't solid black but flecked with chips of amber. "Perhaps the deal was also to know you better as well."

She forced her gaze onto her lap. "Well, Kentro is the heart of Enomenos and has the best nightlife. The best music troupes frequent their taverns. Avato to the north has the most curious people, mainly miners, who spend their days underground." With a coy glance, she turned to the King. "Remaining underground most days changes a person."

"I can imagine," he murmured, amusement lighting his eyes.

"Then Rotamu offers the best ale by far—my top suppliers came from the river city-state. But the beaches in Notos are to die for, right on the coast of Evgeni Sea. I was planning a trip to visit my parents there before…" Marietta hesitated, swallowing hard before continuing. "It still doesn't compare to the love I have for Olkia. For the array of shops and curious creators that make its vibrant markets."

"Like you with your bakery," he said, drawing her gaze. "Or Tilan with his smithy."

Marietta didn't dare breathe. "How do you know that?"

He chuckled, his hand falling on her leg. "Ah, you haven't answered my question. Which city is your favorite?"

Gods, Keyain said no one was aware of Tilan, of her bakery. "Olkia," she answered in a shaky voice. "It's my home, my community. And you attacked it. You hurt the people I care about."

"No wonder you hate Keyain," he said with a raised brow. "Though he swears he loves you, he still attacked your home city-state and killed your husband."

Her face blanched. "Keyain said you didn't know. How do you know about the bakery? About Tilan?"

"Keyain told me of Tilan, though through my sources, I learned you married the human willingly. Keyain made sure to leave that part out." He paused, glancing at her ankle. "He also hid that you left your traveling business to start a bakery."

The Queen knew that information. Was she playing Marietta a fool, feeding everything she said to the King?

The cold touch of his fingers fell on her ankle. "What are you doing?" she hissed.

"I'm only checking, I promise." He lifted her ankle, the fabric of her skirt falling to the sides.

He turned back to her, his brows furrowing. "Are you feeling alright? You're breathing quite heavy," he said. "And your eyes are dilated."

Marietta went to snap the fabric over herself, but the King caught her hand, leaning close to her. "Do I make you nervous, Marietta?" His deep voice and the closeness of his face made heat creep across her cheeks.

She hated it, hated that a smirk crept onto his lips.

"If not nerves, then what is it?" he asked.

"Perhaps I'm a bit flush," she answered, refusing to break eye contact as she swallowed hard. A full smile came to his lips. It was wonderful and frightening, and Marietta couldn't look away.

"You are very fun to tease," he murmured, his gaze dropping to her mouth.

Then she heard the approaching footsteps and the hushed voices that followed. Elyse came into view first, stopping at the sight of Marietta with her leg on the King's lap. Her face blanched as Keyain appeared next to her.

Marietta leaned away from the King, and he sat up straighter, pulling back from her face. For once, she was at a loss for words.

Keyain stood, mouth tightened to a line. He took in her dress, the slit that revealed her thighs. His nose flared when he saw her leg, the King's hand caressing her ankle. His features darkened as he glared at him, grinding out, "Hello, Wyltam. Marietta, my love."

She went to shift her leg from his lap, but the King's hand stayed true. "Keyain, Elyse, what a lovely surprise." His face settled back into its icy demeanor, its warmth and humor disappearing. "Care to join us?"

"Why?" Keyain said, his gaze locked onto the King's hand.

"Marietta injured her ankle. I was being a dutiful king and making sure it rested before she placed weight on it. Isn't that right, Marietta?"

With wide eyes focused on Keyain, she nodded her head, avoiding Elyse's uncomfortable expression.

"I'll take her if she's injured," Keyain said through the grind of his jaw.

"Nonsense. Either join us or continue your walk." He gestured to the path they walked on with his unoccupied hand.

Elyse was the first to answer. "As much as I would love to join you, my King, I have plans this afternoon. Keyain was just escorting me." She glanced at Keyain as he took a deep breath.

"A shame. Carry on then." He waved a dismissal.

Elyse started walking away, glancing back at Keyain, who remained rooted in place, glaring at the hand on Marietta's ankle. She cleared her throat. He tore his eyes away and stormed off.

"Perhaps that was too far," she said after a moment, unable to breathe.

"I disagree," he said, releasing her ankle. "Elevating it helped; the swelling has gone down. Though I didn't mean for it to appear so scandalous."

The ice in his expression melted into an amused smile. Marietta hated how easily he could shift into and out of his mask. She hated it even more that he removed it for her.

With a sigh, she shifted her leg, setting it down in front of her. She tested a bit of weight, and though it was uncomfortable, walking was an option. She stood, favoring her uninjured leg.

"I told you it would work," King Wyltam said.

Marietta shot him a glare as she hobbled away. "It'd be best if I go find Keyain."

"You can't chase after him every time he's angry."

She flipped her dark hair over her shoulder, looking back at him. "I'm not chasing after Keyain; I know him and his anger. He's going to take it out on Amryth, and I'd rather not have my friend receive the brunt of his rage, Your Grace."

"You have a kind heart." He paused, considering his words. "Keyain never deserved to hold such a heart."

His words froze her in place as regret settled into the pit of her stomach. "That's why I took it back." Her voice was only a whisper, unsure if the King could even hear her.

After a moment, he said, "You're dismissed, Lady Marietta."

It shook her from her thoughts. Though she already stood to leave, King Wyltam saw it fitting to dismiss her. Irritated, she sighed, earning a chuckle from him.

A storm cloud was a correct depiction of him—dark, beautiful, and unpredictable. The smiles that broke through were lightning in her chest, his laugh a rolling thunder that caused her heart to skip a beat.

As she left the King sitting on the bench, she cursed herself for being so foolish. He was the King. A murderer. He stood for everything she wanted to tear down. She should hate him—should despise his very being.

Yet, she didn't.

Chapter Fifty-Four
MARIETTA

Marietta returned to the hallway lined with statues, finding Keyain red-faced and pacing. She hobbled forward, her steps slow. He stopped when he noticed her.

"Where's Amryth?" she asked, taking another step towards him.

"Don't walk any farther." His lumbering form approached. "I dealt with Amryth." In a fell swoop, Keyain braced Marietta's back and scooped her up behind her knees.

As expected, the fabric slipped from her legs, their length exposed by the slits in the skirt. "Stop it—put me down," she snapped. "Amryth did nothing wrong. Let me guess. You took your anger out on her."

The muscle in Keyain's jaw flexed as he stared ahead, carrying Marietta down the hall. "She has a duty to protect you."

"Like she would tell the King to fuck off." Marietta shook her head, then struggled against Keyain's grip. "Let me down right now."

"You can't walk."

"I can walk just fine!"

"If you're injured enough that the King—" He snapped his mouth shut, taking a deep breath. Marietta marveled at how his teeth hadn't cracked.

He carried Marietta to an exit, stepping into the Central Garden. The afternoon's heat hit like a wall, jarring from the chilled interior of the palace; yet the temperature didn't slow Keyain's pace as he trekked onto the garden's paths.

"Keyain," she warned, wiggling her body.

He gripped tighter.

"I swear to gods if you don't let me down right this instant—"

Keyain paused on the path, the rapid rise and fall of his chest pressing into her side as he stared out into the garden, unwilling to make eye contact. "He went too far."

"For the love of all the deities, there was nothing malicious about King Wyltam's actions." She struggled once more but Keyain's grip held.

"Not once did he touch Elyse." He swallowed hard. And though he blinked them away, tears swelled in his eyes. "You are my wife but he touches you as if you weren't married." His gaze shifted to Marietta, the pain clear across his features. "And he has done it twice to you, knowing that I haven't had you in years. Knowing—"

His voice heightened as he stopped himself, swallowing back his emotion. "I lost you. You were the gaping wound in my chest, and he knows this. Now that you're here, he can't give us a moment of peace." A single tear slid down his cheek.

If the King knew that, then their deal was all the more cruel. Marietta brushed the tear away, her hand tentative. For a moment, a sliver of sympathy slithered out, watching the hardened man she knew beginning to break.

She had wanted this—wanted it to be so much worse—but to witness such raw emotion was more than she expected. Keyain was controlling, raging to a fault, but he cared for Marietta. He wanted to protect her and wholeheartedly believed that he was doing as such. Her hand cupped his cheek. "I know," she whispered, "but I'm here now, aren't I? I'm right here."

It happened in slow motion. Keyain turned his eyes to Marietta as she leaned into his face, her lips brushing gently on his. She held them there for only a breath, but it seemed like a lifetime. A kiss they hadn't shared in nearly a decade.

The tension in his face eased, his shoulders relaxing. Keyain stared at Marietta with parted lips and widened eyes. She knew that look. Hope. It was a damning feeling.

Keyain set Marietta on the ground. She turned to him, wrapping her arms around his middle as Keyain enclosed her with his arms. She dared to look up into Keyain's face, still slacked with awe.

"You kissed me," he said, blinking. "And not just on the cheek."

He leaned in, kissing her again, more desperately, as if the moment was fleeting. Marietta hadn't intended a second, but didn't dare pull away. The plan, she had to stick to the plan; yet, with Keyain's fingers lacing her hair, his tongue plunging into her mouth, a wave of nausea rolled through her. He killed Tilan. He attacked Olkia. Abducted her. Married her without her consent.

And now she was kissing him.

The plan—stick to the plan. Marietta couldn't pull away, not without further damaging Keyain, so instead, she imagined. They were in Kentro, about to head to an inn. The day was hot, but the promise of a cold drink was not far away, and she was kissing *that* version of Keyain. The one who guarded her but let her grow her business, let her be herself.

A pointed cough came from behind her. Keyain pulled away, wrapping Marietta tight to his body. "Lady Tryda, Minister Dyieter, apologies."

Marietta looked over her shoulder, glimpsing an older elven man with slicked-back white hair, and at his arm was Tryda.

"Will you stop that?" Tryda chided as they neared. "I've known you since you were a babe. No need to call us by our titles."

Keyain's grip loosened enough that she could turn and offer a proper greeting.

"Marietta, I'm thrilled to see you're feeling much better." She had a glint in her eye as if she expected such a display. Her stomach stirred at the thought. "If you ever need a thing," Tryda continued, "don't hesitate to ask. And you, Keyain, you best be treating her well." Tryda patted his shoulder as they passed.

"I wouldn't dream of treating her any less," he said while pulling Marietta in closer.

Marietta tilted her head, curious.

"Tryda and Dyieter were close friends of my parents," he murmured, looking over his shoulder towards the couple. "Dyieter is the King's Council with me as Minister of Law, while Tryda was the Lady-In-Waiting to late Queen Olytia."

"And not to Queen Valeriya?"

Keyain gave a dry laugh. "I guess she is the Lady-In-Waiting for Valeriya, too. Yet the new queen is more… aloof. No one here trusts her, and you shouldn't either, for that matter."

Marietta wished to defend her but thought better. "Queen Valeriya seems to love her schemes."

"You don't even know half of it." His grip around her loosened, and he offered his arm. "Are you sure you're okay to walk?"

"Yes," she said, exasperated. "We'll just take our time. That is, if you can take your time. Shouldn't you be in meetings?"

He shook his head. "I sent a message along to cancel them for the day." He bit down his anger and set a slow walking pace.

The corner of Marietta's lip tugged upward, batting at his chest. "You took a break from work for me."

"I know I'm not a good husband or a good partner," he said, taking a deep sigh, "but I'm trying to be better. Even if I'm a slow learner."

"Slow learner is one way to put it." She smiled at Keyain's eye roll. "Always a pain in my ass."

A smile crept to his lips, causing him to glance down, then back at her. "You haven't said that to me in a long time."

Gods, she hadn't meant to, the loving phrase being her favorite to toss at him back when they traveled. "Some things never change, I guess."

Though it took longer, Keyain helped Marietta to the Noble's Section; he even let her walk up the stairs herself. More than likely, Keyain wanted to carry her, but he restrained himself. That was new.

Before, Keyain's rage and stubbornness always triggered their fights, and the longer they were together, the more protective he became of her. The last time Keyain returned to Satiros before she ended their relationship, he wanted to have a friend be her shadow. Go to her meetings, sleep in her room—always within arm's length. Of course, he had lost that fight.

Marietta nearly broke it off right then. Now that same man was learning that he was wrong. What would have become of them if he had learned that sooner?

Back in the suite, Keyain insisted Marietta lay in bed with her leg propped up to rest. Before their dinner, a nurse stopped by to check her ankle, claiming that raising it right away saved Marietta some healing time. The comment made Keyain clench his jaw, but he said nothing. When Marietta had asked the nurse about healing magic, she explained that only the temple of Therypon could heal instantaneously, but they could speed up the process with medicine. The liquid Marietta took from her tasted awful, but edged away her pain.

After dinner, he made her get into bed but had a surprise for her. At some point in the afternoon, he had a servant stop at the library to select a handful of books. When she read the titles, she could only laugh. "*Heart of Thirst? A Rose by Any Other Name*? Keyain, did you have them pick out smut books for me?" She tossed her head back with a laugh, falling into the pillows stacked behind her.

"I gave them the book you read last week and asked for them to grab some based on it." His smile split his face, eyes shining as he leaned against the post of the bed. "I didn't expect they'd only bring bodice rippers. You just read the last one so quickly after complaining about my books."

"There's a reason for that," she said, raising a brow with a smirk as she read the other titles. "*Rough and Ready*? This one has to be a joke."

"If there's nothing you like, I can send for more."

"No," she said, looking up with a smile. "These will do. I'll start with *Honorable Intentions*. It reminds me of you." She held up the book so he could see the cover.

Keyain tilted his head down as if to hide his bashful smile, and his eyes glanced at her. "And do you want to think of me while reading smut?"

It was an honest enough question, but her cheeks warmed and her center heated at the thought, both of which surprised her. "I mean," she said, shrugging, "we do have that history."

"We have a lot of history in that regard." His gaze darkened as he took in the nightgown she had changed into, the low cut of silk and lace. He swallowed hard and turned away.

Could she go down that path? After everything, could she be intimate with Keyain? It would further their plans, their goals. If it built Keyain up higher, it meant he had farther to fall. With a steadying breath, she set the books to the side, looking at Keyain. "I heard history repeats itself."

"It does." He turned back to her, but he didn't seem to breathe.

He was waiting for her to invite, for her to initiate. "Then maybe let's repeat it."

"Are you sure?" he asked, approaching the edge of the bed.

"Who is this Keyain who asks when I'm sure after inviting you into bed?" she said, smirking. "Yes, I'm sure." But truly, she wasn't.

Keyain pulled his shirt off over his head, ignoring the buttons that strained over his shoulders. If anything, at least she found him *physically* attractive. It made the whole ordeal easier.

Careful of her ankle, Keyain got onto the bed, muscular arms flanking her as he lowered himself with a kiss. He grabbed the hem of her nightgown and tossed it to the floor. To feel him so close, a familiar stranger, made her stomach churn. And when his fingers rose up the inside of her thighs, she forced herself to still, to not pull away.

At least they were gentle, soft. Like the King's hands on her ankle. Marietta jerked away from Keyain with that thought—at the heat that flared in her. Gods, why did she think of the King?

"Did I hurt you?" Keyain looked down at her with furrowed brows.

"No," she said, pulling him back to her face. "Just tickled, that's all."

She brought his mouth to hers before he could answer. Keyain's hands crept higher, brushing against the outside of her center. His mouth traveled from her lips to her neck. When he ventured lower, his teeth biting her breast, she moaned with an arch of her back.

Keyain moaned into her skin. "Can I go further?"

"Yes," she said, breathless, as she shifted her hips with the movement of his hand. And when he entered her, she moaned again.

His mouth moved to her other breast, and he laughed while filling his mouth. He bit again and Marietta arched into him.

"Fuck," she cried out, wanting more.

"Such a filthy mouth."

Marietta paused, taken back at the exact words the King told her just earlier that day.

"Perhaps I should make my mouth just as dirty." His kisses trailed down her stomach.

Deities damn her. Why did King Wyltam keep coming to mind? Sure, he had a handsome face and a wonderfully deep voice, but he was the enemy, wasn't he?

Gods, so was Keyain.

"Mar," he said, lifting his face from her and drawing her attention. "We can stop if you changed your mind."

Perhaps she should. It was one thing to fuck Keyain, something she's done numerous of times. It was another to think of a different person while with him. But she could block it out; she could go through with this. "Don't stop," she said, pushing his head lower.

His smile was sinister as he buried his face between her legs, his lips kissing against her with such fervor that she nearly melted then. With a flick of his teasing tongue, he put his whole mouth against her most sensitive spot, sucking.

Marietta's thighs squeezed against his head as he continued, his fingers plunging in and out of her. After all that time, he remembered exactly how she liked it. Keyain withdrew his fingers, both hands pinning her legs to the bed. Gods, he remembered everything, even as his grip tightened on her thighs, as his mouth explored, his tongue teasing against her. She cried out, savoring the touch, so familiar to the last time they were intimate that it wasn't hard to imagine it was the old Keyain, especially as she kept her eyes clenched shut.

His grip slipped from her thighs to her hips, pulling her closer to his face as her breaths quickened, her core tightening with the nearing release. Keyain must have sensed it as well, for his fingers found their way back inside her. The movement of his fingers and the stroke of his tongue built her tension, snapping it as Marietta crested. Her center pooled from Keyain as she melted into his tongue, her limbs numbing with waves of pleasure.

"Fuck, Marietta," he groaned, his fingers teasing against her.

"Now." A simple demand from her. It was all she had to say for Keyain to reach for his pants, hastily undoing them and tossing them over the edge. Careful of her ankle, he bent her legs, pushing them farther apart. He rubbed the length of himself against her, his gaze locked on to between her legs with furrowed brows and parted lips.

Without warning, he plunged into Marietta. She moaned from the pain—from the pleasure—mixed into one where she couldn't tell where one started and the other ended. Keyain's hand landed on her center, rubbing as he thrust. Her core tightened again, feeling the tension rise within her with each thrust, with each swirl of his finger.

He murmured to Marietta, his voice deep and breathless, but the words were lost to her. No, she wasn't thinking about Keyain with her eyes closed. As much as she resisted, she only heard King Wyltam's deep voice. *You are very fun to tease.*

It was the King she imagined on top of her, pleasuring her. The King was the one moaning her name. And when she crested again, the tension ripping through her with such intensity that her vision went white behind her lids, she clamped her lips together so she wouldn't call out King Wyltam's name.

Keyain lowered himself to be flush with her, his hips not missing a beat. He moaned in her ear, calling out her name. Marietta's nails dug into his back as he finished, thrusting deep inside.

Still slick with sweat, Keyain rolled over, laying on his back next to Marietta as he panted. Marietta lay next to him with her stare fixed on the canopy of the bed, still shocked at what had happened.

Gods, why did she think of the King? What in all the hells was wrong with her? Stupid, he was no better than Keyain. No—he was worse. King Wyltam had the power to create change and enabled Keyain's actions.

"Are you alright?" Keyain's hand found hers, pulling it to him for a kiss.

She shook her thoughts, rolling onto her side to face him. Gods, don't say the King—anything but that. Think of the plan. "I wish you spent more time with me." The lie came smoothly and through Keyain's post-sex haze, he didn't seem to notice.

"I wish for that, too."

"Can you promise then?" She rubbed her thumb against his hand. "Promise you'll spend more time with me?" More time to win him over, to distract him.

"I would do anything for you, Mar." The sincerity in his gaze with his words made guilt sit in her stomach like a rock.

After readying for bed, Keyain wrapped his arms around Marietta, sleep finding him quickly. She didn't have such luck. Instead, her mind sifted through her troubling thoughts, of the King who had no business being stuck in her head. Why did she think of King Wyltam? Was it that she thought him more attractive? Was it because he was kind to her?

And then she realized, for all that she despised the King for his action and inaction in Satiros, Marietta still didn't hate him as much as she hated Keyain.

Chapter Fifty-Five

VALERIYA

Valeriya sat at a small desk in her room, lost in writing. A cool breeze blew through the open balcony doors, white gauzy curtains twirling. To ease her anxious thoughts, she wrote them down in a journal. In Satiros, she had no one to confide in; everyone was an enemy in her game. Only her written words relieved her of her thoughts. Sometimes she wondered what her life would have been if she was the eldest, if she were born the Queen of Reyila. As a princess, Valeriya had ample opportunities and was better off than almost anyone, but there was one thing she always wanted—her name immortalized through history.

Growing up, scholars taught her and her sister of the late Queens and Kings of Reyila, spanning thousands of years. The idea of not being forgotten by future generations was intoxicating, and Valeriya knew she had to do something to gain it. Her sister was handed such an opportunity; Valeriya made sacrifices for hers. Becoming Wyltam's Queen Consort had been and continued to be difficult. Since the first day, he drew the line of how Valeriya would rule, which was to say not at all.

She left behind everything and everyone she knew to get what she wanted. Valeriya had thought that would be enough of a sacrifice. No Katya, no training as a mage, no sister. Valeriya was alone, but she wouldn't be long. After waiting for years for Wyltam to change, she eventually yielded to her sister's plan and together they would change Satiros.

Valeriya looked out the window, the sun dipping below the horizon. She should get ready, needing to drop the financial documents off still. Beside her bed was a loose brick in the wall, which she removed to reveal a

small hollowed place for her to store items. She pulled out the documents and tucked them deep into her pockets.

As she went to exit the suite, Wyltam entered. Of course, he only ever showed up when it was inconvenient. "Wyltam," she said with a dip of her head, hoping to dismiss him and be on her way.

"Valeriya," he answered, pausing as he shut the door behind him. "Going for a walk?"

"What else would I be doing?" she asked, bristling. There was nothing else for her to do in that cursed palace.

"You shouldn't walk by yourself at night."

"I'm perfectly fine," she said, reaching for the handle. "Unless you think Keyain has done a poor job securing the palace."

Wyltam eyed her with an icy expression. "It's unusual for a queen to walk unattended. Even my mother—"

"I'm not your mother." Her words came out sharp, her irritation growing.

He stared at her with an arched brow, the only hint of emotion. "Obviously. I offered to assign you a Queen's Guard."

Valeriya laughed as she perched her hands on her hips. "Oh, yes, there is nothing I'd love more than to have Keyain's guards trail me day and night."

"As I said, you could pick them out yourself."

"If you are so accommodating, then why couldn't I keep my guards from Reyila?" Bitterness laced her voice with more emotion than she had intended. They had been her one hope at having familiar faces in Satiros, but Wyltam killed that small joy.

"I have my reasons."

"Do you now?" Valeriya took a step towards her husband, not hiding her scowl. "What reasons would those be, because that would be the first I've heard of them."

A ripple of irritation swept through his expression, the brief furrowing of his brows and lips tugging downward. Looks like her husband was capable of showing emotion. "Go on your walk then." With that, he turned from her and took off down the hall.

That's what she thought—there was not a real reason. Always a pleasure and a delight to talk to her husband. The door slammed harder than she intended as she stepped into the hall. How dare he act like she was the unreasonable one? What did he forfeit in this marriage? What life did he have to leave behind? He lost nothing and only had an alliance to gain. How unfortunate for him that Valeriya and Nystanya were working against that boon.

The night air remained warm, though darkness shrouded the Central Garden. She nodded her head at a group of courtiers enjoying the evening, offering a small smile. Vile, most of them. Clawing their way to the top of their menial hierarchy. Perhaps that was why she had a soft spot for Elyse. Though skittish, the girl never showed interest in gaining Valeriya's favor for a higher standing. If the situation between her and Az resolved, then she would be a wonderful asset to her future court.

At the center of the garden, Valeriya checked for persons nearby, satisfied when she saw none. She stepped off the path and into the shroud of trees that blocked her from sight.

Closing her eyes, she pulled at the aithyr around her as she cleared her mind of all thoughts and emotions. A twig snapped, causing her eyes to pop open. For a moment, as she stared at the direction the sound originated and saw the face of an unfamiliar male with dark skin and black hair pulled back into a tail. The next moment, he was gone. She knew that blip, what it meant. Shit. A mage was trailing her.

Chills raced up Valeriya's spine as her heart thundered in her chest. Keeping her eyes on the spot where the male had been, she focused enough of her attention on the aithyr around her to send a message to her contact. *No drop tonight. I'm being followed.*

Chapter Fifty-Six

MARIETTA

Marietta woke the following morning, still naked and curled up on Keyain's chest as golden morning light filtered into the room. She brushed her fingers over his muscles. She shouldn't have thought of King Wyltam; she should've stopped when he wouldn't leave her mind. The game she played with the King was already dangerous. To then think of the King when he wasn't present—when another man was inside her—was troubling. More than troubling.

"Good morning, my love," Keyain said, his voice gravelly with sleep. She pushed herself up onto him, sitting on his stomach. "Didn't get enough last night?" Keyain smirked as his hands reached up and held her hips.

"I will never get enough of what happened last night," she said, technically not lying.

Keyain lifted his hips against her, his eyes sleepy but ready for more.

"Don't you have to leave?" she asked. "You're usually long gone by now."

Keyain jerked up, his arms wrapping around her to keep her from falling. He swore, realizing the time. "I need to go."

He left the bed and walked to the bathroom. Running water filling the tub sounded from the room, followed by a loud thud and Keyain's swearing.

"Anything I can help you with?"

"No, I just have a meeting I need to get to," he said impatiently.

A few minutes later, he left the bathroom and dressed. Keyain was still pulling on his shirt as he walked into the dining room. Marietta

threw on a gauzy robe from her closet and followed him.

In his office, Keyain unlocked a drawer and dug through its contents, pulling out a stack of files. "You'll need to wear something else, so you don't tempt me to skip this meeting and spend the day with you," he said with a smirk, glancing up at her.

"Perhaps that's what I'm hoping for," she teased, leaning against the doorframe. It wasn't, but the comment deepened Keyain's smile.

When he finished, Keyain closed the desk drawer and strode over with a kiss. "When this war is over, I promise to give you every second of my time."

"And until then? You'll be better about not leaving me alone all day, every day?" Marietta smoothed the fabric on his chest.

"I promised you last night, didn't I?" Keyain kissed her again and then walked past her back into the dining room.

"Will you take me into the city?" she asked, following.

"Into the city? Why?"

"I'd like to go to a play or dinner," she said, twirling the end of her hair. "We could have Elyse and Brynden join us."

Keyain set his papers down on the dining table, looking towards Marietta. "That's a very random request. I don't see the point since they're no longer to be married."

"Doesn't mean Elyse wouldn't like to see him again. It would make her happy, would it not?" Marietta needed to play into Keyain's soft spot for her. "And you'll be there to supervise. What's the worst that can happen?"

"Plenty," he said, turning around and walking into the bedroom. "But I'll see what I can do. Elyse always enjoyed getting out of the palace."

Marietta rolled her eyes—of course she enjoyed getting out of the palace. Who in the hells would want to be trapped here all the time?

As she leaned against the table, Keyain's files pulled her attention. Intrigued, she peeked into the other room to check that Keyain remained distracted before lifting the top folder. An alphanumeric name titled the page, and the document listed dates from a few weeks prior. The name Olkia stood out to her but Keyain's heavy footfalls approached. She let the folder fall back into place, noting he didn't lock the drawer of his desk.

Keyain walked back in, pulling on a pine-colored jacket over a white button-up shirt. "I'll be back by dinner tonight." He picked up the files and kissed Marietta. With his empty hand, he cupped her face. "You are mine. I love you, Mar. Please, stay out of trouble today." With one last kiss, he left the suite.

Anticipation thundered in her chest as she darted back to Keyain's office, seating herself in his chair. The wooden desk had drawers to either side, with a series of smaller drawers along the top. She tried the center most top one first, sliding it out. What she found made her heart stop. Half hidden among the charcoal and extra sheets of paper sat the nymph dagger—the one Tilan made her.

With shaky hands, she pulled it out and turned the blade over in her hands. Though it had been cleaned, dried blood caked some of the details of the hilt. Her stomach churned, remembering the blood that coated her hands. Marietta shut her eyes, taking a deep breath as she cradled the dagger. So many memories were tied to it; only the last had been traumatic. To leave it in Keyain's possession felt wrong, an insult to Tilan's memory. She placed the blade on the desktop, deciding she would keep it if not for herself, then for Tilan.

Marietta took a breath and focused back on her original goal. She opened the drawer to the left first, finding rows of files. The first folder she checked had rows of equipment, weapons, and other miscellaneous inventory for the army. The date listed at the top was from a few months ago. She pulled another one out at random, finding more of the same. Though inventory might be nice to know, it was not the type of information Valeriya needed. If Marietta had exclusive access to Keyain's information, then there had to be more than just equipment lists.

Cursing, she switched to the other drawer, also finding it unlocked. Foolish of Keyain, already letting down his guard. She pulled out a file from the middle. The page had a series of notes referring to something as *the creator*. Curious, she quickly read through the files. Most of it was nonsense, just gibberish mentioning the creator and its progeny. It almost read like an interview, but she couldn't find meaning in the words. It had to be some sort of code, some sort of hidden meaning beneath the wording. She set the document off to the side.

Digging deeper into the drawer, she removed a file from a different section. The document inside was labeled "TR-1128." Marietta opened it, looking over a series of reports, all dated eight years ago. The location was listed as Olkia, that it was some meeting. There was dialog from... no. Her heart skipped a beat in her chest, her breath pausing. Tilan. Direct quotes from Tilan from a meeting. If Keyain had notes from an Exisotis meeting, then that meant Satiros had a spy in the Exisotis.

Marietta dug for a file with a similar name, finding one dated a few months ago. She flipped it open on the desk to find detailed notes of Tilan's movements, including when he headed home, the time of day, when he saw Marietta, and when he was at Exisotis meetings. Like the other file, this one had quotes from the meetings they held.

Keyain had an informant tracking Tilan. Marietta searched the drawer again, finding a file labeled the month he took her from Olkia. The document shook in her hands as she opened it, knowing it was Tilan's last moments before Keyain murdered him. As she read, she remembered his long nights in the smithy, clearly marked as Exisotis meetings. According to the papers, they were planning an attack on Satiros. It was clear from the notes that Tilan played a crucial role, but it didn't say how.

How would Tilan have had a vital part in their plan? In all the years they had been together, she had never seen him fight. Maybe it was his weapons? If Tilan took part in planning an attack on Satiros, then he was no better than Keyain.

Marietta scrubbed her face, unsure what to make of the information. Valeriya would want to know about this, as well as the coded document. Why would they hide insignificant information in code?

A thought hit her. If the Exisotis had a spy and the Queen of Satiros claimed to be working with the organization, could she be the one handing information to Keyain? Marietta rubbed her temples. The court games and schemes were dizzying. No, Valeriya wasn't a spy—she would never side with Keyain or Wyltam. Let alone how would she listen in on their meetings when she was in Satiros?

A quick knock rapped on the front door, followed by Amryth announcing herself. Marietta slammed the drawer shut and grabbed the papers and dagger, hurrying to the living room. She managed to shove the items under the cushions of the couch when Amryth came into view.

"Underdressed today, are we?" she said with a raised brow. Marietta forgot she had only thrown on a gauzy robe.

"Oh, I didn't have time to change after Keyain left. You just missed him." Marietta crossed her arms, trying to give herself some more coverage as she passed Amryth to the bathroom and started the bath.

"You wore that in front of Keyain, the same male that stole you from your home? The one that secretly married you, legally claiming you in Satiros because of some backward law against pilinos? The same Keyain who almost attacked Therypon's paladin because you were getting help?" She stood in the doorway, her back to Marietta as she got into the bath.

Gods, how did she not expect Amryth to find out? Marietta could trust her with most things, but treason would be too much, too big of a risk.

"The same Keyain I used to love and found attractive? Yes. It's... complicated." Marietta said as she lowered herself into the bath, cursing herself. From Amryth's point of view, Marietta looked like a fool.

Amryth gave an unimpressed look. "Right. Complicated."

"He's problematic—and I'm not proud of it—but that history is still there."

"Sure," Amryth said skeptically. "And what was the fallout from the incident with the King yesterday?"

"That was the fallout," she murmured while trying to wash quickly.

Amryth sighed. "Don't trust him, Mar. Promise me you aren't trying to have kids. Are you taking anything?"

Marietta paused, not having thought of that. Swearing, she earned an exasperated sigh from Amryth.

"The guards get their drugs in the garrison infirmary, so I'll be back." Amryth pushed off the doorframe, her face half turning toward Marietta. "Try to be dressed when I return. I'm going to the temple, and I'm following up on a promise to bring you with me."

After sending Keyain a note that she wished to visit the temple, a handful of guards escorted Marietta and Amryth to a carriage. Though she preferred to walk, despite the scorching heat of the day, she didn't wish to fight with Keyain so soon. Otherwise, she would have undermined her own efforts.

The city blurred by in shades of white and green as their carriage wove through the streets. When they neared the temples, their pace came to a crawl along the crowded lane as people walking outside the carriage passed them.

At first, Marietta wished to throw open the doors and walk the rest of the way; yet, the slowdown meant she could inspect each place of worship as they passed. To one side sat a temple made of pale-yellow stone. Golden yellow banners stamped with a chimera hung between ornate columns. Like the other temples, this one had an extensive set of steps leading to the top, adorned with shrubbery and statues decorating the path.

The statue out front brought uneasiness to Marietta's chest, the figure's features obscured with what was carved to be a veil. She marveled at the sculptor's ability to chisel fabric from stone, to look as if a body peeked through the veil—neither man nor woman. It was ominous, almost shifting.

"Oramytiz," Amryth said. "Deity of reality and deception."

"The statue is stunning." Marietta placed her hand upon the glass, wishing to be closer.

"You should see the other side."

Marietta turned her gaze to the temple across the way. Taupe-colored stone, much to the same style as the others, with light gray banners divided by a lightning bolt, rose before her. The statue was of a woman with curled hair twirling over her head as if a gust twisted it up. At her feet was a false cliff face, the stone carved to look as if stones crumbled away from the base. A stirring woke in her chest, ever so slightly, like the goddess' twisting hair.

"Seidytar, goddess of chaos and order." Amryth leaned forward, looking to the following building. "And that," she said, pointing, "is Kystrorgiste, god of creation and destruction."

The vibrant red stone was shocking next to the gray, with the familiar flame inside a water droplet on crimson banners. Before them rose the statue of a long-haired god, one arm raised with water expelling from the hand, and the other curled below with flames. "I know this one." A smile pulled at her lips, the memory returning a crackling, heated sensation to her heart. "I had a handful of friends sworn to this deity."

Amryth snorted a laugh. "You had friends who were attendants, yet you never asked about their god or temple?"

Marietta shrugged. "I was never one for religion."

As they neared the last temple before Therypon's, Marietta marveled at the black stone temple, ominous against the bright blue sky. Statues of people in pain, of the elderly, of those collapsing into the arms of another, lined the steps. "Those are ghastly."

"That they are. Zontykroi, god of life and death."

A black crescent below a thin circle outline marked bright white banners that flapped in the breeze, contrasting with the temple's dark facade. The darkness reminded her of the King's eyes, yet they were missing the amber flecks. Marietta shook the thought from her head, startled it even came up. Thinking of the King when he wasn't present was a habit Marietta didn't want to make.

The statue before the building was plain. A man with short-cropped hair and made of white stone was stark against the dark stone structure. His face was handsome, austere yet solemn. A heaviness filled her, like a weight on her chest. From that distance, it was hard to see, yet Marietta knew she wasn't mistaken. "They didn't carve ears."

"None of the deities' statues have ears," Amryth noted, "to show that the gods belong to no race. Plus, no one knows what they would be in a mortal form."

"Do they have a mortal form?" Marietta squinted as they passed, her eyes scanning the temple.

"Some scriptures say they do but no one has ever seen them." She shrugged. "Lastly, of course, there's Therypon, goddess of healing and pain." A smile lined her lips as she stood.

"Now that we brought up the ears, I can't remember if Therypon had them during my prayer. I remember her dark skin and hair, but not her ears." She wracked her brain, trying to remember.

Amryth's grip stilled on the handle. She turned slowly, brows furrowed. "You saw the goddess?"

"Yes, last time when—"

Amryth silenced her with a hand, peeking out from the carriage. "Say nothing about this until we're inside the temple."

Curious, Marietta bit her tongue. Wishing to ask Amryth why, Marietta refrained as they left the carriage, and the guards closed in. Unlike last time, they escorted Marietta up the steps, only stepping away when she entered the antechamber.

The temple was peaceful, the chapel quiet, with pious folk sitting in prayer to the goddess. Instead of sitting at the benches, Amryth led her off to the side of a hallway. After a few turns, she stopped at the door, knocking.

"Come in!" called a familiar chipper voice. Inside, Deania sat behind a desk, her long, dark hair loose and cascading over her cerulean blue tunic. She bit at her nails, reading a paper before she finally looked up. "Oh! What a surprise," she said, jumping to her feet. She skipped from around her desk, embracing Amryth on her tiptoes to make up for her lack of height.

The cleric turned her bright eyes to Marietta, arms opened. "It is wonderful to see you!" She wrapped Marietta in a hug before she responded. All she could do was laugh and embrace her back.

"Deania, will you knock that off!" chided a voice behind her. Coryn stepped into the room with a half-hearted scowl on his face. "You'll scare off another one."

She released Marietta, spinning on the spot. "For the last time, I did not scare him off!"

Coryn gave a face that said otherwise.

"Trust me—she isn't going anywhere." Amryth flagged them in, her smile faltering, giving way to tight lips.

The office was roomy and bright, with white walls, a small window, and blue tapestries. Next to Deania's dark wood desk sat a couch and few chairs, of which Amryth took a seat.

Coryn closed the door behind him as he ushered Marietta into the room. As before, he wore his blue tunic beneath his armor. "Saw you two walking up the steps but I was surprised when you weren't in the chapel."

Amryth pursed her lips, waiting as Marietta took her seat. "Mar, can you tell them what you told me in the carriage?"

"That I can't remember if Therypon had ears?" Marietta narrowed her eyes, confused on why she'd have to repeat it. "Why'd you tell me to stop talking in the carriage?"

"The other part." She crossed her arms, leaning into the couch.

"That I saw her when I prayed?"

Deania and Coryn exchanged surprised glances. "You saw Therypon during your prayer?" Deania said, scooting to the edge of her chair. "You're sure about this?"

"Well, yeah, she looked identical to the statue. And when she spoke—"

"She spoke?" Coryn interrupted. "As in, she told you something?"

"She told me a few things," Marietta said, turning to him. "We had an entire conversation, but it was in my mother's herb garden." Marietta turned back to Amryth, who looked as if she'd be sick. "Is that not normal?"

"No," Deania answered, her grin growing. "Marietta, only those who are Iros receive visions like that."

"And even then," Coryn said, leaning forward with his arms resting on his knees, "not every Iros converses with the goddess, let alone does it on their second time praying."

"I don't know what Iros means." Marietta's heart skipped a beat at their range of emotions.

"Iros are paladins of the gods, chosen to be their elite warriors for unique causes." He rubbed the scruff on his chin as his gaze was lost in thought. "Usually only those who are an attendant to a god or goddess are claimed as an Iros. It's a rare honor and holds the highest respect in the temples."

Coryn shifted to the end of his seat and reached for the hem of his shirt, pulling it up to expose his torso. Gods, he was muscled. It took her a moment to notice that inked onto his dark skin were two intertwined snakes through a lattice of X's. The tattoo extended from below his hip up to his neck, ending in twin snake heads. "Those of us who are Therypon's Iros share the goddess's mark inked into our flesh. The sign of the Iros is this, the goddess's serpents." He let his shirt drop and leaned forward on his knees once more. "Once that ceremony is complete," he said, holding out his hand before him, "we gain control over both of Therypon's domains—healing and pain." White light emanated from his fingertips, then gave way to black crackling energy.

"That's a lot to hear," Marietta said, blinking at the magic. Her friends in Enomenos had never shown her that. "But I'm not an Iros. I'm not an attendant." She craned her head to Amryth. "I'm not any of that."

Amryth shook her head with a shrug. "You're a lot of things, Marietta, but I can honestly say I know no one else who's had a vision that early."

"She should pray in the hand!" Deania said, jumping out of her seat. "Right now, actually." She pulled Marietta up from her seat.

"In the hand?" Marietta asked.

"Yeah, in the goddess' giving hand within the chapel! It's normally what attendants do when they're seeking a more meaningful prayer with the goddess." She led Marietta to the door, Coryn and Amryth in pursuit. "All Iros are claimed in her hand."

Returning to the silent chapel, fewer devotees occupied the benches. At the front, the statue of Therypon loomed over Marietta as she approached.

"All you do is kneel in her hand," Deania said, guiding her over. "Then you pray as you did on the bench. Got it?"

"Not really." Gods, what did they think would come of this? Perhaps

Therypon knew Marietta needed help, so she had manifested. Marietta wasn't an Iros, couldn't be. The idea was ridiculous.

Stone bit into Marietta's bone as she knelt, the pain not unbearable, but she was unsure if she'd be able to clear her mind enough to speak to the goddess. She tilted her head back, facing the statue. With her mind focused on ignoring her uncomfortable seated position, she let her conscious fade, reaching for the Therypon's warmth. The pain in her legs subsided, and her vision went white.

First came the eucalyptus and peppermint scent, then the white faded and she stood in the center of her bakery's kitchen in Olkia with Therypon standing across from her. A choking sob built in her throat at the sight of her home, at the place she felt most herself. A knowing smile came to the goddess' face, her onyx skin glowing and her long black waves blowing though there wasn't any wind.

"Welcome, Marietta." Her tone was still affectionate and earthy, comforting and familiar.

"My goddess," she said with a bow of her head. "Thank you for giving me a direction." She looked up, glancing around the kitchen, her hand falling onto the wooden countertop. "For giving me one last time to see my home."

"Who said it would be the last time you saw it? Things, as they are now, won't be as they are in the future—nothing is set in stone."

Marietta's heart skipped a beat. "You said you know my future. Will I return to Olkia? Will I be free of Satiros?" At her anxiety, the goddess glowed with golden light. A comforting warmth settled deep into Marietta's chest, and she held onto it, savoring it.

"That will always be a possibility, but only if you seek the truth. You came to me today, not for your goal, but answers. What do you seek?"

She reflected on the conversation she just shared with Deania and Coryn. "They say I might be an Iros because you speak to me. Is that true?"

"You are, and have always been, one of my Iros, my chosen."

"But why?" Marietta asked, her heart stricken. She had never been religious; she never paid the gods much attention. "Why do I deserve to be your Iros?"

"It is less what you deserve and more what you will do—what you are and who you become."

"What do you mean?"

"Your future decides the fate of many, your lifeline entangled with those you do not know."

Marietta tried to bite back her surprise. "My future? How will that decide anything?"

"It is your choice of future that shall decide. Death will be a known friend to you."

Well, that was ominous. Marietta's chest tightened, but the warmth of the goddess soothed her uneasiness. "Can I prevent the deaths? Are those the decisions I'll need to make?"

"Death will follow any decision you make. Some choices will bring more and others will lead to less."

"But what will I do? What is my goal that makes me a chosen one?"

"Seek the truth. Answers follow. You have already learned this."

Exasperated, Marietta asked, "Is that my only goal?"

A smile tugged at the goddess' lips from Marietta's impatience, as if her emotions were amusing. *"Stay true to who you are. Forgetting yourself will affect the choices you make."*

"What will happen now that I'm one of your chosen?"

"You've always been my chosen one. The only change is that you're now aware."

"But what will change? What do you expect of me?"

"Train and learn. Follow the other Iros, the one named Coryn. Devote yourself to me, and you will earn the strength to deflect your enemies."

The warmth faded from her body. "What of the King? My husband? What will happen if either of them knows I'm an Iros?"

"They will kill you." The voice was a whisper in the back of Marietta's head. Her entire body shivered, twitching.

Marietta's eyes opened, facing up at the statue of Therypon.

Chapter Fifty-Seven
MARIETTA

The goddess' warning echoed in her head as the temple came into
view around the statue. Being in Keyain and Wyltam's grasp
already put her in danger. Now the goddess shared that her being
an Iros, which was completely ridiculous, put her in peril. Gods, Keyain
hated the temples, calling the attendants cultists. What would he do if he
knew her status? That she was now a deity's paladin?

Perhaps Therypon made a mistake. Perhaps Marietta was
hallucinating. What if she never woke up from the drugs that Keyain put
her under? The sudden thought sent chills across her body. With a hard
pinch, she determined that no, this was real. She had conversed with a
damned goddess who claimed her as her paladin.

Marietta turned towards her friends, who stood off to the side. Deania
silently cheered for Marietta while Coryn smiled and beckoned her to
follow them. Amryth stood between them, mouth agape.

"You should've seen you!" Deania whispered in the hallway. "You
were glowing with the goddess's light with your hair floating around you
like you were underwater! Oh, Marietta, this is so exciting!"

"Deania, hush. Wait until we're somewhere private," Coryn chided,
though a smile still lined his face.

After a silent trek back to Deania's office, Coryn shut the door, turning
to Marietta. "So we were correct; you are an Iros." Coryn clapped her
shoulder as he walked past, propping himself up on the edge of Deania's
desk. "Congratulations, Marietta."

"This was all meant to be! Coryn, you get to tell her about the Iros!"

Deania bounced on her toes, unable to contain her excitement.

At a loss for words, Marietta turned to Amryth, who stood with a bewildered expression. "Mar, this is not good. I mean, it's incredible, but still not good." Amryth shook her head and sat on the couch, her gaze feverishly shifting back and forth in thought.

"She's right," Coryn added, crossing his arms. "This is incredible, but complicated. The King and his court don't worship the gods. Ever. They oppose those who seek them, which puts you in a dire situation."

"What does this mean to be an Iros? What will I do?" Marietta asked.

"Therypon deemed you worthy of her gifts. Usually, devotees need to train, pray, and seek the deities to gain their favor. Deania has been an attendant for many years now but she never received her ability from Therypon until she completed her cleric training a few years ago." Coryn shifted his weight as he crossed his arms.

"So I can do magic." Marietta stared at her hands.

"Not quite." Coryn's gaze shifted to the ceiling. "You'd have to go through the ceremony first, get inked with the serpent's ash, but this," he said, pulling down his collar, "is quite noticeable. I'm unsure how the crown would react. The tattoo makes it impossible to hide."

"They'll kill me," Marietta said in a small voice, her eyes staring at the marble floor. "Therypon said if they found out, they would kill me." Her gaze rose to meet Coryn's, his lips tugging into a frown.

"I would doubt that, but if the goddess said it, then maybe they're worse than we thought. A noble becoming an Iros…" Coryn laughed dryly, rubbing his hands on his face. "Therypon sure has a sense of humor, gifting this information after we just received instructions to join Enomenos in the war that Minister Keyain controls."

"Coryn, that's not very funny." Deania chided him that time, frowning.

"I know, and I'm sorry, Marietta. Gods, this is such a mess." He shook his head. "Communication is sparse between us and the temples in Enomenos, since Satiroan soldiers still occupy Olkia. I'm not sure when we can hold the ritual, so there's time to figure this out. Therypon wouldn't have made this so obvious if she didn't mean for you to become a fully-fledged Iros."

"But what if I don't want to become one?" Marietta asked, her throat tightening. It was as if they claimed her choice, just as Keyain did.

Coryn shot a glance at Deania. "We would never force you to become an Iros, but the goddess doesn't converse with even the best of us." He stepped toward Marietta, placing his hand on her shoulder. "Marietta, you're an enigma. We've never had someone like you."

"Can I think about it?" She searched his dark eyes, finding confusion and hurt. "It's not that I don't want to, but it's overwhelming. My life has already changed so much." Coryn stepped back as she fidgeted with a strand of hair. "First losing Tilan, then adjusting to life here."

"Mar," Amryth warned.

Coryn and Deania exchanged looks. "Who's Tilan?" Deania asked.

"Don't." Amryth's tone was resolute, her expression stern.

Marietta glanced at her friend. "Some things are best kept secret."

"Perhaps another time then." The serious look on Deania's face was off-putting for her cheerful demeanor. "So you are aware, the temple can claim you and protect you, even against the crown."

"Granted that you don't break any laws," Coryn added with a sad smile. "If you ever feel unsafe, you have us."

Marietta nodded. Not a day has passed where she's felt truly safe ever since she arrived in Satiros. But Amryth was clear—some secrets need to be left unsaid.

"I heard about them finding the other missing pilinos," Marietta said to Deania. "I'm so sorry for your losses."

A tight smile came to the cleric's face, as if forcing a smile through such pain was familiar. "May they finally find peace. Life in Chorys Dasi wasn't easy for any of us."

Marietta's eyes slid to Amryth. "I didn't know they were all from Chorys Dasi."

"There isn't an official record kept of pilinos refugees' home city-state," Amryth said. "Per law, Keyain can't base any of the findings off of word of mouth, but he's trying. He's following up on full elven persons who came to Satiros from Chorys Dasi."

"And any luck?" Coryn asked.

"No." Amryth frowned as she stood. "Nothing official, even with the tip about horns and wings."

Deania's face darkened to an expression that didn't fit her features. "The guards laughed at them, said they were crazy."

"And this friend, they were from Chorys Dasi as well?" Marietta said, sensing Deania's mood change.

The cleric nodded her head, a smile returning. "Yes, they served an elven family, as I did. We came from a long line of servants to a wealthy family."

"Yet, here you are in Satiros, cleric to the goddess Therypon," Marietta said. "I don't understand how anyone would want to serve a Syllogi elf like that."

Deania laughed. "There's good money in it, you know. The elven designed Syllogi so half-elves have little room to grow. Servitude is one of a few lucrative jobs choices for pilinos."

"Then why'd you leave?"

"Well, it was fun until it wasn't," she said with a sheepish smile. "I fled to Satiros because I made the family angry, and then had to join the temple for immunity. The family sent the Chorys Dasi guard after me."

"King Wyltam told me that they don't allow other city-states' guards into the city," Marietta said with furrowed brows. "Why would you *have* to join a temple once you made it to the city?"

Deania hesitated, glancing at Coryn.

"Well," Coryn said, running his hand over his chin, "that doesn't prevent the city-states from hiring elven civilians to, uh, apprehend refugees inside the city's walls. It's a loophole."

Marietta's heart sank to her stomach. "Why would they come after refugees? What's the difference between a refugee and a pilinos moving to Satiros?"

"The laws state anyone can move between the city-states of Syllogi, but only with the proper paperwork." Distaste laced his features as he locked eyes with Marietta. "Of course, that process is unending and most pilinos never get the paperwork approved."

"Does that mean pilinos can't even visit the other city-states?" Marietta said, anger tinging her tone. She thought of her life in Enomenos and how often she would travel freely and regularly.

"Again, with the proper paperwork, they can, but must follow a strict set number of days to return by," Coryn said. "Which most pilinos use that time to give themselves a head start to flee if their situation merits it. Others don't even get that approved and leave the city themselves."

"Once they arrive," Deania said, pulling Marietta's gaze, "only some are hunted down. Not allowing guards into the city slows the process and protects those who have committed no crime; yet, those of us who did, they send bounty hunters for us. Our only option is to join a temple." She gave a weak smile. "Not even the Queen Agnyssa of Chorys Dasi would go against the temples, so we gain immunity."

Gods, what crime could Deania have committed? But did it matter? No, not when the elven forced pilinos to the city-state in which they lived. Not when stealing was, unfortunately, some people's way of surviving. That much, Marietta could assume.

"The pilinos who went missing, are the bounty hunters taking them?" Marietta paused, hesitant to add, "And killing them?"

"We consider all visitors suspects at the moment," Amryth said. "The guard is investigating all possible legal avenues."

"We're lucky Minister Keyain has a soft heart for pilinos," Deania added, the corner of her lips curling. "Without you, Marietta, the whole situation could've been worse."

Marietta stilled, her breath caught in her chest. "But they're being attacked because of me."

Deania gave a small, dry laugh. "I can understand why the guard thinks that, but I'm sure you're just a convenient distraction. Something else is going on." She shook her head. "You should get back. Keyain will be worried."

Coryn clapped her shoulder again, walking to the door. "As for becoming an Iros, you have time to decide. Just don't take too long. I'll reach out to the others so they can arrive in time for the ceremony." He gave Marietta a weak smile. "That is if you decide to accept."

Iros. A paladin. To a goddess.

The thought was laughable. Unbelievable. Utterly ridiculous. But she saw Therypon—again. Her deep onyx skin, long raven hair. Gods, even the *scent* of her was so vibrant, as if Marietta truly saw the goddess in her bakery.

What did it mean? Therypon said she would be of importance, at the thick of it all—that her choices would lead to death.

In the carriage, she rubbed her palms on the skirt of her dress. Death, no matter the cause, was never easy. Even deaths from old age left marks on Marietta's heart, lingering longer than she wished. To think that death would be so known to her that Therypon called it her friend was nauseating.

The goddess was clear. Marietta was only her Iros for the person she was yet to be, for decisions she had not yet made, and to know that any choice she'd make would end in death paralyzed her.

Devote yourself to me and you will earn the strength to deflect your enemies.

Was it possible that becoming an Iros would save her? Impossible when the obvious tattoo would lead to Keyain and the King finding out. They would kill her. Her breath hitched as she steadied herself on the carriage wall, the cab suddenly too small and suffocating.

"It is incredible," Amryth said, breaking the silence. "This is just my opinion, but it isn't the worst idea, becoming Therypon's Iros." She paused, offering a smile. "If you claimed immunity from the temples, you could leave Keyain and the palace. You could go home to Enomenos."

Marietta closed her eyes, mustering a deep breath. Home.

Her home was Olkia, with Tilan. Returning without him, without retribution, would be unsatisfying. As long as Satiros occupied Olkia, what home did she really have?

"If King Wyltam keeps approaching you—"

"The King is fine," Marietta said, cutting her off. "He's kind to me." As kind as a foreign king who attacked her home and maybe slaughtered its population could be. Gods, she shouldn't defend him, yet he understood Keyain. *You can't chase after him every time he's angry.*

How many times had the King done as such? If he loved Keyain, then he knew the temper. Chasing after him only enabled his behavior, and she was aware of that.

She ran after him for the same reason she didn't want immunity from the temple—the Queen's plan. Her proximity to Keyain gave her the perfect opportunity to widen the rift between Keyain and Wyltam, to damage and tear down their court from the inside.

"Did you catch what they said about the war?" Amryth asked, stirring her from her thoughts.

Marietta frowned, looking out the window. In the afternoon's bright light, the reflection from the buildings was near blinding. "The temple of Therypon is moving against Satiros," she said. "I thought the temples stayed out of political matters."

"They do. If the temple of Therypon chose a side, I wonder if the others have, too." Amryth paused, following Marietta's gaze. "The temples have pilinos attendants who tried to flee Syllogi for Enomenos. Satiros attacking Olkia would upset many of them."

Marietta turned to her. "Yet they said Therypon gave the instructions. She has temples in the Enomenos, right?"

Amryth nodded. "I wonder if the army touched the temples. Some of my fellow soldiers are religious, but most hold the same beliefs as the court. Many are taught to, at least."

"Would Therypon enter the war as a retaliation? What would happen to the temple here?"

Amryth shrugged her shoulders. "I don't know. Nothing like this has ever happened. Nothing like you has ever happened, either. Gods, if Keyain finds out, he'll lock you up again. I won't be able to get you out a second time."

"Then I'll have to keep it a secret," Marietta said, knowing it was just one more she'd keep from Keyain.

Chapter Fifty-Eight

MARIETTA

BEFORE

Marietta swore under her breath. Keyain was two hours late to meet for dinner. Again.

Hunger gnawed at her stomach as she paced back and forth in their room at the inn. The asshole. Never courteous of her time, but gods forbid if she were more than a minute late for him. It was always about him and what he needed. The selfish prick.

As her anger grew with her hunger, she left a note saying she'll be at the Firewater Tavern, picking his least favorite place in Rotamu. Served him right. If he wanted a say in the matter, then he should have been on time. With a huff, she left the inn, heading down the main street parallel to the Halia River.

His tardiness was a new development recently. Though he was messing up, his protectiveness of her rose to a new high. Even meeting with a client was next to unbearable for him, let alone the meetings that went longer than she anticipated. Often she would find him pacing outside of whatever business she worked with. Embarrassed didn't even begin to cover how she felt about it. Gods damn prick. Always a pain in her ass.

The winter sun had already sunk below the buildings, painting Rotamu in shades of dull gray as delicate snowflakes drifted to the cobblestone street. Against the chill, she drew her wool cloak tighter around her body, thankful for her thick leather boots.

Marietta took her time walking, savoring the icy burn in her lungs,

puffing clouds of air out her nose, though her stomach growled at her speed. Deities damn Keyain for making her that hungry, for turning her mood sour from a late dinner. Marietta sighed as she walked into the tavern.

"Oi, Marietta!" called a short human male from the far side of the room. He wore a red tunic from one of the temples. Marietta could never remember which one.

"Meruk! It has been some time since we ran into one another," she said, approaching his table. Meruk was an old acquaintance, a cleric to a god. Like herself, he appeared to be familiar with many around Enomenos.

"That it has! Are you alone? Care to join us?" Meruk gestured to an open seat between a human and a half-elven woman.

"I'm supposed to meet my partner but I can sit with you while I wait." Marietta sat next to a man who also wore red.

Meruk and his companions caught Marietta up on the news of Rotamu. It was the typical gossip she expected to hear—rumors of a popular singer's troubled love life. The local drunk had disappeared for a few days. A young girl ran away in the middle of the night. The one shred of news that surprised her was a fire burning down an alchemist's building in the North River district. The owner, an elven woman from Syllogi, had died inside.

Marietta placed a hand over her heart. "That's terrible. Any ideas on what happened?"

Neither Meruk nor his companions answered. Instead, they stared over Marietta's shoulder.

"Mar, a moment?" Keyain's strained voice said as he gripped her shoulder.

Marietta closed her eyes with a sigh. His tone was the only warning she needed. "Excuse me," she said to the table.

Not sparing Keyain a glance, Marietta walked to a quiet corner void of other patrons. With a cross of her arms, she glared at Keyain.

"So much for waiting for me." The veins in his neck bulged as he ground his jaw, lips tightening to a thin line.

"You were late. Again."

"I was busy and came as soon as I could." Keyain gestured toward Meruk's table. "What are you doing with the cultists?"

"Don't call them cultists. Meruk is an old acquaintance, and he asked me to join them when he noticed I was alone, since you couldn't bother to be on time."

"I don't owe an explanation," he said through his teeth. Despite the freckles dotting his cheeks, he was terrifying, almost scary; but Marietta knew he was all bark, no bite.

"I'm tired of this, Keyain. You're always late, treat the people I talk to like they're rubbish, and your attitude is piss poor at best. If you're going to act like this, then go back to the room."

"Watch your tone with me." His face was feral as he forced himself to take a deep breath. "Mar, I'm under a lot of stress, okay? I'm sorry. Please, let's go."

"Sure, you're stressed, but you won't share why. Again. What are you hiding?" Marietta stared him down, refusing to yield.

"We've been over this. If I could tell you, I would. Now let's leave the cultists here and go." Keyain grabbed her arm, pulling her towards the door.

Marietta ripped free from his grasp. "Enjoy eating alone, Keyain." She returned to Meruk and his friends with an apology, the tavern door slamming shut behind her.

Keyain would be furious, but at that point, Marietta didn't care. The increasing possessiveness and his attitude grew tedious, always getting antsy to let her out of his sight for too long. Marietta hated it, and hated his new behavior. To grab her as he did? That sent her over. Keyain deserved to eat alone.

As an added insult to Keyain's anger, Marietta stayed for an extra ale. When she returned over an hour later, he had torn apart the room, their possessions scattered everywhere and sheets ripped from the bed. Strewn across the floor were the contents of her bag, the fabric shredded. Keyain sat on the bed, his head in his hands.

"What did you do?" she whispered.

Shame coated his ragged expression when he looked up. "I'm sorry,

Mar. I want to tell you everything, but I just can't right now." Keyain's gaze faltered, falling to the floor.

Marietta walked over to him, placing a hand on his back. "You can't keep losing your temper like this."

"I know. When I see you with them, I just can't control my anger."

"What do you mean by 'them?'"

Keyain stumbled over his words. "Uh, them, the humans—err, the temple. You know what I mean."

"For someone who insists on traveling Enomenos, you sure have little tolerance for pilinos." Marietta crossed her arms. "Stop saying derogatory things, or I'm leaving you."

"Mar, if you knew what I knew—"

"Then tell me!" she yelled, throwing her hands in the air.

"I can't! Okay? I can't tell you." Keyain stood up, grabbing her shoulders. He took a deep breath and leaned his forehead against her own, holding her face with both his hands.

"Please, Marietta, move with me to Satiros."

"What?" She pushed away from him.

"Move with me." Hope filled his eyes as he repeated himself.

"You said you wouldn't ask that of me," she hissed, jerking away. "I will not move to a city-state where I'm considered a lesser citizen. Are you out of your mind? Do you think I'm a lesser person?"

"No, Mar, of course not," Keyain said, grabbing her hand. "You're not like *them*. Please, I love you so much, and the thought of losing you crushes me. I can't keep this up. It would be so much easier if you moved with me, please. I'm begging you."

"The only way I'm moving to Satiros is if you drag me there against my will. If you expect a future where we live together in Satiros, then we should talk about not continuing this relationship." Marietta pulled her hand out of his grasp.

Tears welled in his eyes, and his mouth tugged into a frown. "Mar, please. I can't let you go. We'll figure something out."

"I don't think we will," she whispered.

Keyain wrapped his arms around her. "I'm not letting you go," he murmured into her hair, followed by a kiss.

Tears fell from her eyes. Four years together, and that was what they had to show for it. Keyain was well aware she didn't want to move to Satiros—that she would never go.

Though she wasn't sure where their relationship would lead, Marietta was okay with it. Keyain would leave for six months of the year, sending her the occasional letter, and they'd be back on the road together for the other six. It worked for her, but clearly, it wasn't working for Keyain.

Despite the love she had for him, a part of her knew she should leave him. His attitude, his actions were unfair to her; yet, he always apologized, always reeled her back in. The back and forth was nauseating. One minute, Marietta was ready to grab her bags and leave. The next, she was hugging him as she cried from his apology. The funny thing about love was that it didn't need to make sense. Marietta had little reason to stay with Keyain, but every time she stepped away, he would pull her back by the strings attached to her heart.

However, the longer their relationship continued, the more her love altered. In the beginning, they spent their nights with friends as they drank and danced and lived their lives. Now, most nights were spent in their room at an inn. Marietta was happy to have the alone time with him, but her friends had tried to intervene, saying that she wasn't acting like herself when he was around. Part of her thought that was her lifestyle changing, that part of her wanted to settle down. A deeper part of herself knew she changed for Keyain, for what he wanted.

It was tiring to love someone like Keyain. The constant push and pull of emotions, the constant fights and rage. With his new effort to move her to Satiros, she could only feel dread about the idea. Not only would she have less freedom, but not having months of a break from Keyain's anger would be too much. He was too much.

Marietta couldn't predict the future, but she knew one thing that was for sure to happen—she would eventually leave Keyain. The only question was when.

Chapter Fifty-Nine
VALERIYA

Valeriya bit her nail as she paced back and forth in her bedroom. The longer she held onto the papers with Marietta's findings, the more the war slipped in favor of her husband. She couldn't prove that the mage who followed her was from Wyltam, but she wasn't going to discount it either. How would he know to have her followed? How did he even have mages? It would be the first she had heard of the Satiroan crown having mages.

Unless it wasn't Wyltam.

Maybe she was crazy, or maybe Wyltam was just paranoid about Valeriya's activity at court. She liked to scheme, and Wyltam realized that. Otherwise, he wouldn't have asked her to look into Marietta, but following Valeriya was new—something she didn't like.

Valeriya sighed, leaving her suite for the lavish halls of that forsaken palace. In seven years, she still hadn't grown comfortable in it, as if she were in someone else's home. Reyila's castle stood atop the mountains with only the sky and wind. Nestled into the rolling hills and city of Satiros, Valeriya felt like a sitting duck. Whoever built the Satiroan palace was a fool, for it wouldn't hold up long in a fight.

As she stepped out of the Royal's Wing, she felt the hairs on her neck stand. How often did the mage follow her? For how long? Perhaps they knew of her plan. Perhaps they were onto Valeriya.

No, she sounded crazy. If Wyltam suspected her of something nefarious, he wouldn't have hesitated to throw her in the dungeons for treason. The fact that she still walked freely and wore her crown was proof

enough that he was unaware of her handing off information.

The intense summer sun burned as she wound her way through the garden. Valeriya sighed as the warm breeze blew past, offering relief from the afternoon heat. The bruise on her chest had faded enough that Valeriya covered it with makeup and wore appropriate dresses for the temperature. The sooner it disappeared, the fewer questions Wyltam would ask.

Outside the palace section that held the Minister's Chambers, Valeriya stood admiring the wisteria. If the mage still followed her, they would be talented without a doubt. To hold invisibility for that long was an impressive feat.

The doors to the building opened as Keyain came striding out in conversation to one of his captains, a blonde female with an impressive scowl. Valeriya smiled. Keyain was so predictable. He didn't see her as he walked down the steps. "Oh, Keyain! What are the chances of seeing you here?" she said in a honeyed voice, eyes wide and innocent as the minister walked into the courtyard.

Keyain stopped mid-sentence, turning to her. "Ah, Queen Valeriya," he said with a bow, "I would say the chances are high considering I work in this building." Annoyance tinged his tone that made his captain flash an anxious expression. Such insolence towards her, and in front of his own subordinate, too. Oh, she loved being under his skin.

"Of course, Keyain." Valeriya slashed a smile at him. "Care to join me for a walk?"

As he ran his hand through his hair, it was clear he didn't want to, but he wouldn't turn her down. Keyain sighed. "Of course, my Queen." He turned to his captain. "I'll find you in a bit to finish this conversation. Go grab lunch in the meantime."

The captain entered the building as Keyain offered his arm to Valeriya. "You're quite busy these days, Keyain. I'm happy you found the time for a silly walk with me." She smirked as Keyain's annoyance rolled off him.

"I am quite busy, Queen Valeriya. Satiros is in a war that takes up most of my time."

"What of your poor wife? Marietta has been here, what, four months now? Are you making time for her as well?" she asked, knowing which wounds to poke. With the war on top of his regular duties, Valeriya was aware he had little free time.

Keyain ground his jaw. "Marietta is doing well. We're happy."

"But you spend so much time away from her, so she must get lonely. I'll make more of a point to invite her for tea."

They followed the path over a bridge coated in thick, green vines with black and white flowers. Below the creek flowed by, the occasional frog croaked.

"Marietta is fine." Keyain's voice strained to remain polite. "I'm sure you didn't want to pull me away from my duties to talk of just my wife."

"Just your wife?" Valeriya playfully batted his chest, earning a scowl. "Marietta is your love! She has shared so in conversations with me. To think a noble in this day and age married for love!" She smirked, watching Keyain bristle. He almost made it too easy.

They approached the creek with its water gurgling down a shallow cliff face, crashing into the stream. The noise covered their voices as she spoke. "What I'm actually concerned about is the palace's safety," she said with her voice low. If she were being followed by a mage, then the surrounding noise would mask her words.

Keyain glanced at Valeriya, then back at the path ahead of them. "I assure you that the guards are keeping a close watch on the palace, my Queen."

"Oh, I don't doubt that your guards are capable," she said, patting his arm. "However, what if someone broke in through magical means?"

"There are systems in place to prevent that," Keyain answered, his tone uninterested.

"But could magic be used to break in? For example, what if I were to say someone trails us as we speak?"

He glanced at her again, biting the inside of his cheek. "Magic can't break through, and no one is following us. Perhaps you're feeling paranoid."

"That may be true, but what if someone were? I thought Enomenoans didn't use magic."

"They don't."

"So if the Enomenoans don't use magic, and if someone was trailing me by magical means, they would be from Syllogi, correct?" she asked, pretending to pick fuzz off her dress. It was a trick she picked up from her husband, who has mastered the art of disinterest.

"Yes, all the Syllogi city-states have magic where Enomenos does not."

"Of course, that includes Satiros as well? I would assume we possess ways to spy."

"Valeriya, is there a reason you're questioning me on this?" Keyain said with a sigh, dropping her title.

"Oh, just in case. One could never be too sure. I feel safer knowing that such defenses are in place. That means if I were being followed, it would be by you or Wyltam." Keyain glanced at her again, realization setting in on his features. "Of course, neither of you has a sound reason to treat a queen as such," Valeriya said, smirking as Keyain looked away, nostrils flaring. She could play this game with him all day.

The path they walked down led to the Glass Gardens, the lofty doors opening to the Glass Garden. Keyain stopped and turned to face Valeriya.

"You know Wyl. If he wanted information from you, he would ask directly," Keyain said, dropping her arm from his and bowed. "But I apologize. I have somewhere to be, my Queen."

Valeriya brought her hand to her chin as Keyain walked away. The confirmation had been obvious in his expression—Wyltam was on to her. She needed to hasten her plans.

Valeriya hadn't met privately with Gyrsh in quite a few months, not since the Chorys Dasians arrived. She had decided it was safer to distance themselves in order to draw less attention to their plans. However, if Wyltam or Keyain were having her followed, then it was time to move. She only needed to give the word.

As Valeriya stepped into Gyrsh's suite, the minister's gaze took in the low cut of her dress and her neck elongated by her hair, neatly pulled back.

"Hello, Gyrsh," she murmured as the door closed behind her, offering him her hand.

He caught it, thumbs brushing over her knuckles. "Hello, my Queen," he said, bringing her hand to his mouth for a kiss.

She ignored the disgust that rose in her stomach. The male was as vile as Syllogian males come; yet, he was useful. The more he believed there was a chance for him to hold Valeriya's favor, the more compliant he would be. The male foolishly thought an affair was a real possibility, that Valeriya would make him her secret lover and rise with her power after their plan was brought to fruition. Perhaps he got the idea from Keyain. After all, it was his secret affair with Wyltam's mother, late Queen Olytia, that got him his position. When she had heard the rumor, she hadn't waited a moment to share it with Gyrsh.

Gyrsh offered his arm, and she placed a hand on top for added effect. The golden tone in his brunette hair shone brighter against the navy of his shirt. Did he purposely choose Reyila's colors? She bit back a laugh. Gyrsh was trying too hard.

In the living room, he opened his liquor cabinet, turning to her. "What would you prefer, my Queen?"

"Just Valeriya," she said, leaning back into the couch, "for tonight at least." A slow smile spread across his handsome face, the one so similar to Elyse's that it was unnerving. If someone had told her they were siblings, Valeriya would have believed them. "And a whiskey, please."

His brows rose in surprise. "Of course, though I have a rare bottle of wine set aside if you'd prefer that."

Which meant he had planned to drink it. Valeriya could have laughed, knowing the male hated his whiskey. "Kind of you to offer, but I'm looking forward to the *bite*." A smirk came to her face, pulling Gyrsh deeper into her web.

With a grin tugging at his lips, he poured the drinks and sat down across from Valeriya, his honey eyes locked onto her. "To what do I owe the pleasure of your company this evening? It's unlike you to make such last-minute visits."

Valeriya shifted, crossing and uncrossing her legs, letting her dress' slits show their length. "With this new privacy of yours—" she gestured to the surrounding suite "—I figured we could discreetly go about our business."

"And what business would that be?" As he brushed back his shoulder-length hair, he took a sip of his liquor, his sultry expression hardening with the alcohol's bite.

Valeriya fought a smirk. Toying with Satiroan ministers would never grow old. "Well, there are a few things but some will have to wait until later." Gyrsh did nothing to hide his gaze roaming over her. Valeriya wanted to laugh, to roll her eyes at his obliviousness to her teasing. "But I'm being followed."

Gyrsh spat out his whiskey, looking wide-eyed at Valeriya. "What do you mean, followed?"

"Keyain and Wyltam have grown *suspicious*. A mage is trailing me." She sat up straighter, letting the seduction subside. "It's time to go."

"They're not ready," he pleaded, running a hand through his hair. "Are you sure they have someone trailing you?"

"Keyain just as much as confirmed it this afternoon."

Gyrsh swore, throwing back the rest of his whiskey, not bothering to hide his expression of disgust.

Valeriya tapped her fingers against her glass. "When were the Chorys Dasians to leave?"

"In a month—"

"Cut that time in half. You have two weeks to close the deal."

"Valeriya, that's not enough time," Gyrsh said, exasperated.

"We're out of time." Valeriya threw back the rest of her whiskey, staring down Gyrsh. "Two weeks."

Gyrsh shook his head. "Az won't leave in two weeks. He's been writing Elyse these foolish love letters, but she still isn't interested in marrying him. If she isn't going with them, then Az won't leave at all."

"That is on you," Valeriya said, giving him a leveling stare. "You lost her as your heir, knowing that Az pursued her hand. Perhaps you should have respected your only child more." She let the insult sink in, Gyrsh realizing she knew the extent of his parenting. As she said before, he was vile.

Valeriya had hoped that after Elyse called off the betrothal that Az would set his sights on someone new. However, Elyse made it into a chase, and Az loved to win.

"Well, not all hope is lost. Keyain contacted Az. The plan is for them to take Elyse and the cl—" He covered the slur with a cough as Valeriya glared. "And Marietta out for dinner in the city."

An interesting development. "Does anyone else see the problem with Az being alone with Keyain after the incident in the Central Garden?"

Gyrsh shook his head. "Az confirmed with Sauntyr and Sylas that he'll be on his best behavior."

"What little good that means."

He laughed at that, sitting back in his chair. "Az wants her. This is our chance to make sure that he leaves in two weeks, to make sure Elyse is with him."

"True." Valeriya wondered if her sister knew of this issue. She'd have to message her later. "How likely do you think Elyse is to accept his hand once more?"

"Before the King took a special interest, I would say without a doubt." Gyrsh stood, offering to take Valeriya's glass, and then walked to refill them. "Now that the King has her studying magic, I can't be for certain."

Valeriya held her breath. "He's doing what?"

"Teaching the girl Fulbryk's principles." Gyrsh poured the spirits and returned Valeriya her glass. "Az found a reader in Wyltam's study. He said that when Elyse held it, it was unlike any other reading he had seen."

Valeriya closed her eyes, thinking of the face she saw for a moment in the Central Garden. She wasn't crazy. She wasn't paranoid. Somehow, Wyltam knew enough about magic to teach Elyse. "Is she like her mother then?"

A vacant look held his face as Gyrsh stared across the room. "She's exactly like Anthylia. And if that's the case, then she's doomed to her mother's fate."

Anxiety washed over Valeriya, remembering the story of her death. It was a mage's worst fear. "Then why does Az insist on pursuing her?"

"The potential is there. He and Sylas are convinced she could surpass her mother in talent."

If that was true, then protecting Elyse would become a new priority for Valeriya. After all, she had been keeping the girl under her wing for the better part of five years. To lose her now to Wyltam would hurt her future—and the court she planned to build in Satiros.

"Then let's hope Az can safely get her out of Satiros before anything is enacted. Come," she said, softening her features and patting the seat next to her. "Tell me of happier things, Gyrsh."

A smile slid its way back onto his face. Even if Valeriya found males attractive, she would never choose someone like Gyrsh. He was handsome, with his strong chin, golden features, and glittering smile, but his actions as a father were deplorable. He did, however, keep himself useful with his minister position and his familial ties back to Chorys Dasi. Gyrsh became a weapon in her arsenal, one to go about her plans right beneath Keyain's and Wyltam's noses. With Marietta wearing down Keyain's resolve and distracting him from his duties, the divide grew between the two. Plus, Marietta was the perfect diversion while they completed the deal with Chorys Dasi.

Valeriya didn't have to fake her smile as she slid her taunting hand across Gyrsh's chest. The time had come. Valeriya would get everything she wanted in just a few weeks' time.

Valeriya returned to her room later than she had hoped, the alcohol making her mind fuzzy. Exhaustion pulled at her focus, threatening to take time away from what she needed to accomplish. She pulled out a small vial of clear liquid, downing it before heading into the bathroom. There was still much to do that evening, and she couldn't let alcohol affect her progress.

She spent a couple of hours with Gyrsh, letting the minister kiss her neck, gliding his hand around her body. Truly, she wished to shower and scrub the memory of his hands off her. After she practiced, she would do as such.

However, a major problem threatened her future. Valeriya was being followed, and she had a strong feeling it was Wyltam. She was out of time—they were all out of time. Hidden away in her room was the information she had to pass on, plus meet with Marietta again to see if she found anything additional. She had hoped to have more time using her in court, but things would progress faster than she anticipated.

Valeriya strode over to her balcony doors, throwing them open to the evening air and letting the warm summer breeze encase her. What if it didn't work, if two weeks wasn't enough time? What if Wyltam caught her and learned how deep her scheming went?

If only Katya were here. She had an impeccable way of helping Valeriya push past her self-doubt, to keep moving forward with her head held high. Without Katya, this game Valeriya played grew tiresome and lonely. To look upon her face, to kiss her one last time. Valeriya should have begged Katya to come to Satiros.

If the plan worked, if the deal went through, then perhaps she'd be seeing Katya in just a few weeks. After seven years apart, she could only hope the half-elf hadn't moved on, that she would still love her. That was if Valeriya succeeded, and to do so, she needed to focus.

With a heavy sigh, she closed the balcony doors. Invisibility was demanding, but the mage trailing her could hold it for hours. Valeriya only needed a few minutes of invisibility to slip past them, long enough to hide and take on her servant's visage.

Valeriya closed her eyes, clearing her mind of thoughts, of doubts, of emotion. She pulled at the aithyr around her, letting it fill her body as she shook with the effort, trying to contain it. And she practiced turning herself invisible until the sun came up.

Chapter Sixty

MARIETTA

The first gift came two days after her visit to the temple, a bouquet made of golden daffodils, sweet-smelling elderflower, flowing vines of honeysuckle, and lavender. Days of selecting fresh-cut flowers with her mother at the market flooded her memory. King Wyltam had no clue how the gift touched her. Along with the bouquet was a brief note.

All beauty is frivolous, yet through you, I'm learning to enjoy such frivolities.

Marietta hated the smile it brought, the swoop that moved through her stomach. King Wyltam wasn't a man of many words, but he was efficient. The gift did its job.

Keyain didn't eat dinner with her after seeing the vase of flowers on the table, the leash on his anger slipping when he saw the note. Instead, he locked himself in his office for the evening. Marietta coaxed him out a few hours later with a kiss, followed by yet another intimate night. Since their first night together, they made a habit of it, Marietta remembering exactly how much she enjoyed that side of Keyain.

A couple of days later, another present arrived. A box the size of a dinner plate tied with a ribbon surprised Marietta one afternoon. Fixed atop was another note from the King.

I'll save you the boredom of this bakery's long history, but know it's the oldest in Satiros and a favorite for a reason.

Marietta tore at the ribbon and lifted the lid, surprised to find slices of custard pie with candied lemon slices. A traditional pastry which made sense if it was the oldest in Satiros.

Her custard pie was a wedding favorite in Olkia, the lemon and cinnamon-infused syrup she drizzled overtop being popular among the masses. It was one of the first recipes she learned.

She bit into a piece, unable to wait. The custard center melted on her tongue, thick and sweet between the thin layers of crisp and flaky dough. The syrup had a nutty flavor, indicative of honey, which was the traditional ingredient. Her last bite with the candied lemon was perfection.

Gods damn the King for not sharing with her the name. Marietta wished to visit, to meet the baker, doubtful she knew them if they ran the oldest bakery in Satiros.

Another thought hit her. There were other bakeries in Satiros—ones she had yet to experience. Gods, her friend Grysella owned a bakery there. How did she forget about that? One day, she'd visit. Marietta would see them all, whether as Keyain's wife or as an Iros to the goddess Therypon.

Keyain tried to ignore the sweets that evening. After Marietta hounded him to try one, he claimed through clenched teeth that he could request something better from the palace kitchens instead. Blinded by his jealousy, he didn't realize how wrong he was.

His anger snapped the night the King's note arrived, a servant handing it to him instead of Marietta. "This is too far," he yelled, slamming his fist and stirring Marietta from her book.

She looked over her shoulder from the couch to where Keyain stood near the dining table. "What's too far?"

The note crinkled in his fist as his stare found Marietta. "It doesn't matter. You're not going."

Marietta snapped her book shut, setting it on the seat next to her, and stood to face Keyain. "What's in the note, Keyain?"

"You're not going, so it doesn't matter."

"So the note is for me?"

"Yes."

"And you won't give it to me?" She crossed her arms, raising a speculative brow.

"No." He walked to the liquor cabinet, pocketing the note as he reached for a decanter.

Marietta approached from behind. "Of course, you aren't," she said, plucking his just-poured glass of whiskey from his hands and taking a sip. "Otherwise, you wouldn't have control over me."

"Mar, that's not—"

"It is." She turned towards the living room, looking back at Keyain. "Does it feel good?"

His mouth parted, unable to form words, though he tried. Things had been good between them, despite the King's taunting presents, and she knew Keyain didn't want to spoil it. It was cruel, but so was attacking her home. Abducting her.

She felt no remorse as Keyain wiped his face and poured himself a fresh glass of whiskey. "This is different. The King—"

"So it was from the King."

"Who else would it be?"

"Exactly." She walked back into the living room, returning to her book with her drink in hand.

As expected, Keyain followed her, exasperated. "The King isn't your friend, Marietta."

"You're right," she drawled, not looking up from the pages. "He's yours."

"So, him giving you inappropriate attention—"

She jerked her face toward him. "Inappropriate attention? Keyain, he's making sure I am well-adjusted in Satiros, especially after...." She gestured with her hands at the suite, referring to the days spent rotting away.

"A king shouldn't be the one to do so."

"You're right," she said, softening her expression. "But someone had to."

The insult landed. Keyain's eyes fluttered closed as he took a deep breath. Gods, if he gripped the glass any tighter, then it'd shatter.

"Come sit," Marietta said, patting the seat next to her.

Keyain trudged over, taking a hefty swig as he sat. Her fingers played with the short brown waves of his hair, the touch easing his jaw.

"I know you're not *trying* to control me," she murmured, "but you must realize that's what you're doing. King Wyltam is your friend, and he's extending that friendship to me." Keyain faced forward, unable to see the lie plain on her face. "Please, give me the note. It wasn't yours."

With a deep sigh, Keyain dug into his pocket and handed the crumpled-up paper. Scrawled in the King's handwriting was another short and simple note.

I have made arrangements for us to visit the Ertwyrmer Sculpture Gardens in the morning if you still wish to visit. It would be my honor to give you your first tour. I await your reply.

Marietta fought the smile that her lips wanted to form. During their carriage ride, the King mentioned the sculpture garden. She had said she'd love to visit. He remembered.

"It's unsafe for both of you to be in a public garden," Keyain said, watching her closely. "Too many hidden areas, dense underbrush. Even if guards sweep the gardens before you arrive, it'll still leave an opportunity for you to be abducted."

She should have held her tongue, but anger blossomed at her center. "Ah yes, it would be *wrong* to abduct me."

Keyain shot her an annoyed glance. "I thought you've been enjoying your time here with me. My apologies."

He went to stand, but she caught his arm, sitting him back on the couch. She folded his hand into hers with a kiss. "I'm sorry," she lied, "but I don't like not making my own decisions. I want to go. The King won't put me at risk." She pressed a kiss onto his cheek.

He sighed, finishing his drink before placing the empty glass on the table. "Come here," he murmured. Marietta set her drink and book to the side, climbing into his lap. "I love you, Marietta."

She shouldn't say it. To tell Keyain such a lie would be the most cruel. "I love you, too."

He pulled back, staring at her face. "What did you say?"

"I love you, too."

Keyain's mouth found hers, his arms pulling her close as he pushed her onto her back. Not bothering to move to the bed, Keyain unzipped her dress, hastily pulling the fabric away.

Marietta started on the buttons of his shirt, but Keyain grabbed the bottom hem, pulling it off and tossing it to the side. His pants came off just as quickly, and then he was inside her, both moaning from the touch, the release.

Perhaps it was too far to say those words to him, but they worked. Marietta was wedging herself between Keyain and the King faster than she ever anticipated. And as Keyain whispered the words into her neck as he thrust, she felt no remorse as she repeated them back.

Though it was well before noon, the weather was hot and dry, summer fully coming to fruition. To appease Keyain, Marietta wore a relatively modest dress of light white fabric. The handmaids helped tie Marietta's curls into a loose knot on top of her head to keep her hair off her neck. On her feet were sandals instead of slippers.

The King's outfit surprised Marietta, though perhaps it shouldn't have. He wore all black despite the heat, but his shirt was of a thinner fabric. He left the top buttons undone to let a section of his chest show.

The carriage ride to the Ertwymer Sculpture Gardens was quick, she and the King exchanging short pleasantries. When they arrived, the King emerged first, offering his arm to Marietta. Guards stepped up closed around them as she left the carriage and her jaw dropped when she saw the garden's entrance.

Between the buildings of Petal Row, the sculpture gardens stood in contrast with its sweeping canopies, thick blooming flower beds, and sculptures of creatures. More sizable than any living being, two statues of females sunk into the trunks of stone trees, hair twisting into the meticulously carved bark, the branches of each reaching across the top of the gate to form an arch.

"Dryads," the King said, bent down to murmur in her ear.

"They're beautiful." Her eyes scanned each one as the guards escorted them into the gardens.

"Wait until you see the others."

A thin, wiry elven man approached them, his nose long and lips curled into an unnatural smile. "King Wyltam," he said with a sweeping bow. "My honor to have you back at the Ertwymer Statue Gardens. Will you need assistance today or—"

"With me is a noble lady you forgot to greet." King Wyltam's deep voice cut through the entrance, the guards at the sides stilling as the King's mood shifted.

"Apologies," he said with another sweeping bow. "I didn't realize the clip—"

"I suggest your next words be a proper greeting for her. You know exactly who she is."

The elven man cringed, swallowing down his words. "Of course, my King. Lady Marietta," he said, the words coming out choked, "an honor to have you visit our gardens." He gave a stiff bow. "I hope your first visit is enjoyable."

Surprised at the King's intervention and authoritative tone, Marietta furrowed her brows at the man. He was aware of who she was, the King not offering her name. "Your hospitality knows no bounds," she said dryly.

From the corner of her eye, she saw the King smirk, his arm tightening on her grip. They stepped forward, passing the elven man who paled on the spot. "Next time I hear that word, I will have you replaced," the King added. "Understood?"

"Yes, Your Grace."

As they entered the garden, lush flower beds greeted them in an array of colors and shapes, bees buzzing from bloom to bloom. Smaller, less impressive statues of feline creatures with wings darted the landscape.

"Apologies, Marietta," the King said, leaning towards her ear. "If I knew Hermyn would be so discriminating, I would've had someone else greet us."

"It was good to see what your city thinks of me, Your Grace." She tore her gaze from the gardens, finding his dark eyes. In the bright morning light, the flecks of amber were vibrant against what she could see was dark brown, not black, and utterly stunning. "I didn't think you could be so authoritative."

He gave a small laugh, turning to the guards. "Some space, please."

A broad-shouldered elven woman stepped forward, dropping to a knee with her hand over her chest. "My King, we have orders—"

"I understand Keyain's hesitancy to let Marietta enjoy herself," he said with a drawl, "but my own personnel swept the gardens before we arrived. They're secure."

The guard nodded her head. Off to the side, Marietta caught the narrowed gaze of a slender woman guard with a plait of long, ash blonde hair. Her eyes darted between Marietta and the King, laced with suspicion. With a reluctant step and crossed arms, she moved back with the other guards.

"As much as I enjoy your brash way of speaking, try not to be so obvious in front of others," the King said, guiding Marietta further down the path.

Above them, tree branches laced together to block the harsh sun. A slight breeze pushed through, offering relief from the already hot day, tousling the King's hair. "I didn't mean it to be an insult," Marietta said.

With the guards fanned out around them, the King didn't fight the smile that curled on one side of his lips. "I know, but I'm a king, the meaning of authority." His face grew wary for a moment, Marietta catching the far-off stare, the falter in his smile.

"You hate it, don't you?"

His gaze slid to Marietta.

"You hate being the King." She narrowed her eyes with a smile.

"I am what I need to be." He paused, eyes lost in thought.

Marietta let him think through his words, admiring the closest statue. Hooved and on four legs, it was like a horse with a single spiraling horn protruding from the forehead, similar to a unicorn; yet, instead of a horse's mane, curled, shaggy fur surrounded its neck. Round, cub-like ears were nothing of a horse, and neither was the stub of a tail.

She drew closer to the edge of the path, King Wyltam following, though he let her arm slip away. Under scrutiny, nearly stepping into the purple forget-me-nots surrounding the statue, she shook her head. "I thought it was a unicorn, but it isn't."

"A monoceros," the King said, standing at her side with his hands clasped behind his back. "Unlike the unicorn, it has the head of a stag and the tail of a boar."

Marietta turned to him, but his gaze wasn't on the statue. It was on her.

"Deemed the quickest hooved fey creature, scholars say they were impossible to catch."

"I've never heard of such a creature," she said in awe. "They were never mentioned in my father's stories. How do you know all this?"

"I spend much of my free time reading," he said, dropping his gaze for a moment. "Many fey creatures have popped up in my texts."

How peculiar that a king read about fey creatures that much. A thousand questions surfaced at once, but the King offered his arm and took her down a small path to one side, the guards trailing far behind them on the winding path.

Peonies lined the way, each shrub bursting with magenta and white blooms. "Those shouldn't be in season still," she noted, turning to the other side of the path. "And hyacinth should definitely not be in bloom." She turned to the King.

"Ever-blooming is more than just a pretty, symbolic phrase for Satiros," King Wyltam said. "We also sit at an apex for magical energy. Many researchers believe that aithyr, the energy used in magic, saturates the soil beneath our feet."

Marietta slowed her gait, stopping to sniff one of the hyacinths, the powerful floral scent just like the ones at her parents' house in Notos. "Impossible," she said. "Do they remain in bloom through the cold months?"

"They do, even when the frost freezes over. Of course, the blooms die over time, but new ones grow in their place." The King leaned over to look at Marietta's face while she inspected a peony. "That's also why we have a wide variety of flowers and plants throughout Satiros."

"That's fascinating. Fresh herbs and vegetables year-round," Marietta said. "Imagine fresh berries all the time!" She grabbed the King's forearm as her excitement spiked. "Well, any fresh fruit, really. The possibilities for fruit tarts would be endless. Or pies. Or spoon sweets!"

The King laughed, placing his hand over Marietta's. "What are spoon sweets?"

"You've never had a spoon sweet?" she said, gawking at him. "My gods, King Wyltam, if I ever get access to a kitchen again, I promise to make it for you. They're whole pieces of fruit, like grapes or cherries, cooked with sugar and honey. Sometimes, depending on the recipe, I'll add various spices into the syrup. But you eat the fruit whole on a spoon."

The King raised a brow, a full smile coming to his face. "Hence the name spoon sweet."

"Yes!" Marietta said as he led her down the path. "I've made them from sour cherries, pomegranates, figs, even with rose petals or tomatoes. It depends on the season. And you can eat it off the spoon directly, sometimes with coffee if you can afford it. Coffee was a luxury in Notos, sailors bringing the beans on ships from the south. If not coffee, then usually with a glass of water to wash it down. Or you can serve it over yogurt or with sweet bread."

"Consider me intrigued," he said, amusement hinting in his deep voice. "I will hold you to that promise, considering you've used the palace kitchens twice."

Marietta paused. "And is that a problem?"

"Not at all," said the King with a soft voice, his thumb brushing over her knuckles.

Surprised, Marietta dipped her head with a grin. At least the King had no issue with her in the kitchens. If only Keyain understood how happy it made her.

"And as much as I'm enjoying your excitement for spoon sweets," he said, his eyes turning towards the path, "I'm more excited to show you this statue."

The King took a narrow path that jutted to the side through thick bushes. Marietta slid her arm from the King, his hand landing in her own. She pulled back for a second, startled by the action, but it was pleasant, comforting. From behind, she had to crane her neck to see the back of the head, not realizing he had almost a half-foot in height on Marietta. Compared to Keyain, everyone seemed small.

He gave her hand a quick squeeze as the path opened up, revealing a monstrous statue of a giant scaled beast, about four times the size of the largest horse Marietta had ever seen.

A reptilian head with pointed teeth topped its neck, which was carved with twisted vines or roots. From its jaw and chest hung stone textured to look like moss. Even from afar, it looked as soft. Thick legs ended in sharp daggers for claws, and a mass of a tail curled around it. Horns branched from the top of its head like a mature tree.

Marietta gasped, gripping the King's hand as she stared up at the statue. The creature tugged at her mind, recalling a memory she couldn't drum up. Without thinking, she walked towards it.

"Careful," the King said at her side as she stepped into the purple flowers that filled the clearing around the statue, "you won't want to crush such flowers."

"Asters," she said in a breathy voice. "They're resilient and can handle us stepping through them. Just try not to crush the stems and bases."

"How do you know so much about flowers, Marietta?" the King said above her shoulder.

"My mother and I would purchase them at the market for my father." She paused, her hand stroking the smooth stone. "He said it always reminded him of his sister, who he left behind in Satiros. Now that I'm thinking about it, he had shared stories of how his sister used to create these elaborate flower displays when they were younger. Allegedly, people requested her to arrange flowers all the time, but I assumed my father exaggerated. Especially after she passed away." She paused a moment, remembering her father's grief after losing his only sibling. She sighed and added, "My mother also loved plants and herbs—she's an herbalist in Notos."

Upon her touch, the statue seemed to shift under her fingers, though the stone remained still. Curious, she turned to the King.

He stood staring at her, lips parted and brows raised. With a swallow, he managed, "That's fascinating."

"Are you alright?" she asked, leaving the King to walk around the creature, her hand dragging across the skin carved like bark.

The King followed close behind. At his silence, she turned to find him with an aster bloom in his hand. "May I?"

She nodded, holding her breath as he tucked the flower behind her ear. "And how does it look?"

"Unbelievable," he whispered.

She snorted with a laugh. "How could a flower behind my ear look unbelievable?" With her back to the King, she bent down to examine the tail of the statue. "And you never told me what this statue was."

"A forest drakon." She jumped, not hearing the King approach. As she turned to him, his hand found hers.

Marietta made to pull away with a question, but the King's awed expression made her pause.

"Keyain is beyond undeserving of you."

She laughed nervously, avoiding his gaze. "Well, you know the truth of our situation."

"But you don't," he said, stepping closer. "Keyain has robbed you of so many opportunities, of potential happiness. I can imagine it now, the woman who you would be without him."

Her breath caught as he brought her hand to his lips, the space between them inappropriately close. "I was very much happy without him."

The King's stare fell to her lips, his free hand cupping her face. She leaned in, wishing to know how his lips would feel on hers.

Gods, he was the King—the enemy. The goddess had been clear: if the King knew she was an Iros, he could kill her. Kissing him wouldn't help any of the mess she was in. Marietta pulled away as his lips were about to brush against her own. "We are both married. Such action is beyond inappropriate."

The King pulled back, his emotion slipping under his expressionless mask. "And if we're both in marriages that makes us unhappy? If my wife finds me unappealing for more than just personal reasons?"

"It's still wrong," she said, savoring the grip of his hand.

The King gave a small, dry laugh. "Valeriya doesn't even like males."

Marietta blinked, his words registering. "What a sad life you both must live. I can't imagine bonding myself to someone who could never want me."

"And here I consider your situation sadder," he said. "To be forced into a marriage without choice or knowledge."

Marietta grimaced, slipping her hand from his. "Says the man who upholds the law allowing it."

"And if I were to annul your marriage?" he asked. "Is that what it takes to make you happy?"

"No," she said, turning back to the statue. "I want independence, freedom." And revenge.

"And if I could give you that? All that and more?"

She turned her head back towards the King. "And what freedom would I have? Could I just return to Enomenos amidst your war?" She shook her head. "Enough of this."

Once more, the statue pulled her attention, walking through the flowers to inspect each angle. When she gained sight of the path back to the main walkway, the blonde guard stood at the entrance, arms crossed with a sneer on her face.

"Is there a problem, Adalyn?" the King asked, stopping behind Marietta.

"Not at all," said the blonde, her voice rougher than Marietta expected. Her gaze raked between the two. "Keyain gave me special instructions to not let her—" she jerked her chin at Marietta "—out of my sight, no matter what orders."

"Head back with the other guards," the King demanded, his hand coming to rest on Marietta's lower back.

Adalyn's eyes shot to the movement. "Perhaps it's best I stay. For Keyain's interest, of course."

Marietta fought the cringe that forced its way into her expression. Adalyn must be part of the Elite Guard, just like Amryth.

"Do not test me today, Adalyn," the King said, a threat underlying his tone. "You're a talented soldier but I will request Ryder for our next outing if this is how you behave."

Adalyn's sneer dropped to a look of annoyance, her eyes rolling with a sigh. "Yes, my King." And with that, she turned and walked down the path.

"I knew she would follow." The King walked past her, his stare focusing on the drakon statue. "She'll tell Keyain about how we almost kissed, which plays into our deal."

Marietta's heart fumbled. How stupid of her to think he actually wanted a kiss. Gods, what was wrong with her?

"What do you think?" he asked.

"Of kissing you?"

The King smiled up at the statue, glancing back at her. "Of the statue."

"Oh," she said, fighting back her embarrassment. "Well, it's fantastic. Everything is so lifelike, and when I placed my hand upon its side, it was as if it shifted."

"Interesting," he said, turning to her. "Do you believe in feyrie tales?"

"I would like to." She paused, staring at him. "Do you?"

"All stories come from some truth."

"And here I thought you were a sensible man."

He laughed at that, a full smile touching his lips. "Come, there's more to see."

Each statue was as thrilling. A hydra with seven heads all tangled together. A couple of griffins, their eagle wings outstretched, beaks crying to the sky, resting on their lion hind legs.

One of the more fascinating statues was the tarandos. The creature was new to Marietta, with its ox size, long hair, intricately curved antlers, and cloven hooves. The King explained it was an herbivore that dwelled in dense forests, like the one that grew in the land Satiros came to occupy. What Marietta found the most fascinating was its ability to camouflage itself by shapeshifting.

"Shapeshifters are common in feyrie tales," Marietta told the King. "My father often told me stories around changelings and their ilk."

"Odd, they weren't that common." The King stared at her with a frown. "Perhaps your father had some fascination with them."

For a moment, Marietta felt a touch of anger in the King's words. It quickly passed as they stepped to the next statue, a sphinx. With the head of a woman, the wings of a bird, and a body of a lion. Her father shared the stories of such cunning creatures who would kill those who could not solve their riddles.

The morning slipped into the afternoon as they wove their way through the gardens. "It's impressive how much you know," Marietta noted. "Not only did you have a name for each statue's creature, but you knew what they did."

The King huffed a laugh. "You mock me."

"Not at all." Marietta searched his face, his gaze dropping from hers. "Your knowledge is fascinating. I could listen to you and your theories every day."

"Then you're kind-hearted," he said. "Often I'm too analytical, too cold because I see the world as it is, for how it works."

"And yet here you are, believing in feyrie tales."

"As I said, there's truth to every story." He paused in the path, brushing a loose hair back from Marietta's face though the guards approached. "And because I seek the truth, it's seen as a distraction from my duties as king."

Seek the truth. King Wyltam's words brought forth an image of Therypon, the goddess' orders. Heat flared in her chest at the thought. How likely was it that the King would say those exact words?

"Are you alright?" he asked.

"Of course," she said, letting the comparison slip away. "But are these feyrie tales why you ignore the living conditions of pilinos in Satiros? You'd rather explore that than change the laws that suppress people like me?"

The King's features darkened, his stare fixed on the path ahead.

"Truth for a truth, King Wyltam," she continued in his silence. "Tell me why you could defend me but not the pilinos population?"

"I think I'll pass today," he said, his movement becoming rigid as the guards assumed their proximity. "You've already shared all I wish to know."

"Such a change in mood," she said under her breath so the guards wouldn't hear.

"Everyone has their reasons for their actions, Marietta," he said under his breath. "Perhaps you understand less than you let on."

"Perhaps I'd know more if I had my freedom."

"Enough." The commanding tone of his voice made Marietta clench her fists. "We've had such a lovely morning; no point in spoiling it now."

Silence settled between them as they returned to the carriage, both remaining so for the ride back to the palace. After an enjoyable morning, the mood shift between them was nearly suffocating in the carriage. Marietta couldn't wait to be free of his presence.

Sure, she wanted to know what it was like to kiss him, to feel his body against hers; but even with his apt knowledge of fey creatures and saying she's too good for Keyain, the King was dangerous. Yet, as she stared at the King pondering out the carriage window, she found her hate replaced with something else.

Something she wouldn't dare name.

Chapter Sixty-One

ELYSE

First came the flashing lights, the crescent-shaped bow of lightning and bright white lines in Elyse's vision, the room around her shifting in a disorienting manner. Then came the muscle weakness, her slurred speech, and body so heavy that she couldn't move. The handmaid tried to help Elyse to the bed, but they only made it to the couch from her study.

That was two days prior.

Still curled up on the couch, a servant lifted another cup of water to Elyse's mouth, goading her to drink. When the water reached her stomach, nausea roiled again, and the liquid came back up. The throbbing on the side of her head was excruciating, the effort of vomiting making it worse. The handmaid said something about getting a doctor, but Elyse didn't want one. She didn't want to take Choke.

Even with the drapes drawn over the living room windows, the morning light was still too bright for her. The lavender scent of soap was too much, let alone the smell of food. Elyse could keep nothing down as her head pains made a horrid return. It had been years since she had one of that severity.

She told the handmaid that the head pains would pass. And it was true—they would. But the longer Elyse went without eating or drinking water, the worse they grew. Perhaps she should take Choke. Perhaps losing control of herself was worth more of the pain; yet, every time the handmaid insisted, Elyse turned her down.

Elyse had been studying magic in her suite's office when it first

hit. After weeks of steady practice, she could draw aithyr to her body consistently. With the help of Wyltam's books, she could perform small magical feats. Creating wind, moving objects across the room, and heating her tea were all second nature to her at that point, but that was before Elyse lost a couple of days of practice.

With sleep being nothing more than brief moments of unconsciousness and a slight reprieve from the pain, Elyse spent the last two days fretting about falling behind, about not practicing her mental exercises. The head pain needed to subside soon.

During one of her moments of brief unconscious relief, a quiet knock sounded on her suite door, followed by someone entering. Odd, considering the handmaid didn't bother knocking the past day.

"Oh, Elyse," whispered a voice, a broad male body approaching in her fuzzy vision. Sylas' face took form as he knelt next to her. "Keyain said your head pains came back. Do you trust me? I have something to help—something that isn't Choke."

Elyse tried to speak, but her mouth felt foreign, like she had never spoken before. The left side of her head throbbed as she tried to nod.

A moment later, a glass vial pressed against her lips, the contents runny and sweet filling her mouth and throat, causing her to gag. Sylas held Elyse's head, brushing back her hair, hushing her. The pain eased, as did Elyse's mind as she drifted off to sleep.

Elyse woke in her bed, the curtains drawn around the four posters covering her in darkness. She sat up, and though she was dizzy, the pain in her head disappeared.

Because of Sylas.

Her legs wobbled as she stood, blood rushing to her head with the effort. When she looked down, Elyse noticed that someone had finally changed her clothes. A simple white tunic and soft, tight pants were preferable when she studied alone in her room. The handmaid must have changed her.

The central room of the suite grew dark with the setting sun, the only light coming from the study. Elyse approached to find Sylas sitting at her desk, looking through her notes.

"Sylas," she choked out, her voice raw from vomiting and thirst.

He turned around, worry knotting his brows. "Are you feeling better?"

She nodded and gestured to her desk. "What are you doing? Why are you here?" Sylas owed her nothing. Elyse was thankful for his help, but playing messenger between her and Brynden was already a burden—taking care of Elyse shouldn't be another.

Gods, the last time she saw Sylas, she cast him away because of his date with Lydia; yet, there he was. He came to help.

"I looked for you the past couple of days to drop off Brynden's letter," he said, standing up from the desk and facing Elyse. "After the library study remained empty, I had a moment to talk to Keyain. He mentioned that your head pains returned. I convinced him I could help, and he let me into your suite—with guards posted outside, of course."

"Thank you," she said, pulling at the hem of her shirt. "But why are you still here?" Elyse bit inside of her cheek, the words coming harsher than she meant.

"I wouldn't leave you alone," he said with a smile tugging at his lips. "I wasn't sure how you'd react to the drugs, but they seem to have worked." Sylas paused, turning to pull the papers on her desk. "Sorry for looking at your notes—curiosity got the better of me. Your drawings are incredible, Elyse. How far have you gotten?"

In her tired state, she wasn't sure if she could do magic. With a deep breath, she cleared her mind and attempted. A gentle gust of wind blew past Sylas' head, earning a surprised look.

"Is someone mentoring you?" he asked with furrowed brows.

Elyse leaned against the doorway, the magic stealing what little energy she had. "Not exactly. Someone provided the readings, but I've been doing the mental exercises and reaching out to aithyr on my own."

Sylas shook his head, looking back down at the notes. "We're heading back to Chorys Dasi in a couple of weeks. If you have made it this far with your own practice and materials offered here, then you should stay in Satiros."

"That's still my plan."

Sylas studied her face, her clothes, her slumped posture against the door. "Brynden will try to convince you to join us. He'll try to make it work. If he does, you shouldn't throw this away." Sylas held up her notes. "I might be Brynden's friend, but I know him and what he acts like. Despite the head pains, you look better—comfortable in your own skin. Don't let him take it away."

"Why are you so nice to me?" she asked, pushing off the doorway, turning towards the living room. "Especially after the Lydia comment."

Sylas laughed and followed her. "You were right about her being the worst." His hand fell on her shoulder. "Friends warn each other, even if it isn't what they want to hear."

Elyse turned to him, staring up into his face. Broad chested, Sylas was thicker than Brynden but still taller, and with his usual scowl, he looked like he was carved from stone—solid. But his face softened, a smile hooking his lips. What blossomed between them was friendship, and with them leaving in a few weeks, it wouldn't give it enough time to take root.

That evening would be one of their last to see each other, the thought making her chest ache. If given the time, perhaps Sylas could have been her friend like Marietta. "Will you stay and eat with me?"

"A chance to dine alone in your suite? Absolutely," Sylas said, his smile settling into a smirk. "It'll drive Brynden crazy."

At the old table in her suite's common area, Elyse sat across from Sylas. Though it was just them, Elyse felt at ease as they slipped into conversation.

Servants had delivered a meal of steamed fish with lemon, vegetables with chickpeas, crusty bread, olives, and boiled eggs. Elyse ate heartily after days of nothing. Sylas stared at her with curiosity.

"I thought you didn't eat meat," he said, gesturing to the fish.

"I don't. Steamed fish is all I can stomach." That was the truth. "I can't stand the flavor of anything roasted or burnt, so apologies for the steamed everything."

"A peculiar diet," he teased. "Are you as picky with all your food?"

"I'm not picky," she said defensively. "There's a reason I can't stomach it."

"Enlighten me then."

Elyse hesitated. "Do you promise not to tell Brynden? The reason is quite morbid."

Sylas laughed as he took a bite. "First dining alone and now sharing secrets? I would love to keep it from him as payment for playing his nursemaid."

Elyse snorted a laugh. Then the humor died in her throat, her tone growing series. "You seem to know of my mother."

"I do."

"How much do you know of her death?"

Sylas' smile dropped, his gaze studying her. "She deteriorated physically, and then took her own life."

Elyse nodded, feeling her throat tighten. "And I was the one to find her at the base of the tower."

Blood drained from Sylas' face, his sympathy knitting his features. Elyse couldn't stand the sight of it, so she focused on pushing around the food on her plate. "My father made me stand at her funeral pyre until her body was nothing but ash. Do you know how long it takes for a body to burn?" She glanced at him, then back at the table. "Five hours."

Sylas set down his fork, his full attention placed on her.

"My father told me to watch, to see what became of my mother because of magic. He told me if I were ever to practice, then that would be my future—that I would be someone's burden and eventually reduced to ash." Elyse swallowed hard at the memory. "The smell, Sylas. It was too close to meat. I couldn't..." her voice tapered off.

Sylas offered her his hand across the table. She hesitated but placed her own in his—a silent comfort. Tears were quick to fall from her eyes.

"Though my father isn't a very traditional male, I was to wear the traditional mourning veil through the burning. He also made me wear it for the mourning period after, not allowing me to have it washed." Elyse's voice guttered, and Sylas squeezed her hand. "He said the scent that clung to my veil was my reminder of what my future could be. Ever since then, anything burnt or roasted or of meat brings back those memories."

Sylas rubbed his thumb across her knuckles, considering his words. "No one deserves what you went through, Elyse. Trauma builds on trauma, and you carry that with you every day. Despite the horrors your father has brought onto you, you still have the will to study magic, to gain your independence, and those prove you're more resilient than anyone I've ever known."

"Like a raw diamond," she murmured, remembering Brynden's words from the townhouse.

"That's not a bad comparison," Sylas said, running his free hand through the curls of his hair. "I'm surprised to hear you make such a reference."

"Brynden told me I was a raw diamond—that I'm resilient and full of potential."

Sylas stared for a moment, then released her hand and resumed eating. "Of course he did. He isn't wrong. Have you ever seen a raw diamond?"

"No," she admitted.

Sylas laughed, swallowing a bite. "The reference is specific. Raw diamonds are unrefined, neither shaped nor polished. The lands I lord over are in the mountains of Chorys Dasi, and my people mine the black and white diamonds for the city-state's export."

Elyse forced herself to eat once more, happy for the change in subject. "I assumed you were just an emissary."

"I'm a lot of things," he said with a shrug. "I've made myself useful in Chorys Dasi. When I'm away at court or working for the Queen, my sister picks up my slack. Though we bring in much gold from mining diamonds, our population is quaint and easier to manage." A smile came to his lips as he thought.

"You love it there," she noted, smiling to herself.

"I do. I miss the fresh air and pine scent of the mountains. When I have free time, I hike up to the waterfalls, sleeping out under the stars in the summer."

Pine scent—she tilted her head. "Is that why you smell like pine? Because it reminds you of home?"

Sylas went still. "What do you mean?"

Elyse ripped a chunk of bread as she remembered back to the day in the townhouse. "When you tied my dress, I smelled amber and pine cologne on you."

His brows raised as he forced a laugh. "Correct, which is why I wear it. Every time I leave my family's lands, I count down the days until I can return to the mountains."

"The mountains must be beautiful," she said wistfully. "Perhaps I could visit you one day."

"If you can leave this palace, then of course." Sylas shifted back in his chair, his arm resting atop the empty seat next to him. "Do you wish to leave Satiros still?"

A complicated question. "I do, but I may have found a way to leave on occasion." Visiting the other courts on behalf of King Wyltam would at least get her out of Satiros.

"Would you like to leave for forever?" Sylas set down his fork, his expression growing serious.

"I don't think marrying Brynden is a good idea."

"There's another option," he said, raising a brow. "I offer my hand to you if you wish to be free of here."

Her silverware dropped with a clatter to her plate. "What?"

"Hear me out," he said, holding up his hands. "Not for any nefarious reason, but simply so you have a chance to be free."

"I—what?" Elyse took a steadying breath, attempting to wrap her head around the idea.

"Be warned that being married wouldn't prevent Brynden from pursuing a relationship, so also take that into consideration." Sylas shifted in his chair, his lips pulling into a frown. "Regardless if you want to be with him, he will fight for you."

"But you just said that I should stay in Satiros to study," she said, exasperated. "Now you're asking me to marry you?"

"I said that you should stay in Satiros if Brynden tried to change your mind," Sylas said, dropping his arm to lean forward. "No matter what promise he makes, there is no guarantee that he can marry you. But if you wished to leave, by your choice alone, if you wish to visit Chorys Dasi and see the mountains, if you want to escape this city-state, then I offer you a chance to be free."

"And what about studying magic?"

Sylas huffed a dry laugh. "If you haven't caught on," he said, raising his hand. "I'm a mage, Elyse. I would teach you, though I have fewer resources and time." A gust of air blew gently across her face from his hand.

Elyse stared at him, pulling her thoughts together as she remembered Sylas walking her through magic at the townhouse, or him looking at her notes. If he was an emissary but also a mage…. "Are you a spy?" Her eyes were wide as she pushed her chair back. Was Sylas what Wyltam wanted her to become?

"What?" he said, a scowl coming to his face. "What made you think that?"

"You said you're an emissary and a mage—you're capable of magic."

"So is Brynden, though he doesn't excel at it, not enough to be considered a mage. Oryck is competent, too," he shook his head, laughing. "Satiros is the only court where the lords and ladies don't study magic, don't learn to control aithyr. King Wyltam's mother was a paranoid ruler."

"You would teach me?" Elyse could have an alternative to Wyltam's plan.

"If that's what you want," Sylas said, leaning back. "I figured out who's guiding your lessons. Though it's a closely guarded secret, I know how talented King Wyltam was when he was younger, when the Circle of Mages still met."

"What's the Circle of Mages? And you shouldn't know that about the King," she whispered.

"It's alright; I won't even tell Brynden." Sylas considered her for a moment. "It was smart of him, considering your mother's skill. You have a raw talent that goes wasted, and with the right training, you could surpass your mother. The King understands what happened to her as well, so he'll be aware of the signs if aithyr affects your mind."

"How do you know all of this? Why are you offering to help me?" Elyse shook her head.

Sylas was silent a moment before sitting forward and resting both his arms on the table. "The Circle of Mages was a group dedicated to studying aithyr and overseeing the ethical practices of magic. About a century and a few decades ago, the group disbanded. Your mother was a member, as was the King."

"I never knew that," Elyse said, attempting to remember her father ever mentioning such a thing. "How did you learn this?"

"I was in the Circle of Mages before they joined—before I had more responsibilities in Chorys Dasi."

Before they joined? "Sylas," she said, gripping the arms of her chair, "how old are you?"

"Older than I appear," he said, frowning. "Older than both King Wyltam and your mother."

"Yet you're friends with Brynden, who is young."

Sylas stared at her, saying nothing.

Because Brynden wasn't young.

"But he's younger than my father," she said, panic rising in her throat. Oh, gods, she knew nothing of him. "Both of you seem younger than him—I don't understand."

Sylas sighed. "People assume we're younger than we are. Brynden didn't wish to tell you and you never asked for his age."

No, she didn't. What else didn't she ask? How close was she to marrying a stranger?

"I told him to be honest with you," Sylas added. "He told me he wasn't lying, just omitting the truth."

"I know nothing about him," she said, her throat tightening. "I'm a gods damned idiot." Elyse cradled her head in her hands.

"Hey," Sylas said, drawing her gaze between her fingers, "you're not an idiot—never say that about yourself. Brynden intentionally misinforming you does not make you idiotic."

"But not asking is idiotic," she retorted with a sigh, slumping back into her chair.

"I would argue it's ignorant—" she shot him a glare "—something you learn with the more people you meet. It's not like you've had the best guidance."

Elyse stared at the plate of half-eaten food before her. Sylas, who was older than her parents—older than the King, offered to marry her, after Brynden, who was just as old, had wanted to marry her. A different kind of pain formed in her head. "What else don't I know, Sylas?"

"What do you mean?"

"You Chorys Dasians, what are you hiding?"

"Nothing, Elyse."

"There are too many things—me having a scent, your age, his mysterious family making all the decisions for him." The food settled in her stomach like a rock, suddenly feeling sick once more.

"That's a dangerous line of thinking, and one I suggest you don't go down." Sylas stared down at his shirt, picking something off it. "I'm guessing it's a no to my proposal then."

Elyse gave him an exasperated sigh. "Of course, it's a no!"

Sylas looked up with a smile. "Good, that means you're learning." Elyse glared at him as he pulled a paper from his pocket. "Now I can give you this last letter from Brynden."

Elyse yanked it out of his hand and left it unopened before her. Did she want to read what he wrote? Gods, did she even want to see him again? Brynden was a stranger—he was her humiliation.

Reluctantly, she opened it.

To see the body of a goddess makes me a lucky male. To forever have it immortalized by her hand makes me blessed. Your talent knows no bounds, and you have entangled my heart in ways I could never free myself. I have no dreams of that release and would suffocate on your love if given the chance. Death by your hand would be the sweetest ending.

My goddess, my darling, Elyse, you have me now and you will have me always, regardless of if you ever forgive me for my transgressions. A male who has sinned against a goddess deserves the torment he brought onto himself, and I am a male who suffers. The thought of losing you, to never hold your talented hands, to kiss the sweetness of your lips, is torture.

What keeps me up late into the night is a single thought, however: a lifetime of opportunities we will miss if we are not together. The missed opportunity of having you at my side. The missed opportunity to watch you grow into your full power. The missed opportunity to worship at your temple every day. There is nothing I wouldn't do to have you as mine, my goddess. I would tear down the world around us if it meant keeping you by my side.

My time in Satiros nears its end, and I have no wish to leave you behind. Refuse me as you must, but don't allow yourself the continued suffering of this cursed place. Though I hate the idea with such a seething rage and burning pride, I ask you to consider an alternate marriage. It threatens my very existence, the thought of you marrying my closest friend, but I would endure millennia of pain if it meant you would feel none.

At this point, I'm sure Sylas has made the offer. Elyse, my goddess, I ask you not to make your decision now, for I understand it is jarring. But the gods may have their eye on you—we will get one last evening together before I go. Through the work of Keyain and his wife, we will journey into the streets of Satiros under their watchful eyes. Though I loathe him, I would take any chance I had to be with you. Any. Until then, my dreams will be of you in gowns of Chorys

Dasian red with black and white diamonds at your neck. Of sunny walks holding your hand along the shores of The Mavros Sea. Of you in my arms, where you belong.

Elyse squeezed her eyes closed, unable to stare at the letter. It was Brynden—every bit of him she knew—baring all for her. "You told me all of that on purpose. His age, his sister, all of it because you figured it'd end like this."

"No, I thought this would end with Brynden breaking into the palace and stealing you."

Elyse paled at the comment. Brynden wouldn't do that, would he?

"He cares about you in ways I haven't seen with the others," Sylas continued. "He refused to leave Satiros without you, so a marriage to me was his solution."

Her heart paused, unable to take a breath as his words hit her. "The others?"

Sylas watched her for a moment, his eyes shifting around her face. "He's courted females prior to you, though only betrothed once."

He might as well have slapped her. "So, I was never his first choice."

"Elyse," Sylas said, pulling her gaze. "They were a very long time ago, before you were born. As I said, he was only serious about one of them, and even then it was nothing like what he feels for you."

She nodded her head, fighting the constriction of her throat as tears threatened her eyes. Stupid. So stupid to think she was someone special to him. "What happened to her?"

"To who?"

"The female was betrothed to. Why didn't they marry?" she paused, taking a deep breath. "Or did they marry?"

Sylas rubbed his chin with a sigh, looking anywhere but at Elyse. "Simi died when they were still betrothed."

Sadness struck her heart at the thought of loving someone to only have them die. "How tragic."

"Listen, he should've told you this, not me," Sylas said. "He didn't have much time to tell you about it, so don't be angry."

Anger wasn't the right way to describe how she felt. Disappointed. Foolish. Sorrowful. Those feelings washed over her as she watched Sylas.

His expression was soft, concern furrowing his brows. "Please share what you're thinking, Elyse. I don't like seeing you like this."

She hesitated, unsure what to say. "I feel humiliated." Tears trailed down her cheek as she tried to blink them away, staring at the ceiling. "For the first time in my life, I felt like I was special to someone. I felt—" her breath caught, stalling her words. "I felt like I wasn't alone. That I had a future. And now, I realize how foolish I've been."

"The fool isn't the partner who was tricked, but the partner who intended to deceive. He could've told you when he offered his hand, but instead he..." Sylas' voice trailed off, letting the implication sit.

"He tried to fuck me."

"I mean," Sylas said, brushing back the hair from his face, "that he did. It didn't change his decision, though. Even now, he wants you, Elyse. He wants to fight for you. Just know this: you are special without him. You are more important, more powerful by yourself than he is without you. Don't let him make you think otherwise, even for a second."

Elyse swallowed hard, taking in his words.

"Brynden is a lot of things, but he will always be the fool, not you." He lifted his chin as he regarded her.

The tears started anew. Sylas barely knew her, but she believed each word from his mouth, believed that he meant it. Such truth made her heart swell. "But he's your friend."

"That doesn't mean I'll sit by and watch you degrade your self-worth over a fool." A smile hooked his lips. "If you don't accept my offer of marriage—which there's no need to answer now and no pressure to accept—then I hope you consider dinner with him, Keyain, and Marietta."

She laughed mirthlessly. "Why would I entertain such an idea?"

"Because you deserve the closure." Sylas took her hand in his. "And you deserve to enjoy yourself. Let Brynden dote on you for one last night before you say goodbye."

True enough, it would be enjoyable. Marietta and Brynden together would be entertaining, to say the least. She thought back to Marietta, discussing which lines of Brynden's letter would make Keyain the most uncomfortable. It brought a smile to her face as she laughed.

"What is it?" Sylas asked.

"I think going just to watch how Marietta and Brynden interact would be reason enough."

Sylas huffed at that. "I'm sad I'm going to miss it. Marietta seems like she's fun."

"She is." Elyse hesitated and added, "I'm happy to call her my friend."

Sylas nodded with a smile, glancing down at the table. "Did he gift you anything by chance? When you two were still courting?"

"Yes, a necklace of black and white diamonds."

"Bring a gift the day you see him—don't be indebted to him, okay?"

"But it was a gift—"

"Nothing is as it first seems, Elyse," Sylas warned. "Trust me. Bring something of equal value. If you need money, I can help."

Elyse narrowed her eyes. "But then I'd be indebted to you."

A full smile cracked on his face. "A quick learner. But Brynden anticipates a reply. I can come by in—"

"Or I can give it to you right now," she said, standing up and going to her desk. A moment later, she returned with a folded paper, handing it to Sylas.

With furrowed brows, he opened it and laughed. "As I said, you're a quick learner."

Sylas stood from the table, pocketing the drawing. Elyse's emotion scattered as she followed, keeping her gaze to the floor. Sylas and Brynden were hiding something—beyond Brynden's former partners. Something didn't sit right, but at least she'd get one last chance to question Brynden before he left.

"One more thing before I go," Sylas said, carrying over a clinking wooden case. Inside were rows of glass vials of various colors and sizes. "The top three rows are for head pains—at the first sign, take a quarter of the vial. If the pain persists, finish the bottle." Sylas took out a vial from the last row. The contents were dark and amber-hued. "This is a liquid form of Mage's Eye—highly potent and concentrated. You only need a few drops."

"Sylas, I can't take this—this is too much."

"Not for the favor I'm going to ask," he said with a smile.

Nerves knotted in her stomach. Of course, there was a catch.

Sylas pulled out a scrap of paper with lines of text scribbled on it. "I don't have time to search the library here for these texts—can you find them for me when you have a moment? Preferably in secret?"

Elyse took the paper, reading the names.

Goodnight Feyries: Bedtime Stories from Feyrie Tales.
Statues and Sculptures of Syllogi.
Beyond the Tefra Forest: An Outsider's Guide to The Disputed Lands.
Aithyr and Air.
History of the Fey.
Myths & Legends of the Akroi Region.
Fulbryk's Guide to Chorys Dasi.

"I'll try, but I'm not sure if I'll find them all within two weeks." The library was extensive, and not having the librarians' help would slow the search.

"That's alright, just find what you can." He turned away to head to the door but paused. "Prioritize finding *Fulbryk's Guide to Chorys Dasi.*" Sylas looked over his shoulder with a conflicted stare.

"Okay," she said. "Sylas, thank you for everything."

He shrugged, placing his hands in his pocket. "It was nothing. I'm happy I had the time with you."

Elyse couldn't help but smile. Sylas scowled, rolled his eyes, and pretended not to care—but he did. She closed the space between them, throwing her arms around him. The amber and pine scent consumed her, causing her to think of his home in the mountains of Chorys Dasi.

Sylas embraced her, his chin resting on her head. For a moment, they stood there and Elyse sighed into him, happy to have stopped crying. He pulled away, cupping her face. "I'll find you before we leave, so this isn't goodbye yet."

She nodded and dropped her arms, letting Sylas go to the door.

He looked over his shoulder one last time. "And remember, bring Brynden a gift."

Her head spun with the information that dinner yielded hours after Sylas left. One thing had become clear to her: she knew very little. Very little of Brynden, of her mother, of the world around her. It was heartbreaking to think that she had lived almost three decades but missed so much. Perhaps she should consider Sylas' proposal, since living in Satiros had been a disappointment in that regard. But then there was the King. If her mother had trained him, then he had her best interests at heart, right? Gods, maybe he didn't. She knew so little of her mother before she passed. Her mental state already deteriorated by the time Elyse was old enough to comprehend what was happening.

What hurt the most was Brynden's truth. He was significantly older than her and failed to mention his previous betrothal. Though she supposed he didn't owe her anything to share such a heartbreaking tale. Who was Simi? Why did she die, and was Brynden still in love with her? The questions haunted Elyse late into the night.

Chapter Sixty-Two
MARIETTA

Marietta tried the desk drawer every day, hoping Keyain slipped up again; yet, he didn't. She wished to explore more of his files, to see if anything else would be useful. The documents she stole were nestled deep in her wardrobe with the nymph dagger, waiting for the next time she'd meet with Valeriya.

Though she's had no luck with the drawer, she's managed glimpses of papers and file names while tangling herself in Keyain's arms every morning, asking him to stay. All lies, of course, but he didn't realize that. Every morning he acted as though he was heartbroken to be leaving her each day, but he enjoyed the begging, especially after the incident in the gardens with King Wyltam.

The guard, Adalyn, had seen enough of Wyltam's actions that Keyain insisted she shared every detail about the garden. When she got to the part of their almost kiss, Keyain lost control of his temper, leaving the suite so Marietta wouldn't see. When he returned later with a calmer mood, Marietta pestered him until he admitted to hunting down King Wyltam and working out his frustrations. Did that mean he hit the King? She wasn't sure, but it thrilled her to know the plan worked.

So, she played the part of the doting wife, of needing one last kiss, of wanting one more minute with him. Keyain was wrapped around her finger and didn't notice her glances at his files. The information she gleaned wasn't much. Just file names labeled *TRM-Exp* followed by a series of numbers. A few files mention Notos. It wasn't solid, but perhaps they planned to target the southern city next.

It became her new obsession, waking up early with Keyain each morning and playing that game. Her attitude softened him enough that he had arranged for a day in the city with Elyse and Brynden. She was excited to meet Elyse's fervent worshiper and to switch up her dragging routine. Even with the expansive sprawl of the Central Gardens, she could only take so many walks before they grew tedious. Fortunately, Valeriya invited her for tea once again. Sitting in a room for hours with the Queen's Court wasn't her ideal fun, but she would accept whatever break in the routine she could get.

Donned in an olive green off-the-shoulder dress with jeweled flowers lining the neckline, Marietta felt prepared for tea with the ladies, yet she still complained. "They're just going to gossip about people I don't know."

"Well, what did you expect?" Amryth laughed beside her in her guard's uniform, escorting her through the halls of the Royal's Wing.

Golden sunlight shone through the tall windows of the hall as they walked. Even after a few months in the palace, Marietta still felt uncomfortable next to its grandeur. Amethyst inlaid floors, gold-gilded pillars, and silk tapestries hanging from the walls were things unaccustomed to her.

"I don't know—perhaps a riveting conversation that doesn't involve insulting people for two hours?"

"You can check the guards with me instead."

Marietta laughed, swatting the air. "Can you imagine how upset Keyain would be if he heard we did that?"

Amryth cut her a quick smile. "Oh, he'd be furious with us."

"I'd rather deal with a furious Keyain than tactless peacocks for two hours," Marietta said as they reached the grand staircase that had thick green carpet running down its middle. At the top, a few ladies of the Queen's Court lingered in the hall, catching sight of Marietta.

"Too late to turn back now," Amryth said with a nod towards the ladies.

"Gods, I don't want to go up there. I don't recognize anyone." Marietta stood on her tiptoes to see who arrived. "This is why I didn't prefer to be fifteen minutes early."

"If you're not early, you're late," Amryth said with a shrug.

"If you're late, you're fashionable. And you don't have to have forced awkward conversations with clucking hens."

Amryth laughed, shoving her hands into her pockets. "How Keyain traveled with you in Enomenos is beyond me."

"Hey, I kept to his schedule," Marietta said, batting her arm. "Well, most of the time anyway." From down the hall, Elyse poked her head around a corner. "Thank gods, Elyse. Wait—where is she going?"

As soon as she appeared, she darted back out of sight. Like hells, she would sit through tea without her, especially if she had gotten any more of those letters. "Come on," she said, pulling along Amryth.

"Elyse!" Gods, she walked fast. "Elyse, it's Marietta." That got her to spin on the spot, her eyes wide.

"Oh, sorry about that." She found a rogue lock of hair to play with that fell from her knot.

"Cute dress," Marietta said, leaning to see it from the side. The flowy black material hugged through her chest and waist but loosened on her legs, ending above her ankles to show a pair of green embroidered slippers. Peculiar, she hasn't seen other ladies wear such a style. "And I love the shoes."

"You think so?" she asked, looking down at herself. "I thought it was a mistake, so I—"

"Went to go change? Nonsense, you look stunning. Plus, you can't leave me up there all alone."

Elyse hesitated. "I can't go—I can't deal with the embarrassment."

Marietta exchanged a glance with Amryth. "What do you mean?"

"I haven't been to tea since the very short betrothal with Brynden and the emancipation from my father. Grytaine will be more unbearable than usual."

Marietta snorted, looping her arm through Elyse's. "If she says anything, I'll toss it back at her. After all, she's married to an elderly man, and you had a dashing, young foreign lord writing you smutty letters after the betrothal ended. Let her say something. I'd love to mention that."

Elyse turned wide-eyed towards Amryth.

"Oh, I forgot to introduce you two—"

"We've met," Elyse murmured. "Keyain introduced us years ago."

"Then why that face?" Marietta asked, gesturing to her expression.

"Because it's embarrassing to talk about that letter when Keyain is like a brother to me and Amryth works for him."

"It's alright," Amryth said with a crooked smile. "The other day, I walked in on Marietta with just about no clothes on after a sensual night with Keyain. I didn't even blink."

"Oh, my gods," Elyse said, clenching her eyes as her face turned red. "I don't want to think about Keyain having sex."

Marietta snorted, pulling her down the hallway back towards the stairs. "You were with him for five years. What did you two do during that time, if not sex?"

"It was never like that," she said, grabbing Marietta's arm.

Marietta caught Amryth's bemused grin. "It's alright. Even if you did, it wouldn't be your fault. You didn't know I existed." Marietta didn't even know she was married to Keyain. "So, what did you do when you spent time together?"

"Read most of the time, though Keyain's books were boring," she said, a smile cracking her face. "Who wants to read about war tactics when they're not working?"

"Thank you!" Marietta raised her free arm for emphasis. "I told you, Amryth! Keyain has the worst taste in books."

Amryth chuckled, shaking her head. "As if I don't also enjoy those books."

"I'd always bring my own," Elyse said. "Two—to make sure I wouldn't need to borrow one."

"And were they smutty like that lovely little letter?" Marietta asked, teasing with her brows flicking up and down.

"I should ask Keyain to select some more smutty books for the suite," Amryth said with a sly grin. "Maybe then you'll make it more than two paragraphs before daydreaming."

"I can make it more than two."

"Two and a half." Amryth gave Elyse an unimpressed look that caused her to laugh.

"That's still more than two." Marietta smiled, the warmth flaring in her chest. "How did you ever respond to that letter? I've been dying to know."

"Well," Elyse said, hesitating with her cheeks still red. "I may have drawn a portrait of myself. Topless."

Marietta whooped with delight. "Elyse, I don't know if Brynden could handle such an image of his goddess. His guided hands will be doing a lot of nightly prayers."

"His what?" Amryth stopped, bent over from laughing. "Does that male seriously call you the goddess?"

Elyse smiled through her blush as she told Amryth the story at the bottom of the staircase. Marietta, of course, chimed in with quotes about his effective ways of praying.

"Gods, I'm going to have to stand guard over you four when you go into the city." Amryth shook her head.

"I didn't even think about that," Marietta said with a laugh. "Do you think you can hold a straight face when I ask Brynden about his prayer schedule in front of Keyain?"

They busted out laughing, paying no mind to the other waiting ladies—or the lack thereof.

"Ladies," Queen Valeriya called. Marietta turned to see her standing at the top of the stairs with a smile. "Teatime is about to start."

Chapter Sixty-Three

VALERIYA

To think the two have grown so close in just a few short months. Though Valeriya wished to be a part of that friendship, her time would come when she set her new court. With Elyse's strength as a mage and having Marietta remain as a lady well after Keyain was removed, she would have that time to bond with them. In the meantime, it excited her to watch the two together—proof that Satiros could blend like Reyila.

Tryda sat across from Valeriya, much to her displeasure. Technically, she was her Lady-In-Waiting, but she couldn't stand the female. When she first arrived in Satiros, Tryda had advised how Queen Olytia ruled, thinking Valeriya would follow suit. Never had someone been so off base.

Valeriya instead turned her attention to Marietta and Elyse once more. Marietta would lean over every once in a while and whisper something to Elyse that would make her laugh. In the years that Elyse had been on the Queen's Court, she had never looked so comfortable. She couldn't help but smile.

"Queen Valeriya?" Tryda said, placing a hand on her forearm.

"Apologies," she said, tearing her gaze away from the pair. "My mind often wanders these days. Can you repeat that?"

"Of course, your grace," said Grytaine, flicking her blonde hair over her shoulder. "Do you think you and the King will try for a second child?"

Valeriya's smile became forced. "With the war efforts going on, not anytime soon." Or ever. Mycaub was all she ever needed.

"A shame," Grytaine said with a frown that didn't match the glint in her eye. "And what of you, Marietta? Has the war stopped you and Keyain

from trying for a child?"

Marietta coughed on her tea, her eyes wide. Valeriya knew her answer, understood how much Marietta hated Keyain. Valeriya smirked over the rim of her teacup.

"Oh, well, I would be lying if I said there hadn't been opportunities." Marietta flashed a grin with a flick of her brow. "Many opportunities, in fact."

Laughter came from the ladies of the room, but Valeriya paused. She hadn't considered pregnancy when she met with Marietta and told her to seduce Keyain essentially. The idea of Marietta having a child with Keyain nauseated her. It would not differ from her and Wyltam.

"Well," Grytaine answered, her hand falling to her abdomen, "if you keep that up and find yourself with child soon, we would be expecting around the same time."

"Oh, Grytaine!" cried Tryda with a clap of her hands. "That is so exciting! Congratulations. I'm sure you and Royir are excited."

Valeriya smiled and said her best wishes, but knew it was just one of many children Royir now possessed, though most were illegitimate. Poor Grytaine.

Apparently, she wasn't the only one to have thoughts about the announcement. Valeriya's focus narrowed on Marietta, who whispered to Elyse again. The two stifled their laughter while Grytaine and the ladies spoke of the pregnancy.

A pang of envy rattled her at the sight, wishing to swap such comments with a friend. Valeriya had been alone in Satiros for so long that she forgot what it was like to have someone like that. Nystanya had always been that person until she married Auryon. She loved Katya deeply, but their relationship didn't replace friendship. Her sister was her first friend, and she assumed it would always be that way.

Valeriya sighed and swallowed her emotions, plastering on a smile for her court. Once she proved herself, Nystanya would come back around regardless of Auryon's presence. They could be sisters once again, making history with one another. Their time would come.

Chapter Sixty-Four

ELYSE

For the first time, Elyse found herself enjoying tea with the ladies. Of course, it was because Marietta whispered her entertaining commentary in Elyse's ear. She couldn't remember a day she laughed so much.

Perhaps the last time was at the Chorys Dasian townhouse. Elyse glanced at Marietta sitting next to her, who half paid attention to what the ladies said. She was unexpected, a friend that Elyse didn't know she could have in Satiros. A smile crept onto her face as Marietta leaned over again. "Gods, we haven't yet gotten to the baked goods and I can't pay attention."

"Perhaps if they were talking about smut, then you'd listen."

"Elyse," Marietta said dramatically, "I am a lady of this court and don't find such foul things entertaining."

Elyse laughed, drawing Grytaine's attention to the other side of Marietta.

"You two seemed to have grown close," she said, her beady gaze narrowing on them. "Elyse, you've missed out on tea a few times now. Unfortunately, we didn't get to ask of your betrothed before that ended, just like your first one."

Heat rose to her face, the words lodging in her throat. Gods, it was just as she thought—

"No, not like her first one." Marietta leaned over, offering a saccharine smile. "Brynden doesn't have a secret wife." She paused, smirking at Grytaine's uncomfortable expression. "And he still writes the most poetic letters to Elyse."

"Oh, is that so?" Grytaine turned her gaze to Elyse with a tight smile.

"It is," she choked out. "Brynden, um, still wishes to marry me."

"Lord Brynden calls her his goddess," Marietta added, waving her hand out in an arc. "To think, so close to marriage but a story riddled with heartache." She snatched her hand back to her chest.

A few ladies nodded at Marietta's words.

"What about you, Marietta?" Grytaine turned the focus away from Elyse. "I heard Keyain had released half the guards into the city after you ran away from the palace. Is everything alright with Keyain?"

"Gods, that," Marietta said, placing her hand on Grytaine's arm. "Communication is a fickle thing, is it not? I had been so ill that my guard needed to take me to the temple for help and the note sent to my husband never reached him."

Grytaine nodded, failing to hide the disgust on her face at Marietta's touch.

"Can you believe how much he loves me?" she continued, speaking to the room. "Sent out half the guard to make sure I was safe."

Her words awed Elyse, the way she flipped Grytaine's attacks. Marietta had the ladies wrapped around her finger, hanging onto every word—even Queen Valeriya.

Where once the Queen would have to step in and save Elyse, she now had a friend who thrived off Grytaine's comments. The idea thrilled her—not having to interact with Grytaine, to fumble on her words. Marietta was on her side and supported her.

"After all this time, he would still go to every length for me. I don't think his heart could handle losing me again." Marietta crossed her hands over her chest as the room offered their replies.

The Queen nodded her head, smiling, almost looking proud. She then looked at Elyse with a wink. Her heart sputtered at the acknowledgment, that something was going right at tea.

Servants interrupted her thoughts by setting a piece of cake in front of her. The brown sponge was sticky, sliced almonds adorning the top. From across the veranda, one lady exclaimed about the cake, and when she took a bite, she had to agree. It tasted sweet and nutty, perfect for summer.

Elyse turned to Marietta, the words dying at her expression. "What's wrong, Marietta?"

She smiled, but tears lined her eyes. "This cake reminds me of home, that's all," she whispered.

Home. Enomenos. Elyse forgot she had lived there for so long. "Well, if this is what your home tastes like, then I hope you'll share more with me. Because this," Elyse said, pointing to the cake with her fork, "is delicious."

The beaming smile on Marietta's face warmed her heart as she nudged Elyse. "I'd love to show you more one day," she said, taking a bite. "There are so many things I wish to tell you, my friend."

My friend.

"But," she continued, "only if you keep showing me those letters from Brynden."

"Gods," Elyse laughed. "You're never going to let me live it down, are you?"

Marietta pointed with her fork as she spoke. "Never."

Chapter Sixty-Five

VALERIYA

Valeriya felt jittery as she waited inside her bedroom. Over the past week, she managed to hold invisibility for ten minutes. It wasn't long enough to get her outside the palace, but it was long enough for her to sneak past whatever mage followed her. At any moment, a servant would arrive and Valeriya would slip out behind them. No one would be the wiser.

She kept Marietta's findings in her pocket. It had been so long since her last drop that she probably had additional information for her, or at least, she hoped. With the mage following her, she thought it would be best to distance herself. Better to not implicate either of them.

Checking the time, Valeriya reached for the aithyr, letting the energy flow up her invisible limbs, and pulled a sizable amount into her, just like she practiced. The aithyr flowed to every inch of her body, the sensation similar to submerging into frozen waters. The process already took its toll on her, threatening to break free at any moment.

She made her way through the common area and to the door to the hallways. As the door opened, the invisible Valeriya slipped past the servant and darted down the hall. Valeriya's focus was on maintaining the encasing magic around her body, hurrying to the Central Garden. The longer she kept it up, the more exhausted she would be.

Down the stairs and out the door of the Royal's Wing, Valeriya didn't feel the sun warm her skin, only the unyielding icy presence of magic. Was it the magic making her cold? Or was it the sun's heat not making contact with her invisible skin? Valeriya had to admit she didn't know how magic

worked at a distilled level. The time to ponder such questions was lost to her.

Valeriya's grip on her invisibility began to slip, feeling the pull against her body. Her breathing turned ragged as she darted through the courtyards and into the garden. As she reached a dense patch of trees to conceal herself, her magic dropped, and she collapsed to the dirt, panting. Though exhausted already, she couldn't help but smile. Conquering a new skill always brought a smile to her face.

However, she had little time to celebrate. There was no telling when the mage could show up, if they knew how to find her at all. That didn't mean they couldn't. It didn't mean that there weren't multiple mages trailing her.

Focusing, she stood and pulled at the aithyr around her once more. If she hurried, she could change into her servant's visage, leave the palace, and return all before anyone realized she was gone. Digging deep within herself, she drew aithyr to her once more. When she opened her eyes, her body appeared as the familiar shape of a serving girl. She strode out onto the path and made her way to the gates and to the city beyond.

Satiros was bright in the summer sun, alive with people going about their business. Valeriya wished to live like them, meandering through the streets without a care in the world. She had never had that luxury, that freedom. She always had a goal or a plan to enact. No one made it into books by sitting around and enjoying themselves.

On the far side of the Halia River in Greening Juncture sat Birdsong Park, the decided drop location. The old oak that she searched for had a hollow facing away from the main path, nestled between two blooming hydrangea bushes.

With a glance to determine she was alone, Valeriya stepped off the path and hid behind the thick trunk of the oak tree. She pulled the papers out of her pocket and slid them into the opening. Her contact would be by soon to pick them up, and she wanted to be far away when they did.

Valeriya sighed in relief when she walked back towards the palace. She handed the information off, her part completed. Soon she wouldn't need to sneak anymore. Wyltam would fall, and the crown would pass to her. It was time to end wars, and to make the pilinos equal citizens under the law. The information she handed off would help ensure that.

It didn't take her long to return to the palace. In the garden, Valeriya dropped her disguise and took a deep breath. She was almost done. Just one last bout of magic and she could breathe. With a shaky pull at the aithyr, she filled herself with the energy and felt the magic shroud her body.

With a hurried pace, she made it to her suite door while shaking once more. If she had the stamina, she would wait to see if anyone came in or out; yet, she didn't. She'd have to gamble that the mage (or mages) following her happened to not be in the hallway. Without another thought, she opened the door and stepped into the suit.

As soon as her invisibility dropped, she noticed Wyltam's voice carrying from his office. Odd. Wyltam never yelled. Valeriya quietly approached the door, listening.

"—couldn't pick up on her trail again?" Wyltam's deep voice rumbled.

"Wyltam, I'm sorry. I wasn't aware that she does that kind of magic, none of us realized—" Wyltam cut off the raspy voice. That must have been the mage following her. Strange that they didn't use his title.

"She doesn't have that level of magic. You messed up. To think I trained you myself."

Valeriya's heart stilled. Wyltam could do magic? How did he keep that hidden?

"I'm sorry, Wyl—"

"Enough. It's too late for apologies." Wyltam cut him off once more. "Don't lose her again. Understood?" Wyltam's voice was demanding, the most kingly Valeriya had ever heard him. Apparently, Wyltam did possess the ability to be a king, but only when it suited him.

Valeriya withdrew from the door, treading down the hall before retiring to her room. Wyltam knew magic. He trained the skilled mage who had been following her. How was she not aware of the threat her husband posed to her? Valeriya assumed Keyain would be the larger issue, but it was clear her husband was a force for which she was not prepared. Wyltam was too much of an unknown. If he sent a mage to trail her, then he had an idea she was doing something. But how much did he know?

Her plan could still work. She could still be queen. Instead of waiting in Satiros for Wyltam's rein to fall, she'd have to take Mycaub and flee.

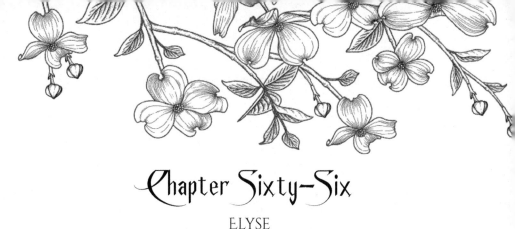

Chapter Sixty-Six

ELYSE

Elyse took a calming breath, remembering the instructions from her studies. *Inhale deeply through the nose and out through the mouth.* She breathed deep, once, twice—over and over until she stood outside the palace gates with Marietta and Keyain. In her hand was a velvet pouch, a present she had Keyain buy on her behalf.

Asking Keyain for help had been embarrassing. He had made it clear he was always there to support Elyse in whatever she needed—he and Marietta both. Though she understood that, she felt guilty about borrowing the coin. Keyain made her promise not to worry about paying him back, but she wanted to be indebted to no one, especially after he paid for a tailor to make a dress for that evening.

What was worse was not knowing what to gift Brynden. Elyse wanted something engraved, but when she had asked Keyain to buy a dagger, he scoffed, saying he wasn't giving an unhinged male a weapon. In the end, she went with Keyain's idea of a new clock that was small, handheld, and ran off of aithyr. Elyse shook her head; she couldn't even find a present for him on her own. Nerves knotted her stomach as her fingers clutched the velvet bag.

An evening in the city should have been thrilling—why did Elyse only feel dread? Perhaps it was the looming answer she'd have to give Brynden, that she wouldn't marry Sylas, that she would remain in Satiros while he returned to Chorys Dasi. A goodbye she never wanted to say.

At the main gate to the palace, Oak Boulevard stretched before her, the street lined with shops, gardens, and pedestrians going about their

day. In the distance, the tall buildings gave way to the winding Halia River.

Elyse only turned back once after realizing Marietta, Keyain, and their guards waited near the gates. Marietta smirked, shooing Elyse ahead. Gods bless her for giving her privacy.

Elyse's breath caught as she noticed Brynden leaning against the carriage. His crooked smile softened into a look of awe as he stood up straight. He'd tied the length of his hair back in a knot, a black shirt dipping low into his abdomen, tucked into black pants with embroidered gold filigree. The outfit brought a smile to her lips. Brynden looked every bit himself.

As Elyse approached, Bryden blinked, his stare roaming her body. "My dreams have come true," he said. "The goddess comes to me in a gown of Chorys Dasian red."

It was a near-replica of what Elyse wore the night they met, silky fabric tight to her frame and a square neckline that emphasized her chest; but instead of black silk, the gown was crimson with the necklace Brynden gifted at her neck.

He opened his arms, wrapping them around Elyse as she stepped into him. Brynden's face nestled into her hair as he inhaled. "You are of another world, my goddess, and I am your most fervent worshiper."

"And you truly are one for poetic proclamations," Elyse said into his chest, careful not to smudge her makeup.

Brynden pulled back to look at her. "If anything, I am dramatic."

"I've heard that before."

He smiled down at her, hand rising to cup her cheek. "May I kiss you?"

"You don't have to ask."

"Well, the last time I kissed you, you were still my betrothed. And this time," Brynden said, kissing her deeply before pulling back, "I don't know what you are."

Elyse let the words hover between them for a moment before revealing the velvet bag.

"What is this?" he asked, taking it.

"A gift."

He shook his head. "Elyse, I needn't a gift."

"Please, just open it."

Brynden hesitated, then undid the drawstring on the pouch, letting the golden metal fall into his hand. No larger than his palm, the outside was smooth metal with a clasp. Brynden pried it open to reveal the glass face of the clock, the twitching hands, and scrollwork numbers. The engraving on the lid pulled his focus, and he read, "*To dream and hope of a future that could never be.*"

His smile faltered, glancing up at Elyse. "This sounds like you've decided."

"Brynden, I—"

He held up his hand, stopping Elyse. "Give me until the end of this evening. Then you decide our fate."

Staring into his wide, hopeful eyes and crooked smile, Elyse didn't have the heart to tell him no. A single evening with Brynden wasn't enough to make up for the lies and it wasn't enough to learn who he was beneath them.

When she hesitated, letting the silence settle between them again, Brynden cleared his throat. "Your drawing led me to believe bringing you to Chorys Dasi was still a possibility. Or should I say lack of drawing?" He kissed her forehead. "My goddess is quite the creative."

"I meant to show I didn't know what my future will be," she said, trying to step out of his arms, but he held her close.

"Yes, I discerned that from the blank paper with only 'Future' written across the bottom. But it could also mean you cannot predict the future, which includes you becoming my wife and living in Chorys Dasi."

Elyse shook her head. "I don't see how it's possible. Even if I marry Sylas—"

"Please," Brynden said, taking her hand and kissing it, "one more evening. Give me one last night; that's all I ask."

What chance would he have? There were countless unknowns, like

Brynden himself. Elyse sighed, kissing him again. "I know you're lying to me."

"What are you—"

"And I don't care," she said, cutting him off. "The lies are yours to keep. There are plenty of odd things about you, and Sylas, and the Chorys Dasians. Information conveniently left out, like your age or being betrothed before me. Too many things that you are unwilling to explain."

"Then let me explain—"

"We don't have the time." Elyse looked over her shoulder at the approaching Keyain, Marietta, and the rest of their entourage. "Perhaps later, but just be aware that I know you're lying."

"Okay," Brynden whispered as he kissed her once more. "Then be aware that I will win your heart today, Elyse."

Despite her better judgment, her heart fluttered with the words. She knew she shouldn't get her hopes up, that somehow he could explain it all in the span of one evening and earn her forgiveness; yet, that didn't stop her heart from aching for Brynden. He was a future that could never be.

~Chapter Sixty-Seven

MARIETTA

"**W**e're going to be late," Keyain said for the fifth time as they walked down the steps toward Elyse. In tow were a handful of guards, including Amryth, who looked like she wished to be anywhere else. Marietta hated that she worked while they enjoyed themselves.

"Do you wish to be down there during that?" Marietta gestured to Elyse, locking faces with the dreamy Lord Brynden. Gods, even from afar, she could see how attractive the elven man was, a bit boyish for her taste, but the cheekbones and cocky demeanor worked for her. To think such a male wrote filthy letters as well. Elyse was a lucky lady.

Keyain bristled at her arm. "I wasn't expecting them to drag out their reunion this long. If I did, then I wouldn't have waited at the gate. I'd rather them be uncomfortable with no privacy than late to dinner."

Marietta patted his bicep. "Perhaps you're feeling cranky because you wore a jacket when it's the middle of summer." The day's heat was near stifling, even as the sun dipped low over Satiros. His green jacket with gold embroidery looked sharp on him, but at what cost?

"I thought having a thinner undershirt would help, okay?" he snapped, followed by a sigh.

Her gaze drifted to his dress shirt—again. Tight to his body, the thin white silk hid nothing underneath. "Well, at least I'm enjoying it. All the Satiroan women will swoon on the streets for Satiros's greatest warrior and his abs," she said with a flick of her brow.

"Quit mocking me."

Marietta looked up at him with furrowed brows, her hand reaching to rest over his heart. "I'm not mocking—the shirt is making me swoon as well." Her hand drifted down his chest and onto his hard stomach.

"Mar," he warned, though a smile lined his lips, "not in public, okay?"

Marietta pulled her hand back. "You're going to make me wait until tonight?" she said with a mocking pout. It became clear to Marietta that Keyain hadn't had sex with anyone after they broke up, which was surprising. Even before his betrothal to Elyse, she had thought a war-hero-turned-minister could sleep with whoever he wanted.

"Get this out of your system now, please," he said with a sigh. "I just want a nice dinner—no dirty comments or innuendos."

Marietta thought back to the filthy letter riddled with innuendos and laughed to herself. Keyain was in for a treat. "There you go, taking away all my talking points before we even get to dinner," she said with a dramatic sigh. "Always a pain in my ass."

He smiled with his gaze fixed on her, at the phrase often said to him when they traveled around Enomenos together. "I already can't wait to take that dress off you, so any dirty reminders might tempt me to end the night early," he murmured, lowering his mouth to her ear.

Marietta batted him away, yet she liked the attention. Sure, Keyain was an ass, but she forgot how fun he could be. The banter and teasing were the basis of their relationship, and it had been easy to slip back into both. Though, during sex with Keyain, she still thought of the King or imagined they were Enomenos. What was the harm of pretending when she'd get the information to help the Exisotis?

"If that's supposed to dissuade me, then find a better reason. Perhaps we skip the dinner altogether and you can strip this dress off me right now," Marietta answered with a wink. Keyain rolled his eyes, his smile growing broader.

As they approached Elyse and Brynden, she couldn't hide her smile. That morning, Keyain surprised her with the stunning gown. Lavender chiffon with a sweetheart neckline emphasized her chest, with sleeves that hung off her shoulders and pearls studded along the length of the dress. Heavy? Yes. Uncomfortable to sit in? Most likely. Was the dress worth it? Absolutely. Keyain had outdone himself.

"Satiros's Greatest Warrior and the First Half-Elven Lady," Brynden said, pulling away from Elyse. Marietta bit back her surprise, not realizing she had her own moniker. With a deep bow, he added, "A pleasure to share this evening with you both." The lord stood back up, his arm hooking around Elyse's waist.

"And you," Marietta said, cutting Keyain off, causing him to bristle. "Glad to meet such a supplicatory male in the flesh."

Brynden's brows rose, his smirk deepening as he turned to Elyse. "I see you have shared my sacred texts with a friend."

Elyse's face turned a shade similar to her dress. "She was with me when Sylas delivered the second letter."

Keyain sighed, his patience running thin. "Brynden," he said, holding out his hand. "We can talk about this on the way to the restaurant. If we don't leave now, we're going—"

"To be late," Marietta said with a wave of a hand. "If I hear you say that one more time, I will purposely make us late." Keyain shot her a warning look before she continued. "Come, Brynden, tell me all about yourself. I've been dying to meet you."

After Keyain ushered them into the carriage, his guards taking their posts outside, Marietta finally got to see the man who held Elyse's heart. To call Brynden charming would have been an understatement. The Chorys Dasian captivated her within moments; his ability to engage with strangers rivaled her own.

Even Keyain was smiling. He lowered his guard as Brynden spoke of his military days, talking with grandeur, every line poetic, gesturing with his hands. In many ways, he embodied how a royal would act.

The entire ride, Elyse's smile didn't fade. With Brynden's hand clamped in her own, sitting with hips and knees touching, Marietta could read the attraction they had for one another. Elyse even seemed at ease, her eyes glittering when Brynden gazed down at her.

In stark contrast, Keyain's only contact was his grip on her knee, opting for space between them. How funny she forgot his aversion to public displays of affection, even when alone with friends. She was his wife, and he still couldn't hold her hand.

Sylas's warning from the garden stuck with Marietta as she searched Brynden's mannerisms and words. None of his actions fit that of an obsessive person, though who would pursue a lady after an ended betrothal? Was it love or obsession? Where did that line get drawn?

Pondering that distinction, Marietta gazed outside the window to the city beyond. Curious onlookers stared into the carriage. Mostly elven, though she glimpsed a few half-elven people.

Having seen the white buildings that lined the cobblestone streets a few times now, she decided they were, in her opinion, boring. Only those with plants growing up the facades had any color. In Olkia, the buildings were anything but white.

Last summer, Marietta had convinced Tilan to paint their own a bright shade of golden yellow. Tilan hated it. At least she hadn't painted it pink or teal, like the buildings flanking the bakery. Her heart ached at the memory of Tilan's dislike, then acceptance, because it made her smile.

As the carriage turned onto a side street, Marietta gasped. Thick bloomed wisteria covered the corner building facade from foundation to roof. Containers flanked the wide oak door, flowers spilling out onto the cobblestone sidewalk. More blooms sat on tables outside, elven folk chatting with pastries and tea. Above the door, in clear lettering, was the business' name.

"Stop the carriage!" Marietta said, her hand flying behind her to Keyain's arm.

"What is it?" Keyain asked, his tone laced with annoyance.

"The Flour Shop!" Marietta turned to him with a smile. "We have to go."

"We're already behind schedule—"

"Keyain," she said exasperated, "you don't understand—stop the carriage." Her friend, it was her shop.

With a curious smirk, Brynden hit the carriage wall, and they came to a stop

Keyain glared at him. "What are you doing?"

"Your lady wished to stop," Brynden said, standing and offering his hand to Elyse. "So we stop. I'm always one for a spontaneous adventure. Unless Elyse wouldn't like to go?"

She hesitated, looking from Keyain to Brynden. "Well, I've heard the ladies talk about The Flour Shop during teatime, and I've always been curious."

Marietta could've kissed her.

Keyain sighed, giving in. "Alright, but make it quick. We shouldn't be too late for dinner. And stay close to the guards."

As they stepped out of the carriage, the guards flanked their party. Excitement bubbled in Marietta's gut. Grysella had visited her bakery in Olkia just a year prior, waltzing into Rise Above and ordering one of everything. Marietta watched in awe as she proceeded to sit and sample them all right there.

The Flour Shop was more impressive than Grysella had led her to believe. Tall glass cases lined the walls, filled with loaves of bread, cookies, pastries, and more, all shaped to look like flowers. From the ceiling hung more wisteria, vines, and blooms. Marietta remembered questioning about how she kept bugs from the food, her answer being magic.

Her hand grazed the dark-stained wooden border on the glass cases, ones enchanted like her own back in Olkia. The Flour Shop had higher quality cabinets with fine wood that matched the countertop by the register, though Marietta paid a similar price for her basic ones. The extra cost for magical items in Enomenos was ridiculous.

A door from the back opened, revealing a spindly elven woman whose curly black hair fought against its tie. "Hello, welcome—" A look of confusion crossed her face, then her eyes grew wide with recognition. She stopped mid-step, dropping the rag from her hands. "Marietta Reid?"

Marietta winced at the name, hearing Keyain exhale beside her. That would be a later problem.

"My gods, Marietta!" Grysella came running from behind the counter,

Marietta walking to meet her. The two embraced in a hug, laughing. "Of all the people I'd expect to walk into my shop." She stepped back, holding Marietta's hands. "Look at you! And—" Her attention fell on the group lingering at the entrance, the smile fading from her face.

"My husband and friends." Marietta turned, gesturing to them.

"Well, welcome to The Flour Shop. It's not every day our Minister of Protection visits," Grysella said, her smile forced. So she knew what happened to Tilan and her. During the few weeks she had stayed in Olkia, Marietta and Tilan met her almost every night, the three growing close. During the day, Grysella would stop by and experiment in the kitchen.

Marietta grabbed her arm, eyes wide. "I tried the blue cheese!"

"As did I," Grysella said, shifting to put her hand on her hip. "And how did yours turn out?"

"Gods, awful. Did you learn how to make it work?"

Her eyes glistened. "Yes, I paired it with fig and honey—"

"I did the same!"

"But the secret was boiling the honey with balsamic vinegar and it—"

"Cut through the richness," Marietta said, finishing her sentence with breathless excitement. "Why didn't I think of that?"

Grysella laughed. "I actually have a few prepared in the kitchen. Come, help me grab it for you and your friends."

Marietta started to follow when Keyain asked, "Where are you going?"

"In the back—I'm helping to bring out some samples. I need to try this."

Keyain's jaw tightened and Brynden leaned over, saying something Marietta couldn't hear. Elyse stood next to him, with his arm looped around her waist, her brows furrowing. Marietta would have to explain it all later, forgetting even Elyse didn't know about her baking days.

The kitchens were as exquisite as the bakery's front. High-end ovens lined one wall, the heat rolling off them with the yeastiness of fresh bread. Scattered across the countertops were kitchen gadgets, some that Marietta recognized. One of them was the magic-powered mixer she saw in the palace's kitchens.

Grysella led her to the back of the kitchen, away from any of her workers. Confused, Marietta turned to her. "Why would you keep samples—"

Tears lined Grysella's eyes. "We've been trying to get you out." She placed both her hands on Marietta's shoulders. "Forgive us for not succeeding, for letting you suffer at their hands."

Marietta shook her head. "What are you talking about?"

"This is the closest anyone has been to free you, to help you. You can't leave now, but we could sneak you out of the palace if you meet—"

"Stop it," Marietta said, breaking from her grasp. "What in the gods are you talking about?"

Grysella dug into her shirt, pulling out the flat golden pendant on her necklace, flashing the 'X,' pressed into the back. "I'm with the Exisotis. We've been trying to free you since the attack on Olkia. The temple of Therypon wouldn't let us take you—"

"Did you know the entire time—about Tilan?" Anger laced Marietta's tone, frustration from the gods' damned organization tied so deeply to her.

Grysella looked over her shoulder towards the front. "Yes, but we don't have time. I can explain it to you tonight if you can get out of your room." Once more, Grysella placed her hands on Marietta's shoulders, but she hit them away.

"All this time, you were one of them. You knew *everything.*" She spat the word. "Were you part of mine and Tilan's arranged marriage as well?"

Hurt flashed across the baker's face. "Tilan loved you so much, Marietta."

"So much that he built our relationship with a lie?"

"So much that he took that lie to his death to keep you safe." A tear fell from her eyes, anguish laced in her features. "Please, just listen to me. I can get you home—you could leave Satiros and go home."

Marietta shook her head, looking around the kitchens and attempted to steel her nerves. How interlaced was the Exisotis in her life? How many friends of hers were in the organization?

Shame settled in the pit of her stomach from being back in a bakery and seeing Grysella after meeting her in Olkia. Life in Satiros became normal to her—almost as normal as her life at home. Her true home. How had she forgotten all of this? How did she forget her love for Tilan? To fuck Keyain so easily?

Her breaths grew sharp, her vision tunneling as she remembered the glint of the knife, the fear in Tilan's eyes. Now she was fucking his murderer.

There wasn't enough air in that kitchen—enough air anywhere. Marietta gasped, holding her sides, shaking, her vision going fuzzy at the edges. Heat suddenly flared in her chest, the calming presence of Therypon nestled against her heart and lungs. She sank her emotion into the warmth, the goddess soothing away the panic. A voice rang in her head. *Seek the truth.*

Grysella looked down at her in equal panic, glancing back at the front. "Marietta, it's alright. Please, meet me tonight—"

"I can't leave." Marietta stood and took a deep breath.

"What do you mean you can't leave?" Grysella's hands fell.

"I'm working with the Exisotis, getting information no one else is privy to."

"You're the one stealing that information? I didn't even think of that." She paused for a moment before reaching for Marietta's hands. "In Enomenos, they see you and Tilan as martyrs. If freedom isn't what I can offer you today, then I will ensure your sacrifice is known."

"Gods, I'm not dead, Grysella."

"Not yet," she said with a frown. "The game you're playing is dangerous—the crown is dangerous. If they ever catch word of what you're doing—"

"Then I'll die. Yes, I know." She paused, taking her friend's hands. "But we need to go back out there and act as nothing happened." Grysella held her a moment longer, then nodded.

It didn't take long to cut the flatbread. Grysella opted for puff pastry as the base with crumbles of blue cheese, sliced fig, and the honey balsamic glaze across the top. Marietta's dour mood left her less than ecstatic to try it. It felt wrong that people saw her as a martyr, all while sleeping with Keyain,

Four months had passed since Tilan's death, but it felt like a lifetime ago. Her entire existence in Olkia seemed like a different life, and in many ways, it was. Though she would always love Tilan, always love her friends, she couldn't shake the feeling that many people knew her proximity to the Exisotis. How many times had they lied to her? Hidden the truth?

A pit of shame sat in her stomach, growing harder as they returned to the bakery's front when she saw Keyain, saw his anger. How did she stand being near him—gods, sleeping with him—after killing Tilan? After he ripped her away from everything and everyone? There she was, forgetting herself because he was a good lay and bought her fancy dresses. It was as if she suddenly woke up from a fevered dream.

Self-hate settled at her center, spoiling her mood. Through forced smiles and fake banter, she shared the flatbread with their group. Keyain kept glancing at Marietta and she kept up the charade of being okay, but somehow, he sensed something was wrong.

At that moment, she was fortunate for Elyse and Brynden's presence. Keyain would never ask what happened in front of them, and she was glad to put off his questioning for as long as she could.

With a brief goodbye to Grysella, the group got back into the carriage and headed to dinner.

Chapter Sixty-Eight

VALERIYA

Wyltam was hiding more than just mages. That afternoon, after tea with Tryda, she returned to the suite, slamming the door to her room so Wyltam would think she paid him little attention. Instead, she hid in their shared living room, waiting to see what Wyltam does when he thought he was alone.

Not having been on a scouting mission since her days in Reyila, her legs ached from staying crouched behind the couch. Back when she still trained, she could sit unmoving for hours before the stiffness set into her limbs. With only twenty minutes passed, her knees begged for a new position as her feet felt like pins and needles. As she went to shift, the indistinct murmur of Wyltam's voice carried from down the hall. Muffled, she inched closer to hear.

"Patrol the streets around the restaurant and watch the carriage," Wyltam said. "I have Marietta and Elyse guarded; I'll know if something goes wrong."

Valeriya's stomach sank. Remembering overhearing their conversation about going into the city, she was confused to why they would need extra guards. Was there an attack on Marietta? Her heart stilled in her chest.

"Can do, sir," said a throaty voice, so like Katya's that it unnerved her. Her former lover kept creeping into her mind at the most unfortunate moments.

"Watch the Chorys Dasian. Make sure he doesn't do anything too unexpected. They're hiding something." Wyltam paused. "You're dismissed."

Valeriya hurried to her hiding spot as she thought the visitor would exit, but no one left the room. Her mind raced. Wyltam was suspicious of Az and the fool was alone with Keyain. Gyrsh had reassured her the situation was covered. Who decided 'having it covered' meant leaving Az unsupervised with that group after the incident in the Central Garden?

Valeriya knew who just to ask.

After changing into a sleek black gown of silk and lace, the neckline dipping to her naval at the center, Valeriya made her way to the Noble's Section. Someone needed to answer for the oversight on Az. Just how foolish were they to leave him alone?

Voices and silvery music carried into the hall from a common room, golden light from inside spilling onto the floor. On occasion she would join these get-togethers, reveling in the gossip and making the nobles sweat. Her favorite way to pass the time was toying with the noblemen. However, she wouldn't do as such tonight; there were more important things to take care of.

A dozen light globes lit the common room, hanging above the groups of bodies with the cloying scent of floral perfume clotting the air. Nobles stood in clusters, drinking various shades of alcohol from crystal glasses. In the corner, she spotted her target encircled by the younger available females of court.

As she approached, swiping a glass of whiskey from a passing servant, her target caught her eye, his lips twitching down at the corners. He dressed in all black finery, one arm draped across a lady with long black hair. The other girls vied for Sylas's attention, none more than a blonde at his shoulder.

Valeriya gave him a subtle nod as she walked past, not wishing to make it obvious to whom she needed to speak. Instead, she settled on an easier target, one who stopped flirting with a younger lady the moment she stepped into the room.

With his handsome-as-ever smile, Gyrsh approached Valeriya and offered a deep bow. "My Queen, what an honor for your unexpected presence this evening."

"Hello Gyrsh," she said, extending her hand. The minister brought his delicate lips to her knuckles before she snatched it back. "The evening grew too quiet for me, and it was between coming to this get-together or going out for a night in the city." Unease flashed across his face before it settled back into his usual calm confidence.

"Then I'm lucky you chose this get-together."

"Luckier than you understand," she said with a fake smile. As tempted as she was to leave the palace and track the Az situation, she thought it'd be best to check in first. "Perhaps you could introduce me to some of your contacts from Chorys Dasi?" She let her gaze drift to Sylas, who still held his position with the group of ladies.

"Have you met Lord Sylas?" he asked, taking her arm, his shirt silky on her skin. "Quite a nice male."

"Haven't met him, but I hear he's quite levelheaded."

"One of his many talents."

Valeriya held her smirk as the corner of Gyrsh's mouth lifted, guiding her through the throng of people. Conversations stopped as she passed, the partiers presenting a quick bow or curtsy before returning to their groups.

As they approached Sylas, he dropped into a low bow. "Queen Valeriya, a pleasure to have you join us." The surrounding ladies curtsied, a few offering their greetings, yet she ignored them.

"May I introduce Lord Sylas Tygenbrook, Emissary to Chorys Dasi?" Gyrsh said.

"Wonderful to meet you," Valeriya said with a quirk of her lip. "Is it true you're an avid reader?"

Sylas blinked, his expression calming. "That would be true."

Gyrsh cleared his throat. "Ladies, perhaps I can introduce you to my other contact from Chorys Dasi. Come, let Lord Sylas meet our Queen."

With a few reluctant glances in Gyrsh's direction, and one of relief from Sylas, the ladies followed Gyrsh across the room, leaving Valeriya alone with Sylas. The last time she was alone with him was years ago, before her sister married Auryon.

"Have you read the book about a strong-headed bull loose in a village?" she asked, keeping her expression pleasant though she seethed inside. "When the farmers failed to keep an eye on it, it rampaged and did irreparable damage."

"I think I did read that one," Sylas said, pausing to sip his clear liquor. "Except the bull never rampaged and was not left unsupervised. The farmer's neighbors kept it calm."

"Funny, I've recently heard differently."

"Which version of the book did you read?" he asked with a slight raise to his brow.

"One by a writer who was more interested in the girl accompanying the bull instead of the bull itself." She paused, smiling at a pair of nobles who passed before continuing. "Some say he had a vested interest in her future."

Sylas paused, his eyes glancing to the other Chorys Dasians. "Didn't know that writer knew the tale to begin with, but I assure you that isn't the story I'm talking about."

"How sure?"

"Positive." His unwavering gaze was as confident as his words.

"Even if I tell you that the writer is rather *guarded* about the story?"

Sylas met her stare, comprehending what she meant. "Even then. The story still remains as the bull getting loose in the village and it returning with no damage dealt."

Valeriya narrowed her eyes. "I'll have to take your word on it." Sylas seemed too calm about Az, but he of all people would know best. She did have one other question she wanted to ask. "That writer I mentioned, have you heard about his other stories on magic?"

Sylas slid his gaze across the room. "Now those stories I have read. The girl with the bull is in one of those, and the writer uses his own proficiency to reveal her magical prowess."

If Sylas already knew Wyltam was capable of magic, who else knew? Was Valeriya the last to know? "I know about the girl," she said before taking a hefty swig of her drink. "I only recently found out about writer's proficiency with magic."

"Perhaps you aren't as well read as you thought, Valeriya," he said, giving a knowing look, mouth hidden behind his glass. "The girl's competency for magic was what caught the bull's attention."

Valeriya raised her brows at that. It explained why Az tried so hard for the girl.

Sylas frowned as he lowered his glass. "But now I fear the girl will stay in the village, which will keep the bull there as well. We're hoping for the girl to return with the bull to its rightful owner."

That was their end game with Elyse? For her to bring Az home to his sister? "I'm sure the girl's father is thrilled to hear that."

"Partially, though he's more interested in the owner's reward for the girl. If the girl leads the bull home, the plan is to test her magical abilities."

A chill raced through Valeriya. That wasn't part of the plan. Elyse was to stay in Satiros, to be a staple in her court after Wyltam was removed. Az's sister couldn't just take Elyse away from her. "You can't be serious."

"I am." Sylas threw back the remainder of his drink. "The girl will become another bull in her pen."

Nystanya didn't share that information, and if she wasn't aware, then Valeriya promised she would be soon. The Chorys Dasians' deviation from the plan did not bode well—what else was Valeriya missing? What was her sister missing?

"I know that look," Sylas said. "The girl will be fine."

"Perhaps the girl should stay home," she offered, failing to hide the bite in her voice. "That was original to the story, anyway."

"You are no writer." Sylas gave her a serious look, his lips barely moving as he spoke. "You control none of this story. It's out of your hands now."

Blood roared in her ears as Sylas bowed and took his leave. They intended to cut her out—cutting Nystanya and Reyila out. Chorys Dasi was betraying them. Her sister needed to know—immediately.

Chapter Sixty-Nine

ELYSE

Seated on a balcony overlooking the Halia, The Waterway was one of the best restaurants in Satiros. A few years prior, Keyain took her to the restaurant as a night away from the palace, back when they were still betrothed. Now Elyse sat across from Keyain's wife and next to a male who was desperate to marry her. Funny how time could change such things.

For how normal the evening started, the mood shifted to uncomfortable. No one at the table addressed it. Keyain remained quiet, not being his chatty self, leaving Brynden and Marietta to fill the silence—something in which they were both adept.

Elyse convinced herself that she misheard the baker call Marietta a different surname. She was Marietta Vallynte, not whatever name she spoke. Perhaps that was her maiden name; yet, Keyain's uncomfortable silence, paired with his warning to Brynden to ask no more questions, left Elyse believing it was something else.

If the name wasn't odd enough, Marietta also had a deep knowledge of baking—the bakery owner even knew her. When they disappeared into the back, Keyain had grown antsy, pacing, not saying a word. Brynden had asked why a noble lady would know a baker, to which Keyain threatened to ban him from the city if he asked any more questions. That had angered Elyse, but what upset her more was Marietta. Even as she talked, she had a sense of discomfort about her that lingered since she returned from the bakery kitchen. What was going on?

Marietta downed her third glass of wine, and her mood shifted into

something lighter. Perhaps she should do the same. Elyse drained the rest of her cup, earning a glance from Brynden, whose hand slid to her knee with a squeeze.

To pull Brynden's attention away from her drinking, she turned to Marietta. "Have you been back to the temple? I know you were visiting Therypon for a moment there." She thought it was a civil enough question, but the look Keyain shot her suggested otherwise.

"Not for two weeks now, though I should make a point to visit again soon," Marietta said, her gaze slipping out towards the river.

"A noble lady devoted to the gods?" Brynden asked, a playful smile across his face. "Was being the first half-elven lady not enough of an anomaly for you?"

Keyain went to speak, but Marietta cut him off. "Of course not. I'm trying to collect as many titles as possible. How silly would it be just to have one?"

"Silly indeed. 'Lady Marietta Vallynte, the First Half-Elven Lady, Favored by the Gods' has quite a ring to it."

"It just slips off the tongue," Marietta said, a smirk wrapping around her lips. "From what I hear, you've found yourself your own goddess to pray to, a fervent worshiper in your own right."

Heat came to Elyse's face at the comment as Brynden's thumb brushed against her leg. Must they talk of this?

"Do you not believe in the goddess?" Brynden asked, giving Elyse a slight squeeze.

"Oh, no, I do. She can do anything she sets her mind to," Marietta said, her smile sharpening. "However, you won't catch me supplicating at her temple."

Elyse caught Keyain's confused stare, and her face grew hotter. Gods, he didn't need to hear that—she didn't want him to hear it either.

"A shame. I'd love to see a female supplicating at her temple," Brynden mused, swirling the wine in his cup. "I am but a devoted male to my goddess, always ready to sing—and share—her praises."

"Who knew being a devoted male made one so poetic?" Marietta said, placing a hand over her heart. "But I must ask, what's your best method for praying? With your hands or by your mouth?"

Brynden's smirk deepened, sipping his wine. "In my experience, both simultaneously are the best form of worship."

Amryth, who stood on guard next to the door, covered her laugh with a cough. Marietta forced down her own chuckle as well. "A devoted follower indeed."

"What are you two talking about?" Keyain asked, his glare passing between Marietta and Brynden.

Marietta leaned back into his arm looped around her seat. "Brynden refers to Elyse as the goddess."

Though Keyain was bright, it took him a moment to replay their words for understanding to reach him. "For fuck's sake," he said, his face turning red as he drank from his glass.

Elyse must have been an equal shade of red. "Sorry," she muttered.

"Trust me," he said, shooting a look at Marietta, "it's not your fault."

Marietta shrugged with a smirk, eying Brynden, which caused Keyain's jaw to clench so hard that Elyse thought his teeth would crack. Never had she seen him so on edge, yet Marietta seemed thrilled with herself.

By the time dessert came out, Keyain's mood continued to sour, but he took it upon himself to fill the gap. He asked Brynden of Chorys Dasi, about his family and what part of the city-state he grew up in. Elyse bit back her irritation—it felt more like interrogating than civil chatter.

The server set slices of white cake before them, layered with cream and strawberry slices. Elyse's bite melted on her tongue, the sweetness from the layers almost overwhelming.

"They added too much sugar for the filling," Marietta murmured as she took a second bite. "If the baker would have tasted the strawberries first, they would've known how sweet their shipment was. Overall, not bad."

"I have to ask," Brynden said, drawing a glare from Keyain. "How does a noble lady know so much about baking? I'm ever so curious."

Marietta shot a smirk at Keyain, then leaned in. "During my captivity, I learned to bake. Became an expert in my own right."

"Ah, yes. The Exisotis captured you, hence why no one knew of Keyain's half-elven wife," Brynden said, furrowing his brows. "The humans have a weird way of treating their captives."

Marietta opened her mouth, but Keyain snapped. "Enough, Marietta. Learn to keep quiet for once."

Keyain's raised tone panicked Elyse, staring at him with wide eyes. His behavior was so odd compared to his calm and collected demeanor. The only time she'd seen him snap was during his fight with Brynden in the Central Garden.

Brynden sat back, regarding Keyain. "A husband must never speak to his wife in such a manner."

Marietta batted a hand in Keyain's direction, earning a glare from him. "Keyain just gets grumpy when I enjoy myself. Despite his hostility today, he had his moments of rowdiness back in the day. Would you believe I got him to dance on a table at a tavern in Avato?"

Elyse cocked her head at Keyain, trying to imagine him dancing at a tavern, let alone on a table.

"Mar," he warned, gripping his glass.

"It took quite a bit of alcohol, but sure enough, he got up on the table with the locals. Do you remember how much they could drink, Keyain? Gods, that's how we even convinced you to drink so much—you felt like it was a competition."

Keyain's tongue ran over his teeth as he looked out over the city, ignoring Marietta. Beside Elyse, Brynden leaned in with fascination.

"If you don't remember that, then perhaps you recall the time that chatty bard wouldn't stop following us as we traveled from Rotamu to Kentro? You feigned falling in love with him, and we had a pretend lover's spat that got him to leave. Gods, what was his name?"

Keyain sighed, sitting back in his chair and running a hand through his hair. "I don't remember, but you only referred to him as Bard-tholomew."

Marietta grinned, laughing. "Yes, one of my better nicknames."

"I hated him and his awful singing," Keyain muttered, looking back at Marietta. "From the bottom of my heart, I hope his career was short-lived."

"He was a lousy singer and an even lousier travel companion."

"I didn't realize you two traveled so much together," Elyse said, laughing. "And that you two lived such an adventurous life." And she was envious of that, never given the opportunity to meet rogue travelers and dance on tables.

"Yes, funny how that is." Brynden leaned back, removing his hand from her thigh to hook it across her shoulders. "Whatever caused you guys to stop? Was it marriage?"

The amusement in Keyain's expression faded, his icy gaze turning towards the city. "Not something we can disclose."

Marietta's hand struck out to Elyse's arm from across the table. "We should go to a tavern tonight!"

"Mar, no," Keyain said with a sigh. "It's neither a good nor a safe idea for you to be out in the city."

"But it'll be just like the old days," she said, patting his arm. Gods, that was their first contact since the carriage ride.

"Actually," Brynden said with uncharacteristic hesitation in his voice. "I would like to walk along the river with Elyse. Alone, if possible."

Elyse caught his stare, heat growing on her face. Not for the romantic gesture, but for the inevitable end to their night—the breaking of their hearts.

"First poetic letters, now romantic walks along the river? You are quite the dreamy man, Brynden," Marietta purred with a flick of her brows.

"Satiros might be a safe city-state, but we are at war," Keyain said, frowning. "It wouldn't be safe now that the sun had set."

"Not a problem," Brynden said, offering Elyse his hand to stand. "Not only am I a trained warrior, but Elyse can handle herself."

Keyain scoffed. "No offense, Elyse, but you don't have a lick of defense training."

"Ah, but she knows magic," Brynden said, grinning. "Show them."

Elyse reached out to aithyr, second nature to her already, and transferred the magical energy into her hand, creating a flame. Both Keyain and Marietta jumped back in surprise.

"Stop that," Keyain hissed, looking around the balcony and the street below. "You know you can't do magic so openly."

Brynden laughed, shaking his head. "That's only true in Satiros. Chorys Dasians do their magic in public and often."

Keyain sighed again. "Fine, go. When you're ready to return to the palace, please send for a carriage."

"Well, of course," Brynden said, bowing his head.

After a few departing words, Elyse glanced back at the table towards Marietta and Keyain. Already he was whispering something to her, his expression furious. Marietta just swirled the wine in her cup and took a sip, ignoring him. What in the hells was going on between them?

Chapter Seventy

ELYSE

Elyse held Brynden's arm as they walked along the river path. The sun dipped below the buildings, the orange already fading into black as stars twinkled. Light globes hung in the air, setting the willows planted along the path in a golden glow. In the distance, a bard played a tune on a lyre, his deep voice rolling along the river. As she looked up at Brynden, her heart skipped a beat.

He stared down at her with a serious frown, concern in his eyes. Brynden turned to her, coming to a stop as he caressed her face. "This feels too much like an ending. I'm not enjoying it."

"All things end, Brynden."

"But not before they start," he said. "Elyse, what lies do you speak of? Please, tell me all you want to know, and I will tell you all I can. Please, I'm desperate."

Elyse bit her cheek, wishing that they didn't need to have that tough conversation. "Well, you can begin by telling me about your previously betrothed, Simi." The name became awkward on her tongue after repeating it in her head so many times.

Brynden paled. "What did Sylas tell you?" he asked, anger biting his tone.

"That I'm not the first you've been serious about. What happened to Simi? Do you still love her?" Elyse regretted the last question as soon as it left her mouth.

"No," he whispered. "I don't love her, and I ended our betrothal right before she died." He closed his eyes for a moment, then gazed back down

at her. "What I feel for you is more intense than anything I had with her, I promise you that. I'll talk of any other lies you know of, but please let this one go for now."

Guilt tossed her stomach from the sad tone of his voice. "Well," she said, hesitating, "could you tell me your age?"

"That wasn't a lie."

"No, just a convenient assumption."

Brynden sighed, his hand falling from her cheek. "I'm much older than I appear, a blessing from my family traits."

"How old?"

"Very. More than twice whatever you assumed."

"Brynden," she protested.

"Come to Chorys Dasi, and I will tell you my age."

Elyse shook her head, frustrated. That just confirmed what she already knew. "Explain the scent, the smelling."

Brynden hesitated, brushing back a lock of her hair. "This one is difficult to explain. Lean into me; tell me what you smell."

She leaned into his chest, his arms wrapping around as her nose filled with his juniper and citrus scent.

"You smell it, don't you?"

"Your cologne? Yes, I do."

"No, Elyse," Brynden said, stepping back with a sad smile. "Some elves have unique traits passed down from their families, ones that only similar types of elven can detect. You are the same as me."

"What are you talking about?" she asked, furrowing her brows. Was he always that crazy, but she never saw it?

"You detected my scent, as I did yours. I've confirmed with your father. Like me, you are not just elven, not by traditional standards at least."

So her father was aware he was different, that Brynden was hiding something—that she was allegedly different, too. "And Sylas?"

"He's the same as us, as are Oryck and Daryn, hence the smelling disturbance at the townhouse. They couldn't believe you were one of us."

Elyse's head spun, remembering the incident and smelling pine and amber on Sylas. "I don't believe you. How are we different? Is it just the scent?"

"It's very real, my goddess," he said with a sad smile. "Range of life is a difference, as is the ability to wield aithyr; it comes more naturally to our kind. Think of us as some higher decree of elven."

"I've never heard of such an elf. This is just another lie," Elyse said, stepping out of his arms. Gods, she should have gone back with Keyain and Marietta. Alone with Brynden seemed like a good idea at first, but that changed. How did she not realize that he was crazy? Keyain was right—Brynden was unhinged.

"How would the world react to such an elf?" Brynden said with a crooked smile. "Our bloodlines are already small. There are fewer families of our kind left, and breeding with normal elves dilutes the traits."

Elyse scoffed—breeding? "So that's why you're so obsessed with marrying me," she said. "I'm useful for your bloodline, just to breed." Her breathing grew heavy, anger darkening the edges of her vision.

"Elyse, no," Brynden said, pleading. "I'm obsessed with marrying you because I could love you if given the time."

She thought back to Sylas' words from under the willow. "Obsession isn't love."

"Someone once told me that love could make even the smartest a fool," he said desperately, grasping her hand. "Perhaps it's less an obsession and more brazen foolishness because I am falling in love with you, Elyse."

The words hung between them, Brynden's eyes wide as his gaze roamed her face for a sign, one she didn't give. He shook his head, dropping to one knee, and pulled her hand to cup his cheek. She gave an anxious glance to a passerby, hating the display they put on.

"Elyse, I promise to tell you everything, to explain every detail to you, if you come to Chorys Dasi." Brynden turned his head into her hand. His lips were soft against her palm, cradling her hand as if he cherished it—as if he cherished her. Elyse's breath hitched as he continued. "I promise to do everything within my power to marry you and to love you with my whole being." He kissed her palm again. "I promise to bring down the world around us if it means spending an eternity with you by my side, living and loving freely."

Tears formed in Elyse's eyes at his words, at the desperate look on his face. Brynden was ostentatious and brash; he would grow bored with her. Yet down on one knee in his desperation, Elyse could see their future again, one where she sat next to him while they laughed with friends, an easy life she had never known. She saw happiness with him, the warmth that his happiness brought. No, Elyse didn't love him, but she could see it. How easy it would be to love Brynden.

"Elyse, I promise each day I will fall more in love with you than the last, that I will cherish you more than a goddess, because you are beyond a divine being." Brynden kissed her palm again. "I promise it will never fade, that I will be yours until my dying breath." With his last kiss, he lingered in her palm, pressing hard against her skin. A tingling sensation radiated from her palm to up her arm.

The lump in her throat wouldn't allow her to speak. Elyse wanted it—wanted to move to Chorys Dasi, to do magic in a city-state that allowed it, and to fall in love like her books. Sure, she was young, but would a chance at love happen again? Under the orders of King Wyltam, would she ever be allowed to love, or choose who to marry?

Her life goal wasn't to wed some high-ranking male; it was always to be free. However, the chance of loving, of having someone hold her heart, and of having her freedom, was a dream. Brynden was that dream. And it scared Elyse that one day she would wake up, realizing none of it was true. That Brynden was a facade on display, that what he felt was only his obsession.

But what scared her more was that she might never dream again. "Okay," she whispered, wiping away the tears that escaped her eyes.

Brynden's head jerked up. "Yes? You say yes?"

"Yes, I'll go to Chorys Dasi," she whispered. "I'll marry you, but I don't know if the King will release me."

Brynden jumped to his feet, pulling Elyse into a tight hug and kissing her deeply. The heat in her stomach curled with his passion, savoring the feel of his kiss. He pulled back with a wide smile. "As soon as we're on Chorys Dasian soil, I'm marrying you, Elyse. I will be your husband, and you will be my wife, regardless of blessings." His kisses were as fervent as his words, pulling her in tight, not letting go.

Married. To him.

The girl she was at the ball would never believe that such a male would chase her down, praise her, fight for her hand; yet Brynden did. Despite all her shortcomings, he wanted Elyse for his wife. The thought was scary, to step away from Wyltam after he'd been so generous. But was it generous? Or was it an obligation he felt to her mother? Elyse saw within herself the magical potential she had—she could become an accomplished mage. Wyltam had seen that, believed that because he worked with her mother; but remaining in Satiros would mean freedom at the length of a leash.

With Brynden's promises and Sylas to teach her magic, going to Chorys Dasi was almost too ideal. It scared her that leaving him tonight would somehow change that future, and she understood she didn't want to leave him, not yet. Elyse wanted Brynden—wanted to enjoy that moment where they decided to be with one another. She wanted to experience life with him, everything life offered.

"I don't want to go back to the palace," she whispered.

"What would you like to do then, my goddess?" Brynden said, cupping her face.

As he stared into his eyes, she knew in her heart how much she wanted him, wanted to be with him. Her heart skipped a beat, thinking of a lifetime of him and his worshiping. "Pull me into your lap and kiss me until your jaw aches."

A smile grew on Brynden's face as Elyse beamed. "How did I become such a lucky male that my lady quotes me so?" He kissed her again. "I'll send for the carriage and we'll go to the townhouse."

Chapter Seventy-One

MARIETTA

Keyain warned Marietta not to say another word until they reached the carriage. For once, she listened. When the cab door snapped shut, he released his rage. "Are you out of your *fucking* mind?" Keyain yelled, sitting across from her as the vehicle moved forward. "First the bakery, then your attitude at dinner." He shook his head, face red with veins bulging in his neck.

Marietta rolled her eyes and turned her gaze outside the window. "Let's talk about your sulking attitude at dinner instead."

"My attitude?" Keyain scoffed. "How in the hells was I to explain to Brynden and Elyse that my wife, a noble lady, befriended a baker? Learned how to bake?"

Marietta laughed, glancing at him. "You could've just said your basic clip wife came from humble beginnings. A life away from such pageantry." She gestured to her dress, which she realized was frivolous; a stupid object from Keyain to adore. Just like how she was stupid enough to let her guard down around him.

"What happened in the back of the bakery?"

"Nothing," she responded, watching an elven couple hold hands as they walked along the sidewalk.

Keyain's fingers appeared in front of her face, snapping. "Look at me, Marietta."

Out of stubbornness, she continued to stare out the window.

Keyain grabbed her chin, jerking her face at him. "What happened? And don't say 'nothing.' How do you know her?"

Marietta fought against his grip, but it held true. "I was a baker, Keyain! A gods damned good one, too. I made a name for myself—even the chef at the palace knew of my bakery."

She wasn't sure what grew wider—his alarmed eyes or his flaring nostrils.

"And why would you know that?"

She cut him a sharp smile. "Because I've used the kitchens to bake."

"You did what?" he growled, his grip tightening.

"Twice."

Keyain's breathing turned ragged, his face a violent shade of red. "I've been protecting your past this whole time, lying to everyone about how you were in Enomenos. And now you're telling me you're baking in the palace kitchens, pretending to be a baker?"

"I am a baker," she snapped.

"Not anymore, Marietta. I had your building condemned in Olkia—it was the first thing I did when the dust settled. You are my wife, you are a noble lady at the court of Satiros, and you must act like it." He drew his face close. "For both your sake and mine, realize how dangerous our positions are."

Marietta gripped Keyain's chin with equal strength. Surprise flashed across his features. "I am a merchant, a baker, and a noblewoman. You can erase my scars, can pretend my past wasn't real, but you will never take away the former versions of myself. Do you understand?"

Keyain's breathing turned rapid, his eyes searching her expression. And then he kissed her, pulling her forward into his grasp. His hands caressed her head, her hip, then her ass, frantic and searching for something that wasn't there.

Marietta pushed him away. "Don't you dare," she hissed, moving to the cab door. She hit the wall where the driver was, the carriage coming to a halt. "Sex won't fix this fight, Keyain." She threw open the door and stepped into the night.

How dare he touch her like that, in the middle of a fight, no less? With all her strength, she slammed the carriage door, partially surprised

Keyain didn't jump out after her. Before Marietta could start walking down the street, Amryth was at her side.

"Where are you going?" she asked, placing a halting hand on Marietta.

"To a tavern."

"And what tavern is that, Marietta?" She gave her usual unimpressed expression, but Marietta saw the concern lying beneath it.

"Who knows? Take me to the safest tavern in Satiros, I guess." Marietta wanted something—anything—to feel like her old self.

Amryth sighed, looking back into the carriage. "What happened with him?"

"He grabbed me, so I left."

Amryth's expression darkened before looking at the other guards. "I'm taking her to the Snapdragon." Then she looped Marietta's arm with hers. "It's a bit of a walk, but you might need it. It's been a while since I've seen you so upset."

Marietta only nodded her head, not having the heart to tell Amryth it was because she forgot herself—forgot who she was.

The day's heat gave way to a comfortable evening, warm with a gentle breeze casting the sweet floral scent of wisteria in the air. The glow from the light globes drifting above the city street gave the buildings a golden hue, reminding Marietta of her bakery's facade. If anger didn't pollute her attitude, then perhaps she'd take a moment to appreciate it.

To sour her mood further, denizens strolling the city gawked at her, arm in arm with a guard, donned in a pearled dress and finery. Without a doubt, they realized who Marietta was. What other half-elf would have such a gown or guard at their arm?

A moment later, Marietta sensed someone approaching from behind. She turned, expecting to find Keyain, but it was the other soldier. An elven male with similar bulk to Keyain, but he moved with feline grace and quiet steps. Tied into a neat knot was his curly brown hair, a few locks breaking free around the top of his high cheekbones; his eyes were a shocking shade of blue, as pale as ice. A thick scar forked from the top of his left cheekbone to the corner of his mouth.

"Three makes a party," Marietta said, dismissing him and continuing down the street.

"The phrase is three makes a crowd, Lady Marietta," he said, amusement in his tone as he came up to her side.

"Well, with how much I plan to drink, it'll be a party. What's your name?"

"Wynn."

Marietta turned to Amryth. "And how well do you know this Wynn?"

"I don't," she said, her gaze narrowing at him. "Wynn is one of King Wyltam's guards, if you will."

Marietta turned her attention back to Wynn, taking him in. "Why would the King send one of his soldiers with us this evening?"

"The King warned me you'd ask a lot of questions, but also told me not answering them would make you bristle," he said, with his lips tilted up to one side. "And I wasn't aware we'd be deviating to a tavern. If my judgment serves me well, Keyain will be here in a moment."

Marietta rolled her eyes. "Just because he has a piece of paper saying we're married doesn't mean I'm going to listen to his demands."

Wynn considered her words, smiling. "I was also told you'd be quite brash."

"Some call it brash. Others call it independent. Pick your interpretation."

Amryth huffed a laugh beside her. "I'd call it both."

"They're not mutually exclusive," mused Wynn.

"Then let's add it to my title. 'Lady Marietta Vallynte, First Half-Elven Lady, Favored by the Gods, and Brashly Independent.'"

The guards laughed as Marietta heard Keyain's heavy footfalls before he reached their group. "That's far enough." His tone was authoritative as if she were one of his soldiers; but she ignored him, continuing to walk.

Keyain's hand gripped her forearm, jerking her around. "I said that's far enough, Marietta." She expected to see the red-faced Keyain from the carriage, but he had collected himself. Based on the grip on her arm, he still fumed on the inside. Behind him were a handful more guards from the carriage, who exchanged glances with one another.

"Let go of me," she hissed, trying to pull out of his grasp.

Wynn reached out, grabbing Keyain's wrist. "It'd be a wise decision to let go of Lady Marietta. King Wyltam already gave his blessing for her to go to a tavern."

Marietta shot him a confused look, to which he responded to tapping his temple, whatever that meant.

Keyain glared at him, removing his hand from Marietta. "Fine. If Wyltam deems it *necessary*, then we'll go to Marietta's little tavern."

"Good," she said, turning her back to him. "Amryth, lead the way."

The tavern wasn't much further, a couple of blocks, and then a turn down a side street. Amryth's smirk caught her attention as they arrived. "Keyain's reaction should be pleasant." And she pushed open the door, the inside clean and airy, but the typical casualness she would expect. Seated at long tables were elves clad in green uniforms, all with jackets undone. Marietta smirked as Keyain swore behind her.

"Don't you want the safest tavern in Satiros for your wife, sir?" Amryth asked. "The safest is one filled with your soldiers." She kept her face serious, nothing to hint at the smirk from moments ago.

Marietta wanted to hug Amryth; it was perfect.

"Watch the entrances," Keyain said, turning to the guards that traveled with them. "Nyx and Allyn, take the back alley. Wynn, I want you inside, but near the door. The rest, keep a close eye on the street."

The guards placed their fists over their hearts before departing, all but Wynn, who had a bemused stare at Keyain. He clasped his shoulder as he passed, Keyain scowling at the action.

Marietta stifled her laugh as she wove through the tables, choosing a table at the edge of the dance floor at the center of the room. Keyain hastily pulled out her chair as she sat, then took the one next to her, hand gripping her thigh.

"Amryth, sit, please." Marietta gestured to the seat across from her, earning a look from Keyain. "We're doing things my way now. Loosen up a bit, will you? Always a pain in the ass."

He glowered at her, anger radiating from his gaze. Gods, even saying that line didn't crack a smile on him. Good, let him stew in his anger.

Their arrival caught the attention of the tavern dwellers. Soldiers from the other tables glanced over, some paying and leaving the tavern. The musician troupe changed from casual tavern songs to a more melodic and formal tune.

A barmaid wandered over to the table, smoothing out her apron before she approached. "My lord, my lady, a pleasure to have you in our establishment this evening. What can I serve you?"

"Two shots of your strongest liquor for each of us, a mug of ale each, and the next round for the guards in the tavern," Marietta spoke up before Keyain, earning a glare from him.

The barmaid paused with a slight smile curling to her lips. "Certainly, my lady," she said with a dip of her head before heading to the bar.

"Really?" Keyain hissed. "The next round for my soldiers?"

"Look at them," she said with a sigh. "They're all on edge because you're here."

"I'm on edge because I'm here, too." He glared at Wynn over his shoulder.

"Trust me. The gesture will go a long way." She reached for his hand, the action calming him a bit.

"Sure, because everything you plan always turns out fine." Sarcasm laced his tone as she dragged a hand through his hair.

Marietta turned to Amryth. "This is where guards come to let steam off after their shift, right?"

She nodded. "One of the main taverns we'll go to, at least."

Marietta turned back towards Keyain. "Let them realize that you also need time to unwind, like a normal person."

"I'm their superior. I have to show restraint."

The barmaid approached, setting down the drinks before heading off to the other tables, letting them know Keyain paid for the next round. A few lifted their glasses in response to their tables. Keyain offered a wave and a tight smile in response.

"See? Now," she held out her shot glass to the center of the table, "to a night like the old days."

Keyain sighed, picking his glass up before clinking it with Amryth and Marietta's. They threw back the shots, the alcohol burning more than she expected.

"Never thought I'd be sharing a drink with you at the Snapdragon, Keyain." Amryth shook her head, mouth puckered from the shot.

"Never thought I would sit in a tavern with Marietta again." Keyain looked over his shoulder. "I'm going to excuse myself for a moment. Another one of my captains is at that table, so I should say hello." He got up, taking his other shot, bringing his ale with him.

Amryth raised her brows at Marietta. "I didn't think he'd let this happen."

Marietta took another shot. "Gods bless the King for his timely intervention."

Amryth chuckled in response, pushing her second shot aside.

Marietta looked at the music troupe with a frown. "If I'm going to dance tonight, then I need something livelier. I'm going to chat with them."

Amryth rolled her eyes but didn't stop Marietta as she stood, approaching the musicians and their sweet, lolling song. Unlike back in Enomenos, they had metal devices attached to a funnel that amplified their sound—another benefit of magic.

As the song ended, Marietta clapped, saying, "Beautiful, you are all quite talented. Have you played in Enomenos?"

The lyre player bowed, her blonde hair spilling to the floor. "Oh, no, my lady. Our troupe hasn't been together long." A blush crept across her cheeks.

"I would have never guessed," Marietta said with a smile, watching the uneasiness fade from their features. A spindly elven man held an aulos, a red face elven man fidgeted with a horn, and a burly elven woman sat before two drums. "I've heard my fair share of music troupes back in Enomenos, and I can see you four have a natural bond with one another."

"You are too kind, my lady," she said again with a bow.

Marietta forced her smile, wishing the musician didn't feel the need to be so formal. "However, also in my experience, taverns prefer livelier music."

"Apologies, my lady. Those songs would be inappropriate for you and Minister Keyain." She gave a nervous glance behind Marietta, likely to where Keyain stood.

"Will you please play a tavern song, at least one for me? I promise it'll be okay. Lord Keyain enjoyed his bawdy tavern songs back in his day," she said with a daring smile. "And I would love to dance and sing to your music."

The musician seemed unsure but exchanged her lyre for a fiddle. "I'm happy to play for you, my lady. Any requests?"

Marietta narrowed her eyes in thought, looking over at the tables of soldiers that filled the bar. "Are there any songs you can play that the soldiers would know but are also known in Enomenos?"

The musician paused, thinking. "There's The Male From Rotamu. Do you know it, my lady?"

Marietta smiled, knowing the song well, though in Enomenos it was 'Man,' not 'Male.' It was the very song Keyain got on a table to dance to back in Avato so long ago. "In fact, I do. Perfect choice."

Marietta let the elf tune her instrument, heading back to the table. She grabbed her ale and drank, thankful to be back in a tavern. The ale wasn't the best she had tasted, but Satiros wouldn't get shipments from Rotamu. Pale in color, it was hoppy with low maltiness and a lingering bitter aftertaste.

Amryth eyed her over her drink. "You're up to something."

"How well do you know the words to The Male From Rotamu?"

She narrowed her gaze as she set down her drink. "Quite well."

The opening part of the tune started, the tavern patrons looking over to the musician. Marietta slung one arm around Amryth, the other one holding her drink as she sang the opening lines. "*Oh, there once was a male from Rotamu who loved his ale more than any brew. His drinking led his wife askew, sleeping with an elf who was passing through!"*

The beat picked up, the following lines coming faster. Reluctantly, Amryth joined her for the next verse, side-eying Marietta as the tavern's eyes turned to them.

"There once was a male from Rotam-o," they sang, their voices growing louder to compete with the instruments. Keyain stood frozen next to a group of guards, his wide eyes locking onto Marietta as red crept up his neck. *"Whose wife we knew from long ago, blessed by the gods they did bestow, a nice big ass to give us a show."*

Marietta sang as she walked over to a table of soldiers and offered a hand to one of them, who sang along. He took it, standing to dance with Marietta.

Keyain's eyes burned as they moved about the open space. Within moments, a few more soldiers joined in, swapping spots to dance with Marietta. She kept her ale in one hand, her other on the waist of her dancing partners, her face heated from laughing and effort.

The song finished, and the room began clapping and cheering as the next song began, one Marietta didn't recognize. The soldiers erupted into singing, Marietta keeping pace with them as they danced. A few songs passed with new people entering the tavern, and more than just soldiers joined them.

Amryth found Marietta on the floor and danced with her as well. It was nice to see her stern demeanor drop, her smile wide. She deserved a break. After all, she'd been through so much as well.

Despite sweat sticking to her body and the gods damned heavy dress threatening to fall every two steps, Marietta felt as if she stepped back in time. The dancing, the ale, the people—it all proved that Satiros could be like Enomenos, that elves could dance with a half-elf. If only they understood Satiros could be equal, like her home, then maybe Marietta could learn to love this city-state too.

Lingering in the back of her mind was the truth. She was Keyain's prisoner, and they considered her a lesser person for being a half-elf. At that moment, there were those in Satiros suffering for what they were born to be.

Alcohol and dancing numbed her brain, distracting her from the truth. For one night, she wanted to just be Marietta. Not a goddess's chosen, not a nobleman's wife. She wanted to pretend everything was still normal. So she drank, and she danced, and she avoided Keyain.

Chapter Seventy–Two

ELYSE

Time moved too quickly during the carriage ride back, perhaps because Elyse spent it in Brynden's lap, her mouth locked on to him. "This is the longest you've gone without talking," she said into his collar.

"Do you wish me to talk more, my teasing goddess?" he said, lifting his chin so she could better kiss his neck. "I could tell you all the filthy things I wish to do to you."

She laughed into his skin. "I'd prefer if you did those filthy things to me." Dangerous words, but she meant them. Kissing Brynden was intoxicating. Was all kissing like that, or was it because they were a unique version of elf?

Elyse tried to block the topic from her mind, but it kept coming back. How did he learn that of her? How in the gods didn't she know?

And if *breeding* with normal elves diluted the bloodline, did that mean both her parents were this variant? One would assume being better at aithyr would have protected her mother's mind against the magical energy, but it didn't. Perhaps it made a person more susceptible to it, which meant she—

"Goddess," Brynden murmured, "I can hear you thinking. What is distracting you at a time like this?"

Her mouth hesitated, pulling away from him. "So this other type of elf we might be—"

"That we, in fact, are."

"Okay, that we, in fact, are. How is that a secret? How are we different?

It makes little sense."

Brynden took her hand, kissing her palm. "With due time, I will explain, but realize this: our community is small, hidden from outsiders, but we're scattered throughout Syllogi."

"And reproducing with normal elves dilutes whatever traits we get from our elven variant."

"Correct, my studious wife-to-be," he said, kissing her nose.

"So then my parents were this type of elf."

Brynden hesitated. "Well, yes and no. Your father's grandfather was the standard type of elf, diluting that bloodline. Gyrsh only has partial traits."

"And what of my mother?"

"Ah, she was from an extraordinary family. Many were furious when she chose Gyrsh as her partner, saying she had thrown away her breeding potential. But then we got you." Brynden cupped her face, gazing from eye to eye. "As extraordinary as she, if not more so. I think that's why your father despises you—you look like him, but you will amount to greater things than he ever could hope to be." He laughed, shaking his head. "I keep telling Sylas you take after your mother, but he doesn't believe me."

"And that's how Sylas knew my mother—beyond the Circle of Mages?"

Brynden blinked. "I didn't realize how much he told you, goddess. But partially, yes."

"And did you know her?"

"No, I never met her. Our social circles never mixed, but enough with this," Brynden said, peering out the window. "It looks like we've made it to our destination, and I only want to think of my goddess." Brynden kissed her again, his fingers sliding into her hair, his tongue into her mouth. He pulled back, biting her lip. The only response she managed was her quickened breath and a nod of her head.

Brynden helped Elyse out of the carriage and up the front steps to the townhouse. He leaned down, kissing her passionately as he opened the door. As it shut, Brynden pushed Elyse back against the wall, one hand caressing her neck, the other squeezing her hip. Gods, what did she do with her hands? Did she put them on his hips? His neck?

Someone cleared their throat and Brynden tore away from her. In the living room, his uncle stood with her father before a group of Satiroan nobles. She knew all of them, the males who worked under her father.

Elyse's face grew hot as Brynden laughed. "Apologies, I forgot your meeting would still be underway." In a fell swoop, he picked up Elyse and threw her over his shoulder. "Hope you all have a wonderful evening."

A few chuckles came from the other room as Brynden started on the stairs.

"Put me down," she hissed.

"I'll put you down when I have you in my room, goddess."

"You should at least go say hello."

He chuckled. "I have more pressing things to take care of."

"Well, they're all going to know *why* I'm here." Gods, she could imagine the rumors already.

"Good," he said. "Then they'll know that you're *mine*."

Elyse watched as Sylas ran up the stairs behind them, as if the situation couldn't be more embarrassing.

"Is everything alright?" he asked.

Brynden turned around, the sight of Sylas replaced by the stairs. "Nothing could be better."

"Hello, Sylas," Elyse added, trying to look over Brynden's shoulder.

"Hello, Elyse," he said. "I'm guessing your night went well then?"

"My friend, I have my lady over my shoulder and am on route to my bed. Do you truly think this is the time for such questions?"

"But she wants to?" Sylas said. "Elyse, are you alright?"

Based on their last conversation, she looked like a fool. She had made it clear she intended to not fall for Brynden's promises, yet now she would marry him. "I'm alright."

"Better than alright," Brynden said. "I believe congratulations are in order."

There was a moment of tormenting silence as Elyse squeezed her eyes shut. Perhaps she was a fool.

"Congratulations, indeed."

"Now, if you'll excuse us."

"Elyse," Sylas added, "I'm sure Keyain is expecting you back at the palace at some point."

"Always playing the caretaker," Brynden said as he turned around and started on the stairs. "Now, back to the important part."

Elyse came face to face with Sylas. His brows were knitted together, a frown tugging at his lips. Then he tapped his temple as his voice sounded in her head. *"Is this what you want? Are you alright?"*

It took her a moment to realize he did magic. Elyse nodded her head. Brynden was what she wanted.

"If you need anything later, my bedroom is down the hall." There was a moment of silence and then she heard, *"Whatever comes of this marriage, know that I'll be there if you ever need me."*

His words brought a smile to her lips, gaining one in return from him. She hadn't yet moved to Chorys Dasi, but she already had a friend. With a final look, Sylas turned around and went back down the stairs.

They reached the top floor and started down the hallways. "Goddess," Brynden murmured, "you stopped petitioning for me to set you down. I don't know if I should be delighted or worried."

"Delighted," she said. "I'm just a bit nervous."

"Of course, my goddess. I promise to take care of you." His hand rubbed down the length of her back, causing heat to blossom at the bottom of her stomach.

When they arrived at his door, he kicked it open and brought her inside. Once the door was shut behind them, he finally set her down. The room was spacious but cozy with its thick carpeted floor, lush red curtains flanking a fireplace before it sat two chairs and a small table between them. To the other side was his bed, draped in black fabric and red pillows. Elyse walked to it and drifted her hand along with the silky fabric, uneasiness filling her. Gods, she had never done this before.

"Goddess, this is a very surreal moment." Brynden drew her attention, his gaze roaming Elyse's body. "I have imagined you in my bedroom a thousand times over, yet to see you stand here, next to my bed." Brynden swallowed hard, walking to her. "You are not of this world, my goddess. Let me prove to you I can be worthy."

Her heart skipped a beat as he leaned in, caressing Elyse's face with a kiss as he pulled her closer to him. Brynden's touch set her alight and his words made her swoon. He was everything she never thought she could have, and more. His love meant freedom, a life that only existed in dreams. Brynden fought for her, and now she couldn't imagine not being his. "What if you're already worthy?" she whispered.

Brynden silenced her with a deeper kiss, his tongue sweeping across her mouth as a hand moved to her chin. With a finger, he tilted her head, kissing down her neck. "Well, I want to make sure I am. Let me make you feel incredible, my goddess," he murmured into her.

Elyse's hands found his shirt, tugging him closer as her breathing turned ragged. His soft lips brushed over her collarbone, Elyse shuddering from his touch. Brynden's hand slipped behind her back to her zipper. "May I?"

Heat flared at her core, and she managed a nod. The fabric slid down, encouraged by Brynden's hand, and she stood nude before him. His gaze turned liquid as he took her in.

Elyse reached for his shirt, lifting the fabric up over his head. Underneath, Brynden's body was hard, his chest broad, his stomach lined with muscles. She placed a hand on his heart, causing him to shiver.

"Surreal," Brynden murmured, pulling her tight to his body, his skin against her. The closeness took her breath away. "And incredible—I'm the luckiest male in Syllogi to see this bit of you. I only ask that I can have more. I want all of you, Elyse."

"I'm yours," she said, kissing his chest.

"Say it again."

"I'm yours, Brynden."

"Call me Az."

Elyse pulled back to give him a look. "Your childhood nickname?"

"The name that only my closest friends call me. And I want you to be closer to me than anyone."

"Okay," she whispered, kissing his chest again. "I'm yours, Az."

He growled, fingers lacing her hair as he grabbed the back of her head, kissing her. In a swift movement, he swept her up and laid her back on the bed, the silk smooth against her skin. Az laid himself on top, his muscular arms flanking either side of her as he kissed her lips, her neck, moving down to her breasts. Elyse lifted her hips against him with a breathy moan, meeting his thrust.

"Goddess," he murmured into her skin between kisses on the planes of her stomach. His hands reached up, caressing her breast as his mouth nipped at her hips, causing her back to arch. "Let me be your most fervent worshiper," he said, dropping to his knees next to the bed. With his hands on her hips, Az pulled her to the edge, draping her legs over his shoulders. "All I wish is to please my goddess," he said into the inside of her thigh with a kiss. "And to pray at her temple."

The heat of his mouth washed over her, flicking his tongue slowly until Elyse shuddered with a whimpering moan. A deep laugh came from Az as his tongue licked up her center, her body arching from the bed. With his third teasing flick, Elyse grabbed the back of his head, his eager tongue sliding inside.

It was like nothing she had felt before, to be so barren in front of someone, to be pleasured so fervently. A moan escaped her as she melted between her legs, her head growing light. Her toes began to tingle as her stomach contracted, a deep thrumming coursing through her body. It was like a moment of weightlessness, where she could hardly catch her breath.

Elyse's mind grew hazy as he slipped in his fingers, feeling the curl inside her while his tongue circled the top of her center. The feeling turned sharp and her body tightened. As she lifted her hips, Az's free hand reached out, pinning her to the bed, holding her writhing body.

Her breaths turned to pants as her body surged with pleasure, the sensation snapping through her in a way she hadn't felt since that evening in the piano room. She came in shattering waves as Az grew hungrier, more impatient. His tongue and fingers frantically moved against her.

When she couldn't take it a moment longer, she grabbed his hair, causing him to look up with a wet smirk. "Az, please," she whimpered,

"That's what I've been doing," he said, flicking his tongue against her, causing her to shudder. "Pleasing you, my goddess."

"Az," she moaned, deepening his smirk.

"Tell me what you want, Elyse," he said, his voice rough.

"You."

"And how do you want me?"

"Az, please," she begged.

He kissed between her center, his fingers teasing. "Say it, Elyse."

Exasperated, she said, "I want you inside me, *please.*"

Az's fingers slipped in again, causing her to grip the sheets with a moan. "Like this, goddess?"

Elyse stared down at him with ragged breaths. "I want your cock inside me, Az."

His smirk turned devilish, and he pulled himself on top of Elyse, kissing with the taste of herself still wet on his lips. "And where inside do you want my cock?" Az teased, a free hand undoing his pants.

Elyse hesitated, hating that he led her along, that he could predict what she wanted, so she decided to be unpredictable. "My mouth."

Az pulled back in surprise. "Goddess," he whispered, gaze heavy on her lips. "Only if you want to."

When she nodded her head, Az's breathing deepened as he clawed to remove his pants.

Elyse knelt before him, knees on the carpeted floor with his legs hanging over the edge. Propped up on his elbows, he looked down at her as she regarded his cock. Suddenly, she regretted her choice—what was she supposed to do with it?

"There's no pressure, Elyse," he said, his chest rising and falling with heavy breaths. "You can change your mind at any point, no questions asked."

"But I want to," she said, placing a hand on his knee, looking between his legs. "I just don't know how to do it." Elyse hated the heat that crept on her cheeks, the smirk that came to his face.

"Well, you just… put it in your mouth, whatever fits. The rest grip with your hands. Avoid your teeth, move your tongue, suck."

With a hesitant hand, she grabbed him, his body shuddering. "Like this?" she said, lowering her mouth to his cock. It didn't taste like much, which surprised her a bit. What she wasn't expecting was the stiffness of it, nor its length.

Az moaned her name, grasping the sheets on the bed. When she looked up at him, Az furrowed his brows, his mouth parted. "I've imagined this a thousand times as well, and I didn't think I'd be blessed with such a sight tonight."

His head dropped back as she went deeper, gliding her tongue along him. Elyse watched how his body reacted, how his breathing changed as she pulled his cock out and flicked her tongue against it. He moaned her name, over and over, shifted his hips to meet her at the back of her mouth.

When tension seemed to coil in his body, he jerked away from her. "If you keep doing this, I won't get a chance to put it anywhere else. Elyse, I am completely unworthy of you."

She wiped her mouth and crawled on top of him, straddling his stomach. Elyse's limbs shook with nerves, but she wanted it. Wanted *him*. "Don't say that—you're worthy. More than worthy."

He shook his head, wrapping his arms around her as he shifted to be on top. "Elyse, you are incredible—and not just because of this," he said, gesturing to her naked body. "You're intelligent, talented with magic, and singing, and drawing. I love that you're always thinking, that you surprise me in so many ways. Long before tonight, I gave myself to you, my whole heart. It is yours to keep and each day I promise to earn yours." He tucked a loose piece of hair behind her ear.

"You already have it, Az." Staring into his gaze, she knew he'd had it since the night of the ball, since that first kiss. Elyse couldn't let herself believe it, that she would give it to a stranger, even when he chased after her. With a clear head, missing the self-doubt and hate that used to pollute it, she stared at him as a new person. Elyse didn't love him, not yet, but he held her heart.

Az kissed her, his body becoming flush with hers. "It'll hurt at first—so you know; but it'll pass. If it's too much, please say something."

Elyse nodded, and he kissed her, cupping her face.

Az was gentle as he eased his cock inside her, a spark of pain causing her to hiss. He stopped, letting her adjust, and continued when she nodded her head. It took a few moments, but the pain subsided, heat filling her center as he thrust his hips. Elyse gasped with a moan, arching off the bed as her nails dug into his back. The way she felt full sent her head spinning.

"Elyse," he moaned. "Goddess, you're incredible."

His body over top of her was strong, and she watched the way his shoulder muscles shifted with effort, watched the way the pleasure changed his expression. Even in the low light, his russet eyes seemed to glow near red the longer he moved.

The deep thrumming within her started again, aided by Az's thrusting, with sharp breaths and nails at his back. He smirked down at her as his pace changed, faster, rougher, and her back arched underneath him with a whimper. The tension was near unbearable as he kissed her, tongue sweeping across her mouth.

He pulled back, his forehead resting on hers as he continued to move. "Do you trust me, goddess?" Looking from eye to eye, she nodded through the haze of her pleasure.

Az slowed, shifting his weight to one arm as a hand moved to her chin, tilting her head to the side. He lowered his mouth to her neck, kissing from her jaw to her collarbone as his hips moved faster, panting. Without warning, his nails grew sharp against her chin, his body tightening as he bit down on her neck.

The scream in her throat released in a quivering moan as the sudden sharp pain in her neck gave way to pleasure. Everything else faded away, her body only aware of where Az touched her. His mouth at her neck, his hips as he came close with every thrust, his cock deep inside her.

Something beyond chaos filled Elyse—thoughts emptied her mind, and there was only her and Az, his moan in her neck as he continued to move, his own breathing ragged. Elyse's orgasm crashed through her body in thundering waves. Her vision faded to white, nails clawing into his back as she cried out for him.

With the utterance of his name, Az lost himself, his body holding her tight against him, his teeth still digging into her skin as he moved faster. He groaned as release found him, only removing his mouth when his body stopped shuddering.

His lips met where he bit with a kiss, her body going lax. Elyse melted into him as Az collapsed to the bed. She looked over at him, sweat slick on his brow and breathless. "Elyse," he whispered, cupping her face, his slacked with awe. "You're mine, and I am yours."

Elyse stared into his russet eyes, knowing that it was true. "You're mine, and I'm yours," she repeated, causing him to close his eyes with a shudder.

"Don't leave tonight. Stay with me." He kissed her deeply.

"But Keyain is expecting me back—"

"Don't go back to them, ever. Stay with me," Az whispered. "We can leave for Chorys Dasi in the morning, you and I."

"Az," the name was awkward to say as her haziness lifted. "I can't just leave."

"What's stopping you?"

What was stopping her?

Guilt that she could make Keyain angry? Disappointment from the King? Was leaving on a whim such a bad thing that they couldn't forgive her? Perhaps the King couldn't, but Keyain was like a brother—he'd always forgive her, right? "Nothing."

"Then stay, Elyse. We can be married in a week, as soon as we're in Chorys Dasi." Az kissed her, the promise on his lips sweet as she held his face.

"I'll stay," Elyse whispered. "I'll be your wife. Just one more week."

Az smiled and it was the most beautiful thing, with his eyes aglow. "A dream that came true. A future that can be," he murmured into her hair.

The decision was impulsive, but that's what she wanted. Az was what she wanted. In her gut, Elyse knew he was her future, that she would see all Chorys Dasi had to offer.

Thoughts of walks along the beaches of The Mavros Sea, of holding his hand in the streets of Chorys Dasi, of doing magic in public filled her mind as she nestled into Az, sleep taking hold of her. Freedom was at her doorstep. Elyse just needed to cross the threshold.

That night proved she could.

Chapter Seventy-Three

MARIETTA

On her fourth trip to refill her drink, Keyain finally intercepted Marietta. "Are you fucking kidding me?" he ground out, stepping in front of her.

Marietta sidestepped him like she would do any guy approaching her at a tavern, looking at him over her shoulder. "Something wrong?"

At the bar, she set down her emptied drink on the counter and flagged down the barmaid. Customers swamped the lone worker as the tavern became packed throughout the night.

"Yes, something is wrong. You're out there making a fool of yourself—of me." Keyain placed a hand on her hip, the touch more possessive than sweet.

With a dramatic eye roll, Marietta glared up at him. "Look around you, Keyain. When we walked in, people were leaving because you made it uncomfortable. Now the tavern's packed, and your soldiers are dancing, having fun. They'll tie that positivity to you."

"No, they're amazed that a noble lady could ever stoop so low. Pay attention to your gown; you aren't dressed to be dancing like that."

She glanced down at the pearl-studded gown that continued to slip on her chest, shifting it up with two hands. "Funny you have a problem with it, considering you picked it out." She turned towards the barmaid. "Two more shots and another ale, please."

The barmaid nodded her head and ducked behind the bar.

Keyain glared at her, annoyance clear in his features. "Do you need

two more shots?"

"No, I don't." Marietta turned towards him, placing her hands on his chest, grabbing the front of his jacket. "But you do. Listen, you need to lighten up. You're dealing with people, so act like a person for once."

Keyain rolled his eyes, but his expression softened, wrapping his arms around her. "You will be the death of me."

She smirked as the barmaid set down the drinks on the bar. "At least you'll die having fun then." She handed the shots to Keyain, watching as he threw them back.

An elven man with feathery auburn hair that contrasted with the green of his uniform approached with a grin. "My eyes must deceive me. Is that the great Keyain Vallynte at the Snapdragon, taking shots?"

Keyain's face lit up with a smile. "Ryder, how am I not surprised that you're here?" The two embraced. His name sounded familiar but Marietta couldn't place it.

"All those times I've invited you out," Ryder said with a mocking pout. "Then to think that after I raced here when word spread at the garrison that you were buying drinks, I find you taking shots without me. You wound me, my friend."

Keyain rolled his eyes but kept his smile. "Trust me, this night wasn't my idea." He gestured to Marietta, pulling her close to his side. "This one insisted."

"Ah, the infamous Marietta." Ryder's grin sharpened.

"And you, the mysterious Ryder." With furrowed brows, she stuck out her hand. Ryder grasped it, wincing as she shook.

"Quite the grip," he said, raising his brow at Keyain. "She lives up to her brash reputation."

"Ryder, not now," Keyain warned.

"Curious, you're not the first person to call me brash tonight." Marietta matched his sharpened grin.

Ryder took a step closer, looking at Marietta from head to toe. "Unsurprising. Though, Adalyn had something different to say about you."

Marietta's stomach dropped at the mention of Adalyn, the scowling guard with blonde hair. That's where she had heard his name before, at the sculpture garden with the King. Ryder knew about the almost kiss. "Well, I can say that I've known Keyain for a decade now and this is the first I'm hearing of you." A saccharine spread across her lips. "Your reputation does not outlive you."

"Oh, that one hurts," Ryder said, grasping Keyain's shoulder. "How does your wife know about your best friend?"

Marietta narrowed her eyes on the pair. She was under the impression that King Wyltam held that title.

Keyain sighed and went to speak, but Marietta cut him off. "Don't be hurt," she said, placing her hand on his arm. "Keyain didn't share most of the details about his life, including his friends." The glare that Keyain shot her was scathing; she couldn't help but smile sweetly at him.

"I've actually needed to ask you something about your unit," Keyain ground out, lowering his voice. Ryder's previous lighthearted attitude dropped to seriousness as he listened to Keyain.

Marietta's attention turned to the crowded room. A flash of bright blue caught her from the far side, finding Coryn from the Temple of Therypon leaning against the wall, arms crossed, gaze locked onto Marietta.

Marietta excused herself, dodging Keyain's hand as he went to stop her from moving. The nerve he had to grab at her. Slipping through the crowd, she made her way towards the grimacing Coryn.

"When I heard a noble lady was dancing at The Snapdragon, I thought there was no way it was Marietta," he said, his expression softening to an easy grin. "Yet, here we are."

"If anything, I can make my presence known."

He laughed. "An understatement. I've known you but a brief time, yet whenever you step foot outside that palace, people know where you are."

"Like the Exisotis," she muttered, taking the spot next to him on the wall, looking out at the crowd.

Coryn raised a brow, looking down at her with his rich brown eyes. "I heard you found Grysella at The Flour Shop this evening."

"You just know all the gossip, don't you?"

One side of his mouth ticked up into a deeper smile, revealing a dimple. "Deania does, actually." He nodded his head to the dance floor where the tiny cleric, clad in her blue tunic, danced with Amryth, the two red-faced and laughing. The sight brought a smile to Marietta's face.

"Grysella had a lot to say. I have more friends in Satiros than I thought."

"Come by the temple this week and we'll talk about that." He glanced at her, rubbing a hand over his stubbled chin. "We also heard the noble lady had quite the beautiful singing voice, bringing the soldiers to their knees with tears in their eyes."

Marietta snorted, looking at the crowd in amusement. "That's partially true, except I brought them to tears with my terrible singing. Can't be both a goddess's paladin and a skilled singer. I can only be so many things."

Coryn shook his head, laughing. "I don't know about that. You're also quite the noble lady."

"Yeah, right. I'm a business owner and a baker, not fit for positions of power," she said, dragging her gaze back to Coryn. "Though my husband would never let me have any power."

"He's a fool if he doesn't. Look around—you know how to rally people, how to win their hearts. The stories coming out of The Snapdragon were entertaining. 'Lady Marietta makes Minister Keyain palatable,' was my favorite." The light caught his gleaming eyes and his handsome face.

The music slowed, the sound melodic as the dancers took a reprieve from the fast-paced songs preceding. "That wasn't my intention. I just wanted to dance," she said, looking off to the dance floor wistfully.

Coryn held out his hand. "Then dance with me."

"How do you think my husband would react to me dancing to a romantic tune with another man?" she asked, placing her hands over her heart.

Coryn shrugged, pushing off the wall. "Let's find out."

Marietta's grin sharpened, placing her hand in his. "Good idea."

They made their way to the dance floor, guards dancing with people not in uniforms. On the edge of the crowd stood Amryth and Deania, the cleric talking fast, using a lot of hand motions, and Amryth bent over with laughter.

"I don't think I've seen Amryth smile this much." Marietta nodded in their direction.

"She smiles like that anytime Deania's around," Coryn said, placing his hands on her hips, Marietta wrapping her arms around his neck. "They'd make a cute couple."

She hadn't considered such a pairing. Amryth's wife died the same night as Tilan, but was she ready to move on? When did enough time pass? Marietta may have lost herself with Keyain, but at some point, her heart would heal enough to enjoy another's company, or so she hoped.

Coryn moved her across the floor, Marietta smiling at his dancing skill. His footwork was smooth, graceful. She held his gaze, his skin shining with golden light, his brown eyes near glowing. An Iros, like her. They'd be working together in the future, whatever that may be. On instinct, Marietta reached to Therypon's warmth in her chest, heat blossoming within her.

Coryn furrowed his brows. "Did you do that?"

"Do what?" she asked as a hand fell on her shoulder. Confusion washed from Coryn's face, replaced with a smirk. Marietta already knew who it was.

"Mind if I cut in?" Keyain ground out.

"Not at all, thank you for letting me borrow your wife," Coryn paused, "for this dance, of course." He winked at Marietta as he walked off.

The insinuation would only add to Keyain's anger, but what was one more thing? A fight from the evening's antics loomed over her already.

Keyain placed both his hands on her hips, gripping her as his gaze followed Coryn.

"Easy there, you're going to bruise me if you squeeze any tighter."

His hands loosened, but his jaw remained taught. "Why is he here?"

"Don't worry about him. Just enjoy this moment with me." Marietta placed her head on his chest, letting the music carry them. How easy it was to pretend they were in Kentro, that Marietta still helped businesses and Keyain remained a mystery. Those days were forever gone, and she knew better than to dwell in the past. It was time to let them go.

The song ended, the pace picking up with a new tune, forcing Keyain to dance faster. She smiled at him, remembering when she finally got him to dance back when they traveled. It had taken a few months and alcohol, of course, but he would dance. It seemed silly that such a prominent politician would be self-conscious. A voice yelled over the crowd, announcing the last call at the bar.

"Is it that late already?" she asked, wiping sweat from her brow.

"It's been hours, Marietta," Keyain grumbled.

She laughed, stepping off the dance floor. "Time flies when you're having fun."

"Right, fun." Keyain waved down Amryth, still with Deania, who gave her a quick hug before darting back into the crowd. At the door, Wynn and the other guards fell into step as they left the tavern.

The summer night was refreshing compared to the stuffiness inside of the crowded tavern. Keyain didn't send for a carriage, which Marietta was thankful for as she leaned against Amryth, walking the streets of Satiros. That evening was her reset—her reminder of the freedom, of the life she had prior, a reminder for why she worked with the Queen, getting information for the Exisotis.

Life with Keyain would end—likely her friendships at court, too. Perhaps Elyse would want to leave Satiros, if not going to Chorys Dasi with her dashing man. With Amryth, they could turn their backs on the crown and live in Enomenos together.

Marietta could return to Olkia with the friends who helped heal her heart, who made her jail cell feel like home. She could imagine showing them all the sights of Enomenos. Elyse would love the artistry in Olkia, and Amryth would love the taverns in Kentro.

Perhaps, after everything, Marietta would come out stronger. Yes, losing her husband shattered her heart, her resolve, but she'd come back more resilient than before, proving that Keyain couldn't break her. To show that Satiros could not break Enomenos.

Grysella was right; Marietta was a martyr, and she would make herself the symbol Enomenos needed.

Chapter Seventy-Four

MARIETTA

Energized by the different people she met, danced, and sang with, Marietta felt sure of herself. Confident. Amryth walked arm in arm with her, both giggling at Wynn's jokes, most at Keyain's expense. If his mood at the tavern was dour, it only further deteriorated while returning to the palace. Even a few of his guards couldn't hold back their snickering. If only she had met Wynn sooner.

The palace was only a few blocks from The Snapdragon. Keyain navigated them towards the main gate, leading the party with a scowl. Flanking the palace's entrance were two female forms, hair twisted into branches, like statues guarding the sculpture garden. Except they scaled higher than any person or tree that Marietta had seen and reached above the wall's height.

Beyond it rose the white stone of the palace. Columns were carved into the side of the soaring walls. In between were trees that spanned five stories chiseled to look like old, gnarled wood. Marietta squinted as they made their way up the steps, seeing a face etched in with the bark texture. Enamored by the details, she nearly ran into Keyain's back, Amryth pulling her back at the last second. Reaching behind, Keyain grabbed for her wrist and dragged her to his side.

Marietta struggled from his grip. "What are—" The words died in her throat as she saw him. Dressed in all black, King Wyltam stood at the entrance with hands tucked into his pockets. "About time you returned, Keyain," he drawled.

"It would've been sooner if—"

"That's enough. Wynn?" he asked.

Wynn approached the King, leaning to speak into his ear. King Wyltam nodded, his gaze landing on Marietta. Maybe it was the alcohol altering her perception, but a smile hinted at his lips. Her heart skipped a beat.

"Interesting," the King said as Wynn stepped back. "Amryth, follow Wynn. He has a few questions for you."

Without hesitation, Amryth clamped her fist over her heart and bowed her head. "Of course, my King."

The guards didn't make it past the grand foyer before Keyain snapped again. "I need to get her inside, Wyl."

"You need to meet with your team. The Exisotis made a move while you were out." The King walked towards them with an unhurried pace. "I suggest you take the rest of your guards and learn what happened."

"After I get Marietta to our room." Keyain jerked her forward, but she resisted.

The King tilted his head. "I'll be more than happy to escort Marietta. You have a duty to our city-state to—"

"I have a duty to my wife." Keyain's grip tightened on her wrist. Marietta hissed, trying to pull out of his hold again.

The King's expression darkened, anger slipping from his expressionless mask. "Go now, Keyain, or I will make an example of what happens when people challenge my authority."

Beside her, Keyain's breathing became strained, but he released her, turning to his other guards and motioning them to follow. "We'll talk after, Marietta." Though she leaned away from his touch, he kissed her forehead and stormed off into the palace.

The absolute nerve that man had. Marietta met the King's gaze, ignoring the pain that lingered at her wrist.

"Are you alright?" he asked, approaching Marietta.

Was she alright? Was anything alright when she was trapped in a foreign city-state and married to a man she didn't want to marry? Admitting she was not alright would be a betrayal to herself; but to continue pretending before a man who knew the truth, who knew her pain, who likely went through similar pain, seemed foolish.

"No," she said, refusing to let her voice falter. Despite giving herself one night, a reminder of the person she used to be, Marietta still needed to say it. A confession for the man who realized when she needed help and reached out. "Nothing is alright. None of this is alright."

"It takes a strong person to admit such truth," the King said, nearly a whisper. "I'm happy you can share your honest feelings." He paused, his dark gaze roaming over her. "Would you like to walk with me before I take you back to your room?"

"I want to be anywhere but that suite," she said, hating the emotion that bit at her throat.

He considered her for a moment, nodding his head. "Understandable." The King held out his arm, and Marietta took it. "Before *that*," he said, leading through the entrance, "did you enjoy your evening?"

"For the most part," she said, offering a tight smile. "I'm thankful for your intervention and glad you sent along someone to play nursemaid."

"Nursemaid?" the King chuckled, a smile coming to his lips as they started down a dim hallway. "Wynn is one of the most deadly mages I've ever worked with."

Marietta stopped and turned to him. "A mage? To protect our party?"

"To protect you." King Wyltam placed a hand over hers that gripped his arm, a smile touching his lips.

Marietta's breath caught. Not wanting to acknowledge the King's implication, that he protected *her*, that he thought of *her*, she said, "I've never met a mage before."

"That's the funny thing about being a mage," he said. "We can be anyone, and you would never know."

"We?" She furrowed her brows. "You're a king, not a mage."

"To be one doesn't mean I can't be the other." His hand brushed back the dark hair that fell into his face. "Mages can be beyond deadly, definitely dangerous, and a complete secret."

"And is that what you are, my King?" she teased. "Deadly? Dangerous?"

She looked him up and down, a smirk curling at her lip. "Because I find you to be neither."

King Wyltam chuckled as he untangled himself from her. Then he disappeared, the spot he occupied becoming empty. Standing before her one moment, gone the next, Marietta had a second to register what she saw before she was pinned to the wall. A scream died in her throat as King Wyltam reappeared, his hands firm but gentle, holding her to the stone. His breath fell on her skin, his mouth inches from her own. She swallowed hard, cursing her heart for betraying her as it thundered in her chest. "I guess that proves your point," she managed to say.

"You have never called me your King, Marietta." He brought his hand to her chin, tilting her face towards his. "Is that what I am? Your King?"

"What if you are?" Stupid. Foolish. She should push him away. Marietta should end the conversation, but she wanted more—she wanted him. His lips were so close; she imagined the softness of them brushing over her skin.

"Then I wouldn't be deadly or dangerous to you. For you, I would be loving," he murmured, his hand coming to rest on her cheek. "For you, I would be tender."

She stared at his mouth, wishing it on her own. "Show me how tender you can be, my King."

His breath slowed as he leaned in. "If I show you now," he said, lips brushing against hers, "then I fear you'll never return to your suite." He pulled back enough that she could look him in the eye.

"And why is that?"

"Because I won't stop kissing you once we start." His thumb brushed over her lips as he released a slow breath. "Because once I have you, I won't want to let you go."

Marietta lifted her face to his, whispering, "That seems better than the alternative."

"And what's the alternative, Marietta?"

"Being in that gods damned suite."

A laugh escaped the King, and for a moment Marietta thought he would kiss her, but he stepped back and offered his arm once more. "Come. We'll take the long way back."

Disappointed and breathless, Marietta continued down the hall with the King. Stupid, he was married, as was she. But Keyain didn't give her a choice in the matter. And the King? Well, if what he said was true of Valeriya, then what harm did it cause?

That's beside the point—it was wrong. Gods, it was for the best that the King stopped such a kiss. It would have been both wonderful and terrible, equally terrifying and thrilling, and utterly reckless. She forced herself to stare down the hall, ignoring the King's gaze upon her.

They walked in comfortable silence. Holding onto the arm of the King, she savored the closeness of him, for it would be as close as she could ever be. Beyond the inappropriateness of kissing him, it simply made little sense. King Wyltam was vexing, often stoking her temper or leaving her frustrated. Though, often he seemed to leave her breathless as well. He was confusing and contradictory, as unpredictable as a storm cloud, yet she wouldn't trade his company for any other. Such a confession made her chest lighter.

The halls remained empty as they walked, devoid of any person. "Is everyone asleep?" she joked, breaking the silence.

"Not quite," he said with a smile. "I just know the best ways to avoid people."

"That sounds like you." Marietta laughed, and turned to him with a grin. For a moment, Wyltam's smile faltered into a look of awe before he cleared his throat and looked ahead.

"You know," she said, attempting to get his attention once more, "I like that about you. It's entertaining, the way you are a public leader but hate the public."

"I don't hate the public. I hate the attention."

"All attention?" she teased. "Even mine?"

"Never yours."

"Good, because I like giving it to you."

He laughed, glancing down before looking at her. "I'll take every drop of you I can get."

Locked together, their gazes refused to drop as they approached the door to the Noble's Section. The King paused a moment, then turned and held the door open for Marietta.

Grasping his arm once more, they made their way to the stairs as voices sounded from a room. "Looks like not everyone is asleep," she murmured. In the doorway to one of the common rooms, a few people watched them make their way to the stairs. What a sight for them to behold: a pilinos at the arm of the King. She laughed at the thought. Perhaps they should get used to that.

The voices faded as they climbed the dark stairwell to Marietta's floor. On one of the landings, the King stopped. He hesitated, then placed his hands on her hips. Out of instinct, she tried shifting away, but he held tight. "Entertain me for a moment, Marietta."

In the dark, she could see the faint details of his face. Without another thought, she brought her arms up around his neck. "Is holding me your idea of entertainment?"

A smile curled onto his lips with a laugh. "Wynn was right—you are acting quite brash this evening. But please, I enjoy being close to you," he said. "Just enjoy this moment with me."

"That's all you want—a pleasant moment with me in a dim stairwell?"

"I'm a simple man; I'll take any moment with you."

Marietta's heart skipped a beat at his words, making it hard to hold herself back from him. "Aren't you a male, not a man?" she asked, attempting to change the subject.

"Don't you say man and woman?"

"So you've noticed."

"Of course, you're from Enomenos, Marietta," whispered the King, his hands squeezing her hips. "Practically the Princess of Enomenos."

"Princess?" She shook her head with a laugh. "I'd rather be its queen."

The King stilled with his lips parted. His hands slipped from her hips and up her back as he pulled her closer to his body. A thought trickled into her mind from his treatment of her, from his words. If he could be tender with her, then what prevented him from treating pilinos better? Perhaps there was a part of him that could understand, that would push for change.

"I wish you cared as much about the half-elves and humans of this city as you do me," she whispered. "Perhaps if you cared about being king—"

King Wyltam's hands released her waist, one coming to her chin. "I care more about Satiros and its people than you understand. Change cannot be sweeping with such hate deeply instilled in the elven community, Marietta." His free hand reached up, brushing a hair from her face. "I've been King for less time than you've been alive, and I've made small, gradual changes working towards a better future for the pilinos who live here."

"You're lying—"

"I'm not, Marietta. Look at me." For the first time, he wore his emotions clear on his face, brows furrowed, lines bracketing his mouth. "Your last words to me at the sculpture garden have hounded me day and night. I can't stop thinking about them—about you."

"But the pilinos who are here, who are still hunted by the other city-states—"

"Do you understand how many less used to make it here? In my mother's reign, most who escaped to Satiros from other city-states died. My mother hated pilinos and placed the strictest restrictions on humans and half-elves," he said, his words coming quick. "I act like an apathetic king so it looks like things slip through the cracks, that I'm not paying enough attention to those who seek refuge here."

"You *act* like an apathetic king?" The foundation on which Marietta built her visage of Wyltam began to crumble. Did he truly care?

"I order Keyain and his men to let them come, let them join the temples, that it isn't worth the resources to stop them—but it's because I want them to be safe. I do not have them chase down those who flee to Enomenos; I do not cut down those who hide in The Weeds."

She laughed mirthlessly. "How can you say that but then attack Enomenos and claim it's for unity—attacking a city of free people?"

"I told you I wanted to force the conversation between Enomenos and Satiros," the King snapped. The anger in his features, his scowl—his frown—made Marietta's heart skip a beat. It made him ordinary, approachable, utterly like a typical person. For a moment, it was as if he didn't wear his crown. For a moment, it was as if he trusted her with seeing his emotions. "Do you know why Keyain was in Enomenos all that time with you?" When she didn't answer, he continued. "He was searching for the leader of the Exisotis, The Shepherd. I want to work with them, to unite Satiros with them. Gaining their trust would aid Satiros in becoming an Enomenoan city-state."

"So, what happened during all this time? People continue to suffer because of your inaction. While you slowly implement change, your laws still consider pilinos lesser people."

"But I make changes so that their children and grandchildren will know peace. It is the best I can offer." The King stared into her eyes, the hurt of his situation obvious to Marietta, but she ignored it.

How could he do nothing? "Just make them equals now."

"You don't understand the type of destruction that would cause—for the elves who hold wealth in the city and with the other city-states of Syllogi. Marietta, know this: I wish I could." His thumb brushed across her cheek, still caressing her face. "Do you want to know why I found you so curious?"

"Is this truth for a truth, Wyltam?"

"I don't need our deal to be honest with you," he whispered, his gaze on her lips. "When Keyain brought you to court, your existence shocked us because you were half-elven. Many saw that as a sign of weakness from Keyain, but want to know what I saw?" He leaned in, stopping before her lips. "Hope," he murmured. "That those in this city-state with the most tainted views can change. Hope that you are just the beginning. So, I seek you out. I ask you questions. I keep you safe—because you are the future of Satiros. You are the change."

Breathless, she stared at him with parted lips. "I'm your symbol."

"No, Marietta," he said. "You are my future."

Marietta held her breath. Was it true? Did the King want to help the pilinos citizens of Satiros? Marietta saw his emotion plainly in his face, the mask lifting and smoke clearing. The elven man who stood before her attempted to hide none of what he felt. If his words were honest, then Marietta could help him.

The change was incremental, but what difference would Marietta's position at court make? Other nobles might be bold enough to marry a pilinos, to include them in court. Perhaps one day soon, Satiros could have both women and pilinos in positions of power.

Marietta searched the King's face, his expression raw with furrowed brows and wide eyes. King Wyltam wasn't a monster—just a man doing the best with the cards he was dealt, slowly playing his hand; and she was his hope to win, his hope of change. "Wyltam—"

The King kissed her, pulling her hard against him, both hands caressing her face. Letting go of all thoughts, she sunk herself into the feeling of being kissed by a man trying to change the world for the better. Marietta parted her lips, King Wyltam's tongue sweeping past her own.

Stupid, so incredibly stupid.

But it was better than she imagined.

Marietta matched his intensity and wrapped her arms around his neck, standing on the tips of her toes. His taste, his touch, his need to pull her closer to him woke something in Marietta, something deeper than lust. For that moment, it was just them. He was just Wyltam and she was just Marietta. His touch felt familiar, comforting, and his kissing gave in to her need, leaving her craving for more.

Her heart thundered in her chest, feeling alive as they stood in the dim of the landing. Therypon said to seek the truth and it led her to that moment—being held by King Wyltam, feeling his lips against her own; so she kissed the King and she let him kiss her back. Marietta was his future. Together, they could bring change to Satiros.

Wyltam pulled back, gazing down at her. "I have half a mind to go somewhere a bit more private, Marietta."

"Why don't we?" she murmured.

He gave a breathless laugh as his lips met hers again, pushing her back against the wall. Heat blossomed in her stomach as he kissed along her jaw and down to her neck.

They heard the footsteps on the stairs when it was too late. By the time they untangled from each other, the damage had been done. "No, this is a fucking joke." Keyain stood on the step below the landing with two guards at his side. He shook his head, covering his mouth as he looked away. "Is this what returning her to our suite meant?" he asked, his voice rising. "So you could fuck my wife?"

Marietta didn't dare take a breath. They had made a horrible mistake. In a moment, her plan fell apart, amounting to nothing. Every sweet moment with Keyain, every kiss, every fuck, was for *nothing*.

One of his soldiers placed a hand on his soldier. "Keyain, keep it down." He shrugged off their hand and walked toward them.

Marietta glanced at Wyltam, who held his hand out in front of her. "She doesn't love you, Keyain."

"Clearly."

"Why did you marry her? Why did you do this to her?" His deep voice was a growl, the anger underlying his tone making her want to kiss him again.

"Who are you to question that?" Keyain spat.

"Your King, in case you forgot."

"So you can just fuck anyone's wife?" Keyain's voice rose to a yell as he took another step forward. "If you were anyone else, I would hit you right now."

"You couldn't lay a hand on me if you tried." Wyltam stepped in front of Marietta. "Your behavior towards her has been and continues to be a disgrace. You will always be a terrible partner. Why is she here, Keyain? Why did you marry her only to let her rot away?"

Keyain remained quiet with his jaw clenched and eyes burning. On the stairs, one guard murmured to the other and took off.

"Is it because of your odd fixation with Tilan?" Wyltam asked.

To hear his name on the King's lips—the ones she just had on her own—made her stomach drop.

"Odd fixation?" Keyain laughed. "You sent me there to find the Exisotis."

"I asked you to find The Shepard or his family. What were you doing all that time, Keyain? Why stay in Enomenos for Marietta? Why bring her back here if she clearly means nothing to you?"

"She means everything to me," he growled as he closed the space between them. "I have loved her every day for the past decade—"

"If that's true, then why did she suffer when she came to Satiros?" Wyltam asked. "I've had to check on her well-being multiple times—"

"Does 'checking her well-being' mean fucking Marietta? Pushing her up against the dark stairwell when you're supposed to be returning her to *my* suite?" Keyain yelled.

"I've had enough of this." Marietta stepped around the King, her blood roaring in her ears. "I don't love you, and I often question if I ever truly did. From the beginning, you've treated me like shit, acted as if my feelings are irrational, and let your anger snap whenever you wanted." She stepped closer to him, forcing him to take a step back. Keyain's lips quivered, and she could see the tears welling in his eyes. "How are you going to cry over this? I gave up after I found out about Tilan, about the Exisotis," she said, emotion clipping her voice, "and you left me to rot. You were okay with me wanting to die. How could anyone love you after that?" A hand reached her lower back, realizing the King had approached. The gesture calmed the building emotion. "I hate you, Keyain, and I hate being your wife."

"King Wyltam, a word." At the top of the connecting staircase dressed in a robe, stood Minister Dyieter. Despite serving Wyltam, the elder elf had a commanding presence, likely from the centuries spent judging others under Satiroan law.

"Now isn't a great time." Wyltam stayed his position at her back.

"I think now is the perfect time, considering your voices have carried down the hallways."

She closed her eyes at the realization. Everyone would know. Gods, Valeriya will know.

With that, the King stepped back. "Marietta, if you'd like to stay somewhere—"

"Perhaps she should remain in her own suite, Your Grace," Dyieter said, cutting him off. "Considering the alleged adultery you both have committed."

"We didn't—"

"It doesn't matter. The damage has been done and the rumors have already spread."

"I'll take her back," Keyain said, his voice taking on an unnatural calm.

"No, you won't," the King protested.

"Someone best take her back." Dyieter started down the stairs.

"I want to talk to her about all of this, but I have no intention of staying anywhere near her tonight." Keyain stepped past Marietta. "Come on."

They had already caused a scene. With Minister Dyieter glaring at her, she took a breath and began to follow Keyain.

Wyltam took her hand in his own. "Do you feel safe?"

She couldn't meet his eyes, couldn't look at him. Shame knotted her stomach, realizing everything she had lost by kissing him. "He wouldn't lay a hand on me."

"He best not," the King whispered to her. "Keyain, if there is so much as a scratch on her tomorrow, I will have you detained. Do you understand?"

Keyain didn't bother to turn around as he answered. "Yeah."

The King tried to bring her hand up to his mouth, but she pulled it away. It was too much. Who was she to kiss the King, a married man of the woman she conspired with? The former lover of the man she was married to? The ruler of the city-state she hated? Her words were nearly soundless as she turned to his face and said, "I'm sorry." Marietta followed Keyain up the steps without another word.

Chapter Seventy-Five
MARIETTA

Marietta wasn't sure what was worse—Keyain when he yelled until he was red in the face, or Keyain when he remained silent and calm. His rage was stirring underneath; she had seen as much from his eyes.

When they approached their suite, he sent the guards stationed outside their door to wait at either end of the hall. That was Marietta's second sign that the fight would be different—that Keyain was a peculiar degree of angry.

Once inside, Marietta darted for the bedroom, desperate to strip herself of her dress, but she only made it halfway. "That's far enough, Marietta." The calm in his voice made her hair stand on end. She faced him, trying to steady her breathing as Keyain narrowed the pace between them.

"How long has this been happening?" Keyain's lumbering form towered over her, fists clenched at his side.

"Keyain, I—"

"How long?"

Marietta hesitated, not wanting to share the truth. "Tonight was the first—"

"What about the sculpture garden?" Emotion cracked his voice, tears welling in his eyes.

"Nothing happened at the sculpture garden."

"But it almost did, didn't it? You knew what he was doing the whole time—kissing your hand, your injured ankle." He dragged his hand

through his hair, his gaze landing on anything but Marietta. With a sigh, he unbuttoned the top of his shirt, shrugging off his jacket and tossing it on the back of the chair. "Why?"

She didn't dare to breathe. In all the years she knew Keyain, he has never remained this calm while angry.

"Marietta, tell me why."

At her silence, he stalked towards her, Marietta taking a few steps backward until she hit the wall. Keyain leaned over, bracing himself. "Do you think he loves you?"

"Gods, Keyain. No—"

"Finally, an answer."

Marietta glared up at him, flinching away as he cupped her cheek.

"This is what you want, right? To be pinned against a wall, or is that only Wyltam when you thought you wouldn't get caught?"

Her breath caught in her throat.

"Tell me it isn't true."

She closed her eyes, unable to look at him. Then she felt his lips on hers. Marietta tried to pull away, but Keyain used both hands to pin her in place.

"Kiss me as you kissed him." His voice cracked, and he kissed her again, Marietta not reciprocating with fear lodged in her throat. "Kiss me as you kissed him, Marietta," he whispered, desperation in his tone.

But she didn't.

His forehead rested on her own as he heaved a sob. "It was all a lie. You don't love me; you never fell back in love with me."

Marietta pushed back into the wall, wishing to be away from him and his heartbreak. Tears streamed down his face as he shook his head.

Keyain took a deep breath, stepping away from Marietta, his expression crumpling. "Start talking."

Fear dug at her mind, disabling her words. Where the heat usually flared in her chest came a stirring, like the way wind twists to form a tornado. At first, it added to her fear, but then realized it was a comfort—a sign not to hold back. "Did you think I'd ever love you after all of this?"

she said, squaring her shoulders to him. The whirling in her chest was like chaos, growing faster. "I hate you, Keyain—you are my enemy. How could you be anything more after destroying my life? Taking away my freedom?"

Keyain closed his eyes, a hand covering his mouth as another sob choked him. "So you finally learned to lie." He shook his head, swallowing hard.

"You killed Tilan—"

"Tilan was a monster."

"He was my husband!" Her breaths became ragged with all the anger built since she woke up in Satiros—since the night Keyain had murdered him.

"And what of me? I'm your husband, Mar."

"Is that so? Tell me about our wedding day, then. Who was there? Did I smile when I agreed to marry you?" She stalked towards him, grinning at his silence. "Oh, you can't, because I left you. I decided I wanted to live my life without you in it, but you dragged me back." She laughed, craning her neck to look up into his face. "The day I married Tilan was one of the happiest in my life. Our ceremony was on the shore of Lake Malakos in Olkia, surrounded by our friends—our community. There wasn't an empty seat, and my parents cried tears of joy. They loved Tilan, as did I."

"Stop it," he hissed, tears falling.

"Stop what? Telling you the truth? Isn't this what you want?"

"Tilan lied to you the whole time—"

"And so did you! You were the Minister of Protection, pretending to be a bodyguard! Do you understand how insane that is?"

"I wasn't supposed to fall in love with you," he choked out, wiping away the tears that fell.

Marietta cocked her head. "Excuse me?"

Keyain bit his tongue, eyes burning. He only shook his head. "Things are going to change. You're done running around like you're the Queen of this fucking palace. I'd confine you to our rooms, but then you won't get to see how much you embarrassed yourself tonight."

"Oh, okay—"

Keyain held up his hand. "Marietta, everyone will know. They'll assume you and Wyltam have been having an affair."

The swirling in her chest died at that realization.

Keyain laughed, wiping away his tears. "You're in over your head. You will never keep up with court, Marietta." He gripped her chin, turning her crestfallen face at him. "It's funny that you kissed him so willingly considering he's certain you're on the Exisotis's side."

Marietta stilled the panic that wanted to rise in her face. Gods, the King knew. Or at least, he suspected. Was that why he kissed her? Is that why he was kind to her all along, hoping she'd confess that she's part of the Exisotis? The realization came as a crushing blow to her chest.

"I protected you, Marietta. If you were still in Olkia when we attacked, we would have rounded you up with the other Exisotis families and used you to get Tilan to speak."

"Is that how you justify it?" she said. "Capturing me and killing Tilan?"

Keyain scoffed. "He lied to you, just as I did, yet you can still love him. Why can't you love me?"

"Because you killed him, Keyain!"

"And if Tilan were alive, could you love me?"

"Never."

Silence settled between them as she held her glare.

Keyain shook his head. "You've changed so much since we were together."

"Your idea of me is not my responsibility to live up to."

"This," he said, gesturing between them, "is done. You and I are done. By law, you are my wife and only remain so for my control. From here on out, you will listen to me—"

"I will not—"

He held up his hand, silencing her. "Learn when to stop talking. When this war is over, I'm ending our marriage, and I will leave your fate to the King's Council of Ministers. I protected you, Marietta, but not anymore. Not after this." He shook his head, running a hand through his hair. "I hate that after all of this, after you leaving me, loving Tilan even knowing his truth, wanting the King, and fucking the guard from the temple—"

"What? I never—"

"Does it matter? It might be a rumor but it's not outside of your nature." She glared at him with new fury.

"After everything, I still love you, Marietta; but I can't be near you." He turned, heading to the door. "I'm stationing extra guards at our door. No one comes in or out until I'm back. If you try anything—to leave or escape—I will have you thrown in the dungeons for treason."

The door snapped shut behind him, leaving Marietta alone, dumbfounded. She should have accepted Grysella's help. If she had, she'd be with the Exisotis, safe from this court and Keyain's devices. Tomorrow, she would go to the temple. Deania and Coryn could help, could protect her against the crown. They said as much during her last visit.

Gods, but she still had the papers for Valeriya.

Marietta scrubbed her face, then yanked her hair free of its bind. If sleeping with Keyain was to help get information to the Exisotis, then she wanted to make it count. She'd ask the Queen to meet again, dropping off the papers. Perhaps she could get one last piece of information from Keyain.

Keyain only opened his desk in the morning before leaving for his meetings and in the evening when he returned them. Though she couldn't break into the desk, they must discuss those papers within their meetings. Trying to overhear them would be a risk, but the situation changed. If Keyain caught her, what's the worst he could do?

Chapter Seventy-Six

ELYSE

E lyse woke to the sun creeping in through the blinds. Wrapped around her was Az, holding her close under the silk sheets that covered them both.

A knock sounded on the bedroom door, startling her. "Good morning, goddess," Az said, his voice heavy with sleep. He kissed her neck at the spot he bit last night, causing her body to melt into him. His hands rubbed down her hip, Elyse realizing she was still naked. Heat came to her face as Az murmured, "Perhaps we should try it again."

The knock turned into a pound on the door.

"Busy," Az called out, his hand gliding to Elyse's center.

The door flew open, revealing Sylas. "Irresponsible—both of you."

"Sylas, my friend, my lady is in my bed—"

"And Keyain is at the door. Just about knocked it off the hinges with his rage," Sylas said, turning his gaze to Elyse. "You never went back last night, never sent a message saying you were staying, and he is furious. I suggest you get dressed and go, Elyse."

But she would not go—she was staying. Elyse and Az were leaving for Chorys Dasi. She turned to Az, at a loss for what to do.

"I've got this," he murmured, pressing a kiss into her temple. "Just stay in bed and rest, goddess." Az rose from the bed fully nude and strode towards the door.

"Put some damn clothes on," Sylas said with a scowl.

"I've got nothing to hide," Az teased with a wink. For as angry as Sylas was, Az seemed optimistic, but he yielded, grabbing his underclothes.

He stepped outside with Sylas, leaving the door cracked. As Elyse lay in bed, she realized Keyain wouldn't leave until she talked to him—until she proved she was okay.

With a sigh, Elyse stood, unsure what to put on. All she had with her was her gown from the night prior. Determined to find something, she walked to Az's wardrobe and dug through his shirts. Most were sheer or had a neckline so deep that they were no better than being naked. Towards the end of the rack, she found a black silk tunic, simple by Az's standard, and slipped it on, the hem hitting the top of her thigh.

Sylas and Az's bickering carried into the room, then Sylas yelled, "What?"

Perhaps she should wait a moment, let Sylas calm down. As she inched towards the door, the words became intelligible. "You don't even know if she can shift, Azarys!" Sylas said, anger dripping in his tone.

Azarys? Elyse must have heard him wrong.

"But I do know. I'm telling you, she takes after her mother—I felt it last night."

"I'm sure you felt a lot of things last night," Sylas snapped, followed by a sigh. "We don't know how strong the traits are in her—"

"I do," Az said, pausing. "What if I confirmed it?"

Only her breath sounded as the males stood in silence.

"Azarys, what did you do?"

There it was, that name again. Elyse pulled open the door, her brows furrowed.

The males gaped at her as Az's face paled. "I said to wait in bed."

"Why is he calling you Azarys?"

He said nothing, just shaking his head, running a hand through his hair.

"Answer me." She hated the emotion choking her voice. Deep down, she knew Az being a childhood nickname was most likely a lie. Stupid, how was she always so stupid?

Sylas' breath caught, his eyes growing wide. "Tell me that isn't what I think it is on her neck."

Her hand flew to the spot Az bit, touching nothing but smooth skin.

"As I said, I confirmed it." His hand reached out to Elyse, but she recoiled.

"One of you answer me right now," she demanded

Sylas laughed, the humor not reaching his face. "Even for you, this is too far. You are the most foolish person I have ever met." He shot a scathing glare at Az. "I'll let Keyain know she'll be down in a minute."

"She won't be down. We're leaving today—"

"Look at her face; she's not going to Chorys Dasi." Sylas gave her a sad stare, shaking his head. "At least, I wouldn't if I were her."

"Go," Az demanded. Sylas took off down the hall. "Elyse, I can explain."

"You best start."

"My real name is Azarys."

Tears fell from her eyes, emotion choking her throat. Of course it was.

"Don't cry, goddess," he said, stepping towards her. She moved away from him, his expression falling.

"You lied to me all this time. Who are you?"

"I can explain more when we get to Chorys Dasi."

"I'm not going with you, not when I just learned your actual name," she said, exasperated. Az grabbed for hand as she backed into the room.

"Elyse, please don't do this."

"What else was a lie? The 'special elves' and wanting to be my husband? Falling in love with me?"

"None of that was a lie. Please—"

"Stop," she said, ripping off the borrowed shirt and slipping into her gown. "I gave you the opportunity to be honest with me last night, yet you still didn't tell me your real name. If you lied about something as basic as that, then you lied about other things." She thought back to her dinner with Sylas, his warning now strikingly clear. *The fool isn't the partner who was tricked, but the partner who intended to deceive.*

Az came up behind her, placing a hand on her arm. "I am falling in love with you, Elyse. Please, look at me."

She jerked from his grasp. *"Azarys,"* she hissed, "I can't trust you, let alone move to an unfamiliar city-state with you." Elyse hated the tears that fell, hated the hurt she felt.

Keyain was downstairs. She needed to get to him, to go back to the palace. Her breath shook as she walked to a mirror that hung on the wall to make herself decent. Elyse paid little mind to the tangled mess on her head and the black splotches that marred under her eyes. No, the massive red mark on her neck drew her attention. Her hand flew to it, gasping.

Az came up behind her, a hand falling on her shoulder.

"What did you do?" she whispered.

"Elyse, please—"

She twisted away from him, holding the unzipped dress to her as she stumbled into the hallway. She was so stupid. How could she hide that from Keyain, from anyone at the palace?

Az grabbed her wrist hard enough she couldn't pull out of it. "Please. Is this what you want?" His lips trembled as he spoke, emotion choking his words.

"Brynden!" Sylas bellowed from the first floor.

"You're a stranger," she whispered.

"I'm the same male," he pleaded. "As dramatic and self-loving as ever. I'm the same male who wrote you letters, who praised your drawings. Elyse, I'm still me."

"But who are you? I know nothing of you. And after the other type of elf nonsense that you spouted yesterday, I know you're lying to me. About everything!" She used the heel of her hands to wipe away the tears. "I'm going back to the palace."

She turned, but he grabbed her hand. "Okay," he choked out. "If that's what you want, I won't persuade you to stay." He took a steadying breath. "But you can't tell anyone about my name, or about our elven heritage. They will kill you if you talk, Elyse, and even I don't have that much power to prevent it."

"Who are *they?*"

He shook his head. "Promise me, please. You leaving is tearing me apart—" he squeezed her hand "—but I cannot handle you dying. The end of you is the end of me."

Elyse shook her head. "You're crazy," she said, taking a step down the hall, but his grip held her back.

"This is breaking my heart." He closed the space between them, his hand caressing her cheek, brushing his thumb over her lips as a tear fell from his eye. He gave a sad laugh. "Now that you're leaving, I can feel it."

She stared into his russet eyes, wishing he would stop talking, that he would leave the words unsaid.

"I love you, Elyse."

She took a shattering breath. Elyse wanted to love him. She wanted to say it back. "I'm sorry."

Stepping out of his grasp, she spared him one last glimpse. To his dark hair, pulled back but mussed from sleep. To his slightly hooked nose, set wrong after an injury in the army. His high cheekbones. His soft lips. Elyse took it all in, imprinting the details to her mind.

Sylas waited in the foyer, leaning against the opened front door, Keyain's voice ranting on the porch step. The expression Sylas gave her was pitiful. She wanted his scowl, his amused smirk, not his pity.

"Wait," Az called, running down the stairs to her. He cupped her face, staring into her eyes, then kissed her. His arms held her close, letting the kiss linger on her lips.

She should pull away, should tell him no, but she wanted his kiss. She wanted to wake up in his bed, the morning just a vivid nightmare. As he pulled back, the reality of the situation hit her.

"Goodbye for now, goddess. I'll pray every day until I make my way back to you." He lifted her hand, kissing her palm. "I will keep every promise I made to you."

"Hurry up," Keyain yelled.

Oh, gods, was he pissed.

She tore her gaze away from Az and walked out the front door. Sweat coated the loose-fitting training clothes that Keyain wore, his hair slick with sweat. He took one glance at her, swearing. "What happened?"

"Nothing, Keyain," she said, making to walk past him, but he caught her arm.

"I am not in the mood for this," he said through gritted teeth. "Tell me what happened—you're crying, and you have a fucking mark on your neck. Did Brynden force himself on you?"

Az appeared in the doorway with a snarl on his face. "Bastard, I would never—"

"Stop," snapped Sylas.

Elyse squeezed her eyes shut, wishing to be far away from Az. "No, he didn't force himself on me. Can we please go?"

"Then why are you crying? And you," he said, turning his anger towards the townhouse. "Do you get off on marking young girls, branding yourself on their necks?"

"First of all, she's an adult—not a girl," Az hissed. She turned to see Sylas holding him back in the doorway.

"If she acts like a child, I'll treat her as one."

"And second, fuck you, Keyain," Az spat. "I'm in love with Elyse."

Keyain huffed a dry laugh. "Both of you are children." Keyain handed her a cloak. "Put that on. Wouldn't want your dress from yesterday to be so obvious when we walk back."

"Take our carriage," Sylas offered, with his hand still on Az's chest as he pushed him back. "It's the least we can do."

Keyain glared at Elyse. "I think she's going to need the whole walk back to explain what in the hells happened. You're a good male, Sylas. Consider switching courts or finding new friends, ones that won't continue to drag your reputation down."

Elyse dared to look at Sylas, who stared at her with furrowed brows. "I've considered it," he said.

"Come on." Keyain fastened the cloak around her and pulled her down the walkway.

"Elyse, I love you. Don't doubt it for a min—" The front door slammed shut, cutting off his sentence, but it didn't snuff the muffled yells coming from the townhouse.

"Talk," Keyain said, his tone demanding. He had never been like this towards her.

"I messed up, and I'm sorry. I should have sent a note—"

"You should have, but I'm more concerned about why you're upset now. If he forced himself on you—"

"I wanted him, Keyain," she said. "I don't want to talk about it." She couldn't talk about it—Brynden was a fake and Az was a liar.

Keyain pestered her for the rest of the walk, questioning her like the night in the infirmary; yet she said nothing—revealed nothing. Frustrated, Keyain tried yelling at her, demanding her to say something, anything. But she remained quiet. Nothing but the truth could explain what happened.

Over the course of the walk back, her heart broke piece by piece, step by step. *I love you, Elyse.* But he didn't love her enough to tell her the truth.

She was so gods damned stupid. Stupid to trust a stranger, to let herself be so vulnerable. Stupid because she was falling in love with him, too, and with each broken piece of her heart, she knew how true it was.

Once back in her suite, she then had to convince Keyain to leave, that she would be fine on her own—because she would be. At least she told herself that.

She leaned against the front door, head tilted to the ceiling as the tears came. Slow at first, then a steady stream. A sob escaped her mouth. Elyse felt dirty, could still feel his hands on her. Yes, she wanted Brynden, but not *Azarys*. He was a stranger, and she let him in.

She pushed off the door, heading to her bedroom, when someone cleared their throat. Startled, she looked towards her study to find her father. "Get over here."

Elyse wanted to resist, thought of running out the door for help. He shouldn't be here. Anger blossomed in her gut—a seething rage because he knew. Her father knew everything.

"Quite a look for you, daughter," he said as she approached. "Pairs nicely with the image you portrayed last night. I hate to ask, but Sauntyr asked me to find out. Are you taking anything to prevent pregnancy?"

Elyse's heat froze, her anger giving way to panic. Gods, she hadn't thought about that.

Her father laughed. "Of course not. Though pregnancy is unlikely, if you carry Az's child, Chorys Dasi would take custody of the babe—"

"You mean if we bred?" she said, repeating Az's terms from the night before.

Her father blinked. "So you know both his name and our true forms." He shook his head, standing up. "A shame, really." From his pocket, he pulled out a vial of Choke. The liquid inside appeared murkier, the vial larger. Her father stalked toward her. Every instinct said to flee, but fear locked her in place. "You're too curious for your own good, and now you've grown close with the King. You're a risk, and we have no reason to trust you anymore." His hand reached out, grabbing where the base of her head met her neck. "Did you enjoy your freedom while it lasted?"

"What are you talking about?" she whispered, shrinking away from him.

"Do you think after all I have done for you that I would allow you to just walk away?" Her father laughed, a smile tugging at his lips. "You are wanted by many and have grown ever more useful to me. You refused Az, and now I have to drag you to Chorys Dasi myself." He shook the vial in his hand.

"No," she hissed, stepping away from his grasp. "You need to leave."

His grip tightened, taking his strength and throwing her to the ground. The smack of her head against the wall made lights dance in her eyes. Her father loomed over her. "Who's going to stop me?"

"You're a terrible father who—"

He kicked her in the ribs, knocking the air from her chest. Another kick landed on her hip. She gasped for air, remembering back to the day she ran from Az when he and Keyain fought in the Central Garden.

"I gave you more than you realize and you disowned me. And for what? So you could fuck Azarys? Study magic? You are the worst parts of your mother, and it disgusts me. No one will be there to take care of you when your mind goes, Elyse. Not Keyain, not the King, and definitely not Az. I'm the only one who will be there when it does."

No, he wouldn't.

Her father would push her to her death, as he did with her mother.

A calm rage washed over her as she stared up at her father. He pushed his honey-colored hair from his face—the same hair as hers. Elyse may look like her father, but she refused to be *his*.

The aithyr came to her easily, curling inside her body and for once not bucking against her control. As her father went to toss the vial at her, she raised her hand. "No," she hissed. "Never again." A gust shot from her hand, the force snapping into her father as he flew backward. There was a sickening crack as his back hit her desk.

Her father hissed and looked at her. "You will regret that, you stupid bitch."

Panic seized her heart. At his tone, at his expression. As she tried to focus once more, she tried and failed to reach the aithyr.

Her father pushed himself up. Before he could narrow the space between them, she jumped to her feet and sprinted from the room. He caught her cloak, the fabric jerking her back at the neck. She reached around, ripping it from his grasp.

"Stop fighting your fate."

Her father followed her as she ran into her bedroom and made for the bathroom. As she turned to slam the door, his foot blocked the jam. "Do you seriously think I'd ever let you go?" He laughed darkly. "Did you think any Satiroan law would prevent me from using you as I intended? You were made from the beginning to help my position rise, Elyse. The sooner you accept it, the sooner we can be done with the drama."

He pushed on the door and Elyse pushed back, her heart thundering in her chest. This was bad—worse than bad. Her father had no intention of letting her go, no intention of letting her be free. She couldn't let that happen.

As her father began to win the push on the door, Elyse focused her mind and let the aithyr creep in. The energy thrummed under her skin.

She reached through the crack, grasping her father's arm, and imagined lightning. Sparks emanated from her hand and shot up her father's arm, causing him to scream out in pain. For a moment, he stepped back and Elyse slammed the door on his face, locking it.

His fist hit the door as she backed away from it. "You fucking bitch." He hit the door again. "You'll have to come out, eventually. I'll be waiting for when you do." The sound of his footsteps faded as he left her bedroom.

Elyse couldn't leave. She wished she could do the magic Sylas had done last night, to message someone to help her. Someone would come eventually. That door wouldn't open until she knew it was safe.

Determined to wait for help, Elyse sat on the edge of her tub. From where she sat, she saw her reflection. Ragged, with a mess of hair, smears of makeup under her eyes, and the mark still on her neck. Her hand shook as she raised it to the redness, checking for a bump. What did he do to her?

A sob worked its way from her chest, spilling out her eyes. Her breaths were quick to come, not enough air filling her. Last night, she had thought she'd be readying herself to leave for Chorys Dasi. Now, she was locked in her bathroom with tears staining her cheeks. Foolish of her to ever think she'd ever be with him.

His name was a curse, neither Brynden nor Azarys in her mind. To think of his being, of his words, were like knives in her chest. *I love you, Elyse.* The pain hurt more than she imagined as she slumped to the floor and tucked her knees into her chest. Those words would haunt her, torment her for the response she would never give him.

I love you, Az.

Chapter Seventy–Seven

MARIETTA

Marietta woke to Keyain ripping off the covers from the bed, to him looming over her. "Get up."

"What are you doing?" she protested, inching away from him.

He grabbed her arm, dragging her to her feet. "I said get up."

She shook free of his grasp, staring at him through sleepy eyes. Anger lined his face, and he wore his training clothes. "What do you want, Keyain?"

"Let's go." He grabbed her again, pulling her from the room.

"Wait—let me change." Marietta wore only a silk nightgown.

"It'll be an encore to your performance last night," he hissed, pulling her through the dining room.

Marietta dug her feet into the carpet. "What are you doing?" She fought his pull, ripping her arm away from him.

Keyain jerked her forward. "Elyse. Something happened and she won't talk to me."

Marietta's heart stopped. "Is she okay?"

"No, she stayed the night with Brynden. Something is wrong."

Gods, she probably got to experience his fervent worshiping, only to find Keyain on the doorstep the following morning. Such humiliation would have been devastating.

Keyain pulled her out the door, and Marietta let him, jogging with the pace. She could feel it, the nervousness under his anger, the way the atmosphere in the Noble's Section seemed to change. A cluster of feelings

crowded her chest—heat, stirring wind, crackling burn, heaviness, unease. She ran faster, ahead of Keyain, causing him to pick up his pace.

Keyain threw open the door of Elyse's suite to find Gyrsh sitting on her couch. Keyain barreled towards him, fists clenched and a snarl on his face. "Find Elyse," he demanded to her. "You're breaching the agreement, Gyrsh."

"I merely had a chat with Elyse after my contacts I've been working with for months had an incident with her," he drawled, inspecting under his nails.

Marietta hoped Keyain punched the smirk clean off his face. She wished to watch it happen, but she needed to find Elyse.

She knocked on the bedroom door. "Elyse?" Upon no answer, she entered the room, closing the door as Gyrsh's grunting sounded. "Elyse?" she called again.

She heard a sniffle from the bathroom and walked to the door. "Elyse, everything okay?"

"I'm fine," Elyse said, her voice nasally, followed by a sniffle. "Don't worry about me, Marietta. I don't want to be a burden. I'm alright."

Though a door stood between them, Marietta knew she lied.

"Something happened," Marietta said, putting her back to the door, sliding down, "and if you don't want to talk right now, that's okay. But I'm going to be right here if you need anything, alright?" She slid her hand under the door. "I'll sit here for as long as you need it."

Elyse didn't answer. Marietta could imagine her pain, the humiliation. Gods knew she had felt it herself.

"You don't have to respond, but I'm going to tell you a story I think you'll want to hear," Marietta said, leaning her head back, staring at the ceiling. "Sometimes we do things we're not proud of—that hurt our hearts and cause our minds to linger." She paused, fidgeting with her hands as the memory came back. "The night I met Keyain, I was meeting with his friend, who wanted a position as my bodyguard for when I traveled. I had no idea that the Satiroan Minister of Protection sat across from me— flirted with me."

Marietta forced herself to take a breath. "His friend was a prick, and I left after he called me a clip. In my anger, I walked down a street I shouldn't have. Alone in the dark I made myself a target. Someone attacked me and almost dragged me into an alley."

Her voice trembled at the memory, at the metal biting into her throat. "Out of nowhere, Keyain appeared, punching the man until he no longer moved. He saved me. Took me back to my apartment," Marietta paused, the swirling emotions in her chest easing. "Gods, I was so scared, so shaken after the attack that I didn't want to be alone." She laughed, wiping away a tear as it fell. "At my apartment, he offered to take the position of my guard. Do you know how I reacted?"

Elyse was silent on the other side of the door, so Marietta continued. "I slept with him, quite literally a stranger I just hired to travel with me after I watched him likely kill a man with his hands. It was the most reckless and idiotic thing I've ever done. He was a stranger from Syllogi, and I made myself vulnerable to him."

A thump hit the door, Elyse sliding down its face. The chaos in Marietta's chest settled as Elyse grabbed her fingers under the door.

With a smile, Marietta continued. "The morning after was uncomfortable. I remember trying to throw him from my apartment, recanting my offer, but he insisted. It wasn't until a few months later that it happened again and that we finally became a couple." She squeezed Elyse's hand. "I was so embarrassed—humiliated—after that first night, but guess what."

"What?" she whispered through the door.

Marietta sighed in relief. Good, she was responding. "Life went on."

There was a moment of silence before Elyse let go of her hand, the door unlocking and swinging open. Marietta shifted, so she faced the door. When it opened, she saw Elyse, face red and blotchy from crying, her hair a mess, still in yesterday's gown. A large red mark marred her neck, the sight jogging something in her memory, but she pushed it back, opting to pull Elyse into an embrace.

Elyse began to cry again, Marietta's shoulder growing wet. She hushed into her hair, rubbing her back. "I know, Elyse. I know and I'm here. I'm not going anywhere."

"It hurts so much," she sobbed.

Marietta's breath caught, emotion choking her throat and blurring her vision. "I know. I know, Elyse. It'll all be okay, I promise." Her pain was so raw. Marietta was the one to push to pursue Brynden for fun, forgetting that this could be the outcome. This was her fault. Marietta pulled her closer as she fought her own tears. She thought she knew what she was doing, thought she knew how to handle the court. Now she made a mess of her and the King. She'd led Elyse to her heart ache. Keyain was right—she didn't understand court life and now other people were paying the price. The realization made her hate Keyain more.

They sat in silence for a few moments as their tears lessened. "Want to know the worst part about my story?" Marietta said, laughing, though she felt no amusement. She remembered her fight with Keyain the night before, all the anger and hate between them. "I didn't know Keyain was the Minister of Protection until a few months ago."

Elyse jerked up, hitting Marietta's head with her own. "What?"

Marietta rubbed her chin, saying, "I didn't even know we were married until I arrived." Elyse furrowed her brows. "Because I'm half-elven, Keyain didn't need my consent to marry me, so he did it without my knowledge."

Elyse sucked in a breath, her body trembling. "Can I tell you something," she whispered with wide eyes, "that you can't tell anybody else?"

"Of course. Your secrets will always be safe with me."

"He lied to me too. The entire time—Brynden's not his actual name. I found out this morning, after we...."

Marietta bit back her surprise. Of all the things she expected Elyse to say, that wasn't it. "What?"

"His name is Azarys. He lied—"

"And he warned you not to tell anyone." The two jumped at the sound of Queen Valeriya's voice. She towered above them with a frown tugging at her lips.

"Queen Valeriya—"

"Enough, Elyse. Az was clear of the consequences if you told anyone." She paused with a sigh. "I trust Marietta with this knowledge, but you both must never speak of this again."

Marietta flinched. The Queen must not have known about the night prior to trust her still.

"You knew?" cried Elyse.

"I did. You both need to listen to me carefully," she said, a translucent bubble appearing around them, muffling the yelling coming from the suite. "If either of you speaks a word of his name, you will be killed. Even I can't protect you," she said, her icy blue eyes locked with Marietta, "regardless of our relationship. Understood?"

"No," Marietta said, anger stirring. "I don't understand—"

"Enough, Marietta. You and I will speak in a week. I'll send you the details."

Confusion crossed Elyse's features, eyes glancing between the two. Marietta only nodded her head.

"Good. Now I'm going to drop the barrier and force Keyain and Gyrsh out of the suite. I suggest both of you lie low for a few days for both of your latest exploits." Queen Valeriya gave Marietta a pointed stare, turning her gut to ice.

Gods, she did know.

Marietta and Elyse remained on the floor as Queen Valeriya left the room. After the commotion from the suite died down, the Queen ushering the men out, Elyse leaned into Marietta. "Does it ever stop hurting?" she whispered.

Marietta's heart shattered, her voice so small and broken, but she didn't have it in her to lie. "No," she whispered back. "You just make room for it."

Pain from love was long-lasting. After she left Keyain, he remained in a forgotten part of herself. Tilan remained as well. For the men she loved were etched into her heart, forever branded there. Yes, both lied and lied continuously, but Marietta still loved parts of them. That didn't just fade away.

Elyse was about to learn that pain, though she quite possibly couldn't love a man she hardly knew; yet Marietta saw how she acted with him. The truth would hurt her, and like Marietta, the love Elyse had for Brynden would remain in her heart. When the silence became too much, Marietta said, "Let's get you washed and into some comfortable clothes."

Marietta spent the day with Elyse, the two lying in her bed. Marietta told her about the rest of her night—told her about the King's kiss in the stairwell. Elyse shared what happened between her and not-Brynden. Marietta didn't have it in her heart to tease her, knowing her pain was so raw, and likely it would remain as such for the foreseeable future.

How fortunate that, despite the awful things that had transpired since her arrival in Satiros, Marietta still had a friend. Elyse was quiet, thoughtful, bashful, and kind. And somehow, in their short time together, they learned they could lean on one another.

Friendship, in its most basic shape, was simply that. To support one another, to uplift and encourage, to listen and be heard. Elyse was her friend, and Marietta was sure of one thing at that moment—she couldn't abandon her.

Elyse could blossom if far away from Satiros, away from all the toxic bullshit that saturated these people. Stunted, they never gave her the proper care to grow. Perhaps they could escape Satiros together.

Chapter Seventy-Eight

VALERIYA

The plan fell apart. Everything Valeriya had worked toward had begun to land into someone else's hands. When did everything shift? How had she not known? Better yet, how had her sister not known?

Now, with Az making his name known to Elyse, the girl was in more danger, especially with her proximity to Wyltam. If he knew the truth, knew his actual name, then he could fit the pieces together. For Marietta to know as well was a damn shame. She hoped they both knew better than to say anything.

Before, Valeriya would've been confident that she could prevent them from getting hurt, from being targeted, but no one could know. Her and her sister's plan was to throttle Wyltam's court, build a new one, and place Valeriya at its head. That was why Chorys Dasi came to Satiros, that was what they had planned. And now? Sylas had been clear. She and her sister were cut out of the picture.

Valeriya trembled at the center of her bedroom, hands flexing at her sides. How could the Chorys Dasians betray them? After they had tasked Valeriya with the dirty work of weakening Wyltam and Keyain and to steal information. They didn't believe in equal standing for pilinos—that was going to be the fight after she controlled Satiros. But now?

She took a sharp breath. Nastanya needed to know. Focused, she ceased her pacing, pulling to the aithyr around her. She thought of her sister's rounded face, her large doe eyes, of her in the castle of Reyila, and formed the message wrapped in aithyr.

"*Chorys Dasi is deviating—they withheld that Wyltam knew magic. Implied we were cut out. Are we being made fools?*"

Through aithyr, Nastanya would have received the message instantaneously in the like of Valeriya's voice. A few moments later, her sister replied, "*Knew about Wyltam. Auryon said to stay your course. We'll be reunited soon.*"

She knew about Wyltam?

Valeriya's breath heaved as the room tilted under her feet. Why didn't she tell her sooner? For fuck's sake, she lived in the same suite as him, yet no one bothered to inform her? Even Sylas knew. Why did she say that *Auryon* said to stay her course? Nastanya was in charge. This was her plan.

A cold dread washed through Valeriya, her chest beginning to ache. She reached out to the aithyr once more. "*Who has the ruling voice in Reyila right now?*" A sickening feeling settled in her stomach. It couldn't be true. Not her sister.

After a few minutes with no reply, she reached out again. "*Nastanya, please. What happened?*"

There was a moment of silence, and then a new voice sounded in her head. "*My uncle and brother will finish carrying out our plan. Enjoy your remaining time in Satiros. You'll return to Reyila after we're done.*"

The smooth voice of Auryon sent chills through her body. Chorys Dasi took it over. They cut them out—cut Valeriya out. Now they were taking her throne away.

Part of her wanted to race to Wyltam, to his ministers, foil the plan entirely, but that wouldn't bode well for her. She'd rather live in Reyila than rot in the dungeons of Satiros. Her hands were tied. Everything she had worked for, had fought for, came crumbling down around her.

The bedroom felt too small, too confined. Valeriya threw open the doors to the balcony and stepped out into the cloudy evening. On the horizon, black clouds churned with streaks of lightning illuminating the twisting dark.

Alone.

Valeriya was alone. Nastanya abandoned her, and now she needed help.

Like an unwanted visitor, the image of Katya crept back in. Their first kiss was on the castle's roof as a summer thunderstorm blew through Reyila. Katya was yelling at her, and Valeriya couldn't pull her focus from her mouth, from how beautiful and fierce she was.

That first kiss was like lightning in her chest—feeling everything and nothing all at once. Katya was her rival, vying for a position Valeriya also wanted; yet, at that moment on the roof where Valeriya grabbed her face, kissing her with years of pent-up aggression and lust, the two became something more, something greater. Katya was her rock, anchoring her to the world. Without her, Valeriya remained stuck in her head. Alone.

Just message her. The rough edge of Katya's voice would be enough to steady Valeriya, to keep her focused. Together, they could find a way out.

Valeriya imagined the short black hair hanging into the glowering face, the intensity of her turquoise eyes. She used to tuck the short strands behind the blunted arch of her half-elven ears. A notch marred her right one from an injury she would never share.

There were a thousand things that she wished to say. Every day she thought of Katya, wondered how she was, often wanting to tell her of her day, of the things that reminded Valeriya of her. A crumpled flower, still beautiful and standing. The way shadows had danced across the cobblestones in the late afternoon sun. The quiet moments in the palace halls, like the ones she and Katya would seek for a moment of peace together.

More than anything, she wished to tell her those three words they never shared out loud. But Valeriya had felt them from Katya. It was in her mannerisms, the way she had concerned herself with Valeriya's troubles. The way Katya had held open doors for her. Her words of confidence when Valeriya had felt discouraged. The never-ending teasing when Valeriya had become lost in her head. The words were there every morning they had laid in bed, fingers intertwined, with the morning sun creeping into the room. Those three words existed in every interaction—unspoken but always true.

Katya held Valeriya's heart, the one that ached every day they were separated.

Just message her.

But what if she moved on? What if she knew her sister's plans had changed? Could Valeriya truly handle that possibility? Likely, no.

In those last days together, when Valeriya left to marry Wyltam, they agreed a clean break would promise a better future for them both; yet there Valeriya was, seven years later, with tears spilling from her eyes on the balcony of her room.

A gust whipped her long, red curls around her as the storm approached. Thick and sticky air gave way to the coolness of the storm, heavy raindrops falling. They hid her tears.

Alone. Valeriya was drowning. The plan was the last thing she had, a goal to change Satiros and rule under a new era. A chance to be immortalized. That dream was ripped out from under her. For all the effort Valeriya put towards helping Satiros, there was a gnawing emptiness inside her chest, replacing the hope that once bloomed there. Everything had a price and the cost of being remembered was her very being.

Sheets of rain cascaded from the sky, soaking Valeriya within minutes, yet she stayed on the balcony, watching lightning dance across the sky. The thunder rattled her chest as she heaved a breath, gripping the railing with her hands.

She couldn't stay.

Soon, she promised.

Katya would hear those three words from her soon.

Part 3

"But as always, you must wait to see the end of a
person, and no one ought to be called blessed until
he dies and his funeral is over."

- Ovid, Metamorphoses

Chapter Seventy-Nine

ELYSE

Funny how much can change in a week. The Chorys Dasians left, returning home after the incident with Az. Elyse didn't ask about it.

As much as she had liked Keyain, that diminished over the past week as well. Keyain tried again and again to get her to say what happened. From what Marietta shared, he threatened her, saying that if she knew and said nothing, that he'd throw her in the dungeons for treason.

Regardless of what happened between Marietta and the King, there was no reason for such threats. If Elyse wanted Keyain to know, then she would have told him.

The worst conversation was with the King. Compared to the shabbiness of her suite, Wyltam looked out of place on her tattered golden couch in his finery. If being alone with him in her suite wasn't enough to make her anxious, then the topic of conversation was. Concerned about her lack of preparation, as he called it, he wanted to have a medic ensure she wasn't with child. Through the heat of her face, she had explained to him she already started her cycle. Thank gods he didn't react. Instead, he just moved on to the next topic.

After her father broke into her suite, the King assigned her a guard to stay with her. Wynn was apparently with them during their night in the city, but Elyse didn't recognize him. In the haze of what was that day, he blended into the background. Little was she aware that Wynn was one of Wyltam's mages, part of the group who would train her.

Wyltam also thought it was time for her to have a mentor watch over

her as she practiced magic. Wynn made her conjure water, filling vessels up to predetermined lines to practice control. He would hold metal spoons, and Elyse would use magic to heat it enough to make it hot but not burn. It was one thing to transform aithyr; it was another to control it, to let it trickle out in the form of the magic one intended or desired to make. By the end of the week, Elyse impressed Wynn with her quick advancement, and he needed to reassess what to teach her next.

Marietta also came by every day, often with Amryth. The first time, Marietta baffled her by greeting Wynn by name. The male joined them at the tavern, which Elyse had missed.

Elyse found herself quiet most days. She laughed at Marietta's jokes, at Amryth's teasing. Wynn's lessons engaged her, and she stayed focused on the task at hand; but during the moments in between, her mind went back to Az, to his last words. *I love you, Elyse.* Stupid, plaguing words that left her awake at night, that haunted her during the day. Despite wanting to yell at him, wanting to curse him for lying, she wanted to know who he was.

Sure, he was Azarys, the same ostentatious lord as Brynden, but did he lie? What else were they hiding? It wracked her brain, never ceasing, but she didn't know where to start—until she found the paper Sylas had written her the day he stayed for dinner. He had asked her to locate the list of books in the library, but she never had the chance. She imprinted the titles into her brain, and she wished to go search in the library, but it scared her to leave her suite, scared of what the courtiers and nobles would say to her.

Once the mark faded on her neck throughout the week, she finally had the nerve to ask Wynn to escort her to the library. He was an intimidating male, towering over most and moving with the grace of a dancer. The gnarled scar on his face helped, too. No one would dare speak to her if Wynn was around.

Elyse hesitated at the threshold of the room, not wanting to leave.

Wynn glanced back at her, offering an arm. "I've got you; no reason to be nervous."

"I have every reason to be nervous."

"That's true if you're a skittering goat," he mused with a smirk.

"Funny." She took his arm.

He smiled to himself, proud of the joke. Somehow it made him more intimidating.

The guard uniform and sword at his waist didn't help. Everyone would stay clear of them as they ventured through the palace. No impromptu conversations, no invasive questions—Elyse could walk in peace. Plus, her outfit would draw some attention. After a week of just pants and blouses, Elyse couldn't get herself to change into a gown. Instead, she donned a black silk shirt that buttoned up the front, tucked into a pair of high-waisted tight pants. The only color came from her green embroidered slippers, the ones Marietta complimented a few weeks back.

Elyse hoped the all-black ensemble was as intimidating as her escort, that it acted as a uniform for the King. Let the court see who she worked for and then no one would bother her again.

She tensed as they passed a group of gossiping courtiers in the halls, their hushed whispers incoherent in the echoing foyer.

Wynn leaned over. "They're talking about your outfit."

"Why would you say that?" she said, fidgeting with the cuffs of her sleeves and hurrying their pace.

"No, I can hear them. They said your outfit is fierce, like you're a real noble. I think they mean as a noble who'd run their own estate, like a male."

"Great, I look like a male. How can you hear that?"

Wynn laughed. "You do not look like a male, but you hold yourself like a person with power. I think it's a compliment."

"Sure."

"So self-conscious," he teased. "I'll have to teach you how to use aithyr to amplify the senses."

"That's a thing?"

"You have so much to learn."

That was the truth. Every day, Elyse felt as if she learned something new, uncovered another secret. For all the bad, Elyse was happy the last few months occurred. Without her father and her pending marriage to Keyain or Brynden, Elyse felt like she had control. Though it was limited control under Wyltam, it was more than she had ever had; so, she walked with her head high, her shoulders back, and prayed to whatever god or goddess listened that Wynn was right about the courtiers' whispers. She wasn't soft, nor was she weak.

Each day, Elyse proved her strength to herself. To not give up, to not give in. Time would come for when she could look in the mirror and be proud. One day, she would love herself.

Chapter Eighty

MARIETTA

Marietta sighed. "Elyse's at the library again? That's the third day in a row."

Amryth looked up from her book on the other end of the couch. "You sound like a clingy lover."

"Not a clingy lover, just a desperate friend." Marietta sighed again, throwing herself back into the cushions.

Ever since Marietta found Elyse in the bathroom, she wanted to check in everyday. Gyrsh was a monster, trying to regain control over Elyse. At least, that's what Keyain shared.

Those were his last words to Marietta. Most mornings, he rose before she woke up and returned after she was already asleep. Unsure if it was to avoid Marietta or if the Exisotis made a move, she was happy Keyain was somewhere else. In the evenings, she ate with Elyse and Amryth—and sometimes Wynn.

Finding Wynn in Elyse's suite surprised her that first day. Not realizing they knew one another, his presence brought Marietta peace of mind—that a talented mage would watch over Elyse and make sure her father didn't return. Or the Queen, for that matter. Elyse had broken some rule by sharing Brynden's real name with Marietta. She hadn't talked to Elyse about it since the day they crawled into her bed, Marietta holding her as she cried.

Though the Queen's warning should have alarmed Marietta, she mostly found it curious. Valeriya knew the Chorys Dasians, knew Brynden's actual name, but why? Perhaps they were also working with

Exisotis. Marietta wanted to ask Elyse questions about Brynden and Sylas—to figure out if they were a part of the group—but didn't want to upset her. In due time, she would.

The documents she took from Keyain's desk still sat in her wardrobe, waiting to be handed to Queen Valeriya. Much to her dismay, Keyain kept his desk locked, Marietta never catching him off guard again. The information she had to give to the Queen was helpful, but it didn't feel enough.

A few days ago, Valeriya had sent a book to Marietta. Highlighted inside were the words 'The revelers meet' on one page, followed by 'just after midnight' on another. A clever system, considering Keyain would likely have the servants bring him any notes sent to Marietta. An irritating thought. At least she would meet with Valeriya tomorrow evening, though she barely gathered anything. What Marietta wished to do was eavesdrop on Keyain's meetings. It would be hard since he kept his distance. Perhaps that would be a suitable cover. She gave Amryth a saccharine smile.

"What do you want?" Amryth said without looking up.

"Are you up for a walk?"

"Of course, but what plan are you hatching?"

"No plan, just a simple walk," Marietta said, toying with a lock.

"Bullshit. What are you scheming?"

Marietta smiled. "Do you remember where Keyain has his meetings?"

"Why?"

"I haven't seen him in a week."

Amryth raised a single brow, giving a leveling stare.

"What? I haven't."

"Why do you want to walk by Keyain's meeting?" Amryth said, snapping her book shut.

"Well, the King mentioned the Exisotis making a move but—"

"You want to overhear what they're saying."

"Yes," she said, sitting up. Not false, she wanted to know what was happening in that regard, but she also wanted more information for the Queen.

"I'm sure Coryn and Deania will have an update when we go to the temple."

"Or, how about," Marietta said, getting up with a stretch, "we happen to walk by their meeting and I happen to hear something about my home city-state."

Amryth sighed as she stood. "This is a stupid idea. Keyain's already upset with you."

Marietta flashed a grin, shrugging. "Then what's one more thing?"

"This is a stupid idea," Amryth repeated beside Marietta. At the front of the palace, in the same section as the entrance, they were on the top floor, looking out to the Central Garden. Noblemen walked about the halls, some exchanging notes, others speaking in hushed tones.

"What? We're just taking a walk," Marietta said, offering a sweet smile to two elven men who stared at them. They nodded and went back to their papers.

"I'm not sure which meeting room he's in, let alone what meeting."

"He's a warmonger in a war—what else would they meet about?"

"He's also on the King's Council of Ministers and attends meetings related to those duties." Amryth sighed again. "I should stop letting you talk me into bad ideas."

"But then your life would be boring."

"Or calm."

"Exactly, boring." Marietta glanced around the corner, finding a few uniformed guards. "Perhaps they know?"

Amryth swore. "They would, considering they're all captains and part of the Elite Guard."

"Like you are."

"Like I was. Keyain and I agreed it'd be best if I transitioned to a different role a few weeks ago, since we spend so much time together."

Marietta jerked her head towards her. "You didn't tell me that."

"Didn't seem important."

"I don't want to affect your career, Amryth."

She batted away the words. "It was my idea to switch. I couldn't stand listening to them," she nodded her head at the soldiers, "gush about how great of a male Keyain is. I've seen the truth."

Marietta placed a hand on Amryth's arm. "I'm glad you have."

"Same." She sighed and rolled her shoulders. "Wait here. I'll say you have an urgent message for Keyain, so prepare some doting response. I'm sure they're expecting it."

Amryth approached a stocky, dark-skinned elven man. Her heart sank when she recognized the other two guards standing with him. One had ash blonde hair pulled into a tail and a sneer on her face—Adalyn, the guard from the Ertwymer Sculpture Gardens who witnessed the King nearly kissing her. The other was Ryder, the guard at the Snapdragon, who Adalyn told about the kissing incident.

Great, just great. The deities had damned her with such luck. All three guards turned their attention to Marietta, who tried to appear as demure as possible with her hands clasped behind her back, head cast down as she looked through her lashes. Adalyn would know, however, that she was less than the doting wife she attempted to play.

Amryth turned with a dour face and waved Marietta over. Marietta kept up the innocent act as she approached, the three guards glaring at her.

"Lady Marietta," the dark-skinned elven man said with a bow, his bald head catching the light. "It's been a while."

"Apologies, I don't think we've met." Unless they met while Keyain still kept her drugged.

"Oh, we have. I wouldn't forget the first time I met you back in Rotamu." He smiled, his mouth wide. "Back then, you were just his partner, not his secret *half-elven* bride."

The gods must have been toying with her. Marietta's smile fell as she remembered the first time Keyain left for six months, meeting his *friends* for drinks at a tavern. The bastard had referred to her as a clip.

"Peryn, that was a long time ago. What happened to the woman you traveled with, Rynka?" Marietta glanced in the hallway, hoping not to see the ill-tempered woman.

"She quit as soon as we returned to Satiros." Peryn gave her a leveling stare, his implication clear. Keyain had crossed a line. "I see you're still a half-elf."

"And what else would I be?"

"Well, you're definitely not good enough for Keyain," Adalyn said, looking over Marietta from head to toe with her arms crossed against her chest.

Marietta clenched her fists, checking her anger. She needed to persevere, get the information she needed, and she'd never see these people again.

"I don't know," Ryder said, running a hand through his auburn hair. He leaned to the side, glancing behind Marietta. "Her ass is as amazing as Keyain said."

With blinding anger, she was ready to snap as he burst out laughing. Amryth beat her to a response. "Marietta is a lady of this court, and you three will treat her as such. Understood?"

Ryder laughed again, grinning. "That was pretty tame compared to what I usually say about the noble ladies. Like that Lady Elyse—if I could get her to ride me like she did that Chorys Dasian—"

"Say that again," Marietta said, taking a step towards him, squaring her shoulders.

He laughed again, eyes shining. "Keyain said it was easy to get you riled. He also said you could scrap in a fight, so come at me, Marietta." He took a step forward, flashing a smirk. "I'd love to pin you down. You don't mind when other males have a go, right? Or is that just the King?"

"Enough, Ryder!" Amryth snapped, but he still approached Marietta.

Marietta stood her ground, her face softening in a sweet smile. "Perhaps the big, great Keyain isn't as big or as great as he would have you believe. Tilan, on the other hand—"

"Enough," Peryn said that time.

It was an order, but Marietta didn't answer to him. "Keyain had his reasons to be jealous, but really there was only one main reason."

"Enough, Lady Marietta," he said again, jaw grinding.

"Oh, I'm sorry. I probably shouldn't talk about the size of Tilan's cock in front of the people who murdered him. Was it one of you who did it? Part of the little mission to save me from Olkia?"

"Marietta," Amryth said, warning in her tone.

"What, they can't handle the truth about Keyain? How about how Keyain enjoyed my presence more when I wished to die than when I was healthy? He'd rather keep me confined and suffocating than speak up for myself."

"Enough!" Peryn yelled, taking Marietta by the arm. "I suggest you learn to stay quiet about sensitive information, especially regarding your rescue, Lady Marietta." He let go and adjusting his leather armor. "Now, why do you wish to see Keyain during his meeting?"

Marietta glared at Peryn. "I need to talk to him."

"You couldn't do that in your suite?"

"He's been avoiding me for a week."

"I would too if I found you kissing the King," Adalyn said with a glower.

Peryn held up his hand to Adalyn, not sparing her a glance. "Well, is it important?"

"Yes."

"What is it?"

She didn't come up with an excuse—shit. "Keyain should be the first to hear," she said, hating to form a lie on the spot.

His eyes narrowed. "Like what? Enlighten me."

Marietta crossed her arms. "It involves the future of mine and Keyain's family." The falsity rolled off her tongue, the guards exchanging surprised glances. "Would you like me to explain further, or can I please find which room my husband is in so I can tell him the news myself?"

Peryn cleared his throat. "Of course, follow me." He turned to his companions. "You two stay here. Not a word to anyone else. I mean it, Adalyn."

They nodded at his order. At least Marietta's lie forced them to quiet. She made a point not to look at Amryth. Even from her peripherals, she could see her glare. They walked down an adjacent hall, turning onto the side hallways. "Third door on the left. The meeting should end any minute."

"You're free to leave," Marietta said with a dismissive hand, irritated to be caught in an idiotic lie.

"I think I should wait—"

"So you can see Keyain's reaction when I tell him you found out first?" He scoffed, turning to Amryth. "You honestly chose her over us?"

Marietta's breath held, not realizing she made such a choice.

"Yes," Amryth replied. "And I would again a hundred times over."

"What of Deyra? How would your wife feel—"

Amryth grabbed him by the arm, wheeling him down the hall, fury in her face. It was subtle, but Marietta caught her glance, her head nodded towards the door.

Taking the cue, Marietta approached, hearing the muffled voices within the room, the words unclear and hard to understand. Carefully, she leaned against the door, her ear pressing against the wood.

"Some delegates reported denizens leaving the city-state proper, specifically the delegates from Wisteria Heights and the Blooming Borough," droned a man's voice. "They've reported many are upset over the current choices made by the King's Court regarding recent... events."

Someone grumbled something, the door dampening the sound.

"Say that again." Gods, that was Keyain. She'd recognize that angry voice anywhere.

"I said," spoke up a new voice, "perhaps if you didn't bring your clip bride into court and spend a ridiculous amount of resources on the missing pilinos, then this wouldn't be an issue. They say they're upset with the King's Court, but we know exactly who is causing the problems."

"Gyrsh, I've warned you for the last time." King Wyltam's deep voice was distinct from the others. She sighed, closing her eyes, blocking out the memory of his words. That evening he'd shown how *tender* he could be but hasn't reached out since. The line between them had been drawn. "The next time you say that word during our meetings, I'll suspend you from your position." He paused, the room in utter silence. "And if we're going to talk about those failing on my council, then perhaps you'd like to share why the Chorys Dasians fled."

"I told you, my whore of a daughter—"

"Enough." King Wyltam didn't need to yell to silence him, the command carrying weight. "Lady Elyse will not be a topic of these meetings."

"Oh, but you'll continue to bring up Marietta and her presence." She didn't need to see Keyain's face to know what he felt. Part of her was surprised he even spoke up for her at all.

"Perhaps I enjoy talking about your wife," drawled the King.

Something thudded. "We are not talking about—"

"My King, Keyain, enough of this," said a hoarse voice. "This is not how we conduct meetings. We decided last week that if we talk of Lady Marietta, it'll be to determine who is leaking information from the court."

Marietta's stomach sank, her limbs going numb. They suspected she was feeding information. They knew.

"I'm telling you, it's not Marietta. I've been monitoring her. One of my best guards is with her when she leaves the suite," Keyain ground out.

"It's not only her, Keyain," the hoarse voice said again. "We also discussed the possibility that Queen Valeriya had contacted Reyila."

They knew about the Queen too. Marietta needed to leave, wanted to move for the door, but she felt rooted in place. Just one more minute—maybe they would share something else.

"Amryth isn't with Marietta every time," the King added. "I think I proved that." Was this how he talked about that evening? Was it only a moment to use against Keyain? To torment him? A spark of anger rose in her. That night—that kiss—meant something to her, but she seemed to be alone in that notion.

There was a moment of silence. "Well, you were with Marietta so you can account for her time," Keyain said, his voice forced.

"I suppose I can."

"Have you followed up on the Queen, King Wyltam?" a nasally sounding voice asked.

"Funny you all keep suggesting our wives. I have my suspicions, and I have questioned her quite a few times, yielding nothing. Even under surveillance, we've still found nothing. If she is doing it, then she's better than I expected."

A muffled voice answered, but she couldn't hear what they said. The scraping of chairs and feet on stone followed. Marietta backed off the door but didn't have time to move down the hall before it opened.

"Oh, Lady Marietta, what a surprise." Minister Royir stood in the doorway, one hand still on the knob.

From beyond the doorway, she could still see King Wyltam lounging in his seat with one knee tucked into his chest. The way he looked at her with cold detachment made her stomach flip. "How curious. I wonder if she's here for me or you, Keyain." His words left her breathless. Was he mocking her for what happened on the stairs?

"Excuse me." Keyain pushed past Royir. "Marietta." Annoyance blanketed his expression as he reached for her arm to guide her down the hallway.

"Please share, Lady Marietta, what you were doing outside the door during our meeting?" The King stood now, approaching at a slow pace. His mask covered any emotion he had, but she remembered his easy smiles, the shyness of his laugh. She hated to remember them, wishing her mind would just forget.

"King Wyltam," she said, holding her chin high. "I was just hoping to catch my husband before lunch to see if he would walk with me. We need to talk."

"Marietta, I'm busy," Keyain said with a warning.

"This can't wait. You've avoided me for a week."

"What is it you couldn't wait to share?" The King asked, approaching her and Keyain. Behind, other ministers and noblemen filtered out of the room, many of whom she didn't recognize.

"I think it's a conversation better held private, Your Grace."

"Come on," Keyain said, gripping her arm and forcing her to walk.

"Marietta, it is not a good look to find you lurking outside our meeting. I think you owe an explanation to all of us here." The King's warning was obvious—they all thought she and Valeriya were leaking information, and they just caught her.

She looked to the King, then to Keyain. "I'm with child."

Keyain blinked. Once. Twice. "You're what?"

"Pregnant."

His face went white, his grip on her loosening. "Pregnant."

"Yes," she hissed, happy the lie stuck.

"How do you know?"

"If you've been around, you would know that I've been sick every morning."

"Excuse us," he said, ushering her down the hall.

"Do you think it's his or yours, King Wyltam?" someone asked, causing Keyain's grip to tighten.

"I guess we'll find out in nine months," the King drawled.

Marietta jerked back. He was feeding into the rumors that they were having an affair? Her patience ran out, having half a mind to unload her anger on the King; but Keyain gripped her arm harder. "Don't you dare."

She swallowed her anger, letting Keyain drag her out to the Central Garden, away from wandering ears and eyes.

Keyain gestured to a stone bench, having her sit. He stood for a moment, then took a seat next to her, hands scrubbing his face. "You're pregnant."

"Yes."

"How?"

"Well, Keyain," she said, forming a circle with one hand, holding out her index finger in the other. "When two people—"

Keyain cut her off as she slid her index finger into the circle. "Grow up, Marietta. I know how—I meant, weren't you taking anything? I assumed you wouldn't want a child with me."

"Slipped my mind."

He glared at her and then slumped back on the bench. "This should be one of the best moments of my life, but all I feel is dread." He closed his eyes, letting his head drop backward.

"So the King is telling people he and I—"

"No, he isn't telling. Wyltam is encouraging the assumptions."

Marietta dug her nails into her hands. Of course he was. Did his sweet words to her mean anything? He had called her his future, and now he fed into the rumors surrounding her affair. A part of her heart began to ache, not realizing Wyltam had found his way in. *I'll take every drop of you I can get.* Had he lied?

"I'm getting you out of here."

"What?"

Keyain looked at her, exhaustion wearing on his expression. "You're going to our estate on the lands we rule."

"Our estate? Lands we rule? I thought you were ending our marriage."

"That was before I learned you were with child. I wouldn't abandon you like that."

"No, you would just abduct me from my home."

Keyain sighed, shaking his head, looking off into the garden. "I don't know what we're going to do."

Marietta did. It was a lie—one he would discover eventually, but she didn't expect to be around when that happened. Between the false pregnancy and Wyltam's behavior, she recognized there was little reason to stay. After the meeting with the Queen, she'd ask for the Temple of Therypon for protection. She would finally be free.

Chapter Eighty-One

VALERIYA

The sun's warmth spread across Valeriya's skin as she walked arm in arm with Tryda, another afternoon spent with the elven female. She was the Lady-In-Waiting to Wyltam's mother for two hundred years; yet Valeriya had never brought herself to trust her. Tryda was kind, offering to guide Valeriya through the transition to Satiros, but she lacked awareness of political intrigue. She was, however, an excellent source for court gossip.

"In other news," Tryda said, her dark skin glistening in the sun, "have you heard about Marietta?"

Valeriya snapped her head out of thought, looking at her. "That depends. What about her?" Did she have another incident with Wyltam? The girl took it upon herself to further irate Keyain through Wyltam, only to make a fool of herself. If she had told Valeriya of her plans, she could have warned her.

"The ministers found Marietta lingering outside the meeting room door while Keyain held his meeting. Royir caught her in the hall." Tryda smirked.

Valeriya stilled the panic that wished to rise in her face. "Why would she be doing that?" she asked, feigning ignorance. Marietta was gathering information for her, and Wyltam caught the half-elf. She steadied her thoughts, not letting her mind run wild with the implications.

"That's the interesting part—Marietta's with child!" Tryda said with a laugh, a broad smile on her face. "She was so excited that she didn't want to wait to tell Keyain. It was sweet. Foolish, but sweet."

Valeriya almost laughed. There was little possibility she carried Keyain's child. After their last tea time together, she had done some digging. Amryth, the guard who was often with Marietta, had been getting contraceptives from the guard's infirmary. Why would a female who was only attracted to females need to prevent a pregnancy? Amryth didn't, of course. More than likely, Marietta took those from her.

"Wow, another child at court!" Valeriya said, feigning surprise. "Just after she and Grytaine were talking about having children."

"I know! Poor Marietta, likely already trying, and we pried into her personal ordeal." Tryda stopped to examine a flower, bringing her nose to the bloom to smell.

Valeriya rolled her eyes at her back. Poor girl indeed, sleeping with Keyain in order for their plan to work. The news of her pregnancy would spread, which could pose a problem. How would the Exisotis react if they caught wind that she was pregnant with Keyain? They'd be outraged, of course, assuming Keyain forced himself onto her. The threat of them apprehending Marietta just became higher. Perhaps it was time for Marietta to leave the palace as well.

Tryda stood and turned to Valeriya. "I just met Dyieter on his break before seeing you. He said that Keyain seems nervous, probably because of *those* nasty rumors going around; yet, when Dyieter pulled him aside, Keyain admitted that it's all he ever wanted. Such a sweet husband."

That would be an issue. Keyain already hovered around Marietta. He would only grow worse now that he believed she was carrying his child. It could still work; Valeriya could sneak her out in the passages under the palace. That was if she would work up the nerve to message Katya. After years of being apart, she hoped Kat still cared for her enough to help her escape Satiros, to give her a place to go.

"I'm happy to hear about his excitement," Valeriya lied. "Do you know how Marietta is handling the news?"

Tryda continued walking down the path, her eyes taking in the scenery. "Excited, but I think she's nervous, with obvious reasons to be. Why else would she not wait until his meetings finished?"

"Perhaps she feels more alone in this court than we realize." Valeriya recognized the feeling.

"I should reach out to her later this week once she's had time to digest the news." Tryda glanced at Valeriya, her eyes crinkling with a smile. "I've seen my fair share of children grow up at this palace. Their child and Mycaub could grow up to be as close as Keyain and King Wyltam, with less drama, of course."

Valeriya knew of the drama she referred to. "It would be wonderful for them to grow up as friends," Valeriya said, smiling at the thought. "If they have a girl, she could be the future queen after me." She bemused the thought of Mycaub and Marietta's non-existent child.

Tryda huffed. "That's impossible. Even if her features lean more elven, we would know she isn't a true elf. Can you imagine a half-elf queen?" She laughed at the idea.

Valeriya forced her soft laugh. "Ridiculous. Wyltam would never allow it."

"The citizens wouldn't allow it. Imagine the uprising," she said, laughing once more. "If the child is born with Marietta's half-elven features, I wonder what fate they will find at court. Hopefully, I'll still be around for it."

Valeriya smiled. "I think you have many years left in you yet, Tryda."

She and Tryda parted ways. Valeriya had to pack a few things while afternoon meetings distracted Wyltam. She smirked. The false news probably hurt him as well. Oddly, she pitied her husband, the male having to be so close to the person he yearned for, yet never getting what he wanted. She imagined Wyltam sitting next to Keyain, who undoubtedly discussed his future child. It's all the pain he deserved. Her only regret is that she didn't have more time to dangle it in front of him.

Later that afternoon, Valeriya sat at her desk and reread her script one more time. For the past hour, she wrote out the best way to convey her message to Katya, of how to ask for help. Now she only had to contact her, but why was it so hard?

It surprised Valeriya how simple it had been to open up to Katya once they became more than rivals. Never one to judge, Katya understood when she should listen or when she should give advice. She always knew what to say or do when it came to her emotions—ever a rock. What made reaching out difficult now? Because seven years had passed. Because there was a chance that Katya had moved on, that she no longer felt the same for Valeriya. Seeing Katya with someone else would hurt, but she would still help Valeriya.

With a deep breath and pounding heart, she reached into the aithyr and drew the energy into her. She imagined Katya's tan skin, the scars that marred her body, her piercing eyes, her black hair tucked behind her ear, and thought of the message she crafted.

"Katya, I know we agreed to go our separate ways, but please realize I wouldn't contact you unless it was necessary. Would you be willing to help me?"

Valeriya collapsed back in her chair as the energy shot out of her body. Full sentences were difficult for her to send, but Katya would always be worth the energy.

A minute passed. And then another. Valeriya jumped out of her seat and began pacing. Katya was probably planning what to send. It had taken her an hour to figure out a few short sentences. She was just thinking it over. Though, what if she wasn't? What if Katya worked with Nastanya and Auryon? How likely would it be that Katya would tell Nastanya and Auryon of her plan after she laid it out for her? No. She would never. Katya was the one hesitant about Auryon from the beginning. If she saw Nastanya hand over power to him, then there would be little to no chance that Katya would tell them.

Well, there was the chance that Katya might not want to talk to her at all. Perhaps she was angry that Valeriya didn't fight to bring her to Satiros. How could she when Katya was sworn to protect her sister? Valeriya's heart paused at that notion. If Katya was supposed to protect Nastanya, but Auryon took over... no, she's okay. Katya was alive and well.

Another few minutes passed. Valeriya bit her nails, walking the same circle in her room, refusing to assume the worst had happened—that Kat was dead. The thought caught her breath, the sudden tears in her eyes. She crumbled to the floor as her breaths came sharp. She couldn't lose them both—not her sister and Katya. It couldn't be true, but as the minutes passed by, her mind prepared for the worst.

Suddenly, the rough sound of Katya's voice filled her head.

"For you? Always."

Valeriya cried with relief, tears streaking down her cheeks as she held her head. It would all be okay. Katya was coming, and she would finally be with her again.

Chapter Eighty-Two

MARIETTA

BEFORE

Marietta smiled as she tilted her head back in the sun, enjoying the blistering heat on a beach off the Evgeni Sea. About an hour outside of Notos, she and Keyain took a day to relax for once, though she still thought about her clients. Tomorrow she had four meetings set up, one of them being a new business. A beekeeper, which was a great client to gain considering how often honey is used in Enomenos, be it mead, baking, or general consumption. Her mother had helped make that connection.

Guilt knotted her stomach at the thought of her parents. She and Keyain were within a day's ride of their country home, yet she made no plans to go visit them. Not while Keyain was with her, anyway. Oh, the fit her father would throw if he found out about him.

Four years together and Keyain still had never asked to meet them.

"This is nice," he said, sprawled on a blanket next to her. "You never take a day to relax."

Marietta laughed at that. "I'd rather be doing something instead of lying around, but I figured one day wouldn't hurt."

"This is peaceful."

"It is," she murmured back. They were by themselves with just the lapping of the saltwater on the sand and the calling of birds around them. She closed her eyes, letting the wind catch the strands of hair that broke loose from her knot.

"Would you enjoy it if it was always this peaceful?"

Marietta opened her eyes at the question, her mood plummeting. Glancing over, Keyain had propped himself up on his side with his legs stretched before him. "We're not having this conversation again," she said, her tone final.

"Mar, we need to talk about it."

"We don't."

"Well," Keyain said, hesitating, "I would like to."

"Fine, go ahead. Tell me of how you want to live in the Satiroan countryside in your big, fancy house and make me push out child after child."

"Why are you like this?" he snapped. "Is having a normal life with me too ridiculous for you? Do you really think we could travel like this for the rest of our lives?"

"No." She cast her gaze out over the water, watching the ships in the distance.

"What is that supposed to mean?"

Marietta swallowed hard, fighting against the bite in her tone. "That I didn't think we'd ever last this long."

For a moment, Keyain was quiet. "I can see it, you know. You being a wonderful mother, living in a home—a real home—together. We would have the two sweetest little girls who'd look just like you."

"Oh, yes, because that's not crazy at all." She shook her head.

"I'm allowed to want a family. I'm allowed to dream of that life with you."

"Go ahead." Marietta turned her burning stare to him. "As long as I'm your partner, then it will stay a dream."

Keyain ripped his hand through his hair as he ground his jaw. "Why are you so difficult all the fucking time?"

She laughed mirthlessly. "Let's play out the scenario, Keyain. We move to Satiros, into your manor, or whatever bullshit thing you call it." Keyain tried to speak, but she talked over him. "We have these children, two sweet little girls. What happens when they have these?" Marietta flicked the blunted tips of her ears, gesturing to the half-elven shape.

"I will still love them, and you know that," he ground out.

"Love doesn't save them from being a lesser citizen!" she yelled. "It sure as fuck wouldn't save me!"

"No one would treat you any differently—"

"You can't promise that!" Marietta had turned to him fully, breathless with her anger. "You can't promise me anything."

He bit back his answer, running his tongue over his teeth. "There's a strong chance they'll look more elven, Mar. There's plenty of couples in Satiros who have elven-passing children, though one parent is a half-elf."

"And what happens when they have a noticeably half-elven child?" she hissed. Marietta couldn't imagine having a child who was deemed lesser than her by backward laws—how could Keyain? "There's still that chance, and I refuse to put a pilinos child's life at risk by living in Satiros. We've been through this."

Silence settled between them, neither wanting to address the disparity in the future they saw for themselves. Marietta didn't want kids. They'd had that fight countless of times. Keyain once got her to admit she'd be more willing to have a family with him in Enomenos, and he took that as she was open to having kids. Correcting him grew more exhausting with each fight.

Perhaps she should have listened to her father's warnings about Syllogi elves. Marietta loved Keyain, but it wouldn't be possible for them to stay together and both be happy.

Finally, Keyain broke the silence. "I would give almost anything up for you, Mar. Why is it you can't give up anything for me?"

A lie. He has never given anything up for her, and she was the one with everything to lose. Marietta refused to answer, tucking her knees tight to her chest. Their future had never been so clear.

"As a reminder, Monty will travel with you to Kentro. After that, I'll send someone else who can stay longer, about a couple of months," Keyain said while packing his clothes on their last morning in Notos, taking off in just a few hours. Marietta would head to Kentro, and Keyain would return to Satiros.

Marietta didn't respond, her throat tightening and her body shaking with what she was about to do.

Keyain was looking over his shoulder at her. "Mar, you okay? You look like you're about to be sick."

"Keyain, can you sit?"

"I've almost finished packing," he said, turning back to his clothes.

"Keyain, please," she begged, her voice cracking as tears filled her eyes.

"Mar?" He turned, his brows furrowed with her expression. With a few blinks, he stood, saying nothing as he sat on the bed. When Marietta sat beside him, Keyain didn't reach out to touch her—he sensed what was coming.

"Keyain, we want two very different futures."

He frowned, his eyes watering. "I would have any future with you, even if it's not the one I want." He brushed a tear away, looking at Marietta with a sad smile.

"I can't ask you to do that. You deserve to live the life you want." Marietta looked down, watching her tears saturate the wooden floor at her feet.

"You don't have to ask. I'd give everything up to be with you."

"Yet you keep bringing up kids. You should have the future you want," she paused, taking a shattering breath. "Keyain, I'm so sorry." Marietta burst into tears, unable to hold back.

Keyain reached over, pulling her into a hug. Even at that moment, he felt the need to comfort her. "Is this what you want? Do you wish to not be with me?"

Those questions were like a knife to the heart. "I'm so sorry," she repeated.

Keyain held her as she cried, his hand cradling the back of her head. "It's alright." He pushed her hair back to study her face, his green eyes glossy with tears, his face flushed with emotion. "I wasn't meant to be happy."

The words cleaved her in two. Marietta loved him, but she needed to let him go. They sat there, holding each other, until finally Keyain wiped his face and got their stuff ready.

Monty met them outside the inn, eyes darting between the two, catching what had happened. Marietta wouldn't meet Keyain's gaze; she held her head high in the opposite direction, trying to have some pride still.

Keyain's heavy footsteps approached behind her, his hand falling on her shoulder. Her lips trembled, turning to him. "I guess this is it, Mar." He fought back his tears, his jaw tightening.

"It is." Marietta looked up into his face, memorizing his features. The spattering of freckles. The cut of his cheekbones. The arch of his lips. Each detail she loved, that she would miss.

"Monty will take you to Kentro. I figured you'd find your own guard after that."

Marietta nodded, tears sliding down her cheeks.

Keyain rubbed his eyes before the tears fell. "I love you so much, Mar, always will."

"I'll always love you, too."

He kissed her one last time, his lips lingering, not wanting to pull away, not wanting the end to come.

Marietta turned from him, gasping for a breath. She couldn't look at him; she would change her mind.

Monty pulled up the horses beside her. "Ready?"

She mounted her horse, taking a deep breath, and kicked her steed into motion with Monty at her side.

Marietta didn't let herself glance back to see Keyain standing alone in the middle of the street. She didn't let herself imprint the pain of his expression into her mind. Their futures were separate from one another, regardless of their love. Or perhaps because of it. She loved him enough to let him go. Keyain would live in his large house with the kids he always wanted, but Marietta would never be a part of it.

Chapter Eighty-Three

MARIETTA

Later that afternoon, Amryth rushed into the suite and released her anger. Of the things that Marietta could have said, why did she say pregnant?

"Are you out of your gods damned mind? They're going to know," she hissed, her voice dropping.

"I know," Marietta hissed back. "It was stupid, but what else was I going to say?"

"Literally anything but that, Marietta. I hope your outing was worth it." Amryth plopped down at the dining table, rubbing her temples.

"It was. Someone is leaking information from Satiros, and I'm one of their suspects."

Amryth dropped her hands with a frown. "Please tell me you're not." When she saw Marietta's face, she sighed. "Better yet, don't tell me. I'd rather not be an accomplice to treason. Are you their only suspect?"

"No, Queen Valeriya is, too."

Amryth laughed. "The Queen seems more viable a suspect than you. I bet they only threw out your name because of the temple."

Marietta leaned away so Amryth wouldn't see her face. She should tell Amryth the truth about how she was helping Valeriya steal information. Amryth wouldn't be against it. She had turned her back on Keyain already; but Marietta couldn't do it there, not knowing who watched them. She'd have to wait until they left the palace. Marietta glanced over her shoulder at Amryth. "I'm not sure, but the King is keeping watch on the Queen and I both."

"What are you going to do when they find out you're not pregnant?"

"By then, I should be an official Iros and protected by the temple."

Amryth nodded her head. "So, you've decided, and you finally have a logical plan."

"Thanks," she said, rolling her eyes.

"If the King and his council think you're committing treason, the temple can't protect you from their investigation, let alone if you're found guilty.

She didn't know that. Panic bloomed in her gut but vanished as warmth flared in her chest from the goddess. "Can we go to the temple in the morning? Coryn and Deania will need to know."

"You'll have to ask Keyain, though I suspect half of Satiros already knows the news." Amryth gave her a leveling stare. "You weren't exactly subtle about your fake announcement."

"Gods, just great," Marietta said, dropping into the seat next to Amryth, staring at the table.

"And if you thought Keyain was bad before..." she trailed off.

"He's going to be terrible now." The one thing Keyain always wanted with Marietta was a child. Now that he was seemingly so close to his dream, he wouldn't let anything rip it away. Such a stupid thing to say as a lie. "I'll talk to him," Marietta said, "but be ready to leave in the morning."

"Of course. Deania and Coryn know the laws better, of how they can protect against the King's suspicions, and if Keyain discovers you're lying."

Marietta turned to Amryth. "What happens if he finds out I'm lying?"

"He might look into any little reason to have you tried or use your lie as incriminating evidence." Amryth sighed, sitting back in the chair.

"But would he? Keyain says that he loves me."

"He loved you when he let you waste away in here. He loved you when he abducted you. Love didn't stop him then, and I don't think it'll stop him now."

Marietta's stomach sank. "And if I become an Iros? Does that make me any safer?"

Amryth's gaze slid to her, narrowing. "We'll have to ask tomorrow, but for your sake, I hope it will."

That evening, Keyain returned around dinnertime and acted more insufferable than Marietta could stomach. No longer was she allowed to lift anything heavier than a book. She couldn't walk more than a few feet without his assistance. Even eating had a new level of interest from him, adding more food to her plate while insisting she needed to eat more for the baby. When she brought up going to the temple, Keyain had a surprising reaction.

He planted a kiss on her forehead. "I'll send word for my guard to escort you in the morning. I think it'll be good for you to go," he said, unbuttoning his shirt.

Perplexed, Marietta leaned against the doorframe of their closet. "You do?"

"Of course. If it helps you relax, then it'll be good for you and the baby." He changed into a pair of sleeping shorts, throwing on a soft shirt, then approached Marietta. "Plus, it'll be the last time you visit."

"What is that supposed to mean?" she asked, her heart thundering as she followed him into the bedroom.

"It means you can tell your little temple friend the child is mine." Keyain walked out of the bedroom, Marietta a step behind him.

"For the last time, I didn't sleep with him," she snapped, grabbing for his arm.

Keyain paused mid-step, turning to her. "Prove to me that it's something you wouldn't do."

Her nails dug into his arm as she clenched her fists. "That isn't my responsibility to prove. I'm not lying to you, Keyain."

"It doesn't matter anyway," he said, slipping his arm from her grip and continuing to the living room. "Whether you did, whether you didn't. Even if he did impregnate you, that's my child you're carrying."

"Keyain, I didn't—"

He turned abruptly to her. "I don't care, and it doesn't matter," he said, no hint of anger in his expression. "Next week, you'll be in the countryside, and you will finally be safe. So, go to the temple tomorrow, say your goodbyes, and be done with all this mess."

Her blood turned to ice in her veins. Keyain planned to take her to the countryside, to his manor. "You just get to decide that?"

Keyain waited in the door of his office, one hand clutching the frame as he turned to look at her. "That's how things will be until I trust you again. Now, go to bed."

He closed the door and Marietta remained dumbfounded, unable to move. Keyain already took so much of her life away, and he planned to do it again. It only solidified what she already decided—she needed to escape, to get far away from Keyain, and she would do anything, including becoming an Iros, to gain her freedom, once and for all.

Sleep dragged Marietta in and out of consciousness, her mind running through all the possibilities of what becoming an Iros would mean. Forever she'd be an attendant to Therypon, to her temple. Sworn to her and bound in ink. The details of being an Iros were murky at best. Would she ever be allowed to marry? To work again? Could she go back to Enomenos and open a new bakery? Gods, would they expect her to be celibate? She hadn't considered any of those questions, but now, with Keyain's controlling hand closing around her, she didn't have much of a choice. She would have to ask Coryn tomorrow.

Marietta imagined that being an Iros meant she could at least see her parents in Notos. Her heart ached for her mother and her herb-scented hands, for her father, who would talk the ear off of whoever would listen. She would give almost anything to hear his stories again, of his years traveling around Enomenos.

Morning came too soon, Keyain waking and readying for the day as the sun crept above the horizon. He kissed Marietta goodbye, saying the guards would come in a couple of hours and she must follow their directions. Marietta only agreed because it got him to leave the suite quicker, and she finally was alone to ready herself.

A knock sounded at the door a little while later, Marietta confused.

Amryth wasn't one to knock then wait. She answered the door, her stomach dropping when she saw who waited.

"Hello, Lady Marietta." Ryder flashed a sharp grin, pushing back the fluff of his auburn hair.

Marietta shook her head. "No." Deities damn Keyain. Of all the guards to escort her, why did it have to be him?

"No, you don't want to go to the temple?" he asked, giving a mocking pout. "After all of us assembled to bring you safely?"

Marietta followed his hand that gestured to the hall, finding more than a dozen guards lingering. "Where's Amryth? She's taking me to the temple."

"Keyain thought it'd be best to have someone he trusts to take you," Ryder said, holding out his arm.

"And why would he trust you after the comment about my ass?" she snapped.

"We are males of similar taste. Who better to trust?" He reached around Marietta, pulling the door shut behind her. "Besides, Keyain wanted his best guards to protect his wife and unborn child."

Marietta lifted her chin, meeting Ryder's stare. "If you're his best, then I worry for my safety."

He laughed, looping his arm through hers. "Gods, you have a sense of humor. Let's hope you do not need to witness how wonderful of a captain I can truly be."

She ripped her arm from him, walking ahead of him down the hall. Keyain understood what he did, placing his most vexatious guard in charge of her.

The remaining guards took positions around Marietta with Ryder at her back. "I could get used to walking behind you with a view like this."

She turned abruptly to him. "You couldn't be more of the boorish Syllogian man stereotype, ready to hump anything that walks in your direction."

"Apologies," he said, grinning. "That wasn't an attempt to sleep with you." He leaned in, looping his arm with hers once again, and whispered,

"Between King Wyltam and the temple attendant, you have enough males competing for your bed."

The guards nearest to them bit back a few smirks. So, they all heard rumors that Marietta slept with King Wyltam and Coryn. The sooner she left that gods damned city, the better.

Ryder and the guards led Marietta in the opposite direction of the temple, instead, to the southeastern gate, none of them answering her when she asked where they were heading. Not when Ryder draped a cloak over Marietta, her face obscured by a hood. And not when they exited through that gate, at the opposite end of the palace from the temples.

Ryder ushered her into a waiting carriage, neither she nor him sitting before the driver had it in motion, the guards armed and in position on the outside. "Keyain took precautions. Three carriages left the palace at the same time. Only two will arrive at the temple."

Marietta rolled her eyes. "This is completely unnecessary."

"Keyain would do anything to protect those he loves, even if that person doesn't deserve it," he said, draping his arm across the back of the seat. He crossed one leg over a knee, smiling out the window at the passing city.

"Apologies, I should love the man who abducted me—"

"I wouldn't continue that sentence, Marietta."

She narrowed her gaze at him as he looked back at her.

"I trust Keyain," he said, "and I'm smart enough to realize I don't know all of his reasonings, but you know what makes a good leader?"

Marietta refused to reply as she held his stare.

"Though I don't have all the details, I know, without a doubt, that Keyain took you back for more than just personal reasons." Ryder looked her up and down. "That's what makes him a good leader—I trust he knows what he's doing and tells us only what's necessary."

Gods, no wonder Amryth couldn't stand being around him. "Sounds like blind ignorance to me."

Ryder laughed again, looking back out the window. "Oh, I like you. I see how you and Keyain could have worked."

Marietta bit back her irritation, realizing that snapping at Ryder would yield nothing but more frustration.

The carriage wove through different side streets to the south. From Marietta's sense of direction, they overshot the distance to the temple, and then wove back. They took a lane parallel to the Halia River, weaving through side streets before pulling into an alley.

The temples rose in the distance, and the black stone of Zontykroi pulled her gaze first. It was as ominous from behind, with a stone wall encircling a courtyard at the back. Above the stone rose spikes of cypress, their boughs still in the stagnant air.

As they journeyed further into the alley, the white stone of Therypon's temple came into view. Bright blue banners waved from the upper floors towering above. Like the temple of Zontykroi, a stone wall guarded the back, filled with trees and other greenery beyond.

"So here's how your visit will go," Ryder said, sitting forward with his gaze sweeping the streets. "We enter through the back, you give a very brief goodbye to the attendants, and then I will escort you to a private prayer chamber. You may take as long as you need, but I will be vigilantly waiting outside the door."

"I sound more like a prisoner," she said, her heart sinking. How would Deania and Coryn help her if Ryder watched her so closely?

"Well, it's mostly for your protection. Word of your pregnancy has spread, and Keyain didn't want to take any chances." He stood, stooping in the low cab as he offered Marietta his hand. "Everything else is because I don't trust you."

"You don't say," Marietta grumbled, ignoring his offered hand to stand.

Ryder laughed as he opened the door, stepping out of the carriage where guards flanked the two steps to the courtyard's entrance. He looked back at her, flashing a grin as if he always found something amusing. "Let's go give your goodbyes."

Olive and oak trees spotted the temple's back courtyard. Beds of echinacea, chamomile, milk thistle, and valerian flourished in patches, the flowers familiar from her mother's gardens in Notos. Foxglove and castor bean plants grew in a few spots, which surprised Marietta that they'd have such poisonous plant life.

A group of armed attendants approached from the doorway. At their front was Coryn, lips tugging into a frown. Ryder stepped closer to Marietta's side, placing a hand on her shoulder.

"Welcome back, Marietta," Coryn said, one side of his mouth lifting into a smile. "Odd circumstances but congratulations on your pregnancy."

Coryn and Deania believed she was actually pregnant. She fought the fear that climbed up her throat, threatening to choke her words. "Odd is one way to describe this," she said, pulling out of Ryder's grip.

"I will let Keyain know you send congratulations to him as well," Ryder added. "He's very excited to be *the* father."

Coryn furrowed his brows. "I don't doubt that he is."

"It'd be best if you remembered that," warned Ryder.

"Gods, Ryder. Enough," Marietta snapped. "Can I please go?"

"Of course," Ryder said, grinning. "Lead the way, attendants."

Deania met them inside, her face lined with worry as she took in Marietta. "I'm happy to see you're alright," she said, her high-pitched voice sweet.

"Why wouldn't she be alright?" Ryder asked, hovering at Marietta's shoulder.

Marietta turned to him, taking a step away with a glare. When she turned back to Deania, she threw her into a hug.

"Everything will be alright," she whispered into her ear.

The panic eased in Marietta's chest. They would help her—Deania and Coryn wouldn't let Keyain take her to the countryside. She pulled away, finding Coryn at her side. As she raised her arms to embrace him as well, Ryder's hand landed on her shoulder, stopping her. "I think that's close enough."

Coryn's eyes narrowed on Ryder. "You're almost as controlling as her husband."

"I'm but an extension of Keyain," Ryder said. "I act on his behalf."

"Great," Marietta said, "as if one Keyain wasn't enough."

"Well, one Keyain didn't stop you from making poor decisions," Ryder replied.

Marietta turned to snap at him, but Ryder spoke over her. "Please show us the way to the private prayer room. We shouldn't dawdle. So you both are aware, this will be Lady Marietta's last visit."

Deania and Coryn exchanged worried glances. "You can't prevent Marietta from visiting the temple," Deania said, taking a step down the hall.

"You're correct." Ryder guided Marietta to follow. "But it'll be hard to visit the temple once she's no longer in the Satiros proper."

The questions they had died on their lips, their stares falling on Marietta. She lifted her chin, grimacing. Aware of Ryder's close inspection, she didn't dare give them any look, any hint of what Keyain had planned, and how she felt about it.

They wove through the temple, Ryder at her back, with Coryn and Deania leading the way. The guards that traveled with the carriage waited at the exit. Ryder gave brief instructions to survey the back, adding that the second team would monitor the front.

The prayer chamber sat at the heart of the temple on the top floor. A window set high in the wall lit the room made of all-white stone. At the far end was a modest-sized statue of the goddess and before it a single bench. "Take the time you need, Marietta," Ryder said, pushing her in.

She glanced back once to Deania and Coryn, concern lacing their features as the door shut behind her. Alone in the room, she took a shattering breath.

She had to escape—this couldn't be her future. Even if she wasn't with child, today only confirmed her biggest fear: if Keyain found out she was lying about being pregnant, then he would ensure it happened after all of this. After the news became so public, he wouldn't risk the embarrassment.

The room felt confined, too small, as her breaths came sharp, sucking nothing into her lungs. Marietta's vision blackened on the edges as she collapsed to the bench, trying to breathe. Keyain would get what he wanted—and it wasn't her on trial. Keyain would get his family. He would make Marietta carry his child. He would force into her the life she never wanted. With a heaving gasp, tears came as she suppressed her sob.

Suddenly, there came the warmth flaring from the center of her chest and easing her breath. "*You never walk alone,*" a voice whispered at the back of her mind.

Through the haze of her panic, she turned to Therypon's statue. The heat flared again, steadying her breath. Marietta wasn't alone. She would be Therypon's Iros, and her friends would help her. Never again would she be trapped.

She focused on her steadying breath. On a count to four, she inhaled through her nose, exhaling slowly through her mouth, until her heart settled and she could breathe again. In her calm state, she shut her eyes, clearing her mind to pray to the goddess. She would know what to do, how to help.

A minute into freeing her thoughts, there was a soft swish from behind the statue. When she opened her eyes, she found Amryth standing at a hidden door in the wall, face taut with worry as she held a finger to her mouth. Glancing at the room's entrance, Marietta stood and walked to Amryth as quietly as she could. When she stepped aside, a man in a similar cloak to Marietta's appeared, his hair long and curled like her own. With a wink, he went and sat on the bench, his back to the door.

Amryth took Marietta's arm, guiding her down the secret passage as the door slid shut. Marietta wanted to cry, to hug Amryth, but she hurried her steps, anxiety rolling off her.

After a few minutes, Amryth paused, listening through the wall, then pulled it open. Beyond was a dark room, lit only by a candle, and within the glowing light, she saw Coryn and Deania. Marietta sighed with relief, pulling Amryth into a hug as the door shut behind them.

"I'm going to murder Ryder, I swear to you," she said into her hair. "As soon as Keyain said he forbade me to take you, I knew what was happening." She pulled back, placing her hands on Marietta's shoulders.

"When does he plan on taking you to his manor?"

Marietta huffed a small laugh, knowing Amryth knew Keyain better than she did. "Next week."

"Then you need to decide," said Coryn, drawing her attention. "We have enough Iros congregated to perform the ceremony right now, but we have a few questions."

"I'm not actually with child," she said, hoping to quell his anxiety. Instead, he exchanged glances with Deania.

"We know," Deania answered. "Amryth told us already. But to give you asylum from the crown, we need to ensure you have broken no laws." She hesitated, fidgeting with her long braid. "Grysella told us you're working with the Exisotis, that you're stealing information. So, when Amryth also shared that you're under the ministers' suspicion for treason…." She didn't finish the sentence, looking at Marietta with wide, hopeful eyes.

Marietta took a steadying breath. "Grysella is correct; their investigation is justified."

Coryn swore, wiping his face. "Then we need a new plan." He paced, eyes darting in thought. "Why do they think you're pregnant?"

Marietta clenched her jaw. "I was trying to listen in on a council meeting after I heard the Exisotis made a move. When Keyain's guards hassled me, it sort of slipped out."

Coryn turned back toward her. "How does that just slip out?"

Marietta sighed, running a hand through her hair. "I don't know—I just wanted to listen in on the meeting, not this. At least it was a good lie. Keyain has always wanted one thing from me."

Coryn whipped his head to Amryth, then back to Marietta. "I'm guessing it's believable because you have been having sex with him?"

Marietta felt the heat flood her face. "Who are you to judge me?"

Coryn shook his head. "The goddess chose you, Marietta. Did you think we wouldn't protect you? They could have caught you listening, and even if you gave no excuse, the temple could claim custody. You didn't need to have this added layer of lies."

" I already had decided that I was going to leave. Keyain planned to end our marriage when the war ended, and I needed to get away before King Wyltam did something else."

"Funny that you bring up the King. Do those rumors hold any merit? Coryn asked.

"Why does that matter?"

"Because some people think you're carrying the King's child." Coryn's lips tugged into a frown.

Marietta looked him dead in the eye. "He and I kissed, but the last time I checked, you can't get pregnant from kissing someone."

Coryn sighed, shaking his head as he looked away. "Why would you even kiss him in the first place?"

She hated the shame that burnt into her cheeks. "I thought he was different," she said, remembering Wyltam's sweet words. "I guess I was wrong."

"Different how?"

"Why are you giving me such a hard time about this?" she snapped.

His expression softened. "Because I care."

Marietta shook her head, hating the truth. "Wyltam said he wanted a different future for pilinos in Satiros, and that I was his hope."

Coryn laughed, the sound filling her with dread. "Don't tell us you believed him."

She glared at him, cheeks burning. "Not anymore." Even as she said it, she felt the lie for what it was.

"And now some people believe that you carry his child." Coryn laughed again. He scrubbed his face, planting his hands on his hips as he turned. "Would you like to know what the Exisotis did?"

"Of course, that was the whole point of listening, besides gleaning information."

"When you stopped at The Flour Shop, the Exisotis attempted to secure you," he said. "That's why Deania and I went to the Snapdragon. Grysella contacted us after you left, asking if we knew you were giving information to the Exisotis. It seems we can confirm it now."

"That was the news?" Marietta closed her eyes with a sigh. "But how would King Wyltam know? It was just Grysella and me in the back of the kitchen—"

"That's what you were doing?" hissed Amryth. "Keyain knew it—he knew something was wrong. You told the baker you're the one leaking information to the Exisotis." She swore, turning her back to Marietta.

"After you refused their help, a few Exisotis members formed a secondary plan for recapturing you later that night," Coryn added. "But someone walked to a tavern instead of taking their carriage. That's the plan King Wyltam and his guards discovered."

"Why didn't they stop when I told Grysella I was helping the Exisotis, though?" Marietta asked.

Coryn and Deania exchanged glances, a silent conversation passing between them. Deania hesitated, then said, "Pelok insisted on saving you, to keep trying since that was the first time you were outside the palace and not at the temple."

Marietta blinked, unable to hold back her surprise. Tilan's friend— her friend—was in Satiros? "Pelok wouldn't keep trying like that."

"Believe us, he was," said Coryn, raising his brows. "He threatened to take you at The Snapdragon as well. That's why Deania and I were there, in case he was stupid enough to walk in and let Keyain see his face."

"We have a few more questions for you," Deania said, hesitating. "Like who was Tilan Reid to you?"

Marietta's heart stopped at the name. "Tilan was my husband, the one I married by choice."

"Pelok didn't lie," Deania said with a sigh. "And who is your contact in the Exisotis? The temple has been communicating with the organization since we claimed a side with Enomenos. No one mentioned you had contact."

Marietta shifted her feet, not wanting to speak.

"Mar, please," Amryth pleaded. "Who was your contact?"

She hesitated, then gave in. "Queen Valeriya."

"What?" Deania and Amryth said in unison.

"We were trying to further ruin Keyain and King Wyltam's relationship in order to weaken their court. It was to help the Exisotis."

Coryn turned to Deania. "Can you send a message to your contact in Enomenos? I want confirmation the Queen is working with the Exisotis."

Deania nodded her head and wandered to the corner, closing her eyes to concentrate.

"Therypon chose you for a reason. Right now, I'm having a hard time understanding her reason." Coryn looked up, lost in thought. "Your best chance at escaping Satiros would be to undergo the Iros ceremony and officially become an attendant to the temple." He paused, his gaze finding her. "We can no longer stay in the city. Pelok will take you and me to Enomenos."

Her heart skipped a beat. She'd go home with Coryn. Gods, Keyain would think she left with her secret lover; the thought sickened her. "Not that I mind, but why would you come?"

"To train you," he said, crossing his arms. "The goddess came to me in a vision, saying no matter what happens, I need to stay by your side to protect you and train you. Therypon as my witness, I swear to do just that."

Heat came to her face as she nodded her head, thankful to have him by her side. "What if I need to go back to the palace?"

"Why would you need to?" asked Amryth. "You could be safe now if you become Iros. They could claim you immediately, and you can leave tomorrow."

Tomorrow. Marietta could go home, but a thought settled like a rock in her stomach. "I have stolen documents at the bottom of my wardrobe. Keyain will find them if I leave now." She hesitated, adding, "And I can't leave Elyse behind. She's in just as much danger."

"She's in a better position now than she was a few months ago," Amryth said. "We can't take her."

"We need as few people as possible to move quickly," Coryn added. "Plus, she would only draw more attention to you escaping."

Deania spoke up from the other side of the room, her voice breathy. "Checked with one source. Queen Valeriya is working with the Exisotis. She has someone meeting with them on her behalf. They last received information from her a month and a half ago."

Coryn sighed, rubbing his temples. "At least that was true for the Queen. What information is on those documents?"

She thought back to the documents, the transcriptions of their meetings. "Proof that there's a spy in the Exisotis and an interview of some sort, though that document was coded."

Coryn swore. "So, information is important. When are you supposed to hand that off?"

"Tonight," Marietta said. "I'm meeting with the Queen tonight, so if I go back, even just for the evening, I can hand over that information. And if I don't, then it was all for nothing."

The three gave her confused looks.

"What was all for nothing?" Deania asked.

"Making Keyain think I loved him, so he'd let down his guard."

"That's why you had slept with him," hissed Amryth. "You've been working at that for months. Why didn't you tell me?"

"Because you're his soldier," Marietta said, frowning. "I trust you, but I couldn't put you in that position."

Amryth shook her head. "I wish you did. If I had known, then we could've had an emergency plan in place."

"Do you want to help the Exisotis?" Marietta asked. "Even if they're against the city-state you're bound to protect?"

Amryth lifted her chin. "I swore an oath to protect the citizens of Satiros, and right now, the biggest threat is the head of state. They uphold the laws that suppress innocent people, but ignore the law when it best suits them. Something needs to change, and I refuse to do nothing."

Deania reached for Amryth's hand, her eyes shining in the glow of the light.

"Then let me help them," Marietta said, looking them all in the eye. "If I can get those papers into the Exisotis's hands, then they can narrow down the spy based on who was in what meeting."

"Okay," Coryn sighed. "Marietta will return to the palace and act as if she's going along with Keyain's plan. Tonight, meet with the Queen. Amryth, you set a meeting point with her and remove her from the palace and back to the temple.

Amryth nodded her head as the plan came together.

"When you return, Marietta, we'll perform the ritual, claiming you as an Iros to Therypon and officially place you in protective custody of the temple," Coryn said. "Keyain won't be able to march in here without starting a civil war in Satiros. It'll buy us time to get you out of the city-state."

Marietta nodded, her gut twisting. She'd have one more night in the palace. Gods, she wouldn't be able to see Elyse before she left, but she could come back for her. Marietta was out of options; she was no longer safe.

Chapter Eighty-Four

MARIETTA

Before returning to the private prayer chamber, Amryth gave Marietta a quick explanation of the tunnels that ran underneath the palace, Marietta explaining that one led to her suite. After meeting the Queen, Marietta would take the tunnels towards the Guards Garrison and find Amryth.

Marietta thought of all the ways the plan could fail, yet there was no other way. She'd convince Keyain to drink that evening, so he wouldn't wake as she crept out of the room. When she finished with the Queen, she'd meet with Amryth, who had servant's clothes in which she could change. It could work. Their plan could work. Tomorrow she could be going home.

Nervousness fought in her gut and not just for the escape. The meeting would be her first time seeing the Queen since the incident with Elyse, not forgetting Valeriya's warning. Marietta decided it would be best not to tell the Queen that she was leaving. There needed to be no excuses, no further reasons to stay in Satiros.

When Keyain returned for dinner that evening, Marietta had a glass of whiskey waiting for him. Each time he had finished his drink, she refilled it. Despite the past week's fallout, he seemed in high spirits, almost proud of himself. Sitting across from Marietta at the dining table, Keyain asked, "Do you hope for a boy or a girl?"

"It doesn't matter to me," Marietta said with a forced smile. If she had been pregnant, then the gender wouldn't make a difference, not to her.

"I'm still hoping for a girl," he said, his smile softening. "Though if

she's anything like you, I'm in for a rough time."

"If there were two of me, life would be much more interesting."

"I'd have a lot more headaches."

She pointed at him with her fork. "And a lot more fun, but our child will still be half-elven."

Keyain rolled his eyes. "That doesn't matter."

"Doesn't it, though?" Marietta tilted her head with a raised brow. "Imagine our daughter at court and whatever noble could have a marriage license signed without her consent, let alone yours."

"My child wouldn't. There are perks to being in positions of power."

Marietta set down her fork, the food turning to lead in her stomach. "So you recognize that it's wrong to do?"

"Well, if it's our child—"

"What if it was me?" she snapped.

"Mar, calm down. Anger isn't good for the baby."

Marietta took a deep breath, closing her eyes. "It's what you did to me, and it happens to pilinos all over Satiros, Keyain. If it's wrong for our child, then it's wrong for anyone. You don't get to pick and choose the use case of your morals."

"This is why we don't get along. Everything turns into a fight with you," Keyain answered, cutting into his food.

She sat back, realizing it was her last meal with Keyain, her last evening with him. As it was in the beginning, he still didn't understand how his views hurt her, or why they were a problem. It was the proof she needed. Keyain would never change.

"What?" he said, catching her gaze.

"Nothing." She forced a smile. "What baby names do you like?"

Keyain rambled on about the non-existent baby until they climbed into bed, thinking it was a safe topic. After settling, Keyain rolled over to face her. "I'm still upset by you, more than you could ever understand, but I'm trying to work past it for the sake of our child. I love you, Marietta, and I'm excited about getting this third opportunity with our relationship."

"I love you, too," she said, the lie coming easy.

In the dark, Keyain leaned over with a kiss. "Life will be easier in the country, I promise." With his last words, he rolled over, making a point not to sleep next to Marietta.

Life on his estate would be easy, away from court, away from the King and Queen. Marietta would never know what that kind of life was.

When Keyain's breathing turned heavy, she slipped out of bed, retrieving the papers from her wardrobe. The nymph dagger rested precariously in her pocket. At the threshold of the bedroom, she looked one last time to Keyain. Leaving in the night seemed fitting, considering it was how he stole her in the first place.

Marietta pondered what life with Keyain would have been like if she married him all those years ago. Would she have learned to love it? Would any of it be different? Perhaps she and Keyain would love each other, filling his countryside manner with kids. She shook her head, her final goodbye to Keyain.

The hidden door in Keyain's office swung open silently, though she struggled to close it in the dark of the stairwell. Marietta didn't risk lighting her light globe until she stumbled down the spiraling staircase, arriving at the adjacent corridor well below the palace. Marietta thanked whatever god or goddess blessed her with a memory for directions as she retraced her way to Valeriya's secret room. After a few wrong turns, she arrived at the door.

With a deep breath, she knocked. No noise came from the other side. She waited a moment and reached to knock again, but the door cracked open, revealing the Queen's face before opening up wider.

"Marietta, I'm so happy to see you," she softly said after she shut and locked the door.

"I don't have a lot of time, Valeriya." The Queen smiled as Marietta spoke her name. "I dug through Keyain's files. I have proof that there is a spy in the Exisotis. I also found this coded message. If they felt the need to hide the meaning, then it's probably worth knowing."

She handed the papers over to the Queen, who glanced through them. "You're right. They have word-for-word documentation from their meetings, a lot of it being from Tilan."

"We need to get this to them as soon as possible. Were you able to deliver my notes on Minister Royir's ledgers?"

Valeriya nodded her head. "I delivered them last week."

"Good." Marietta paused before adding, "King Wyltam and his council know one of us is leaking information." She waited for Valeriya to mention the incident with Wyltam, but she didn't.

Instead, the Queen gave her a sad smile. "This meeting will be the last we can have. I'm leaving Satiros. We're no longer safe here." She paused, reaching for Marietta's hand. "Come with me. I have a way for us to escape."

"Oh," Marietta hesitated, surprised by the offer.

"Don't say yes or no just yet. I have another thing to show you, one last secret. It will probably influence your decision to stay or leave, but you need to see this before I go."

"What is it?"

Valeriya shook her head. "You have to see it. Come."

She unlocked the door and led Marietta into the dark hallway. The Queen held Marietta's hand and gripped the light globe in the other, weaving their way through the underground passages. After traveling for what felt the length of the palace, Valeriya dimmed her light and whispered, "We're almost there. Just stay quiet."

Voices carried down the hall, causing Marietta to panic, fearing that the Queen betrayed her. Marietta's steps faltered as the Queen pulled her ahead.

The voices grew louder the further they walked, but the passageway remained dark. They turned, another long hallway extended in front of them. To one side, there was a jingle of metal and muffled laughs. Valeriya didn't slow; she stayed her pace and continued.

"Here," she whispered when they could barely hear the voices. "There are some foot holes in the wall. Feel around for them and crawl up. There should be a small hole where the light comes through. Just look into it."

Perplexed, Marietta felt her way in the dark with her heart thundering in her chest. Gods, what did the Queen need to show her? Marietta struggled to keep her breaths even as panic set in. She did not know where Valeriya had taken her, no idea why she brought her there.

At the top of the wall, there was a crawlspace where Marietta saw the light Valeriya mentioned. She drew a deep breath and looked through the hole.

It took a moment for her eyes to adjust as a dirty and dingy cell came into view below her. The walls were wet stone; the door was solid metal with a grate over a small window. In the corner sat a bucket filled with excrement. A body laid in the other.

Marietta pressed closer to the hole, trying to make out their details. Rail thin, a mop of scraggly dark hair matted their head, with a thick beard on their face. Only humans grew beards that thick. Why was there a human in their dungeons? Were they a prisoner of war, or someone she knew in Olkia?

The breath left Marietta as she realized who the Queen brought her to see. Biting into her hand, she muffled her cry, resisting the scream that built. Less than ten feet from her was Tilan. Alive.

Her husband was alive.

Marietta took in his features, blinking back tears. In the dungeon, his body wasted to nothing and his mass from smithing lost to inactivity. Without a haircut or bath in months, his dark hair was so matted like a stray dog. As he rolled over in his sleep, she saw his face, still handsome, but it pained her to see the neglect, how gaunt his features had become. The sallowness of his complexion. Tears blurred her vision as anger and guilt battled in her stomach. Tilan was in the palace the entire gods damned time.

He was alive.

Her husband was alive.

The chaos returned to her chest as her fury grew. It took all of her effort to tear away from the hole. When she met Valeriya at the bottom, Marietta grabbed her by the collar and pinned her to the wall. "You knew the whole fucking time."

"Marietta, hush," Valeriya said, placing her hand on top of her own. "Let's head back and then we can talk."

Each step away from Tilan felt like a betrayal. Marietta was so close to him, so close to seeing his face, that smile. The Queen had to drag her along the hallway to get her to move.

She'd come back. Gods, Marietta would return for her husband, and she would tear down the whole gods damned palace with her when she did.

Chapter Eighty–Five
VALERIYA

Valeriya rolled her shoulders, enjoying the unloaded weight of no longer hiding Tilan. Marietta's quiet rage filled the space between them as they navigated back toward the Noble's Section. Understandable, to say the least, though necessary. Of all the details Valeriya hid from her, this had been the most troublesome. If Marietta had known Tilan lived, she wouldn't have been able to seduce Keyain. Even now, there was a risk in showing her, knowing that Marietta would want to save her husband. She'd be a fool to not leave with her.

Her plan with Katya was simple—reveal Tilan, grab Mycaub, and meet Katya in a park a few blocks from the palace. From there, Katya knew a way to slip out of the city. After that, she didn't know; yet, she'd take the uncertainty over Wyltam discovering the truth or bowing to Auryon in Reyila.

Never had she thought it would come to this. In her mind, she could always go home to Reyila if the situation in Satiros worsened. But not anymore.

They stopped near an intersection that would be closer for Marietta to return to her suite if she felt like being a fool. There was nothing but damnation remaining for either of them in Satiros. Valeriya closed her eyes, reaching out to the aithyr, pulling the energy into herself and expelling it into a dome around them.

Valeriya turned to Marietta. "Now we can talk. The barrier will keep our voices muffled as a precaution."

Marietta's tear-stained face shined in the glow of the light globe, her

features contorted with rage. "How long did you know?"

"Marietta, I'm sorry, but we don't have time. I need you to decide, and I hope it's the right choice." Valeriya sighed, taking a step towards her friend. "Will you leave with me?"

"I'm not pregnant," Marietta said with a lethal quiet.

"I know. You should still come with me."

"I'm not going with you," Marietta hissed. "I don't know if I could leave at all now."

"Use your head." Valeriya's gut twisted as she repeated Wyltam's words. "It's only a matter of time before Satiros falls. Please, come with me."

For a moment, Marietta only offered her scathing glare. "Did you drop off the other papers, the ones with Royir's ledgers?"

Valeriya sighed, knowing they hadn't much time before they'd need to leave. "Yes, I did, just last week."

"And who did you give them to?"

"To the Exisotis, of course. Look, Marietta—"

"You're lying." Marietta shook her head. "You haven't given them information in a month and a half."

"And how would you know that?" This escape wasn't going as she had planned.

Marietta opened her mouth to answer as a surge of energy smashed against the barrier, Valeriya gasping as the dome fell around them.

"Oh, how precious is this?" A male elf with dark skin and black hair pulled back into a tail stepped into the light.

That voice.

That face.

Valeriya's blood pounded in her ears. He was the mage who had followed her into the garden, who she had heard in Wyltam's office. She squared her shoulders and bared her teeth as the heat of her rage took over. Rage for her husband, for Auryon's control of Reyila, and for the downfall of her legacy. Despite her emotions, she drew the aithyr to her body and set flame to her fists. "Run, Marietta!"

Valeriya lunged at the male as Marietta turned to escape. The male jerked his chin, and she heard Marietta fall behind her. Valeriya shot fire from her palms, narrowing the space between her and the mage, who dodged her assault. Releasing the aithyr from her hold, she unsheathed the knife at her hip—the one coated in magicsbane—and threw herself into the attack.

He swung a dagger, nearly slashing her face. Valeriya ducked out of the way, spinning with her arm outstretched. Just as she was to plunge into his flesh, the male released a gust of wind, and Valeriya flew backward, landing on her stomach.

Valeriya rolled into a crouching position as the mage sized her up with a smirk. She glanced toward Marietta, gesturing for her to run again, but her legs wouldn't move; the male's magic held her in place. If Valeriya could hit him hard enough, then she could break his concentration. She launched herself at him, blade lashing out with one hand, lightning crackling in the other. He dodged the dagger only to have his arm land in her grasp, shocking his limb.

Valeriya dug deep into the aithyr around them, screaming as she released it as magic. The male's body convulsed with the crackling energy, sparks lighting the surrounding hallway. She grabbed him by his hair, ready to slice his throat, but his legs kicked out from under him and into Valeriya. She dropped the dagger to catch herself from falling.

Adrenaline coursed through her body, aiding her to roll away as the mage lashed a whip of fire towards her. Burnt hair filled her nose as she held back her scream, the tip slicing her face. She breathed through the pain, calming herself.

Focused again, Valeriya pulled at the aithyr until her body shook with the effort of containing the magic. Fire erupted from her outstretched hands, engulfing the male. His scream carried through the passageway as the smell of burnt flesh permeated the air.

"Marietta, run!" Valeriya cried again, readying another attack. The mage attempted to summon water, his energy too low to combat the fire, let alone clear his mind under that amount of pain.

Marietta stood, stumbling backward, and took off down the hall. Good. Now she just needed to finish him, and then she could grab Mycaub and flee to the safety of Katya.

Valeriya stalked toward her attacker, the flames licking at his skin as the aithyr burned from her body. She picked up her dagger, flicking it out, ready to plunge it into the male who enabled her husband's reign. A smile came to her face at the thought of magicsbane entering his bloodstream, at his struggle and fear when his aithyr would no longer reach him. As the flames died down, the mage collapsed to the ground, panting.

"Who knew my husband had such a skilled lackey working for him." Valeriya grabbed his singed hair, looking into his face.

He smiled as she raised the dagger. "Lackeys, actually," he said, laughing.

Valeriya noticed them when it was too late. Two more mages were in the shadows, circling her.

Marietta. She could still escape. Valeriya rolled to the side as the other mages moved in to attack. She focused her mind, her goal clear in her head. She breathed in deeply once more, drawing the aithyr to herself. A ball of fire shot from her palms, striking the top of the hallway.

The flames lit the passageway as the fire smashed into the ceiling, the heat and energy causing the stone to explode then collapse. Now they couldn't reach Marietta.

Hands wrapped around Valeriya as dust and rubble filled the air, a blade biting into her flesh as someone bound her wrists. She reached for her magic, but there was nothing there, the blade's magicsbane taking hold. Her breath hitched. She jerked away from the person behind her.

"Stop struggling, Valeriya," said a throaty voice.

She stilled, not believing who she heard. The mage came into view, her hair black and cropped short, with piercings adorning her blunted ears. "Katya?" Valeriya whispered, her head growing dizzy as she stared at the female she loved. "What are you doing here?"

Emotion rippled through Katya's face. "I'm so sorry."

No.

No, it was wrong.

Katya did not work for Wyltam.

A heaviness pooled in Valeriya's stomach. "You're supposed to be in the park. You were supposed to help me. Kat," her voice shook, "you betrayed me."

"No," Katya answered, "you betrayed Satiros."

Soft footsteps fell from the far end of the hall, slowly approaching where she knelt. With his hands tucked deep into his pockets, remaining expressionless as ever, Wyltam stalked toward her. "Hello, Valeriya."

Chapter Eighty-Six

MARIETTA

Marietta gasped for breath, hearing the thundering boom behind her. She paused in the silent aftermath. Gods, what in the hells was that?

Her mind swam—Tilan was alive, and the Queen knew magic. Marietta nearly wet herself when Valeriya's hands lit into flames, fire racing towards their attacker. She had seen nothing like it. Gods, she had sacrificed herself so Marietta could get away. She sent a prayer to Therypon that the Queen would live, that she and her son would escape as well.

Marietta reached for Therypon in her chest, the warmth spreading, calming her breaths. She and Amryth needed to leave—now. She tried to calm her mind as she remembered Amryth's instructions in her head.

She found her way in the dark, not daring to use a light globe, recognizing the path that led to her room. Her knees burned from tripping along in the dark, the tunnel's rough ground ripping through her dress and into her flesh.

She suppressed a hiss as voices carried down the hall, accompanied by the clinking of metal on metal. Amryth had shared that some personnel knew of the tunnels but also said it was unlikely anyone would be down there. They hadn't planned for it. She needed to keep moving, to find Amryth.

Marietta kept her breaths even, her feet silent as she darted down the path. She peeked around the corner as a guard flicked on their light, Marietta scampering backward and falling to the floor.

"Hear that?" the guard said, the voice vaguely familiar. Footsteps echoed from the hall as Marietta picked herself up and ran to the connecting hallway behind her. As she turned the corner, the light from his globe appeared. She pressed her back against the wall, hearing his approaching footsteps, and then silence.

Marietta held her breath. Gods, was he waiting for her to move?

"C'mon!" called a different voice.

His footsteps echoed back down the hall, his light disappearing.

She sighed, slumping against the wall with relief. Now she just had to work her way to another hall to surpass those guards. Someone yelled from far off, coming from the direction Marietta had left the Queen. A feminine voice answered from the end of the adjacent passageway. Marietta's heart thundered again her ribs—how many were down there? Anxious, she reached for the dagger in her pocket, only to find it missing. She slowly backed towards the hall, where the guard almost caught her. Perhaps they raced towards the person who called out, and then she could slip past.

Metal tinked behind Marietta as she took another step back, causing her to whip around. A golden light suddenly blinded her. She tried to step away, but they gripped her wrist. Her limbs numbed as panic seized her heart, a scream building in the back of her throat. Her eyes adjusted and focused on who grabbed her.

The grip on her wrist tightened as she saw his pallid face and the slow shake of his head. Keyain jerked her closer to him as he hissed, "Marietta, what did you do?"

Chapter Eighty-Seven

MARIETTA,

BEFORE

The sun baked the top of Marietta's head as she bent over a basket of vegetables, her back straining from her position. Though she was technically in the vendor's stall, people bumped into her from the main walking lane of the crowded open-air market at the heart of Olkia.

She was elbow deep when Tilan said, "I didn't realize picking tomatoes could be so tricky."

Marietta scoffed. "It's an art form, thank you very much." She pulled one out and sniffed near its stem. "Perfect."

Tilan shook his head as she added it to their basket. "You're ridiculous. You know that?"

"Says the man cooking dinner tonight. I want to make sure we dine on the most pristine of tomatoes."

Tilan's mouth lifted into a half-smile as he handed the coin over to the merchant. "How would I ever buy my vegetables if you weren't here?"

Marietta brought her hand to her chest. "Why, you would simply just suffer."

Tilan laughed as she handed over the tomato for him to carry with the rest of their items. The way his eyes crinkled at the edges when he smiled sent a swoop through her stomach. Her handsome blacksmith.

She couldn't help but think of the remaining time she had in Olkia—a few days before she left again. Fortunately, Tilan closed his smithy for the

day, and she was sure to book no meetings with her clients. It was a rare event and one she would take full advantage of. Tilan even planned to make her dinner tonight, which was sweet of him. After traveling around Enomenos as often as she did, it was rare that she had a home-cooked meal.

Tilan was thoughtful and kind, always putting her first. But most importantly, he was easy. Easy to love, to get along with, to smile. Nothing felt mundane when she was with him—even shopping for vegetables.

"Did you hear who's playing at The Lonely Dog tomorrow?" he asked, stepping into the crowd.

"No," she admitted, following him. "I forgot to check. Someone good, I'm guessing, if you're bringing it up."

Tilan smirked. "Lexie Tonguetru."

Marietta stopped walking and gripped his arm. "You're joking—no way Pelok got her to play The Dog."

"I promise you he did."

"Tilan, she's my favorite."

"I know this."

A man behind them grumbled for them to keep walking. Tilan rolled his eyes and pulled her along.

"We have to go," Marietta said.

"Of course, we're going. Can you imagine how heartbroken Pelok would be if his favorite customer didn't come to watch such a big act?"

Marietta laughed, her eyes wandering over the stalls. "I think it's least favorite customer but favorite business associate."

"He forgave you for smashing all those glasses, Mar," Tilan teased. "When are you going to realize my friend adores you almost as much as I do?"

"When he stops bringing up the glasses," she grumbled. "Do you think Lexie will have—"

For a moment, the crowd split, revealing a man who lurked near a stall. He was broad in the shoulders with a wave of brown hair, and he stared directly at her. Her chest tightened as she stopped walking again.

"For fuck's sake," cried the man behind them as he barged between Marietta and Tilan.

"It's him," she said, Tilan grabbing her arm and pulling her off to the side.

"It's who? Mar, are you alright?" Tilan cupped her cheek, looking at her from eye to eye.

"Keyain—he's right there. Look."

Tilan glanced over his shoulder, then back to her. "That man isn't Keyain, sweetheart. It's alright."

"No, it is," she said, pushing past him. She looked next to the stall to find the spot empty. Her throat tightened, uneasiness curling out from her stomach. That was the third time she thought she saw Keyain that month.

"It looked nothing like him."

Marietta turned to Tilan, brows furrowed. "And how would you know what Keyain looks like?"

Tilan paused for a moment. He slipped his arm around her waist and steered her in the opposite direction of where the man had stood. "He was a human," he said, avoiding her gaze. "You said Keyain was an elf."

Marietta looked over her shoulder, searching for the man. Her chest loosened at Tilan's protective touch as his eyes scanned the crowd. "You're sure?"

"Positive." He pulled her closer. "How about we go see Pelok at The Dog?"

"Right now?" she asked.

"You look like you could use a drink after that." He glanced at her, his mouth tilting with a smile.

Marietta nodded her head, leaning further into Tilan. She really could use a drink. Part of her thought she was going crazy, seeing things that weren't there. Perhaps after years of undergoing Keyain's controlling patterns, her brain manifested the thing she feared most.

Now a year out from her relationship with Keyain, she could see the unhealthy toll Keyain had caused, the emotional turmoil that he put her through, especially with his anger. Keyain would have never hit her, but not all injuries were physical. Marietta couldn't see it until she left him. Such things were always clearer in hindsight.

Chapter Eighty-Eight

MARIETTA

Keyain paced before Marietta in the living room of their suite with his jaw ground shut. She sat on the couch, her hands clasped in her lap on her filthy dress, torn from where she fell. Red plumed from her bruises, her knees ached and were caked with blood. Despite looking worse for wear, she held her chin high.

"How dare you," he whispered again, his gaze finding her.

"Are you that surprised?"

Keyain laughed mirthlessly. "I said you would be the death of me."

"And I once said I never wanted to see your face again, so you decided to steal me away and attack my city as a cover for your actions. Did you think I would ignore all of that?"

"I suppose I'm a fool for thinking you would." Keyain looked away.

"And you lied to me," she hissed, hot tears running down her face, "I saw him; Tilan's in the dungeons. He's alive."

The muscles in his neck tightened. "What did that bitch do?"

Marietta laughed. "Valeriya gave me the truth—that you are a liar. Why keep him here? To torture him while you fucked me, claiming me as your wife?"

Rage flashed in his eyes as Keyain turned, punching the wall next to him, splintering the wood paneling. Blood ran down his fist, his voice a growl. "Tilan is a monster. How many times do I need to say this?"

"You're just petty and controlling. Does it excite you, having complete control over me? To make me tremble at your anger?"

Keyain glared at Marietta, his fists flexing. He turned, disappearing

into his office, digging through his desk drawer. When Keyain returned, he pulled a few pages out from a file in his hand.

"What's this?" She looked at Keyain with knitted brows.

"Look for yourself."

The papers shook in her hands as she lifted them, her eyes taking in the notes. Tilan's handwriting—she would recognize it anywhere. And gods, those were his drawings, the streaky, sketchy style of his designs, but the machines were... nausea rolled in her stomach. No, Tilan hadn't made these. Not him. Not Tilan.

The first sketch was of a device stretching out a body. The person on the rack had pointed ears, their face sketched in pain. Tilan's handwriting made notes in the margins around the drawing.

"See those machines, Mar? Your sweet Tilan designed those himself, intended to use them against Satiros." He laughed darkly. "I told you he was no better than me; I was just faster than him this time."

Marietta turned the page, letting the first fall to the floor, holding the breath in her chest. Unbelievable—they weren't Tilan's.

The second page had sketches of large wooden blocks loaded with spears. Tilan's notes detailed how black powder launched the spears into groups of people, impaling them. Black powder. Gods, Tilan had talked of black powder with her not that long ago.

"Keep flipping, Marietta," Keyain hissed. "See what your husband created."

The next was a small hand-held apparatus made from metal that, at first, appeared to be harmless. The diagram showed round compartments attached to an elongated frame with notes in the margins that denote the use of black powder to launch a metal casing that exploded on impact.

She flipped through the pages, each machine crueler than the previous. Bile climbed her throat with each sketch. Marietta leaned over the couch, her stomach spilling out to the floor. How could he have designed such evil things? How could anyone have done so?

Keyain approached her with heavy footfalls, his hand on her back. "I hope you understand that this is what your treachery aided." His voice choked as Marietta spit the remaining vomit in her mouth to the floor. "I don't know what Wyltam will do to you, but I might spare you and the baby from death if you give us the identity of your Exisotis informant because I am sure it was you leaking information."

The baby. Keyain still thought she was pregnant. She closed her eyes, resting her hands on her head. It was all too much. She reached to find the warmth of Therypon in her chest, calming her. "I don't know who the informant is," she whispered.

"How do you not know?" He lifted her chin to stare into her face, confused.

Tears blurred her vision as she sucked in a shaky breath. A knock rapped on the door at that second. Keyain sighed and walked into the other room to answer it.

"What?" he yelled. His heavy footfalls grew louder as he walked back towards Marietta in the living room. "Were you with Queen Valeriya?" His voice was stern, eyes wide.

Valeriya had given herself up so Marietta could escape. She said nothing, her gaze fixed on Keyain.

He took a few steps toward her. "Mar," he warned. "They just captured her and found this on the scene." The nymph dagger sat in his palm.

The tears came faster, obscuring Keyain's form. They would kill Valeriya.

"Marietta." He approached, his voice dropping to a whisper. "Say that Valeriya coerced you to help her; say she forced you to steal from me so I can save you and the baby." His hand reached out for her own.

It would doom Valeriya, but if they captured her, she was likely already going to be sentenced to death for treason. Marietta closed her eyes, her breath shattering as she nodded her head.

Keyain ran to the doorway. "Marietta knows about the Queen. Send a message to Wyltam. I'll join them soon." The door slammed.

The message would seal her fate; Valeriya would not come out of this alive.

Keyain looked at her, his shoulders slacked. "I don't know what I'll do with you, Marietta. When this blows over, I doubt I can trust you to be alone, ever."

She said nothing, her face wet with tears. There was no intention to stay—she needed to flee, to find a way to the temple. If they couldn't protect her from the crown, she would run. Marietta would escape to Enomenos.

Keyain went and fussed in the bedroom before stepping back into the living room. "I stationed the guards outside your room and in the hidden passage." His voice dropped so only she could hear it. "Don't do anything," he said. "This is my last chance to save you." Keyain walked to her slowly, planting a kiss on her head before leaving out the front door.

Marietta looked at the papers again with shaking hands. Tilan was alive, but he was a monster. Her head grew dizzy. The room spun.

He was alive but a monster.

Chapter Eighty–Nine

VALERIYA

Katya. Her name was a blessing, her presence a curse. Valeriya walked to her damnation following the female she loved—that she adored. How could Kat have betrayed her? She haunted Valeriya's field of vision as they wove through the underground passages into an unrecognizable section. Never had she ventured so far.

Wyltam had sent the male she battled with to get medical help. At her back was the last mage, a tall male the size of Keyain but moved with feline quiet and grace. Though she knew he remained behind her, nothing alerted Valeriya that she had someone following her.

How had Wyltam gathered such mages? Better yet, how had he learned to be a mage in the first place? It wasn't as if he had a sibling to protect—not like Valeriya. His fate was always to become the King of Satiros, so why did he learn magic?

She watched her husband continue forward towards a perpendicular path. Instead of turning, he continued straight into the wall. Valeriya blinked, realizing the stone was illusioned. She was more blind than she ever imagined; Wyltam was well-equipped.

The path curved away from the palace-proper. If Valeriya had to guess, they were underneath the city by then. They continued downward, and then she saw it. The tunnel ended with a vast, cavernous room, light globes flickering on at their arrival. To one side, pads lined the floor. A sparring circle, she noted, like she and Katya used to train back in Reyila. Racks of knives and daggers of every size sat near the ring. Across the way was a shooting range. Bows, crossbows, and other devices she didn't recognize rested in another rack. At the far end of the room, targets stood,

marred from practice.

Though they were deep underground, the air remained drier than she expected. None of the musk or dust of being subterranean permeated the space. Magic changed the atmosphere.

So, this was how Wyltam kept it secret. Below the city-state, he and his mages would train, no one above the wiser.

Wyltam led the group down one of three hallways, stopping before a door. He motioned for Valeriya to follow Katya into the room and turned to the unfamiliar male. "Send a message when you find her," he said, his deep voice echoing. "And protect her, Wynn. Tensions are already high." The male offered a curt nod before taking off down the hall.

Though underground, the room was comfortable. To one side was a small kitchen area and a table. Katya led her to the other side, to a plush sitting area. Valeriya sunk into the couch. Katya sat at the other end, determined not to look at Valeriya. Her heart ached. Wyltam took the seat across from her, his arm resting on its edge as he propped his head. She didn't bother to hold back her sneer. Of course, he was unable to sit like a king as he sent her to her death.

Sighing, Wyltam shook his head. "You've made a mess of things." He crossed one leg over the other, further degrading his posture. "Stealing money from the crown to help our people is one thing, but sending sensitive information to the Exisotis, your sister, and the Chorys Dasians is something else."

Valeriya sat with her back bone-straight and lifted her chin to look down at her husband. Katya had told him everything then. The crushing pain of her betrayal choked Valeriya's breath. She swallowed hard, managing to say, "Go on with it, then. Send me to my pyre."

Katya's head whipped to him, eyes wide. "Wyltam, you promised you wouldn't."

"I'm not," he said with another sigh. "Valeriya, you've been playing your own game from the beginning. I'm aware that before our wedding, you arrived in Satiros two weeks before your public arrival date. I'm also aware of your magical capabilities. Master Arkym of Reyila spoke highly of you. When you took a special interest in The Weeds, I recognized you would be of help to me, to Satiros; yet, you have been, and continue to be, loyal to Reyila."

Wyltam knew the mage who trained her and Katya? Had known that she knew magic and she snuck into the city? She stilled her expression, her heart racing in her chest. "I'd rather be loyal to a city-state that views pilinos as equals than to a king who works with leisurely care. How many books have you read while your citizens starved?"

"How would I have made a difference when the group of ministers I inherited is already distrusting of me?" Wyltam cocked his head, his dark hair falling to the side. "Tell me how I, the King of Satiros, could do as you did to help the pilinos? Never could I sneak away like that, nor understand the social nuances in The Weeds—but you did. I let you take the coin, and I hid the loss from my ministers. By pretending to be distant and careless with my position, I allowed others to make a difference."

"So, me putting my safety on the line every time I stepped out of this palace was from your doing?" Valeriya spat, feeling her anger rise. "Don't act as if you let me; it was my own doing."

"I see that," Wyltam said, his words clipped, "but I made sure you were safe."

Valeriya scoffed, shaking her head. "You don't care about me. You don't care about your city—or anyone."

"That's not true," Katya whispered, lifting her head to stare at Valeriya.

"Oh, so now you speak." Valeriya hated the anger in her tone, but finally, Kat looked at her. Her sharp nose. Her bright eyes. Even though she scowled, she was stunning. Fierce. Emotion choked Valeriya's voice. "Give me a reason to trust you after… after this."

"Because Nastanya tried to execute me."

Her words fell like a hammer to her chest. That couldn't be true. "My sister would never."

"Auryon would." Katya swallowed, her gaze hardening. "I told you the Chorys Dasi prince was rotten. He's corrupted your sister—corrupted Reyila. Together, they passed a law that moved pilinos to be subservient to the elven, just like the rest of Syllogi. Like Chorys Dasi."

A wave of nausea washed over her. Auryon was a touch sullen, but he wasn't that corrupt, was he? Then again, if he took over ruling Reyila… Nastanya wouldn't allow such a ruling. "I don't believe you." Even as she said the words, Valeriya knew they were a lie. Dread weighed down her stomach, her limbs. Nastanya deceived her because of Auryon—because the plan all along must have been to give power to Chorys Dasi. Her hand shook as she brought it to her mouth, feeling the bile rise

"Why do you think I'm here, Valeriya?" Katya asked, gesturing to the room. "Why do you think I'm working with Wyltam? With Satiros? I had to flee Reyila because your sister and her husband sent mages after me. Master Arkym gave his life to get me to Wyltam safely. All the pilinos nobles of Reyila have been executed."

Valeriya shook her head, furrowing her brows. "Nastanya's closest childhood friend was a half-elven lady. You're saying she executed her?"

"Trylien is dead." Katya swallowed hard. "They're all dead because Auryon planted his seeds of distaste. Reyila is now just an extension of Chorys Dasi. The Reyilan Crown is an appendage of theirs."

Valeriya closed her eyes as the tears welled, dripping down her cheeks. If this was the truth, then Nastanya was in trouble. Her sister devoted herself to their queendom and thrived on the diversity of their people. She was proud of Reyila and carried the crown with that pride. What happened? What changed?

Doubt crept its way into her head, the image of her sister and Reyila shattering. She looked at Katya's intense stare, the passion brimming in her features. She turned to Wyltam, her husband, who never showed emotions; yet had a concerned frown marring his face. And like that, she understood.

Valeriya never ruled the game; she was a player in it.

"How long?" Valeriya asked, swallowing back her emotion. "How long ago had this happened?"

"Four years," Wyltam answered.

Valeriya nodded her head and glanced at Katya. "You've been here for four years and hid from me."

"How could I reveal to you I was here when you'd tell Nastanya?" Katya pleaded. "I know how much you love your sister. Fuck, I loved her, too." She mussed her short-cropped hair as she flung herself on the couch. "I tried to help her, Valeriya. I tried to tell her about Auryon, but it placed a target on my back. If they learned where I was, they'd hunt me down. I uncovered too many of their secrets."

Valeriya closed her eyes as her thoughts raced. If Auryon had corrupted Reyila and now the Chorys Dasi Prince controlled her home, what did that mean for the plan? The sudden panic left her breathless. The Chorys Dasians orchestrated this and now, they would seize Satiros.

Her body felt far away as she spoke, staring at the empty hearth. "If what you say is true, then Satiros is in grave danger. I gave Chorys Dasi everything I took, and they're using it to plan an attack."

"I know," Wyltam said, drawing her gaze. Her husband's stare was unwavering. "What we need to know is what information you passed to them or Reyila."

"And not to the Exisotis?" Valeriya asked.

"I'm curious about that, but what you don't know, Valeriya, is that I've been working towards uniting Satiros with Enomenos. Right now, I am arranging talks with the leader of the Exisotis."

She stared at him, her jaw slacking. "What are you talking about?"

"For the past two decades, I have been working to unite Satiros with Enomenos and the Exisotis. In doing so, I hid everything from my ministers." He shifted in his seat, his dark eyes locked on to her. "I want to break Satiros away from Syllogi and adopt the practices and beliefs of Enomenos so we can grant pilinos an equal station."

"That's ludicrous," Valeriya said, laughing though she felt no humor. "You can't achieve such a thing, not on your own."

"I will achieve it," he said with quiet confidence that Valeriya didn't realize he possessed. "Marietta is the key to that plan's success."

"How does she play into this?" Valeriya asked.

"They're desperate to get her back and will do anything to do so," he said. "And that includes meeting with me."

For a moment, Valeriya could see how Wyltam's plan could work out, how they could leverage Marietta against the Exisotis. The documents she received from them proved how close to the top she stood, but there was one problem. "I let Marietta escape," she whispered, eyes wide.

"She didn't escape," he continued. "Wynn sent a message moments ago that Keyain apprehended her." Wyltam paused, shifting forward to rest his forearms on his knees, staring at Valeriya. "But she leads to our main problem. The ministers know one of you is leaking information. Keyain will do anything to save her. He knows we captured you, Valeriya. He even sent word that you coerced Marietta to commit treason on your behalf."

Valeriya scoffed at the ridiculous notion. "The girl wanted to help the Exisotis. I had not coerced her into working with me."

"I know," Wyltam said, "but your word means nothing against his. Most of the ministers are looking for any reason to rid the court of Marietta. This would give them their reason. Keyain was already desperate to help her and now that she's carrying his child—"

"She's not pregnant," Valeriya said, cutting him off.

Wyltam's eyes fluttered closed as he took a breath before regaining his emotionless expression. She had just thought the rumors surrounding him and Marietta were baseless at best. Given his reaction, what had she missed? "Regardless, Keyain will make sure the ministers find you guilty of treason. I'll agree with him.

Katya jumped from her seat. "Wyltam, you promised—"

"Hush," he demanded. Katya silenced herself with a look of fury. "Marietta needs to remain innocent—thus alive—in order to work with Enomenos. Charging her with treason, which would lead to her death, would only worsen our relations. They must find Valeriya guilty of it."

"Valeriya has lost enough," Katya yelled. "Let the half-elf die." Beneath the anger was something sharper. Fear.

Wyltam's features hardened on Katya. "Marietta's survival means we could aid those in Satiros—"

"Let them all die! I don't care." Katya's chest heaved as she met her stare. "Valeriya's life isn't worth that sacrifice. Not to me."

Valeriya shook her head, remembering Wyltam's words from months ago. "The life of one isn't worth the life of many."

Katya approached her. "Your life means *everything* to me." She leaned over Valeriya, bracing her hands on the back of the couch.

"But I can change everything for *them*." Valeriya raised her hand to cup Katya's cheek, but she jerked away.

"Seven years and you're altruistic as ever," she spat, shaking her head. "Fuck them, fuck this city, and fuck anyone who thinks this is a good idea." Her glare cut to Wyltam.

"Don't be selfish," Valeriya said, exasperated.

"Oh, I'm selfish?"

"Yes," Valeriya snapped, "this isn't about you or me. This is about changing—"

"There you go again about change! Just like before, back in Reyila." Katya stared from eye to eye, her breathing heavy. "You want your fucking legacy! Change is more than a person."

"But one person can bring about change."

Katya laughed, shaking her head as she stepped back. Valeriya grabbed for her hand, folding it into her own. Tears streaked down Katya's face as she glowered at the wall, her jaw set. "Your life is too much to give," Katya said, her glare finding Wyltam again. "You promised you wouldn't execute her."

"I won't," he replied, his face remaining passive.

"But if she's tried for treason—"

"Valeriya won't be." Wyltam stood, clasping his hands behind his back as he paced. "You two are to leave Satiros together. By fleeing, Valeriya will implicate her guilt. Both Valeriya and Marietta will live."

Valeriya nodded her head. "That could work." She looked up into Katya's face. After all this time, they could finally be together.

"What's so special about Marietta that the Exisotis want her?" Katya hissed. "Why must Valeriya give everything she worked hard to achieve?"

Wyltam remained with his back to them, then glanced over his shoulder at them. "She is more important than anyone realizes. She is our hope."

And then Wyltam shared the truth about Marietta.

Chapter Ninety

VALERIYA

After Wyltam left, Valeriya and Katya remained silent. Alone for the first time in seven years, Valeriya didn't know what to say—not after the information Wyltam revealed to them. Never would she have thought this was how it played out.

After sharing the information she handed to the Chorys Dasians, including a packet about Marietta, he had become deadly quiet. Wyltam was convinced that the Chorys Dasians would discover how valuable Marietta was, and that posed another problem. To have seen Wyltam nervous had put Valeriya on edge.

Katya paced like a caged wildcat, anger fueling her movements. Valeriya watched, absorbing the elegant way her body moved, the soft swishing of her hair. At least there was one positive: they would finally be together. Yes, Valeriya must give up everything she had worked for in Satiros, give up the legacy she had been building, but the tradeoff was the woman she loved. That was infinitely better than dying at the hands of the King's Council.

If anything, this outcome was better than she imagined. Well, almost better. She'd have to leave behind Mycaub. Valeriya's breath hitched at the thought, bringing tears to her eyes. That evening would be the last time she saw him until it was safe for her to return—if it ever was. Of all the sacrifices she had to make, that one hurt her the most, threatening to rip her heart from her chest.

"His plan has too many holes," Katya said again. "There are too many ways it could go wrong."

"What other choice do we have, Kat? Chorys Dasi and Reyila now also pose a threat," Valeriya said, sitting up straighter at the edge of the couch. She brought her hand to her chin in thought. "Alone, Satiros can't defend against them. But united—"

"It's still too much!" Katya snapped. "Yes, you gave information away, but you've done more good for this city-state than anyone. Why do you need to flee?"

"Stop with the selfishness, Katya."

With a shaky sigh, her eyes turned toward Valeriya, shining in the light. "For you, I can be selfish."

"No, you can't."

"I can!" she yelled, approaching Valeriya. "You are the only thing I'm selfish for, Valeriya—the only thing I gave myself!" Katya held Valeriya's face, her glare intense as she raged. "I've dedicated my life to everyone else—just like you. But you, Valeriya," she said, shaking, "you are my everything. For you, I am selfish. For you, I fight for your life, your existence. I will die defending you and all the good you bring to the world."

Valeriya didn't breathe as she stared up at Katya, hot tears running down her face. After all that time, her feelings hadn't faded. Their relationship was as it had been—as it would always be. Even now, as Katya raged, the three words were present in every seething word. Three words Valeriya needed to say—that Katya needed to hear. "I love you, Kat."

Katya's face crumpled, the tears falling faster as she pulled Valeriya's face close, kissing her. Gentle and feather-soft, unlike anything else on Katya, her lips pressed into hers with all of her intensity. "I love you, Valeriya."

Her fingers wove into Katya's hair, pulling her into her lap as her tongue brushed along hers, with seven years of built-up affection behind it. To feel her—to kiss her—was enough to give her the strength she needed, for her sacrifice was more than them. So that people like Katya had a future where they could love and live freely. She wished there was something more she could do—a different outcome, a different solution for their problem—yet, the truth Wyltam shared meant Valeriya had to leave everything behind, including her son.

"It'll be okay," Valeriya murmured into her. "I won't lose everything, for I gain a future with you."

"That isn't what you want," she said, her bright eyes lined with tears.

"You were always what I wanted but what I could never have." Valeriya pressed a kiss into Katya's temple. "We'll return when the dust settles in a few years. I'll get Mycaub and my future with you. It's all working out for us."

"But they'll hunt us down—we'll know no peace."

"Wyltam ensured Keyain wouldn't send anyone after us."

Katya brushed back a lock of Valeriya's hair. "And if the Chorys Dasians do?"

"We'll give them the fight of their lives," Valeriya said with a sad smile. "After all, we were Arkym's best students."

Smiling into their kiss, Katya finally conceded. "Okay," she murmured. "If you've made your peace, then I'll stand by your side. Always."

Overwhelming emotion swept through Valeriya, a melancholic joy that brought her to tears. There would be no more legacy. She'd leave her son behind in Satiros. Her home and her sister were both gone. The guiding light through it—the joy—was the female she loved. A crown would no longer hang over Valeriya's head. No responsibilities besides keeping each other safe. Valeriya would lose everything but gain something she always wanted but never thought he could have: a future with Katya.

Chapter Ninety-One

MARIETTA

Hours later, the door to the suite opened, the call of Amryth's voice far off. She came into view, and Marietta stared at her friend, unable to hear her words. Amryth slapped her in the face. "Marietta," she hissed. "Snap out of it. What in the gods happened?"

Marietta shook her head. "A mage attacked the Queen and me, and when I fled, Keyain found me in the tunnel. And Tilan." Her throat constricted.

"Gods, what about Tilan?" Amryth sighed.

"He's alive. In the dungeon. He was alive this whole time."

Amryth swore, her fingers pinching the bridge of her nose. "Marietta, I know you're in pain, but we need to go."

Marietta ignored her and instead shoved the Tilan's notes into her hands. "These are Tilan's creations," she whispered.

Amryth gave her a look before reading the papers. She flipped from the first page, her jaw dropping. "Deities be damned."

She dropped the papers, her own hands shaking. "Marietta, listen to me. I know you're feeling a lot right now, but we need to get you to the temple. They need to perform the ritual to make you an Iros before Keyain advocates for you. Him and the King plan for you to testify against the Queen. We need to go. Now." Amryth grabbed Marietta's hand, pulling her up from the couch.

"How will we get out of here? They're guarding our only ways out." Marietta said, frowning.

"I have an idea," Amryth whispered, edging near Keyain's office.

Marietta stood near the fireplace, waiting for Amryth's signal. Amryth walked into the office, approaching the guard stationed there. "Hey, did Keyain say anything about—" A light flashed, followed by the smack of a body hitting the floor. "Go," Amryth called.

When she turned the corner, Marietta saw Amryth standing over the unconscious body of the guard. "Quick, help me undress him. We only have so much time to disguise you."

Marietta darted forward, taking the armor and clothes from Amryth. Marietta removed her dirtied dress, stepping into the uniform that was too big for her, the elven man's boots too loose, but they would suffice.

"Let's go," Amryth said, lighting the light globe from her pocket. The two raced down the spiral staircase. At the bottom, Amryth held up her hand, listening. The tunnels had quieted, the commotion of earlier calming down. "This way."

Marietta remained close to Amryth as she made her way through the tunnels, staying alert. By some blessing of the gods, no one intercepted them as Amryth slowed her gait, listening on the wall. She pressed her hand against the brick, and a section of the wall shifted away.

They stepped into a closet lined with cleaning supplies and other odds and ends. "Keyain told our unit about the tunnels and the ways to access them. The late queen had them bricked over during her reign, but a few ways to enter and exit remain."

"Convenient for us," Marietta muttered.

Amryth leaned against the door to listen. "Only if his other guards aren't patrolling it."

Marietta sent a small prayer to Therypon that they weren't. Everything else from their plan had gone sideways.

Amryth waved her over as she cracked open the door. A small room with tables and chairs sat beyond. "Act as if you're a guard and stay close." She loosened her posture and walked to the room's exit. Without another word, she entered the hallway beyond with Marietta in tow. Beneath the hood of her cloak, Marietta tried to keep her breath even as nervousness kept her on edge. A few guards milled about, some acknowledging them with a nod. The gate beyond the palace doors appeared as they rounded a corner. She sighed in relief. It was just like the first time Amryth took Marietta to the temple.

The sun crested over the buildings, bathing the city in the golden morning light. Though early, the city beyond the gates bustled. Amryth must have timed their escape for the shift change with the guard as they slipped in with a group of soldiers heading out for duty in the city. Amryth kept her hand on the small of Marietta's back. Marietta held her breath, her eyes wide as the gate neared.

They crossed the exit, the whitewashed buildings coming into view. She exhaled, smiling at Amryth. "How did we do that twice?"

"I don't know, but we need to hurry. We're on borrowed—"

Someone shouted behind them. Marietta whipped her head around to see a guard pointing in their direction. The guards in the group next to them snatched Marietta's arm. "That's them!"

Amryth grabbed her hand, tugging her free, and they sprinted into the city. She dragged Marietta along at full sprint, the too-large boots causing her to stumble. Behind them, the guards neared, closing the bit of lead they had. They raced towards the temple, pushing people in the crowded streets out of their way. Her chest heaved, a stitch threatening her side, cursing herself for not having Amryth's conditioning.

Marietta panted as Amryth slowed her gait, taking in their surroundings. Alarmed expressions from city folk eyed them. "Go on ahead. I'll try to throw them off."

"No, please don't!" Marietta grabbed for her arm. Amryth dodged her hand, turning around to face the guards. Marietta took the opportunity to duck into a crowd. People yelled at her as she hastily made her way through, her gaze searching for guards. A hand grasped her shoulder, yanking. "I told you to spread out." Marietta's eyes grew wide as a stocky elvish man addressed her.

Thankful for her hair covering her ears, she responded, "I think I heard a commotion coming from that direction. I can cover this area if you want to provide backup."

He gave her an odd look. "Aren't you forgetting something?"

"Sir?" Marietta added.

"Don't be disrespectful to your superior officer. I'll deal with you later." He took off in the direction that Marietta had sent him.

Relief flooded her body with a sigh, taking a moment to catch her breath. Though it was still the morning, the summer weather was hot, especially in the full guard's uniform. Marietta wiped away the sweat that stung her eyes.

The temple wasn't much further. If Marietta could gather her strength and make a break for it, granted, she ran into no one else. The goddess must have been watching over her; that interaction with the guard was too close for comfort.

Marietta took off again, jogging down a side street. It should connect her to the road next to the temples if her memory served her right. Ache spread through her legs with each step, swearing to the goddess that if she made it out alive, she would train to never be weak again. Heat flared in her chest, causing Marietta to laugh. Therypon watched over her. As a response, the pain in her legs—even her lungs—subsided, the warmth lingering instead.

She turned the corner and resisted collapsing to her knees. Rows of guards in Satiroan uniforms surrounded the temple's entrance, keeping a clear perimeter around the steps. Already, a crowd formed in the street's square, yelling at the guards.

Gods, she couldn't break through that crowd, not without drawing attention. Marietta swore, staying to the edge of the street, reassessing her position.

Figures of blue stood at the temple's entry, swords drawn and shields raised as a handful of guards approached. In the crowd below, robed attendants from the other temples joined, jeering at the blockade. She leaned against the alley wall, her heart sinking. She tried to remember the route Ryder took when she last visited the temple. Their carriage had traveled from the south, and Marietta was north of the temple. Perhaps if she—

"There you are!"

Marietta jumped, turning to run as Deania peeked up from behind her.

"Deania, thank gods. What's going on?"

"Keyain ordered the guards to surround the temple once he realized you were missing. I'm lucky I found you. Where's Amryth?"

Marietta frowned. Of course, he did. "She used herself as a distraction so I could get away."

Deania nodded her head. "I can get you to the temple. I don't trust the guard to put up with Coryn and the other paladins much longer."

Marietta followed her through the back alleys, ducking behind barrels whenever footsteps sounded.

"They won't expect you to make it this far, so the back alley should be unguarded," Deania murmured, her eyes searching in front of them. She stuck out her head, checking the street that sat between the alley they were in and the one behind Therypon's temple. Deania motioned for Marietta to follow as she took off running.

As they dodged bystanders walking along the street, someone gripped Marietta's arm. "She's here!" a guard shouted. Small but quick, Deania jumped in front of her, grasping the man's exposed wrist. Solid black filled her eyes as dark, crackling energy released from her hand. He cried out in pain, trying to fling Deania, but she held on.

"Run!" Deania screamed.

Marietta sprinted to the alley, leaving her friend behind. Cerulean banners waved from the upper floor of the temple, encouraging Marietta forward. She glanced back, realizing Deania hadn't followed. Gods, first Amryth, now Deania. If they were caught, if something happened to them because of her—no, she had to focus. At the opposite end of the alley, two guards appeared. Marietta swore, her legs pumping faster as she raced toward the temple—toward the guards, too. She was so close to the back wall of the temple grounds. She just needed to get on the property.

Relief flooded her as she reached the gate, pulling the handle. But it wouldn't budge. She frantically tried again, the guards closing in, yet it remained locked. Marietta took a calming breath, staring at the wall. She'd have to climb.

Her nails chipped as they dug into the mortar, her feet slipping as she struggled to find a hold, yet she climbed and continued to rise, cresting the top and seeing the temple gardens from the other side. "Help!" she screamed towards the temple, attendants in blue appearing in the windows.

A hand wrapped around her ankle, ripping her from the brick. Marietta crashed onto the cobblestone with a groan. Shaking off the stinging pain, she lurched to the side, throwing off the guard, but a second seized her, pinning her to the ground. "Run, tell them we got her."

One guard took off running. The other grabbed her by the hair, holding her in place. "You've made quite a disturbance, haven't you?" The guard laughed, pulling her to her knees.

Marietta turned to spit in his plump face as someone's foot slammed into it. The guard released Marietta and Amryth jumped on him, the kick stunning his reaction, and she landed a second blow to his nose with a sickening crunch.

Deania came running up behind her, arms flailing towards the temple. "Open the gate!" she screamed. "Open the gods damned gate!"

Amryth grabbed the guard by his collar, head-butting him, and dropped back onto the path. "Mar, go!"

She darted, but the guard reached out, snagging her ankle. Gravel stung her face as she fell, just as a group of guards charged the alley.

Amryth swore as the guard kicked out at her, and she launched on top of him. "Go!" she screamed again.

Deania grabbed Marietta's arm, helping her to the gate as the group of guards approached, the first meeting Amryth's fist as she held the line. Deania threw Marietta towards the door as she turned to help Amryth.

Marietta dove through, crawling away from the entrance. There was a flash of black, followed by Amryth and Deania racing through the gate.

Deania held up her hands, her fingertips glowing white. "On behalf of the Goddess Therypon, I declare Marietta Vallynte and Amryth Sulyng under our protection!" A white barrier appeared in the fence's gap where the door should be, the guards slamming into it.

"Quick, close the gate," Deania ordered two attendants who remained off to the side, mouths agape. Deania wiped her hands off on her pants and looked up at Amryth and Marietta. "Well, wasn't that fun! I haven't had to fight like that since I fled Chorys Dasi."

Amryth stood, offering Marietta a hand, eyes lining with tears. She pulled Marietta into a tight hug. "Thank gods. We did it. You're safe." Her voice was thick with emotion.

Marietta hugged her back, squeezing, unable to believe it herself. Amryth, who saved her once, had saved her again. "I don't know how to thank you," she said, a lump rising in her throat. "You risked everything for me."

"I couldn't leave you there, not after all you've been through with Keyain. But we did it; you're here. We're both here, and we're safe."

They pulled back, Marietta using the heel of her hand to wipe away her tears. "I'm forever in your debt."

Amryth shook her head. "No, Marietta. You're my friend, and you needed my help."

"I'm here for you, always. Okay?"

Amryth nodded her head, new tears forming in her eyes that fell down her cheeks.

"I know this is emotional, but we need to move and find Coryn," Deania said, her hands ushering the two inside.

They wound their way through the temple, heading underground to a room where they found Coryn pacing.

"Thank the goddess," he said as they walked in, his left eye swollen and red.

"Coryn, what happened?" Deania said, approaching him.

He shook his head. "Keyain's here. There isn't enough time. The ceremony is long and we have just enough Iros to perform it." He sighed, pulling Marietta into a hug. "I'm glad you made it."

"I only did because of these two. Amryth distracted the guards that followed us from the palace. And Deania—what even was that? When you grabbed the guard and then the flash of black?" She turned to Deania as she fussed over Coryn's eye.

"Pain is the other domain," she said, sighing at Coryn's injury. "I expelled energy that flares their nerves, so they feel as if they're injured, in theory."

"Enough." Coryn jerked away from her touch. "Right now, I need to get Marietta to the ceremony. When they learn she made it to the temple, they'll order a King's summons, and I don't doubt they'll try to infiltrate the temple looking for her." He held out his hand for Marietta to take.

She grasped it, looking at Amryth and Deania as she left. "Thank you both again-"

Amryth smiled. "No time, Mar. Get going."

Chapter Ninety-Two

MARIETTA

"Y ou sure like to get yourself into trouble," Coryn said as he led her up a set of stairs, further towards the top of the temple.

"I've been told that before," she grumbled, her body exhausted. It took all her energy to focus on not collapsing on the steps. "When you train me to be an Iros, will there be a physical aspect to it?"

"Like conditioning?" he asked, raising a brow, the smile coming easy. "Oh, yes. Plenty of that."

"Great," she grumbled again.

"You should be excited. The ceremony is a big deal."

"I am, but," Marietta hesitated. "I don't know what the ceremony is, nor do I know if being an Iros will save me from the crown." She paused with a heavy breath. "And I don't know what rules I'll have to follow. Will I have to live at the temple once I'm an Iros? What will be expected of me? Will I have to be celibate?"

Coryn huffed a laugh, dipping his head down before glancing at her. "I've never met an Iros who was celibate."

"Well," Marietta said, "that's good news at least."

With a half-smile, Coryn shook his head. "The only immediate expectation is that you train to learn her powers, how to control pain and healing magic. After you've gained competency, there are tasks we're given. More often than not, we visit small villages on the outskirts of the city-state where medics are less likely to be and offer healing free of cost."

"Charity work?"

"More or less. Plus other things arise usually."

"Like?" Marietta asked.

Coryn hedged, turning his head away. "You'll see."

Annoyed, she shook off his answer. "What should I expect from the ceremony?"

"The head of our temple, Nosokyma, is an Iros, and she performs the inking ritual, like this," he said, gesturing to his neck. "The pain is horrible, worse than a normal tattoo, but that's part of the process."

Marietta's face paled. She had never faced physical pain like that.

"Just trust the process," he said, glancing at her expression. "And trust the goddess. No matter what, you can get through it. You simply must accept the pain."

"Sure," she mumbled. "But what happens? I'm tattooed, and then suddenly I have powers?"

"Therypon's magic blesses the ink. Made from the ash of burnt serpents' skin burnt at the goddess's altar," he explained, turning down another hall as they took another set of stairs. "The needle is a serpent's fang, also blessed by the goddess. During the ritual, the other Iros channel Therypon's energy and focus it back to you, hence needing other Iros here." They came to a stop outside a door. "Ready?"

"No." Her head spun, trying to digest the information he dumped on her. Gods, she should've asked sooner.

Coryn laughed, then knocked once. An elven woman opened the door, her face half-covered in tattoos, her eyes dark, long black hair extended down her back.

"Who knocks at the gate of Therypon?" she asked, her voice like silk.

"One chosen for the duality of pain and healing," Coryn said, pushing Marietta forward.

The elven woman stood aside, letting Marietta pass into the low-lit room, an altar made of white marble sitting at its center. The only light came from a rectangular window set into the ceiling directly above them. Coryn and the elven woman joined the other handful of people who sat crossed-legged around it, all wearing the blue of Therypon.

An older elven woman, who must have been Nosokyma, stood next to the altar, her face lined with many years, the tattoos on her skin drooping with them. "Marietta Vallynte, we welcome you to join Therypon's chosen guardians, the Iros," she said in a deep voice. "The Goddess selects each of us herself, handpicked for reasons only known to her. Do you willingly accept the ritual brought upon you today?" She raised her hands as she spoke, her piercing eyes locked on Marietta.

"I accept," she said, raising her chin and refusing to let her voice falter.

"Come, join us at the altar of Therypon." Nosokyma beckoned her forward.

The altar was a flat stone slab, the same stone that the statue of the goddess had within the chapel. On both sides sat the attendants, including Coryn, with a glazed-over look to their eyes, palms facing the ceiling.

"The duality of Therypon is that of pain and healing. For without pain, one cannot heal. And without healing, the body shall only feel pain. With this in mind, we bestow onto you, new to Therypon's divine Iros, the symbol of the goddess and the symbol of her chosen. Welcome her permanence to your flesh."

Marietta, unsure what to do, bowed her head.

Nosokyma smiled. "New to the Iros, remove your garb. Lay bare with the pain bestowed by Therypon."

Marietta jerked her head in surprise, looking at Coryn, whose gaze glossed over. He had left that part out. She turned back to the elven lady, who motioned her to remove her clothes.

She peeled off the guard uniform and lay upon the stone. The hard surface bore into her, the cold biting into her skin.

"Bring forth the instruments of Therypon."

An attendant brought forth a box and set it in front of Nosokyma. She removed the contents beyond Marietta's line of sight. Her hands touched Marietta, rolling her to the left, exposing her right side.

Nosokyma held up a piece of wood that had a serpent's tooth attached to the end. "Therypon, witness us mark the pain for your Iros!"

Black ink covered the needle, the elven woman holding it over

Marietta's side. The first stab into her body was sharp, burning. Then it spread through her rib cage, the second adding to the pain. Marietta bit her lip to keep herself from crying.

The pain leached into her ribs, pulsing down her body with the beat of her heart. It was deeper than bone; she hurt through to her very center. Again and again, the pain came crashing, each prick worse than the last. The coppery tang of blood filled her mouth as she bit through the skin of her lip.

Marietta kept herself from crying out, but the pain was unbearable. Bile rose in her throat. She steadied her breath, reaching for the warmth in her chest. Tears fell from her eyes as the pain grew worse, the heat continuing to slip away from her. The stabbing sensation cascaded from her neck to her ankle though the needle remained in one spot. Nosokyma hadn't even moved. Marietta steadied her breath and tried again.

She focused on the warmth of the goddess, how it felt to speak with her, the peppermint and eucalyptus scent, the wash of calm Therypon brought. She called out to the goddess to bring her peace. Slowly, the pain in her body faded, and there was nothing for a long while. Blackness encased her vision.

Was she dead? Did she pass out? But all her thoughts were there. Her body quivered as the needle stabbed, but the pain was distant.

Finally, Marietta called out, "Are you there?"

As with before, the answer came from inside her head.

"*I am always here.*"

Thank the gods; she was alive. "Am I on the right path?"

"*That depends. What truth have you found?*"

"My husband lives, but he created horrid machines. Keyain had lied, as had Valeriya."

"*Yes, but what else? Dig deeper.*"

Marietta thought for a second before she answered. "They kept Tilan alive after faking his death. He lives, but I don't understand for what purpose."

"*Another truth you must seek. What else?*"

Her mind drifted back to the Queen. Deania's voice came back to her. The last time the Exisotis had heard from Valeriya had been a month and a half ago. She had said she delivered them last week. "The Queen wasn't just working with just the Exisotis. Brynden—Valeriya's threat of knowing his real name. Gods, she was working with the Chorys Dasians."

"Another truth, one that will cost many lives."

Marietta's breath hitched. "Because of me. Many lives will be lost."

"You had your hand, yes. But redemption will come if you follow the truth."

"Is returning to Enomenos possible? Will Coryn and I make it?"

"It is one of many possibilities, but one that comes with much consequence."

"What does that mean?"

"Your decisions come with the cost of lives. Your goal is to save and heal through seeking the truth. Do you think you'll be effective away from those who suffer? Or at the center of those who decide the fate of many?"

Her heart stilled. Therypon meant remaining in Satiros. "But Keyain will take me away. Or the King will kill me. If they know I'm Iros, they both will kill me."

"Fates change as we make decisions. No future is set in stone. If you go back, you will face your hardest decisions yet but be closer to the truth of everything."

"Is that what I seek? The truth of everything?"

"Yes, the truth that will set many free. The fabric of fate is woven into you because of this truth. The decisions you make will be the decision of many. For that reason, you are my chosen. My hero. Seek the truth, heal the world."

Therypon's last words echoed through her head as the warmth left her body, her mind sinking back to the pain. Marietta bit against the stabbing as it racked through every inch of her body once more. Sweat slicked her brow and above her lip, but she would endure.

That pain was just the beginning. Through the power of Therypon, she would keep seeking. She would find all the truths kept from her. She would save as many people as she could.

Time slipped into a void. There was only the sound of Nosokyma, the prick of the needle, the crashing pain through her body.

Again.

And again.

And again.

Through calm breathing and the lingering warmth in her chest, Marietta focused on nothing, clearing her mind of all thought, all sensations, accepting the pain for what it was.

Chapter Ninety-Three

ELYSE

D ays at the library proved ought for little. Hours spent searching, making Wynn sit around, only to find one book. At least it was the one Sylas said to prioritize.

Frustrated, Elyse looked forward to another day of combing the library shelves, but Wynn sent her a message, waking her while she slept.

"Don't leave your room—danger happening. Will get you when safe."

An ominous warning, as if hearing someone's voice in your head wasn't unsettling enough. To be woken by it startled her so much she couldn't go back to sleep. That was hours ago.

Elyse sat with a mug of tea at her desk, fighting off her late afternoon sleepiness as she read *Fulbryk's Guide to Chorys Dasi*, trying not to think of Azarys—she failed miserably.

Fulbryk described how Chorys Dasi sat on the shores of the Bay of Black in The Mavros Sea, its waters an unsurprising black, but what was surprising was the sand was as well. Pirates populated the waters of the region, excelling at breaking the ice in the winter and plundering cargo transported between Chorys Dasi and Reyila.

Elyse imagined the dark sand beneath her feet, of Azarys at her arm, the salty breeze blowing through her hair.

Stupid, stupid, stupid. Such fantasies were unnecessary. Az lied, and she never learned of his reasoning.

Blank pages filled the center of the book, flanked on either side by chapters. The first half covered geography; the second discussed their histories. One chapter dug into the fabled Bull of the North, who

slaughtered more pirates than any other military member.

She shook the thought from her head, pondering over the blank pages. Elyse inspected them again, eyes scanning as she held them up to the light. And then she saw it. Tucked into the binding's inner crease in tight scrawling letters were the words, *"Histories sealed by blood, the secrets our kind keep."*

The words reminded Elyse of her mother's song, the one that Az and Sylas knew. Fulbryk didn't mean actual blood, did he? The blood from her elven heritage?

No, that's absurd. Magic didn't work that way.

Yet Elyse also learned something new about its possibilities every day. If she could use magic to enhance her senses, as Wynn suggested, then how likely was it that blood could also be magical?

With anticipation growing in her chest, she ran to her room, pulling a needle from her sewing kit. As she sat back down at her desk, Elyse pricked her finger and watched the blood fall to the page.

Nothing.

A stupid attempt, but at least—

The page absorbed the blood, spreading it across in bright red lettering. Breathless, she flipped through the pages that now contained odd portraits and names and titles. Her heart ceased when she reached the last page. No—no, no, no. This was wrong.

She found his picture first. His nose was straighter, his cheekbones sharper, but she knew it was him, even with two large horns protruding from his temples, circling the shaved parts of his hairline. Underneath was scrawled, *"Azarys Vynz, Prince of Chorys Dasi, Twin Brother to the Queen, Beastial Domain."*

Elyse blinked, touching the page to make sure what she saw was real. Flanking the portrait were two more of the same size. A female with an uncanny face to Az held a smirk, horns rising straight up from her forehead. *"Agnyssa Vynz, Queen of Chorys Dasi, Beastial Domain."*

The farthest right was a male, similar to the other two, but with a smaller nose, a delicate chin. Horns circled his head like Azarys's. *"Auryon*

Vynz, Prince of Chorys Dasi, Younger Brother to the Queen, Beastial Domain."

Below were more sketches, smaller and less detailed, showing sharp-cheeked elves with tails, cat ears, feathered wings—beast-like features of all kinds.

Elyse couldn't breathe, couldn't register what she saw. Az was.... Her legs wobbled as she rose, unsure what to do, who to tell. Wynn said to stay in the room, but that book—

The door to Elyse's suite slammed open. She pressed herself against her back wall, gripping at aithyr for defense, letting it fill her. Upon hearing their voices, she collapsed to her knees.

"You're wasting your time." Oh, gods, was that her father?

"Elyse is never a waste of time, Gyrsh." Her heart stopped—that was Az. And he was... Elyse's stomach lurched as she searched the room for a spot to hide.

"Stay focused. The goal is to grab Elyse and get out of the palace." Gods, no. Sylas, too?

They were in her suite; they were there to take her. After Wynn's warning that morning, oh, gods—

Elyse took a calming breath, forcing her mind to calm. She saw the wooden case Sylas had given her. Scrambling forward, she fumbled with the latches. With trembling hands, she grabbed the amber-colored liquid of Mage's Eye and yanked out the cork stopper, taking a swig. The drug took effect, streams of translucent white materializing as they swirled around her body. Calmness washed over her as she pulled in the nearest tendril, the aithyr seemingly eager to enter her body.

Elyse imagined herself as the wall, as the floor. She wanted to become her surroundings—they couldn't find her. When she looked down at herself, she became exactly that. Her body was invisible, the magic coating her in a thin, comforting layer of cold.

"We should focus on rescuing Valeriya," her father snapped.

The Queen? She missed something with Wynn's warning.

She heard rustling in the other room. "I'll check her bedroom," Sylas said, his voice fading.

"For the last time, Valeriya's a lost cause. They have her down in the dungeon, questioning her as we speak." Azarys walked into the study and her heart stopped at the sight of him. *I love you, Elyse.*

Gone were his flowy shirts and decorative pants—he wore the outfit of a Satiroan guard, the leathers looking as if they fit his body better. "With half the guard in the city looking for the clip, this is our only chance to get Elyse." He looked out into the main living area of her suite, glowering.

As he turned to move toward her desk, Elyse took her chance. She needed to leave. She needed to find Wynn. Or Wyltam. Or Keyain.

Anyone.

Gods, Az was a prince—a beastly prince with horns. How did no one know?

Azarys cursed, leaning over her desk as she reached the doorway. "She knows."

Elyse darted out, finding her father standing with his arms crossed, leaning against the table as Sylas appeared from her bedroom.

"Knows what?" her father asked.

She inched along the wall, her hold on aithyr strong, careful not to stumble on her unseen feet.

"My position—our kind. Fuck," Azarys swore, "the blood's fresh."

There was a pause, Elyse almost to the door. She just needed to reach it, and then she could lose them in the castle halls.

"Her tea and seat are warm." Azarys appeared in the doorway. "Goddess, you're here, aren't you?"

Elyse stumbled at his address, not expecting him to guess that.

"Don't be ridiculous," her father said. "Elyse isn't capable of that magic."

"Yes, she is," Sylas said, fear lining his features. His gaze met hers, realization brief on his expression before he turned to Azarys. "But I can't sense her."

Azarys walked into the room, looking around, as her hand landed on the doorknob. She pulled, but a gust of wind from Azarys slammed it shut. "There you are."

Faster than she thought possible, Azarys sprinted at her as she ripped open the door, flooding aithyr into her strength to beat his wind as it whipped past her again. The shifting of focus dropped her invisibility, and she ran into the hallway.

Elyse made it three steps when his arms wrapped around her waist, stopping her even as she flooded herself with aithyr. Azarys grunted with effort before his teeth met her neck, her body going limp as he bit. Confused, she realized it was where he bruised her during sex.

"Goddess," he murmured, brushing back her hair with a hand. "I know you're scared, but I'm here. I'm taking you with me to Chorys Dasi."

The sensation wore off, but Elyse pretended to remain limp as Azarys's grip loosened. Behind her, she heard Sylas and Gyrsh yelling from the other room.

She blocked out everything—her panicked breathing, the yelling voices, Azarys's grip on her—and gave herself to aithyr. The energy flooded her, eager and searching every inch of her body, and then she grabbed ahold of it, thrusting it out as a concentrated gust of wind directed at Azarys.

He flew backward into the wall with a crunch. Elyse turned, watching as he slumped down, unmoving against the cracked wood paneling. She covered her cry with her hand.

Sylas appeared in the doorway, staring from Elyse to the unconscious Azarys. He stepped outside, shutting the door behind him. Flames appeared in his hand, melting the handle. He turned to her. "Run."

Elyse shook, staring at Sylas as he bent over the unmoving Azarys. He looked up, his eyes wide with fear. "Elyse, you need to run. Hide," he hissed, looking over his shoulder as her father began pounding on the door.

A second later, the door flew out, hitting the wall across from it. Her father appeared in the doorway, face laced with fury. "You stupid bitch," he hissed, eyes burning on Elyse.

And she ran.

Her legs carried her down the hall, her father close behind. Trails of aithyr flowed around her, appearing and disappearing into the walls and floor. Some seemed to follow her as she ran. Her father was faster than she realized, unable to lose him, even as she darted down the stairs to the first floor. Not a person was in sight—no guards, no nobles. Gods, what the hells was going on?

Elyse ran through the doors leading to the courtyard, her father snagging her shirt, but she shot lightning at him from her hands as she ran.

Though her breath heaved, she forced herself to calm as she stepped into the garden path. When she reached out to the aithyr, it answered as if to say, "*Here, come here, it's safe.*" She followed the pulling tendril, running off the path and into a dense section of lilacs. A branch caught her shirt, feeling the fabric tear as she ripped herself free. Elyse arrived in a small clearing at the center of the bushes, revealing a massive statue of a canine creature. Its body was made from stone, carved to look like twisting vines, sitting on its haunches and poised as if it would attack. Two large, thorny antlers protruded from its head, ending in elongated spikes.

Elyse listened to its calling, watching the aithyr swirl around the beast. Tentatively, she brushed her hand over the stone. Was it alive? It felt alive.

Her father swore, his footsteps carrying through the gardens away from Elyse. She took a shallow breath, her hand grazing the beast's side. Had it helped her? The stone remained unmoving with her touch. It was just a statue—and aithyr was just energy.

Elyse forced a breath, knowing she had to find someone. Azarys and Sylas couldn't have made it far if Azarys remained unconscious—if he wasn't dead.

Gods, what if she killed him? She pulled her thoughts back with a smack to her forehead. The King needed to know and he needed to know immediately. Elyse knew where to go.

Elyse took off down the path, pulling aithyr into her as she ran, her body becoming invisible once more. If she focused, her plan could work.

Never in her life had she seen the palace so empty—no one, not even guards, walked the grounds. Nervousness bubbled in her gut as she approached the library doors. It was the first time she hadn't seen soldiers posted outside.

Pushing past the entrance, she sprinted towards the King's office. Rows upon rows of books flew by, her eyes scanning the rows for anyone.

When she arrived, the door to the King's office was open. Inside, her father stood, panting. The room should have alerted Wyltam when her father entered, but he didn't come.

With invisibility still cloaking her, Elyse stood in the doorway, considering her options. She could run and find somewhere to hide, or she could face her father and call for Wyltam. The King would come if she screamed his name.

Elyse was not soft.

She was not weak.

And she was exactly like her mother.

She crossed the threshold and dropped her invisibility. "Hello, father."

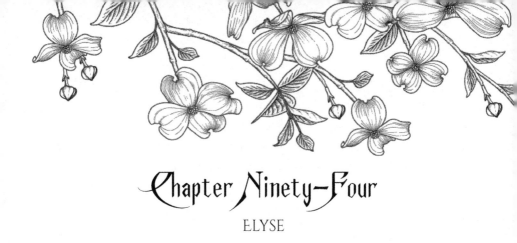

Chapter Ninety-Four

ELYSE

T he King's office looked as it always had. Bookcases lined the room with small glass apparatuses scattered among the volumes. The desk remained covered with Elyse's notes and stacks of books she liked to reference. It was familiar, a home. Something her father had never given her, not truly, at least.

Her father's presence marred her sanctuary, his presence a disease in the first place she felt in control, felt that she had power. To see him stand among it made the aithyr curl deeper inside her body, begging to be released. In the haze of the Mage's Eye, she glared at the male who dared to make her submit. Never again would he be given the chance.

"You," her father hissed, lips curled into a snarl. "I told you he was too good for you. Do you understand why you needed to listen to me? Do you think you could've won his hand on your own?"

Despite his tone, a cool calm remained over Elyse. "Did you ever think that as my father, you should have told me the truth?"

"This is all your fault, you stupid—"

Elyse whipped her hand out, releasing the aithyr as wind, the magic blasting her father to the back of the room. He slid to the ground, shattered glass from the King's possessions around him. Aithyr flooded her again, shifting under her skin, anticipating its release.

"You're going to end up just like her," her father said with a laugh, bringing his hand to his head and seeing the blood she drew. "Right now, I can see what she was in you. As you let aithyr in, it will take control."

"I control the aithyr."

He laughed, tears forming in his eyes. "Elyse, you look like me, but you are your mother through and through. Go ahead; dive deeper. Be a burden just like your mother, and see who pushes you to your death."

An unprecedented rage built at her father's words. To mention her mother's death after *he* was the one to push her from the tower, then lie to everyone that she took her own life, was more than she could handle. Elyse saw it. She had watched her father push her mother before he turned to her and threw her to the ground. Elyse had barely escaped his wrath then. She had fled to her mother at the base of the tower, remaining at her side as she took her last breath. Until now, Elyse had blocked it out. Until now, Elyse forgot the extent of her pain—and the extent of her fury.

"Wyltam!" Elyse screamed, drawing on the aithyr. The air in her father's lungs pulled out of his chest with her effort, slumping him over as he clawed at his throat. And then she released it, letting him catch his breath. "I will be no one's burden—never have I been, never will I be.

He laughed again, and Elyse tore the air from his lungs once more.

"I despise you, father. I hate everything you are and everything you did to me. You're a murderer and a monster. I'm disgusted that I ever listened to you—that I didn't fight back sooner." Her father gasped as she let the breath reenter his lungs. "I will never feel pain caused by you again." Elyse focused the aithyr on her muscles, amplifying her strength as she kicked him in the ribs with a sickening crack.

She screamed, kicking again and again, until her father curled up in the ball, his cries mixing with her own. Elyse hated him, loathed everything he stood for, and using aithyr to bring him that pain felt glorious. So, she kicked. His bones caved in, and she ignored any injury to herself.

When someone wrapped their arms around her, she flailed, screaming, fighting to break free. Sharp pain dug into her hand as the aithyr faded away, slipping from her grasp. "No, no!" she screamed.

"Elyse, stop! It's me!"

She looked up to see Wynn, his hand holding her head. Through the haziness of her rage, she recognized his fear.

"Fuck, this is Elyse?"

Elyse turned to find a half-elven female with short black hair.

Wynn drew her gaze back to him. "Tell us what happened."

"The Chorys Dasians—Brynden. His name is Azarys—he's the prince." Elyse grew dizzy, Wynn holding her up.

"Valeriya shared as much," said the half elf's husky voice.

"My father's working with them," she choked out, black edging her vision.

Wynn spoke, his voice muffled through his chest as she leaned against him.

Control. Elyse had actual control. That was the beauty of aithyr, the key to her future.

As her mind drifted off, Elyse watched the swirls of energy around her, though the aithyr wouldn't approach her body as if she was deterring it. A humanoid form stood at her side, all aithyr and beautiful. It caressed her face, Elyse trying to feel it with her hand.

Nothing had ever felt so right.

Nothing had ever felt so wonderful.

Her hands grasped at the air as she passed out in Wynn's arms.

Chapter Ninety-Five

MARIETTA

The darkness held her vision as the needle pricked along her side. The stinging, unbearable at first, gave way to peace. Though it was excruciating, the pain would fade, but only if she learned to accept it.

So Marietta did; the needle stabbed into her flesh, and she would take a deep breath, over and over until the pricking ceased.

Marietta woke as Nosokyma spoke again. "Hear us, Therypon, she who heals the world, she who brings pain onto us. Deity of Duality, she of healing and pain. Hear your chosen and most faithful, the Iros. Together, we complete the cycle. Therypon brought her pain onto us, her guardians, and now through us bestows her healing." Her voice cried out, arms splayed, head tilted back.

The other attendants stood, approaching the altar with their glazed eyes, reaching their hands over Marietta's naked body. Their hands hovered over her, and they chanted, "Through Therypon, all pain can be healed."

A flash of white extended from their hands, bathing her body in the bright light. Her pain ebbed away. Familiar warmth brought her comfort. Even the skin she bit through on her lip healed. The attendants backed away as Nosokyma yelled, "Rise, Marietta, guardian of Therypon, member of her Iros!"

Marietta lifted herself, coming to a seated position. The tattoo on her side extended from her hip, around her breast, and up onto her neck. Inked onto her were two intertwined snakes through a lattice of Xs. Despite the

freshness of the tattoo, the skin healed enough that there was no pain; Marietta ran her fingers over it.

An elven woman brought over a blue robe to place over her. Marietta looked to Coryn, who averted his eyes as she covered herself.

Marietta held out her hands, noticing the warmth in her chest that crackled with energy under her skin. She called it forth, reaching towards the warmth like she would when she prayed, and bright light extended from her fingertips.

"Peculiar," Nosokyma said, her lined face smiling. "You're already attuned to the goddess's powers. I recommend not using them until you have proper training. Coryn has already volunteered to be your mentor." She nodded at Coryn, who approached.

His warm smile greeted her. "How do you feel?"

"Strange. The same, but different. Like there's energy right under my skin," Marietta held out her hands again as she spoke.

"That's the power she bestows on us. When we reach Enomenos, we can start your training," he said with a frown. "We'll grab attendant's clothes for you to wear on our way downstairs."

Her stomach dropped. "I thought if I became an Iros, we would flee to Enomenos."

"That was before Keyain followed you here, before he had every exit watched with more than a dozen soldiers each." He placed a hand on the small of her back, guiding her out of the room. "The King's summons came with an arrest for treason against Satiros."

"But the temple still has me claimed, right? So they can't hurt me?" Marietta flexed her hands, not used to the energy crackling under her skin.

"Not without starting a riot in the street, more so than what's already out there. Many in Satiros follow the gods, and King Wyltam wouldn't dare cross that line. At least not when he's warring with Enomenos. He'll need to keep the peace at home."

Marietta nodded. It was the confirmation she needed. She could head back with Keyain to the palace, and with her new powers, she would free Tilan.

Keyain paced in the antechamber, wearing metal plate armor of Satiroan green marked with the wisteria crest. "The King's summons came five hours ago. I won't ask again," he growled. "Where is Marietta?"

The doorway to the front framed Keyain, making him glow in the dim of the interior. His back-lit silhouette was ominous, with the cacophony of voices beyond. Ambient calls carried up the temple steps, echoing in the temple. Some chanted; others yelled. All Marietta could discern was the unrest in their tones.

Coryn leaned closer to her. "You must leave with Keyain," he murmured in her ear as they approached, "but they can't lay a hand on you now without serious consideration. Nosokyma will petition on your behalf, but we don't know how long that will take."

They paused at the precipice of the antechamber, hidden by the hall's shadows. In front of them stood a line of Therypon's attendants, adorned in armor and brandishing their swords.

"No matter what happens, we'll be there to support you." Coryn wrapped his arms around Marietta, pulling her close. "May Therypon guide your way."

"Thank you," she whispered into his chest, surprised at the lack of fear in her voice. "For everything you have done and what you have yet to do." She stepped back with her hand clasped in his. Coryn smiled, a hint of his dimple showing, and she nodded her head.

"What's the meaning of this?" Coryn said, stepping into the light. The attendants stepped aside, letting Coryn stand among their ranks. Marietta remained hidden, waiting for him to call her.

Keyain's head whipped to Coryn at the sound of his voice. "Where is she?" he ground out, taking a step forward.

"Where is who, Minister Keyain?" Coryn asked with mocking confusion.

"I don't have time for this bullshit." Keyain stomped forward, and the attendants raised their weapons.

"Of course, you're a busy male," Coryn said. "If you state your business, then we can send you on your way."

Keyain stepped close to him, his jaw tight and his chest heaving. "Where is Marietta?"

"Ah, that's why you're here."

Keyain took a steadying breath as his face slipped into a sneer. Of course, Coryn was taunting him. Marietta felt nervousness pull at her stomach as she watched Keyain's mood further deteriorate.

"King Wyltam summoned Marietta Vallynte to the palace," Keyain continued. "And I came to escort her."

"You talk as if she doesn't share your last name," Coryn said with furrowed brows. "Is she not your wife?"

"Yes, she's my wife," Keyain snapped.

Coryn looked over his shoulder at Marietta, beckoning her forward. "You best remember that as you march her to her demise."

Marietta approached his side, wearing the bright blue uniform of Therypon. Coryn placed a steadying hand on her shoulder.

Keyain's sneer dropped, his jaw slacking. He stared at her neck, the twin snakeheads that now climbed up her skin. With a heavy breath, he stared at her as if she were a ghost, at a loss for words.

"Marietta Vallynte, newest to the ranks of Therypon's Iros," Coryn announced. "Goddess-chosen and protected by the divine."

The attendants of the blockade dropped back their heads, their faces turning towards the ceiling. "Goddess, bless those who brandish your mark," they murmured in unison.

Keyain shook his head, scrubbing his face. "You've ruined her."

"Says the male who upended her life and put her in this position." Coryn's hand fell from her shoulder. "You chose to wed Marietta and to bring her Satiros. All the blame falls to your shoulders."

Keyain's features twisted with rage. "You—"

"Enough," Marietta called out, her voice ringing in the antechamber.

Keyain's words died on his lips as Marietta stepped toward him, staring into his face.

"What did you do?" he whispered, his breaths sharp.

Marietta lifted her chin higher, looking at Keyain from head to toe.

"I saved myself."

She walked straight past him, not sparing him a glance even as he spoke. "Marietta Vallynte, on behalf of his majesty, King Wyltam, I take you into custody for conspiracy of treason, acts of treason, and failure to follow legal protocol."

"We'll see you soon, Marietta," Coryn called out behind her.

Marietta smiled at his words. Coryn would help her—Deania would help her. They wouldn't let them execute Marietta. The goddess would intervene.

Or, at least, she would intervene long enough for Marietta to reach Tilan, to free him. The energy crackled under her skin. Such power felt natural, as if it belonged within her, and with it she could give Tilan a chance to escape.

Marietta stepped onto the temple's front steps, gasping at the sight before her. Therypon's hoplite soldiers lined the front, spears held out with their shields raised, forming a barrier. Two stepped aside as she walked through, emerging to the chaos below them.

The citizens of Satiros packed the square, people standing shoulder to shoulder, yelling and shaking their fists. Some wore the colors of the temples, but many dressed in standard garb. A few groups were pushing against the guards who blocked the bottom of the temple stairs.

Dressed in similar armor to Keyain, the soldiers at the top of the stairs surrounded Marietta as she made her descent. Helmeted with heavy swords in their grasps, they were menacing. Gone was the leather armor suitable for everyday wear. Instead, they were equipped for battle. Keyain joined her, his hand gripping just above her elbow.

At the bottom, the crowd parted for their group as they entered the chaos. No carriage awaited for them, the masses too dense for vehicles.

Many called out Marietta's name. Others sent their prayers to Therypon. Marietta turned to them and offered a genuine smile, locking eyes with a young half-elven girl who pushed her way to the front, eyes watering as she looked up at Marietta with an enormous smile on her face.

Keyain noted the attention and whispered, "Don't. You'll incite a riot."

"Stop, Keyain." Marietta tried to pull her arm from his grasp.

"Let her go!" someone yelled, causing a murmur to ripple across.

Keyain gripped her tighter, his breath quickening as he looked out over the masses. Lines bracketed his mouth as the crowd pressed closer. "For once, please listen to me."

Marietta pulled away again. "I did nothing but protect myself from you," she yelled, letting her voice carry. For all he did, Marietta would never go willingly.

A few men from the crowd pushed against the guards. "Let her go, you bastards!" one cried.

A guard hit the man on top of his head with his sword's pommel, dropping him to the ground.

"Stop," Keyain ordered. "We do not hit civilians."

The crowd pressed in around them, voices yelling, swallowing Keyain's commands. "It's either us or them, Keyain," a guard called back.

"I said, we do not—"

The crowd erupted around them, surging into the circle, pressing the guards close to Marietta and Keyain at the center.

"Form a barrier. Protect Marietta!" Keyain ordered his soldiers, who exchanged nervous glances before swinging at the civilians. Keyain swore as the horror unfolded around them. Their swords cut through men and women alike, slicing through them like a hot knife through butter, clothing being the civilians' only protection.

A man charged forward, screaming her name, only for a sword to connect with his neck. Hot beads of blood splattered across Marietta's face. More guards joined the circle, moving them through the mob of people.

"Stop!" Marietta screamed. They were dying because of her. "Please, stop!" She jerked away from Keyain to pull a soldier off a young half-elven man.

"Marietta, don't," Keyain pleaded, pulling her back as the sword connected with the man's neck, severing his head from his body. Frozen in his lips was her name, his head dropping to the cobblestone.

She shrieked as tears flowed down her cheeks. "Please, stop!"

Keyain grabbed Marietta, throwing her over his shoulder as a pile of bodies and a stream of blood trailed behind them. Her voice turned hoarse, but she continued to yell as Keyain carried her away.

Through the noise of the crowd, Keyain screamed at his soldiers to deal non-lethal blows. Blood continued to spill; the bodies kept falling.

For a moment, the crowd parted, and Marietta saw a tall, broad man of olive skin, a beard thick on his face as dark hair fell into his eyes as he slid a sword from a guard's body. His gaze locked with Marietta, and her heart stopped—Pelok.

"Tilan's alive!" she screamed, clawing at Keyain's back.

"Marietta!" Keyain yelled, holding her tighter. "Stay still, for the love of fuck." Panic gripped his voice as the guards pushed in closer around them.

In the distance, bells started tolling.

"He's alive! Tilan's alive!" she screamed again, hoping her voice carried over the commotion of the crowd.

Pelok gawked at her as the crowd swallowed him whole.

Chapter Ninety-Six

VALERIYA

As a mother, Valeriya never thought she would part with her son. Mycaub was curious, showing intelligence at such a young age, but like his father, he was quiet. Shy. Valeriya thought she would have time to help him overcome his reserved nature, to one day be the King that Wyltam never was, but those plans had changed.

One last day with Mycaub wasn't enough. Valeriya had read him his favorite books and played his favorite games, yet he knew something was wrong. Mycaub was too smart for his own good. Part of her wished he hadn't noticed, that he could be a child for one last day, for the next time she'd see him, he could be halfway to adulthood.

The goodbye to her son was a wound to her chest. Sobbing silently into Mycaub's hair, her sweet son had turned his head to Valeriya, saying, "Mama doesn't cry." His words had been her undoing. Similar words she had always told him, her sweet boy.

Valeriya now waited on the bottom floor of the Royal's Wing for Wyltam to escort her to Katya beneath the palace. They were to leave that evening, heading east to Enomenos. Her future awaited her, one where she and Kat could be the couple they always wished to be. That was if Wyltam ever arrived.

The mixed cities of Enomenos both thrilled Valeriya and brought on nerves. Her mind imagined them being something like Reyila, yet without a monarch. How did such a system work? A thought came suddenly to her—pondering such ideas would be a possibility, for she was no longer a queen. She and Kat could stroll city streets, walking hand in

hand without a care in the world, besides looking out for danger. Still, her heart swelled. Though hurt by her separation from her son, she would have the opportunity to live the life she always wanted—with Katya.

Wyltam burst into the Royal's Wing, Valeriya noting for the first time that no guards waited beyond its doors. Worry lined his face, the emotion disturbing from such a reserved male. "What is it?" she asked, fear twisting her stomach.

"The Chorys Dasians broke into the palace with the help of Gyrsh," Wyltam said, gesturing for her to follow. "They tried to abduct Elyse and flee."

They were here. She could stop their plans.

"Katya and Wynn apprehended Gyrsh—well, I should say Elyse did." He shook his head, taking off down the hall. Valeriya tried to keep in step with him.

"And not Azarys and Sylas?"

"Gone by the time we made it back to Elyse's suite."

Then likely off the palace grounds already. A missed opportunity. She could have redeemed herself. She could have.... Valeriya steadied her thoughts with a breath. Even if she found Azarys and Sylas, the odds of apprehending them would have been low. After all, Sylas was Queen Agnyssa's Mage Master.

Wyltam scrubbed his face, worry and exhaustion ebbing from his features. The sight unnerved her. She had known Wyltam for seven years and never had she seen as much of an expression. He was hiding something. "What's wrong?"

"A riot. Keyain went against my orders and is blocking the Temple of Therypon." Wyltam threw open the doors to the garden, heading for its paths with Valeriya following in his steps.

Her heart stilled. A riot in the streets as well as a break into the palace? Were they enacting the plan? No, if they were, then she would see Chorys Dasian soldiers rushing the grounds. "I take it that's where the guards are. Foolish to leave none behind. Whose order was that?"

"Keyain's," Wyltam ground out. "He deployed every able-bodied soldier into the city to find her. Marietta's friends at the temple got her there safely and tried to claim immunity for her, but Dyieter called a meeting." Wyltam kept his strides long as he rushed through the garden, his words coming fast. "The Ministers decided in a vote of eight to two to try her for treason."

"Two? I'm guessing Keyain voted against it, but who else?"

"Minister Adryan."

She bit back her surprise at both Wyltam's willingness to share the information and to hear that Minister Adryan intervened. As the Minister of Commerce, he had little reason to gain Keyain's favor. A pang of regret shot through her, knowing she would miss the thrill of politics once she was in Enomenos. "Of course, as I'm about to leave Satiros, you decide to speak so freely," she said, bristling.

Wyltam stopped abruptly, turning to her. "My biggest regret is not confronting you about your sister from the beginning. If I could do it over, I would change that detail, and then maybe we'd be in a better place now."

She searched his face for the mocking tone he usually used with her, not finding it.

"I will hold that regret until the end of my days because we could've been great rulers if we were on a united front." Wyltam looked at anything but Valeriya as he spoke. "An apology will never sum up the weight of guilt that I feel, but I hope you find peace with the women you actually love."

Actually love.

Did he know from the beginning that her heart was held by a female? If he knew Master Arkym, the mage who trained Valeriya and Katya, then perhaps he was aware when he asked for her hand. That would explain his actions while trying to conceive. Time and time again Wyltam had tried to stop, to say an heir was unnecessary. She took that as he didn't plan to keep her as Queen, never considering that he wanted to save her from that pain.

"I don't blame you," she said, stepping into his line of sight. "For Mycaub. It was... uncomfortable, to say the least, but never once did I blame you." Her chest lightened with the confession. Those were the two darkest years, trying and failing for a child, having to return to his bed after each bleeding came. "Mycaub was my light through it all." Her voice cracked with emotion, thinking of her son. "Keep him safe."

Wyltam nodded once, swallowing hard before he took off down the path again. Silence settled between them.

From the beginning, Valeriya had thought the worst of Wyltam, always viewing him as heartless, like a corpse. If the past day's events proved anything, it was that her husband had a larger heart than he ever cared to show. For his people. For others. He was a king who would sacrifice his legacy in order to be a better ruler. The lost opportunity forged from miscommunication would haunt her until the end of her days.

"What's the plan now?" she asked, desperate to think of anything else.

"I want to ensure Marietta is safe within the palace before I take you to Katya." They approached the palace once more, Wyltam holding the door for her. "The citizens aren't happy that the crown wished to apprehend Marietta while she sought immunity at a temple. Thousands gather outside waiting for Keyain to remove her."

"Please tell me he has a way to get her out of there safely," Valeriya said. Sweat gathered on her skin from the day's oppressive heat. "In this weather, such a crowd would grow restless."

"Keyain best have a plan to return her safely," Wyltam said. "For both his and Marietta's sake."

Valeriya furrowed her brows. "You're saying you don't know if Keyain has a plan?"

"If he has one, he didn't share it with me."

Fear rose in her throat, but she swallowed it down. "Are Marietta and Keyain still at the temple?"

"No, they're returning to the palace as we speak. I announced the summons hours ago," he said. "The nobles are on lockdown while Keyain deployed most of the guards into the city." He glanced at her. "So, if we keep off to the side, no one will notice us and we'll still be on track for your departure."

She nodded. Last night, something had shifted between them. From the beginning, Wyltam never trusted her. Though that irked her, she understood. Hells, she went into the marriage with the intention to tell her sister everything she could about Satiros. Love from her sister blinded her endeavors and ruined the opportunity she had as queen. Her ambition wasn't for her own gain, but Chorys Dasi's. Never again would she allow herself to be so blind.

They hurried to the palace's front and from the entrance hall, they could hear the screams carrying from the city streets. Valeriya stared at Wyltam, her heart sinking. "We have to see what's going on," she said.

"Agreed." Wyltam walked to the entrance. "Try to stay out of sight. Most of the guards should be—"

He stopped at the center of the doorway, his jaw dropping. Confused, Valeriya joined him and understood. A crowd rioted from the palace gates, all the way to the Halia River, filling Oak Boulevard. Thousands of civilians, more than she had ever seen amassed, filled the cityscape before them.

The gates had swung shut before they arrived. Guards stood at it and prodded the crowd back. Keyain had a guard pinned to the wall, his face red from screaming. Marietta stood alone with a haunted expression on her blanched face marred with blood, wearing a blue tunic from the temple.

"He marched her through the crowd," Valeriya said, pointing to the armored guards wiping blood from their swords. "What the fuck did he do?"

"We need to get Marietta inside the palace. Anyone could attack her out in the open like that." Wyltam took a step forward, but Valeriya held him back.

He was right; with the guard's attention on the crowd, it was a prime opportunity for an attack. "This isn't safe."

"I know it isn't." He ripped his shirt from her grasp as Keyain turned, locking eyes with Wyltam. "Which is why Keyain's priority should have been getting Marietta to safety."

"Have them come to us," she said, her eyes scanning the rooftops visible from the front steps. "Something is wrong." The hair on the back of her neck stood. Somewhere in the distance bells tolled, setting an eerie tone for the scene before them. This riot would be a perfect distraction.

Keyain approached while guiding Marietta forward, waiting until the top of the steps to acknowledge them. "Get inside, all of you." The veins in his neck bulged, his jaw grinding.

"What happened?" snapped Wyltam, his expressionless demeanor slipping into a sneer. He grabbed the front of Keyain's armor, his voice a low growl as the two began bickering in quiet voices.

Valeriya turned to Marietta, who shook where she stood. "Marietta, are you okay?"

Black ink curved up her neck. She took in her clothing, understanding what both meant: she joined the temple for immunity. Shocked, Valeriya forced her eyes to meet Marietta's haunted face.

"They all died because of me," she whispered.

"No, they didn't." Valeriya took her hands and tried to guide Marietta inside, yet she wouldn't move.

Tears streamed down Marietta's cheeks, mixing with the spattering of blood. She looked back at the crowd. "They were trying to free me and Keyain's guards slaughtered them."

"Hush, now." Valeriya pulled her into an embrace. "Let's get you inside." She glanced over her shoulder to the rooftops and she saw a person aiming something at their group. Before she could manage a warning, she saw them release the weapon.

Time slowed for Valeriya. The crowd's jeering muffled as her breath stilled. She watched the trajectory, watched the crackling of electrical energy on what she could now see was a crossbow bolt. She saw where it would hit. Without thinking, she grabbed Marietta and twisted her away from the projectile.

A sharp, agonizing pain pierced her back and took the breath from her chest. Valeriya heard Marietta's shriek, heard the crowd behind her break into a panic. The world felt far away as she collapsed to the ground, the electrical magic causing her body to convulse. Her last thought was of Katya, who waited for her. Maybe in the next life they could finally be together. Maybe then they could both find happiness.

Chapter Ninety-Seven

MARIETTA

One moment, Marietta watched the sea of people riot outside the gates. The next, Queen Valeriya had grabbed her and turned her away from the crowd. There was an impact, the shock of electrical energy, and the heaviness of the Queen collapsing against her. She turned to see her face down with blood beginning to pool around her, the crackling energy seizing her form. Then someone jumped on top of her, pinning her to the ground.

Through her screaming, Wyltam's voice broke through. He cupped her face as a translucent dome formed around them. "Marietta!" he yelled, pulling her attention. "Marietta, are you hurt?" His dark eyes were frantic as he searched her body for an injury.

Outside the palace walls, screams of terror erupted, muffled by the surrounding dome.

"Marietta, please focus," pleaded the King. He brushed back her hair with shaking hands.

Instead, she jerked her head towards Valeriya. She could do something—Marietta could help, but only if she hurried. She scrambled to Valeriya, calling forth Therypon's energy, the warmth growing at her fingertips. With a sobbing cry, she lay her hands on Valeriya. The bleeding slowed, yet she didn't stir.

Gods, Therypon, help her. Help her save the Queen.

Marietta screamed as she pulled the energy from under her skin, as she pulled it from around her body. There was a rush of power that bucked against her control, but obeyed her will as she laid her hands on Valeriya.

Blinding light emitted from her fingertips, her vision seeing nothing but the shadowed outline of the Queen. She trembled with the effort, crying as her skin felt flayed from her body. Marietta forced herself to accept the energy—to expel it into Valeriya. The light shot outward and behind her, the King crying out.

Blackness ebbed the edges of Marietta's vision, but she continued to flood Therypon's healing into her. It wasn't too late—she could save her. Valeriya could live.

Sharp metal bit her arm and the energy she pulled suddenly stopped filling her. Exhaustion seized her mind as the last of the power depleted. Through her haze, she saw Keyain as she slumped backward.

King Wyltam appeared before her, eyes wide in awe as he cupped her face. "What are you?" he whispered.

And then there was nothing.

Chapter Ninety-Eight

ELYSE

The past day passed in a haze of events. When she first woke, Wynn held her head in his lap, talking to the half-elf female with black hair. "You're leaving then?" Wynn's voice rumbled through her.

"I am," the half-elf said.

"For good?"

"Most likely, until it's safe again."

There was a moment of silence, then Wynn said, "I'm sure we'll cross paths."

"We will if you're ever in Enomenos."

Elyse faded out, her mind growing fuzzy. The left side of her head throbbed with the bright light arcing across her field of vision. What a time for her head pains to return. At one point, she was certain she vomited, remembering spitting the bile from her mouth.

When she woke again, she rested on her side and her body stiff from sleeping on a couch. Slowly, she sat up and held her head. What happened? And where was she?

She looked up, finding a dark-haired child staring at her. Elyse blinked, registering Prince Mycaub's face, before scanning the rest of her surroundings. The room was cozy but ornate with wainscoting on the walls, plush carpet on the floor, and elegant furniture. She turned back to the Prince, who half hid behind the arm of the couch. "Hello?"

He said nothing, and continued to stare before running away. Gods, was she in the Royal Suite?

"You're awake."

She turned to find Wynn leaning against the wall with his arms crossed over his chest. A smile touched his lips despite the wariness in his expression. "What happened?" Elyse asked.

He pushed off the wall and walked to her, offering a hand. "Wyltam would like to be the one to explain."

Elyse hesitated, then nodded her head. The King wanted to explain— explain what? Her vision swam as she stood, gripping Wynn's arm for support.

"You alright?"

She nodded, leaning on to him as they left the room, heading down a hallway. Light shined through the only open doorway, Wynn leading her to it. Inside, the King sat behind his desk with his attention absorbed by the papers in his hands. Wynn walked her forward and eased her into a chair in front of the desk. He sat in the one next to it.

Wyltam looked up from his papers. "How're you feeling, Elyse?"

"Like shit."

Wynn snorted at her response, and the King smiled.

"Unsurprising, considering what happened." Wyltam set down his papers and turned his full attention to her. "Elyse, I would like to thank you. What you did took bravery and because of your actions, we secured your father before he escaped."

Secured her father? She frowned, staring at her feet. There was something with her father, but what was it?

"In the face of fear, you chose to denounce the males you once called friends and ensured the capture of your father after the abuse he has brought on to you," he said, drawing her gaze back to him.

Males she once called friends?

"Over the past couple months, you have proved time and time again your loyalty to me and you have my full-hearted trust." He moved a velvet box to the center of his desk, opening it to reveal a golden broach of the Satiroan crest. "With that in mind, I'm raising your status from Lady of the Court to King's Administrator. Similar to the first position I offered, you will be my eyes and ears still, but the responsibilities shifted. You won't just work in foreign courts, but the Satiroan Court as well."

She shook her head. "I don't understand what's happening." She paused, looking at her hands. "I don't remember what happened."

Wynn leaned over, his hand holding the armrest of her chair. "Do you remember the Chorys Dasians attacking you? Or when you were in Wyltam's study with your father?"

Elyse furrowed her brows, her mind catching up to their words. Brynden—no, Prince Azarys—tried to take her to Chorys Dasi. And her father.... Her breath came sharp as it all came back, staring from Wynn to the King.

"Do you remember Fulbryk's second principle?" King Wyltam asked, his fingers tapping against the box.

"*Magic is manipulation of aithyr through the will of the mage, not through the will of aithyr. Don't let aithyr win,*" she recited.

"Aithyr won, and you lost control. When Wynn found you, you were in a frenzy and nearly killed your father." The King sat back, his eyes staying on Elyse. "You're to remain on magicsbane for the next few days to clear the aithyr from your body, ensuring that your mind stays intact, but I have to be honest with you, Elyse. Given what happened to your mother, I'm worried about your sanity."

She remembered the sensation of letting go, of letting the energy take over. Her face heated with shame, realizing her mistake. Now, the King thought she was crazy. Maybe she was. Did she really see Azarys in that book? Was he really a *beast man*? She shook her head, realizing she couldn't tell the King, not without her thinking she was insane. "But you offer me a new position? What if I'm compromised completely?"

"You aren't," Wynn said. "The process can take years, so it just means we need to be conscious of your training going forward. If you want it."

Elyse turned to him; she wasn't too far gone. "Of course I want it."

The King laughed, a slight smile pulling to his face. "Between sitting in on my meetings and mage training, you're going to have a busy few months. Especially with the two wars." His smile faded as his eyes found his papers once more.

"Two wars," she said. "As in, we're now in two wars?"

The King nodded, exhaustion clear in his features. "Not only are we fighting with Enomenos and the anti-Syllogi group, but also with Reyila, backed by Chorys Dasi."

Elyse's limbs numbed. War. With Chorys Dasi. "What happened? Why Reyila? Chorys Dasi isn't attacking because of me, are they?"

"No," he said. "There was an assassination attempt on Marietta. Queen Valeriya sacrificed herself to save her."

"What?" She sat forward, not registering the words.

"Because Valeriya was hit, most believe it was an attempt on her life. Reyila's sources claimed I orchestrated her death because of the rumored affair with Marietta." His jaw ground as he looked at the stack of papers again. "Which is to say it is just that—a rumor. Now, the queendom released an official notice that they are moving against Satiros."

As if losing Queen Valeriya hadn't been enough on top of Azarys, there was also another war. Tears blurred her vision as she hastily wiped them away. Marietta and Wyltam may have kissed, but they hadn't done more than that. Elyse knew Marietta enough to know she would've said something.

"There's one last piece," Wyltam added, picking up the papers. "Marietta is to go to trial for conspiracy of treason, acts of treason, failure to follow legal protocol, and now murder of Valeriya."

Elyse jumped out of her seat. "That's the most ridiculous thing I have ever heard. She wouldn't have done any of those things."

"Marietta is guilty of handing off sensitive information that she stole from Keyain." The King's dark eyes found her. "Now my ministers look to offload the war with Reyila by sentencing her to death."

She shook her head, her hand coming to her mouth. "They can't kill her."

"I agree," Wyltam said. "Which is why your first task as King's Administrator is to help me dig through these documents, if you are well enough for it. Her trial is the day after tomorrow, and I'm running out of time." He paused, swallowing hard. "Elyse, I need your help to save her. Please."

"Anything I can help do, I'll do. What is it we're looking for?"

He pushed the papers toward her. Elyse sat forward, taking them in her hand and reading the first page. "Birth records?" she asked, glancing up at him.

"Proof," he said, handing another pile to Wynn. "We're looking for the last name Fulbryk."

Chapter Ninety-Nine

MARIETTA

Marietta woke with a splitting headache. Light filtered in from above her, hurting her eyes, too bright for such pain. The room spun. Her stomach churned. What had happened?

She forced open her eyes to the small room, the white walls glaring. Glancing down at herself, she saw the familiar shift dress. She was back in the infirmary.

Why?

Marietta pushed herself up, crossing her legs as she cradled her aching head. There had been a ceremony—she was an Iros. Therypon was inked into her skin, giving Marietta her strength. Though dizzy, she focused on the energy under her skin. She found none. Did she lose it? No, she had used the goddess' power. Why had she used it? She shook her head, frustrated as her thoughts felt thicker than honey.

A knock sounded at the door. "Yes?" she called, her voice hoarse.

The door cracked open, revealing Wyltam standing beyond. "Marietta, do you mind if I come in?"

She furrowed her brows at his question. "No?" Why would she mind?

The King took a seat across from her bed. Black marred beneath his eyes, his face ebbing with tiredness. Looking at him pulled her memory, yet she couldn't remember why.

"How are you feeling?" he asked, crossing his leg over a knee.

"Confused, mostly."

A brief smile flashed onto his face with a laugh. "Undoubtedly."

Marietta frowned, staring into her lap. "I can't think."

"It's the sedatives," the King said, drawing her gaze. "Something I had argued against but lost."

"Who'd you fight against?"

"My council." He leaned forward, resting his forearms on his knees. "You're to go to trial for treason."

Marietta nodded her head. "The temple is advocating on my behalf."

"They already have," he said, dropping his gaze. "It didn't go well, considering the latest charge they've added to your trial."

"Even after becoming an Iros?"

The King glanced at her neck. "The risk of offending the temples was offset by another threat."

She shifted, dangling her legs over the edge of the bed as she stared at him. "You're going to need to explain that."

Wyltam began to speak, but stopped, his fists clenching. The reaction stilled her heart.

"You need to tell me what's going on, Wyltam." Despite having no reason to hold herself with such dignity while wearing an infirmary dress, she drew up what confidence she had.

"Do you remember the front steps?"

"Front steps?" Marietta focused on that thought. Dark eyes, his hair tousled into his face. "We were on the front steps. You held my face."

"I did," he said, frowning. "Do you remember who else was there?"

"Keyain."

"And who else?"

Her heart stilled. The faces of the pilinos who tried to help her flashed in her mind. Her next breath came sharply as she remembered the blood. Marietta shook as she looked at Wyltam. "People died," she whispered.

"What do you remember, Marietta?"

"The people—the ones the guards attacked. They—they had—" Her voice trembled as each horrific scene came back.

"They did, yes." Wyltam kept his voice soft. "But what else?"

There was a body under her hands. The King screamed—gods, Marietta shrieked herself. Why? There was intense pain, as if she were being ripped apart at the seams. Marietta's breaths sharpened and the edges of her vision blurred. "Valeriya. Did she—" She gasped. "Is she—"

The King came to her side, placing a hand on the small of her back. "Try to breathe for me, Marietta."

She gasped again. Wyltam dropped to his knees before her. "What color is my shirt?"

"What?" she asked.

"My shirt—what color is it?"

She gawked at him. "Black."

"Right, and is there anything else black in the room?"

Her throat constricted, her breaths merely gasps, but Marietta searched the room. "The chair."

"Right again. Anything else?"

In her panic, she focused on the King, her gaze scouring him. "Your hair." She took in his features. "And your eyes."

The corner of his mouth curled. "Close enough."

"Why are you asking me this?" she asked, leaning away from him.

"I'm grounding you. This is real." He took her hand. "We are real—your thoughts are memories. Now, please, take a deep breath." She followed his orders, breathing deeply through her nose and out through her mouth. "Good."

Wyltam kept her hands in his. "Once again, you've been through a tragedy, and for that, I am truly sorry."

"What happened?" She squeezed the King's hands, trying to control her rising panic.

"Someone attempted to assassinate you." He paused, his thumb rubbing over her hand. "But Valeriya stopped the crossbow bolt from hitting its mark. The details released to the public were wrong, many claiming it was an attempt on the Queen's life. Now, Reyila thinks I orchestrated her death because of our rumored affair."

Her stomach dropped. The rumored affair. It was her fault, because they had kissed. Because she thought she could handle court life. She slid her hands out of Wyltam's grip. "The kiss—we caused this." Her voice struggled. "Then you just encouraged the rumors, as if you planned it all along. Did any of your words carry truth?"

"We caused *nothing*. Valeriya jumped in front of that crossbow bolt for you. Someone intended on you dying." Wyltam's eyes held hers as he took her hands again. "I meant every word I said to you, meant every kiss. There is nothing I regret from that evening."

"Is that why you encouraged the rumors?"

"Not at all," he said. "Keyain was close to terminating your marriage. I was trying to give it the extra push, so you could be free of him for good. When you shared the pregnancy news—"

"I'm not pregnant."

"I know." A slight smile hinted at his lips. "Valeriya told me, though it was a very convincing lie. You've come a long way."

She shook her head.

"My intention was to never harm you, Marietta." He raised her hand to his mouth, brushing a kiss across her knuckles. She savored the touch of him, the intimacy. "I am never a danger to you; I am on your side. Always."

He was the elven King, kneeling before her in an infirmary bed. If he didn't care, then he would have never come. "I see that now."

"We can't fight two wars." He rested his forehead against their joined hands. "The ministers are adding her murder to the list of your charges."

Marietta stared the blue-black strands of his hair. "That's why the temple couldn't help." Her voice was far away. "They're going to execute me."

Wyltam raised his head, his jaw set and eyes burning. "Not if I can help it. You've done nothing wrong."

She offered a weak smile. "Well, I did hand off information."

"Sure, but you thought it was to an ally I'm trying to gain," he said, raising his hand to cup her cheek. "So, I can argue that it's not worth your life. I need to convince my council that an alliance with Enomenos is better than attempting to save relations with Reyila."

"An impossible task." Her stomach sank. "They will never side with

Enomenos, not if it meant changing the laws on Pilinos."

"I think I have a way," Wyltam said, hesitating. "Do you mind if I have Minister Adryan come in while I ask you a few questions? He'll need to witness your raw reaction and answers to them."

"Who?"

"The Minister of Commerce. He was the only person besides Keyain who voted against your treason." Wyltam paused, as if he didn't want to say the next part. "And he was the only minister who didn't vote for the additional murder charge."

The only minister. In the end, Keyain protected himself. "Why did this Minister Adryan vote against them?" she said, not having the heart to bring up Keyain.

"He knew of you before you came to Satiros."

"He did?"

The corner of his mouth tilted. "Said you're a damn good businessperson and had an overwhelming amount of people reach out to him when news of your marriage to Keyain became public."

"What does that have to do with anything?"

"You can ask him yourself, if you'd like."

She nodded in response. Wyltam stood and went to the door, opening it to beckon in Minister Adryan. He stood shorter than the King, with a flock of golden hair coiffed back from his face, and walked as if he wasn't facing someone on trial for murder. His posture was casual and his smile easy. "Marietta Lytpier," he said, holding out his hand. "A pleasure to finally meet you."

She furrowed her brows at her father's surname as she took his hand. "To finally meet me?"

"Keyain has been avoiding me for months." He smiled and placed his hands in his pocket. "Made the mistake of telling him I have friends who have worked with you in Enomenos. Nothing but wonderful things to say."

If she could have furrowed her brows further, she would have. "Why would a Minister of Satiros have worked with people from Enomenos?"

"A question I get often, I'm afraid. Business is business, regardless of who's buying and who's selling," Adryan said. "As Minister of Commerce, I care about the economic stability of our city-state, which means I am open to the idea of trading with our neighbors."

"A progressive view in Syllogi," she said. "Unfortunate that there aren't more of you."

"There's more than you'd think." His smile spread, and he gestured to the King. "We should get this done, though, Your Grace."

The two males sat on chairs across from Marietta. Wyltam nodded his head and asked, "What can you share about your parents?"

"My parents?"

"Yes."

Marietta shook her head. "Why are you asking about them?"

"What do they do for a living?"

"At the sculpture garden, I shared with you that my mother is an herbalist." She paused, furrowing her brows. "My father is a retired traveling merchant."

The King nodded his head. "This is all for Adryan's knowledge, if the questions repeat. Where do they live?"

"In Notos, about an hour outside."

"And which city-state did you grow up in?"

"Does that really matter?"

Adryan huffed a laugh, a smile curling on his lips. "I like her."

The King locked eyes with Marietta. "I like her, too."

Her stupid heart stuttered at his words. Gods, she was about to die and she acted like a foolish girl. She sighed and said, "I was born and raised in Kentro. I lived there until I moved to Olkia with Tilan Reid."

"Speaking of Tilan," Wyltam went on, "were you aware of his position within the Exisotis?"

"Not until Valeriya shared that with me. Keyain confirmed it afterward."

"Can you confirm that you knew nothing of Keyain's work in Enomenos until I told you?"

"What does this have to do with anything?"

"Please answer, Marietta."

She shook her head, meeting his gaze. "He refused to tell me."

"Even to this day?"

"Yes."

"Did you know Valeriya was working with the Chorys Dasians?"

Marietta remembered her revelation the last time she prayed to Therypon. "Not until it was too late. When I agreed to aid her, I believed that the information would go to the Exisotis."

"And last question," Wyltam said. "Why did you steal information from Keyain under the pretense that Queen Valeriya would give it to the Exisotis?"

She swallowed hard, remembering the Queen's intense gaze from their first meeting. "I was angry with Keyain. Angry that he attacked my home city-state. Angry that he signed that marriage contract without my consent."

Adryan's brows raised with the last comment, the humor in his expression fading away. "Do you mind if I ask a question?"

Marietta sized him up, looking from his head to his toes. "Not at all."

"Why would Keyain sign a marriage contract without your consent?" Adryan looked between Wyltam and her as he leaned forward. "Then he dragged you back to Satiros a decade later."

"Keyain said he thought I'd agree to a marriage when I never once suggested, entertained, or considered the idea." Her fists clenched at her sides, letting the anger take over. "Why did you say drag me *back* to Satiros? I've never been to Satiros before Keyain abducted me."

Adryan furrowed his brows, then raised them as his jaw dropped. "That's what you're looking for."

"I think that's enough for today," Wyltam said, staring at Marietta. "Adryan, I will find you later this afternoon."

The minister cleared his throat and stood. "Again, Marietta, it was a pleasure."

She offered a weak smile as he left the room. The space seemed smaller with him gone, the King staring at her with such sadness. Once again, he took off his expressionless mask.

Marietta slid off the bed and walked over to him, standing before his chair. "Are you going to explain or let me speculate?"

Wyltam leaned back, looking amused. "With due time, I'll tell you anything you wish to know."

"Well, it seems like I'm going to die in two—"

He stood and took her hand. "You will not die. I won't let it happen."

Marietta looked up into his face, taken aback by the intensity in his expression. "Why do you care if I die or not? It'd solve your war."

"I'd fight both of them if it meant keeping you safe."

For a moment, she could say nothing. She held his gaze, the impact of his words taking root. "That seems a tad brash," she said, trying to deflect.

"You would know." He looked away as he smiled, trying to hide it.

Marietta reached for his chin and drew his face back toward her to see. She was on death's doorstep and this man, this stranger—a gods damned king—once again wanted to save her. Little did he know she hated needing to be saved.

He leaned in, Marietta's heart racing at the thought of his lips on hers again, but they fell short as he rested his forehead against hers. His hands caressed her cheeks as she closed her eyes and savored the deepness of his voice. "No matter what happens, no matter which way the ruling goes, I'll make sure you live."

"Couldn't you just pardon my crimes?" she asked, pulling her head away. "You're the King."

"I'm a king trying not to be a king. If I ordered people to do as I wish, then how could I justify uniting with Enomenos?" He shook his head. "The balance I have with my current council is that I trust that they will uphold the laws."

"Great," Marietta said. "You have one minister who proves he doesn't."

"Keyain is a fool."

"An understatement."

He smiled again, not hiding it from her that time. "If they vote in favor of your execution," he said, tucking a strand of hair behind her ear, "then I'll get you out of Satiros. You'll live no matter what, so don't lose hope. Please."

His last word was a plea, his emotions twitching his lips downward. Gods damn him for it, for the way she wished to smooth the tension between his brows. For the truth she heard in his words. As it was in the beginning, Wyltam wished to make sure she was alright. Her chest stirred with an emotion she dared not name. "I trust you," she murmured.

A moment passed where he said nothing, just taking in the details of her face. "I'll talk to the nurses so they don't drug you again."

"An order from their King?" she said with a slight raise of her brow.

"A demand, if you will," he said. "As long as I'm the King, no one will touch you or give you anything without your consent. That is my promise."

Marietta dropped her hand from his touch, nodding her head. She watched as he left, as he paused in the doorway to look at her one last time before closing it.

Her head whirled with the information. Valeriya was dead, she was on trial to be executed, and the King wanted to save her. None of it sat right with her, feeling helpless. There had to be some way to gain control, one way to flip it on them. Marietta paced as she reflected on the conversation, determined to find a way out by herself.

Chapter One Hundred

ELYSE

lyse hesitated outside the door, stomach clenched as she twisted the rings on her fingers. Under her arm was *Fulbryk's Guide to Chorys Dasi*, somehow left on her desk after Sylas and Azarys disappeared. When she finally returned to her suite, she expected it to be gone with them; yet it laid open on the page, the ink long since fading back to blank pages.

She couldn't stop thinking about what she saw, couldn't stop picturing him with horns. What in the hells kind of other elf were they? She stood in the mirror for an hour, searching her scalp for protrusions, finding nothing. Not knowing left her on edge, her mind racing with the possibilities. If she could just share it with someone, someone who wouldn't think she was crazy, then it would be enough to calm down.

With a deep breath, she knocked on the door.

"Come in," called a voice.

Entering the room, she found Marietta on the infirmary bed, brows furrowed as she stared at her hands. When she looked up, her face relaxed. "Elyse, it's you."

Elyse ran across the room, tossing the book onto the bed. She pulled Marietta into a tight embrace. "I'm so sorry, Marietta."

"No reason to be sorry." She leaned back with a tired smile on her face. "You have no idea how much I needed this distraction."

"We're trying to find something."

"We?" Marietta asked with a speculative brow. "Helping the King now, are you?"

"I'm working for the King in an official capacity." Elyse pointed to the broach pinned to her chest.

"Of course you are," she said, smiling. "What else have I missed?"

Her gaze turned to the book, Marietta following it. "I, uh, found something?"

Marietta grabbed it and read the cover. "You said that as if it were a question," she paused, raising the book in her hand. "I don't think this will have any smut in it."

She gave a nervous laugh, shifting on her feet. "None that I found at least."

"You're anxious," Marietta said, eying her. "What's wrong?"

Gods, this was stupid. She was about to be on trial for treason and murder. Marietta didn't have time to ease her mind. "Maybe this was a bad idea."

"That means it's a good idea. Now, sit." She scooted over, patting for Elyse to take a seat. Marietta wasted no time flipping through the pages. "Extensive history on Chorys Dasi. Interesting book choice." She flipped to the cover. "By this Lyken Fulbryk. Never heard of him."

Elyse stilled with that, her palms sweating as guilt resonated through her. She wasn't supposed to say anything. "I, uh, wanted to show you the center of the book."

Marietta opened to the blank pages. "Odd choice to leave blank pages in the middle." She began inspecting them as Elyse had, except she found the words faster. "'*Histories sealed by blood, the secrets our kind keep?*' Interesting. What does it mean?"

Elyse removed her brooch and took the book from Marietta, pausing as she held her finger over the pages. If the images didn't show up again, it would be proof that she was crazy. She pierced her skin with the brooch's pin, her blood dripping to the page. Marietta remained quiet, focusing on her blood. Elyse held her breath, wishing for it to spread.

"Odd," Marietta said, taking the book back to her lap. "The blood absorbed into…." She gasped, running her hands along the pages. Her eyes scanned the illustrations, her mouth moving though no words came out. She kept flipping until the last page, her hand rising to her mouth. "Oh, Elyse."

She shook where she sat. "You see it, right? I'm not crazy?"

"Oh, I see it." Marietta gaped at the book. "Two horns circling the sides of his head from his temple." She closed her eyes and took a deep breath.

"I don't know what they are—what I am. They're beasts or monsters. They said I was like them, but I don't have horns. I don't understand." Her breath picked up, unceasing as the panic hit.

"You don't know what they are?" Marietta shook her head. "Gods, what you are?"

"No."

"Beastial domain means nothing to you?" Marietta asked.

Elyse began picking at her nails. "Should it?"

"Fey. Proof that fey exist."

"As in, feyrie tales?" That was impossible. Then again, so was having a distinct scent. So was having horns.

"Yes," she said, her voice rough. "During the height of the pilinos disappearances, there was a witness who reported being attacked by two people. One had a set of gray, feathery wings." She paused, meeting her gaze. "The other had two horns circling the sides of his head from his temple. Elyse, he killed those people."

Time stilled as Marietta placed the book back in her lap. She stared down at the picture of Azarys, the details of his face so familiar, suddenly distorted with this revelation. Elyse couldn't move—couldn't breathe. She was in love with a murderer. "Are you sure?"

"Positive." Marietta grabbed her hand. "If I don't survive the trial, you need to bring this to Amryth."

"Don't say that." Elyse's throat choked with emotion. "I need you here. You're going to be okay. Wyltam said you'll be okay."

"I trust that he'll do everything in his power to help me, but you have to make sure this—" she pointed to the book "—is known by Wyltam and Amryth."

"Wyltam will think I'm crazy. He already—"

"He knows about the fey and can confirm what I'm saying." She shook her head. "This is the greatest discovery of our lifetime, and the only confirmed fey we've met is a murderer."

"But why? How could he have done this?" Elyse took in a sharp breath. "Sure, he lost his temper a few times, but murder?"

Marietta stared across the room with furrowed brows. "If Syllogians already hated pilinos, then it isn't that much of a stretch that the—" she leaned over to the book, reading "—Prince of Chorys Dasi wanted to murder them. Have you ever heard him use the term 'clip?'"

As she went to say no, she hesitated. Az had used that slur, hadn't he? And not once had Elyse corrected him. Acid burned in her throat as she nodded her head yes.

"The bodies they did find had 'clip' carved into their foreheads, Elyse." She reached over, grabbing Elyse's hand. "Chorys Dasi orchestrated those murders, and I wouldn't be surprised if they were the ones saying I killed Valeriya. Gods, they probably were the ones trying to kill *me*." Marietta huffed a humorless laugh. "To think my father told me all those fey stories just for them to brutalize pilinos like myself."

Guilt rattled through Elyse at the mention of her father. Wyltam ordered her to keep what they found a secret, but how could she say nothing to Marietta? Especially after helping her uncover that her formally betrothed was a hateful murderer. The broach weighed heavily in Elyse's hands. "Wyltam had me search through birth records."

Marietta sat back, tearing her stare from the book. "Why?"

"What if I were to tell you that you were born in Syllogi, not Enomenos?"

"I'd say you were crazy. My father left Satiros long before I was born."

She squeezed the broach, letting the metal dig into her skin. This was the right thing to do. Telling Marietta the truth was what she deserved. Elyse summoned her strength, raising her stare to her friend with a deep breath. "Apparently, he came back."

Chapter One Hundred One

MARIETTA

Marietta couldn't feel the goddess's magic thrumming under her skin or the heat of her presence in her chest, but Therypon watched over her. The truth Elyse had brought her shook her very being to her core.

The fey discovery—learning that Az, better known as Brynden, or the gods damned Prince of Chorys Dasi was a fey—seemed impossible. To discover he was the one brutalizing pilinos, carving clip into their foreheads made her furious. They hid inside the court the whole time. At least they had been right about the murderers being from Chorys Dasi. If Marietta's plan worked, if she lived through today, then she would raise all seven layers of hell to bring Azarys to justice.

What Elyse had shared about her father and the truth around her birth explained so much. It gave her an idea of how to leverage herself in court, standing on trial for crimes she both did and did not commit. If her plan didn't work, then at least damage would be done.

Marietta stood between two guards, the doors to the throne room towering before her. How funny her abduction to Satiros ended with her on trial for murder while Tilan lived in the dungeons. She wondered if he knew that she was in Satiros at all.

There was a knock, and then the guards ushered in Marietta. Cavernous, the room appeared as empty as Marietta felt. Her footsteps echoed in the quietness.

Across from the entrance loomed a massive stained-glass window. The light shone through its panes of greenery and swirling flowers, bathing the

room in its glow. Before it, dressed in his contrasting black, sat Wyltam on a golden throne, an ornate crown replacing his usual simple golden circlet. He didn't seem to breathe as she neared.

His ministers fanned out from his dais. Minister Dyieter stood apart, waiting at a podium for Marietta to approach. Keyain wouldn't look at her. Gods, of course, he wouldn't. After all, this was his fault. He should have left her in Olkia, left her to her life. At least he would end their marriage today—that had been one bit of information Elyse passed on.

Besides the ministers, groups of their men watched. Off to one side stood Wynn and Elyse. The latter nodded at her. She knew Marietta's plan, had even helped her run through all the ways it could go wrong. Wynn leaned down to whisper something to her, squeezing her shoulder. Elyse locked her eyes with Marietta as she whispered something back to Wynn.

The attendants of Therypon stood across from them. With a grimace, Coryn shook his head. Next to him was Nosokyma, who glared at the ministers and the King. Amryth was without her uniform, holding Deania, who cried. The sight crushed her. The people who risked everything to keep her safe now had to watch her gamble with her life.

More men stood in the galley's shadows. They spoke in hushed whispers, their voices not carrying, but Marietta saw their lips all the same. Some dared to smile. She wanted to sneer at them but didn't have her usual fire. Calm washed over Marietta as she approached the dais.

She lifted her chin, daring Keyain to look at her. Instead, Dyieter cleared his throat, pulling her attention. "Lady Marietta, the King's Council of Ministers has gathered today to decide your future, but before we get to that, there's unfinished business."

Keyain stepped forward, his stare landing anywhere but on Marietta as he approached her side. He turned, facing the dais. "I move to annul my marriage to Lady Marietta under the grounds of adultery and high treason to the court of Satiros." Adultery. He'd rather slander her name than help save her. Never would she forget his betrayal.

The King watched Marietta as he answered. "Approved." Unlike the day he visited her in the infirmary, he tucked away his emotions.

Keyain walked to Dyieter, signing a paper before stepping in line with the other ministers.

"As it should be. After all, Marietta lied to Keyain about being with child." Dyieter set papers down with a raised brow. "But now," he said with a clap of his hands, "we can begin. Marietta Vallynte—apologies, that's no longer your name."

Vexed, Marietta wished to wipe the smirk clean from his face.

"Marietta Lytpier, you stand on trial for treachery against Satiros and the crown."

So Wyltam had not told them yet. Hope grew in her chest, realizing she could still get the information out before him.

Turning to the ministers, Dyieter added, "We charge Marietta with delivering sensitive information to our enemies, aiding in their war efforts. During our apprehension of her, she incited a riot, and then she conspired in the tragic death of Queen Valeriya."

Marietta bit back her surprise. The riot had not been her fault—it wasn't her sword taking the lives of citizens. She withheld a scoff. They were throwing any charge at her to justify her execution.

"Two of the charges are worthy of death," Dyieter continued. "The other is a serious crime. Without defense, the Ministers of the King's Council will—"

"You didn't ask if she had one." Wyltam's voice echoed across the empty room.

Rage mixed with adoration, for they would not give her a defense. Wyltam had to save her, the idea of both making her heart skip a beat and her stomach nauseous.

"Your Grace, who do you suppose would stand at her defense since I have already denied the temple custody of her?"

The King stood, taking his time to smooth his clothes and walk to the edge of the dais with his hands pocketed. "I stand in defense of Marietta."

The bastard. The stupid, helpful bastard. Marietta dug her nails into her palms as she lifted her chin. "I stand in defense of myself," she responded.

A few chuckles sounded from the side. She caught the gaze of Minister Adryan, who looked delighted by her outburst.

"I don't think you want to do that, Lady Marietta." Wyltam's voice strained as he spoke. "Let me help you."

Minister Dyieter smirked. "It seems she's already decided."

To her left, a squat man with dark hair and tan skin stepped forward and cleared his throat.

"You may speak, Minister Rymos," Dyieter said.

"The rules of conduct state that the person on trial can choose at any moment to have someone stand in their defense, even after rejecting it," he said in a hoarse voice. "Marietta may also speak as needed during her statement with any information that may help better inform us Ministers."

"Well," Dyieter said, "it'll be entertaining, at least."

"Your Grace," Rymos added, turning to Wyltam, "you are our King. If we go against your defense, how do we ensure you won't seek retribution?"

Wyltam glanced at him. "If I wanted my ministers to serve me blindly, I would pardon Marietta without a trial." His dark eyes found her. "But I am not my mother. I ask you all to listen to the information we present and use it for your judgment."

"Of course, Your Grace," answered Rymos. "With that in mind, we can continue."

Dyieter sighed and cleared his throat. "You may begin the defense, King Wyltam."

Marietta bit back her irritation—of course, they would have him start. She took a deep breath and waited for her opening.

"When Minister Keyain shared he took a wife in secret, I decided to investigate, for there had to be a reason he never brought her to court." Pausing, he glanced at Keyain. "And the reason had to be beyond her capture by the Exisotis. Over the past couple of months, I sought Marietta's company, and I would ask her harmless snippets from her life. What I discovered was the truth."

Marietta furrowed her brows, glancing between Wyltam and Keyain, who paled.

"First, I will address the easily disputable charges—at least easy to dispute when you have a defense."

Dyieter stiffened with the comment.

"Marietta did not incite that riot." His voice called in the quietness. "Yesterday, the attendants pleaded on her behalf. We discovered that while a crowd gathered outside, Marietta was within the temple of Therypon, undergoing the ceremony to be named an Iros. My summons for Marietta inspired Satiros's most devoted to the streets. The guards' presence put them on edge." The King paused, gesturing to Keyain. "Though we at court are not ones to follow the deities, it's not a crime in Satiros to worship them or become any level of their attendants—Iros or otherwise."

Murmurs echoed from the galley at the King's words. How easily he dismissed the blatant charge. The ministers orchestrated this, believing Marietta would have no one to defend her.

But she did. She stared at the King with parted lips, raising her brows.

"Second, I was beside Marietta and Valeriya at the time of the assassination. The riot served as a distraction for our guard, leaving high-ranking members of court vulnerable—"

"You and Queen Valeriya had no reason to leave the Royal Suite," Dyieter said, cutting off the King.

"Do you question our loyalty to our city-state? To our people?" Wyltam asked. "I heard they gathered outside from my summons, and as the leaders of Satiros, we needed to witness it."

Dyieter bit down his retort, motioning for King Wyltam to continue.

"As I was saying, Valeriya sensed the attack before it happened, warning us to return inside. Yet when the assassin struck, Valeriya protected Marietta."

"Why would the Queen of Satiros risk her life for a pilinos?" Dyieter asked, drawling out the word.

Marietta went to speak, but Wyltam held a hand. She bristled as he continued.

"Valeriya understood Marietta's death would fuel the riot," he said.

"And she knew it would stoke Enomenos and the Exisotis' vengeance. Before her death, I shared with her the truth of who Marietta is."

"No," Keyain whispered, drawing Marietta's attention. His skin paling further, he now appeared as if he'd be sick.

"Before even that, I would like to address our perilous position." King Wyltam stepped from the dais, placing his hands behind his back. "Reyila claims Marietta had designed Valeriya's assassination." He paced before Marietta, catching her gaze. "They seek vengeance for Valeriya's life lost. On their side, there are the Chorys Dasians, who worked with Gyrsh Norymial to infiltrate and steal information from Satiros, also aided by Valeriya."

Resisting the urge to turn to Elyse, Marietta bit back the blinding anger that wanted to burn. Not only had Valeriya betrayed her, but she worked with the bastard who mistreated Elyse.

"Though the war in Olkia is at a stalemate, we now find ourselves at war with a Syllogian city-state. Likely Amigys and Kyaeri not only will refuse to help but also we cannot trust our past relations with them because of Gyrsh's betrayal." Wyltam stared at the ministers. "Our foreign relations are sullied, caught between two wars with no allies. Enomenos, aided by the Exisotis, will attack, and Satiros will be at a disadvantage. We cannot fight two wars, let alone handle the mutiny in our city." The King gestured with a hand. "Minister Leyland, please explain the current situation within our city-state."

An older man with dark skin and gray flecked through his hair stepped forward. "Much of our wealthiest citizens fled the city-state proper following the riot and death of Queen Valeriya. When Chorys Dasi and Reyila declared war, many fled from Satiros altogether."

He paused, looking at his fellow ministers. "They do not compare to the number of citizens who gather outside the palace gates each day. Most of the population view Marietta's trial as an attack on the temples and that the crown overreached our control. And it's not just the pilinos. The elvish neighborhoods of Greening Juncture and Wooded Ward, our largest concentration of middle-class citizens, gather each night to protest Marietta's charges. The city-state is in an uproar, and many of my subordinates fear a mutiny."

They protested her charges when she was the one that failed to help them. Her stomach churned at the thought of them gathering in her name.

"The city cries for Marietta," the King said, "because even they see through the ludicrous charges against her. Though she committed treason, Marietta said that Valeriya urged her to help, stating that the information was to help the Exisotis—her true home."

"Your Grace," cut in Dyieter, "if she considers Enomenos as her true home, then she's a foreign entity leveling an attack, just as the Chorys Dasians did. And with her marriage to Keyain dissolved, she no longer has citizenship in Satiros."

"That's not true." Marietta held her voice still as she spoke. "I was born in Satiros."

"And what proof do you have?" Dyieter drawled, his face unimpressed.

Marietta turned to the King. "I believe you have the birth record."

"That I do," he said with furrowed brows. From his pocket, he pulled out a slip of paper and brought it to Dyieter. "You should recognize it, though this is the authentic version. Not the one Keyain doctored."

Dyeiter ground his jaw, looking between the paper and Wyltam. "That is a bold claim—"

"I have the fake one Keyain had made as well." He handed over a second paper. "There's a discrepancy in the surname."

So, it was true. Marietta's heart pounded faster. Her idea could work. "Not only did Keyain forge those documents," she said, her voice echoing in the cavernous room, "but I had rejected his proposal of marriage multiple times."

"Per the law, that is legal," Dyeiter said. "You should know that."

"It is, but perhaps you should all be asking why. Why insist on marrying a half-elf from Enomenos?"

Murmurs followed her voice, the ripple of unrest starting.

"I'll presume you'll explain why, then." Dyeiter almost looked bored.

Her heart raced as she looked at Wyltam. He could fill that gap, the part she couldn't figure out as she paced in the infirmary.

"As most of you know, I had tasked Keyain and his team to seek the leader of the Exisotis, otherwise known as The Shepherd. For years, Keyain spent half the year away from court, searching—or so I thought." His deep voice rang through the room.

Keyain trembled where he stood, not daring to speak.

"There was a rumor that The Shepherd had a child. During Keyain's time in Enomenos, I asked him and his team to look into that rumor, thinking if we couldn't find the group's leader, then we could find their offspring." Wyltam glared at Keyain. "Through my conversations with Marietta, I learned of how they met, of how a male named Alyck introduced her to Keyain." The King paused as murmurs broke out. "Keyain found the Shepherd's daughter and married her in secret. For years, he has been married to our so-called enemy's daughter."

The roaring in her ears drowned out the murmurs that grew louder. Wyltam had shared they searched for The Shepherd and his family. Now he was saying... no. That couldn't be true. Elyse hadn't shared that part.

Keyain heaved where he stood, his eyes finally landing on Marietta. He knew. He fucking knew the whole time. He knew her father was the leader of the Exisotis.

"Markys Lytpier, otherwise known as Anthys Fulbryk in Satiros, is the leader of the Exisotis and is Marietta's father." Wyltam stood with his hands clasped behind his back.

The last name alone was shocking—her deceased family member being the founder of magic principles and wrote the gods damned book on the fey. To find out her father also lied about who he was—what he did for his entire life, was devastating. No wonder he and Tilan got along so well. They fucking worked together.

"Do you have proof that she's our enemy's daughter? Or that Anthys Fulbryk is their leader?" Dyeiter held her under a scrutinized gaze as if he were seeing her for the first time.

Wyltam nodded his head. "Bring him in."

Unbound, washed, but bone-thin, Tilan entered, supported between two guards. He lifted his head, finding Marietta. He blinked a few times, his jaw slacking as he stared at Marietta. She couldn't tear her gaze from him. Up close, she saw his hands and cried out. His once sturdy and sure fingers bent and twisted at the wrong angle, mangled beyond use.

"Ministers, this is Tilan Reid, Master Creator for the Exisotis," the King announced. "Tilan, will you confirm for the court who Marietta is?"

Without removing his gaze from her, he said, "Marietta is the daughter of The Shepherd. Markys Lytpier is the leader of the Exisotis. In previous private conversations regarding Marietta's safety, he confided in me that he is Anthys Fulbryk of Satiros."

"Stop!" Keyain yelled, stepping forward. The minister at his side grabbed his arm, halting Keyain's approach. Tears formed as he gaped at Marietta, lips trembling.

Marietta shook her head, turning back to Tilan, who knew the entire time. He knew who her father was and knew he arranged their marriage. Her breaths came sharply as the edges of her vision blurred.

"Marietta, look at me."

In her panic, she hadn't heard Wyltam approach. The King's voice was soft, as if they were the only two in the room. "Remember how I told you that you're the princess of Enomenos? This is what I meant. Your father controls much of the war, and he is pleading for your return." He lifted her chin, earning a hiss from Tilan. Under his breath, the King whispered, "Trust me."

Marietta took a slow breath in as she nodded. She trusted him, but she wouldn't go back to Enomenos.

"Clearly, she had planned this," said a minister, who stepped forward. "This all seems rather convenient to come out while she's on trial for treason and murdering our Queen. How do we know she wasn't working with her father to trick Keyain?"

Wyltam nodded to Adryan, who stepped forward. "I stood to witness Marietta answer a series of questions before the trial. She had no knowledge of the information Wyltam would share today and confirmed that her father hid his true work." He shook his head with a smile. "A traveling merchant was an excellent cover for him."

"You're willing to swear on the law?" Dyieter asked. "If found out you knew she was lying, I will also try you for treason."

"I swear on the law and on my life." He nodded his head at Marietta as he stepped back in line.

"So, we have our enemy's daughter in our hands and proof that she snuck information to them, or at least tempted to," Dyieter continued. "I think that's implication enough for her execution."

"We have no proof that her execution will appease Reyila," Wyltam said, standing at Marietta's side. "We could execute her, and it could mean nothing."

"Who says it isn't worth the risk? She's been nothing but trouble since her arrival." Dyieter spared a glance at Keyain, whose face grew redder by the minute. The minister next to him tried to calm him down but lost that fight.

"I ask the council to consider all the evidence I brought forth today," Wyltam said. "Satiros fights two wars. One with Enomenos and the Exisotis, and the other with Chorys Dasi and Reyila. Our city is in an uproar over Marietta's looming death sentence, and killing a deity's Iros will spike tensions with all the temples. Her death would rally our enemies in Enomenos and with the Exisotis, solidifying her as a martyr. Marietta committed treason, yes, but it would be to our soon ally, protecting us against the greater enemy: the pending assault from Chorys Dasi and Reyila.

"If we return Marietta to the Exisotis," Wyltam continued, placing a hand on her lower back, "we show good faith in an alliance with both the group and Enomenos. We could fight back against Reyila and Chorys Dasi, both of whom used Valeriya to steal information, as we now know."

"They'll never agree to such an alliance," Dyieter spat. "We'll hand over The Shepherd's daughter, and then they'll turn on us."

"It's worth the negotiation," Wyltam countered, his voice hardening.

"We don't have time—"

"I have a proposal." The room fell silent as Marietta turned to the ministers. "I have spent my life working in Enomenos, and I know the cities and its citizens better than most. My love for my home and its people reaches no limit. I have made myself well-known through aiding the people of my city-state." She nodded to Adryan. "If you doubt my notoriety, you can ask Minister Adryan, who knew of my business. You could even ask Chef Emynuel in the kitchens who knew of my bakery."

She paused, waiting to see if anyone would question, but the room remained quiet. Marietta continued, "I am no politician, but I have made myself a staple of my community. Learning the truth of my father only solidifies my standing in Enomenos."

Marietta took a breath, looking each minister in the eye. When she got to Keyain, he broke her stare, staring at the floor. "Each day, the citizens of Satiros riot at your gates, but not for me—for what I symbolize. I am the first pilinos ever to receive a title at court, and I am the first noble to become an Iros.

"So, I stand before you, the Ministers of Satiros, as your subject, the proof being my birth record." She paused, glancing at Tilan, who stared at her through furrowed brows. "Since I lived in Enomenos for more than a decade, I hold citizenship there as well. I sit at a unique intersection of two regions at war, a citizen of both, which leads to my proposal." She turned to Wyltam. His dark eyes watched her, curiosity and awe slipping through his expressionless mask. At that moment, she was thankful to see it. "I propose to unite Satiros with Enomenos and the Exisotis through marriage. King Wyltam," she said, bowing her head. "I offer my hand to you."

"No," Keyain yelled. "No!"

"Someone get him under control," Dyeiter said. With her head down, she heard Keyain's struggles. "How dare you come into my court for treason and murder after being accused of adultery—"

"I accept." Wyltam's finger found her chin, lifting her face to his. Marietta's breath caught with his stare, for the intensity it carried. Her plan was working.

"You can't just decide—"

"I accept her hand. Ministers, vote as you will, but consider the evidence we have brought forth."

Murmurs broke out throughout the room. "Quiet! I will have silence!" Dyieter yelled. "We'll put it to a vote. Your Grace, please return to the dais."

Wyltam squeezed her hand once before stepping away. Her stomach fluttered from both his acceptance and the call to a vote. Before, Adryan had been the only minister who didn't vote for her murder charge. The chances were slim, but she bolstered herself. If they didn't accept her proposal, then it would be their demise. The riots would only inflame, knowing that Coryn and Deania wouldn't let the proposal go unknown. By rejecting her offer, they would cause a mutiny for the city-state. Regardless of the outcome, she had already won.

"Since we have stripped Gyrsh of his title and Minister Keyain is..." Dyieter said, hesitating, "unfit to rule at the moment, the vote will be out of eight for the remaining ministers. All those in favor of a marriage between King Wyltam Grystier and Marietta Fulbryk, step forward. All those against, take a step back."

Adryan stepped forward without hesitation, followed by another minister whose name she didn't know. Dyieter took a step back from his podium, his glare locked on to Marietta. She only raised her chin as her pulse remained steady. Two more ministers stepped back. Royir, Grytaine's husband, was one of them. Unsurprising. He did call her a clip.

Three ministers remained. Marietta turned to Tilan as they contemplated her fate. Tears trailed down his face as he shook his head. Marietta wished a part of her heart to break for the man she had loved; yet, it didn't. With the truth of her father's position, she had discovered how much Tilan hid.

Minister Rymos shook his head and stepped forward, drawing back her attention. The last two ministers seemed to have a silent conversation between them. At the same moment, one minister stepped back, the other forward.

A tie. It was a tie.

The room was dead silent as they all turned to Wyltam, watching as he left the dais and approached Marietta. "I have already cast my vote, and as the King of Satiros, I break ties."

Breath left Marietta's chest as the realization hit. After acting as a pawn pushed around by different people at court, she, at last, became a player.

A smile crept to Wyltam's face, the sight beautiful and haunting framed in the golden light. "All hail Marietta, the future Queen of Satiros."

Pronunciation Guide

Marietta Lytpier Reid
mare-ee-et-ah lit-peer reed
Half-elf from Enomenos. Former business consultant. Owner and baker at Rise Above bakery. Married to Tilan Reid.

Tilan Reid
till-ehn reed
Human from Enomenos. Smith and owner of Reid's smithy. Married to Marietta Lytpier.

Keyain Vallynte
kee-ayen vahl-len-tee
Elf from Satiros. Minister of Protection. Oversees Satiros's city guard and army. Best friend to King Wyltam.

Valeriya Ruuyl Grytsier
vuh-lare-ee-uh roo-il grit-see-er
Elf originally from Reyila. Married King Wyltam Grytsier to become Queen Consort of Satiros.

Elyse Norymial
eh-leese nor-eh-mee-al
Elf from Satiros. Lady of the Queen's Court. Daughter of Minister Gyrsh Norymial.

Wyltam Grytsier
will-tahm grit-see-er
Elf from Satiros. King of Satiros.

Amryth Sulyng
ahm-rith sool-ing
Elf from Satiros. Employed by the Crown of Satiros.

Bryndan Vazlyte

brinn-dehn vahz-leet
Elf from Chorys Dasi. Emissary from Chorys Dasi.

Sylas Tygenbrook
sie-lus tie-gehn-bruhk
Elf from Chorys Dasi. Emissary from Chorys Dasi.

Deania Dinke
dee-ahn-ee-uh deenk
Half-elf from Satiros. Originally from Chorys Dasi. Cleric to the goddess Therypon.

Coryn Niershade
core-inn neer-shayde
Half-elf from Satiros. Originally from Amigys. Iros to the goddess Therypon.

Wynn Styrmer
winn stir-mehr
[Information Redacted]

Katya Timms
kaht-tee-ah tihms
Half-elf from Reyila. Mage Master to Queen Nystania of Reyila.

Nobles & Courtesans.

Mycaub Grytsier
my-cub grit-see-er
Elf from Satiros. Prince of Satiros. Son of Valeriya and Wyltam Grytsier.

Gyrsh Norymial
gee-ursh nor-eh-mee-al
Elf from Satiros. Minister of Foreign Affairs. Father of Elyse Norymial. Husband to the late Anthylia Norymial.

Anthylia Norymial

ann-thil-lee-uh nor-eh-mee-al

Deceased. Elf from Satiros. Lady of the Court. Late mother of Elyse Norymial. Late wife to Gyrsh Norymial.

Grytaine Romyn Lasyda

grih-tayne roh-minn lahs-see-duh

Elf from Satiros. Lady of the Queen's Court. Married to Minister Royir Lasyda.

Royir Lasyda

roi-eer lahs-see-duh

Elf from Satiros. Minister of Coin. Married to Grytaine Lasyda. Formerly married to Lyna Pinyl.

Lydia Rynts

leh-dee-uh rintz

Elf from Satiros. Minor lady to the Court of Satiros. Former friends of Elyse Norymial.

Tryda Tywik

tree-dah tie-wihk

Elf from Satiros. Lady In Waiting to Queen Valeriya. Former Lady in Waiting to the Late Queen Olytia. Married to Dyeiter Tywik.

Dyeiter Tywik

die-ee-ter tie-wihk

Elf from Satiros. Minister of Law. Married to Tryda Tywik.

Leyland Fedyr

lay-land fehd-eer

Elf from Satiros. Minister of Vassals. Married to Magyrite Fedyr.

Rymos Batyst

ree-mohs bah-teest

Elf from Satiros. Minister of Conduct. Married to Ymorea Batyst.

Ymorea Batyst
eh-mohr-ee-ah bah-teest
Elf from Satiros. Lady of the Queen's Court. Married to Rymos Batyst.

Adryan Pytts
ay-dree-an pihts
Elf from Satiros. Minister of Commerce.

Enomenoans

Pelok Fairweather
peh-lock fayr-wehth-ehr
Human from Olkia. Owner of the Lonely Dog Tavern. Friend of Marietta and Tilan.

Tristina Turner
tris-tee-nah ter-ner
Half-elf from Olkia. Friend of Marietta.

Terms & Misc.

Aithyr
ay-thur
Naturally occurring energy that is invisible to the eye that is used to perform magic

Exisotis
ecks-oh-so-tis
Resistance group against Syllogi and their treatment of pilinos. Though based out of Enomenos, the group functions separately
from the government. The group's name isn't well-known to common folk.

Pilinos

pihl-len-nohs
Any persons containing human descent, including humans and half-elves.

The Shepherd
sheh-purd
Leader of the Exisotis. Identity is unknown.

Therypon
thare-ih-pone
Goddess of healing and pain. Associated with cerulean and serpents.

Iros
eer-os
Elite warriors who serve a single deity. A highly respectable position within a temple.

Places

Akroi
ah-croy
Region between the Mavros Sea and the Evgeni Sea. Extends from the Ekrixi Range to the Tefra forests. Includes the
city-state collectives of Syllogi and Enomenos, as well as the Queendom of Reyila to the north.

Enomenos
en-no-mehn-nohs
Collection of city-states in eastern Akroi. Known for is mixed populace of elves and pilinos. Society built without the use of magic. Ruled by the Enomenoan Unification Council, which is a democratic group selected by the citizens.

Kentro
kehn-troe
Capitol of Enomenos. Largest city-state of the collective known

for its nightlife.

Olkia
ohl-key-ah
Western most city-state in Enomenos. Known for its quality craftspeople.

Rotamu
roht-ta-mew
City-state best known for its breweries, distilleries, and wineries. Built around Halia River and Malakos River juncture.

Notos
no-tohs
Southern most city-state in Enomenos. Sits on the coast of the Evgeni Sea. Imports goods from around the world. Common city-state for older citizens to move to.

Avato
ahv-vah-toe
Northern most city-state in Enomenos. Sits at the bottom of the Systada Mountains. Known for mining metals and materials from the mountains.

Syllogi
sill-oh-ghee
Collection of city-states in western Akroi. Ruled by the elven. Pilinos are considered lesser citizens. Society relies on magic. Ruled by the kings and queens of the four city-states in the Syllogian Council.

Satiros
sah-teer-ohs
Eastern most city-state in Syllogi. Known for its lush gardens that bloom all year despite the weather. Surrounded by farmlands that supply food for the rest of Syllogi.

Chorys Dasi

kor-es dah-see

Northern most city-state in Syllogi. Main trading port with the Queendom of Reyila to the north.

Amigys

ah-mihg-gess

Southern most city-state in Syllogi. Major port to the rest of the world. Sits on the sandy shore of Seiryn Bay.

Kyaeri

kai-air-ee

Western most city-state in Syllogi. Settled on the waterfall that feeds the Halia River in the Ekrixi range.

Reyila

ray-eel-lah

Queendom in northern Akroi. Though it is ruled by an elven family, pilinos are equal citizens.

The King's Council of Ministers
THE CITY-STATE OF SATIROS

King or Queen
Currently held by King Wyltam Grytsier.
Crown is passed on to the first born child, regardless of gender. Ultimate rule over Satiros.

The Ministers

Minister of Law
Currently held by Lord Dyieter Tywik.
Oversees the court of law. Provides order to the city-state.

Minister of Protection
Currently held by Lord Keyain Vallynte.
Oversees the city guard and army.

Minister of Foreign Relations
Currently held by Lord Gyrsh Norymial.
Oversees the foreign relations with other city-states.

Minister of Vassals
Currently held by Leyland Fedyr.
Oversees the non-noble population of the city-state and maintains the relationship with the temples.

Minister of Conduct
Currently held by Lord Rymos Batyst.
Oversees court conduct and palace procedures.

Minister of Health
Currently held by Galyn Mydeus.
Oversees overall health and well-being of citizens.

Minister of Commerce
Currently held by Adryan Pytts.
Oversees businesses, guilds, and the economic welfare of the city-state.

Minister of Education
Currently held by Lord Redwyn Horsyn.
Oversees education and educational institutes.

Minister of Infrastructure
Currently held by Gordyn Donyr.
Oversees the maintenance of roads, bridges, buildings, and more in the city-state.

Minister of Resources
Currently held by Lord Asyn Teryp.
Oversees the production of resources for the city-state.

Minister of Religious Affairs
Defunct.
Oversaw the relationship with the temples.

Minister of Mages
Defunct.
Oversaw common magic practitioners in the city-state.

Acknowledgements

Writing A Queen's Game has been the most incredible journey that wouldn't have been the same without the support of a few key people. First and foremost, I'd like to thank Tyler Gace. Before I even had the courage to write a book, you believed in me. Not once did you doubt that I could get it done, and you supported me at every turn. Without you, there would be no book. Without you, I would have talked myself out of this journey. I am forever grateful for your support, feedback, and love. You mean the world to me.

I'd also like to thank Lauren Parks. Even in its roughest form, you supported this project. I've come a long way from those early drafts. Without your support and critical feedback, it would have never gotten to where it is today. I can't wait to return the favor when you finish your book.

Thank you to Lindsey Shadik for your honest and unfiltered feedback. The time you gave to go through my manuscript is priceless to me. Also forever grateful for your advice on the name change. It was the right call.

Thank you to Abbey Kondalski, my fellow smutty fantasy book lover. The hours spent discussing various phallic members from books made this journey much more enjoyable. Your feedback still makes me giggle when I look back on that version of my manuscript. Much love for my one and only omega reader.

To my beta readers, Sarah S. And Anna A., thank you for your time and energy towards this project. I was a no-name indie author, yet you took a chance on me. I'm forever grateful.

To my friends and family, thank you for your support and encouragement. This process was a gentle reminder of how fortunate I am to be surrounded by you all.

A special thanks to all my friends on Bookstagram and BookTok.

You've supported me from day one, making my book publishing journey more gratifying. I hope this book was everything I promised and more.

Lastly, I'm thankful to all the readers who picked this book up and gave it a chance. I hope you saw yourself in this book. And remember, you are never alone.

About the Author

Ever since Eri Leigh was a kid, she's spent her life in her head. Frequent daydreams of different worlds and the fantastical creatures that occupy them were often at the forefront of her mind. She spent years working on various writing projects until one day in 2020, when the world was at a standstill, she found her story.

A Queen's Game, her debut novel, explores themes of seeing individuals for more than their face value and finding freedom from life and from ourselves. Growing up as an anxious kid—and into a more anxious adult—she weaves bits of her experiences into her characters. Mental health is a prevalent topic within her writing, including how symptoms of mental illness can suffocate those who have it.

Though writing occupies much of Eri's life, she is also an avid reader. She spends her date nights either on the couch reading with her fiance Tyler or venturing to the local bookstore to buy more books she doesn't need.

——

Stay connected with Eri Leigh!
Instagram: @author.erileigh
TikTok: @authorerileigh
Newsletter sign up:
www.authorerileigh.com/newsletter

Printed in Great Britain
by Amazon

37418656R00433